MILES MORALES
ULTIMATE END

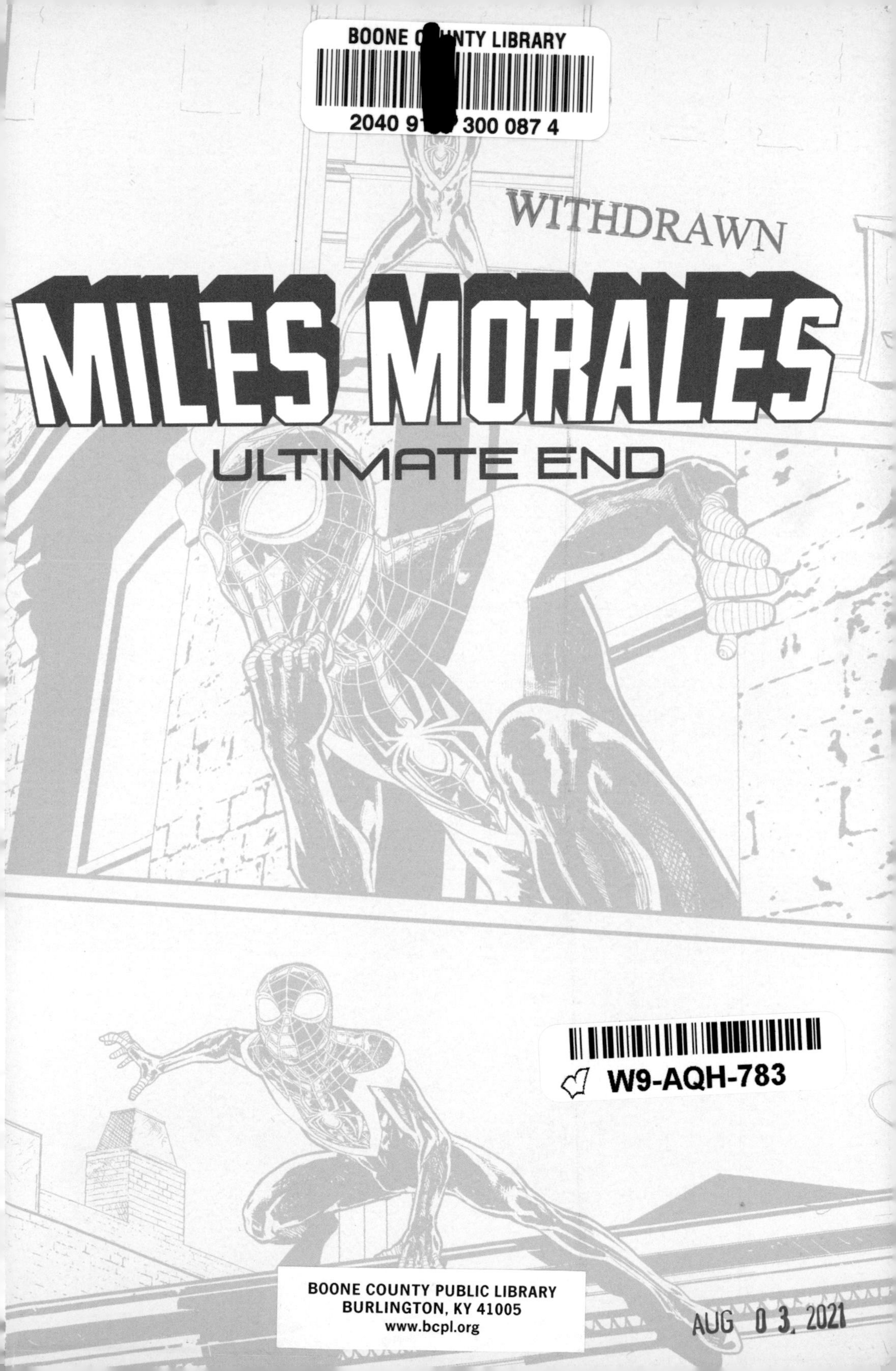

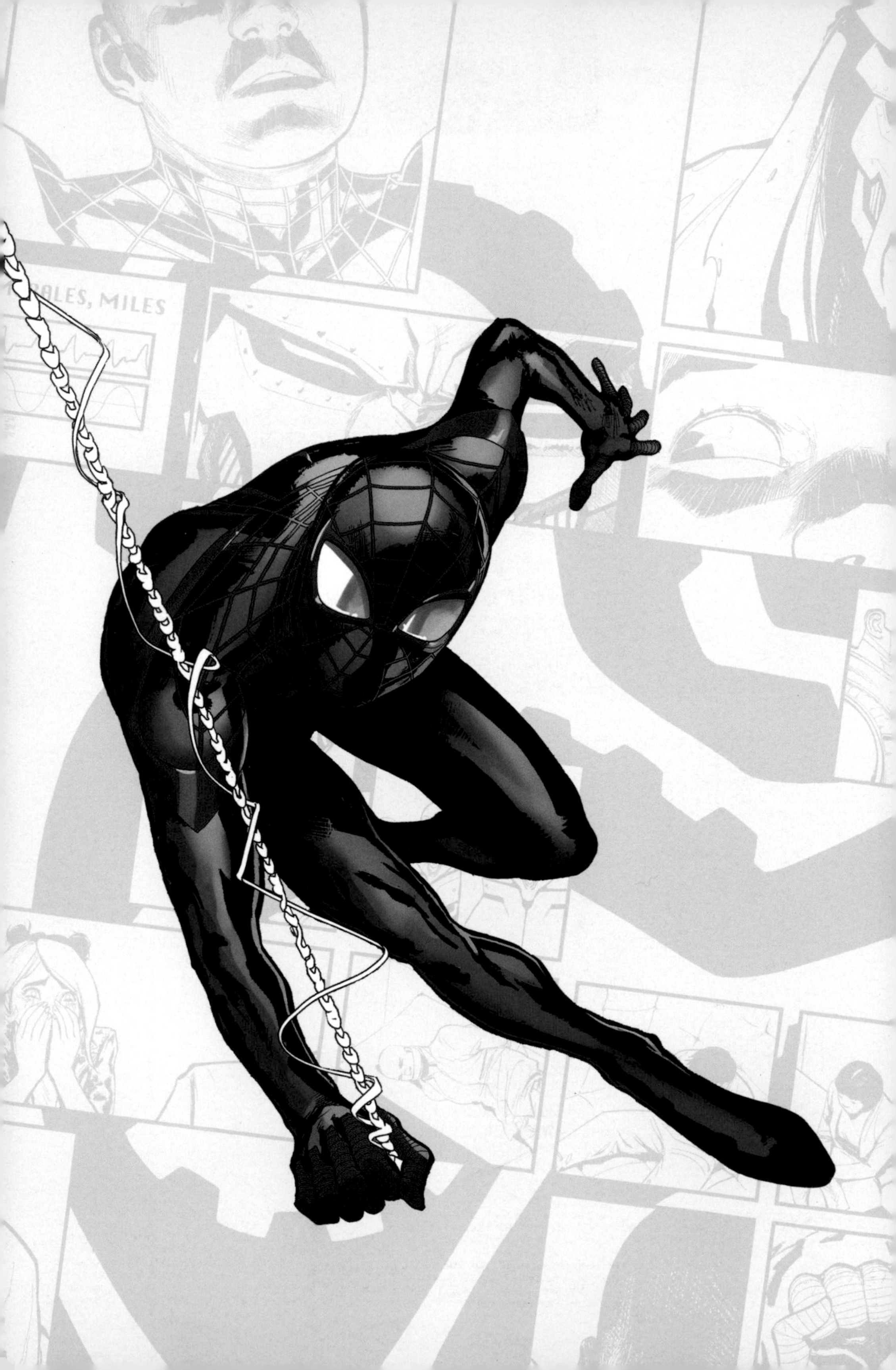
RALES, MILES

MILES MORALES

ULTIMATE END

WRITER
BRIAN MICHAEL BENDIS

ARTIST
DAVID MARQUEZ

COLOR ARTIST
JUSTIN PONSOR
WITH **JASON KEITH** (#6)

LETTERER
VC's CORY PETIT

COVER ART
DAVID MARQUEZ & JUSTIN PONSOR

ASSISTANT EDITORS
EMILY SHAW & JON MOISAN

EDITOR
MARK PANICCIA

Spider-Man created by STAN LEE & STEVE DITKO

collection editor JENNIFER GRÜNWALD • assistant editor DANIEL KIRCHHOFFER
assistant managing editor MAIA LOY • assistant managing editor LISA MONTALBANO
vp production & special projects JEFF YOUNGQUIST
vp licensed publishing SVEN LARSEN • svp print, sales & marketing DAVID GABRIEL
editor in chief C.B. CEBULSKI

MILES MORALES: ULTIMATE END. Contains material originally published in magazine form as MILES MORALES: ULTIMATE SPIDER-MAN (2014) #1-12. First printing 2021. ISBN 978-1-302-92983-1. Published by MARVEL WORLDWIDE, INC., a subsidiary of MARVEL ENTERTAINMENT, LLC. OFFICE OF PUBLICATION: 1290 Avenue of the Americas, New York, NY 10104. © 2021 MARVEL No similarity between any of the names, characters, persons, and/or institutions in this magazine with those of any living or dead person or institution is intended, and any such similarity which may exist is purely coincidental. **Printed in Canada.** KEVIN FEIGE, Chief Creative Officer; DAN BUCKLEY, President, Marvel Entertainment; JOE QUESADA, EVP & Creative Director; DAVID BOGART, Associate Publisher & SVP of Talent Affairs; TOM BREVOORT, VP, Executive Editor; NICK LOWE, Executive Editor, VP of Content, Digital Publishing; DAVID GABRIEL, VP of Print & Digital Publishing; JEFF YOUNGQUIST, VP of Production & Special Projects; ALEX MORALES, Director of Publishing Operations; DAN EDINGTON, Managing Editor; RICKEY PURDIN, Director of Talent Relations; JENNIFER GRÜNWALD, Senior Editor, Special Projects; SUSAN CRESPI, Production Manager; STAN LEE, Chairman Emeritus. For information regarding advertising in Marvel Comics or on Marvel.com, please contact Vit DeBellis, Custom Solutions & Integrated Advertising Manager, at vdebellis@marvel.com. For Marvel subscription inquiries, please call 888-511-5480. **Manufactured between 4/30/2021 and 6/1/2021 by SOLISCO PRINTERS, SCOTT, QC, CANADA.**
10 9 8 7 6 5 4 3 2 1

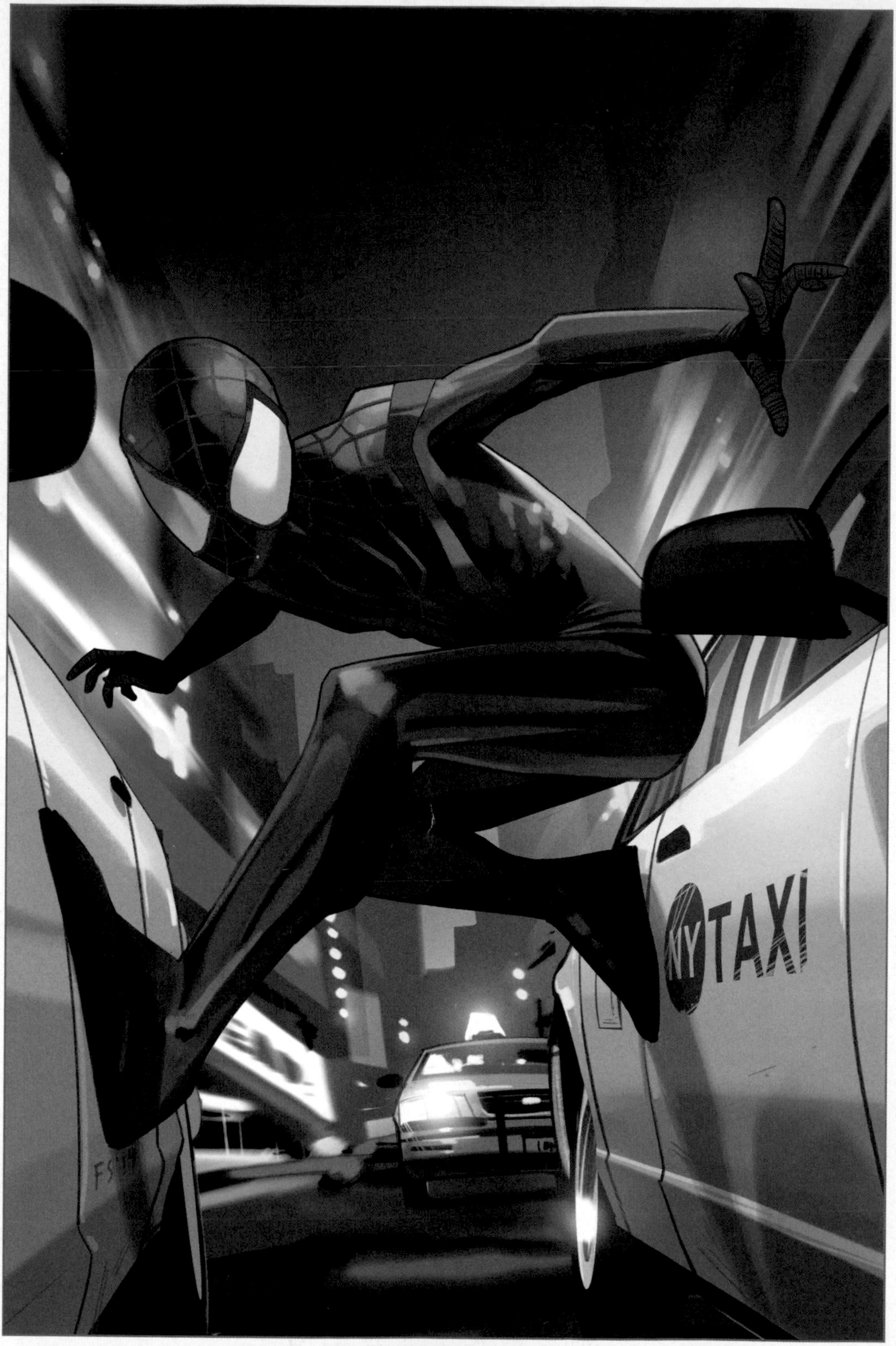
NY TAXI

#1 VARIANT
BY FIONA STAPLES

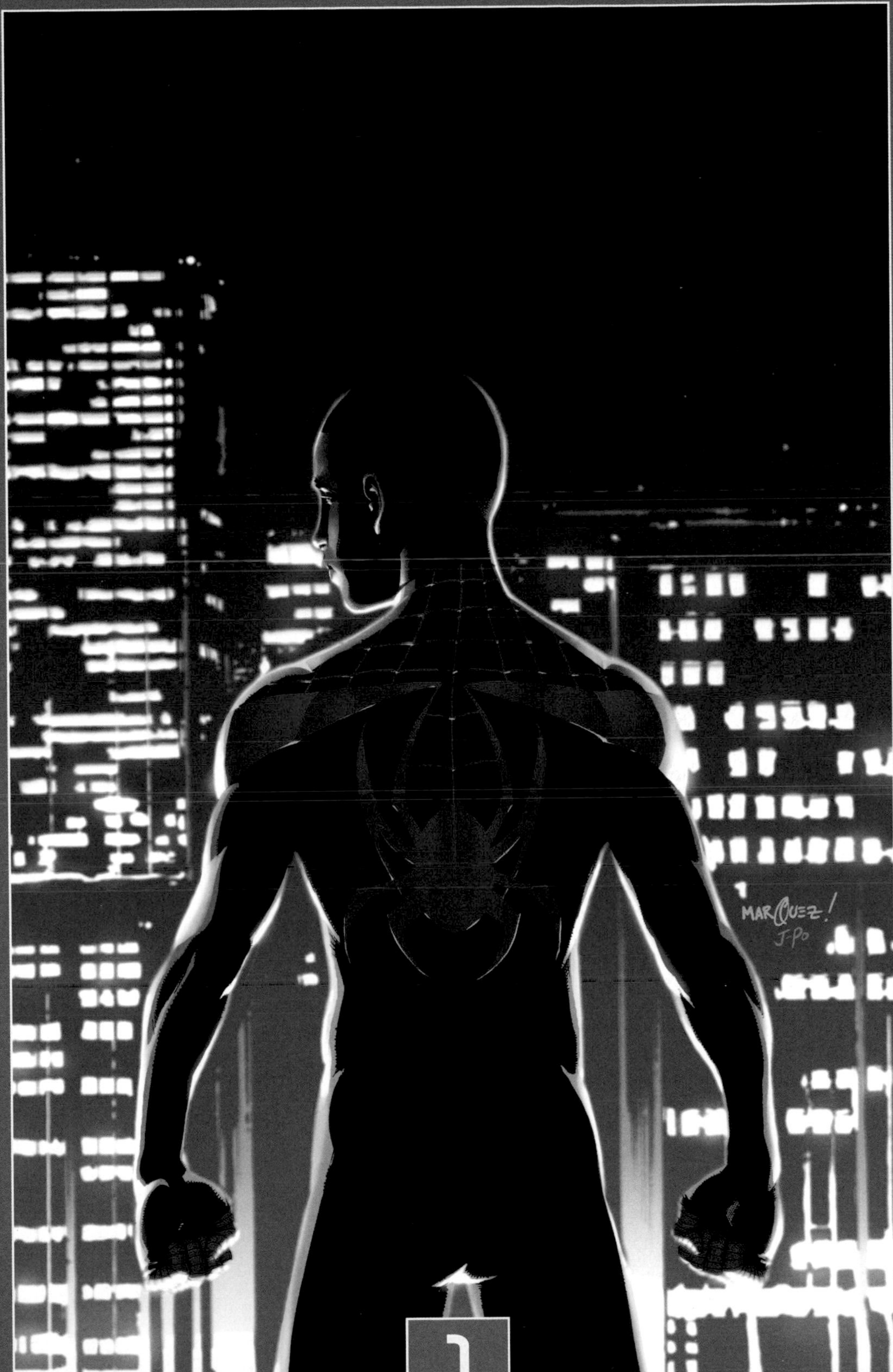
MARQUEZ!
J-Po
1

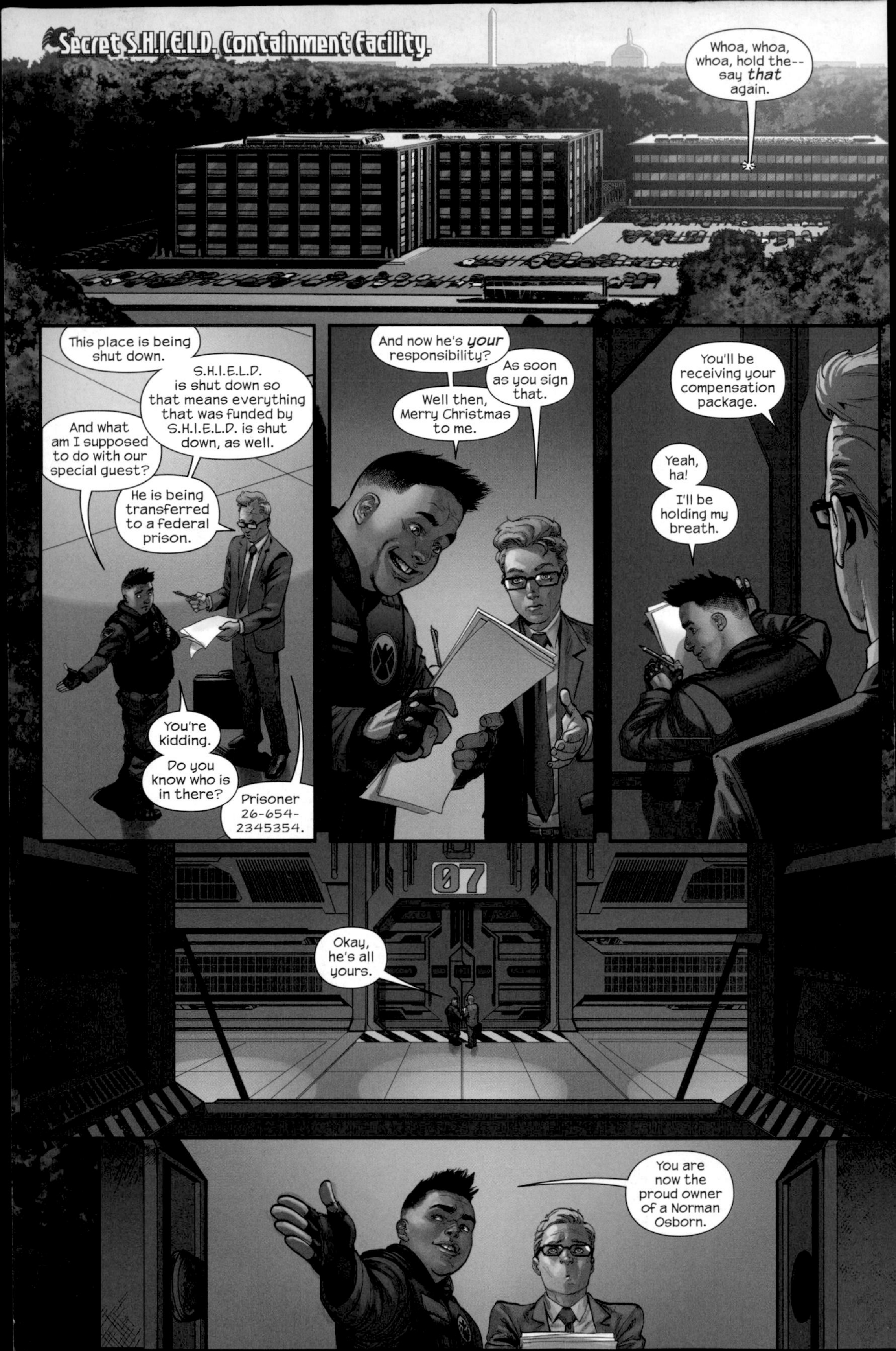
Secret S.H.I.E.L.D. Containment Facility.
Whoa, whoa, whoa, hold the-- say *that* again.
This place is being shut down.
S.H.I.E.L.D. is shut down so that means everything that was funded by S.H.I.E.L.D. is shut down, as well.
And what am I supposed to do with our special guest?
He is being transferred to a federal prison.
You're kidding.
Do you know who is in there?
Prisoner 26-654-2345354.
And now he's *your* responsibility?
As soon as you sign that.
Well then, Merry Christmas to me.
You'll be receiving your compensation package.
Yeah, ha!
I'll be holding my breath.
07
Okay, he's all yours.
You are now the proud owner of a Norman Osborn.

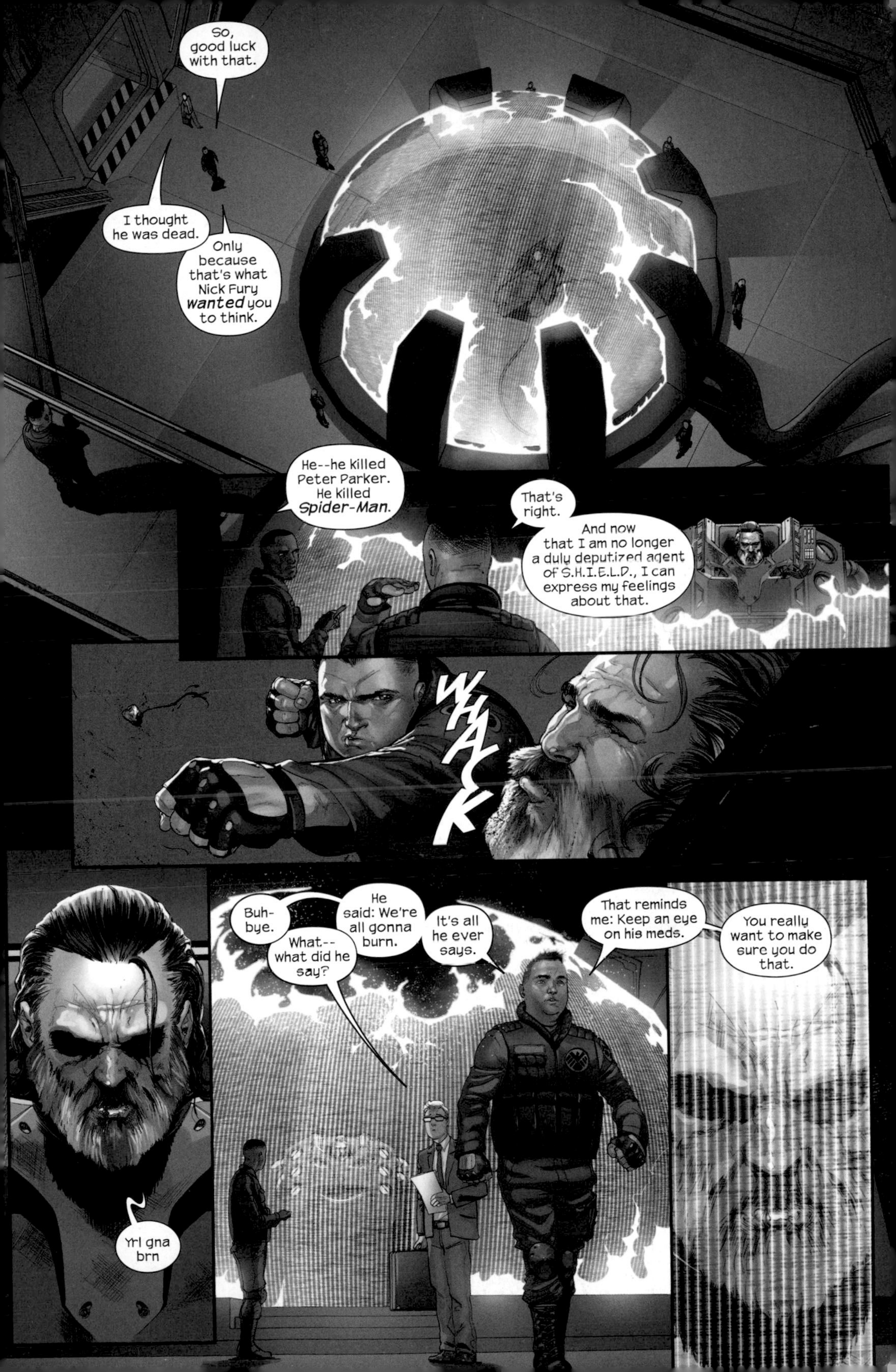

So, good luck with that.
I thought he was dead.
Only because that's what Nick Fury *wanted* you to think.
He--he killed Peter Parker. He killed *Spider-Man*.
That's right.
And now that I am no longer a duly deputized agent of S.H.I.E.L.D., I can express my feelings about that.
WHACK
Yrl gna brn
Buh-bye.
What-- what did he say?
He said: We're all gonna burn.
It's all he ever says.
That reminds me: Keep an eye on his meds.
You really want to make sure you do that.

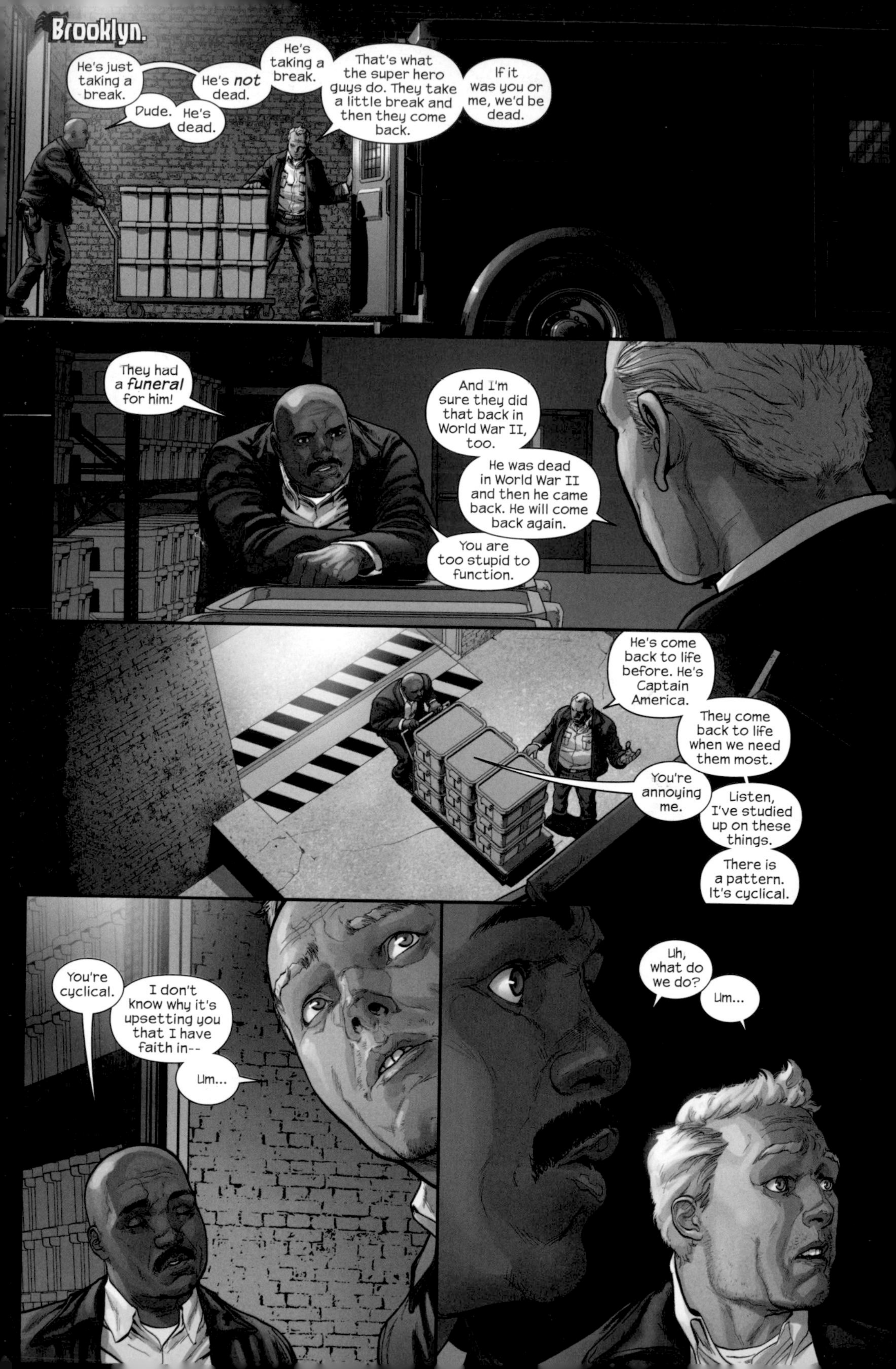
Brooklyn.
He's just taking a break.
Dude. He's dead.
He's not dead.
He's taking a break.
That's what the super hero guys do. They take a little break and then they come back.
If it was you or me, we'd be dead.
They had a funeral for him!
And I'm sure they did that back in World War II, too.
He was dead in World War II and then he came back. He will come back again.
You are too stupid to function.
He's come back to life before. He's Captain America.
They come back to life when we need them most.
You're annoying me.
Listen, I've studied up on these things.
There is a pattern. It's cyclical.
You're cyclical.
I don't know why it's upsetting you that I have faith in--
Um...
Uh, what do we do?
Um...

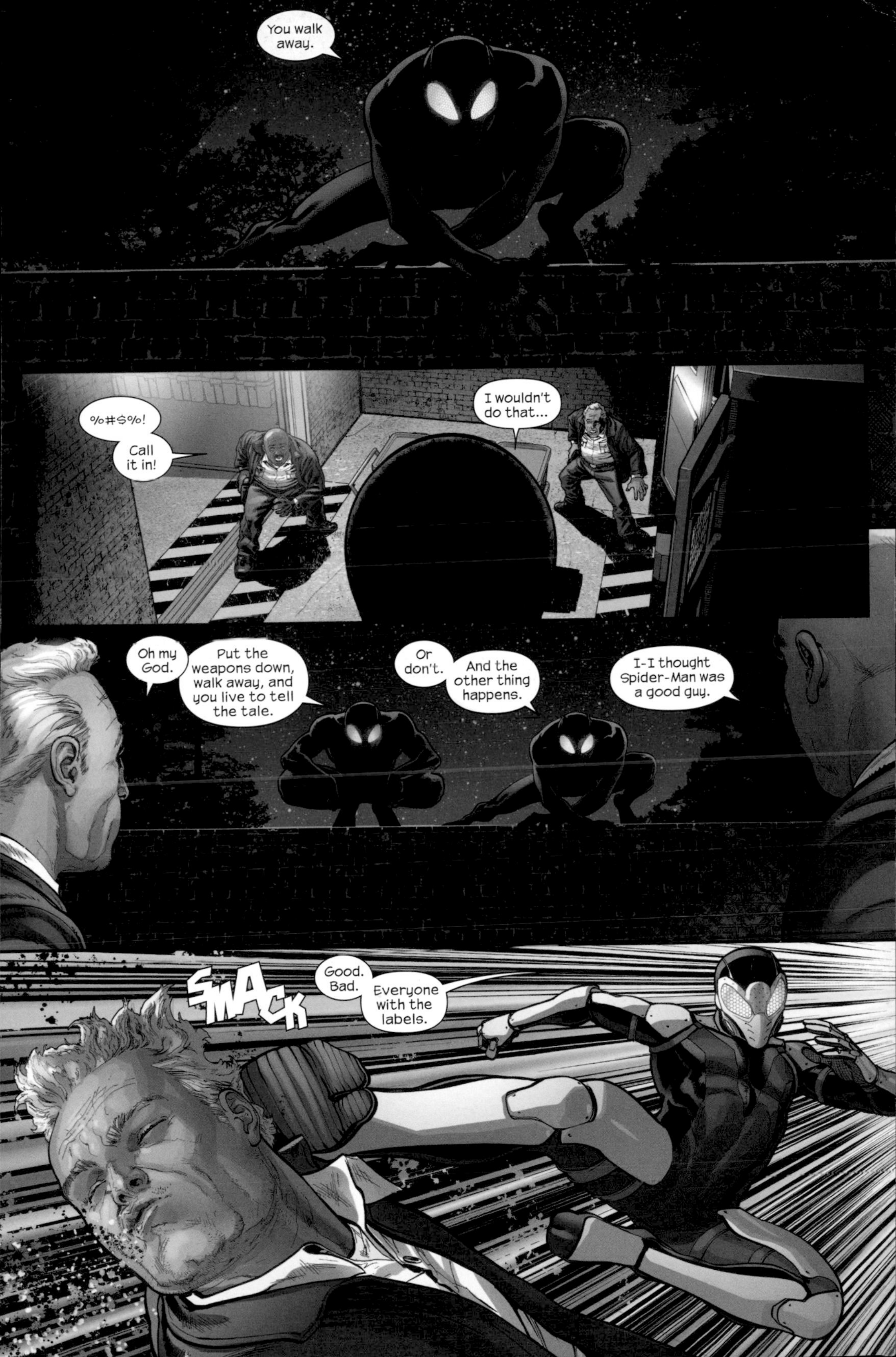
You walk away.
%#$%!
Call it in!
I wouldn't do that...
Oh my God.
Put the weapons down, walk away, and you live to tell the tale.
Or don't.
And the other thing happens.
I-I thought Spider-Man was a good guy.
SMACK
Good. Bad.
Everyone with the labels.

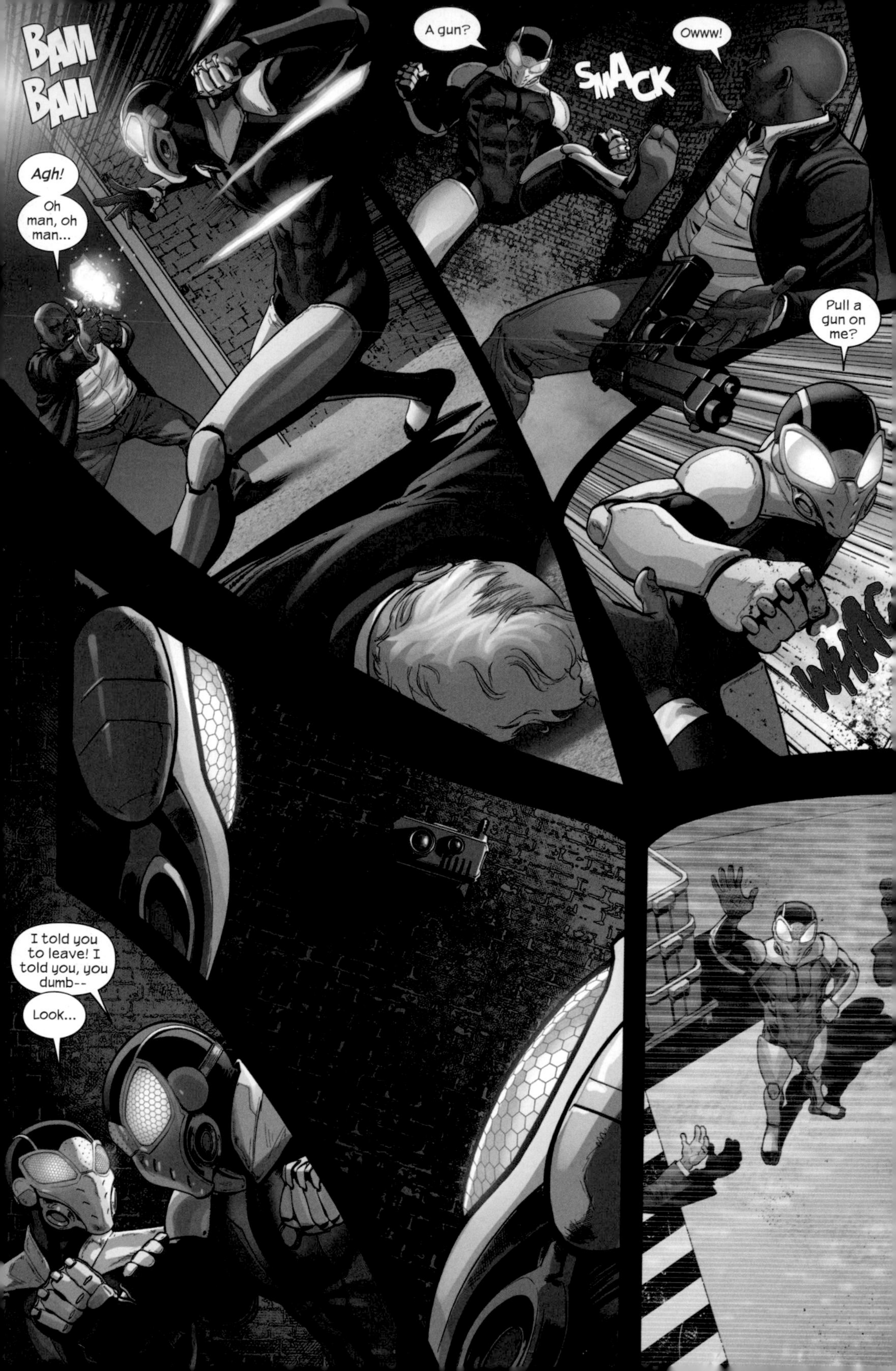
BAM
BAM
Agh!
Oh man, oh man...
A gun?
SMACK
Owww!
Pull a gun on me?
I told you to leave! I told you, you dumb--
Look...

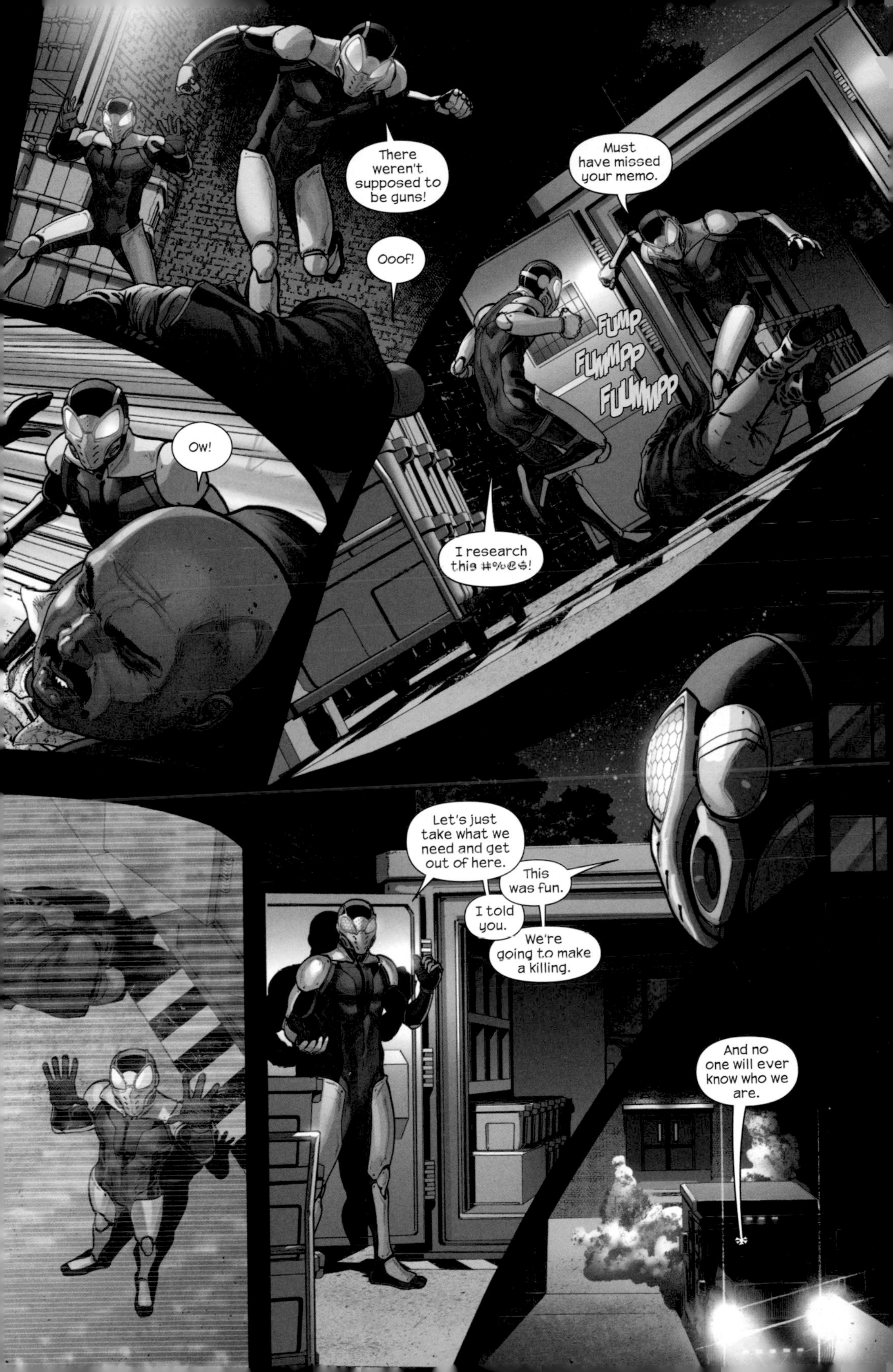
There weren't supposed to be guns!
Must have missed your memo.
Ooof!
FUMP
FUMMPP
FUUMMPP
Ow!
I research this #%@$!
Let's just take what we need and get out of here.
This was fun.
I told you.
We're going to make a killing.
And no one will ever know who we are.

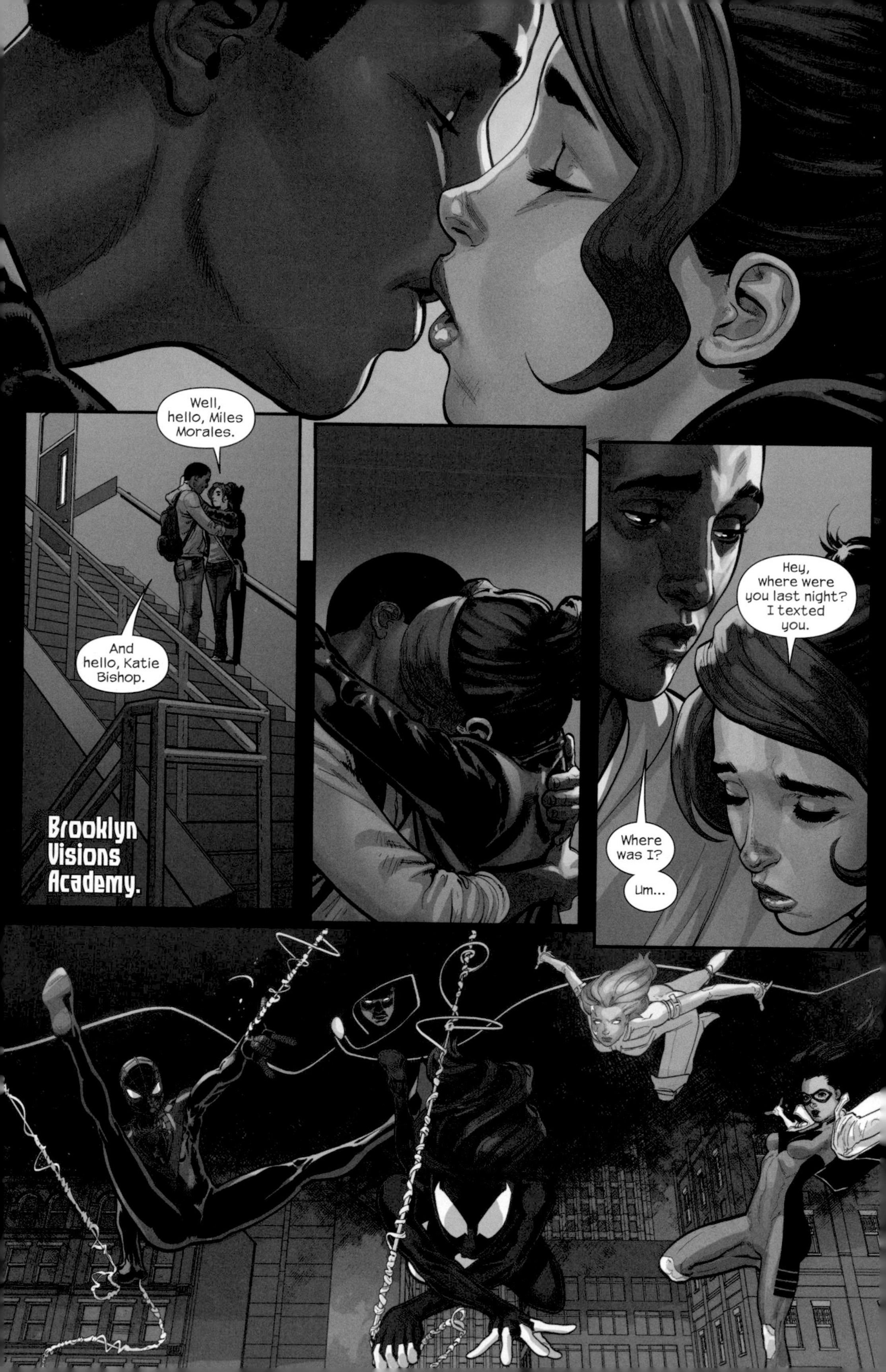
Well, hello, Miles Morales.
And hello, Katie Bishop.
Brooklyn Visions Academy.
Hey, where were you last night? I texted you.
Where was I?
Um...

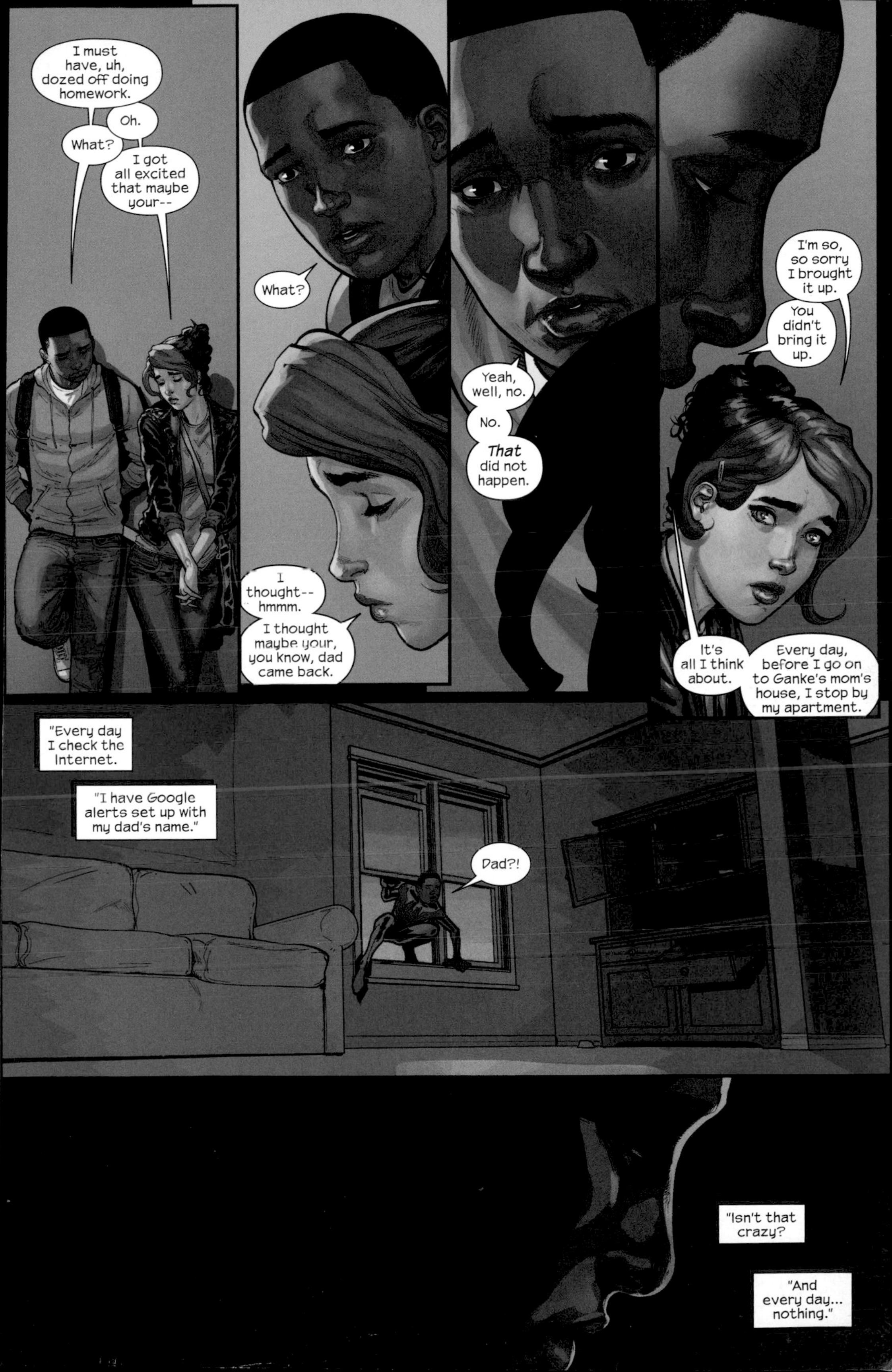
I must have, uh, dozed off doing homework.
Oh.
What?
I got all excited that maybe your--
What?
I thought--hmmm.
I thought maybe your, you know, dad came back.
Yeah, well, no.
No.
That did not happen.
I'm so, so sorry I brought it up.
You didn't bring it up.
It's all I think about.
Every day, before I go on to Ganke's mom's house, I stop by my apartment.
"Every day I check the Internet.
"I have Google alerts set up with my dad's name."
Dad?!
"Isn't that crazy?
"And every day... nothing."

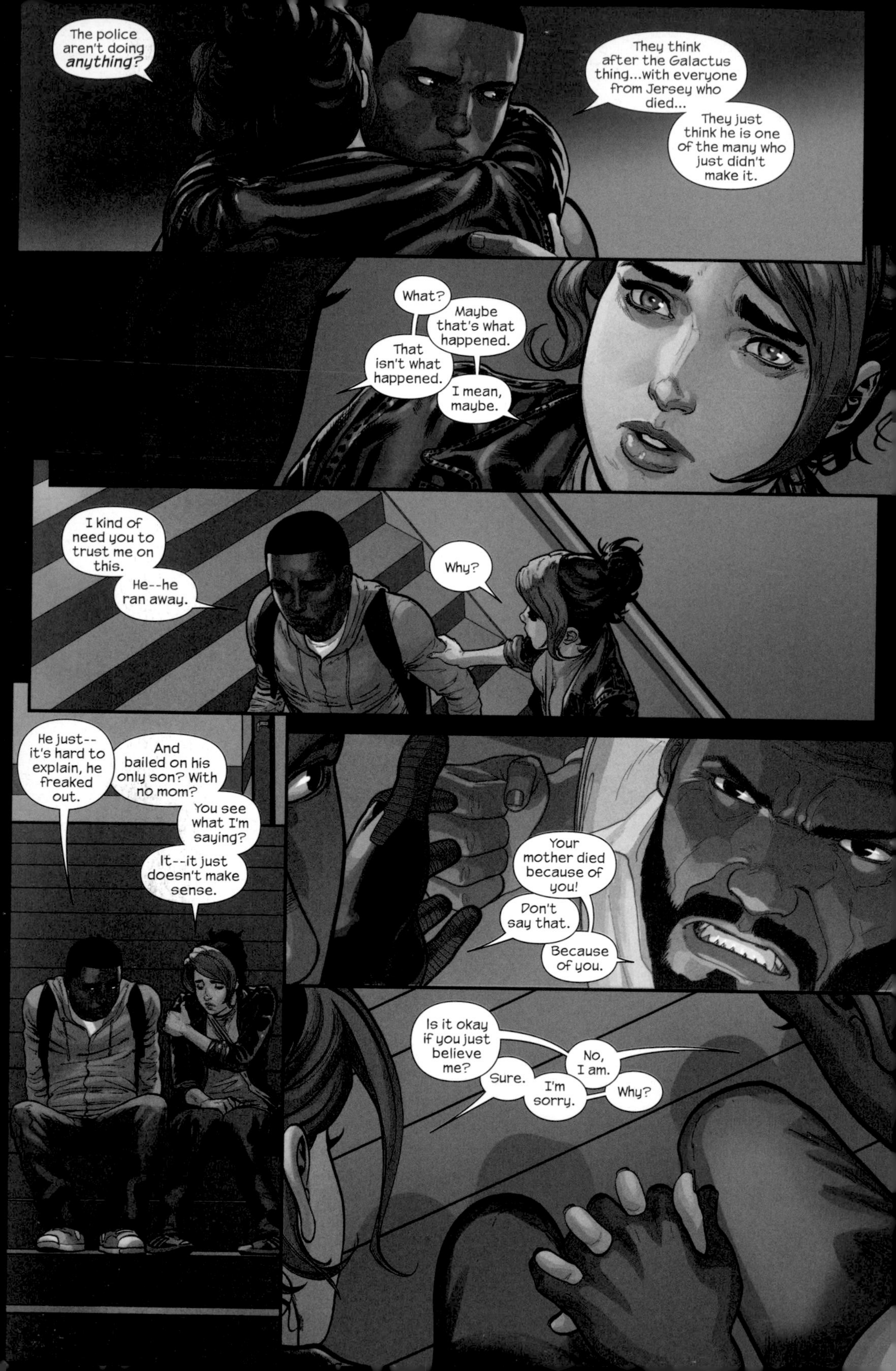

The police aren't doing *anything*?
They think after the Galactus thing...with everyone from Jersey who died...
They just think he is one of the many who just didn't make it.
What?
Maybe that's what happened.
That isn't what happened.
I mean, maybe.
I kind of need you to trust me on this.
He--he ran away.
Why?
He just--it's hard to explain, he freaked out.
And bailed on his only son? With no mom?
You see what I'm saying?
It--it just doesn't make sense.
Your mother died because of you!
Don't say that.
Because of you.
Is it okay if you just believe me?
Sure.
No, I am.
I'm sorry.
Why?

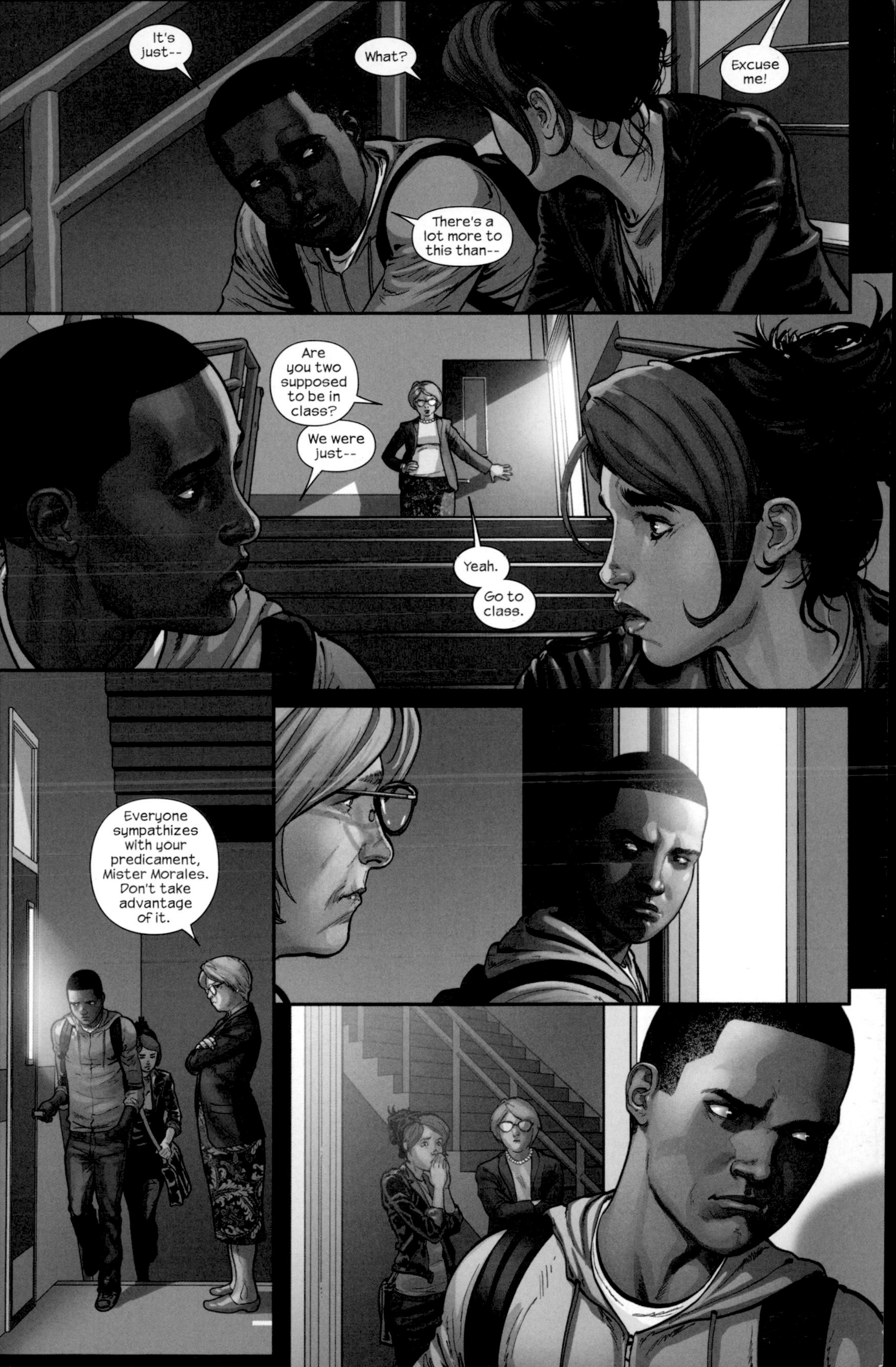
It's just--
What?
Excuse me!
There's a lot more to this than--
Are you two supposed to be in class?
We were just--
Yeah.
Go to class.
Everyone sympathizes with your predicament, Mister Morales. Don't take advantage of it.

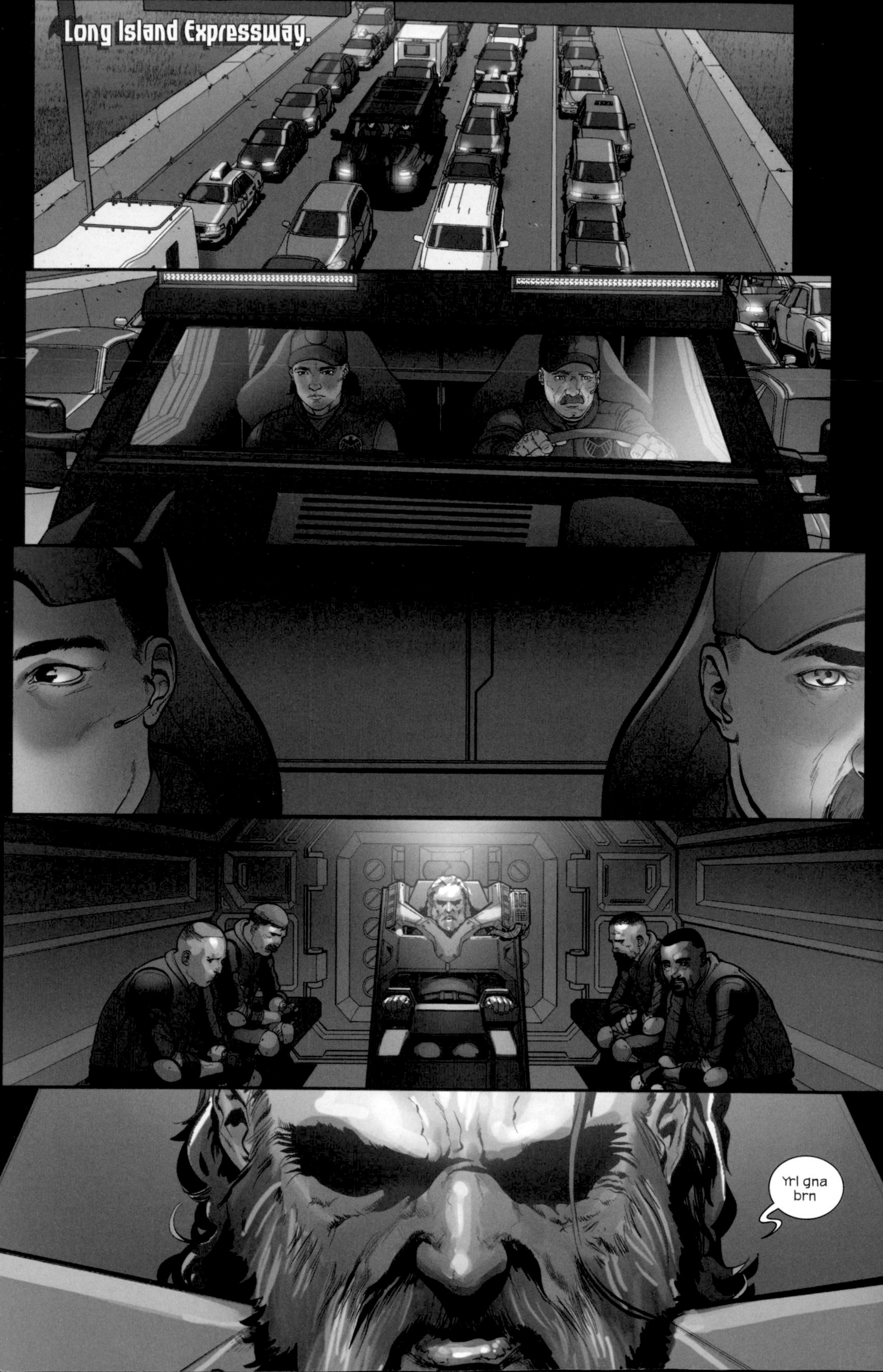
Long Island Expressway.
Yrl gna brn

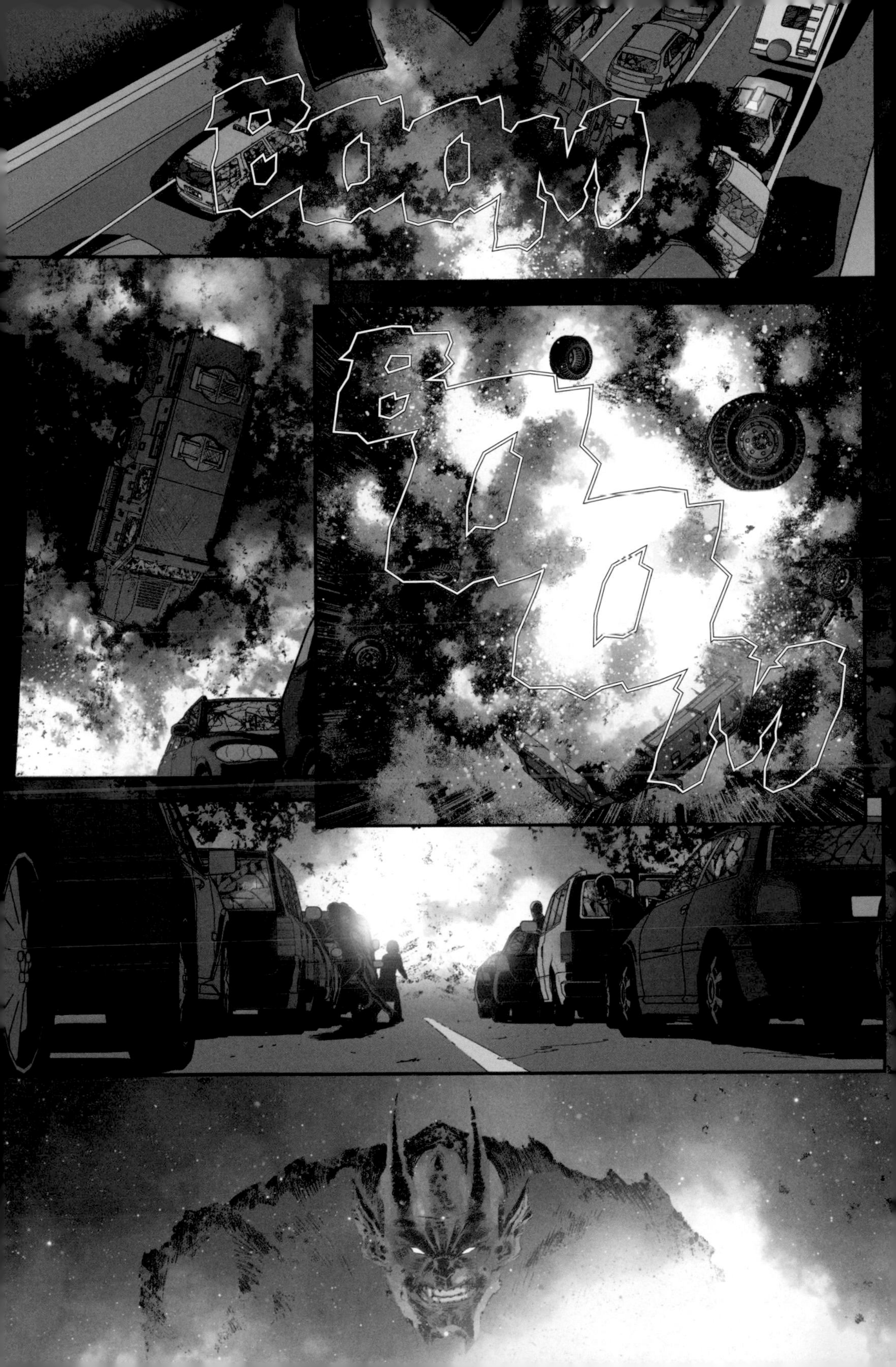
BOOM
BOOOM

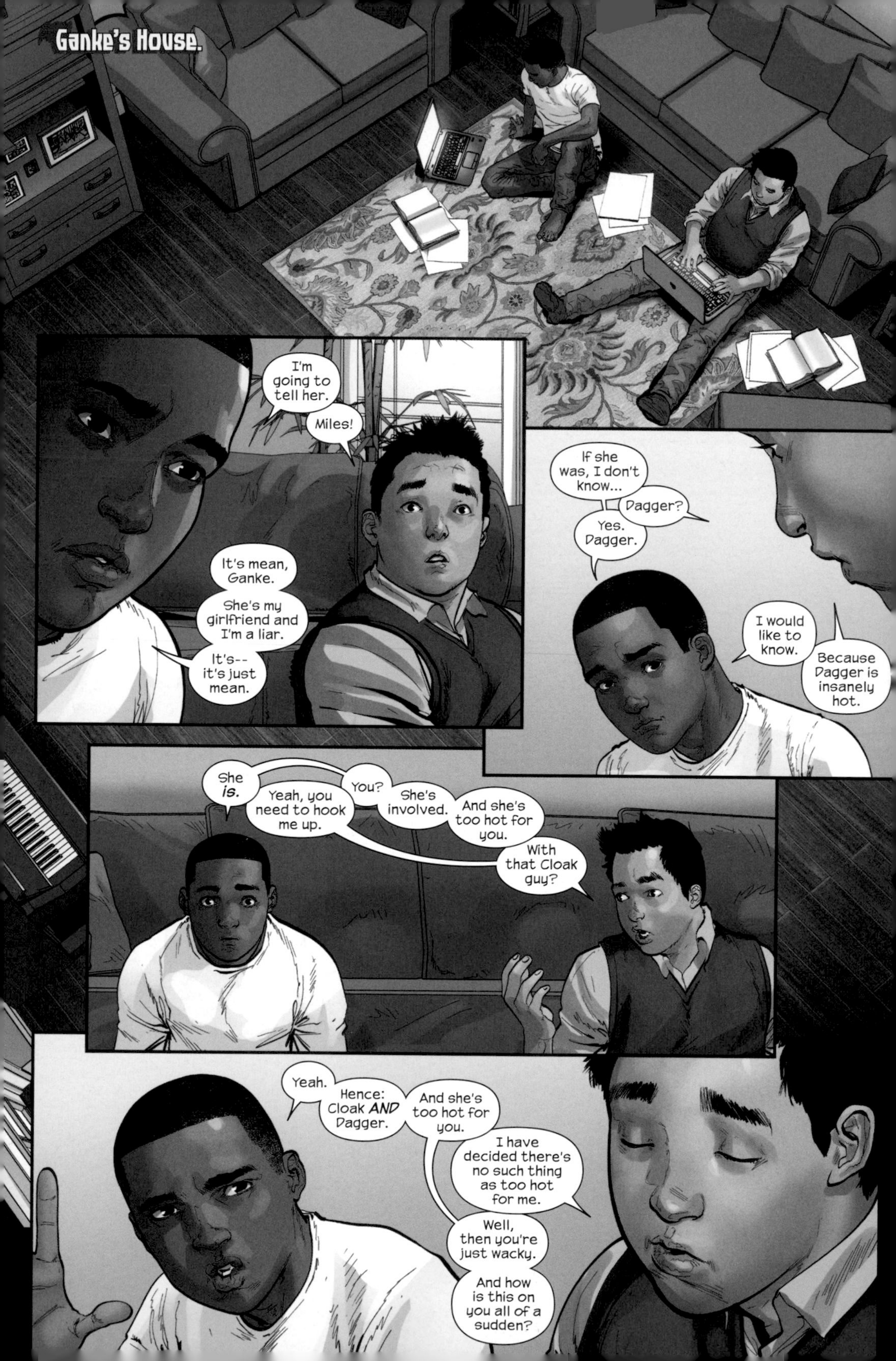
Ganke's House.
I'm going to tell her.
Miles!
It's mean, Ganke.
She's my girlfriend and I'm a liar.
It's-- it's just mean.
If she was, I don't know...
Dagger?
Yes. Dagger.
I would like to know.
Because Dagger is insanely hot.
She *is.*
You?
Yeah, you need to hook me up.
She's involved.
And she's too hot for you.
With that Cloak guy?
Yeah.
Hence: Cloak *AND* Dagger.
And she's too hot for you.
I have decided there's no such thing as too hot for me.
Well, then you're just wacky.
And how is this on you all of a sudden?

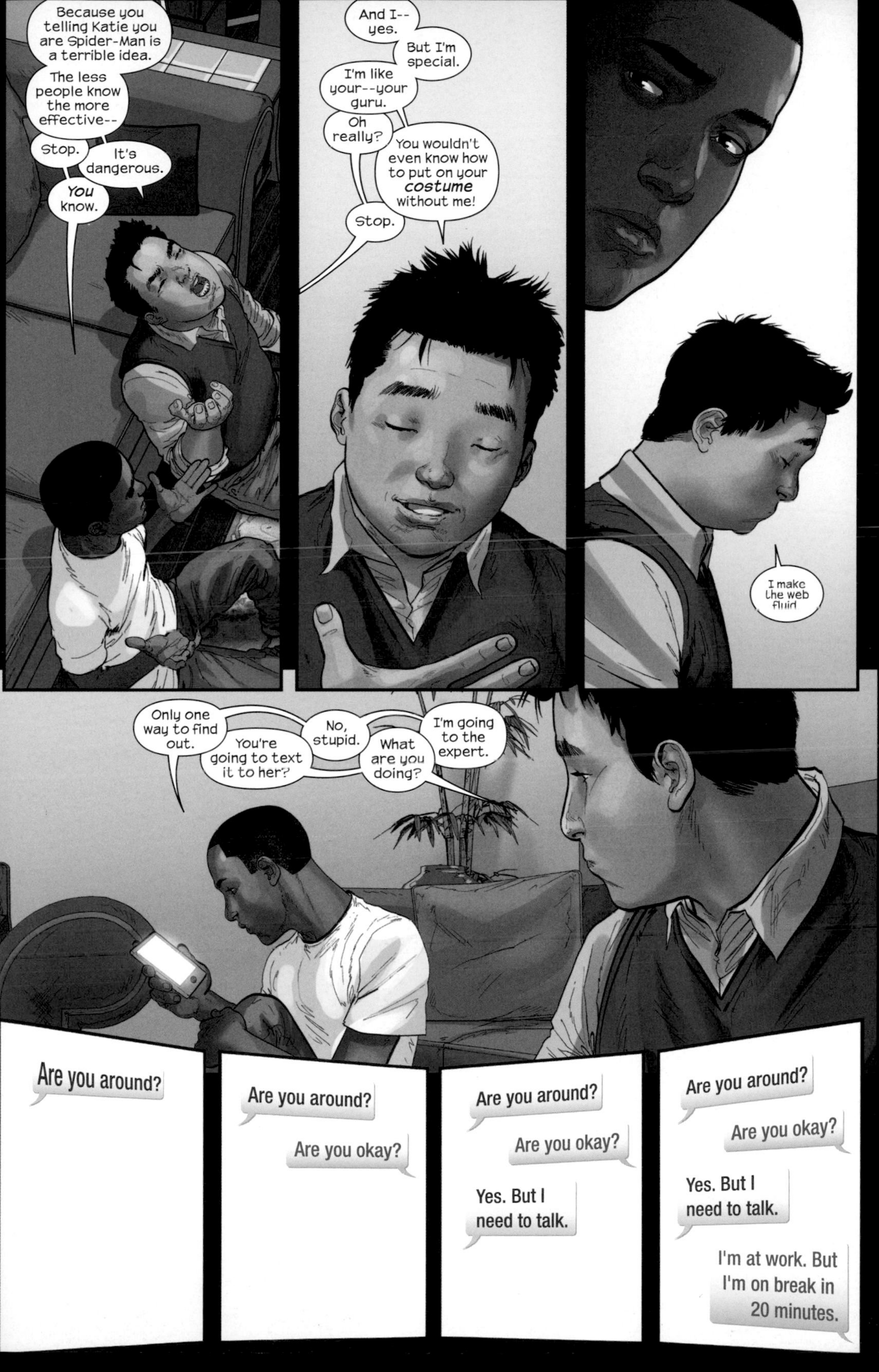

Because you telling Katie you are Spider-Man is a terrible idea.
The less people know the more effective--
Stop.
It's dangerous.
You know.
And I-- yes.
But I'm special.
I'm like your--your guru.
Oh really?
You wouldn't even know how to put on your costume without me!
Stop.
I make the web fluid
Only one way to find out.
You're going to text it to her?
No, stupid.
What are you doing?
I'm going to the expert.
Are you around?
Are you around?
Are you okay?
Are you around?
Are you okay?
Yes. But I need to talk.
Are you around?
Are you okay?
Yes. But I need to talk.
I'm at work. But I'm on break in 20 minutes.

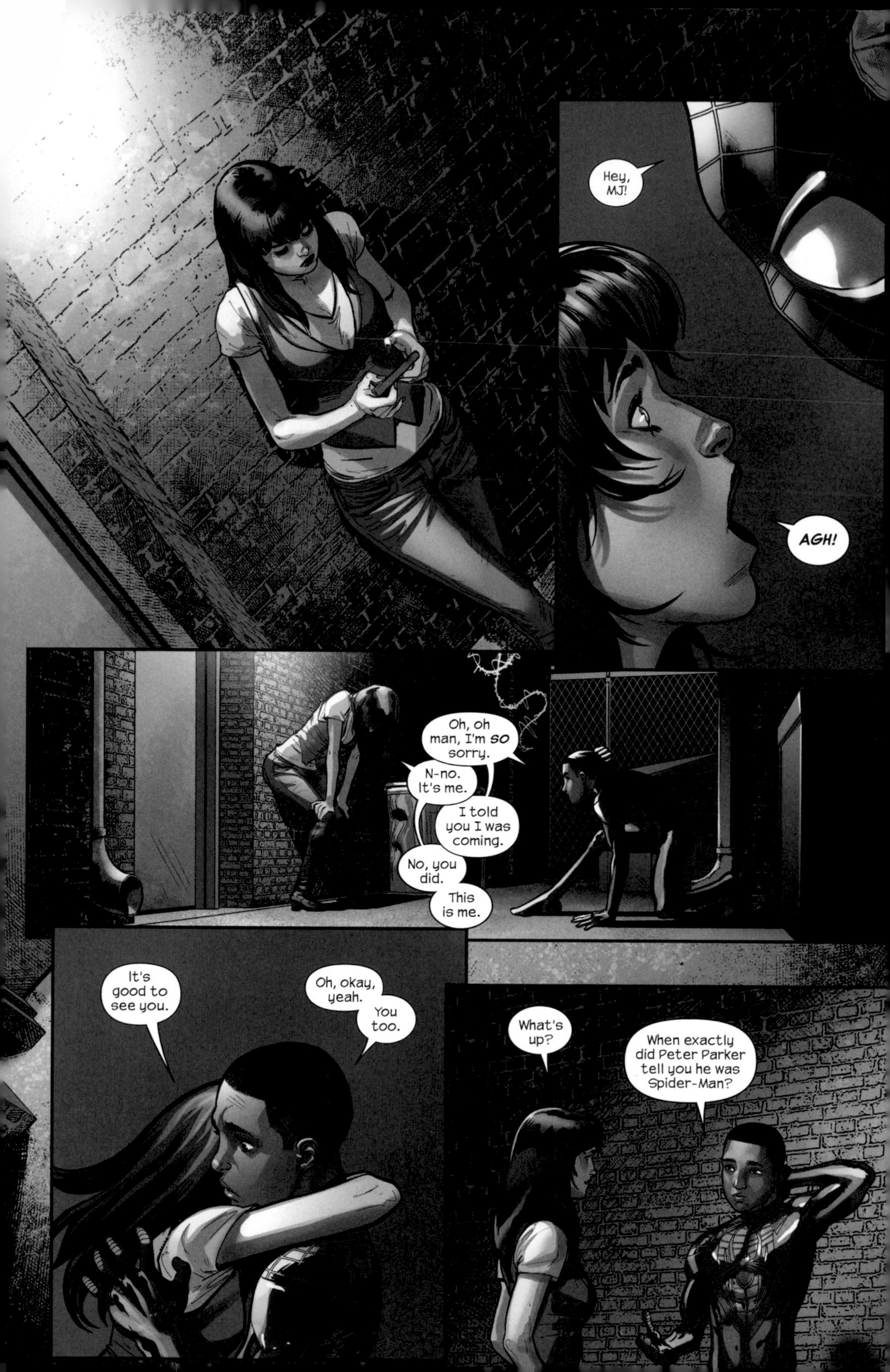
Hey, MJ!
AGH!
Oh, oh man, I'm SO sorry.
N-no. It's me.
I told you I was coming.
No, you did.
This is me.
It's good to see you.
Oh, okay, yeah.
You too.
What's up?
When exactly did Peter Parker tell you he was Spider-Man?

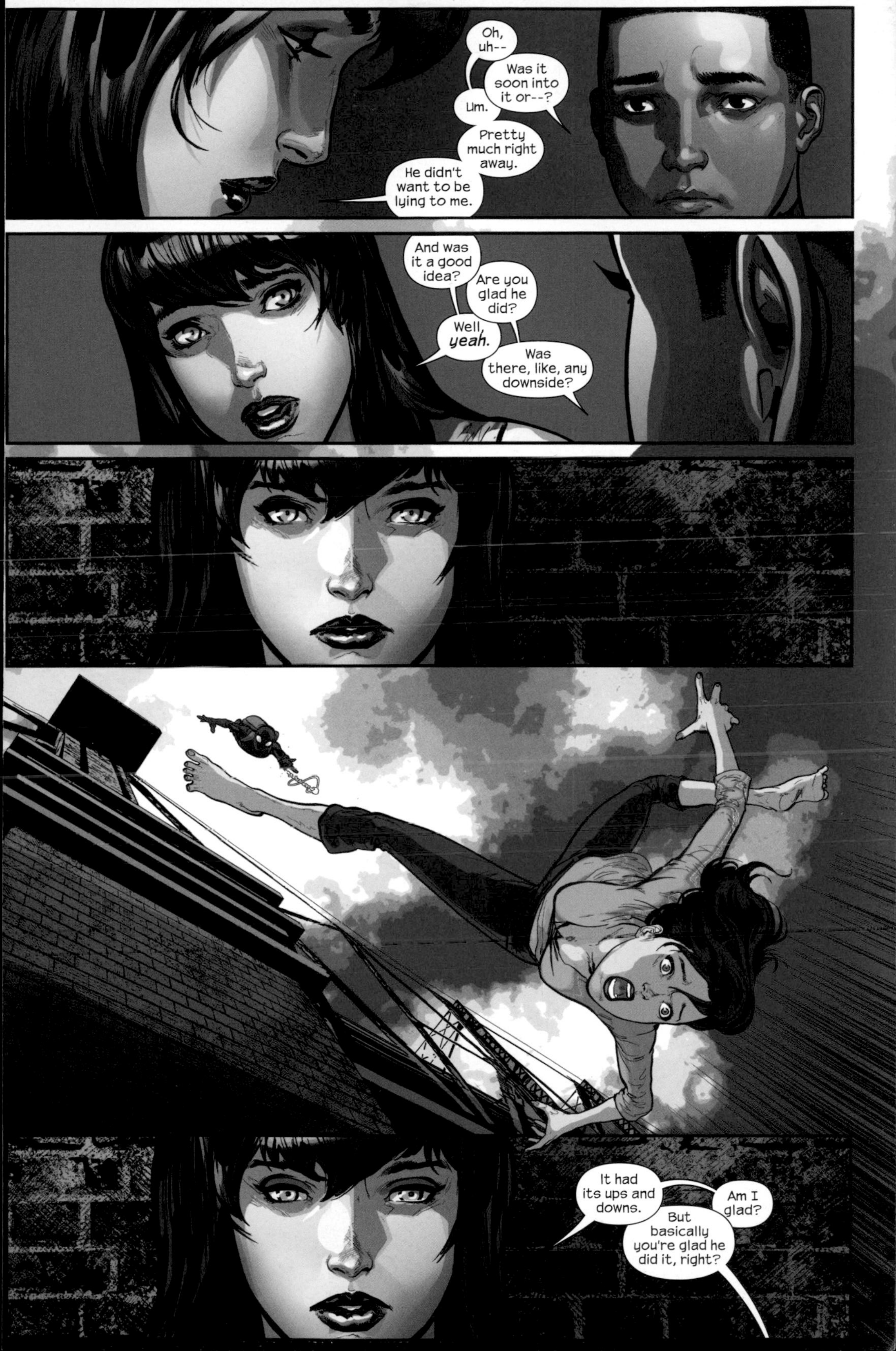

Oh, uh--
Was it soon into it or--?
Um.
Pretty much right away.
He didn't want to be lying to me.
And was it a good idea?
Are you glad he did?
Well, *yeah.*
Was there, like, any downside?
It had its ups and downs.
Am I glad?
But basically you're glad he did it, right?

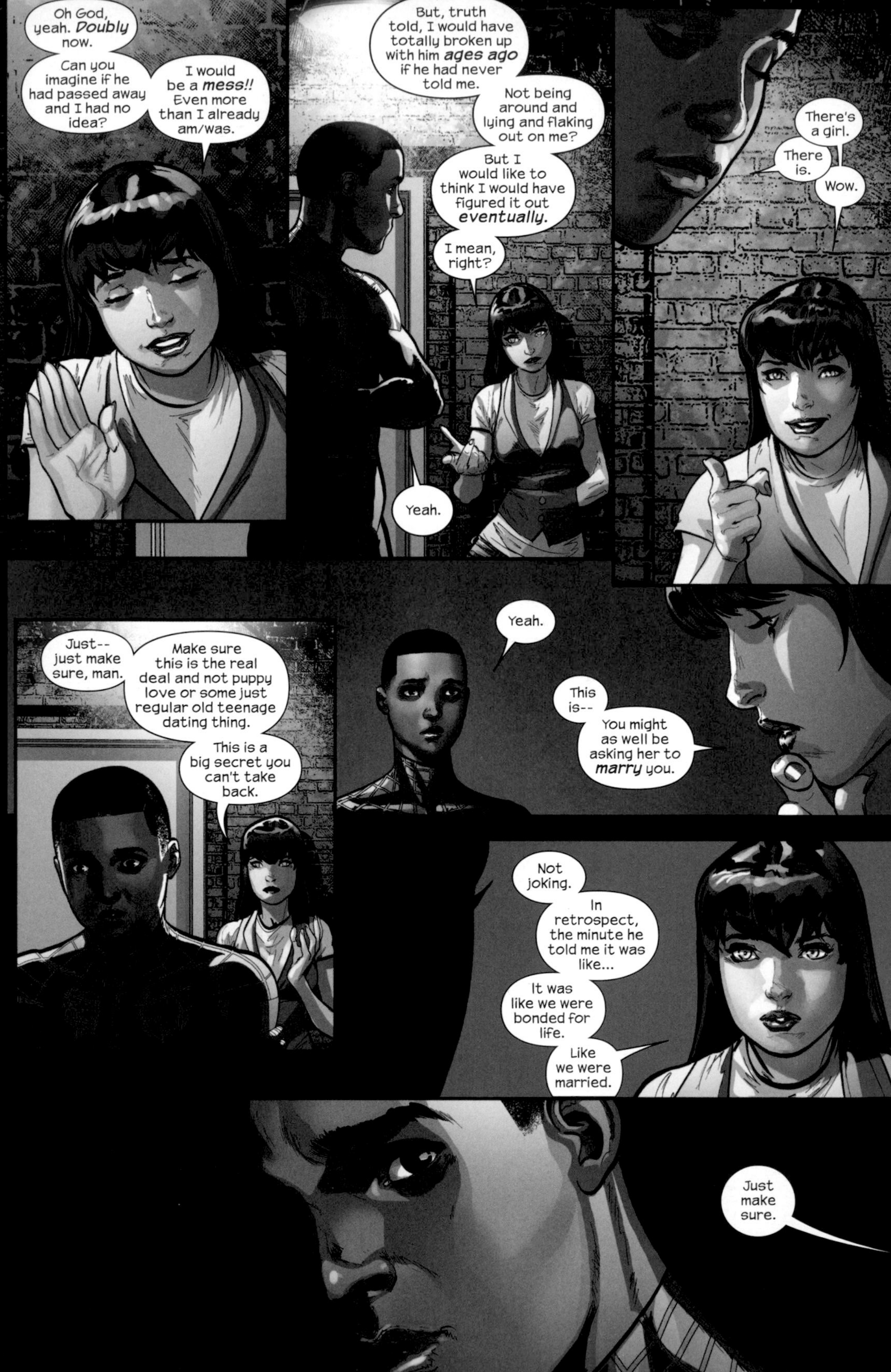

Oh God, yeah. Doubly now.
Can you imagine if he had passed away and I had no idea?
I would be a mess!! Even more than I already am/was.
But, truth told, I would have totally broken up with him ages ago if he had never told me.
Not being around and lying and flaking out on me?
But I would like to think I would have figured it out eventually.
I mean, right?
Yeah.
There's a girl.
There is.
Wow.
Just-- just make sure, man.
Make sure this is the real deal and not puppy love or some just regular old teenage dating thing.
This is a big secret you can't take back.
Yeah.
This is--
You might as well be asking her to marry you.
Not joking.
In retrospect, the minute he told me it was like...
It was like we were bonded for life.
Like we were married.
Just make sure.

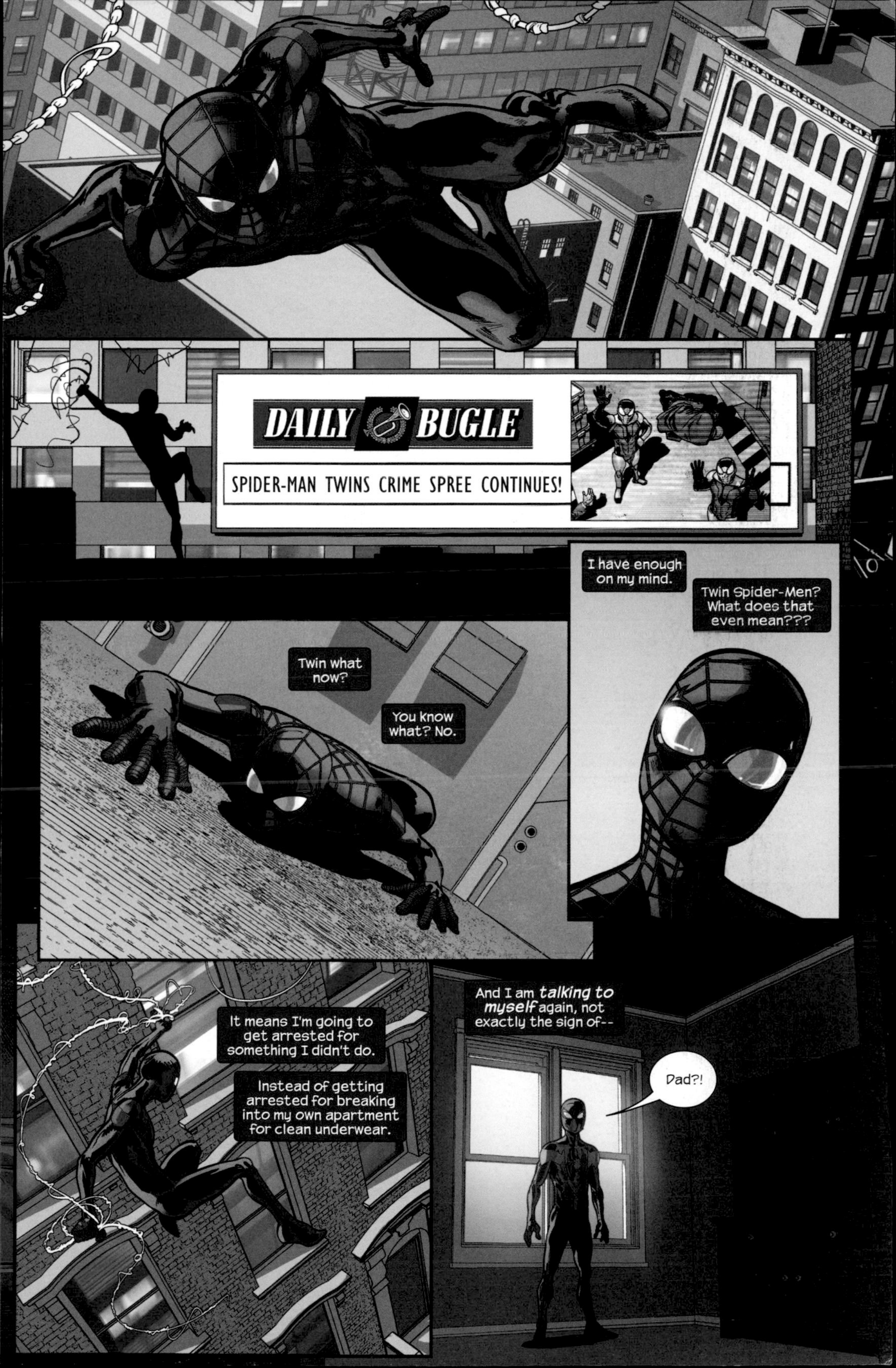
DAILY BUGLE
SPIDER-MAN TWINS CRIME SPREE CONTINUES!
I have enough on my mind.
Twin Spider-Men? What does that even mean???
Twin what now?
You know what? No.
It means I'm going to get arrested for something I didn't do.
Instead of getting arrested for breaking into my own apartment for clean underwear.
And I am *talking to myself* again, not exactly the sign of--
Dad?!

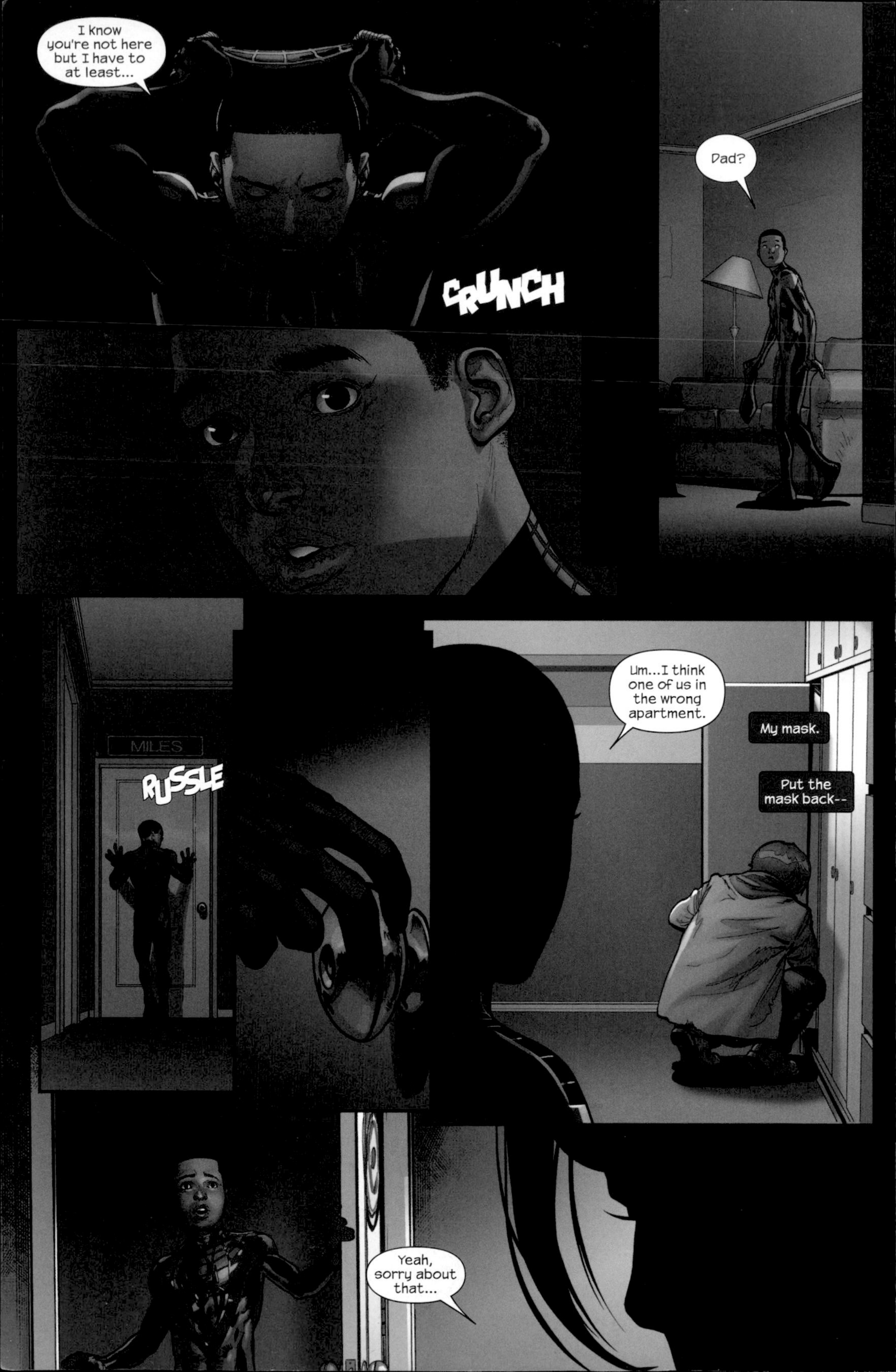

I know you're not here but I have to at least...
CRUNCH
Dad?
MILES
RUSSLE
Um...I think one of us in the wrong apartment.
My mask.
Put the mask back--
Yeah, sorry about that...

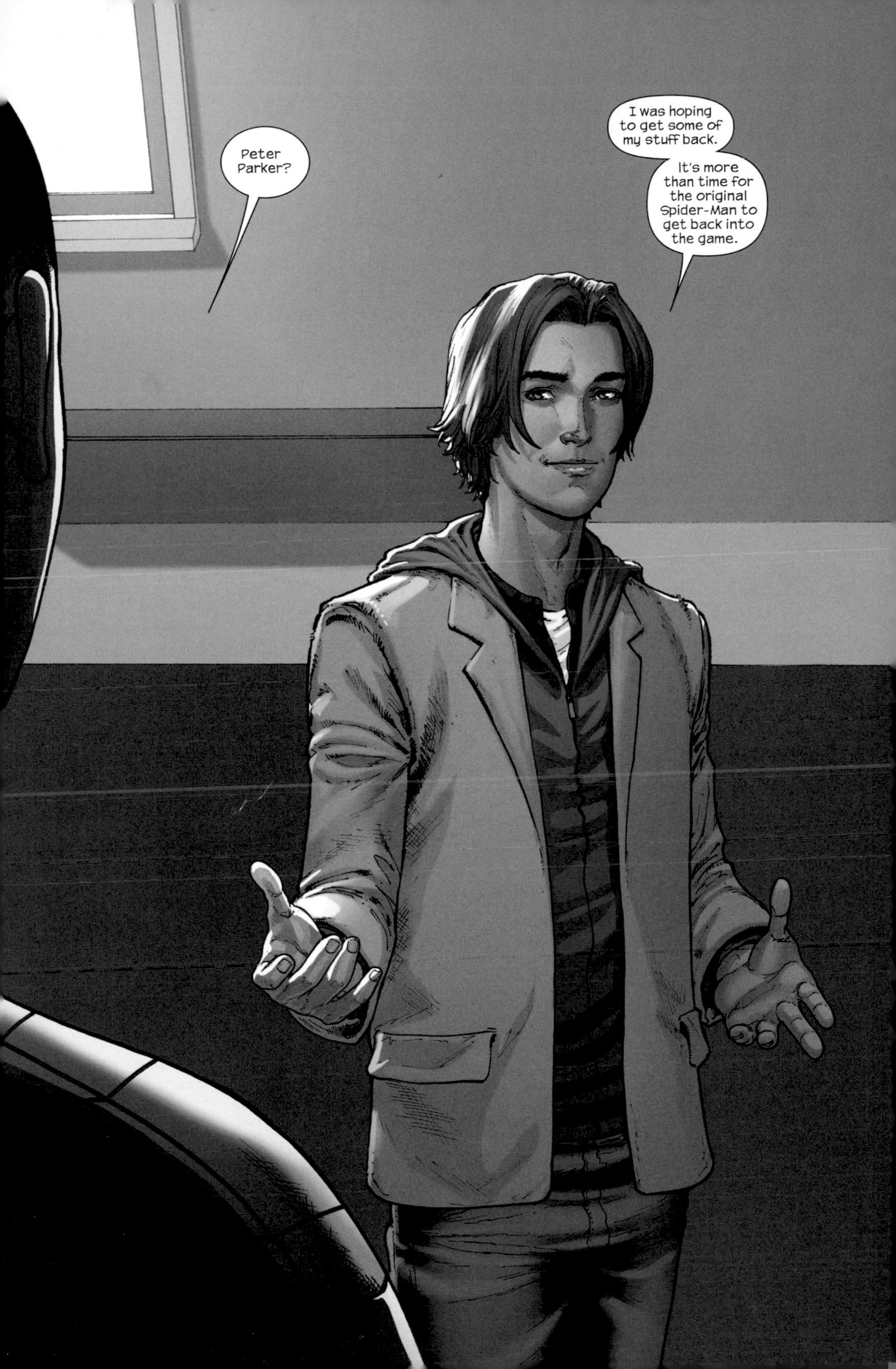
Peter Parker?
I was hoping to get some of my stuff back.
It's more than time for the original Spider-Man to get back into the game.

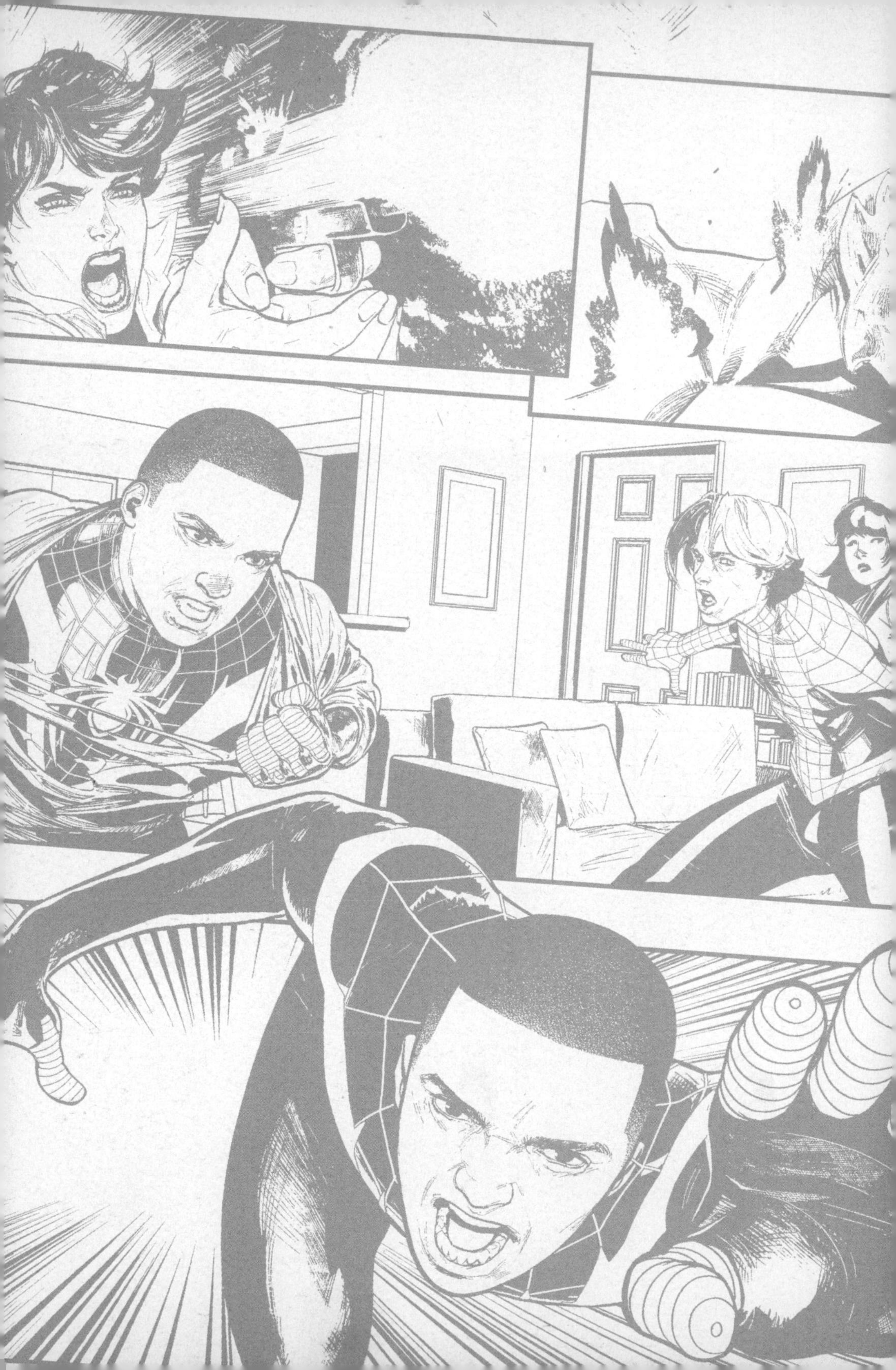

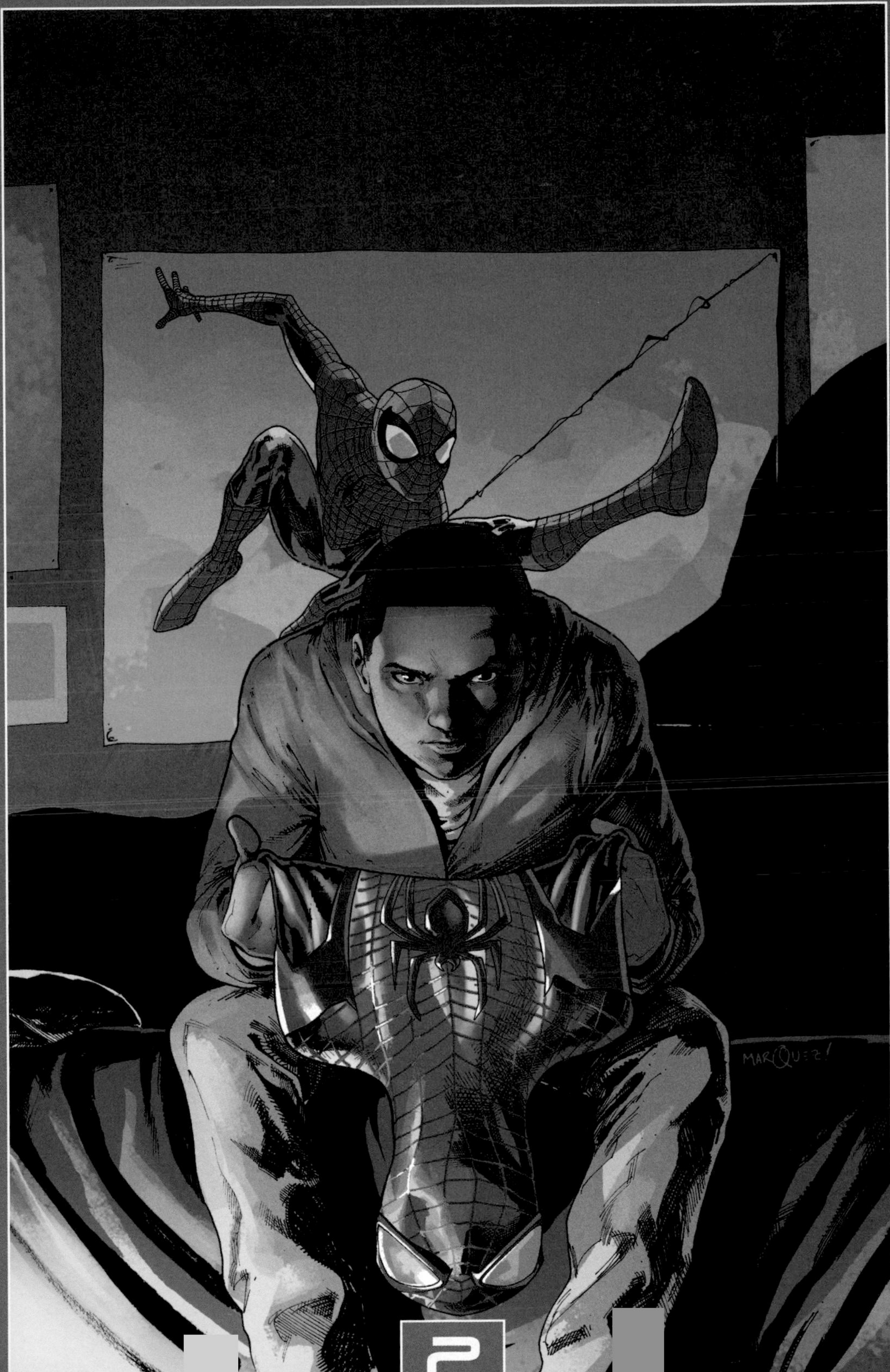
MARQUEZ!
2

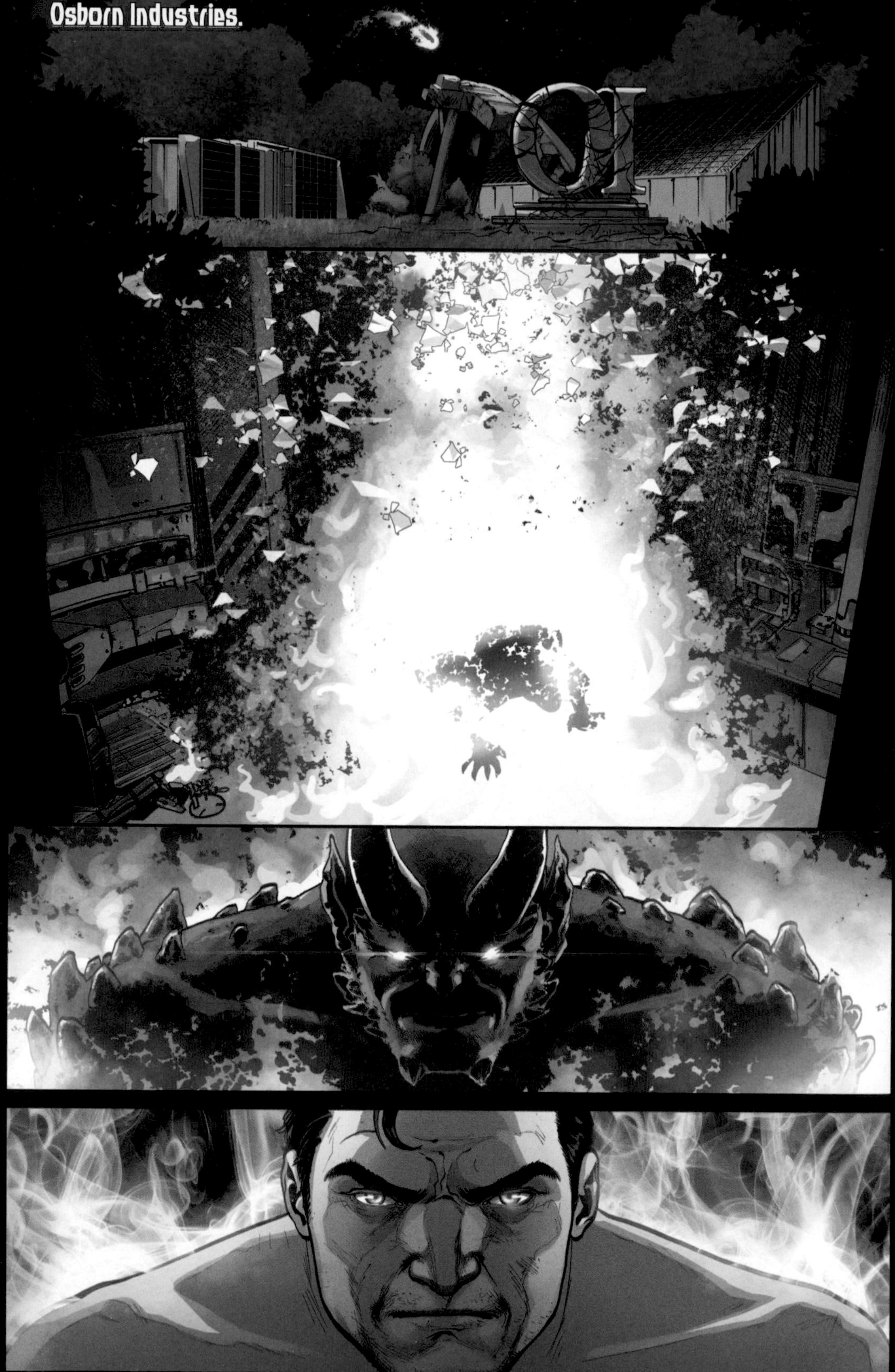
Osborn Industries.

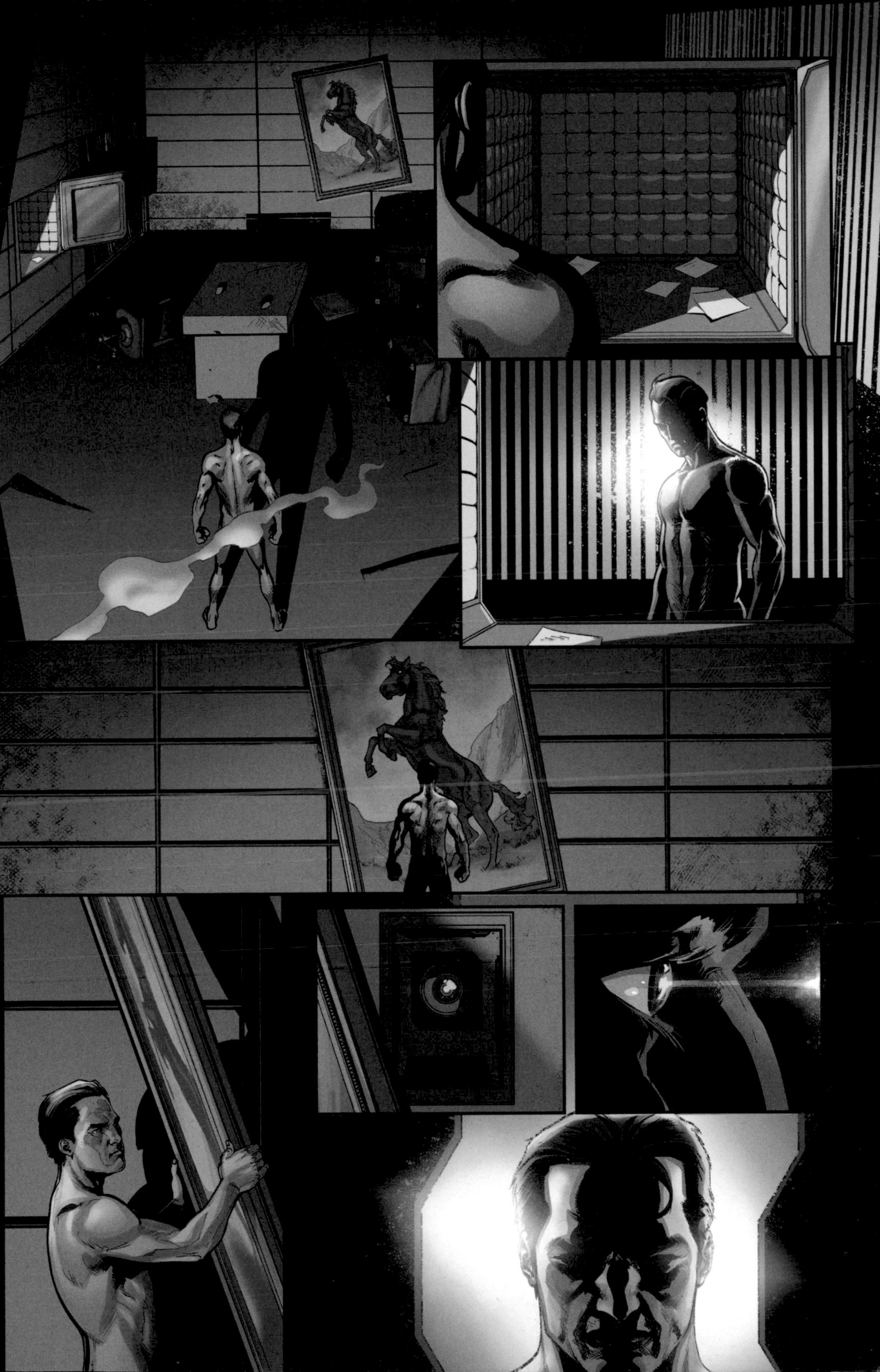

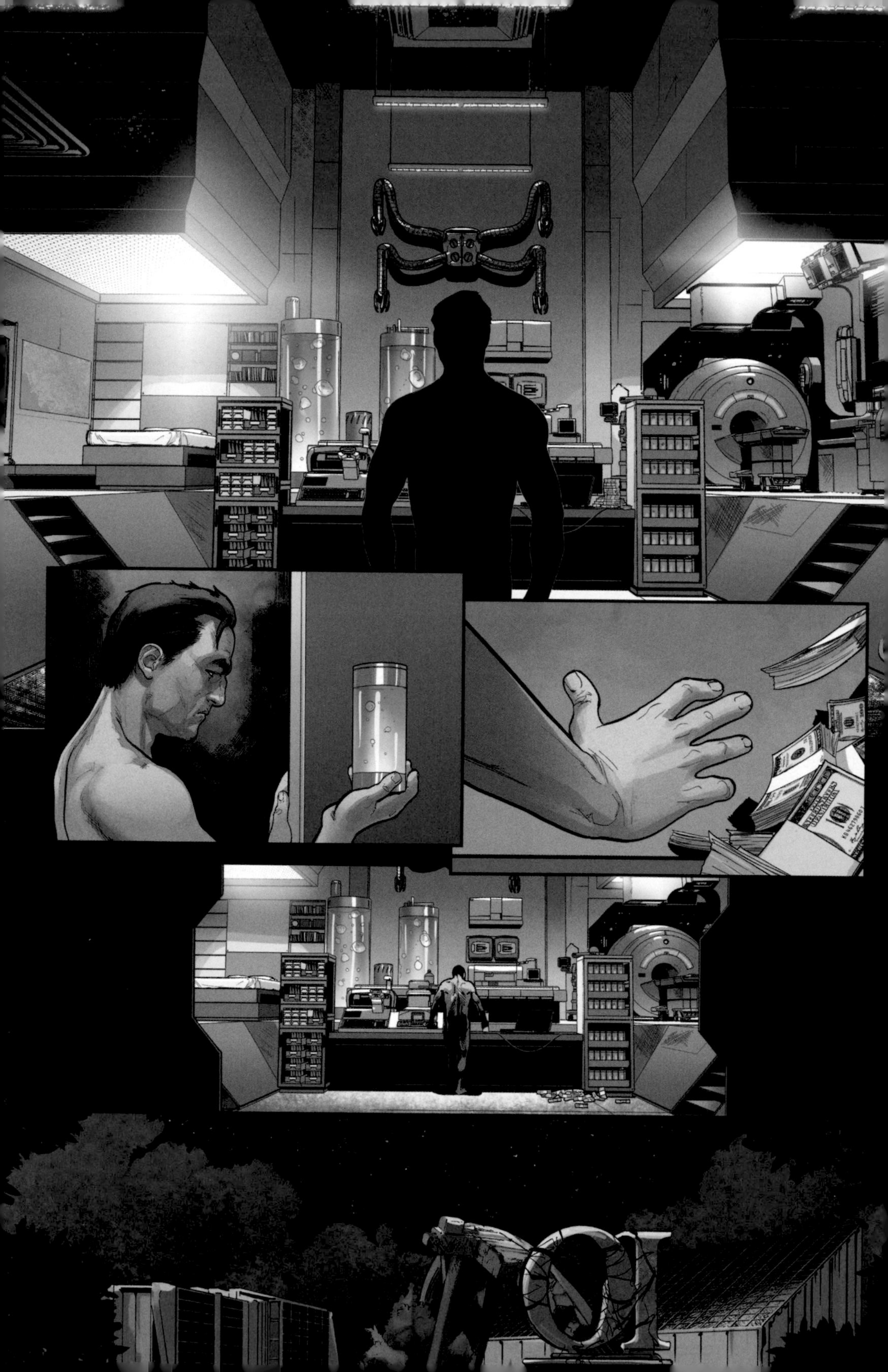

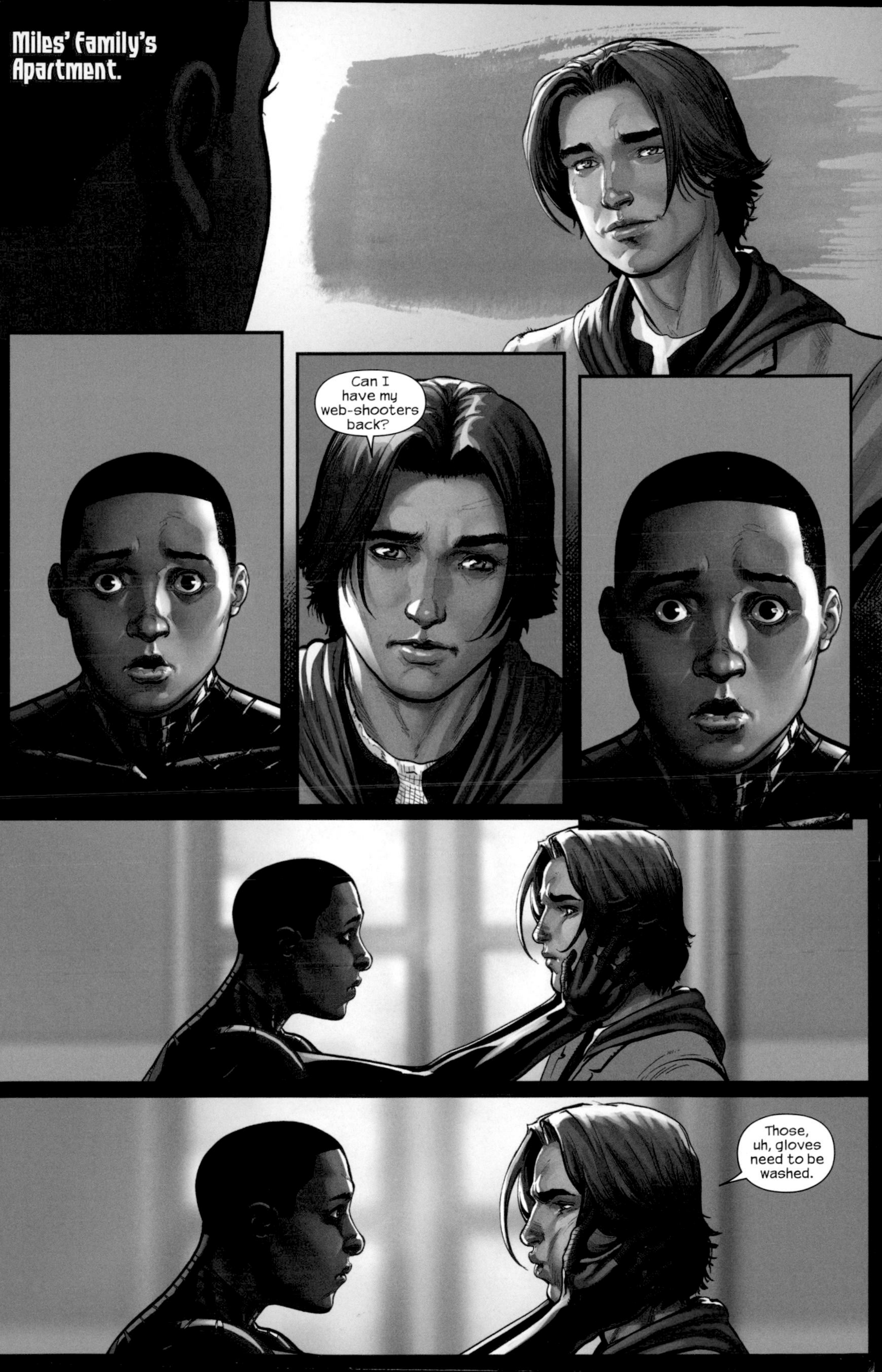
Miles' Family's Apartment.
Can I have my web-shooters back?
Those, uh, gloves need to be washed.

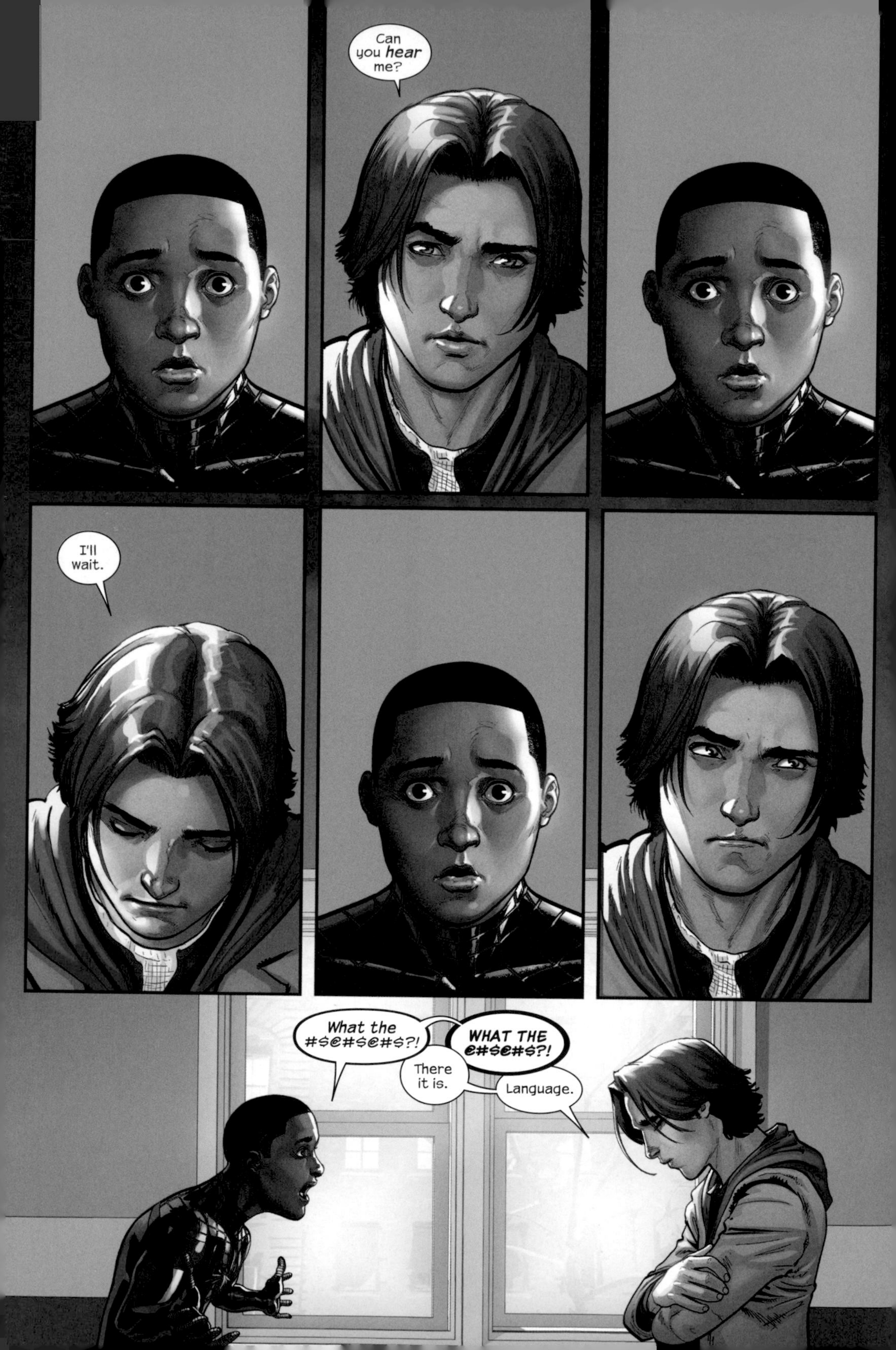
Can you *hear* me?
I'll wait.
What the #$@#$@#$?!
WHAT THE @#$@#$?!
There it is.
Language.

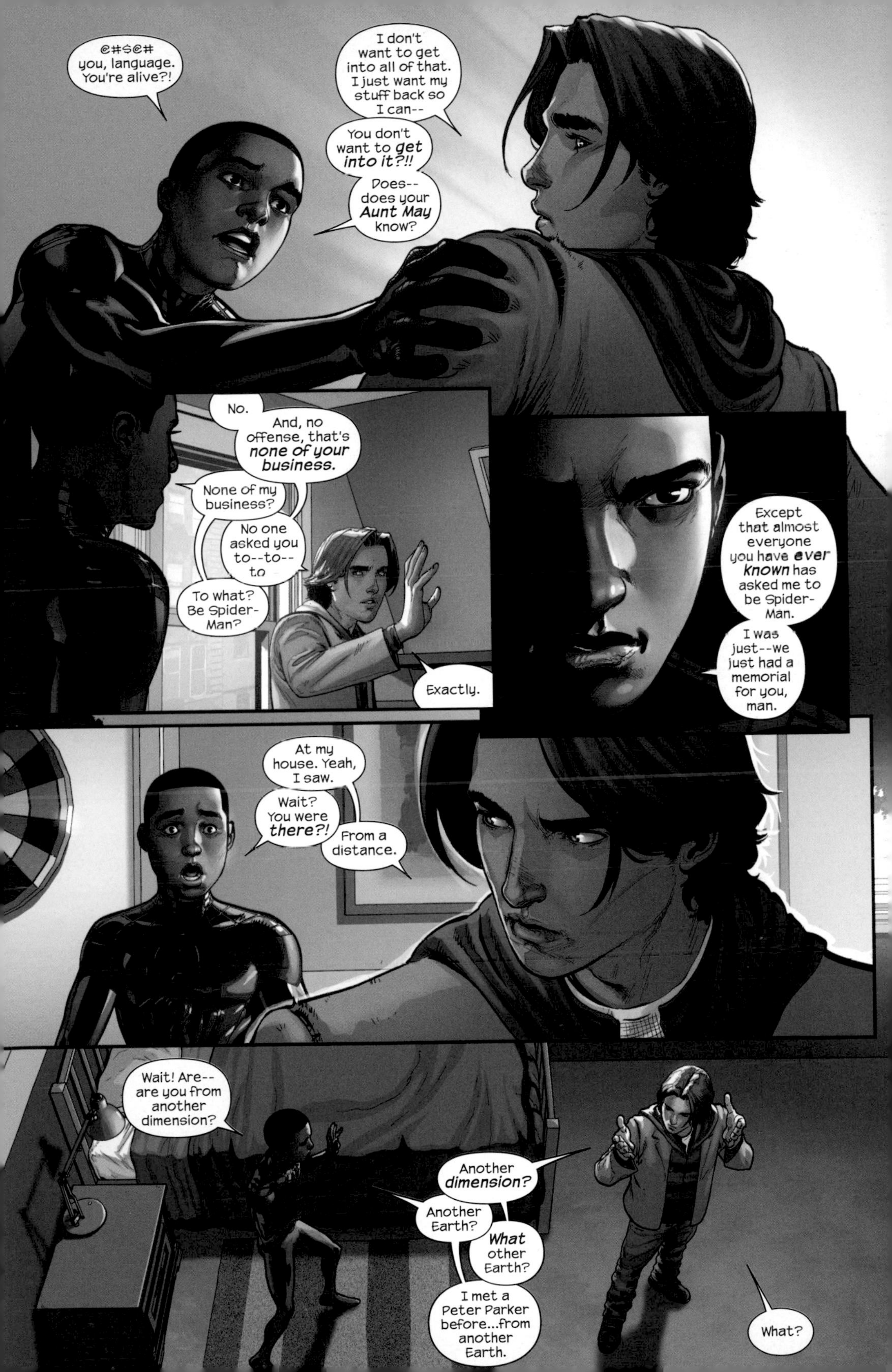
@#$@# you, language. You're alive?!
I don't want to get into all of that. I just want my stuff back so I can--
You don't want to get into it?!!
Does-- does your Aunt May know?
No.
And, no offense, that's none of your business.
None of my business?
No one asked you to--to--to
To what? Be Spider-Man?
Exactly.
Except that almost everyone you have ever known has asked me to be Spider-Man.
I was just--we just had a memorial for you, man.
At my house. Yeah, I saw.
Wait? You were there?!
From a distance.
Wait! Are-- are you from another dimension?
Another dimension?
Another Earth?
What other Earth?
I met a Peter Parker before...from another Earth.
What?

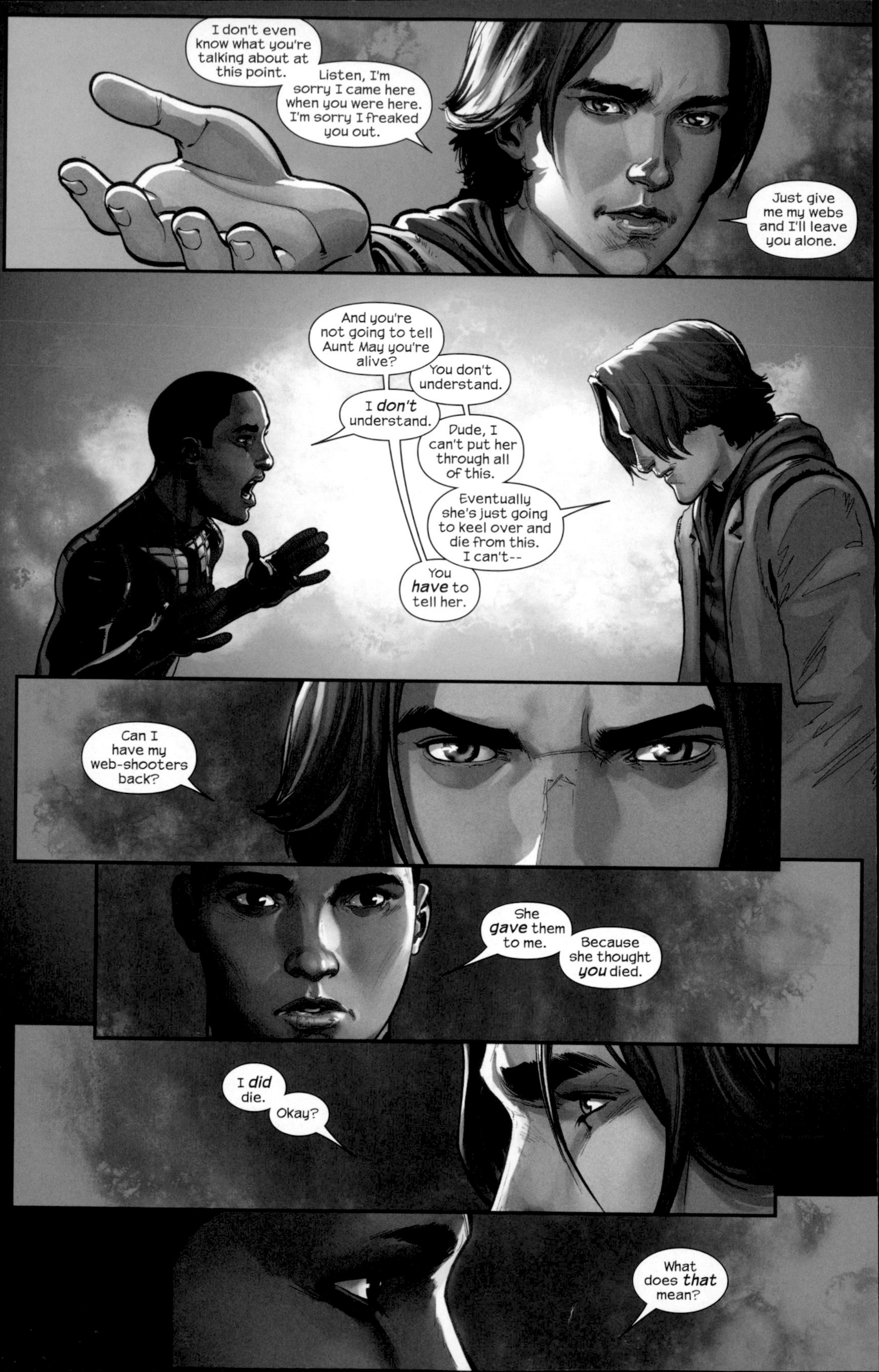
I don't even know what you're talking about at this point.
Listen, I'm sorry I came here when you were here. I'm sorry I freaked you out.
Just give me my webs and I'll leave you alone.
And you're not going to tell Aunt May you're alive?
You don't understand.
I *don't* understand.
Dude, I can't put her through all of this.
Eventually she's just going to keel over and die from this. I can't--
You *have* to tell her.
Can I have my web-shooters back?
She *gave* them to me.
Because she thought *you* died.
I *did* die.
Okay?
What does *that* mean?

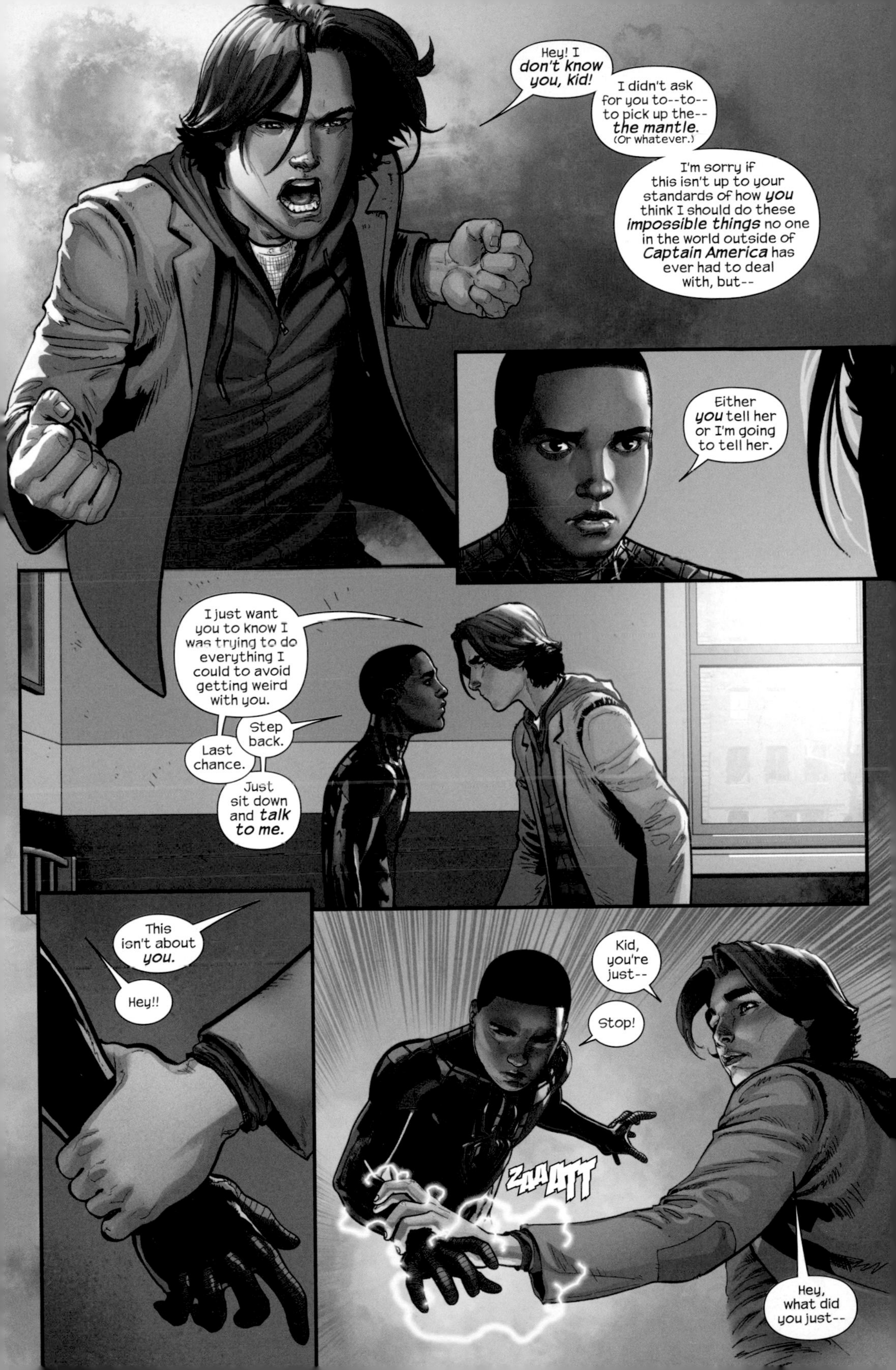
Hey! I don't know you, kid!
I didn't ask for you to--to--to pick up the--the mantle. (Or whatever.)
I'm sorry if this isn't up to your standards of how you think I should do these impossible things no one in the world outside of Captain America has ever had to deal with, but--
Either you tell her or I'm going to tell her.
I just want you to know I was trying to do everything I could to avoid getting weird with you.
Step back.
Last chance.
Just sit down and talk to me.
This isn't about you.
Hey!!
Kid, you're just--
Stop!
ZAAATT
Hey, what did you just--

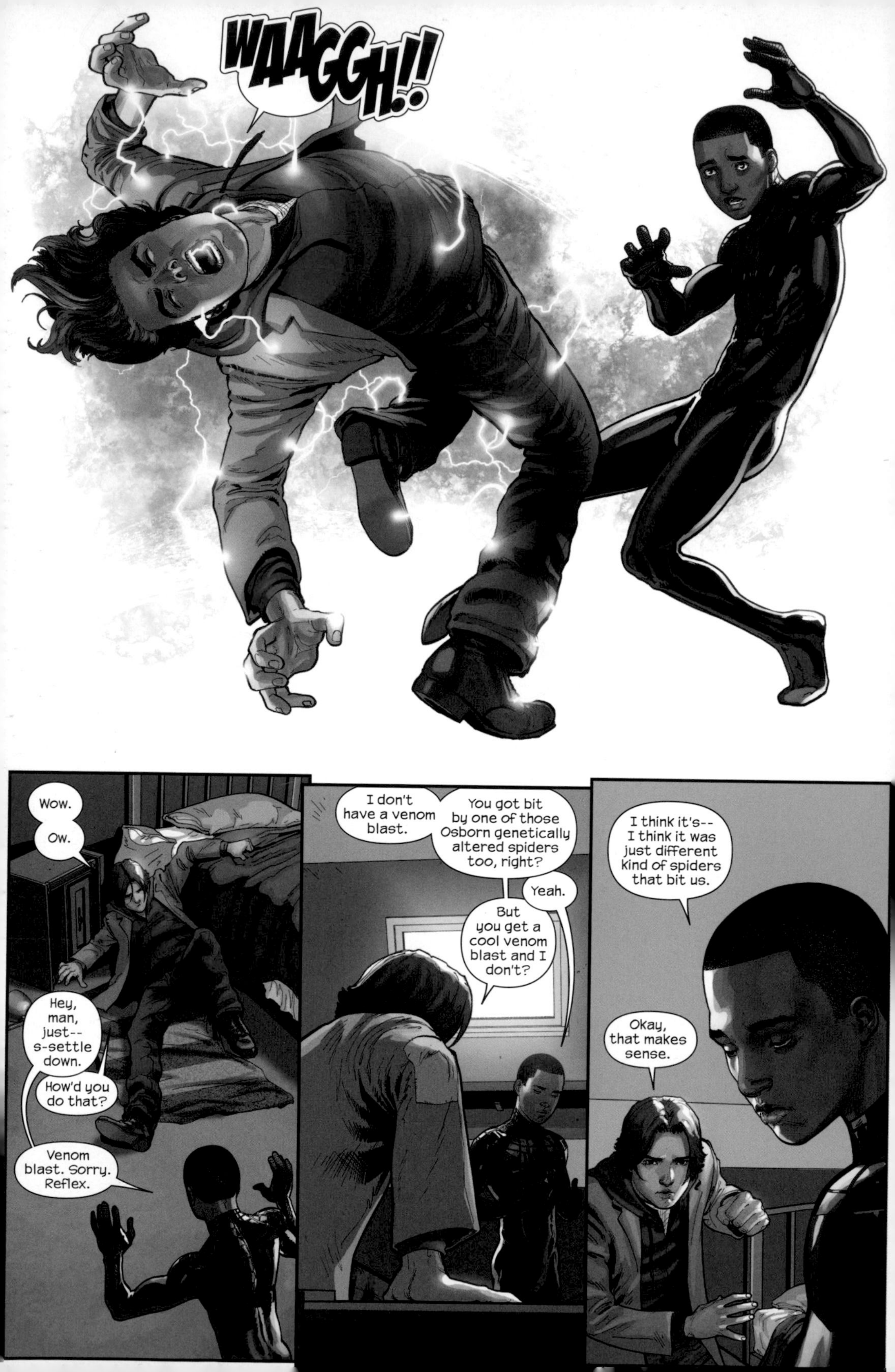
WAAGGH!!
Wow.
Ow.
Hey, man, just-- s-settle down.
How'd you do that?
Venom blast. Sorry. Reflex.
I don't have a venom blast.
You got bit by one of those Osborn genetically altered spiders too, right?
Yeah.
But you get a cool venom blast and I don't?
I think it's-- I think it was just different kind of spiders that bit us.
Okay, that makes sense.

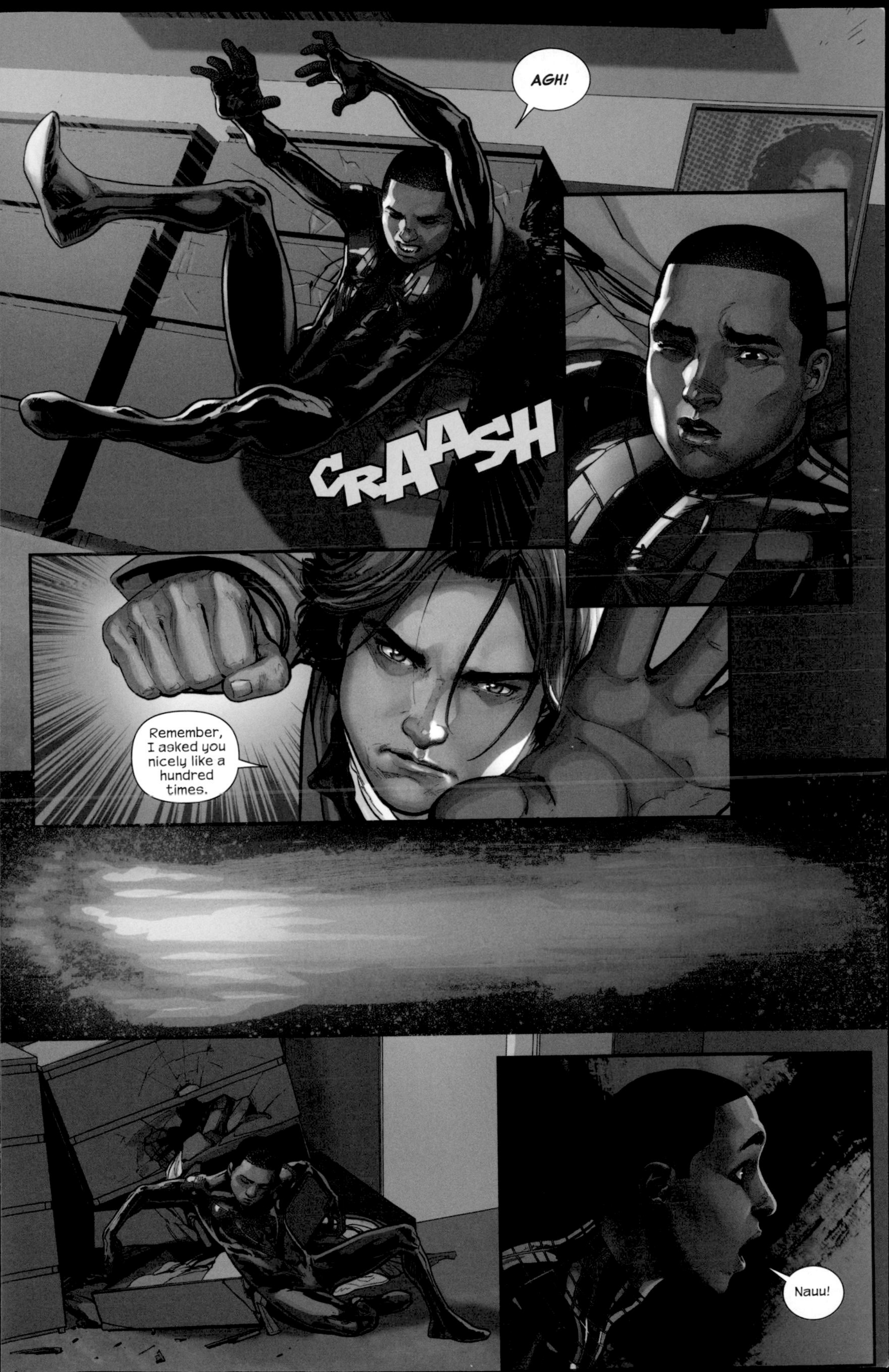
AGH!
CRAASH
Remember, I asked you nicely like a hundred times.
Nauu!

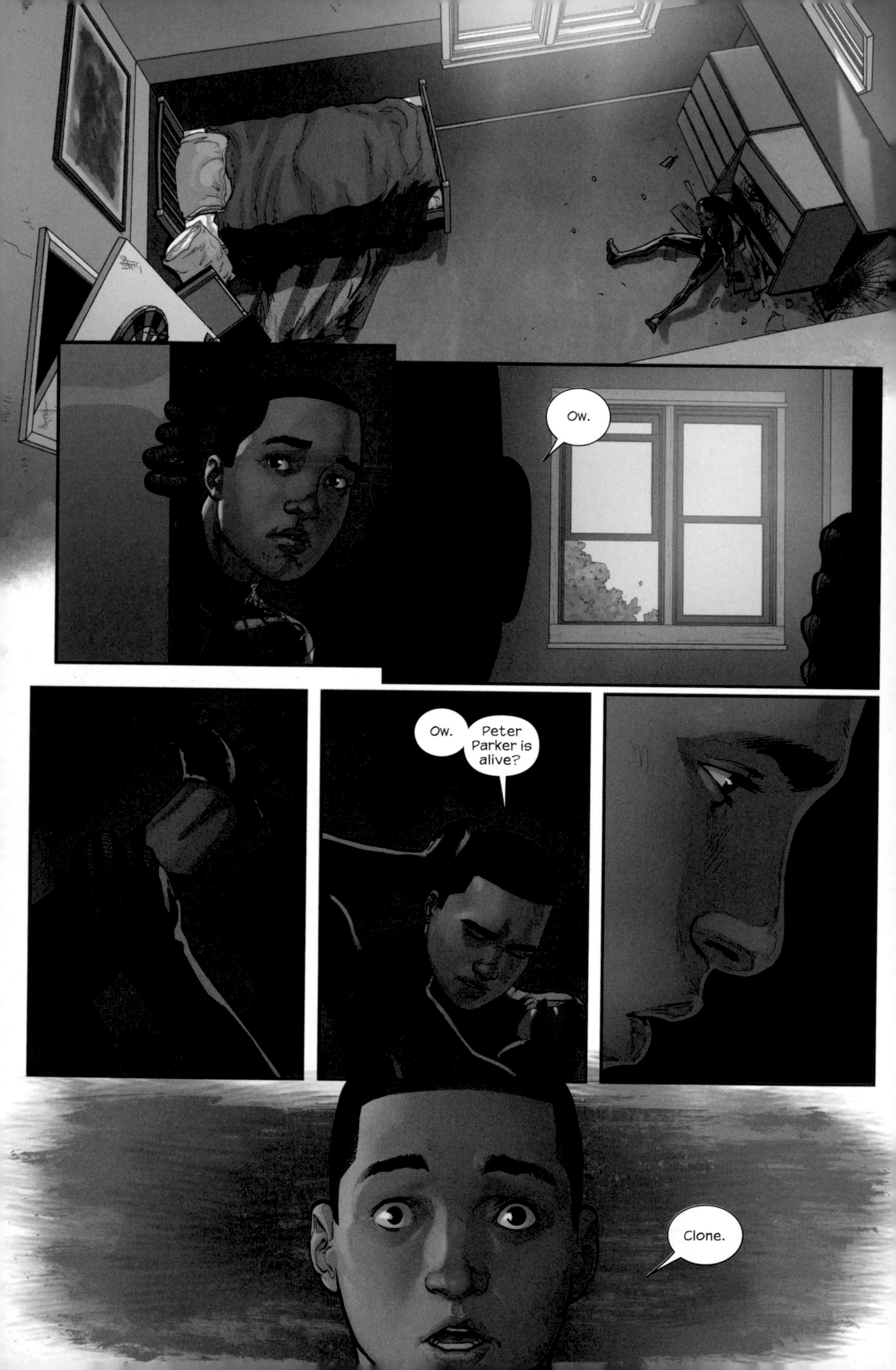
Ow.
Ow.
Peter Parker is alive?
Clone.

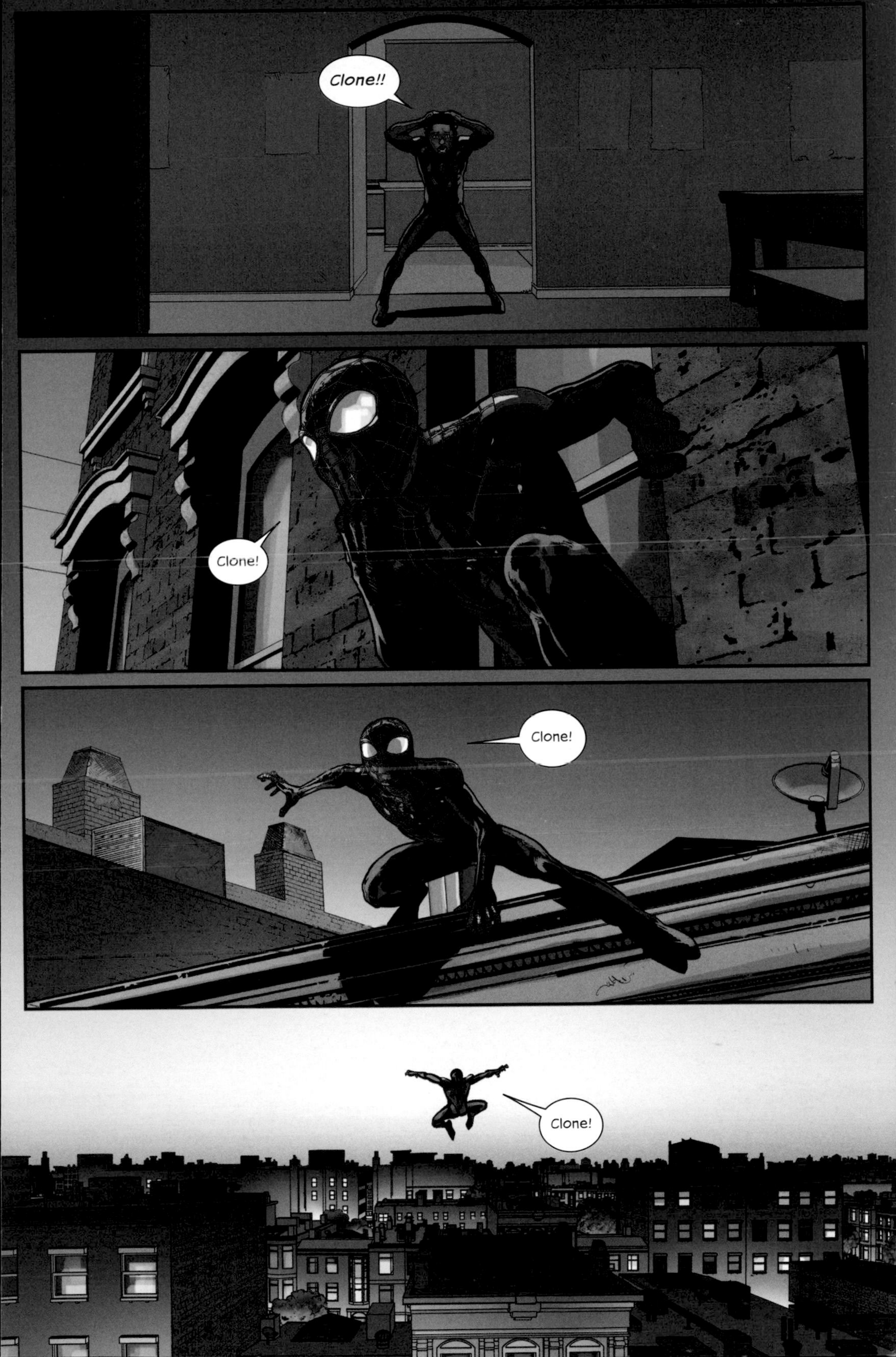
Clone!!
Clone!
Clone!
Clone!

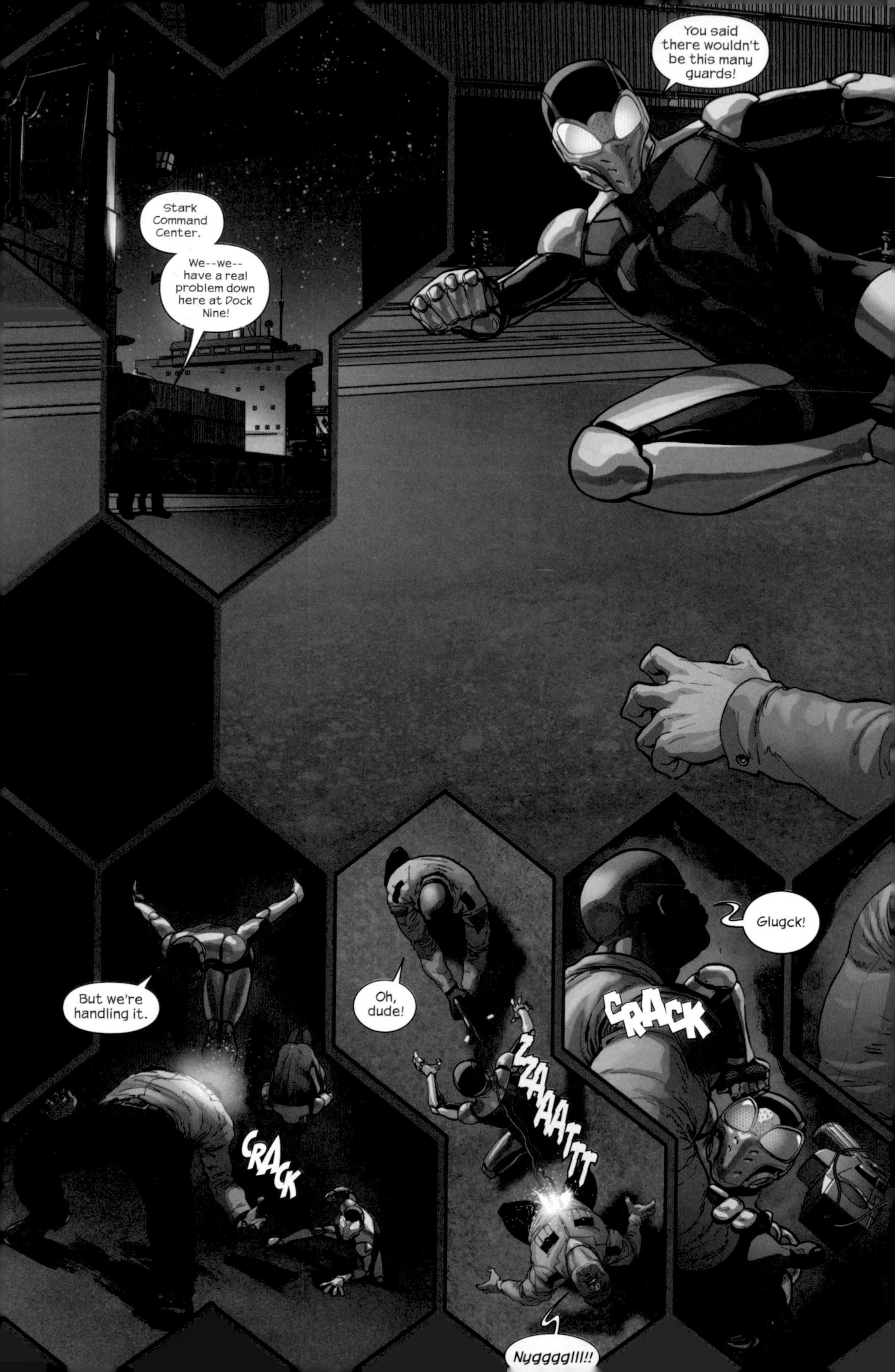
Stark Command Center.
We--we-- have a real problem down here at Dock Nine!
You said there wouldn't be this many guards!
But we're handling it.
CRACK
Oh, dude!
ZZAAAATTTT
Nyggggllll!!
Glugck!
CRACK

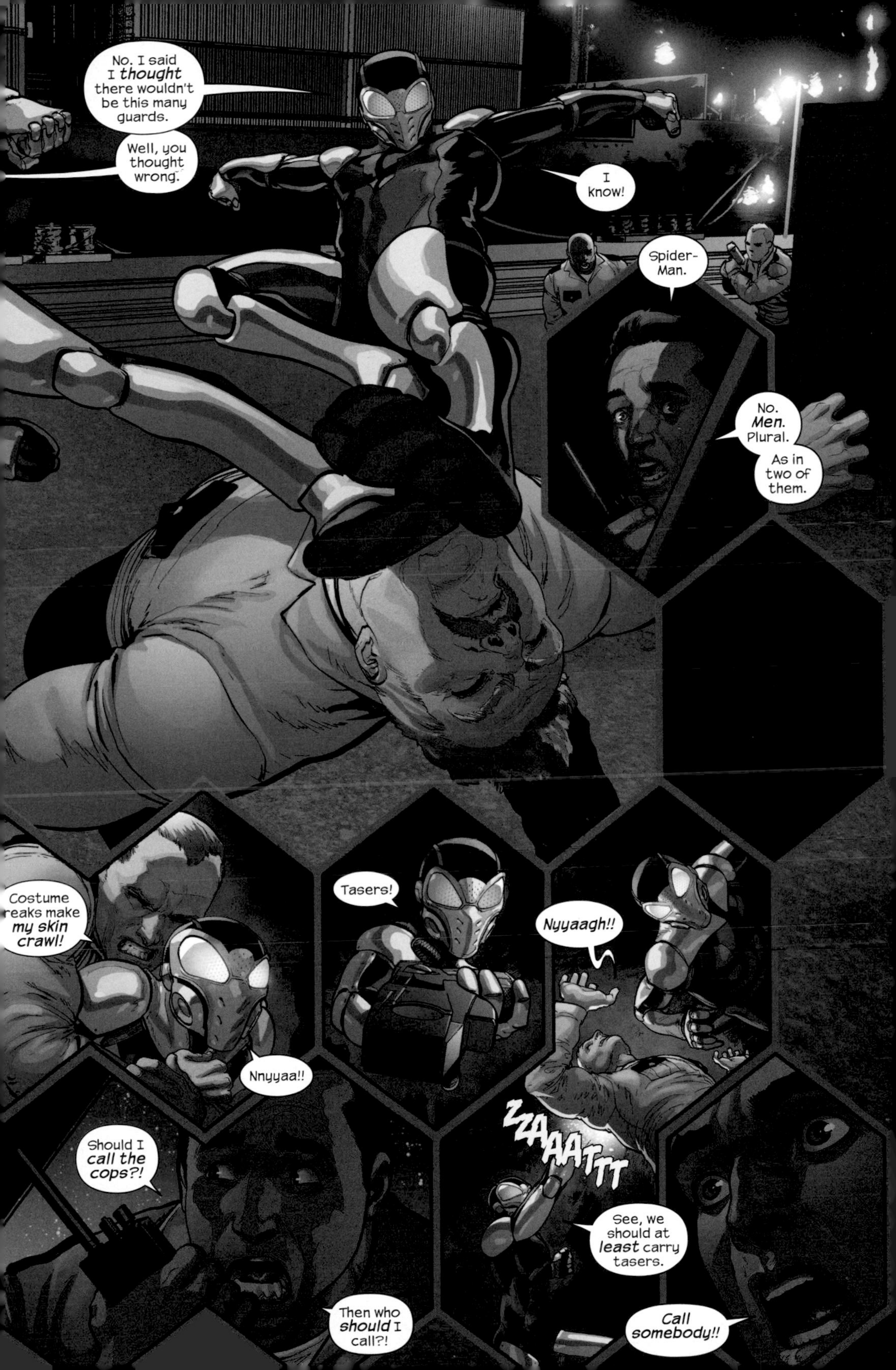
No. I said I thought there wouldn't be this many guards.
Well, you thought wrong.
I know!
Spider-Man.
No. Men. Plural.
As in two of them.
Costume reaks make my skin crawl!
Nnyyaa!!
Tasers!
Nyyaagh!!
ZZAAATTT
Should I call the cops?!
Then who should I call?!
See, we should at least carry tasers.
Call somebody!!

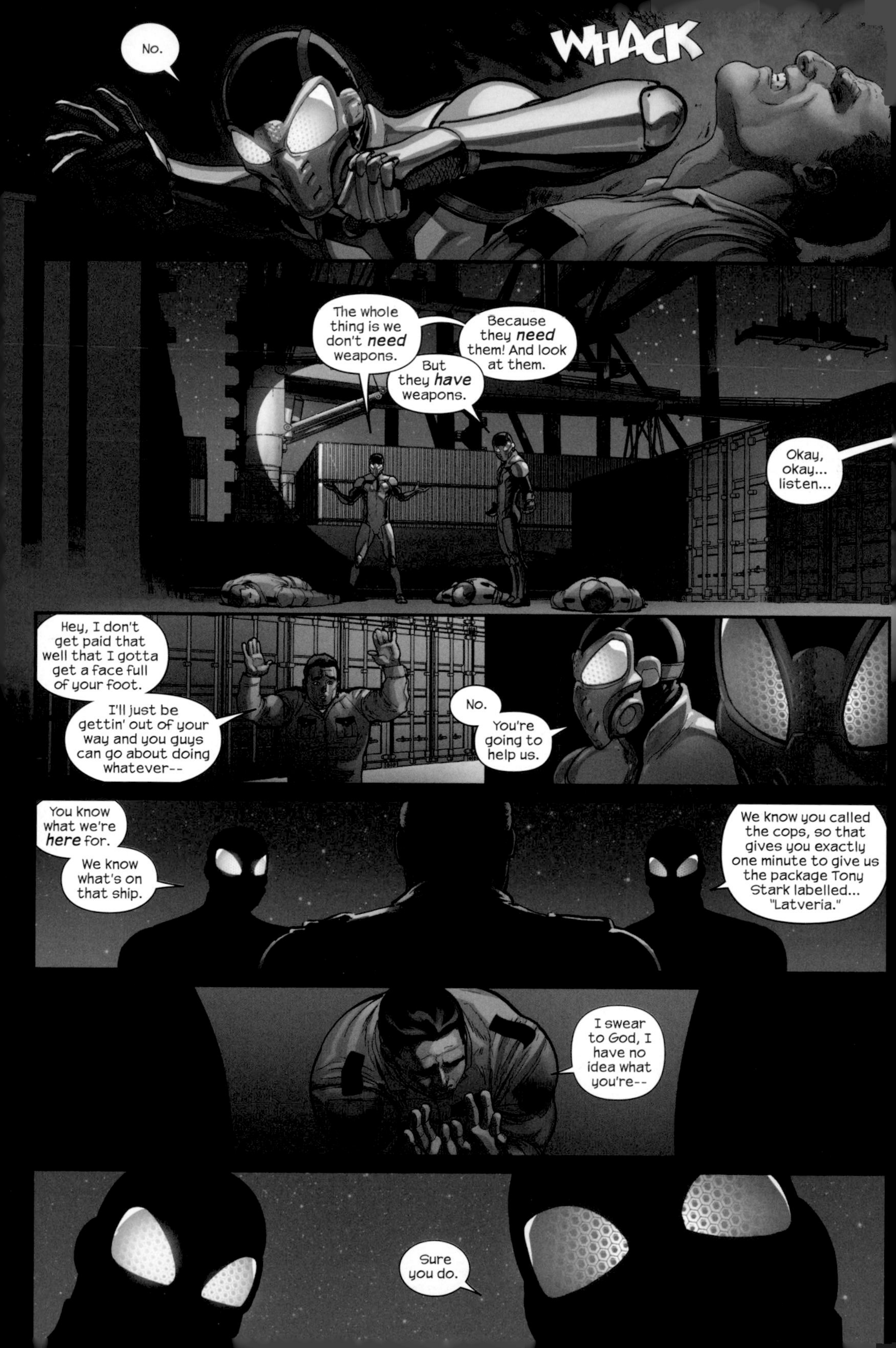
No.
WHACK
The whole thing is we don't *need* weapons.
Because they *need* them! And look at them.
But they *have* weapons.
Okay, okay... listen...
Hey, I don't get paid that well that I gotta get a face full of your foot.
I'll just be gettin' out of your way and you guys can go about doing whatever--
No.
You're going to help us.
You know what we're *here* for.
We know what's on that ship.
We know you called the cops, so that gives you exactly one minute to give us the package Tony Stark labelled... "Latveria."
I swear to God, I have no idea what you're--
Sure you do.

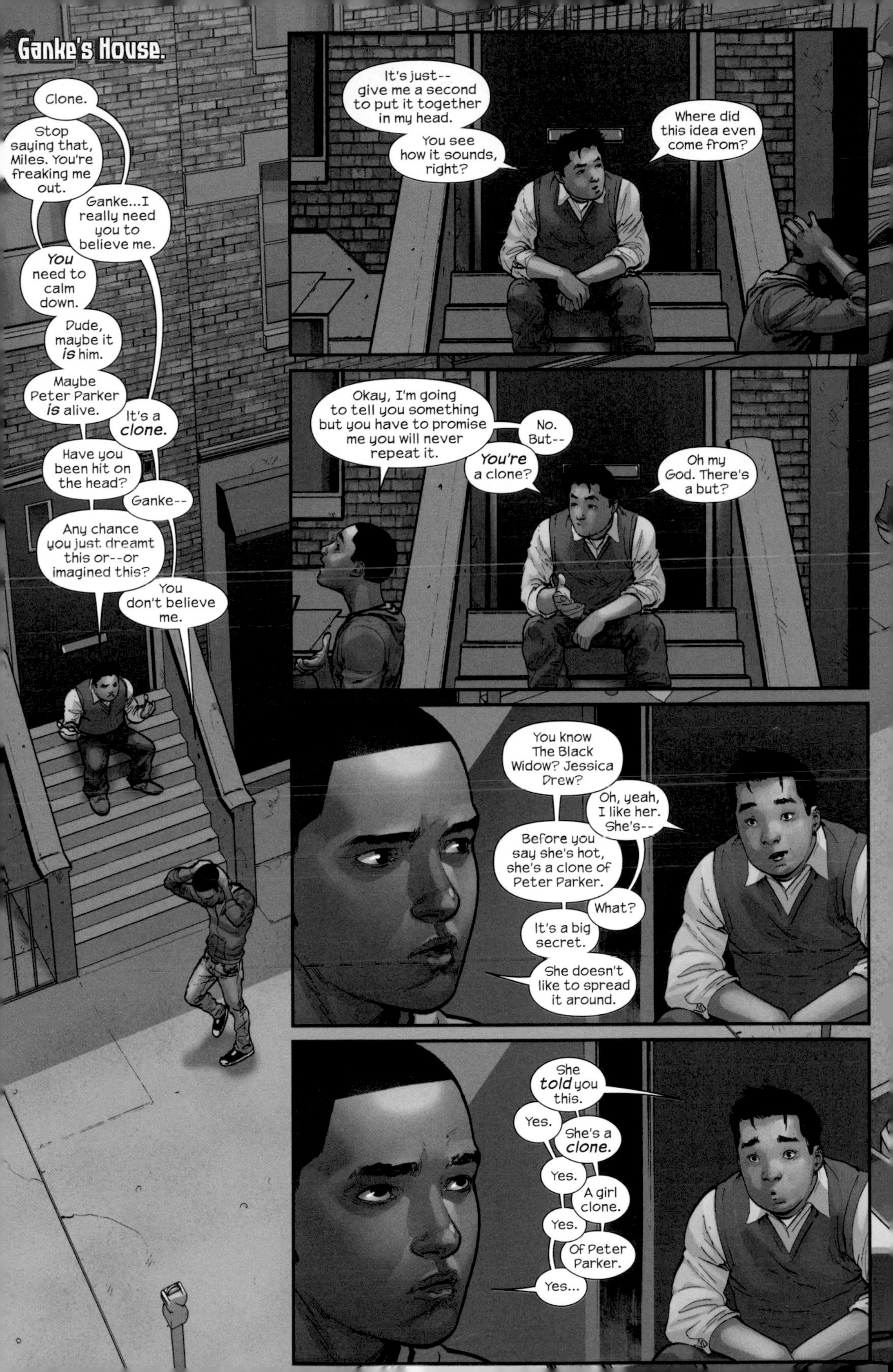
Ganke's House.
Clone.
Stop saying that, Miles. You're freaking me out.
Ganke...I really need you to believe me.
You need to calm down.
Dude, maybe it is him.
Maybe Peter Parker is alive.
It's a clone.
Have you been hit on the head?
Ganke--
Any chance you just dreamt this or--or imagined this?
You don't believe me.
It's just-- give me a second to put it together in my head.
You see how it sounds, right?
Where did this idea even come from?
Okay, I'm going to tell you something but you have to promise me you will never repeat it.
No. But--
You're a clone?
Oh my God. There's a but?
You know The Black Widow? Jessica Drew?
Oh, yeah, I like her. She's--
Before you say she's hot, she's a clone of Peter Parker.
What?
It's a big secret.
She doesn't like to spread it around.
She told you this.
Yes.
She's a clone.
Yes.
A girl clone.
Yes.
Of Peter Parker.
Yes...

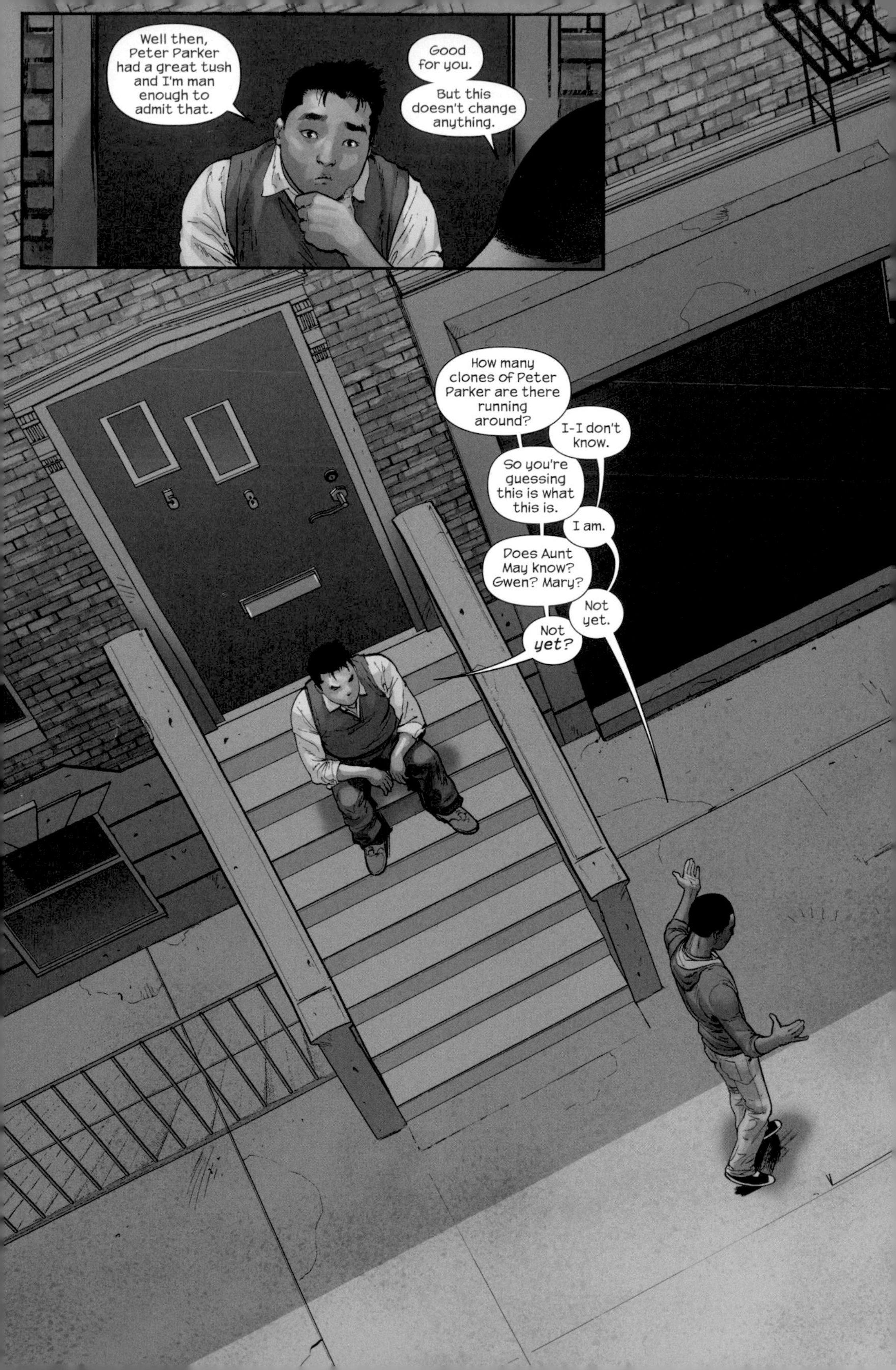
Well then, Peter Parker had a great tush and I'm man enough to admit that.
Good for you.
But this doesn't change anything.
How many clones of Peter Parker are there running around?
I-I don't know.
So you're guessing this is what this is.
I am.
Does Aunt May know? Gwen? Mary?
Not yet.
Not *yet?*

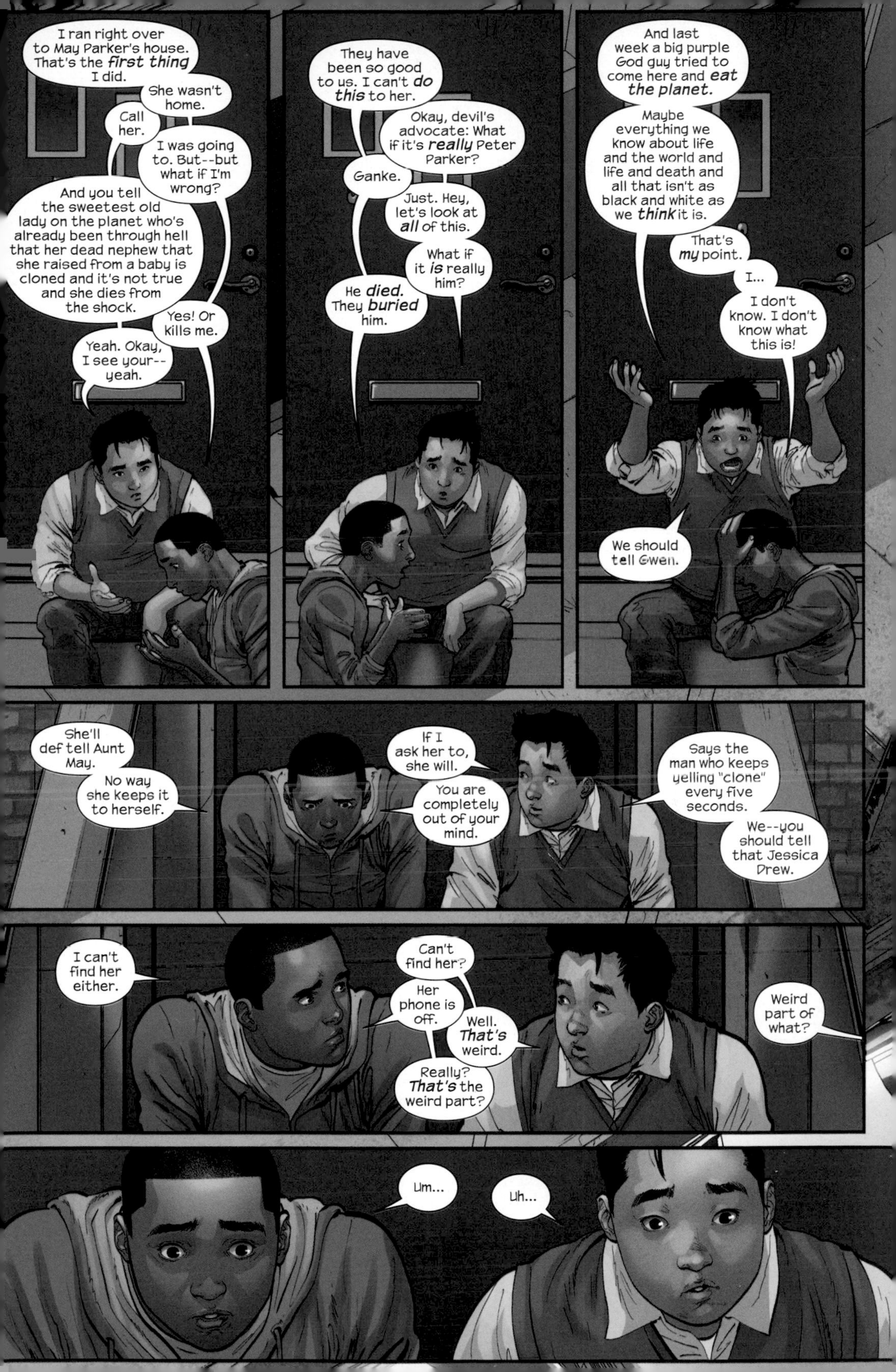
I ran right over to May Parker's house. That's the *first thing* I did.
She wasn't home.
Call her.
I was going to. But--but what if I'm wrong?
And you tell the sweetest old lady on the planet who's already been through hell that her dead nephew that she raised from a baby is cloned and it's not true and she dies from the shock.
Yes! Or kills me.
Yeah. Okay, I see your-- yeah.
They have been so good to us. I can't *do this* to her.
Okay, devil's advocate: What if it's *really* Peter Parker?
Ganke.
Just. Hey, let's look at *all* of this.
What if it *is* really him?
He *died.* They *buried* him.
And last week a big purple God guy tried to come here and *eat the planet.*
Maybe everything we know about life and the world and life and death and all that isn't as black and white as we *think* it is.
That's *my* point.
I...
I don't know. I don't know what this is!
We should tell Gwen.
She'll def tell Aunt May.
No way she keeps it to herself.
If I ask her to, she will.
You are completely out of your mind.
Says the man who keeps yelling "clone" every five seconds.
We--you should tell that Jessica Drew.
I can't find her either.
Can't find her?
Her phone is off.
Well. *That's* weird.
Really? *That's* the weird part?
Weird part of what?
Um...
Uh...

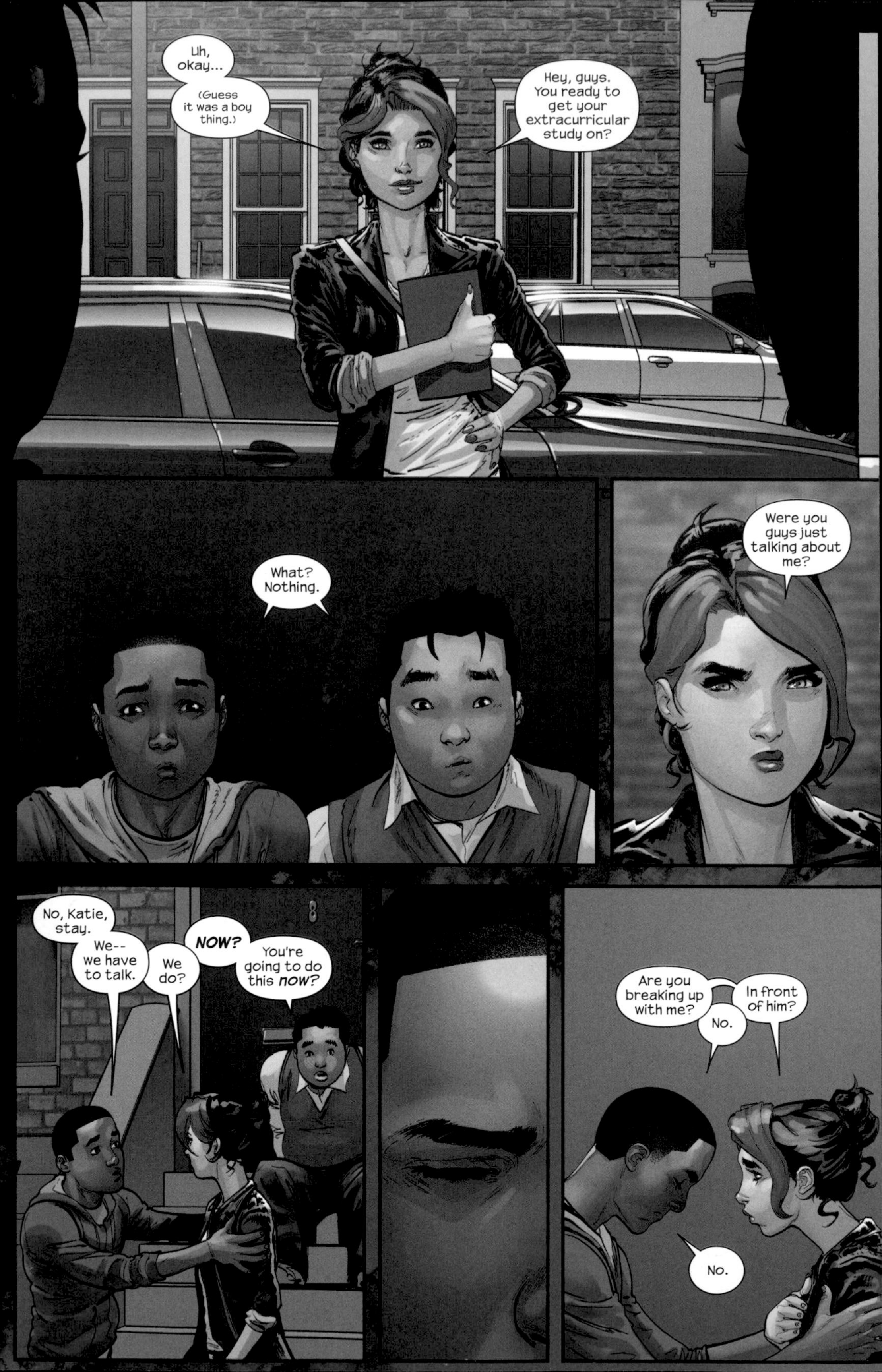
Uh, okay...
(Guess it was a boy thing.)
Hey, guys. You ready to get your extracurricular study on?
What? Nothing.
Were you guys just talking about me?
No, Katie, stay.
We-- we have to talk.
We do?
NOW?
You're going to do this NOW?
Are you breaking up with me?
In front of him?
No.
No.

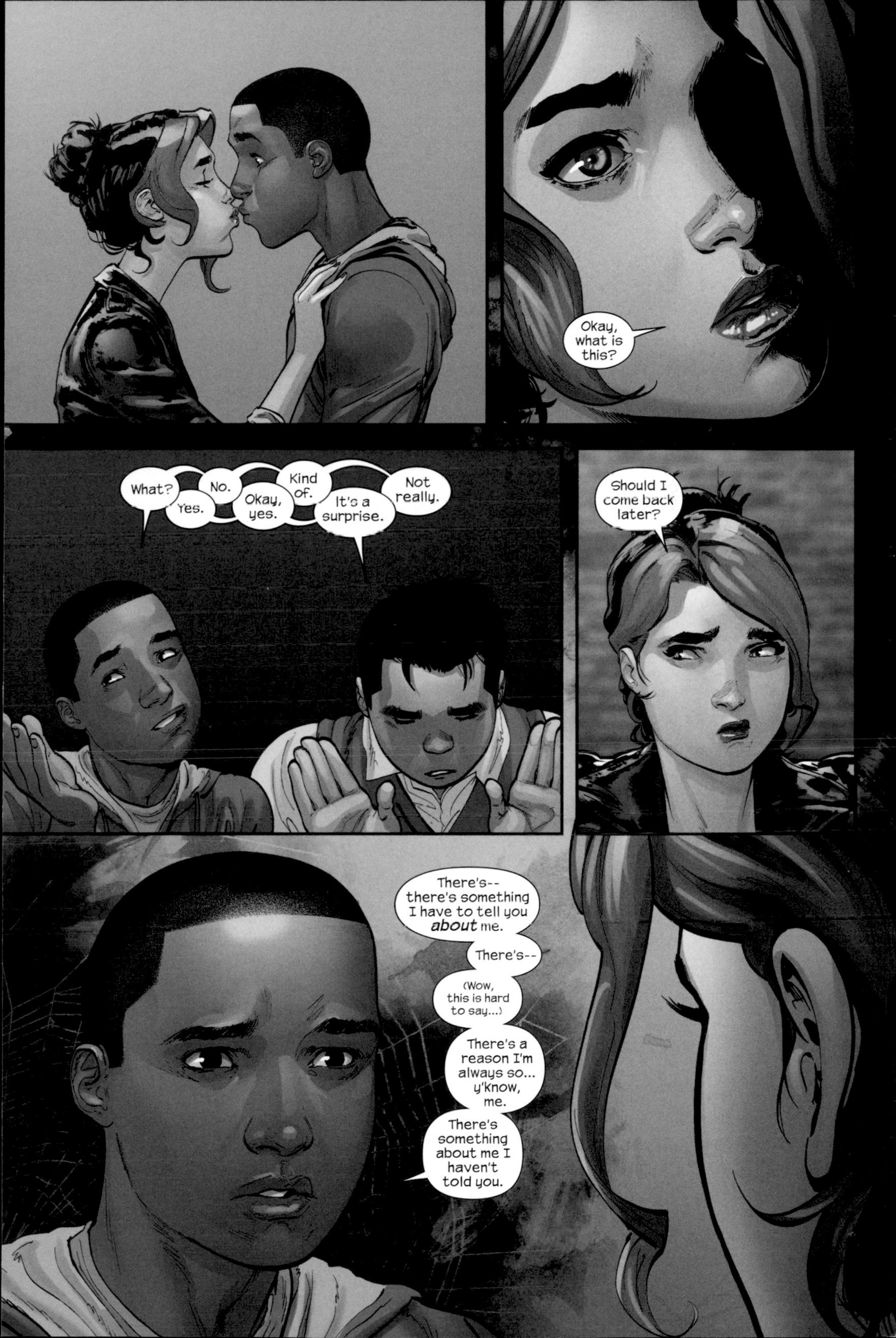
Okay, what is this?
What?
Yes.
No.
Okay, yes.
Kind of.
It's a surprise.
Not really.
Should I come back later?
There's-- there's something I have to tell you *about* me.
There's--
(Wow, this is hard to say...)
There's a reason I'm always so... y'know, me.
There's something about me I haven't told you.

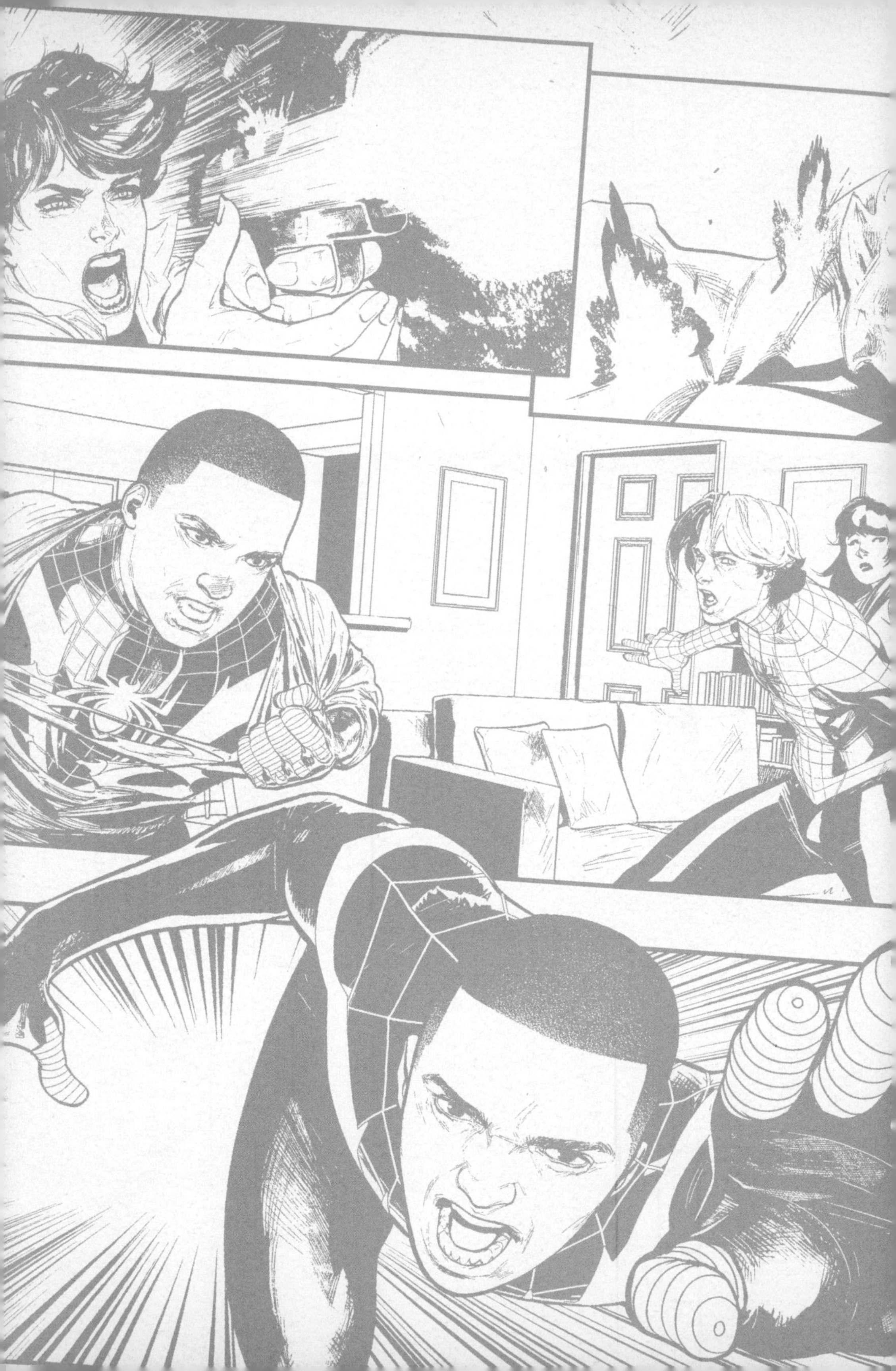

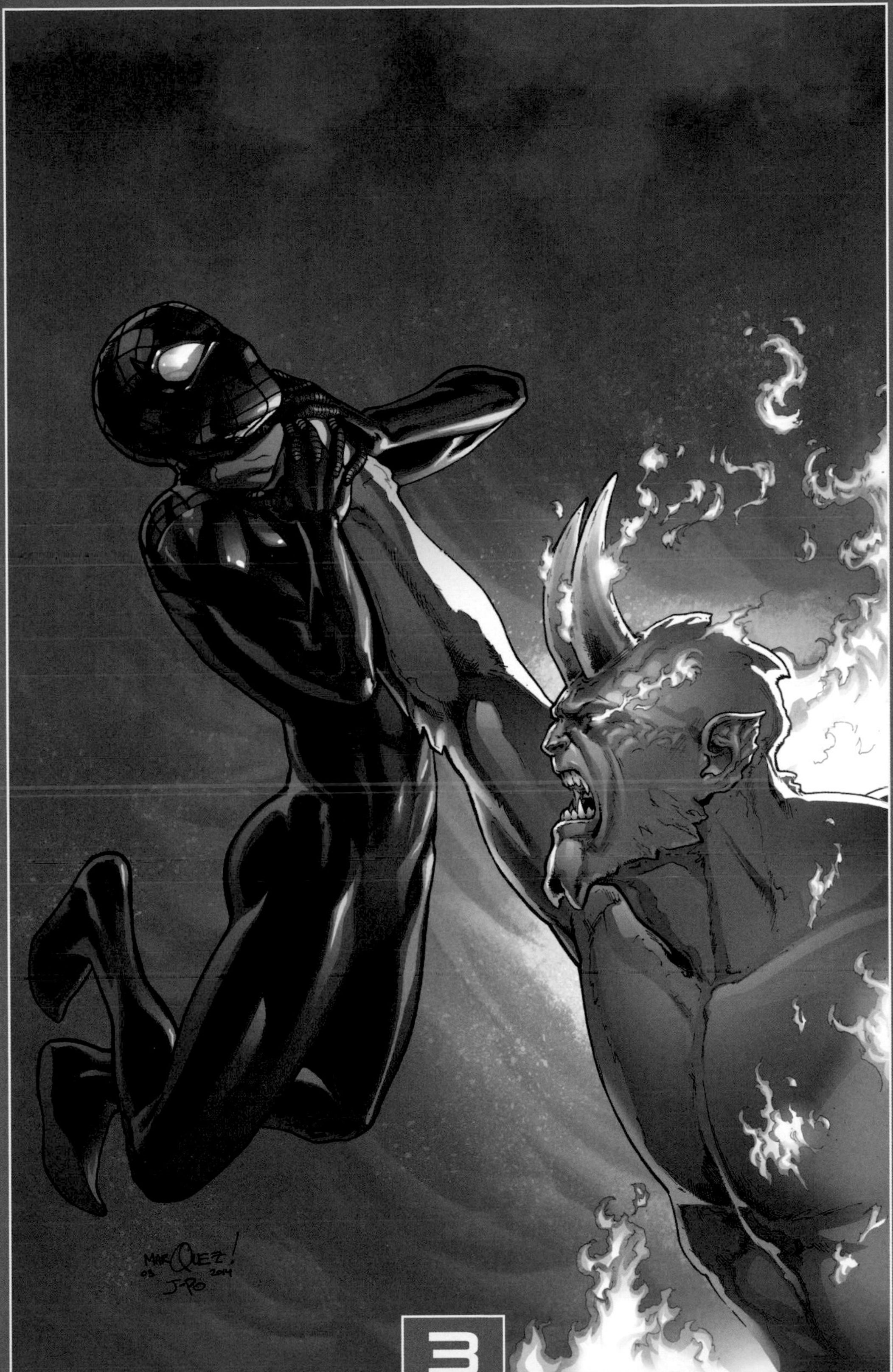
MARQUEZ!
03 2014
J-RO
3

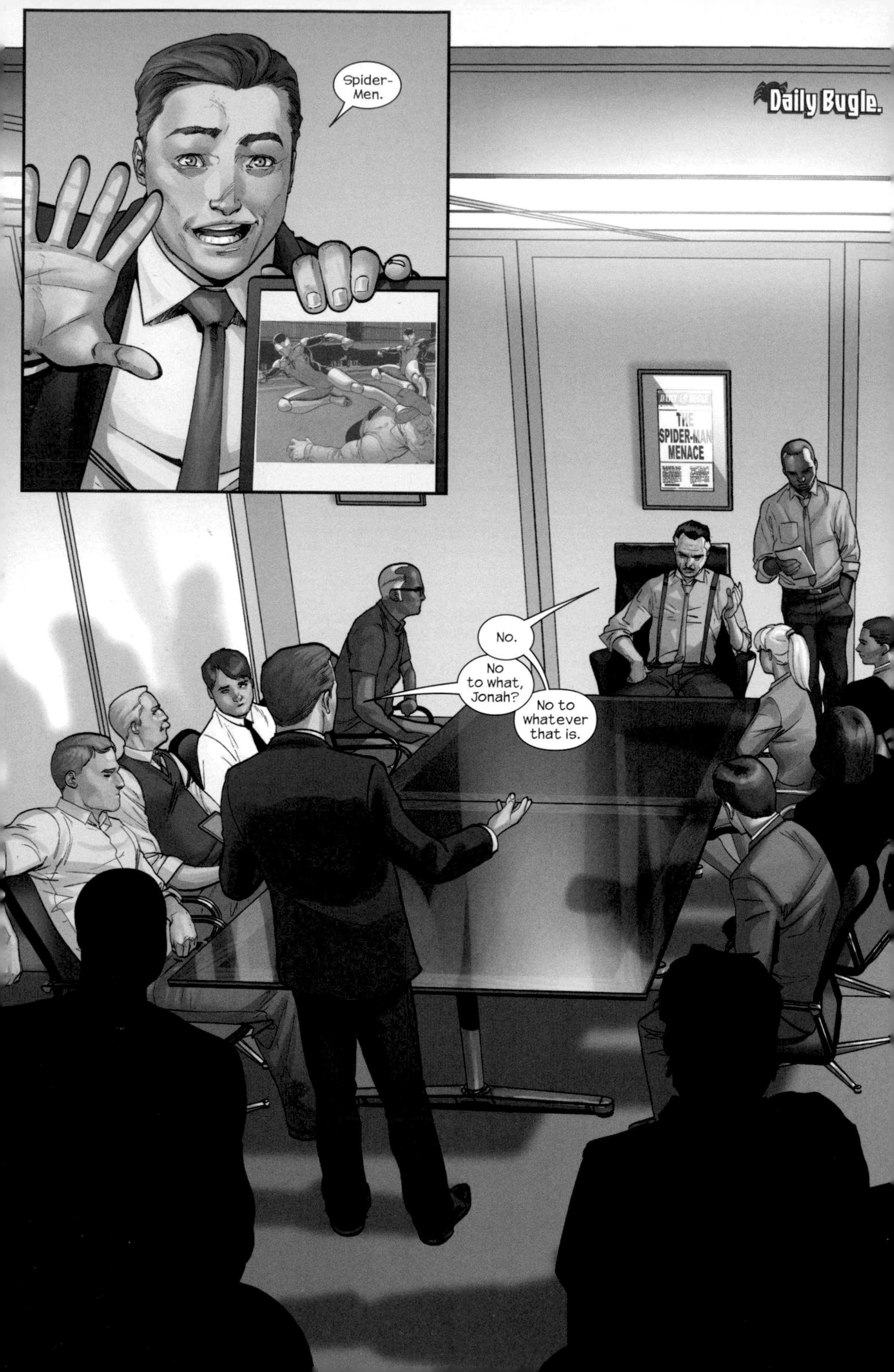
Spider-Men.
Daily Bugle.
THE SPIDER-MAN MENACE
No.
No to what, Jonah?
No to whatever that is.

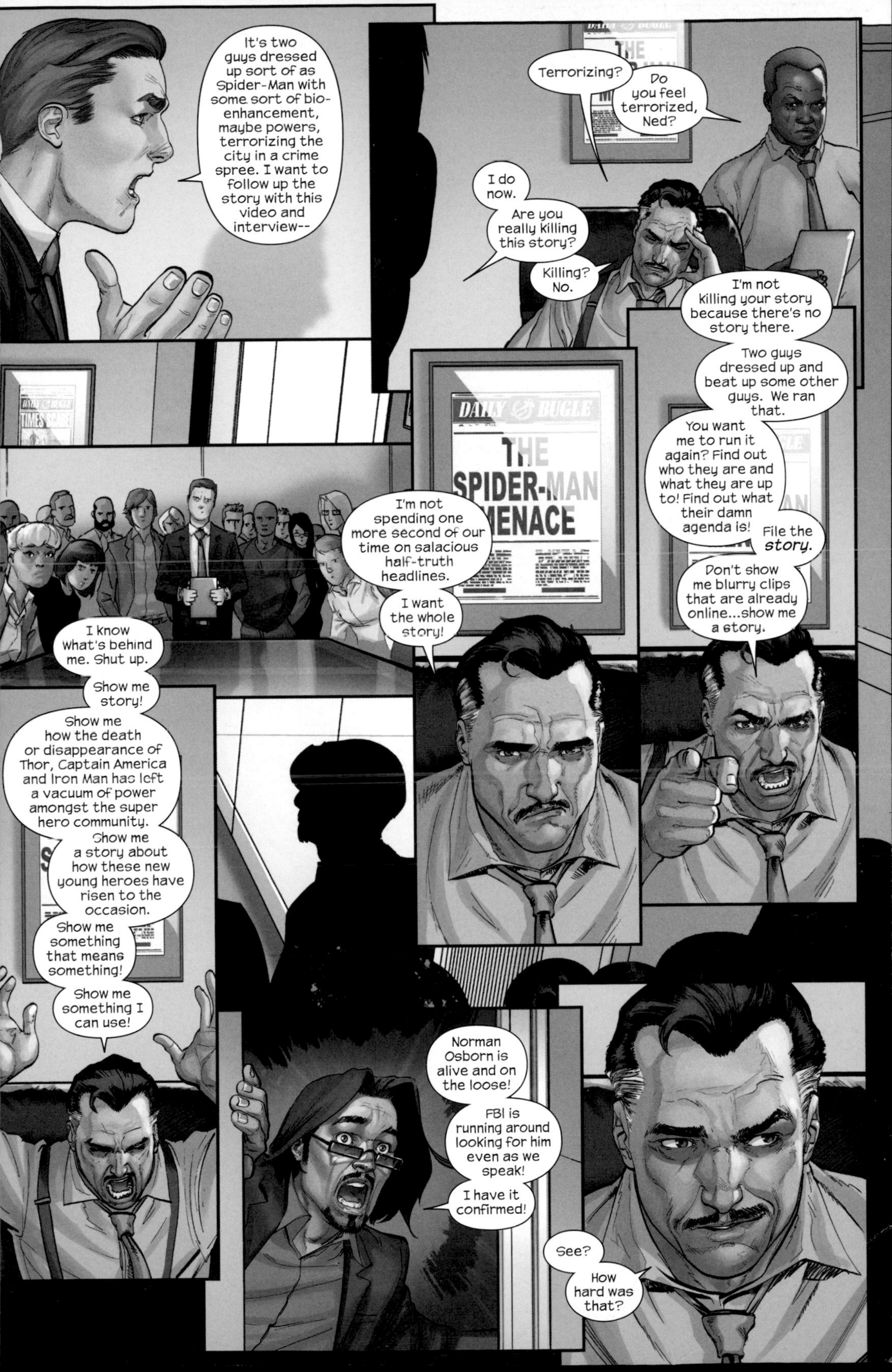
It's two guys dressed up sort of as Spider-Man with some sort of bio-enhancement, maybe powers, terrorizing the city in a crime spree. I want to follow up the story with this video and interview--
Terrorizing?
Do you feel terrorized, Ned?
I do now.
Are you really killing this story?
Killing? No.
I'm not killing your story because there's no story there.
Two guys dressed up and beat up some other guys. We ran that.
You want me to run it again? Find out who they are and what they are up to! Find out what their damn agenda is!
File the *story.*
Don't show me blurry clips that are already online...show me a story.
DAILY BUGLE
THE SPIDER-MAN MENACE
I'm not spending one more second of our time on salacious half-truth headlines.
I want the whole story!
I know what's behind me. Shut up.
Show me story!
Show me how the death or disappearance of Thor, Captain America and Iron Man has left a vacuum of power amongst the super hero community.
Show me a story about how these new young heroes have risen to the occasion.
Show me something that means something!
Show me something I can use!
Norman Osborn is alive and on the loose!
FBI is running around looking for him even as we speak!
I have it confirmed!
See?
How hard was that?

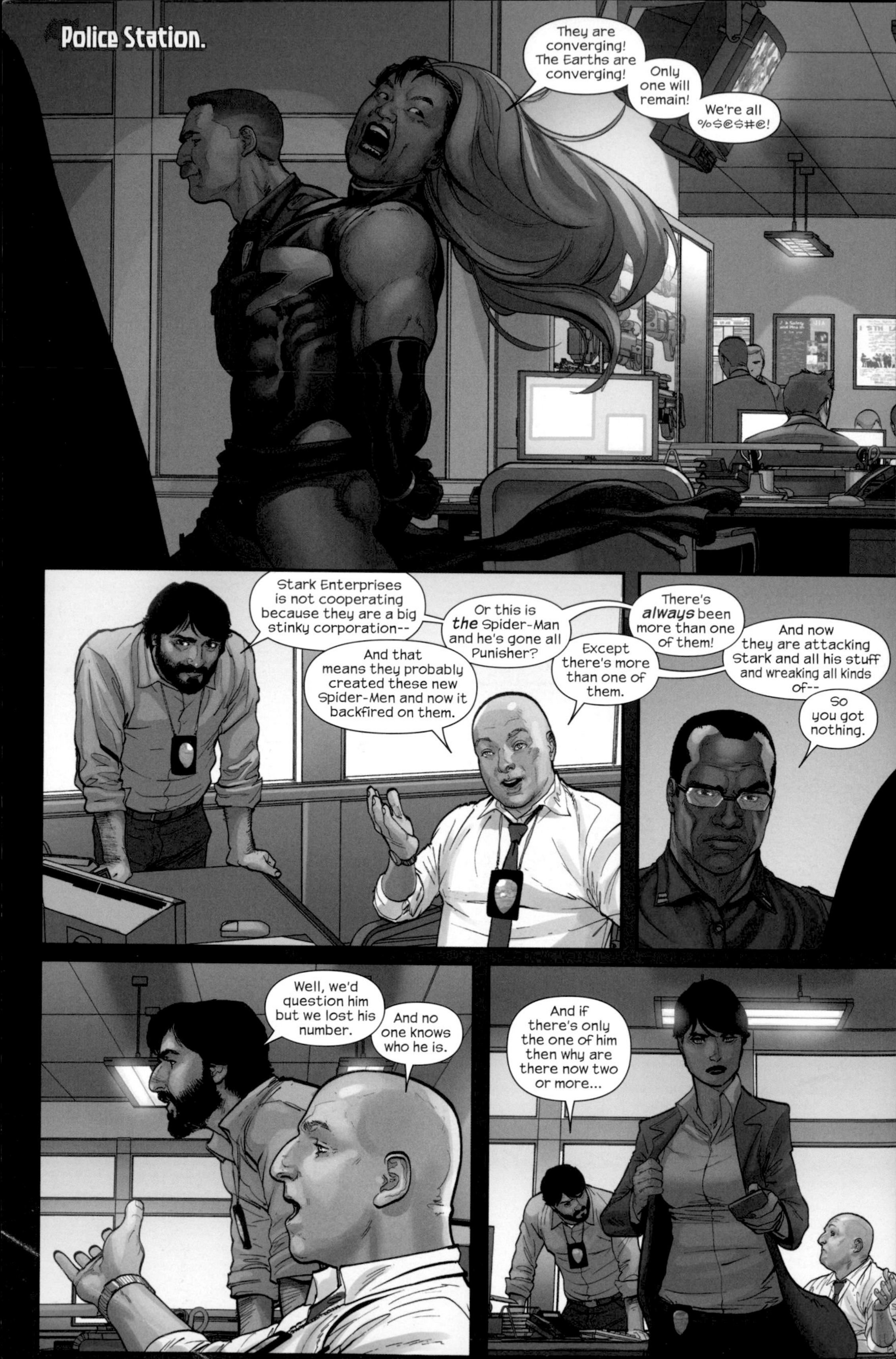
Police Station.
They are converging! The Earths are converging!
Only one will remain!
We're all %$@$#@!
Stark Enterprises is not cooperating because they are a big stinky corporation--
And that means they probably created these new Spider-Men and now it backfired on them.
Or this is the Spider-Man and he's gone all Punisher?
Except there's more than one of them.
There's always been more than one of them!
And now they are attacking Stark and all his stuff and wreaking all kinds of--
So you got nothing.
Well, we'd question him but we lost his number.
And no one knows who he is.
And if there's only the one of him then why are there now two or more...

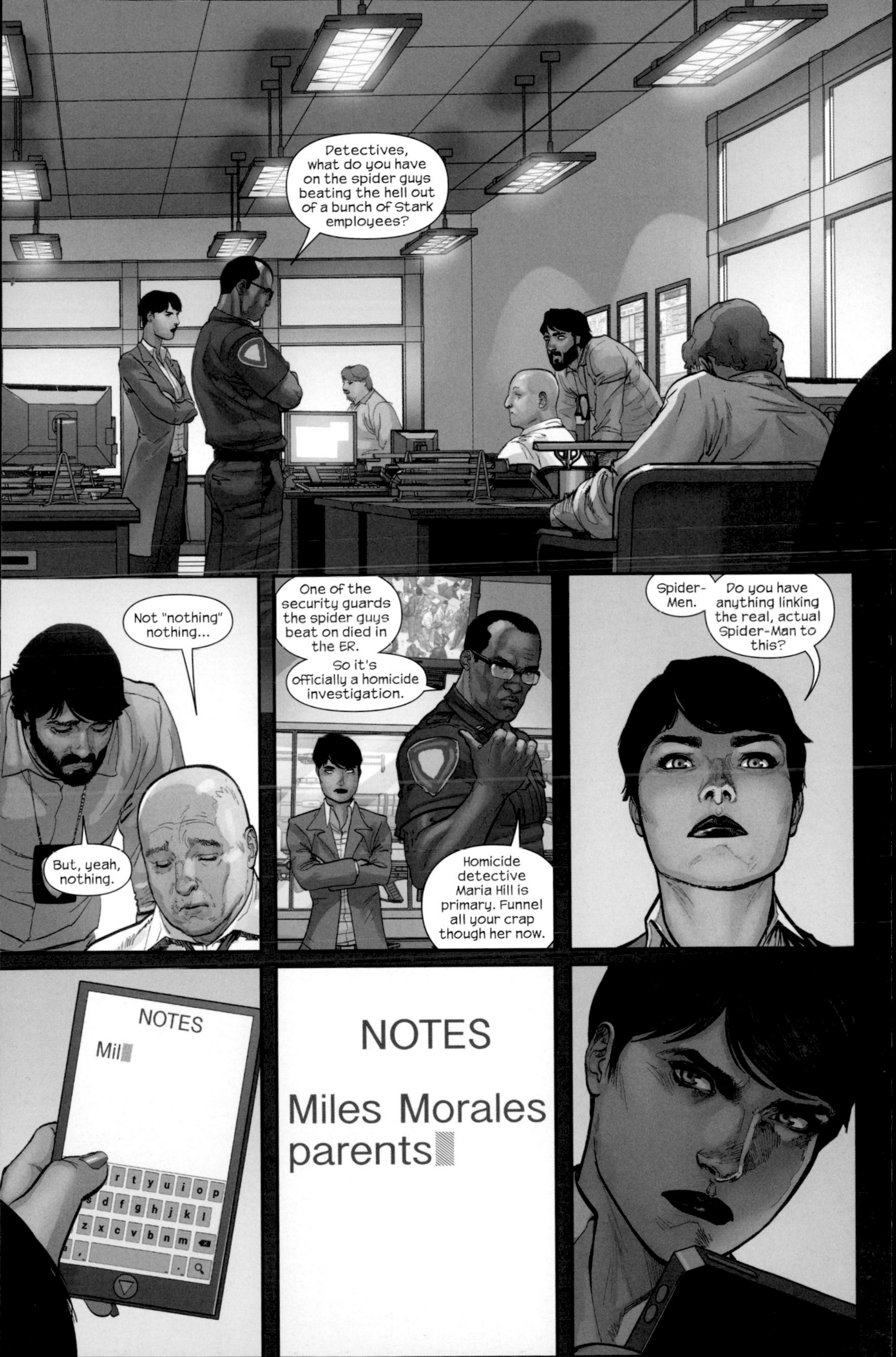
Detectives, what do you have on the spider guys beating the hell out of a bunch of Stark employees?
Not "nothing" nothing...
But, yeah, nothing.
One of the security guards the spider guys beat on died in the ER.
So it's officially a homicide investigation.
Homicide detective Maria Hill is primary. Funnel all your crap though her now.
Spider-Men.
Do you have anything linking the real, actual Spider-Man to this?
NOTES
Mil
NOTES
Miles Morales parents

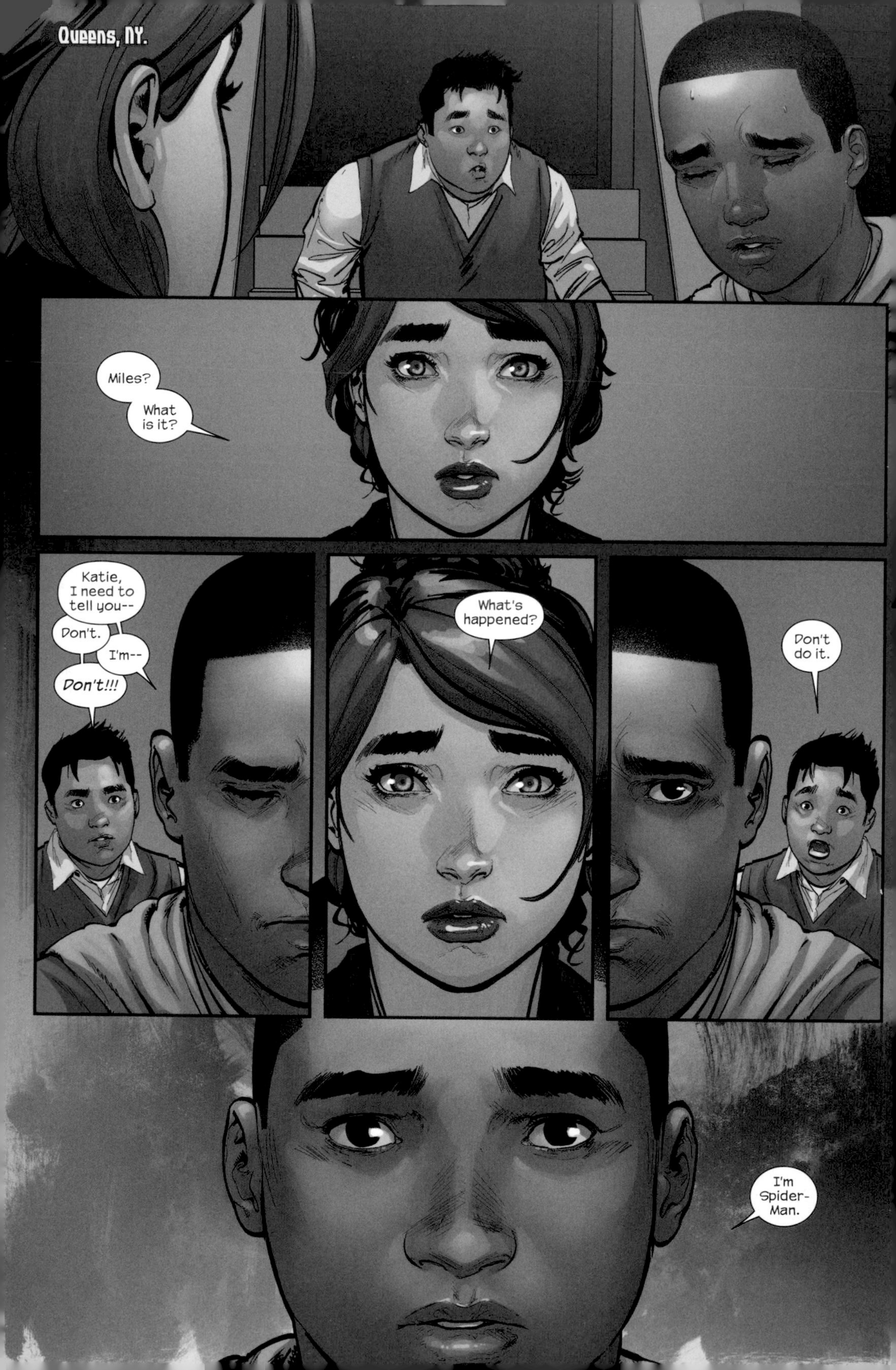
Queens, NY.
Miles?
What is it?
Katie, I need to tell you--
Don't.
I'm--
Don't!!!
What's happened?
Don't do it.
I'm Spider-Man.

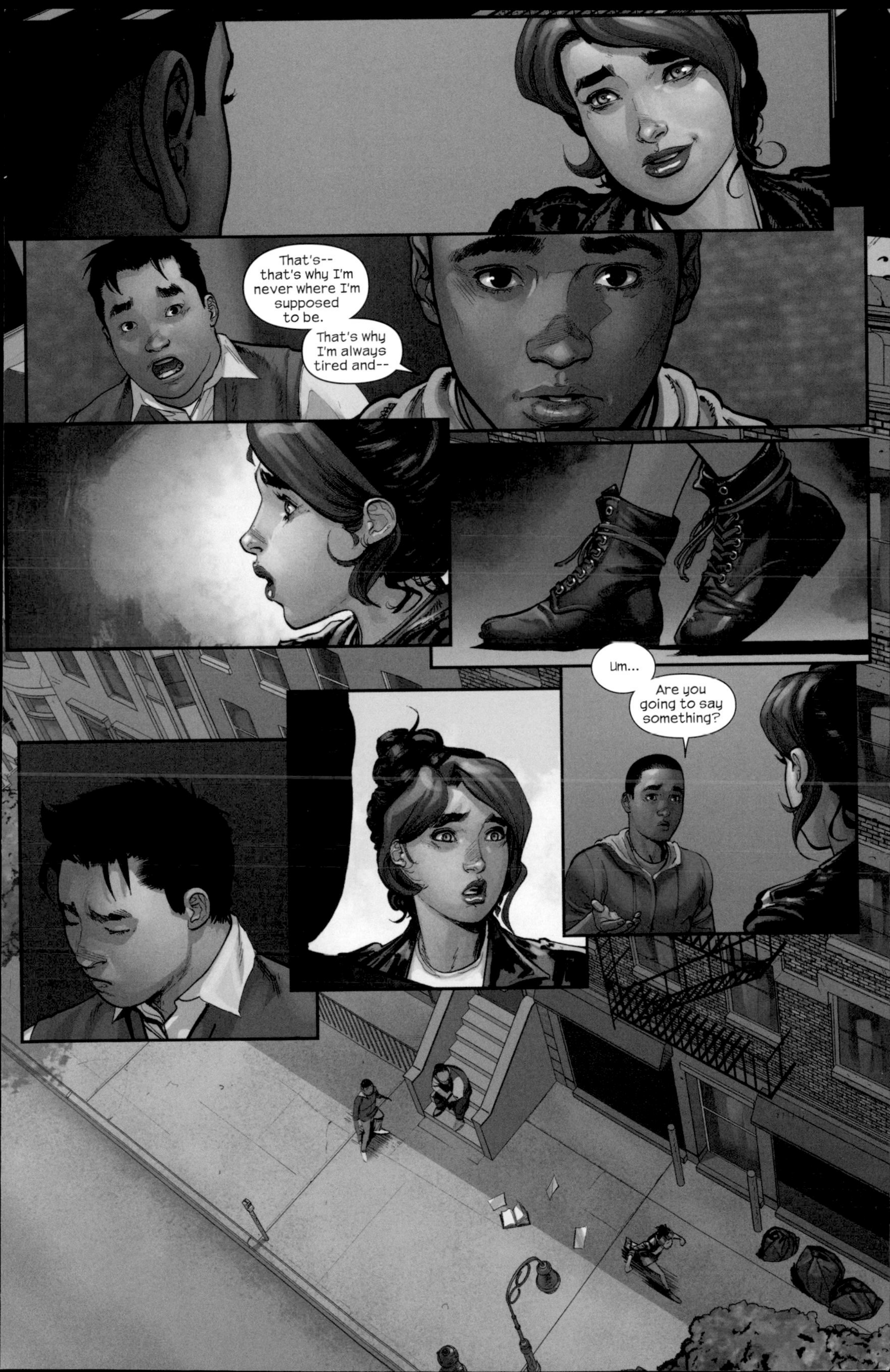
That's-- that's why I'm never where I'm supposed to be.
That's why I'm always tired and--
Um...
Are you going to say something?

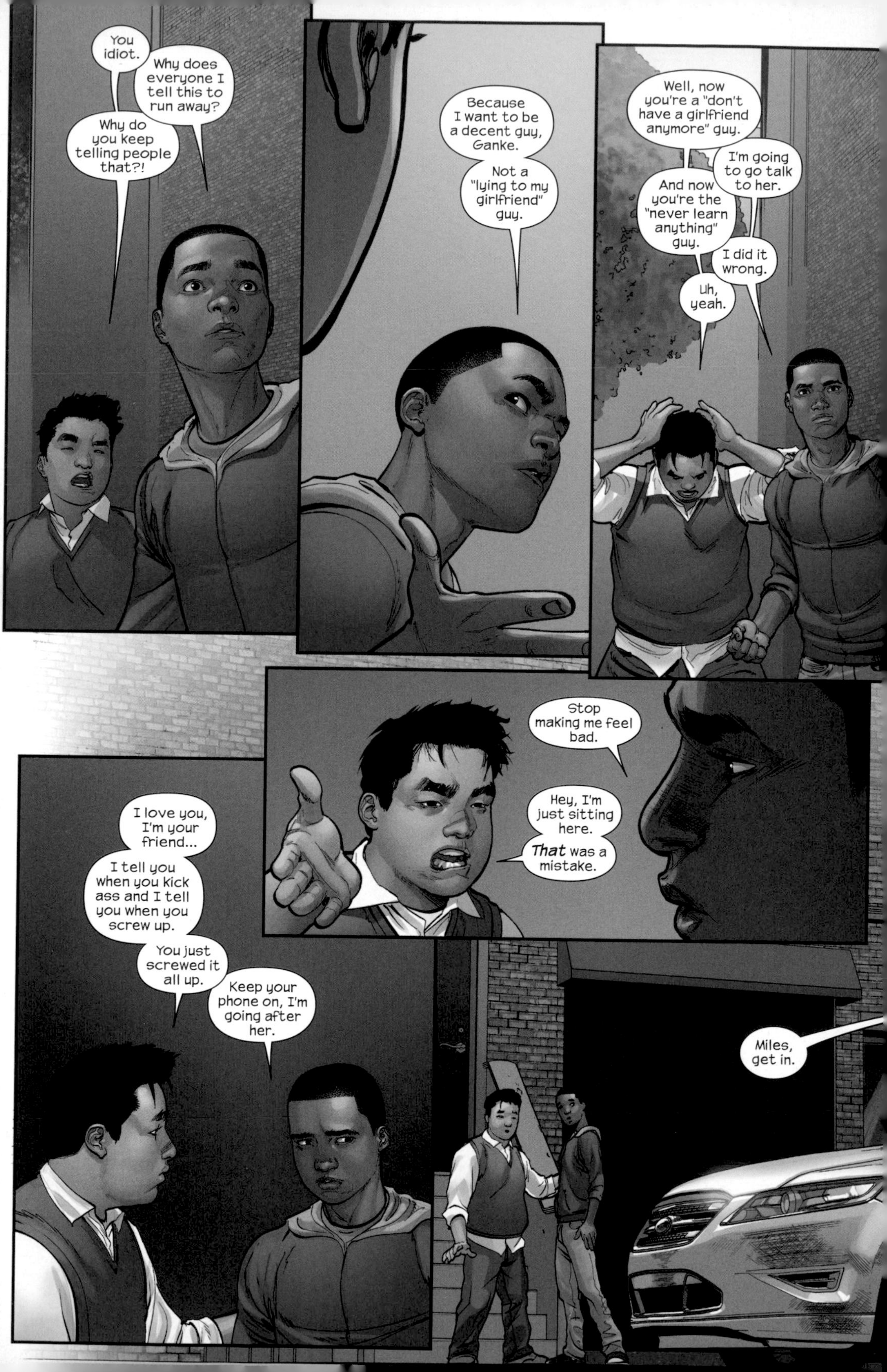
You idiot.
Why do you keep telling people that?!
Why does everyone I tell this to run away?
Because I want to be a decent guy, Ganke.
Not a "lying to my girlfriend" guy.
Well, now you're a "don't have a girlfriend anymore" guy.
And now you're the "never learn anything" guy.
I'm going to go talk to her.
I did it wrong.
Uh, yeah.
Stop making me feel bad.
Hey, I'm just sitting here.
That was a mistake.
I love you, I'm your friend...
I tell you when you kick ass and I tell you when you screw up.
You just screwed it all up.
Keep your phone on, I'm going after her.
Miles, get in.

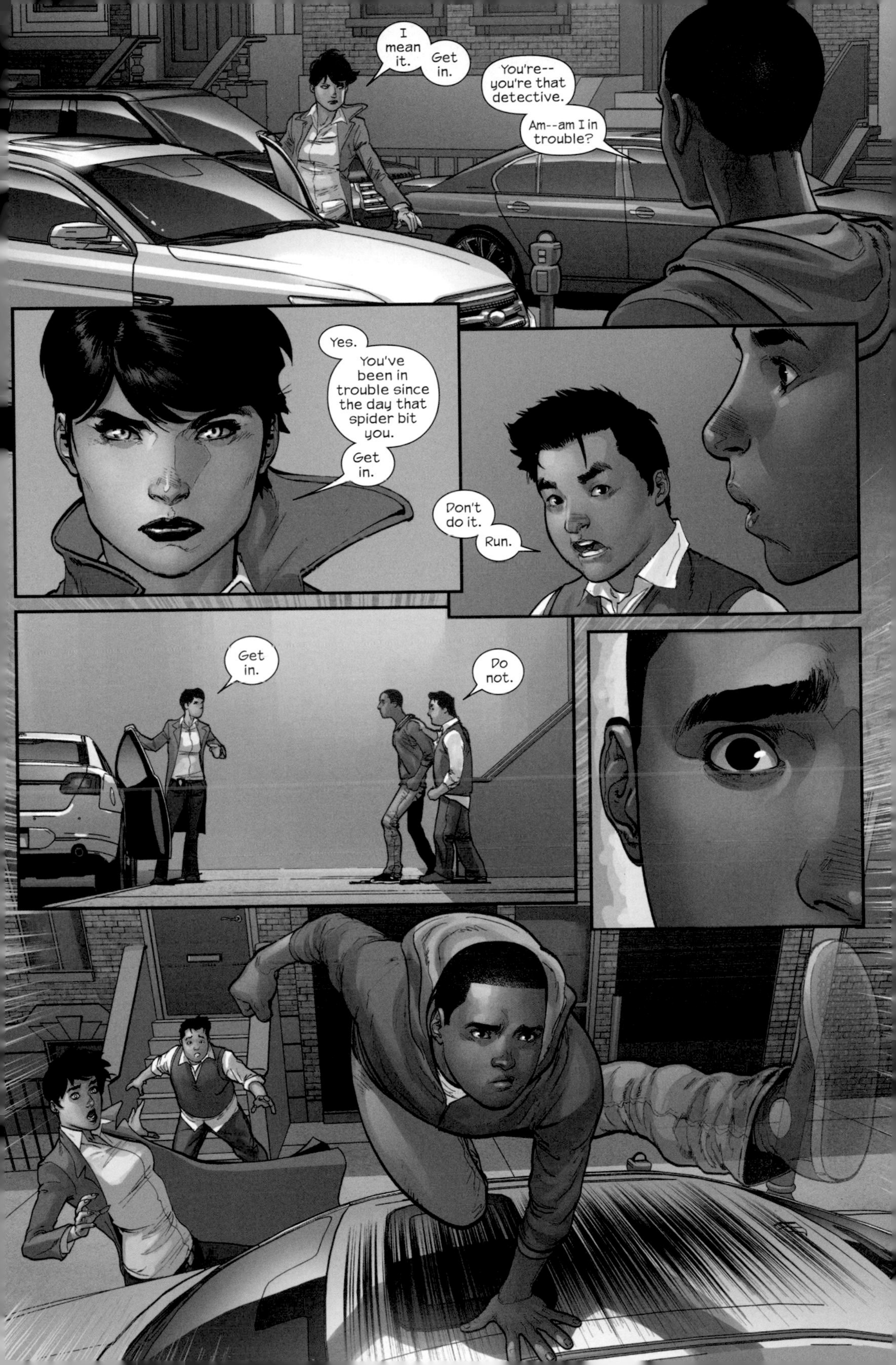
I mean it.
Get in.
You're-- you're that detective.
Am--am I in trouble?
Yes.
You've been in trouble since the day that spider bit you.
Get in.
Don't do it.
Run.
Get in.
Do not.

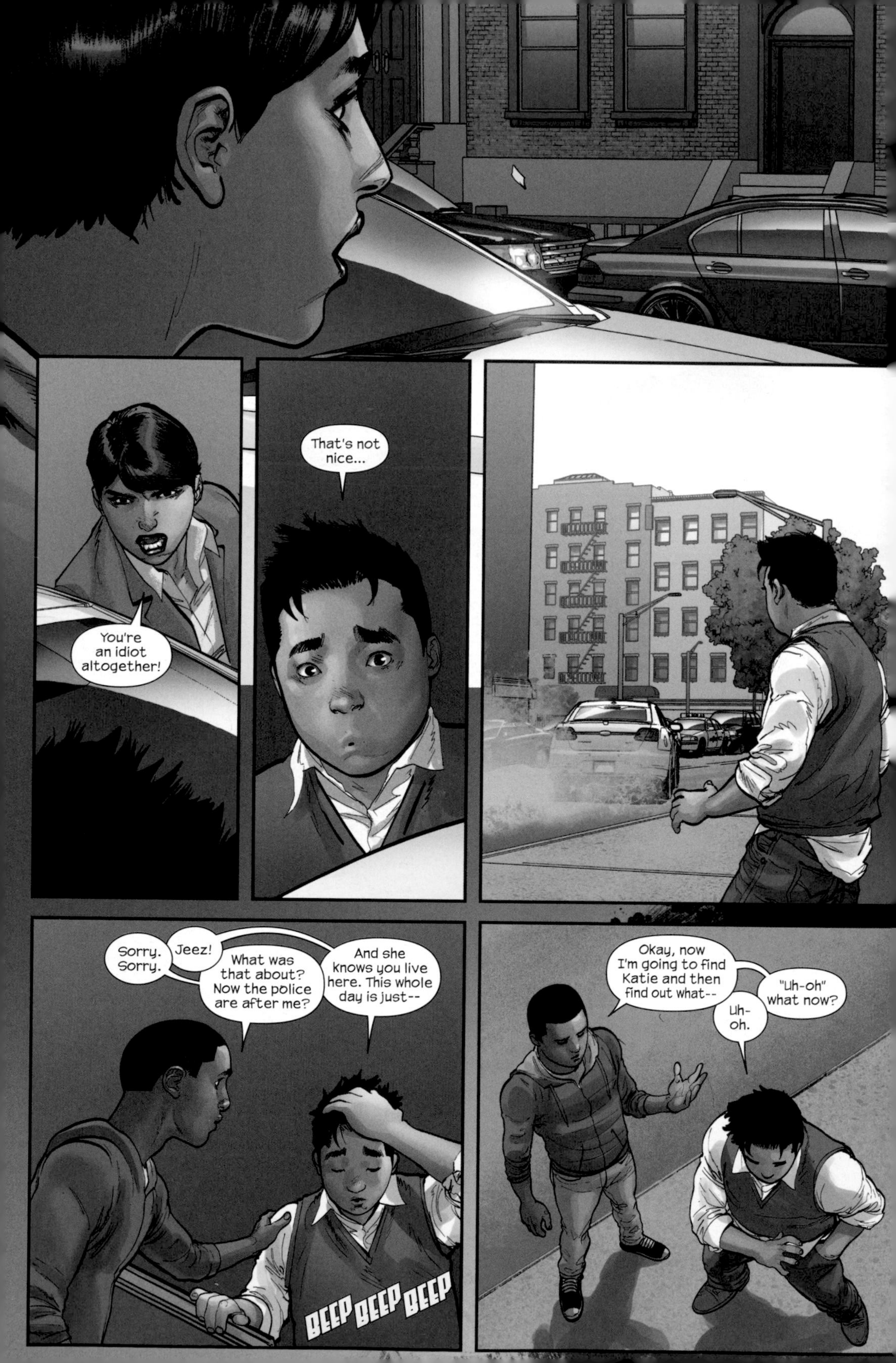
You're an idiot altogether!
That's not nice...
Sorry. Sorry.
Jeez!
What was that about? Now the police are after me?
And she knows you live here. This whole day is just--
BEEP BEEP BEEP
Okay, now I'm going to find Katie and then find out what--
Uh-oh.
"Uh-oh" what now?

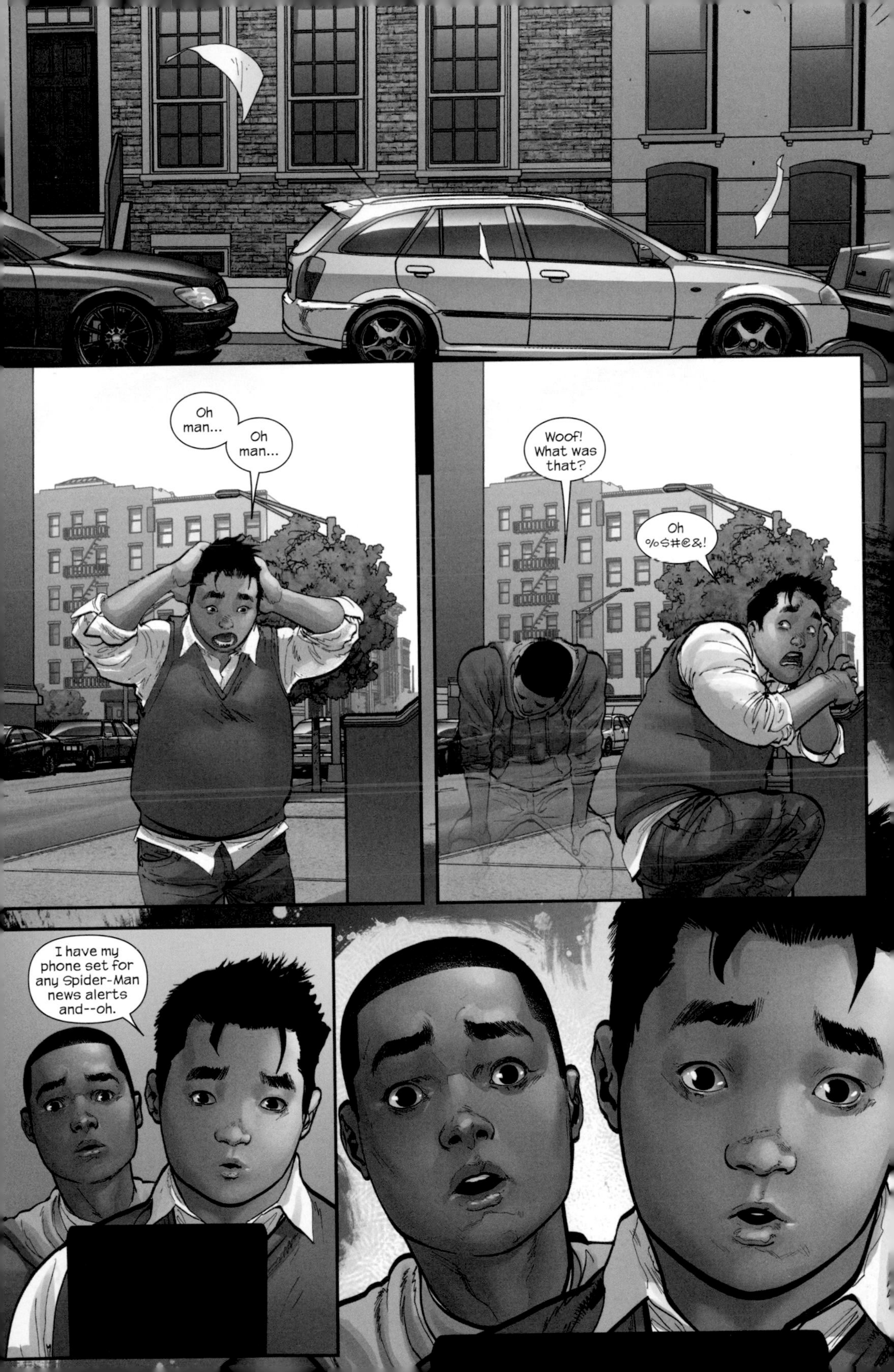
Oh man...
Oh man...
Woof! What was that?
Oh %$#@&!
I have my phone set for any Spider-Man news alerts and--oh.

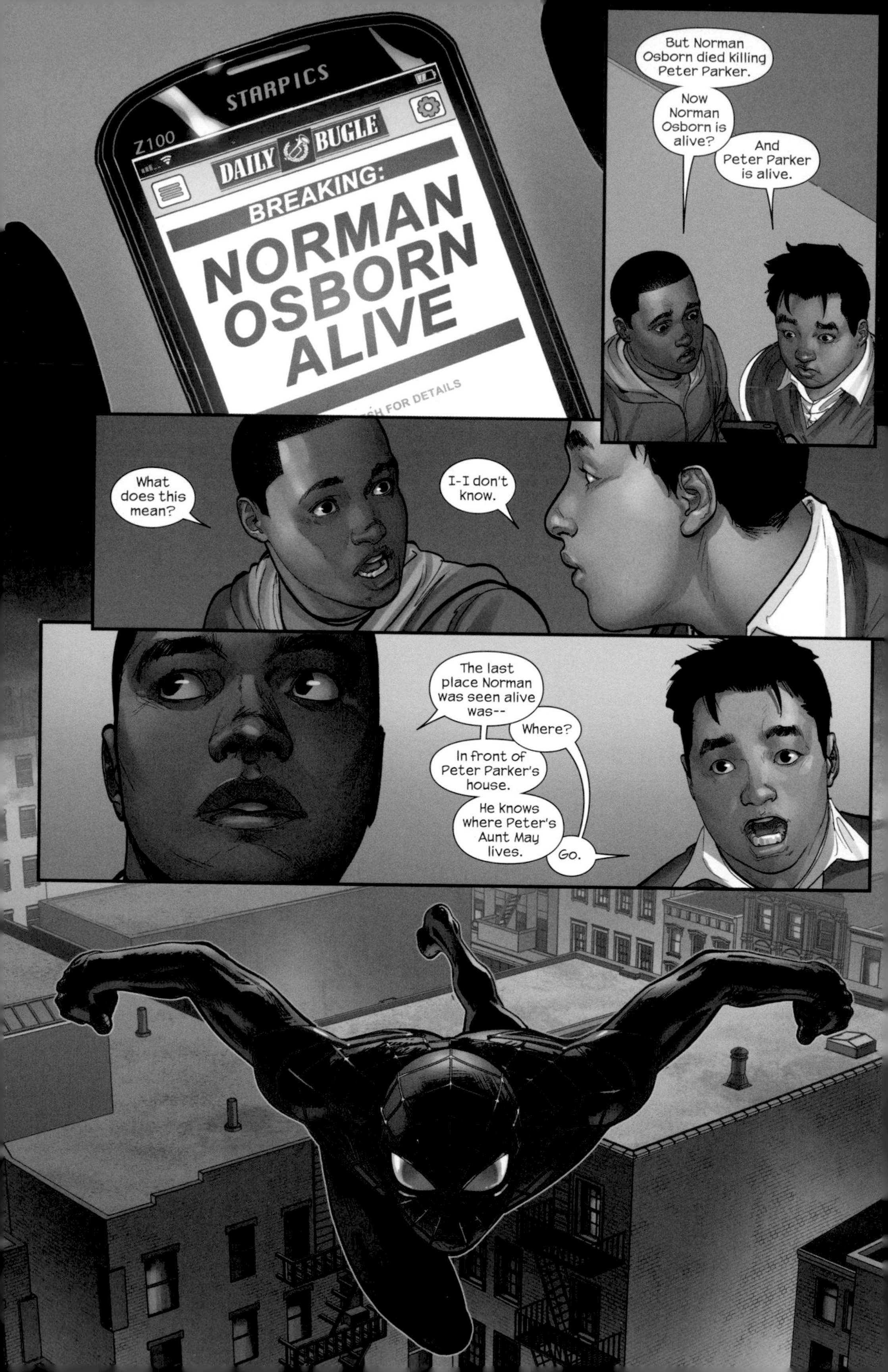
STARPICS
Z100
DAILY BUGLE
BREAKING:
NORMAN OSBORN ALIVE
But Norman Osborn died killing Peter Parker.
Now Norman Osborn is alive?
And Peter Parker is alive.
What does this mean?
I-I don't know.
The last place Norman was seen alive was--
Where?
In front of Peter Parker's house.
He knows where Peter's Aunt May lives.
Go.

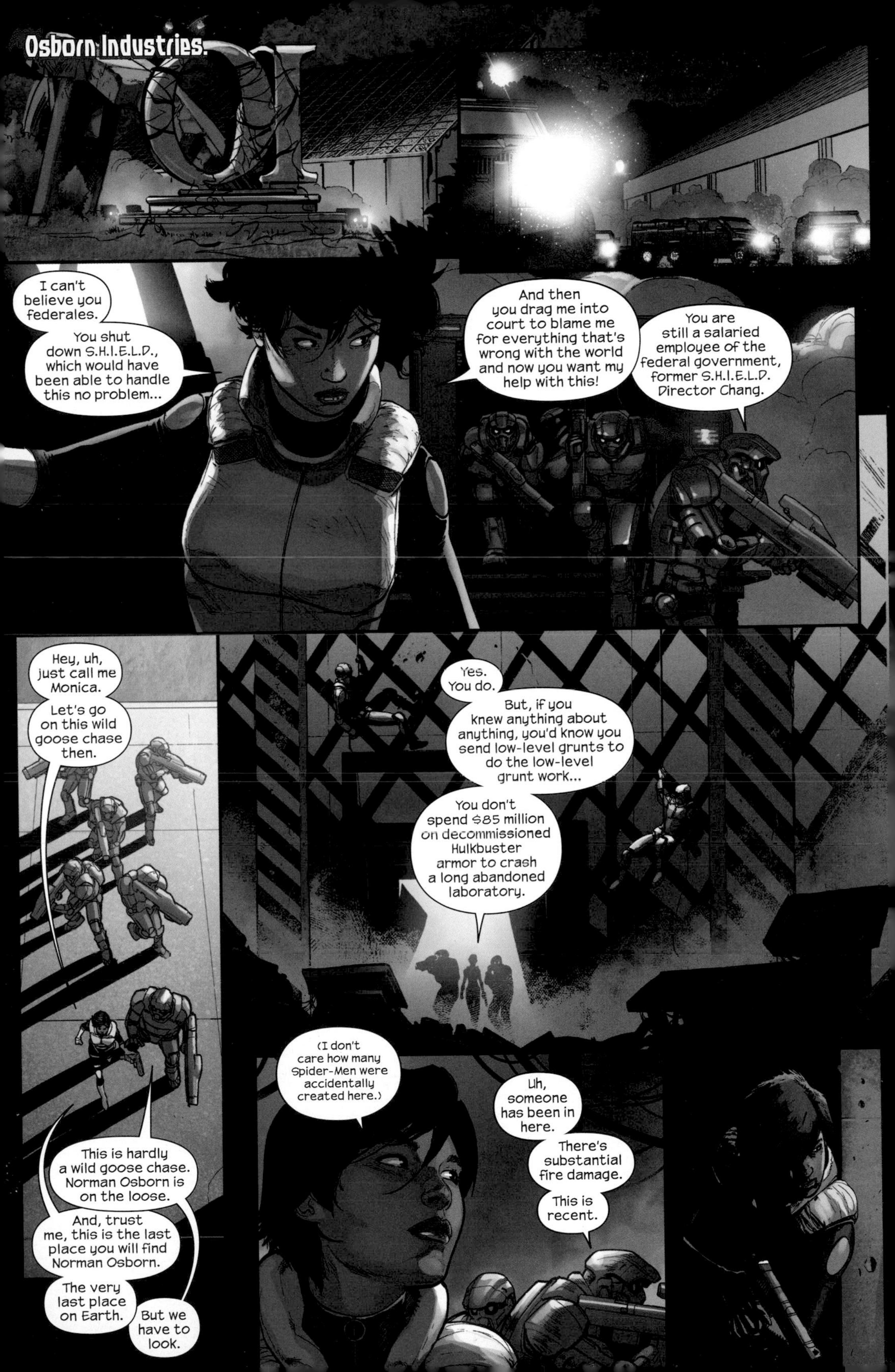
Osborn Industries.
I can't believe you federales.
You shut down S.H.I.E.L.D., which would have been able to handle this no problem...
And then you drag me into court to blame me for everything that's wrong with the world and now you want my help with this!
You are still a salaried employee of the federal government, former S.H.I.E.L.D. Director Chang.
Hey, uh, just call me Monica.
Let's go on this wild goose chase then.
Yes. You do.
But, if you knew anything about anything, you'd know you send low-level grunts to do the low-level grunt work...
You don't spend $85 million on decommissioned Hulkbuster armor to crash a long abandoned laboratory.
This is hardly a wild goose chase. Norman Osborn is on the loose.
And, trust me, this is the last place you will find Norman Osborn.
The very last place on Earth.
But we have to look.
(I don't care how many Spider-Men were accidentally created here.)
Uh, someone has been in here.
There's substantial fire damage.
This is recent.

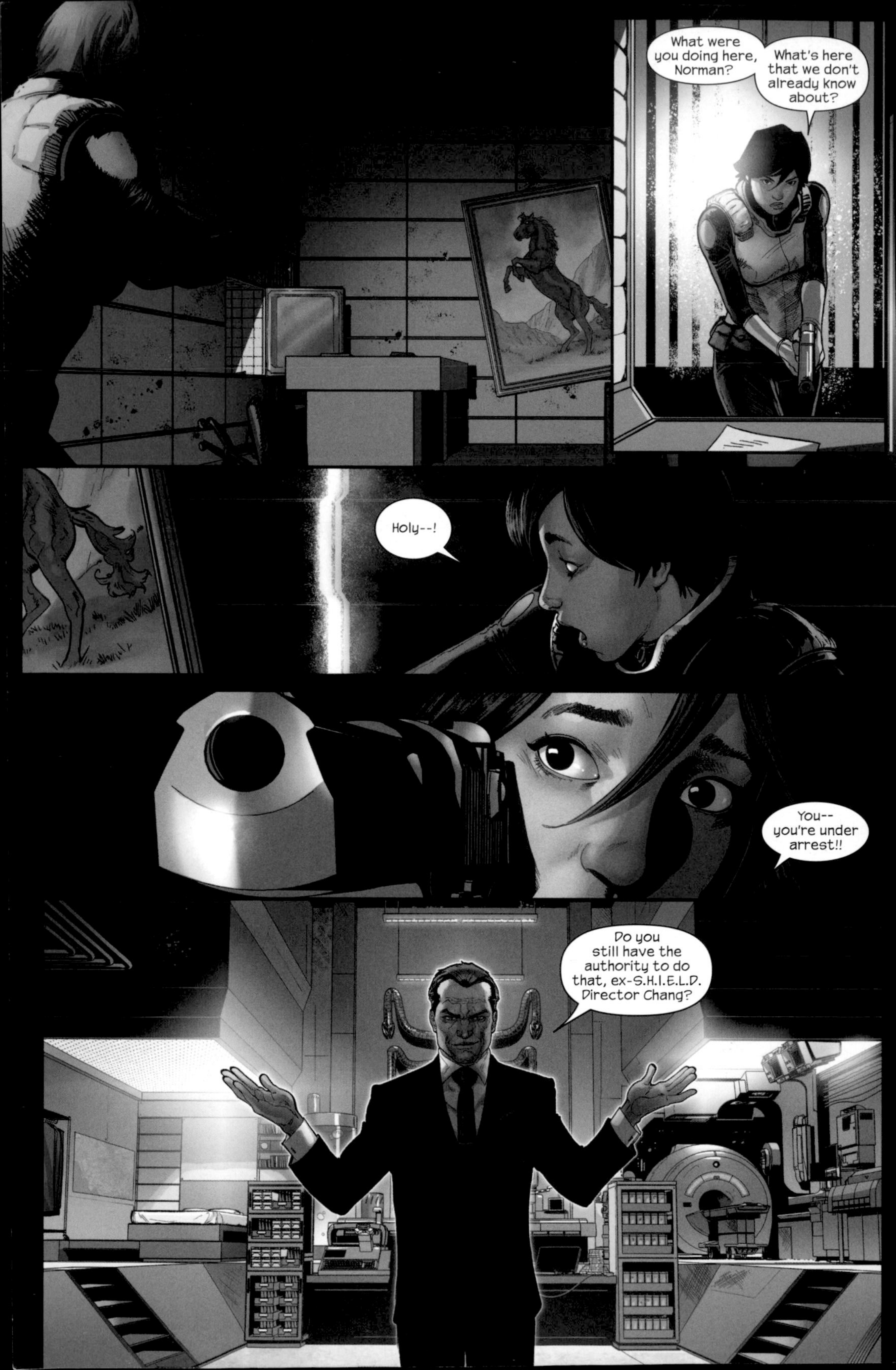
What were you doing here, Norman?
What's here that we don't already know about?
Holy--!
You-- you're under arrest!!
Do you still have the authority to do that, ex-S.H.I.E.L.D. Director Chang?

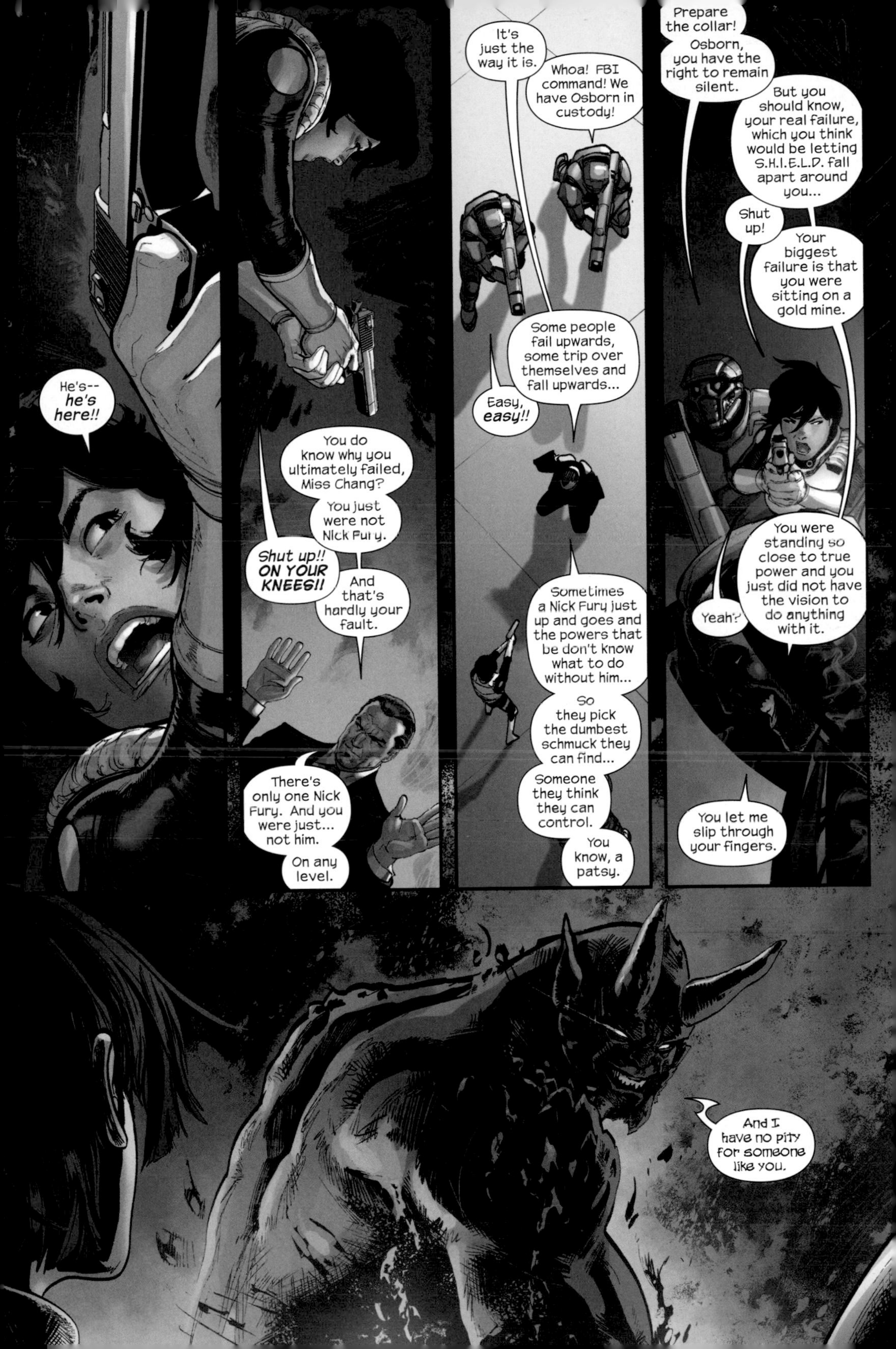
He's-- *he's here!!*
You do know why you ultimately failed, Miss Chang?
You just were not Nick Fury.
Shut up!! ON YOUR KNEES!!
And that's hardly your fault.
There's only one Nick Fury. And you were just... not him.
On any level.
It's just the way it is.
Whoa! FBI command! We have Osborn in custody!
Some people fail upwards, some trip over themselves and fall upwards...
Easy, *easy!!*
Sometimes a Nick Fury just up and goes and the powers that be don't know what to do without him...
So they pick the dumbest schmuck they can find...
Someone they think they can control.
You know, a patsy.
Prepare the collar!
Osborn, you have the right to remain silent.
But you should know, your real failure, which you think would be letting S.H.I.E.L.D. fall apart around you...
Shut up!
Your biggest failure is that you were sitting on a gold mine.
You were standing so close to true power and you just did not have the vision to do anything with it.
Yeah?
You let me slip through your fingers.
And I have no pity for someone like you.

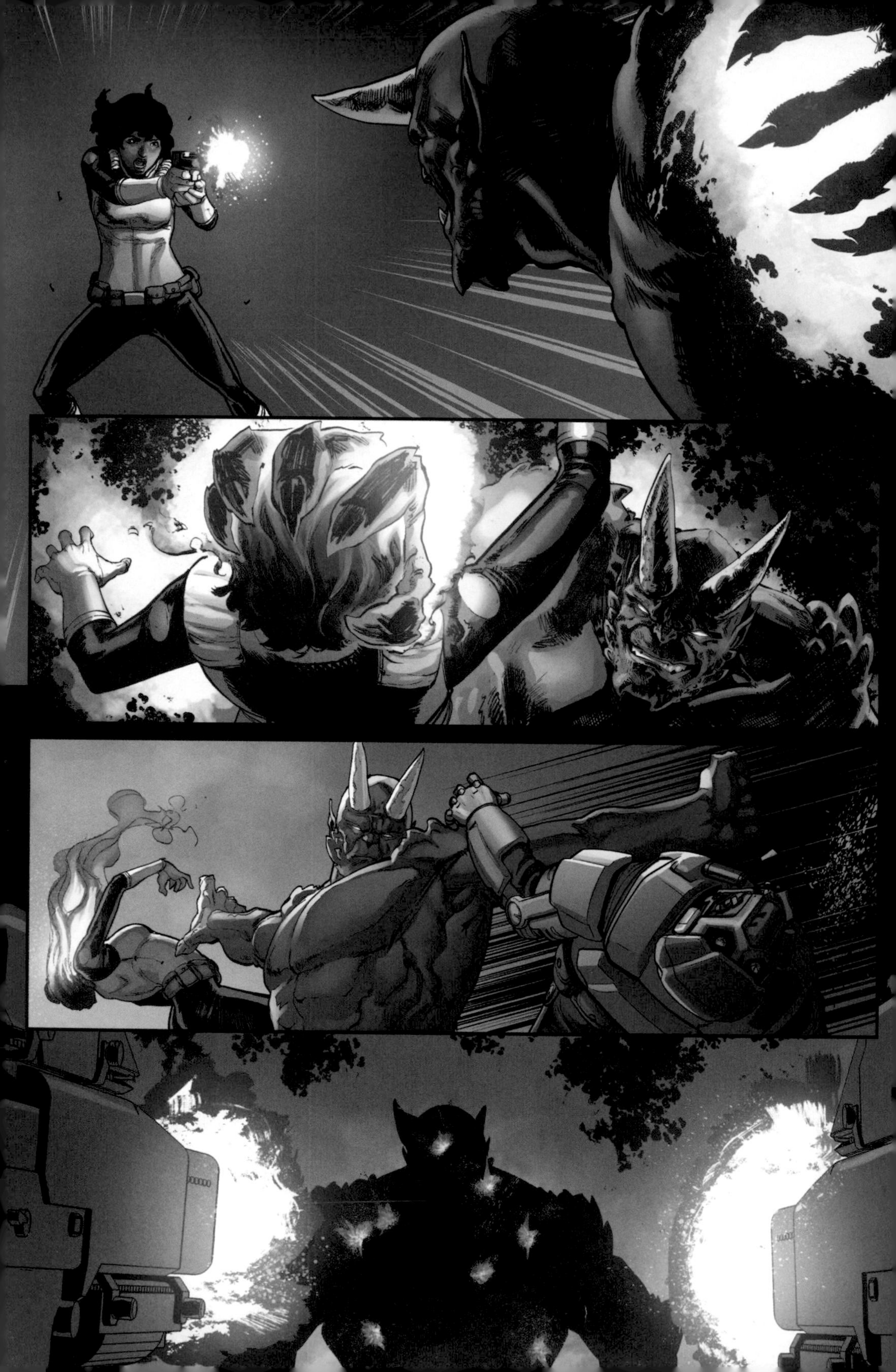

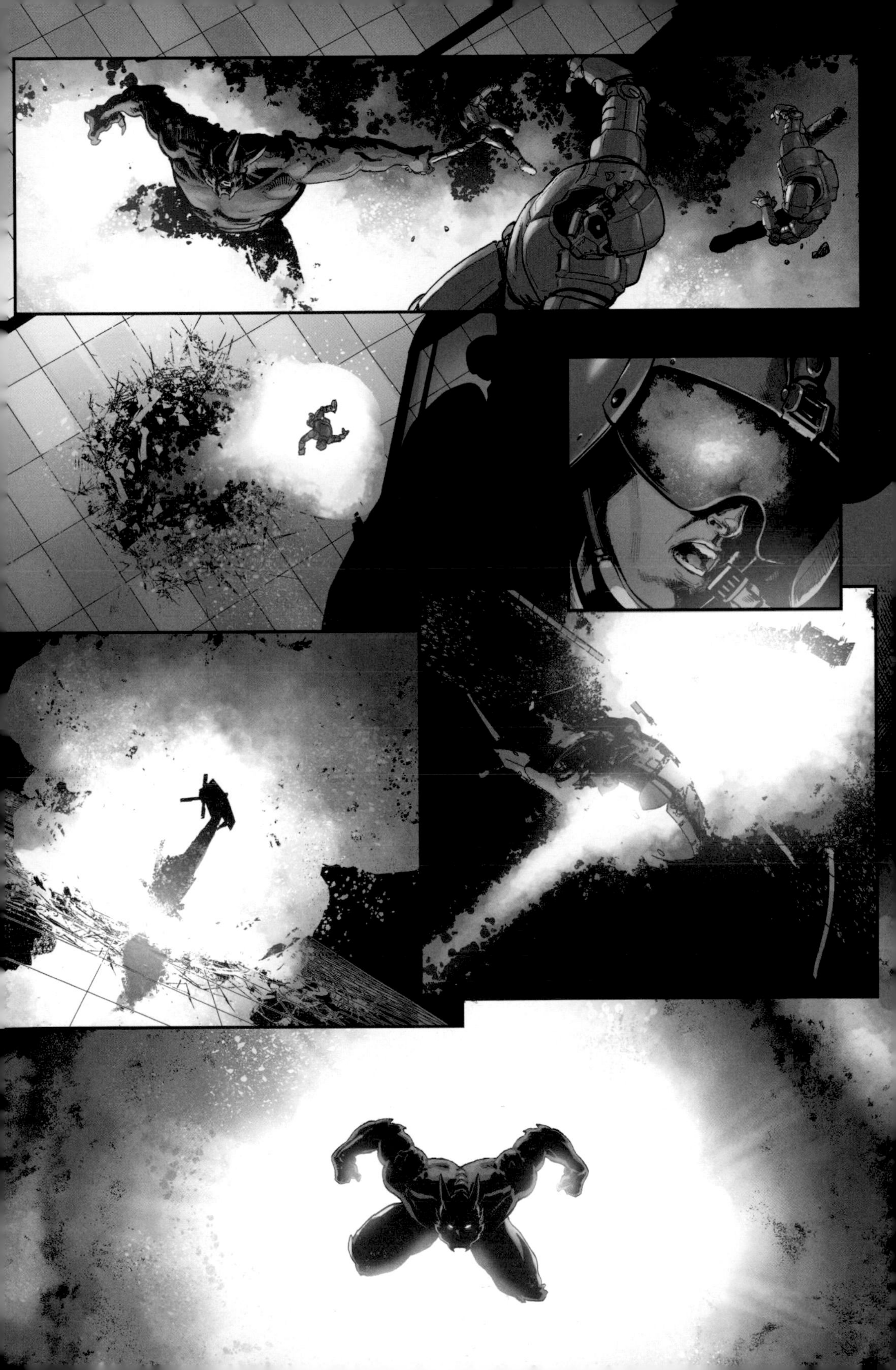

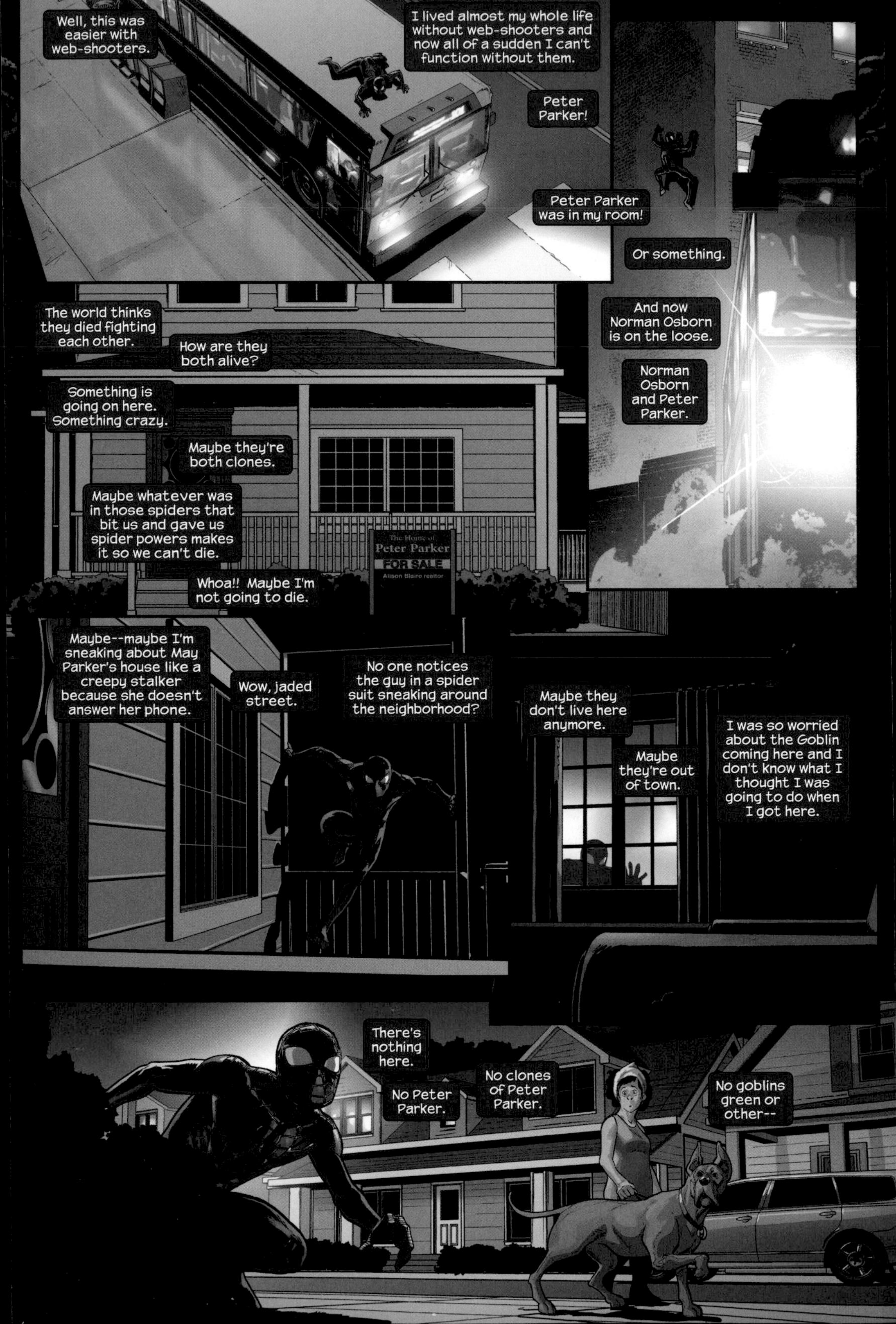

Well, this was easier with web-shooters.
I lived almost my whole life without web-shooters and now all of a sudden I can't function without them.
Peter Parker!
Peter Parker was in my room!
Or something.
And now Norman Osborn is on the loose.
Norman Osborn and Peter Parker.
The world thinks they died fighting each other.
How are they both alive?
Something is going on here. Something crazy.
Maybe they're both clones.
Maybe whatever was in those spiders that bit us and gave us spider powers makes it so we can't die.
The Home of Peter Parker
FOR SALE
Alison Blaire realtor
Whoa!! Maybe I'm not going to die.
Maybe--maybe I'm sneaking about May Parker's house like a creepy stalker because she doesn't answer her phone.
Wow, jaded street.
No one notices the guy in a spider suit sneaking around the neighborhood?
Maybe they don't live here anymore.
Maybe they're out of town.
I was so worried about the Goblin coming here and I don't know what I thought I was going to do when I got here.
There's nothing here.
No Peter Parker.
No clones of Peter Parker.
No goblins green or other--

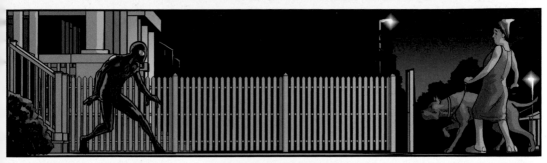

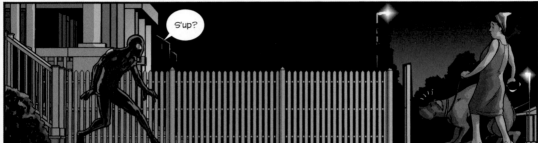

S'up?

What was I thinking anyhow? Norman Osborn killed Peter Parker.

RUFF

He killed him. Right here on this street.

I come here and what? Let him kill me?

RUFF RUFF

RUFF RUFF

Is that-- is that the Human Torch?

RUFF RUFF

RUFF RUFF RUFF RUFF

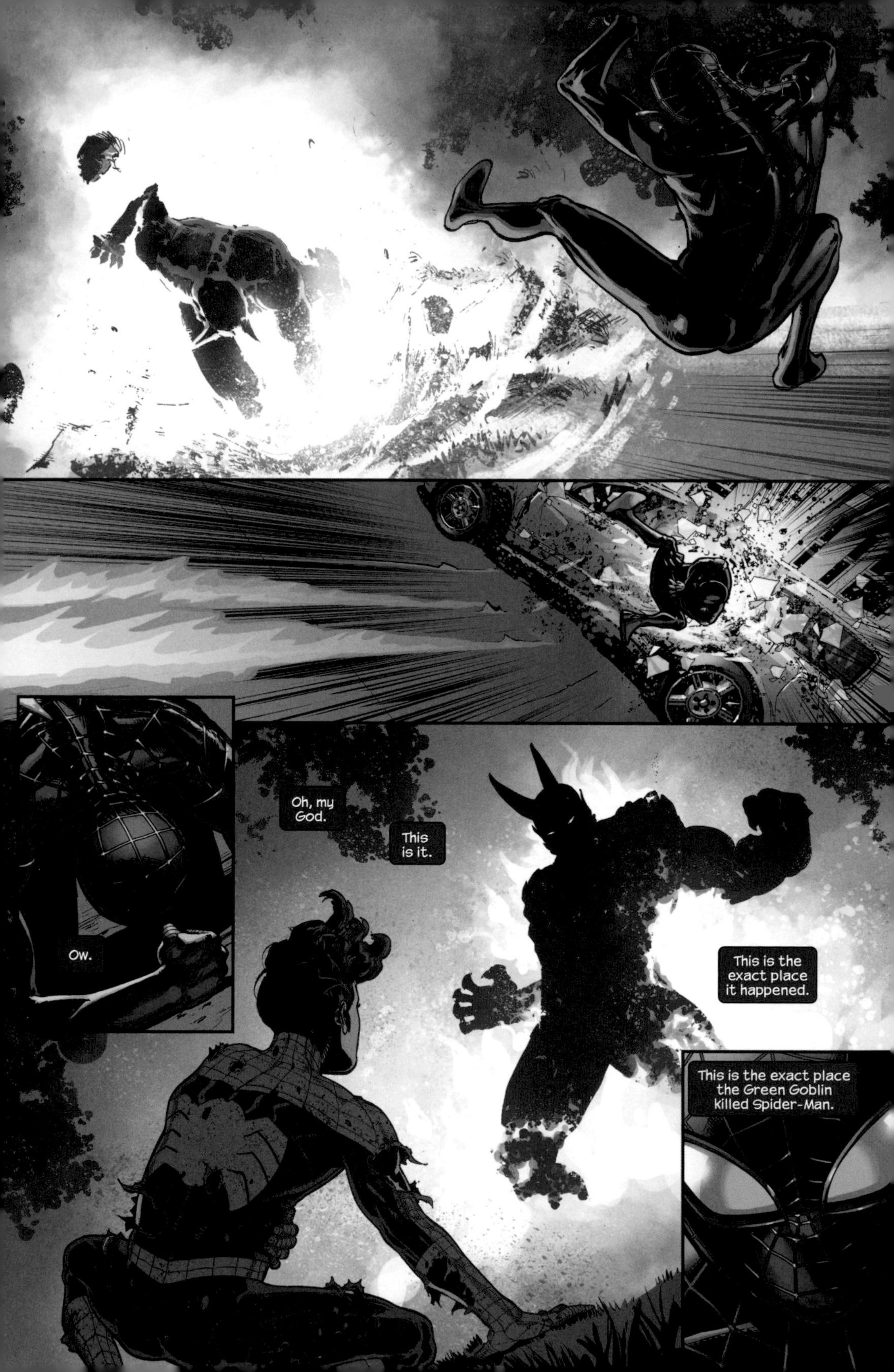
Ow.
Oh, my God.
This is it.
This is the exact place it happened.
This is the exact place the Green Goblin killed Spider-Man.

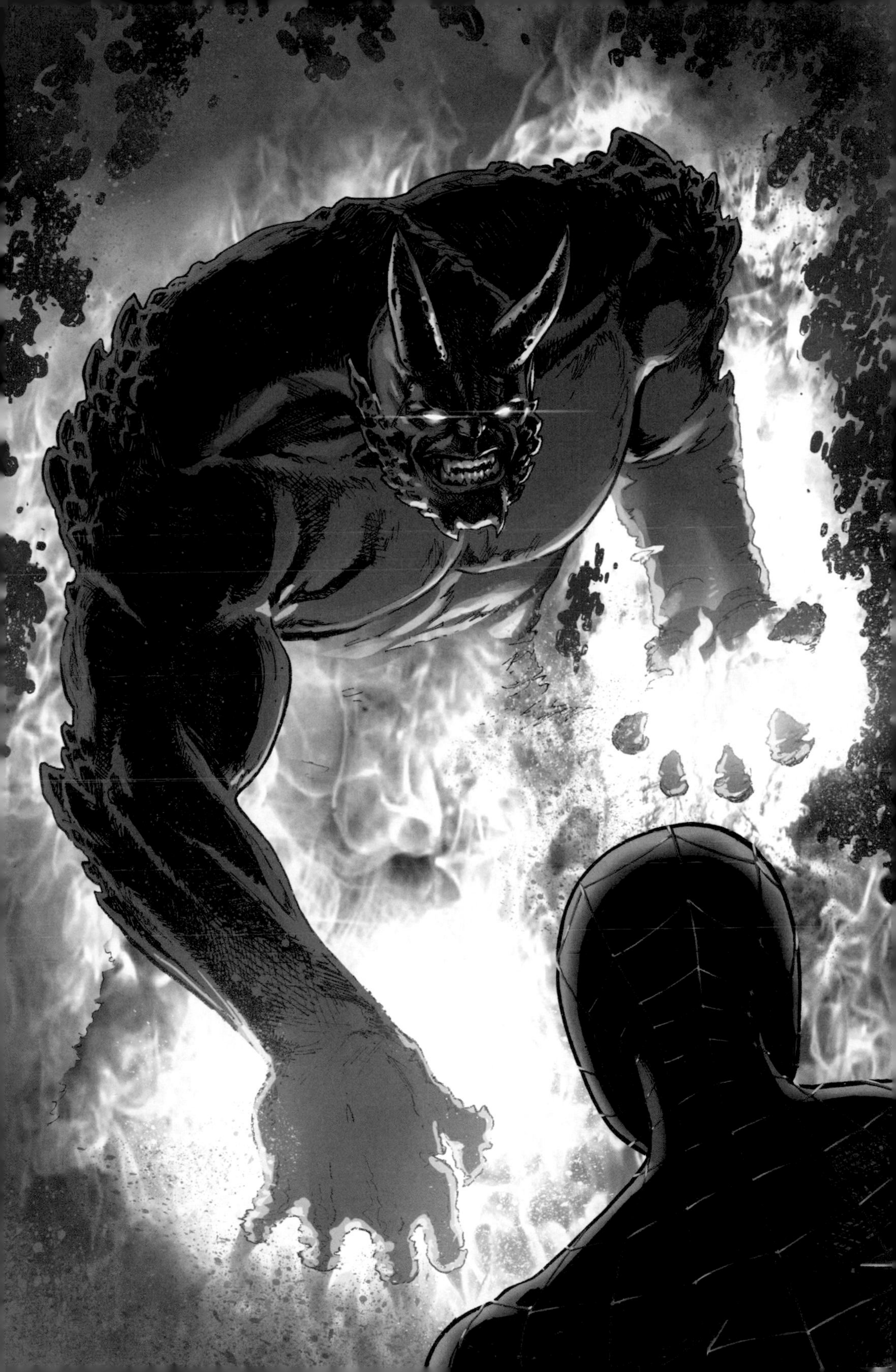

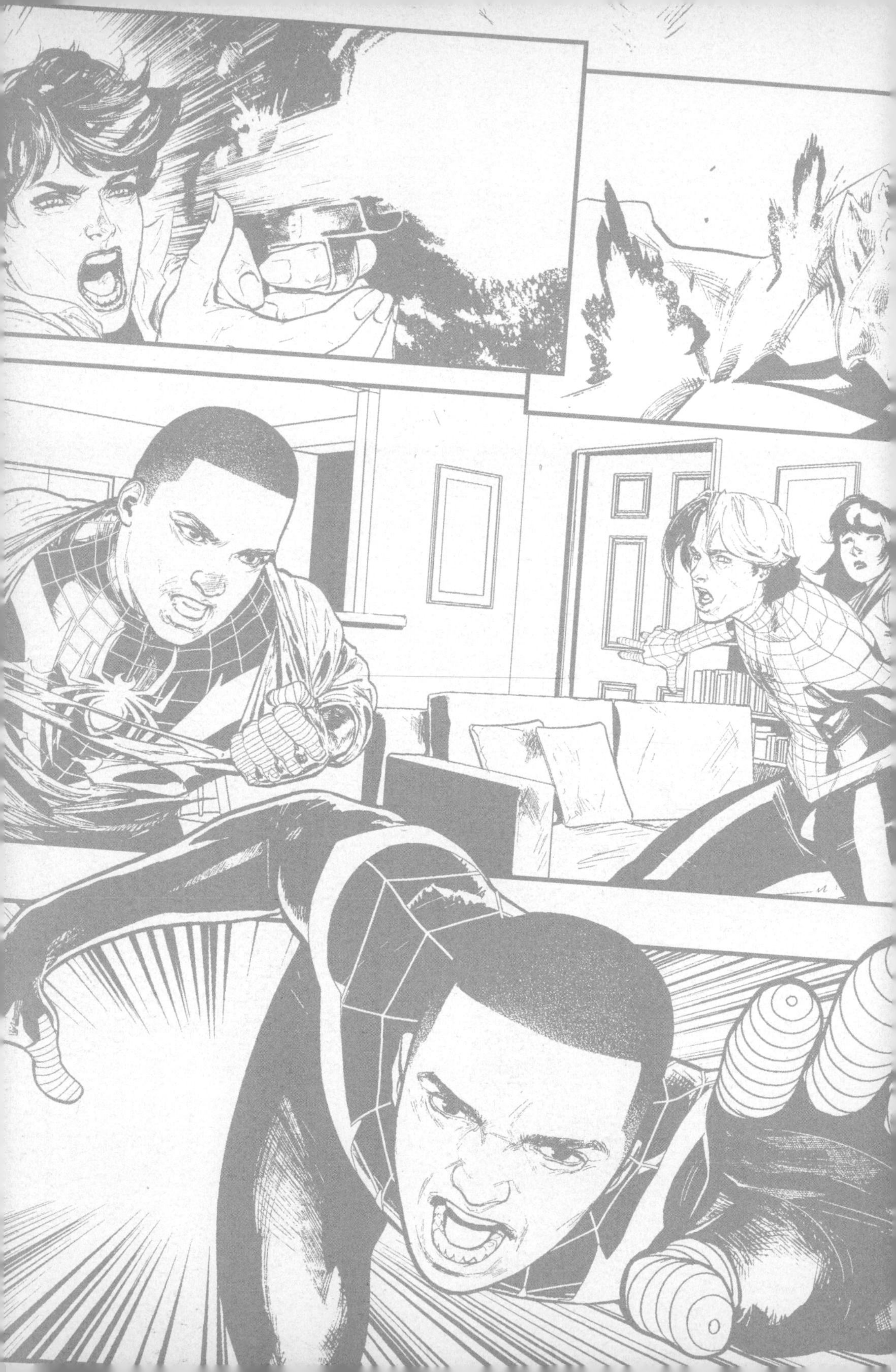

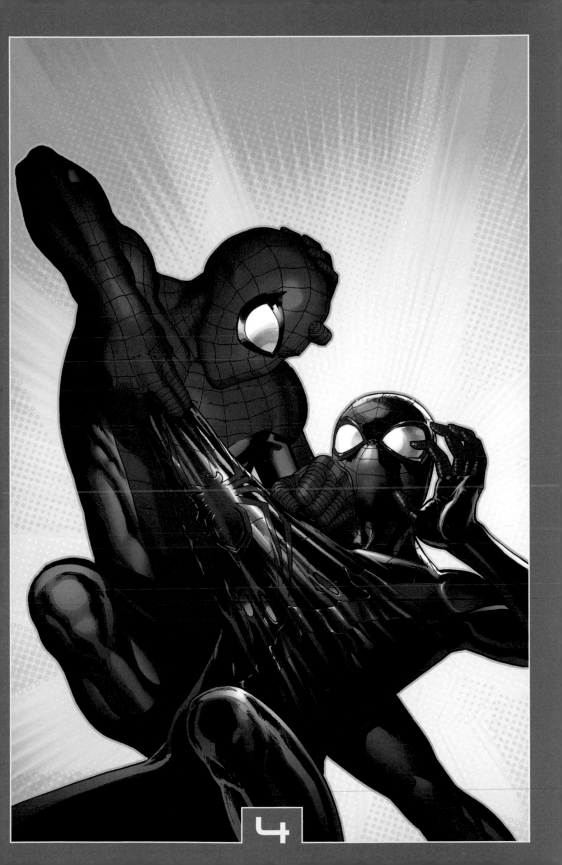

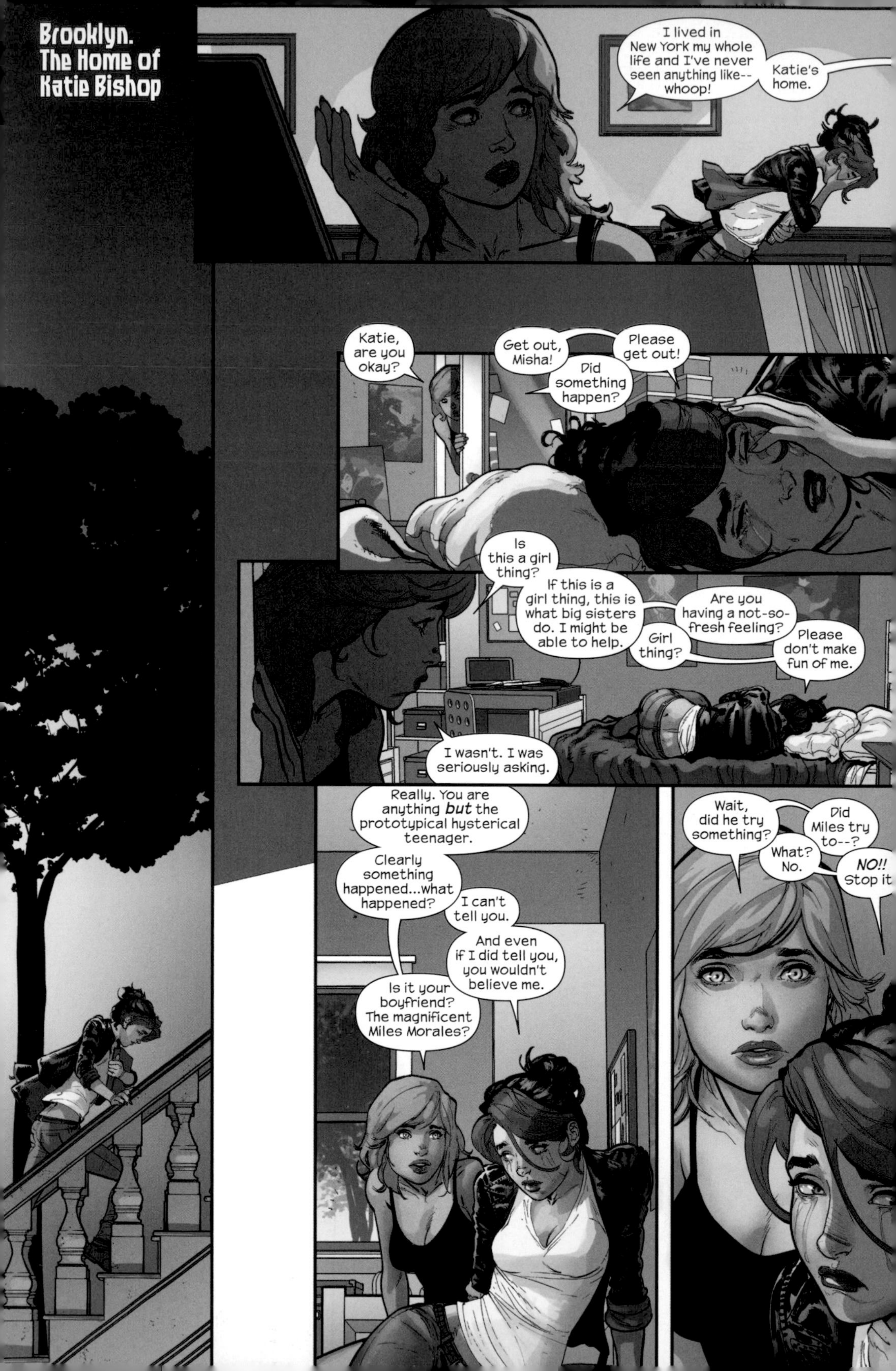
Brooklyn. The Home of Katie Bishop
I lived in New York my whole life and I've never seen anything like-- whoop!
Katie's home.
Katie, are you okay?
Get out, Misha!
Did something happen?
Please get out!
Is this a girl thing?
If this is a girl thing, this is what big sisters do. I might be able to help.
Are you having a not-so-fresh feeling?
Girl thing?
Please don't make fun of me.
I wasn't. I was seriously asking.
Really. You are anything *but* the prototypical hysterical teenager.
Clearly something happened...what happened?
I can't tell you.
And even if I did tell you, you wouldn't believe me.
Is it your boyfriend? The magnificent Miles Morales?
Wait, did he try something?
Did Miles try to--?
What? No.
NO!! Stop it

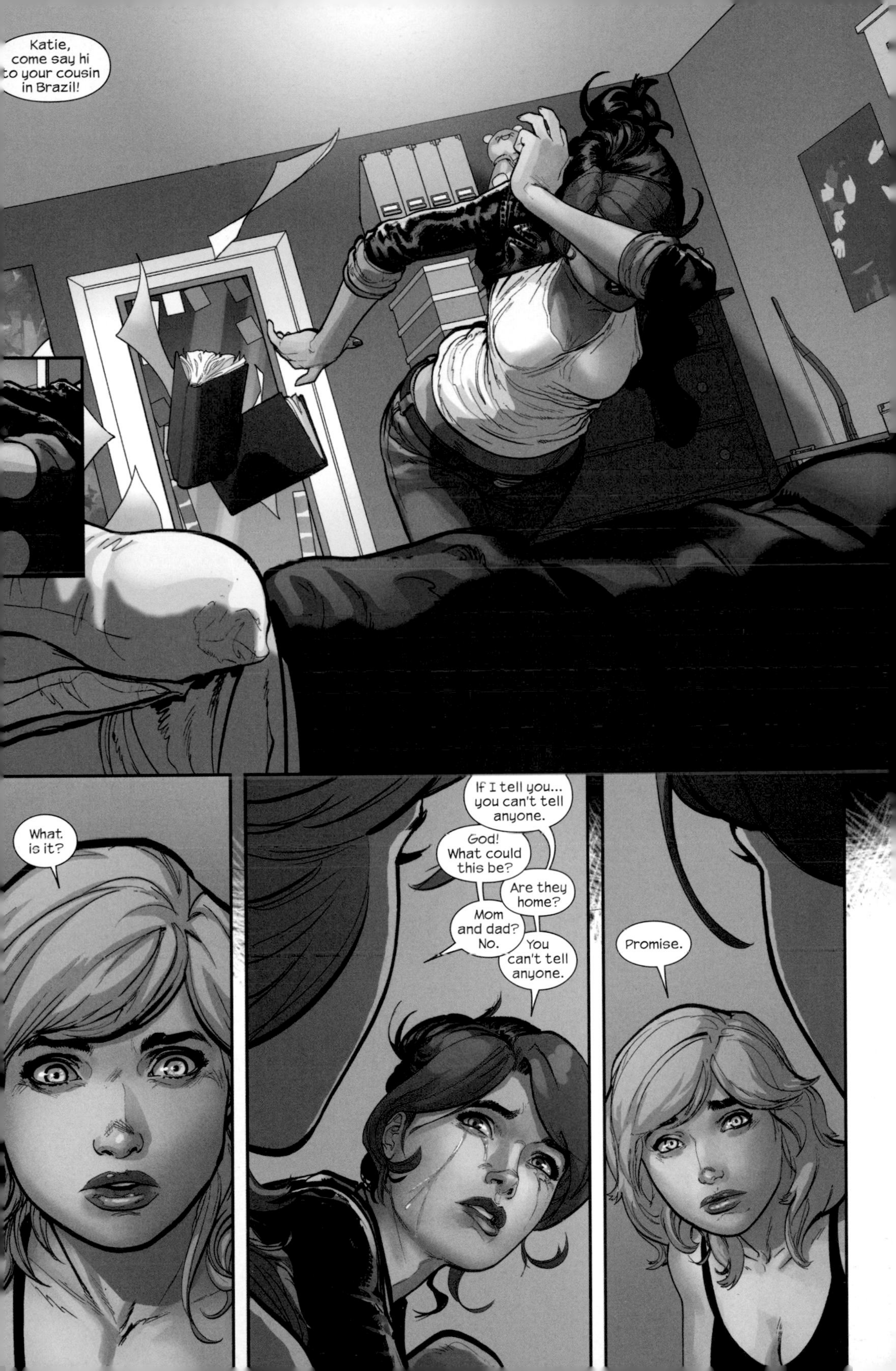
Katie, come say hi to your cousin in Brazil!
What. is it?
If I tell you... you can't tell anyone.
God! What could this be?
Are they home?
Mom and dad? No.
You can't tell anyone.
Promise.

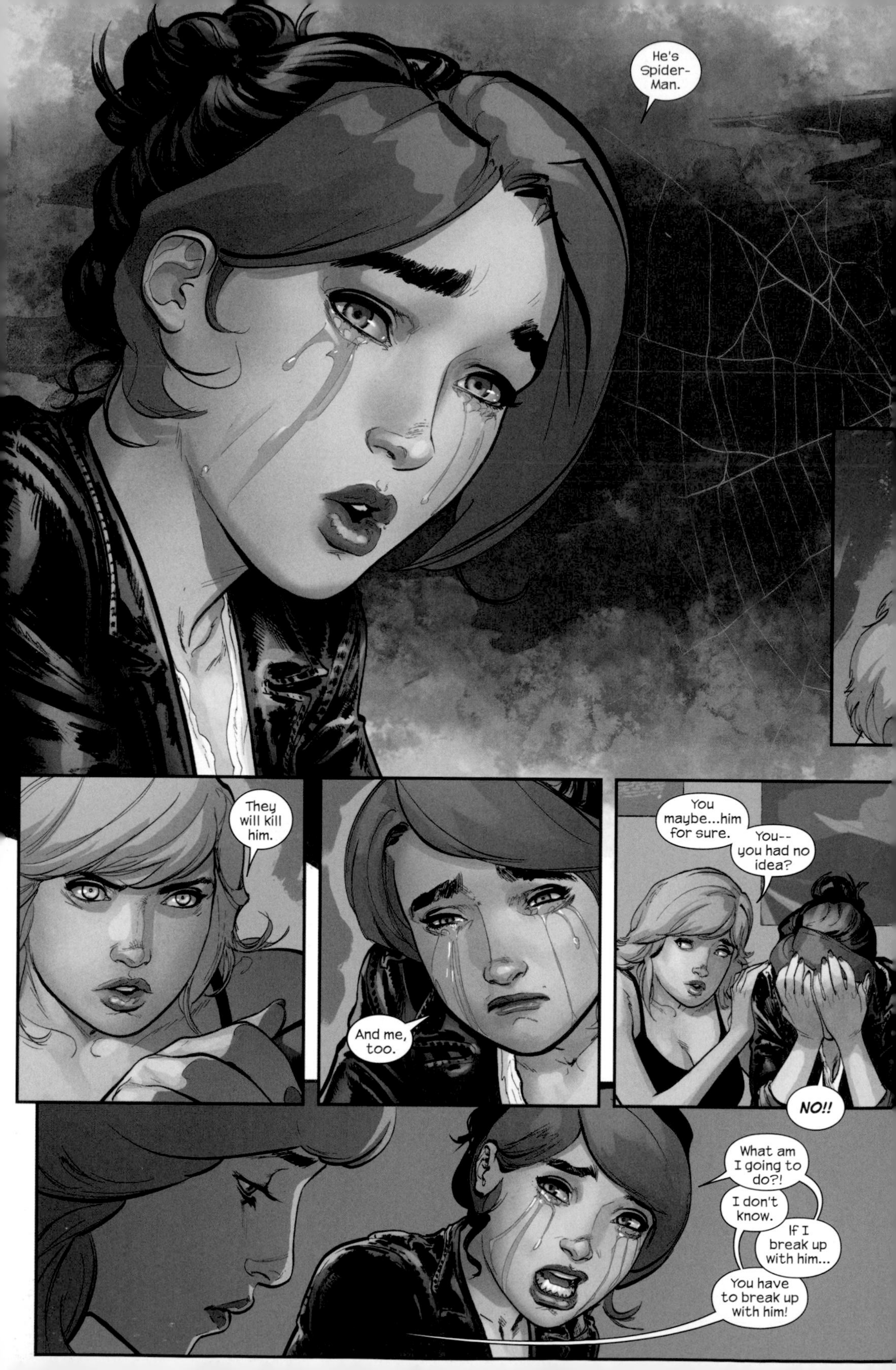
He's Spider-Man.
They will kill him.
And me, too.
You maybe...him for sure.
You-- you had no idea?
NO!!
What am I going to do?!
I don't know.
If I break up with him...
You have to break up with him!

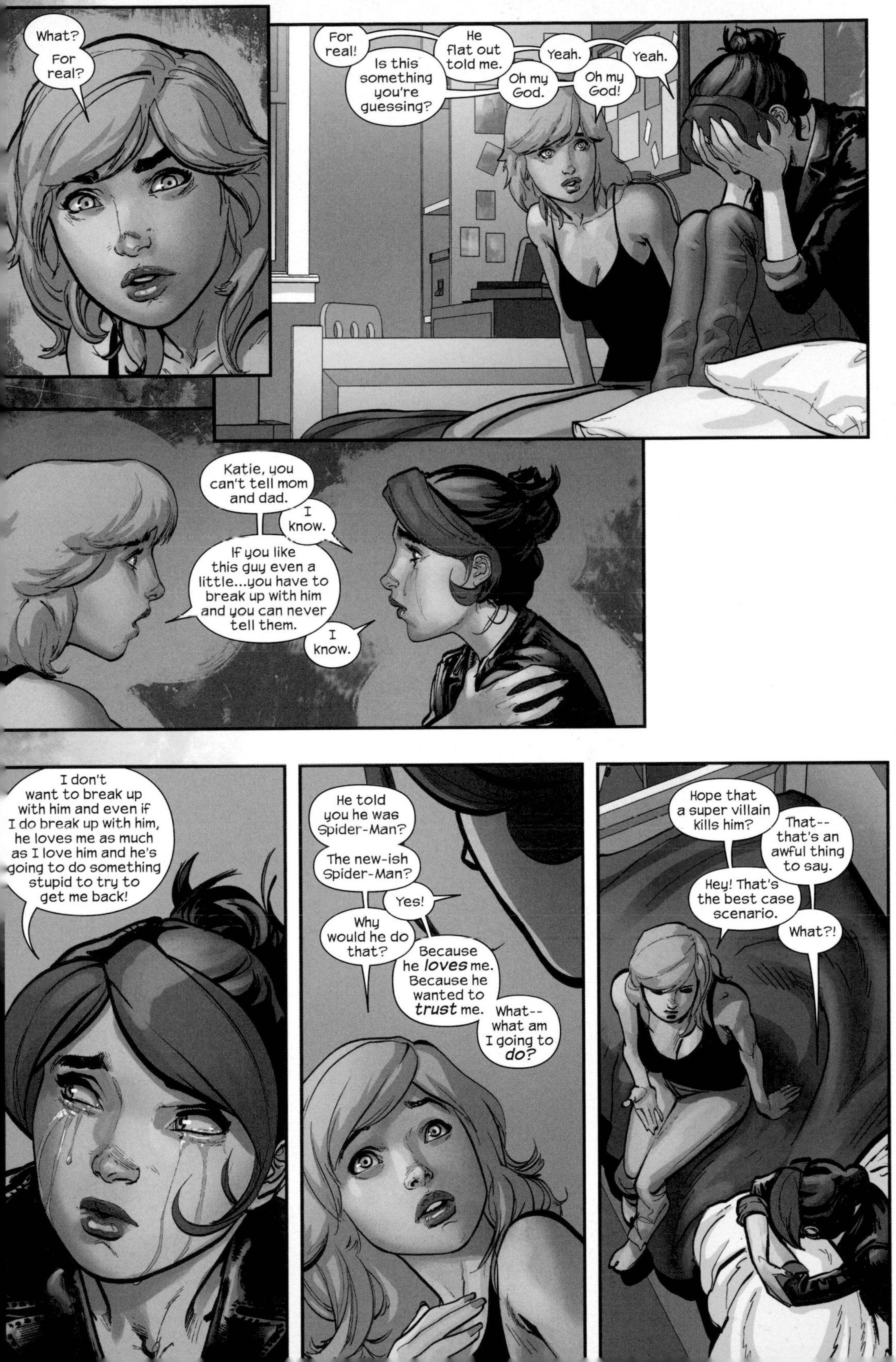
What?
For real?
For real!
Is this something you're guessing?
He flat out told me.
Oh my God.
Yeah.
Oh my God!
Yeah.
Katie, you can't tell mom and dad.
I know.
If you like this guy even a little...you have to break up with him and you can never tell them.
I know.
I don't want to break up with him and even if I do break up with him, he loves me as much as I love him and he's going to do something stupid to try to get me back!
He told you he was Spider-Man?
The new-ish Spider-Man?
Yes!
Why would he do that?
Because he loves me. Because he wanted to trust me.
What-- what am I going to do?
Hope that a super villain kills him?
That-- that's an awful thing to say.
Hey! That's the best case scenario.
What?!

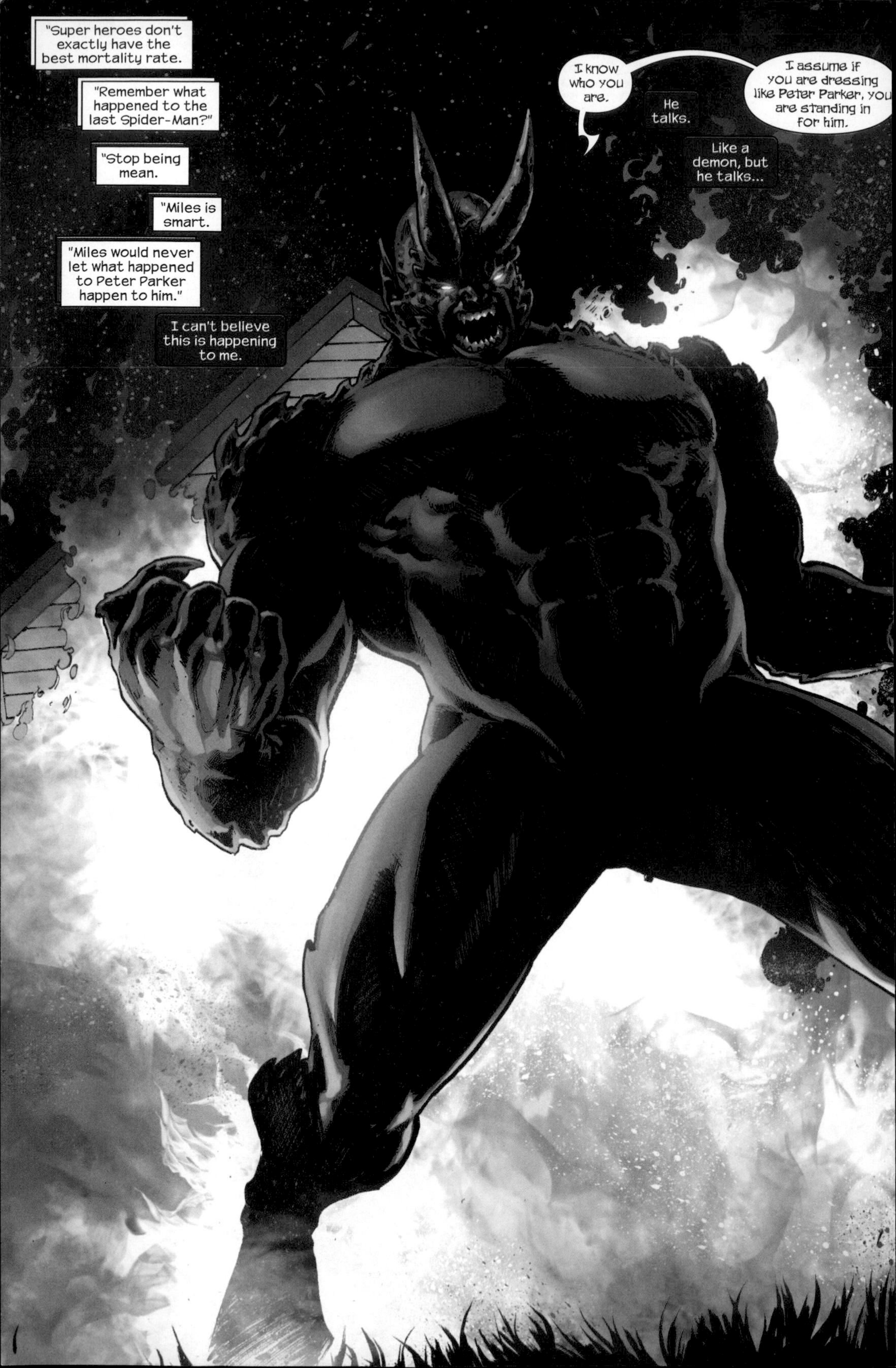
"Super heroes don't exactly have the best mortality rate.
"Remember what happened to the last Spider-Man?"
"Stop being mean.
"Miles is smart.
"Miles would never let what happened to Peter Parker happen to him."
I can't believe this is happening to me.
I know who you are.
He talks.
I assume if you are dressing like Peter Parker, you are standing in for him.
Like a demon, but he talks...

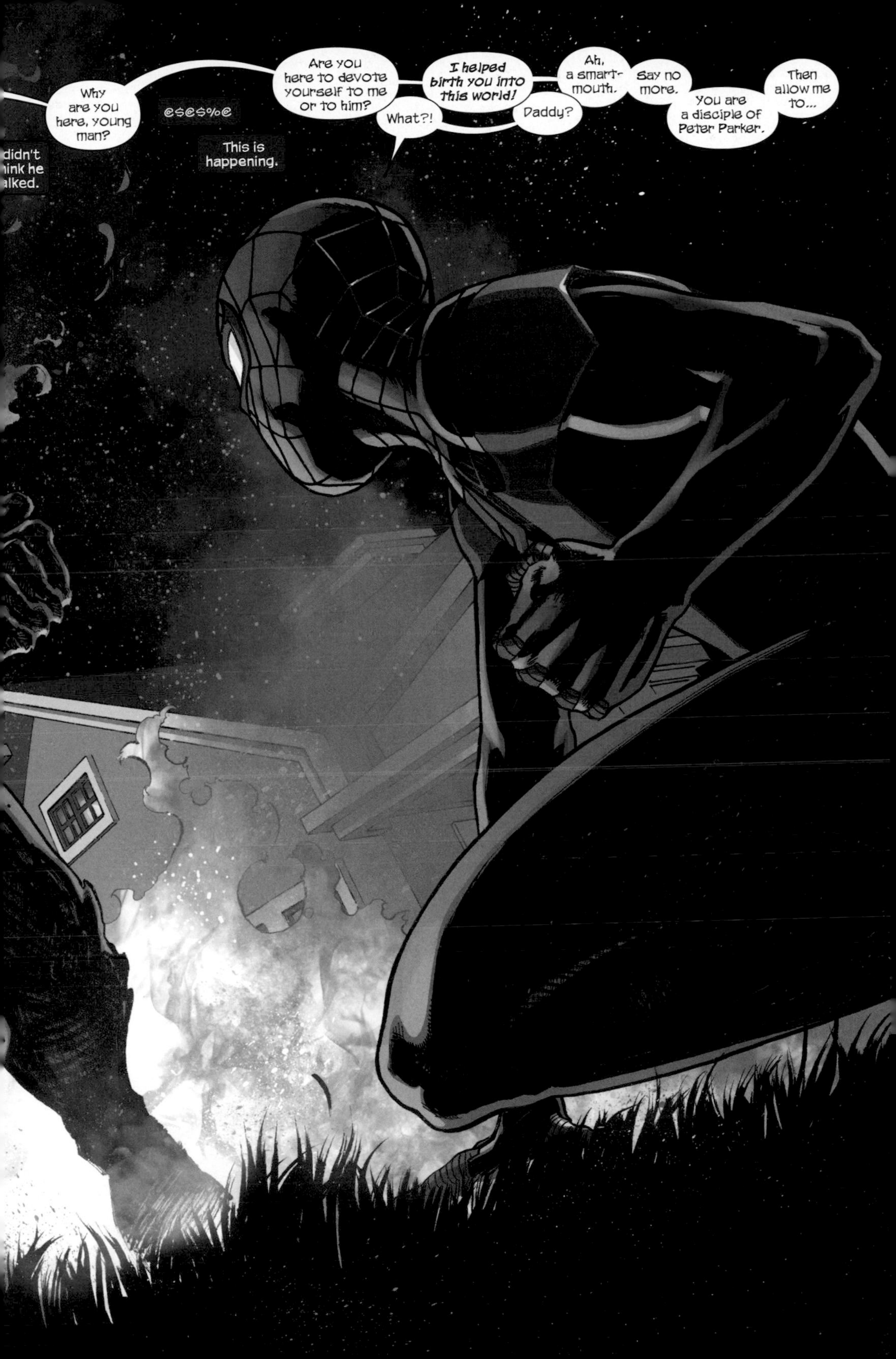

didn't
hink he
alked.
Why are you here, young man?
©$©$%©
This is happening.
Are you here to devote yourself to me or to him?
What?!
I helped birth you into this world!
Daddy?
Ah, a smart-mouth.
Say no more.
You are a disciple of Peter Parker.
Then allow me to...

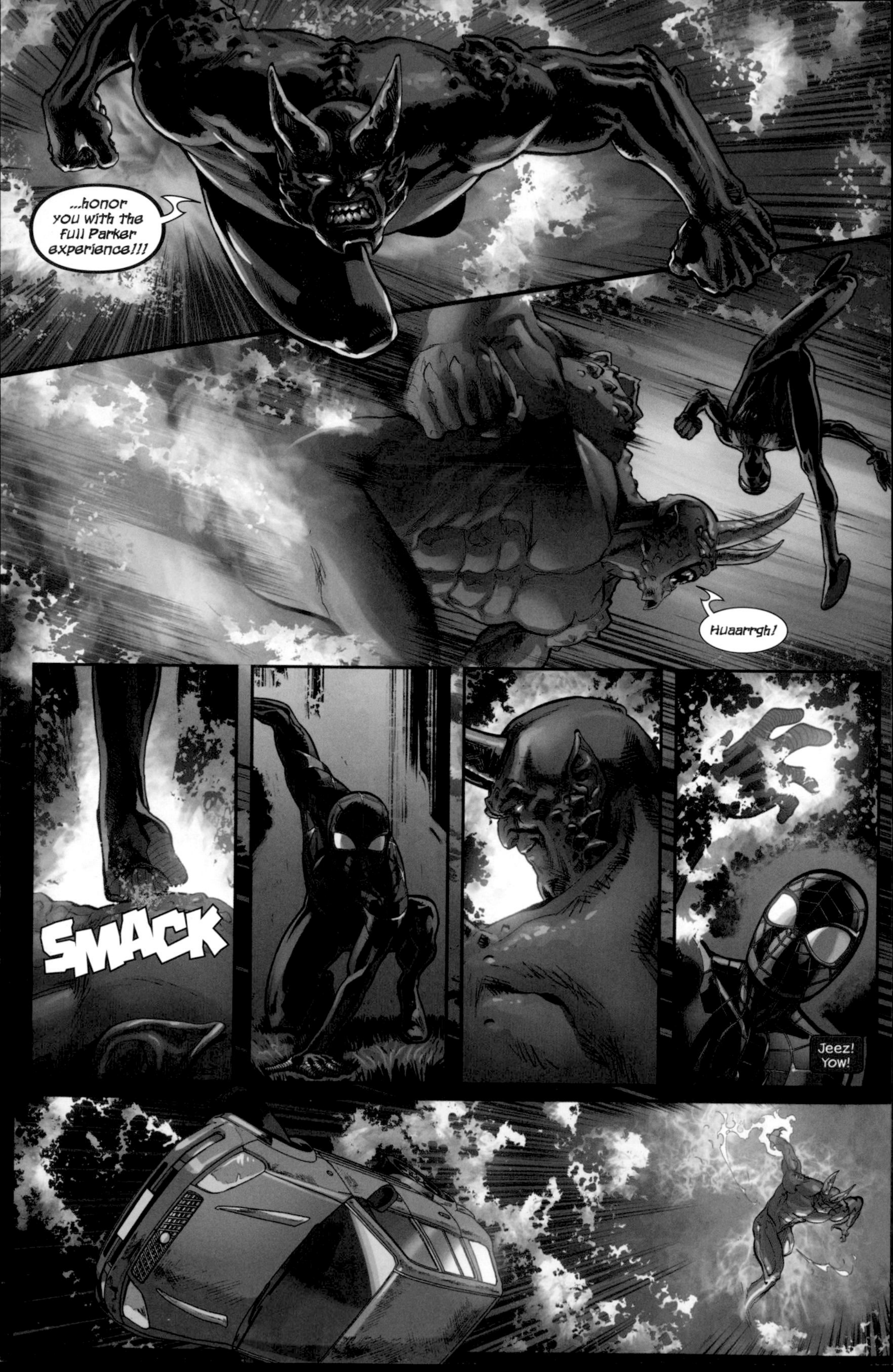
...honor you with the full Parker experience!!!
Huaarrgh!
SMACK
Jeez! Yow!

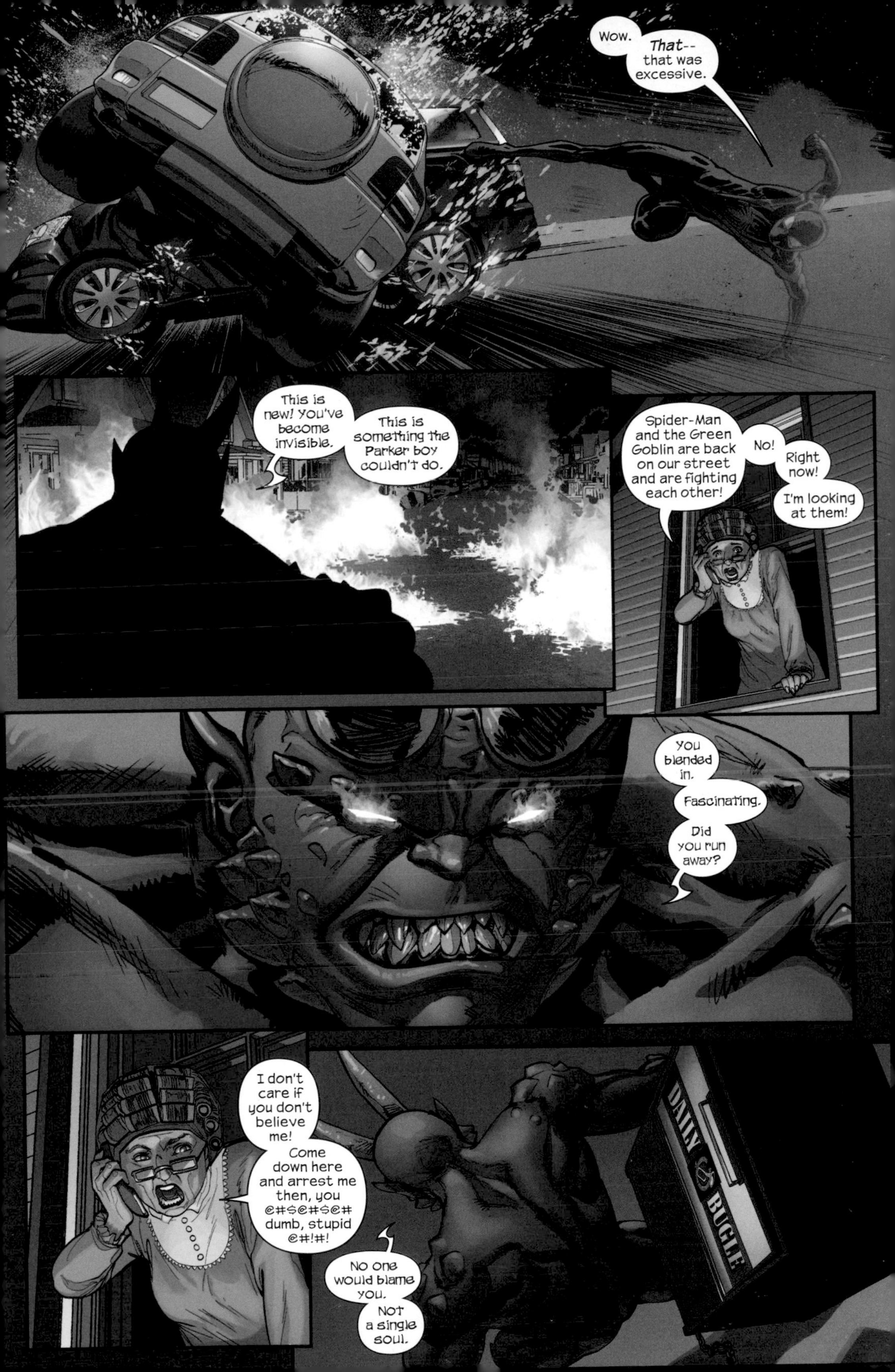

Wow. *That*--
that was excessive.
This is new! You've become invisible.
This is something the Parker boy couldn't do.
Spider-Man and the Green Goblin are back on our street and are fighting each other!
No!
Right now!
I'm looking at them!
You blended in.
Fascinating.
Did you run away?
I don't care if you don't believe me!
Come down here and arrest me then, you @#$@#$@# dumb, stupid @#!#!
No one would blame you.
Not a single soul.
DAILY BUGLE

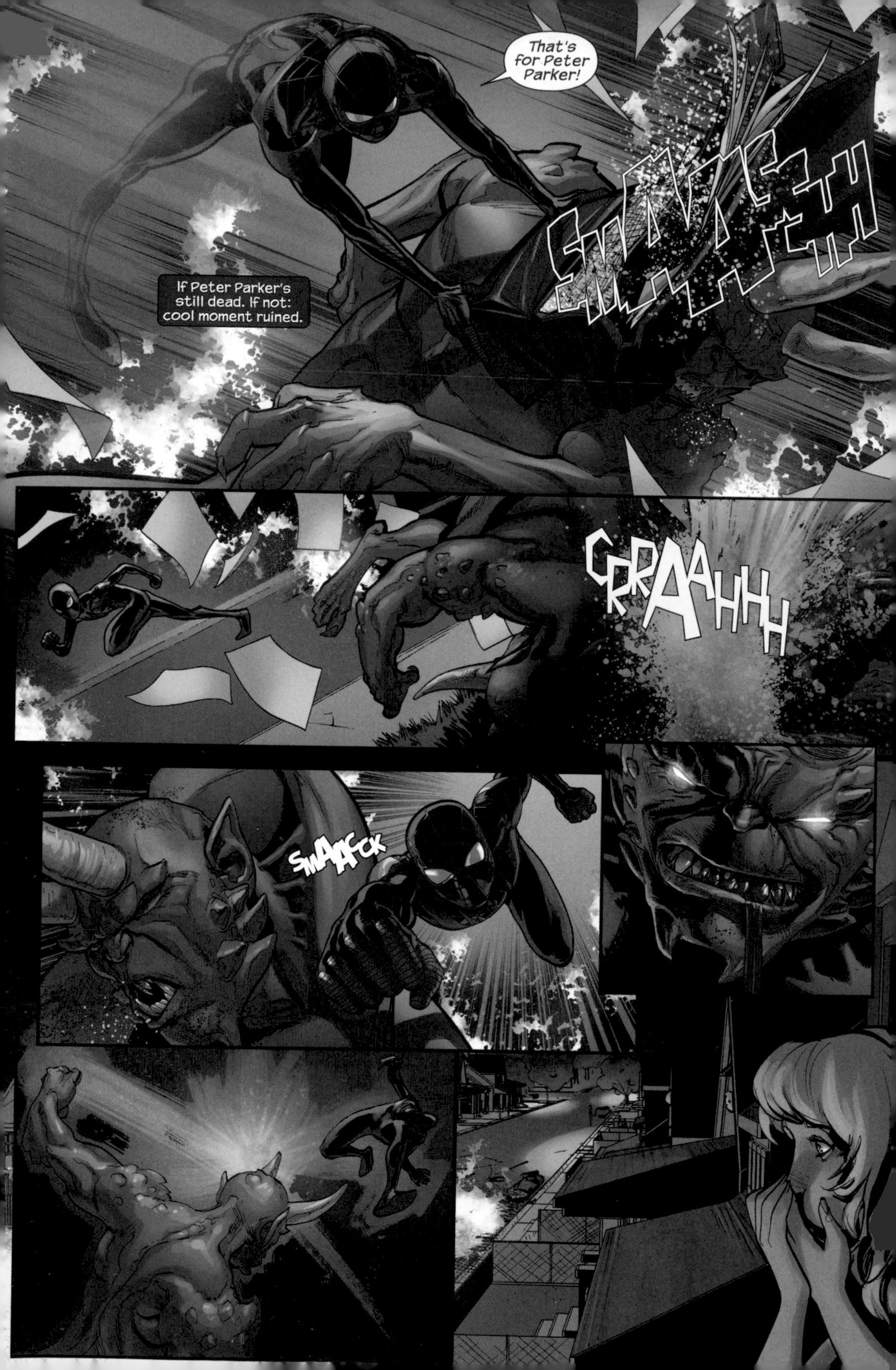

That's for Peter Parker!
SMAASH
If Peter Parker's still dead. If not: cool moment ruined.
CRRAAHHH
SWAACK

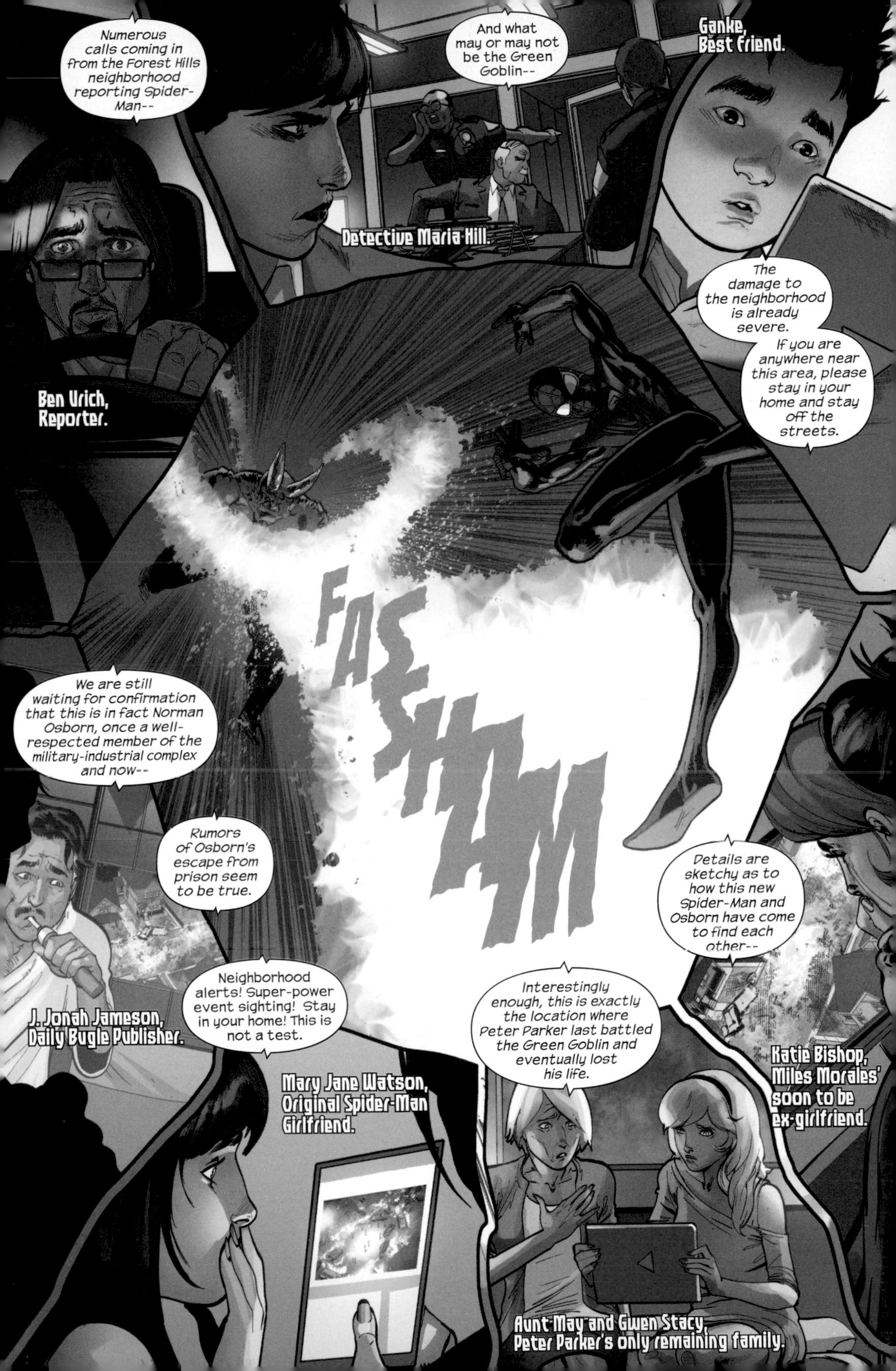
Numerous calls coming in from the Forest Hills neighborhood reporting Spider-Man--
And what may or may not be the Green Goblin--
Ganke, Best Friend.
Detective Maria Hill.
Ben Urich, Reporter.
The damage to the neighborhood is already severe.
If you are anywhere near this area, please stay in your home and stay off the streets.
FASHHAM
We are still waiting for confirmation that this is in fact Norman Osborn, once a well-respected member of the military-industrial complex and now--
Rumors of Osborn's escape from prison seem to be true.
Details are sketchy as to how this new Spider-Man and Osborn have come to find each other--
J. Jonah Jameson, Daily Bugle Publisher.
Neighborhood alerts! Super-power event sighting! Stay in your home! This is not a test.
Interestingly enough, this is exactly the location where Peter Parker last battled the Green Goblin and eventually lost his life.
Katie Bishop, Miles Morales' soon to be ex-girlfriend.
Mary Jane Watson, Original Spider-Man Girlfriend.
Aunt May and Gwen Stacy, Peter Parker's only remaining family.

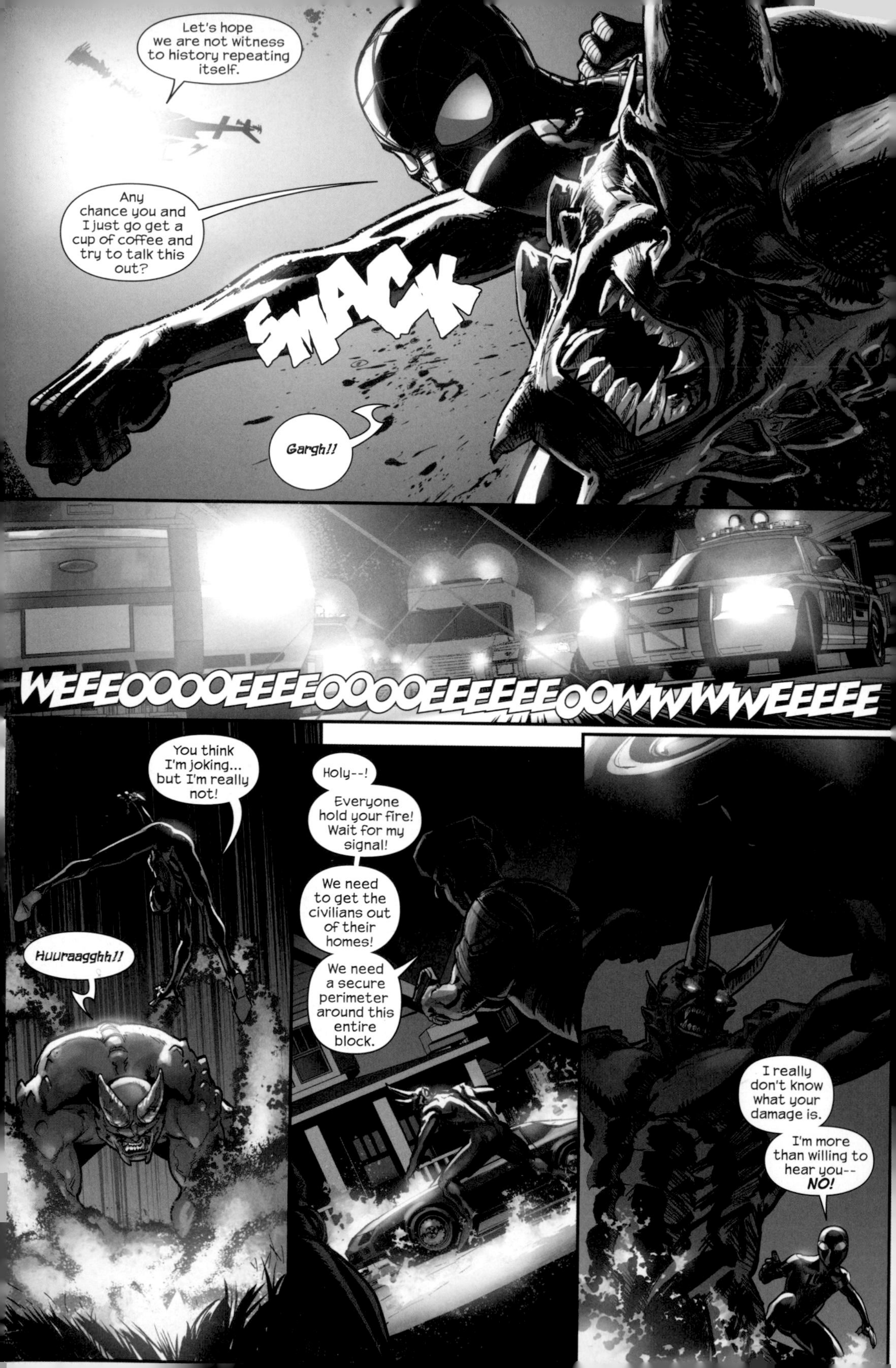
Let's hope we are not witness to history repeating itself.
Any chance you and I just go get a cup of coffee and try to talk this out?
SMACK
Gargh!!
WEEEOOOOEEEEOOOOEEEEEEOOWWWWEEEEE
You think I'm joking... but I'm really not!
Huuraagghh!!
Holy--!
Everyone hold your fire! Wait for my signal!
We need to get the civilians out of their homes!
We need a secure perimeter around this entire block.
I really don't know what your damage is.
I'm more than willing to hear you--
NO!

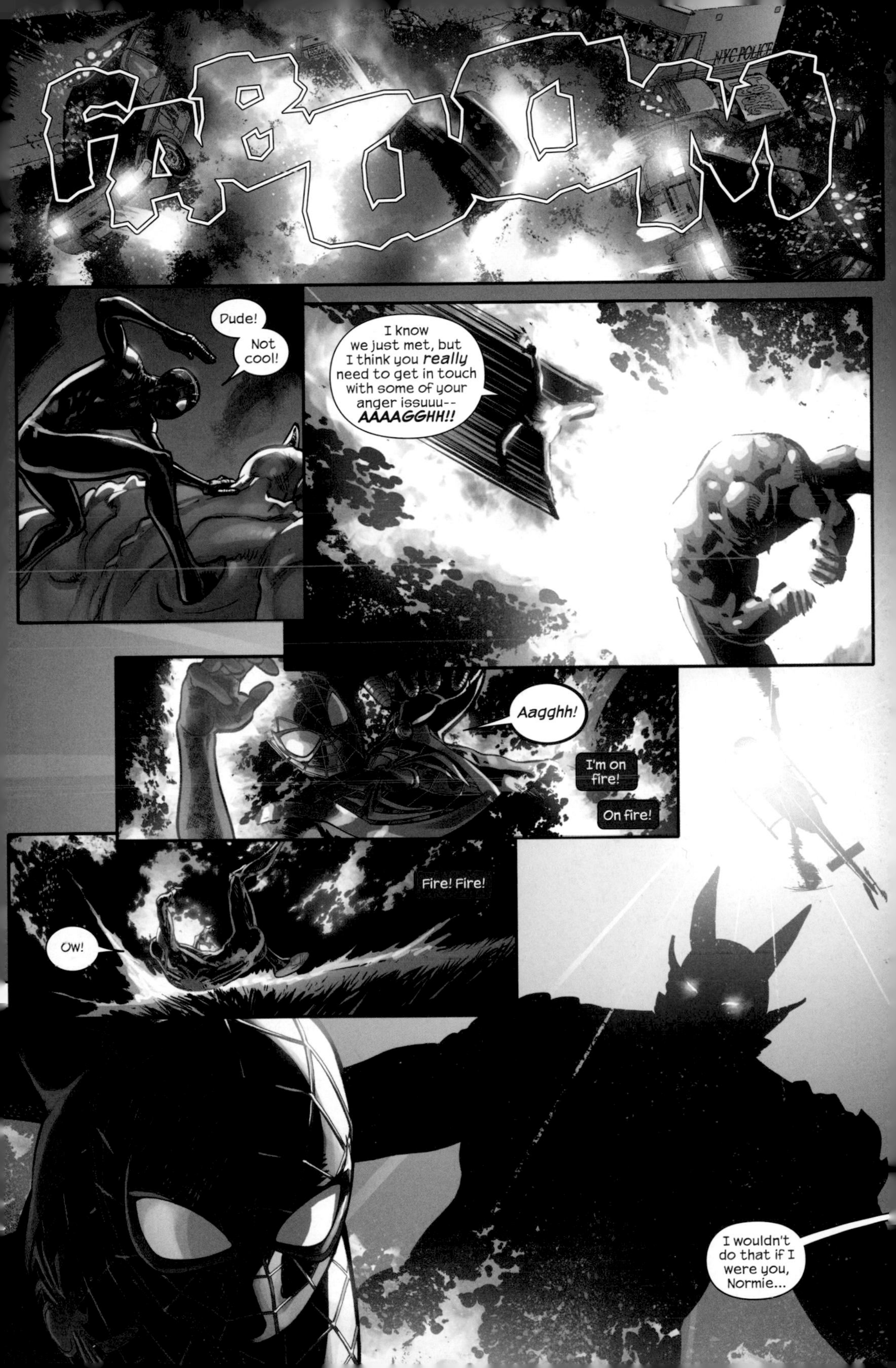
FABOOM
Dude!
Not cool!
I know we just met, but I think you *really* need to get in touch with some of your anger issuuu-- ***AAAAGGHH!!***
Aagghh!
I'm on fire!
On fire!
Fire! Fire!
Ow!
I wouldn't do that if I were you, Normie...

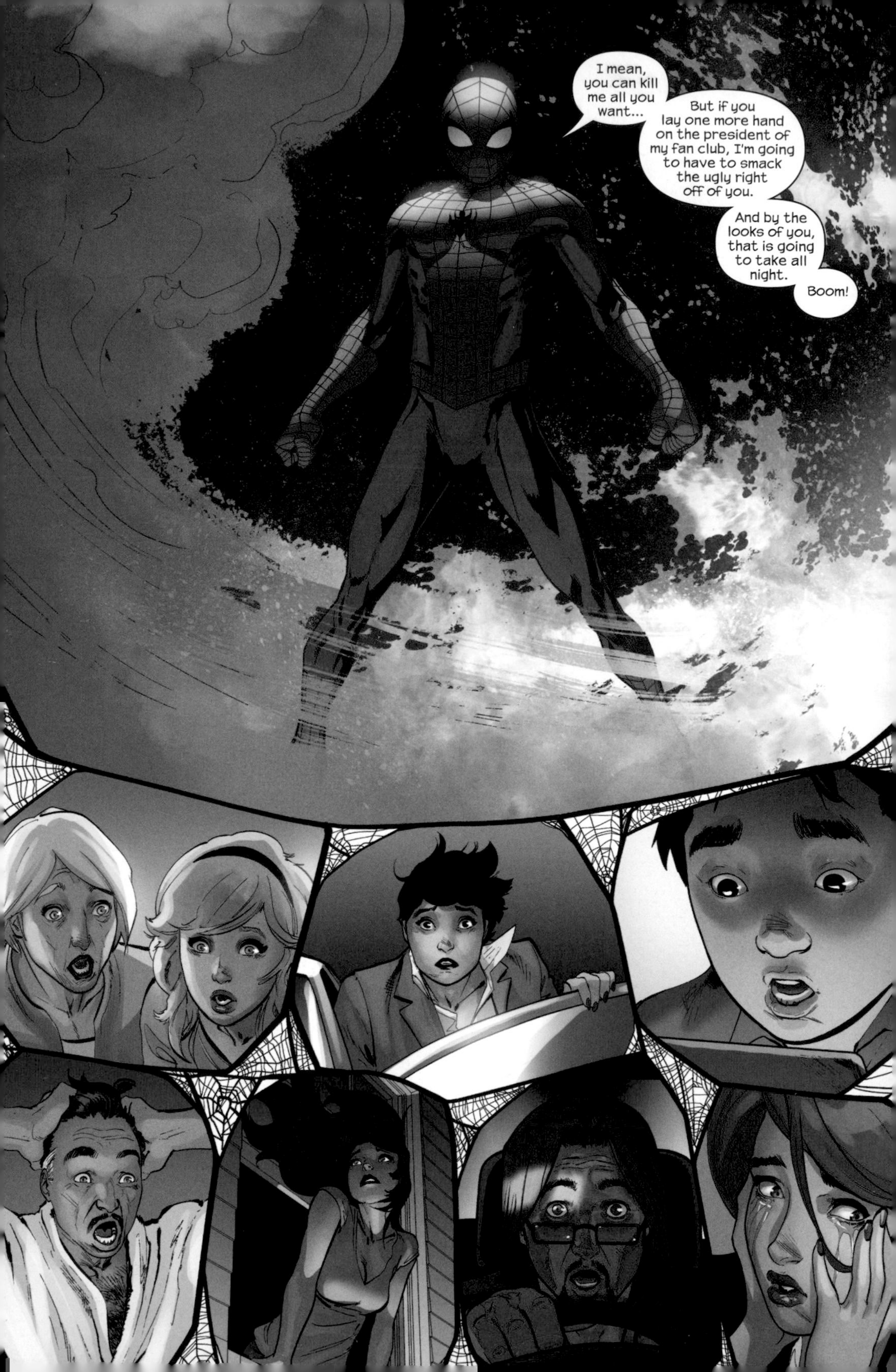
I mean, you can kill me all you want...
But if you lay one more hand on the president of my fan club, I'm going to have to smack the ugly right off of you.
And by the looks of you, that is going to take all night.
Boom!

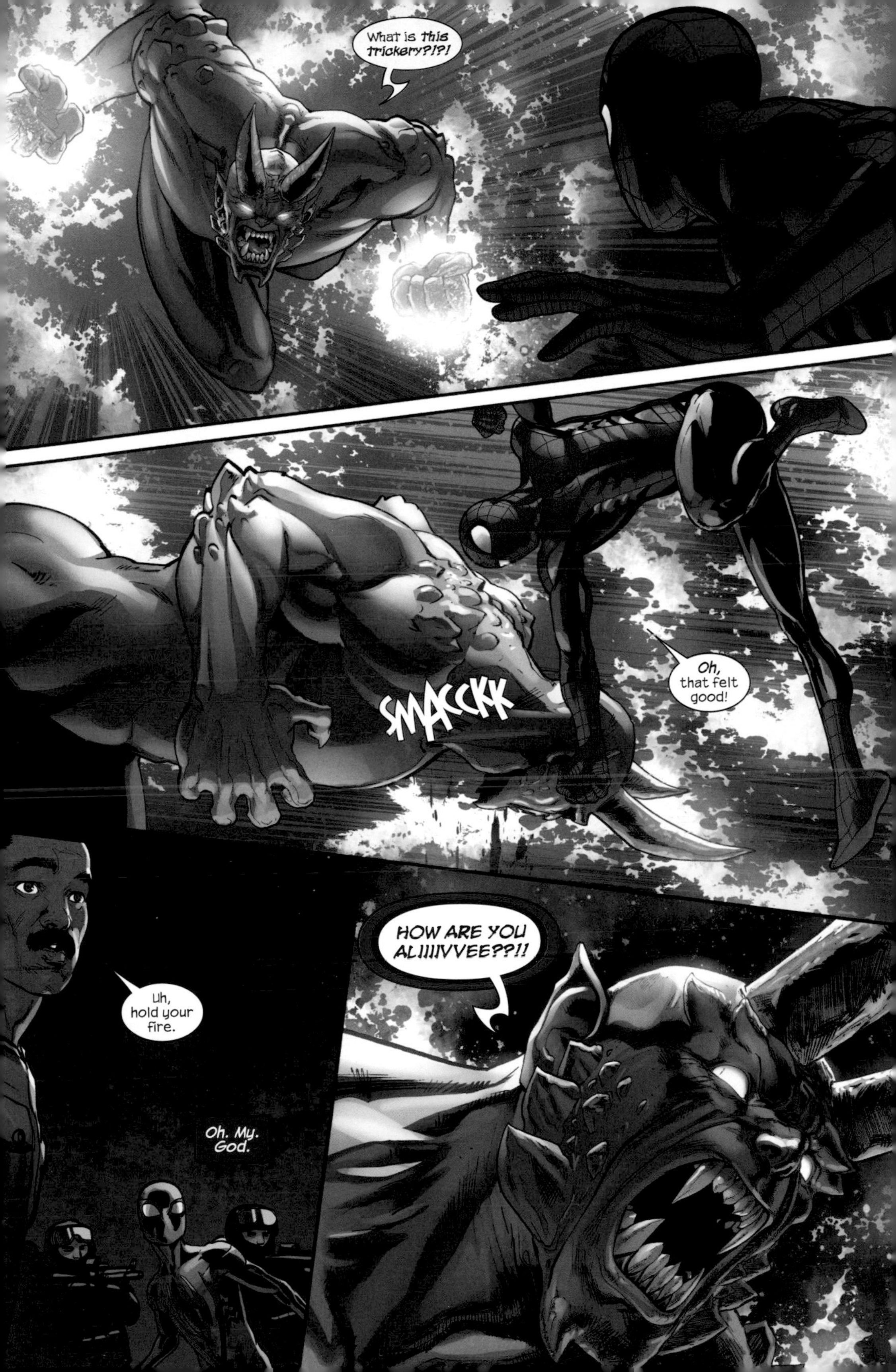
What is this trickery?!?!
SMACCKK
Oh, that felt good!
Uh, hold your fire.
Oh. My. God.
HOW ARE YOU ALIIIIIVVEE??!!

I will not be mocked!

Are you sure? You're *really* good at it!

In position. Do we have the word??

Oh no.

BUDDABUDDABUDDABUDDABUDDABUDDABUD

BOOM

I will burn you all! I will burn this world!

I will watch the flesh of your body bubble and--

THWAP

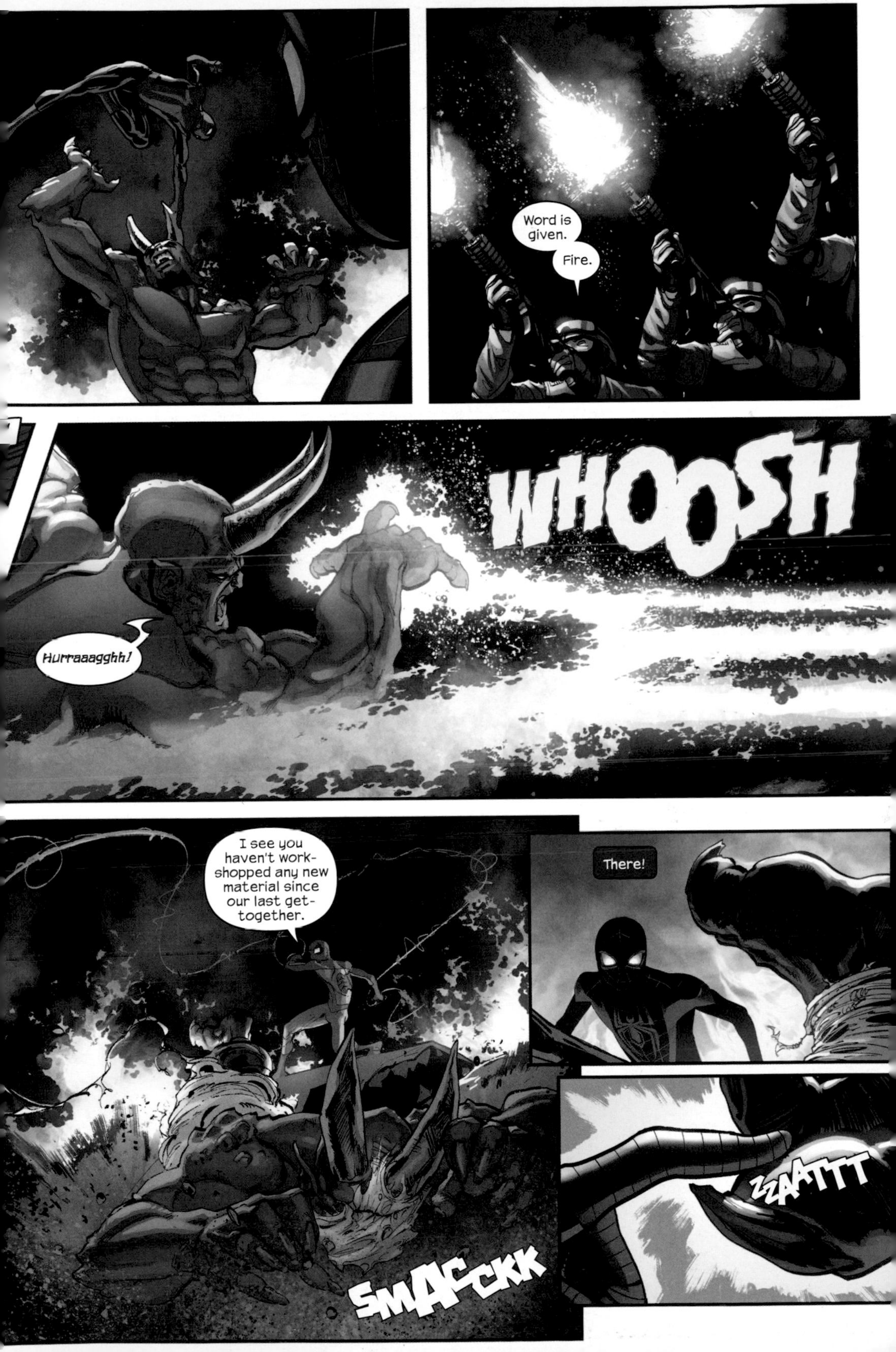
Word is given.
Fire.
WHOOSH
Hurraaagghh!
I see you haven't work-shopped any new material since our last get-together.
SMACCKK
There!
ZZAATTT

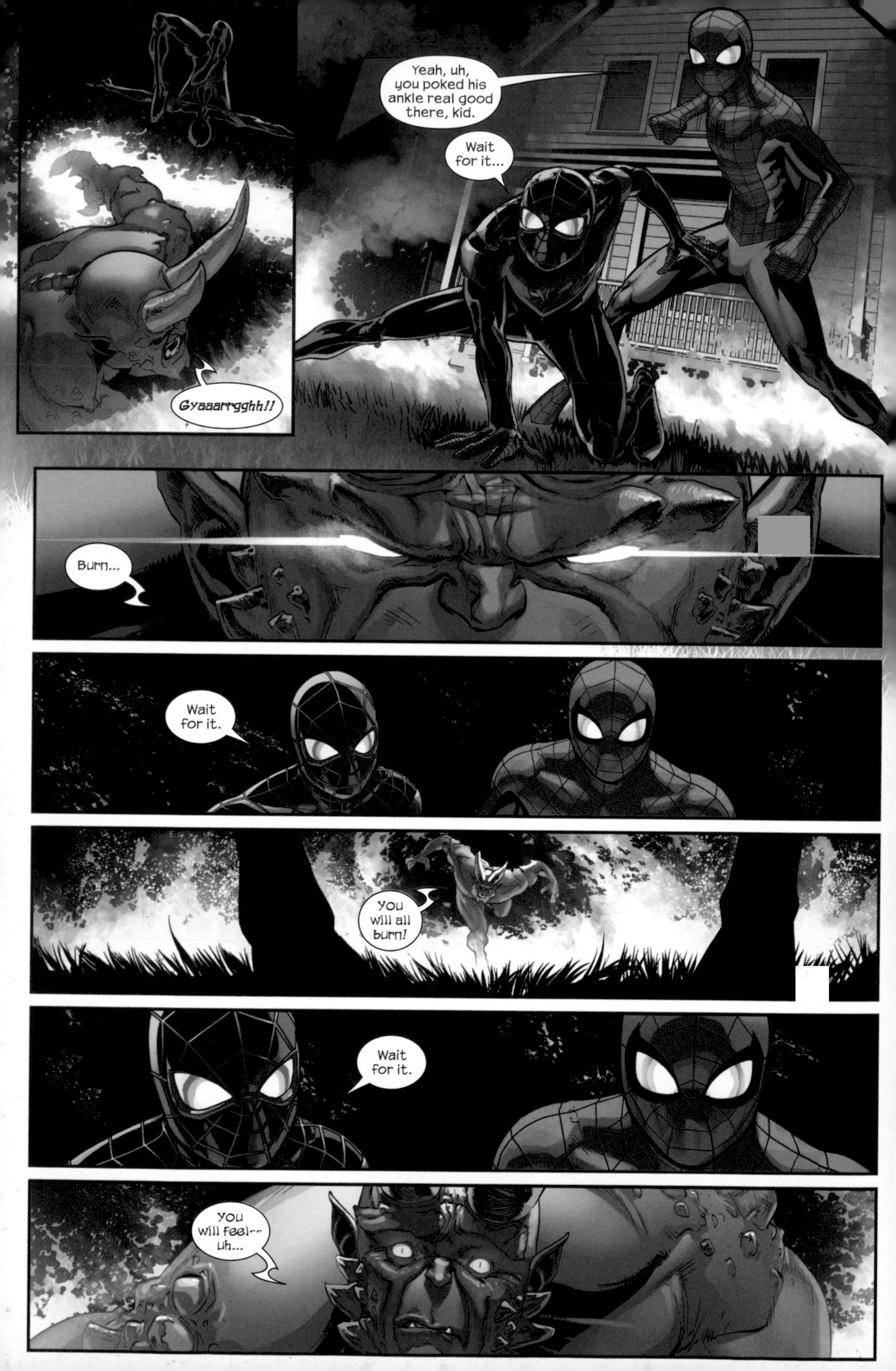
Gyaaarrgghh!!
Yeah, uh, you poked his ankle real good there, kid.
Wait for it...
Burn...
Wait for it.
You will all burn!
Wait for it.
You will feel-- uh...

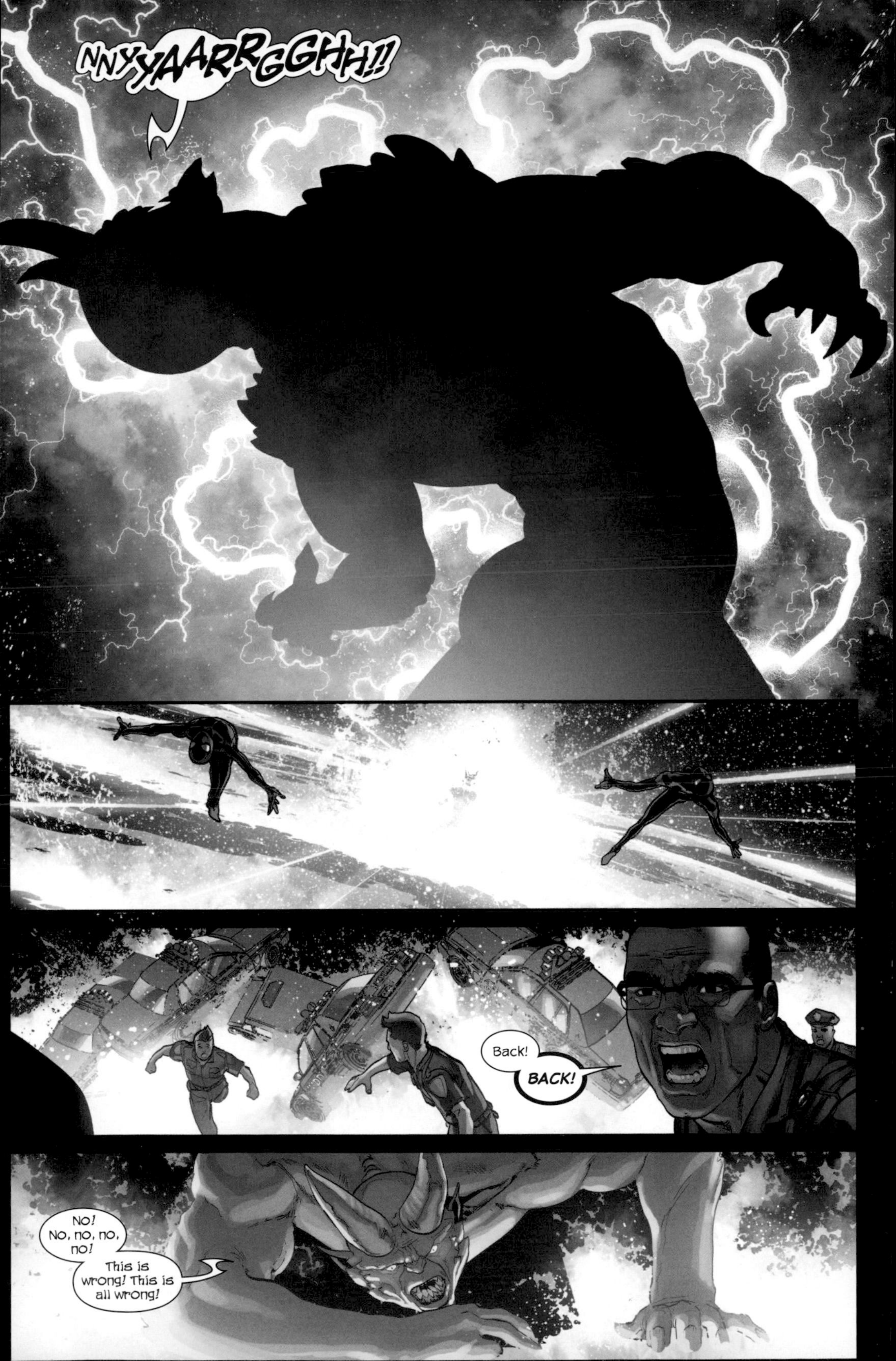
NNYYAARRGGHH!!
Back!
BACK!
No! No, no, no, no!
This is wrong! This is all wrong!

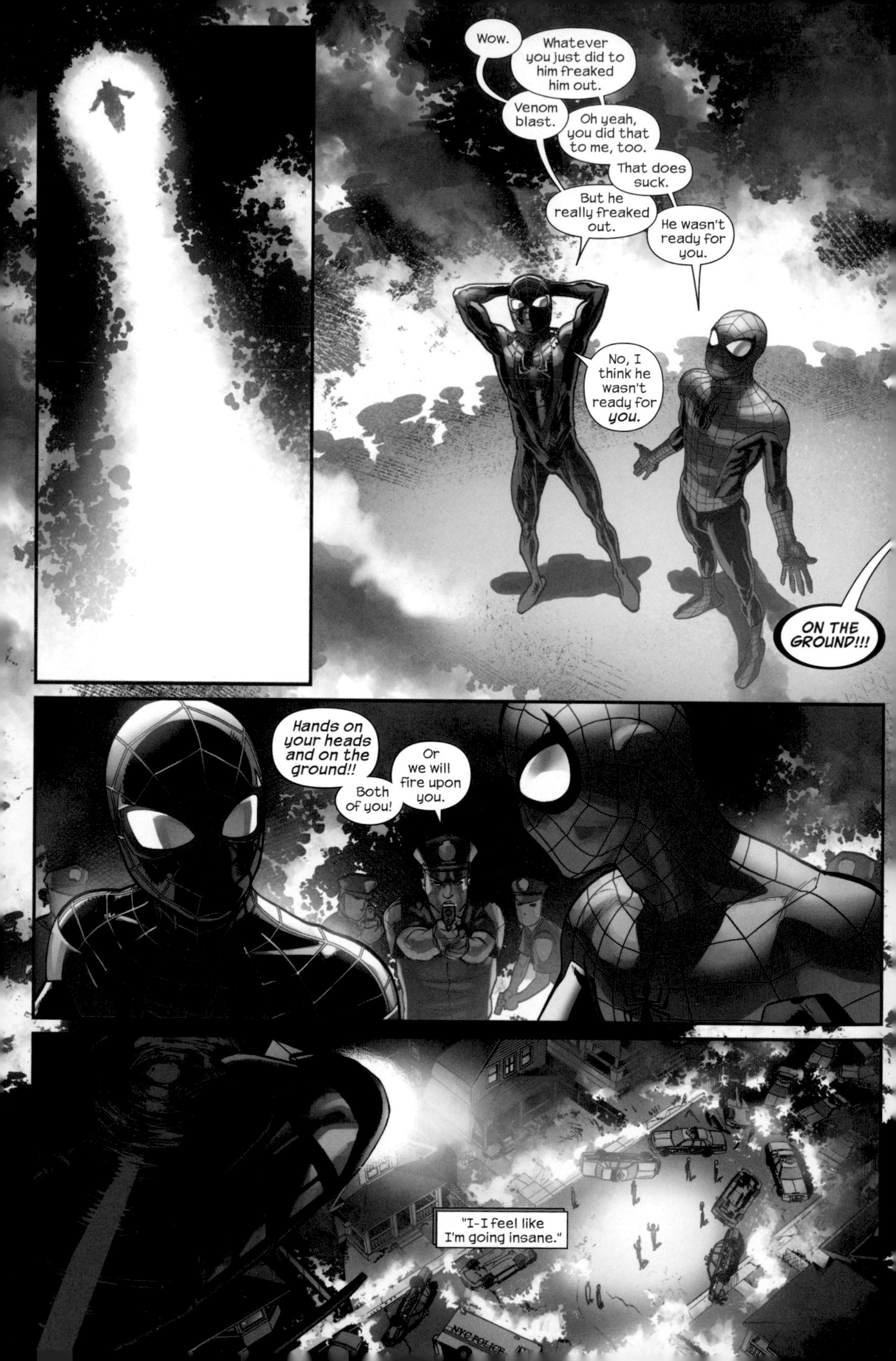
Wow.
Whatever you just did to him freaked him out.
Venom blast.
Oh yeah, you did that to me, too.
That does suck.
But he really freaked out.
He wasn't ready for you.
No, I think he wasn't ready for *you*.
ON THE GROUND!!!
Hands on your heads and on the ground!!
Both of you!
Or we will fire upon you.
"I-I feel like I'm going insane."
NYC POLICE

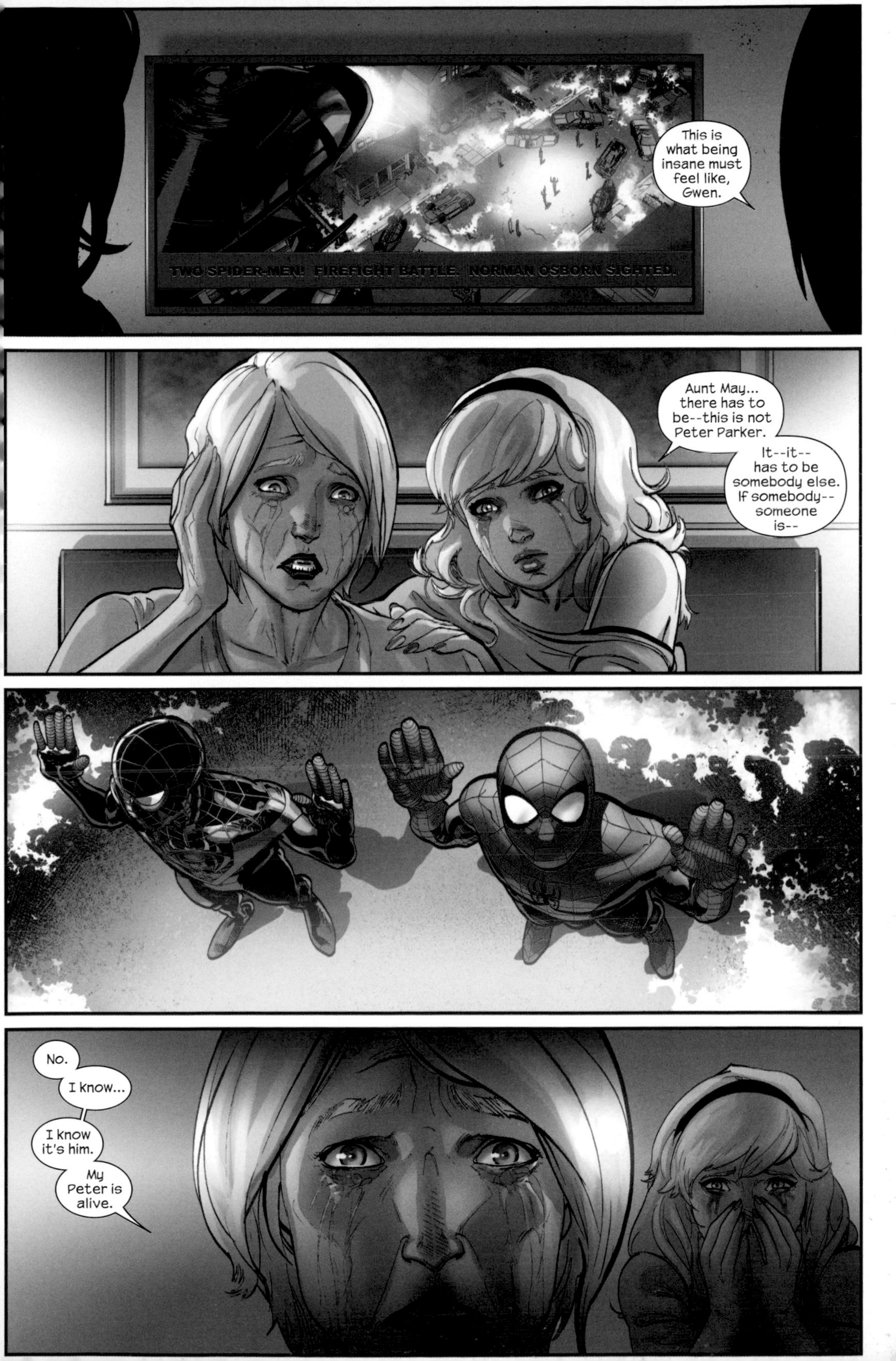
TWO SPIDER-MEN! FIREFIGHT BATTLE. NORMAN OSBORN SIGHTED.
This is what being insane must feel like, Gwen.
Aunt May... there has to be--this is not Peter Parker.
It--it--has to be somebody else. If somebody--someone is--
No.
I know...
I know it's him.
My Peter is alive.

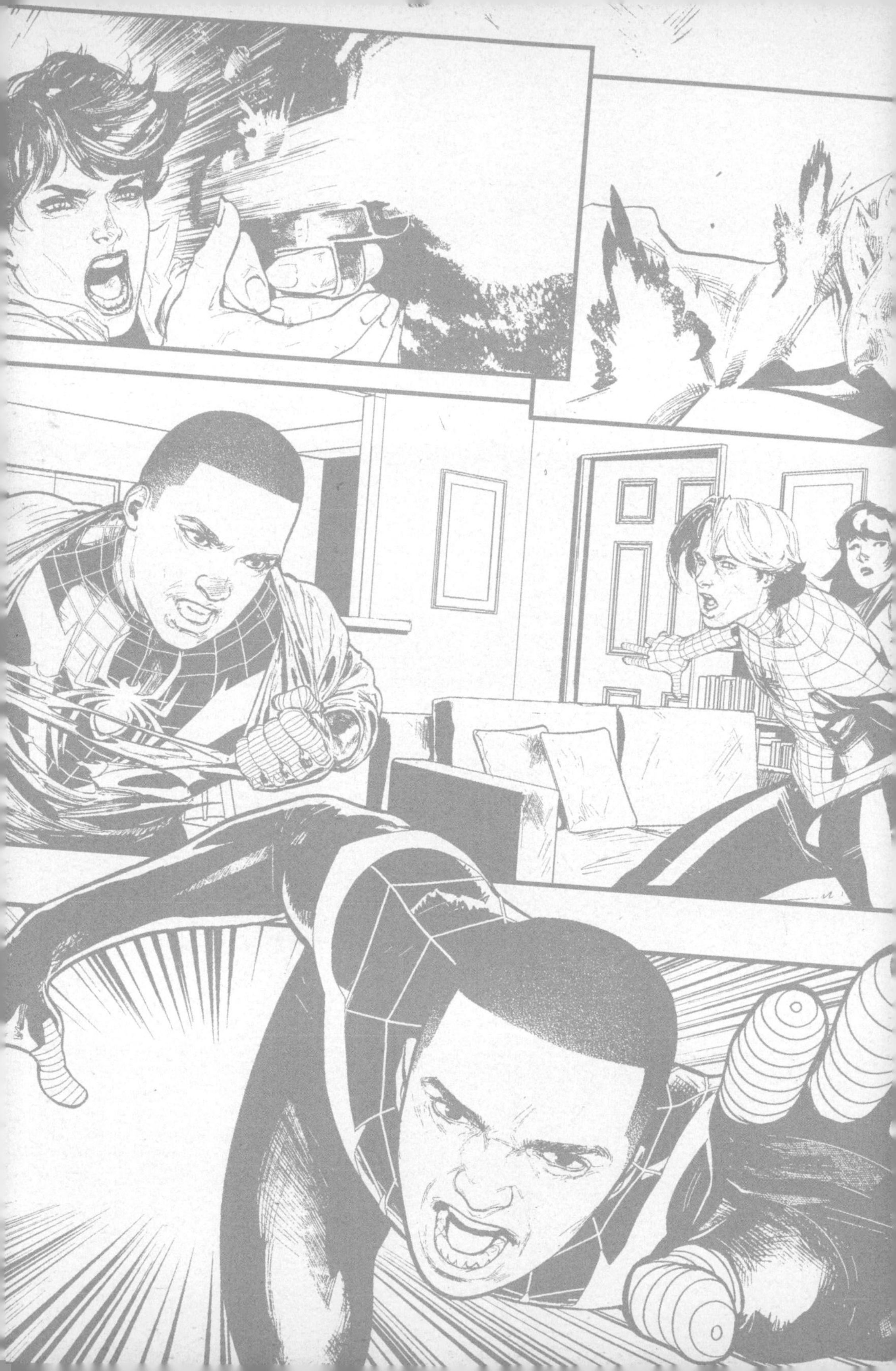

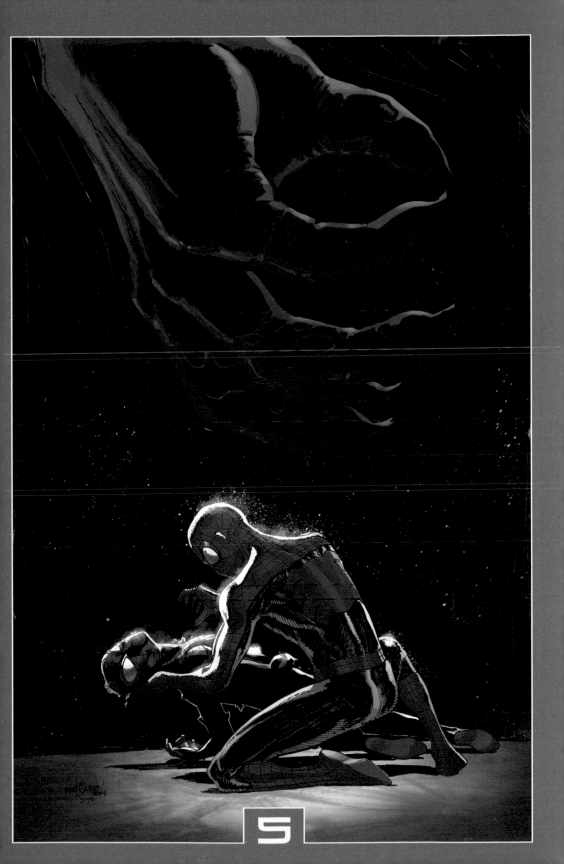

5

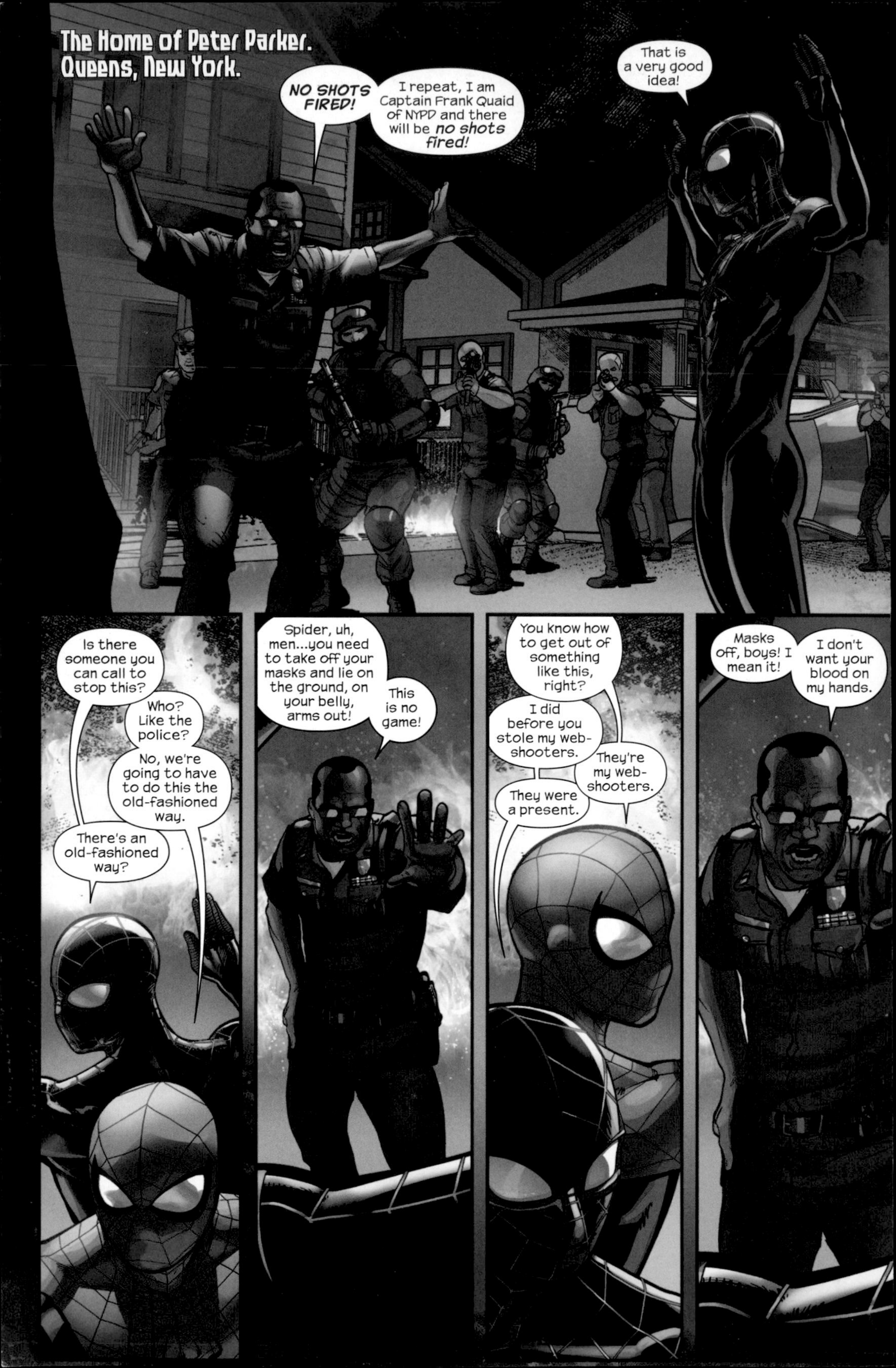
The Home of Peter Parker.
Queens, New York.
NO SHOTS FIRED!
I repeat, I am Captain Frank Quaid of NYPD and there will be no shots fired!
That is a very good idea!
Is there someone you can call to stop this?
Who? Like the police?
No, we're going to have to do this the old-fashioned way.
There's an old-fashioned way?
Spider, uh, men...you need to take off your masks and lie on the ground, on your belly, arms out!
This is no game!
You know how to get out of something like this, right?
I did before you stole my web-shooters.
They're my web-shooters.
They were a present.
Masks off, boys! I mean it!
I don't want your blood on my hands.

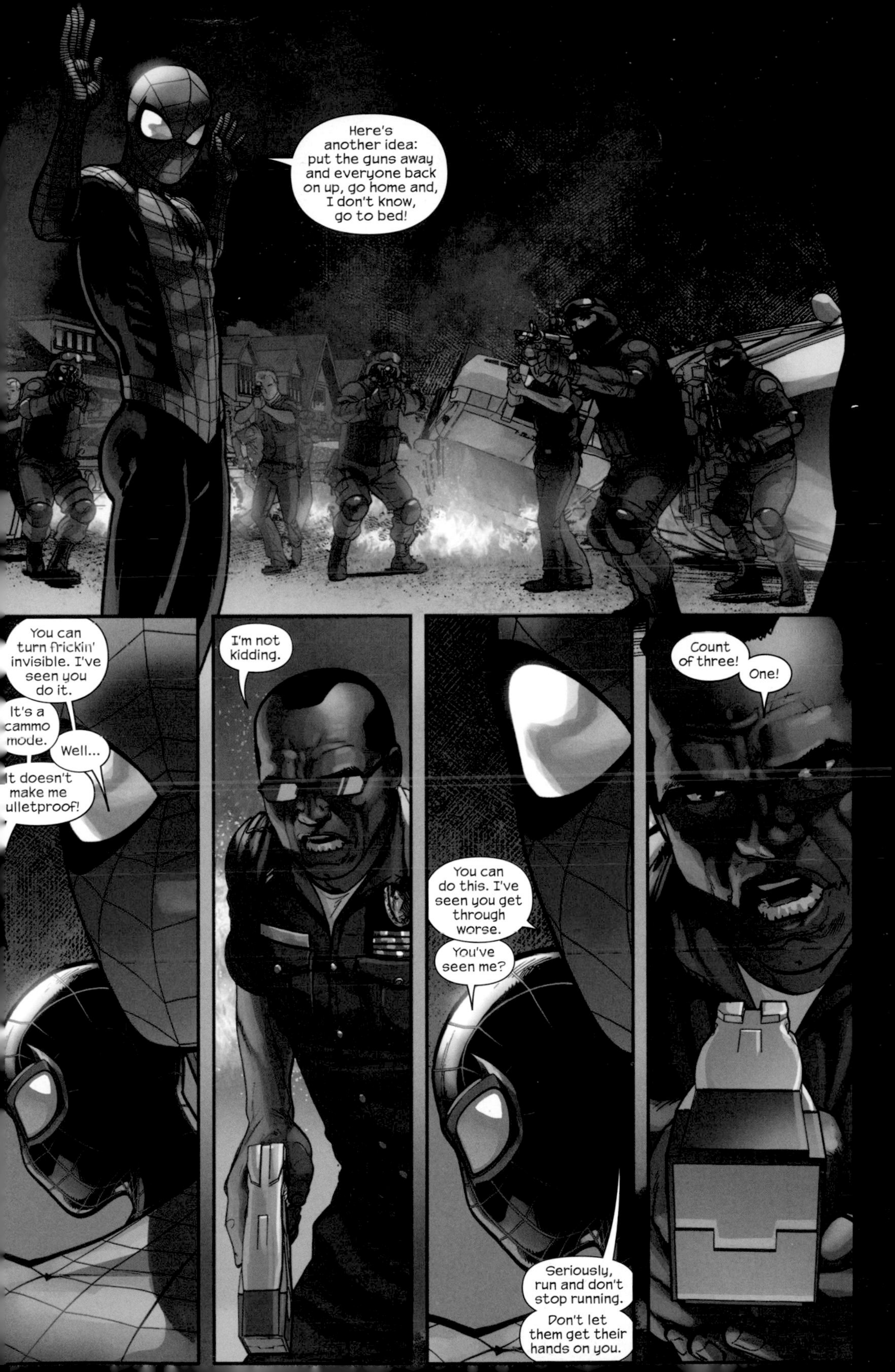
Here's another idea: put the guns away and everyone back on up, go home and, I don't know, go to bed!
You can turn frickin' invisible. I've seen you do it.
It's a cammo mode.
Well...
It doesn't make me ulletproof!
I'm not kidding.
You can do this. I've seen you get through worse.
You've seen me?
Seriously, run and don't stop running.
Don't let them get their hands on you.
Count of three!
One!

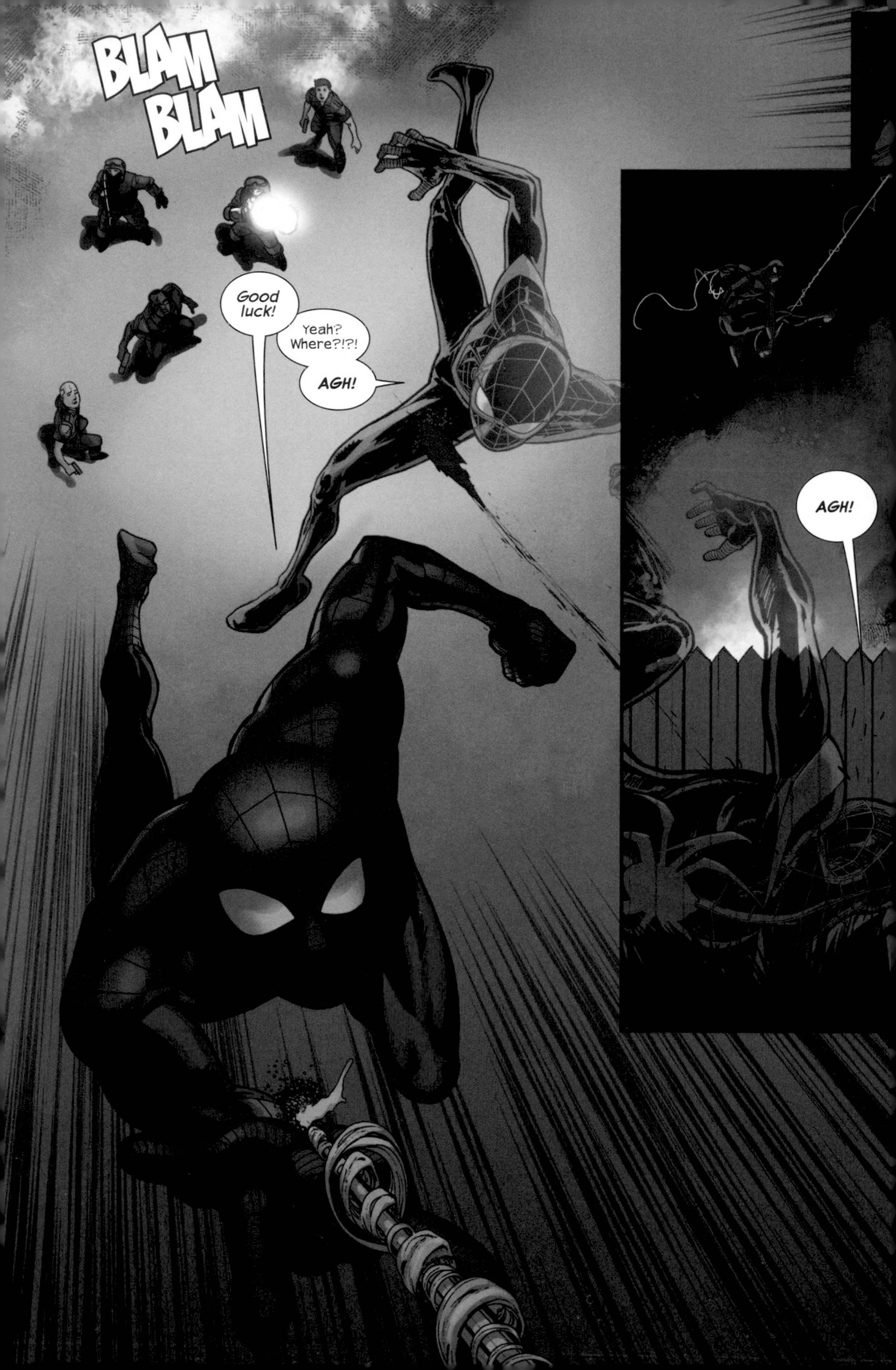
BLAM BLAM
Good luck!
Yeah? Where?!?!
AGH!
AGH!

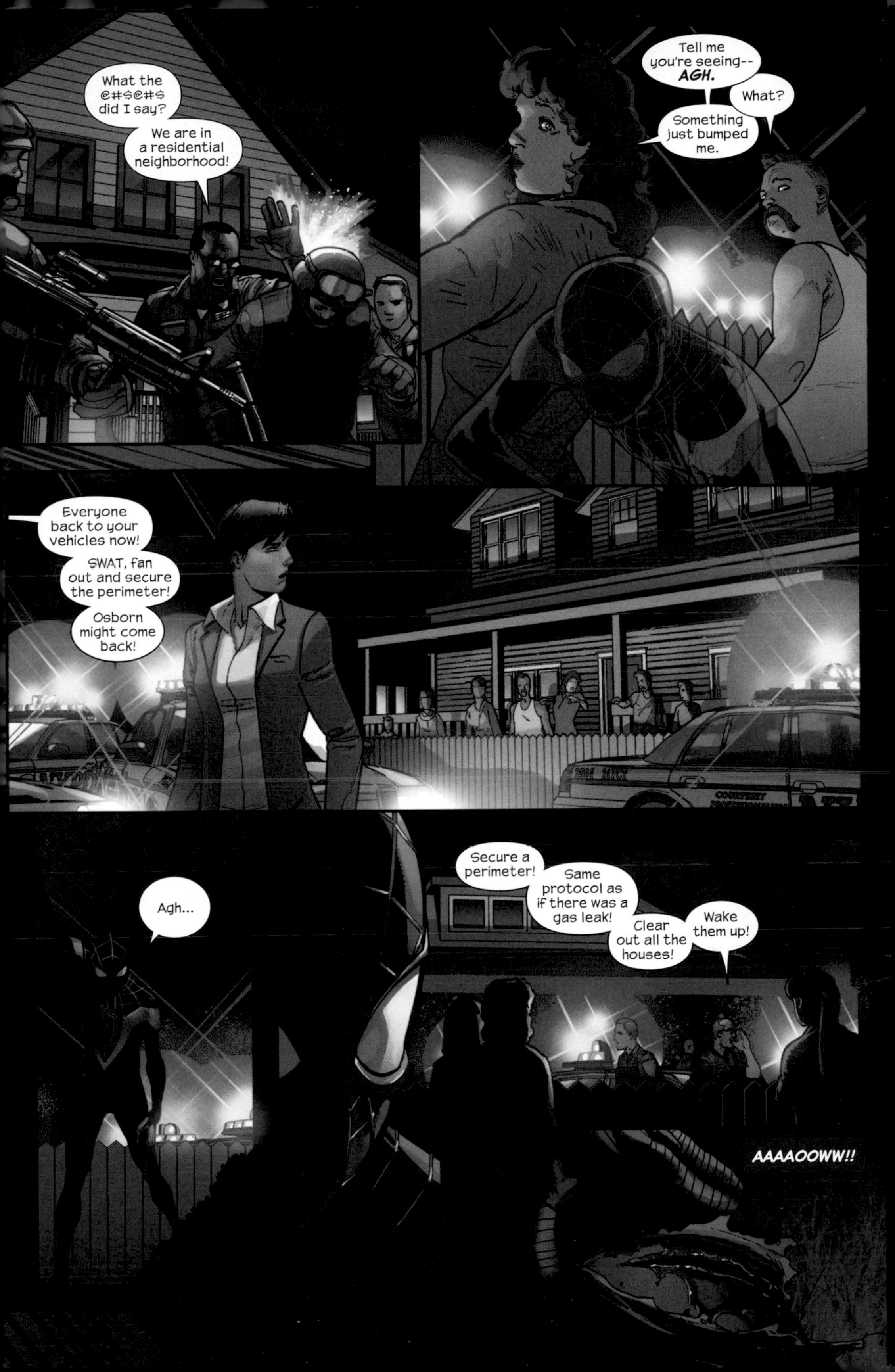
What the @#$@#$ did I say?
We are in a residential neighborhood!
Tell me you're seeing-- AGH.
What?
Something just bumped me.
Everyone back to your vehicles now!
SWAT, fan out and secure the perimeter!
Osborn might come back!
Agh...
Secure a perimeter!
Same protocol as if there was a gas leak!
Clear out all the houses!
Wake them up!
AAAAOOWW!!

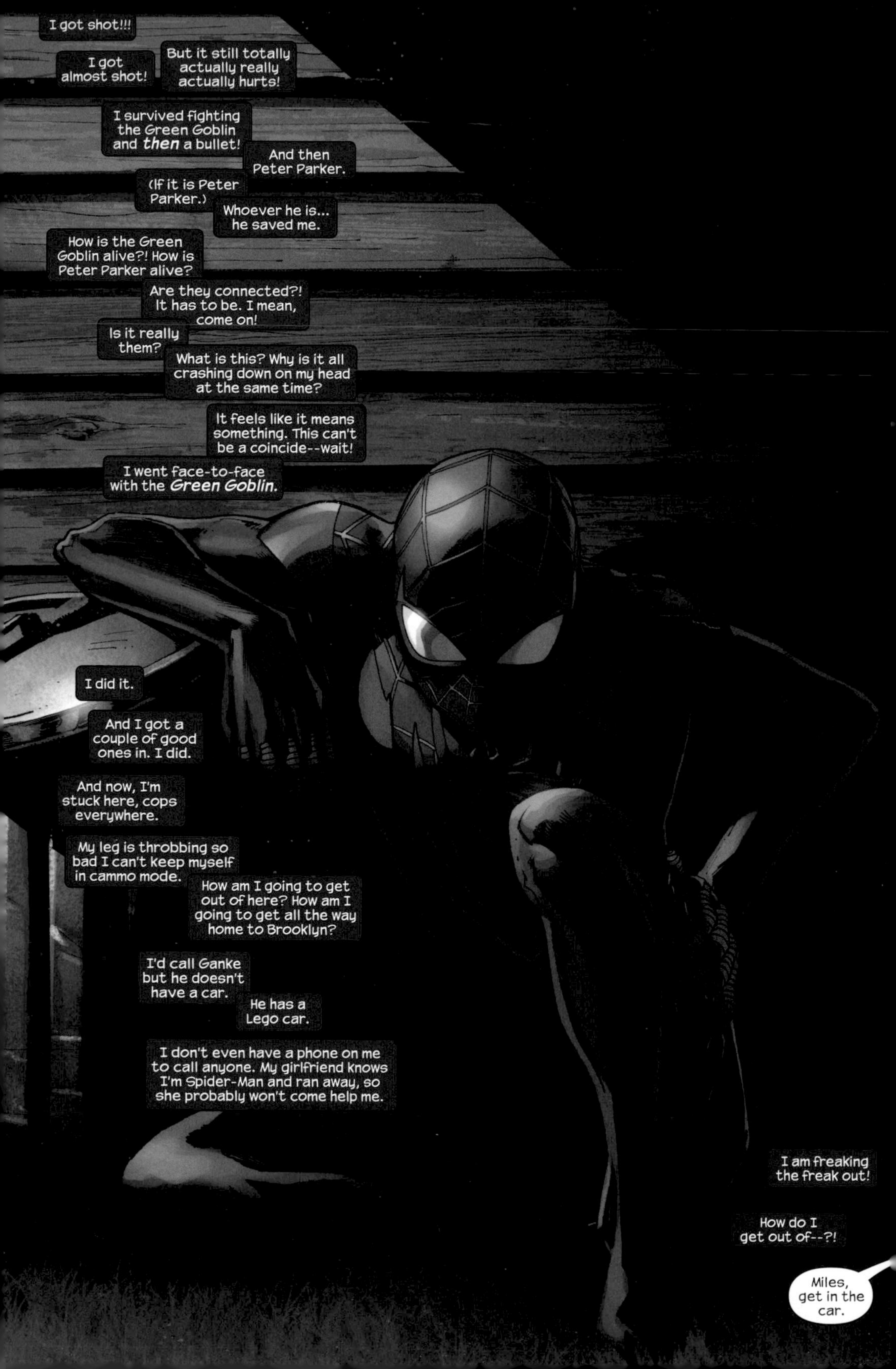
I got shot!!!
I got almost shot!
But it still totally actually really actually hurts!
I survived fighting the Green Goblin and *then* a bullet!
And then Peter Parker.
(If it is Peter Parker.)
Whoever he is... he saved me.
How is the Green Goblin alive?! How is Peter Parker alive?
Are they connected?! It has to be. I mean, come on!
Is it really them?
What is this? Why is it all crashing down on my head at the same time?
It feels like it means something. This can't be a coincide--wait!
I went face-to-face with the *Green Goblin.*
I did it.
And I got a couple of good ones in. I did.
And now, I'm stuck here, cops everywhere.
My leg is throbbing so bad I can't keep myself in cammo mode.
How am I going to get out of here? How am I going to get all the way home to Brooklyn?
I'd call Ganke but he doesn't have a car.
He has a Lego car.
I don't even have a phone on me to call anyone. My girlfriend knows I'm Spider-Man and ran away, so she probably won't come help me.
I am freaking the freak out!
How do I get out of--?!
Miles, get in the car.

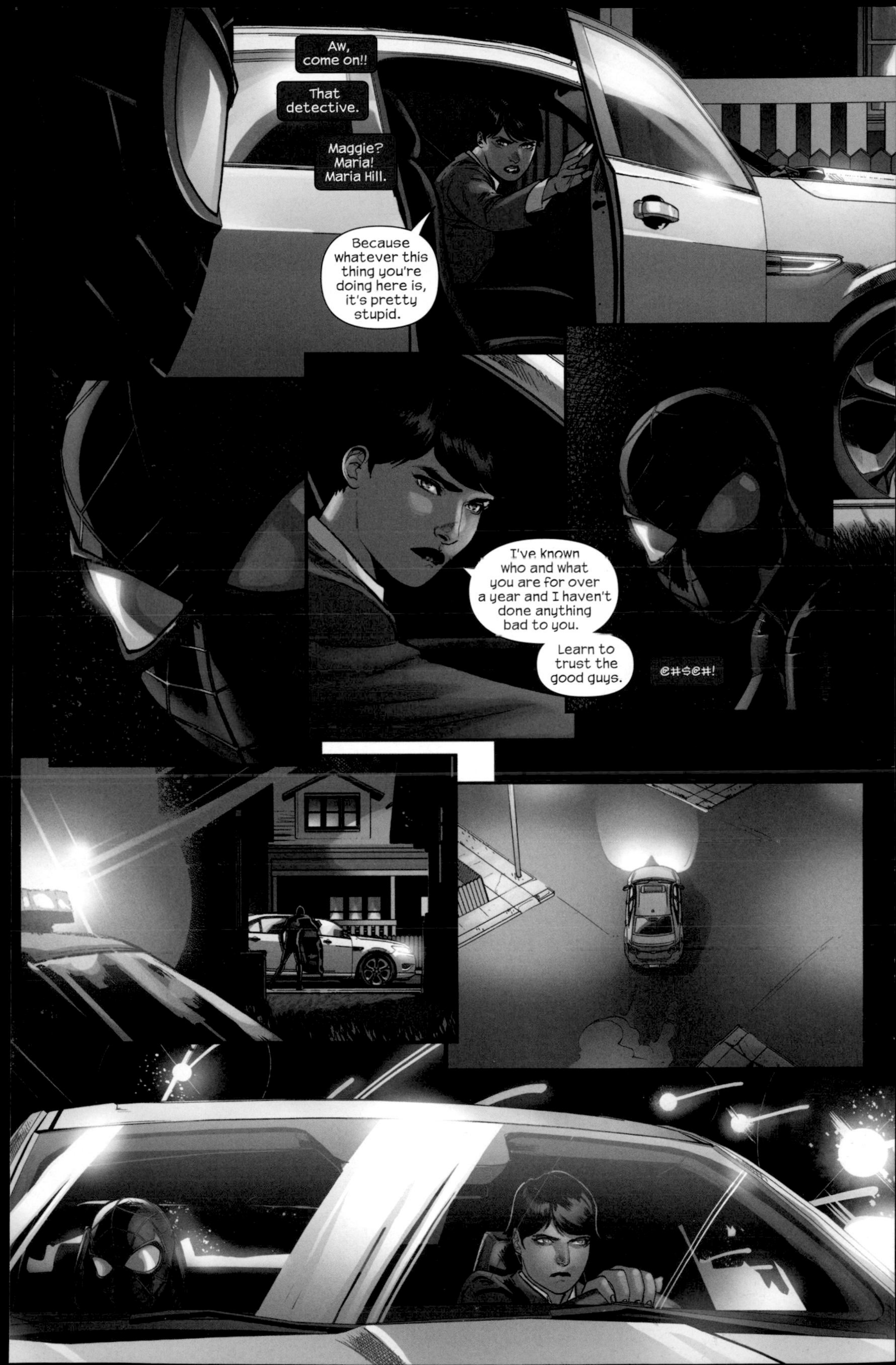
Aw, come on!!
That detective.
Maggie? Maria! Maria Hill.
Because whatever this thing you're doing here is, it's pretty stupid.
I've known who and what you are for over a year and I haven't done anything bad to you.
Learn to trust the good guys.
@#$@#!

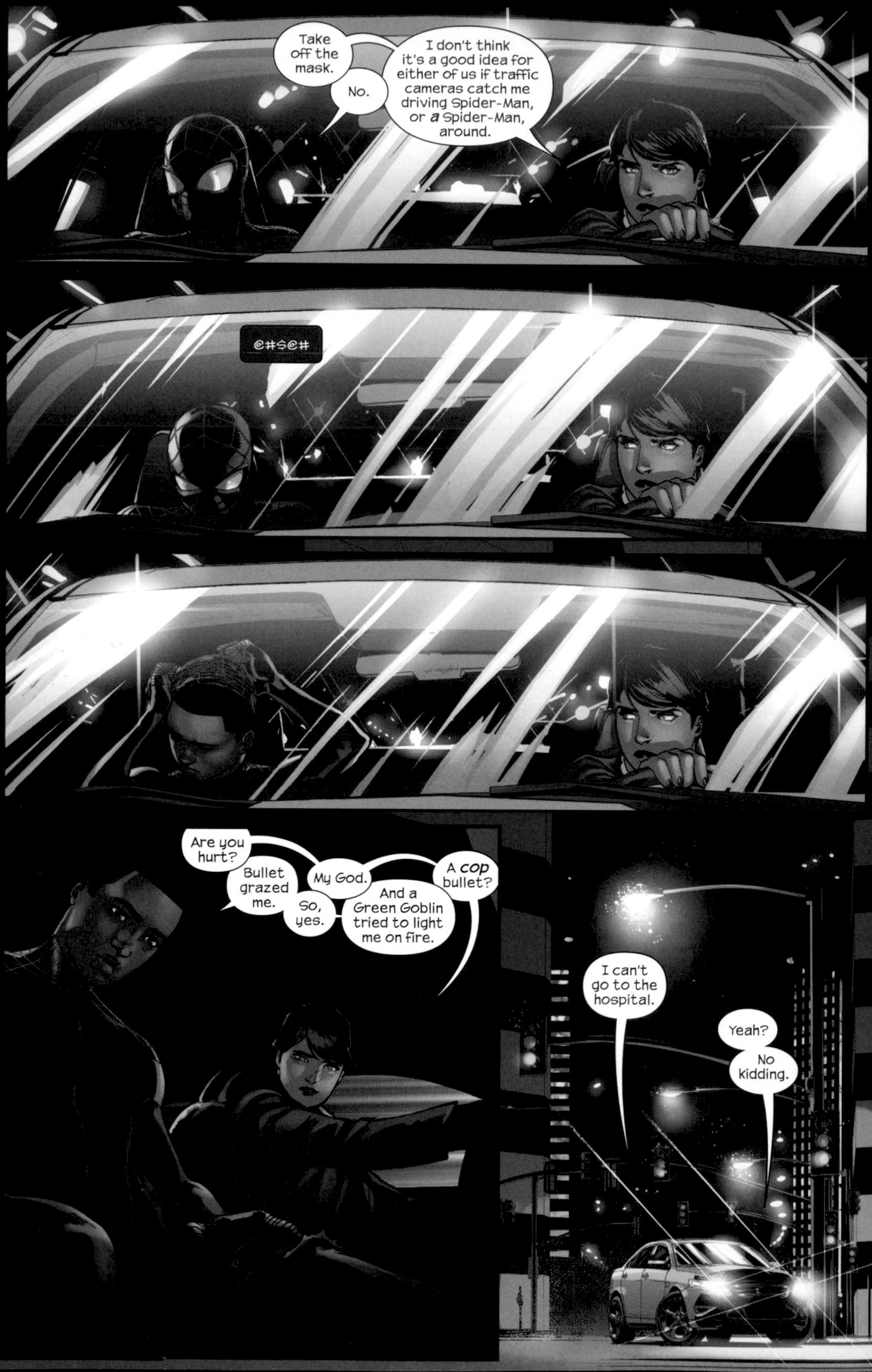
Take off the mask.
I don't think it's a good idea for either of us if traffic cameras catch me driving Spider-Man, or *a* Spider-Man, around.
No.
@#$@#
Are you hurt?
Bullet grazed me.
So, yes.
My God.
And a Green Goblin tried to light me on fire.
A *cop* bullet?
I can't go to the hospital.
Yeah?
No kidding.

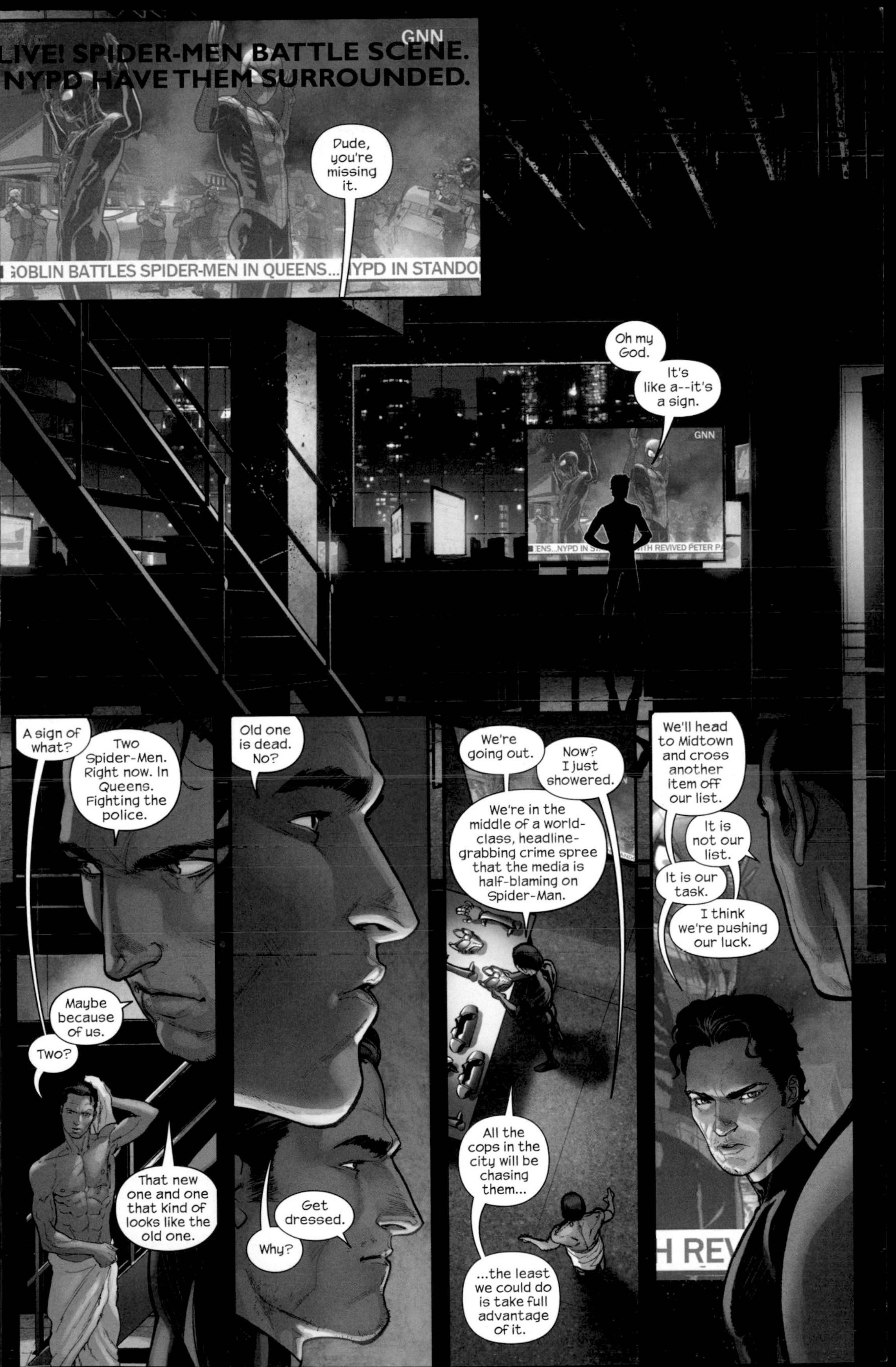
GNN
LIVE! SPIDER-MEN BATTLE SCENE.
NYPD HAVE THEM SURROUNDED.
GOBLIN BATTLES SPIDER-MEN IN QUEENS...NYPD IN STANDO
Dude, you're missing it.
Oh my God.
It's like a--it's a sign.
GNN
ENS...NYPD IN ST... ITH REVIVED PETER PA
A sign of what?
Two Spider-Men. Right now. In Queens. Fighting the police.
Two?
Maybe because of us.
That new one and one that kind of looks like the old one.
Old one is dead. No?
Get dressed.
Why?
We're going out.
Now? I just showered.
We're in the middle of a world-class, headline-grabbing crime spree that the media is half-blaming on Spider-Man.
All the cops in the city will be chasing them...
...the least we could do is take full advantage of it.
We'll head to Midtown and cross another item off our list.
It is not our list.
It is our task.
I think we're pushing our luck.
H REV

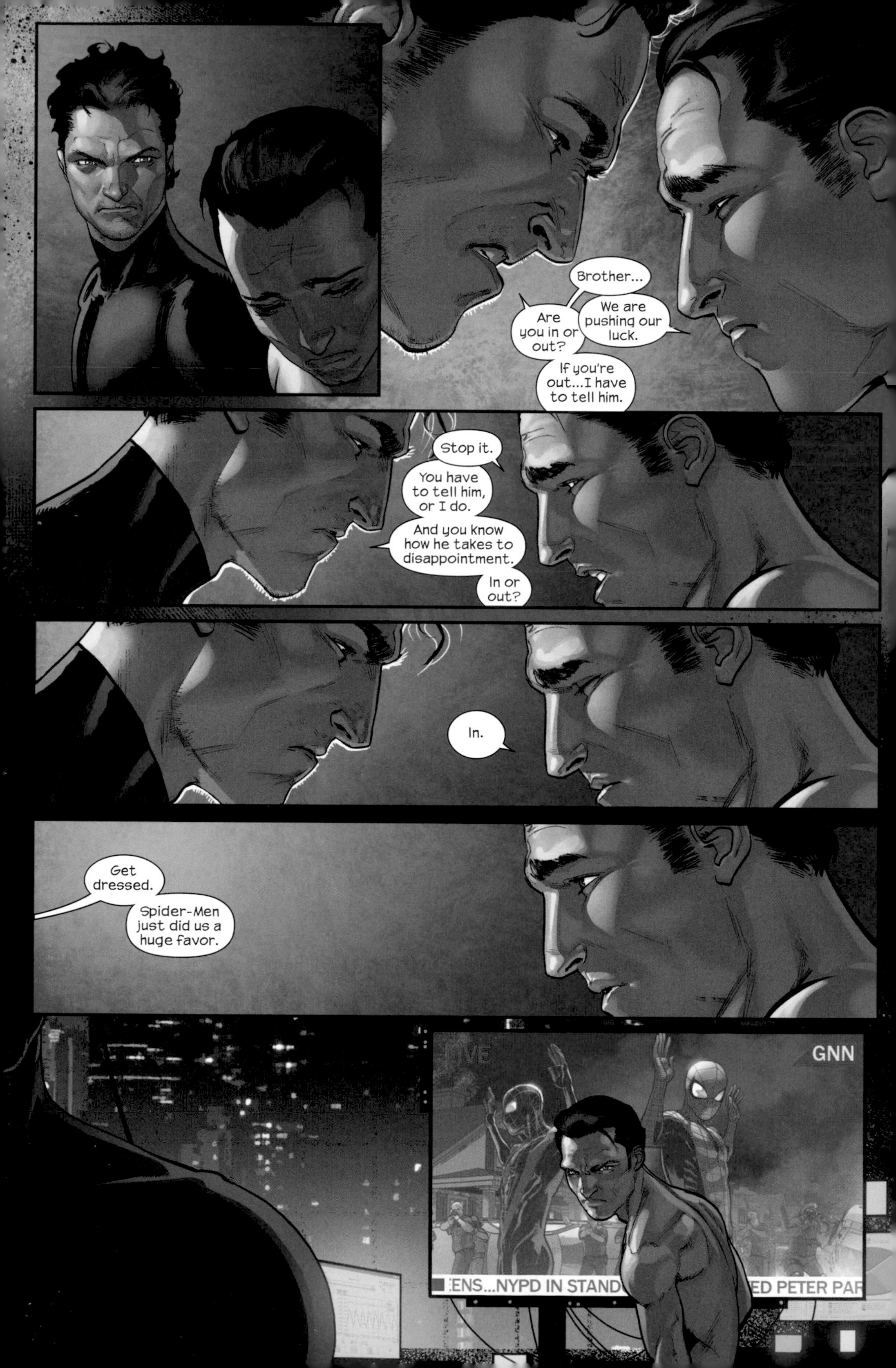

Brother...
We are pushing our luck.
Are you in or out?
If you're out...I have to tell him.
Stop it.
You have to tell him, or I do.
And you know how he takes to disappointment.
In or out?
In.
Get dressed.
Spider-Men just did us a huge favor.
GNN
ENS...NYPD IN STAND
ED PETER PAR

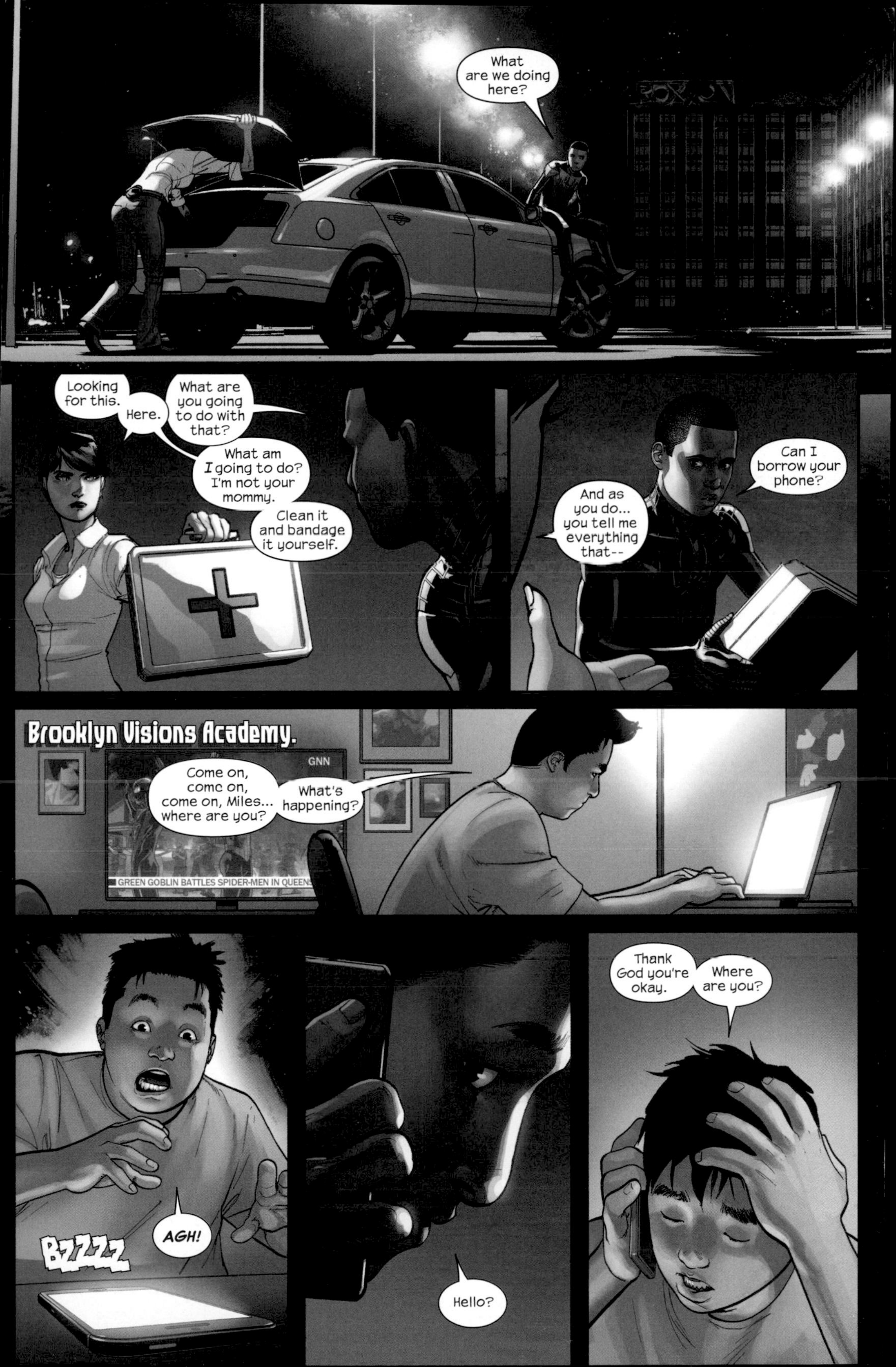
What are we doing here?
Looking for this.
Here.
What are you going to do with that?
What am I going to do? I'm not your mommy.
Clean it and bandage it yourself.
Can I borrow your phone?
And as you do... you tell me everything that--
Brooklyn Visions Academy.
GNN
GREEN GOBLIN BATTLES SPIDER-MEN IN QUEENS
Come on, come on, come on, Miles... where are you?
What's happening?
BZZZZ
AGH!
Hello?
Thank God you're okay.
Where are you?

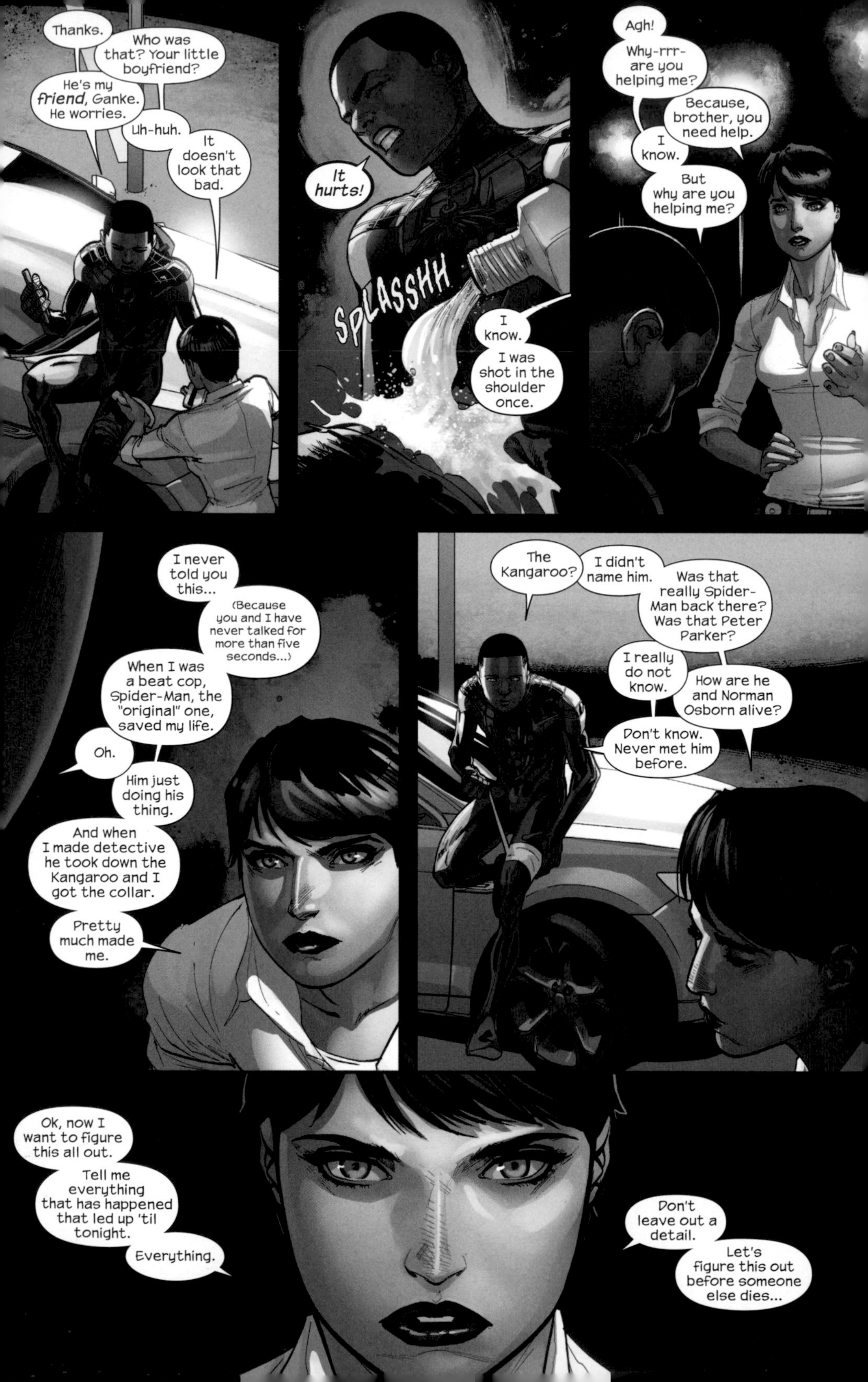
Thanks.
Who was that? Your little boyfriend?
He's my *friend*, Ganke. He worries.
Uh-huh.
It doesn't look that bad.
It hurts!
SPLASSHH
I know.
I was shot in the shoulder once.
Agh!
Why-rrr-are you helping me?
Because, brother, you need help.
I know.
But why are you helping me?
I never told you this...
(Because you and I have never talked for more than five seconds...)
When I was a beat cop, Spider-Man, the "original" one, saved my life.
Oh.
Him just doing his thing.
And when I made detective he took down the Kangaroo and I got the collar.
Pretty much made me.
The Kangaroo?
I didn't name him.
Was that really Spider-Man back there? Was that Peter Parker?
I really do not know.
How are he and Norman Osborn alive?
Don't know. Never met him before.
Ok, now I want to figure this all out.
Tell me everything that has happened that led up 'til tonight.
Everything.
Don't leave out a detail.
Let's figure this out before someone else dies...

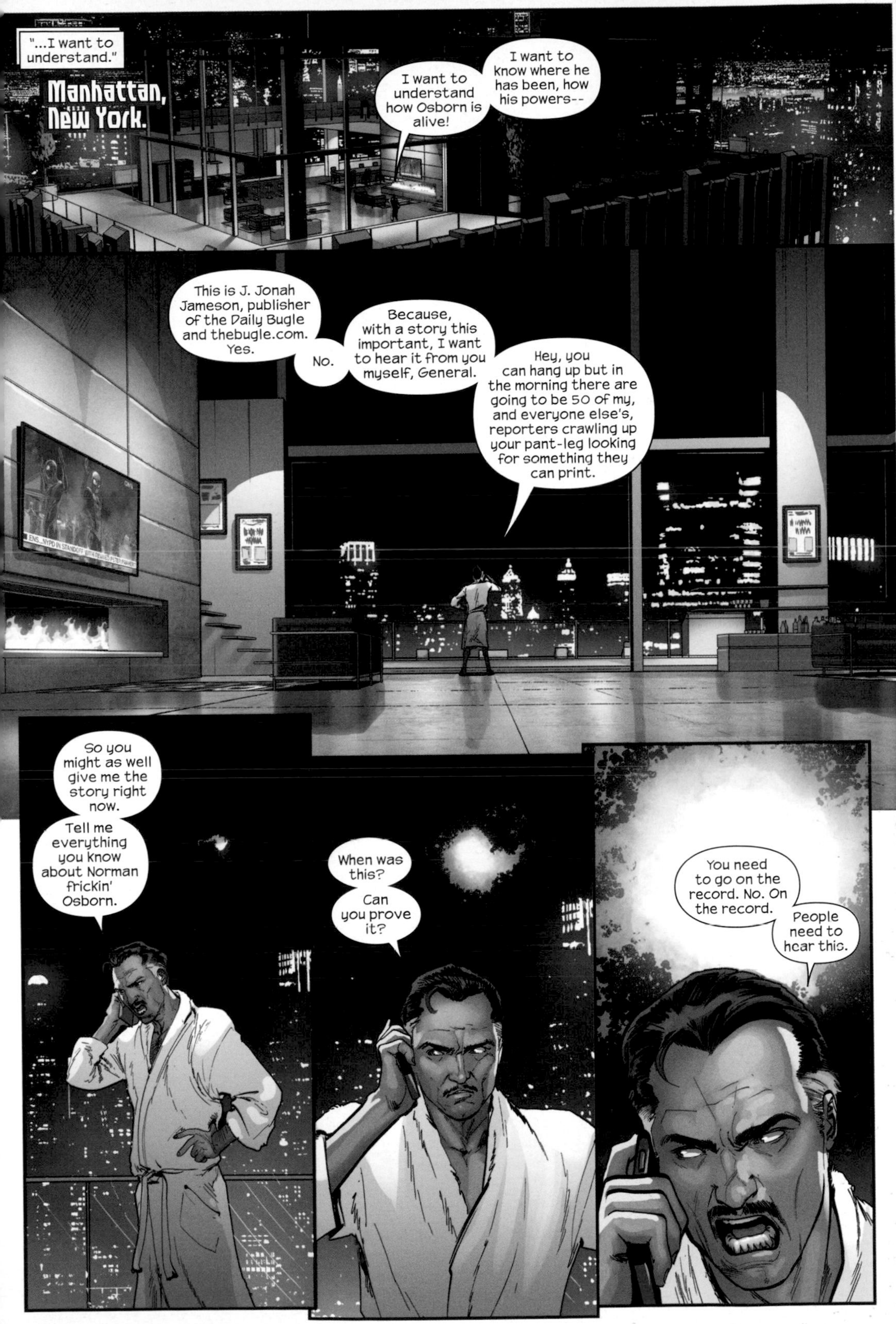
"...I want to understand."
Manhattan, New York.
I want to understand how Osborn is alive!
I want to know where he has been, how his powers--
This is J. Jonah Jameson, publisher of the Daily Bugle and thebugle.com. Yes.
No.
Because, with a story this important, I want to hear it from you myself, General.
Hey, you can hang up but in the morning there are going to be 50 of my, and everyone else's, reporters crawling up your pant-leg looking for something they can print.
So you might as well give me the story right now.
Tell me everything you know about Norman frickin' Osborn.
When was this?
Can you prove it?
You need to go on the record. No. On the record.
People need to hear this.

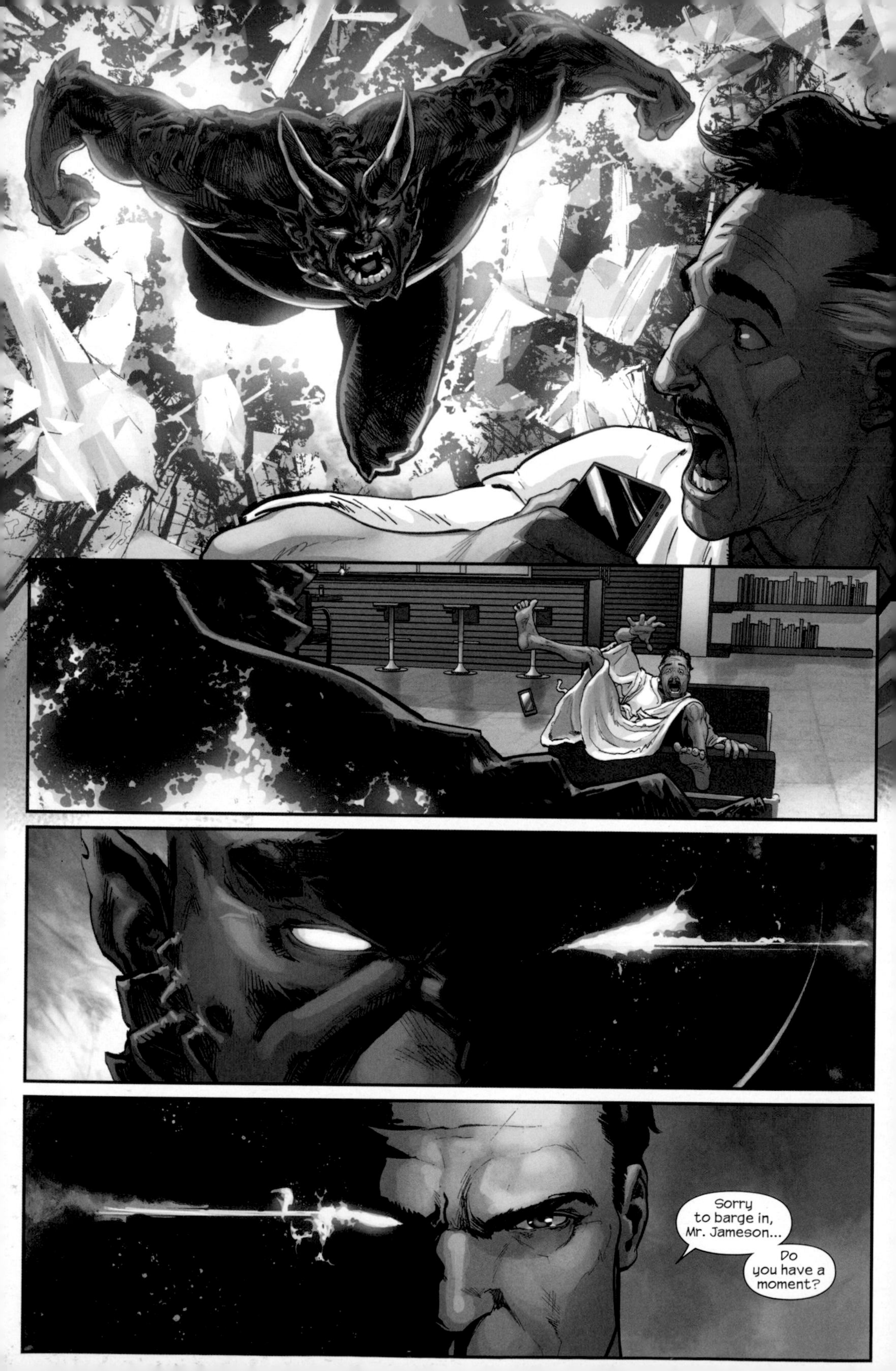
Sorry to barge in, Mr. Jameson...
Do you have a moment?

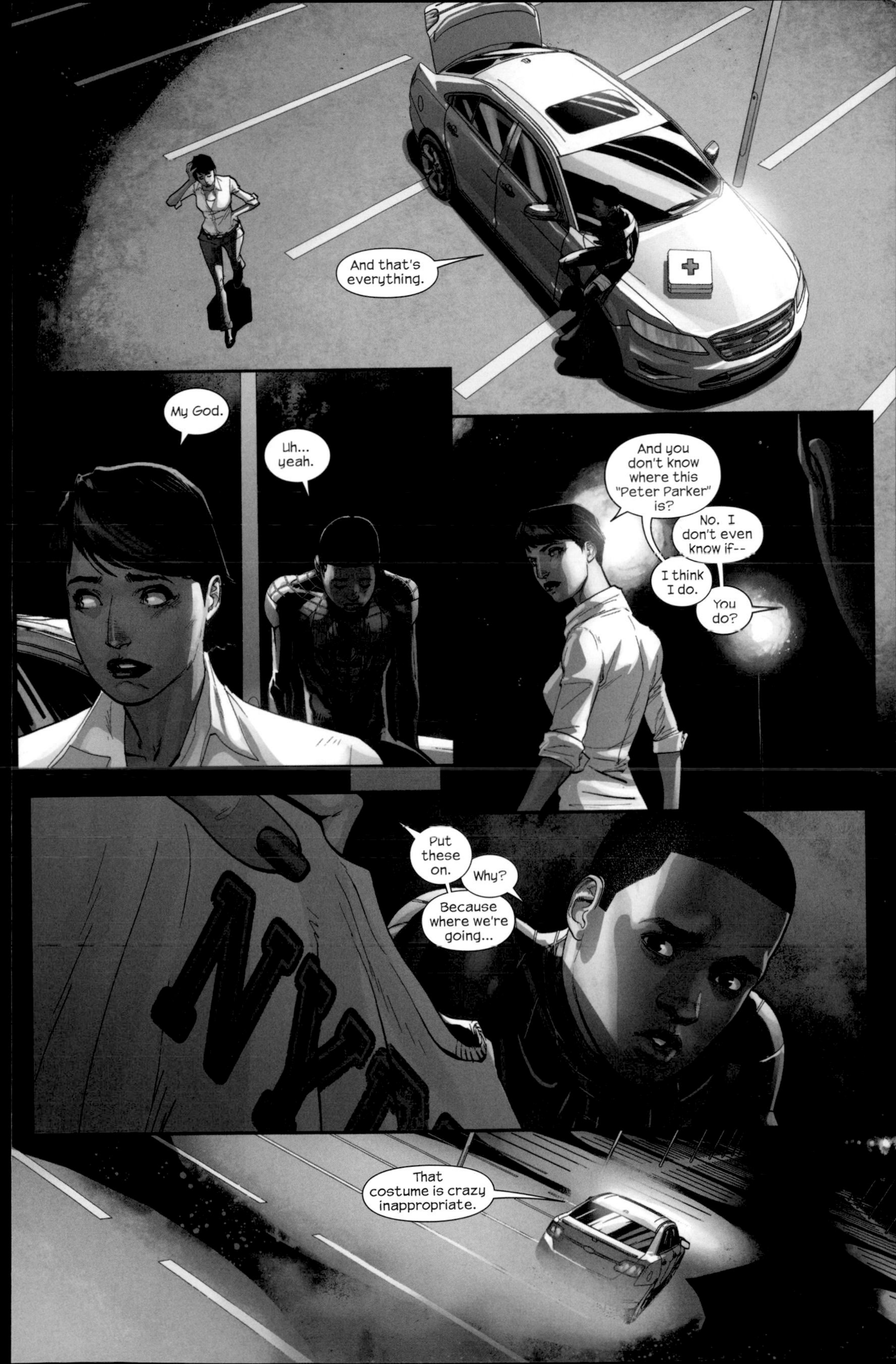
And that's everything.
My God.
Uh... yeah.
And you don't know where this "Peter Parker" is?
No. I don't even know if--
I think I do.
You do?
Put these on.
Why?
Because where we're going...
That costume is crazy inappropriate.

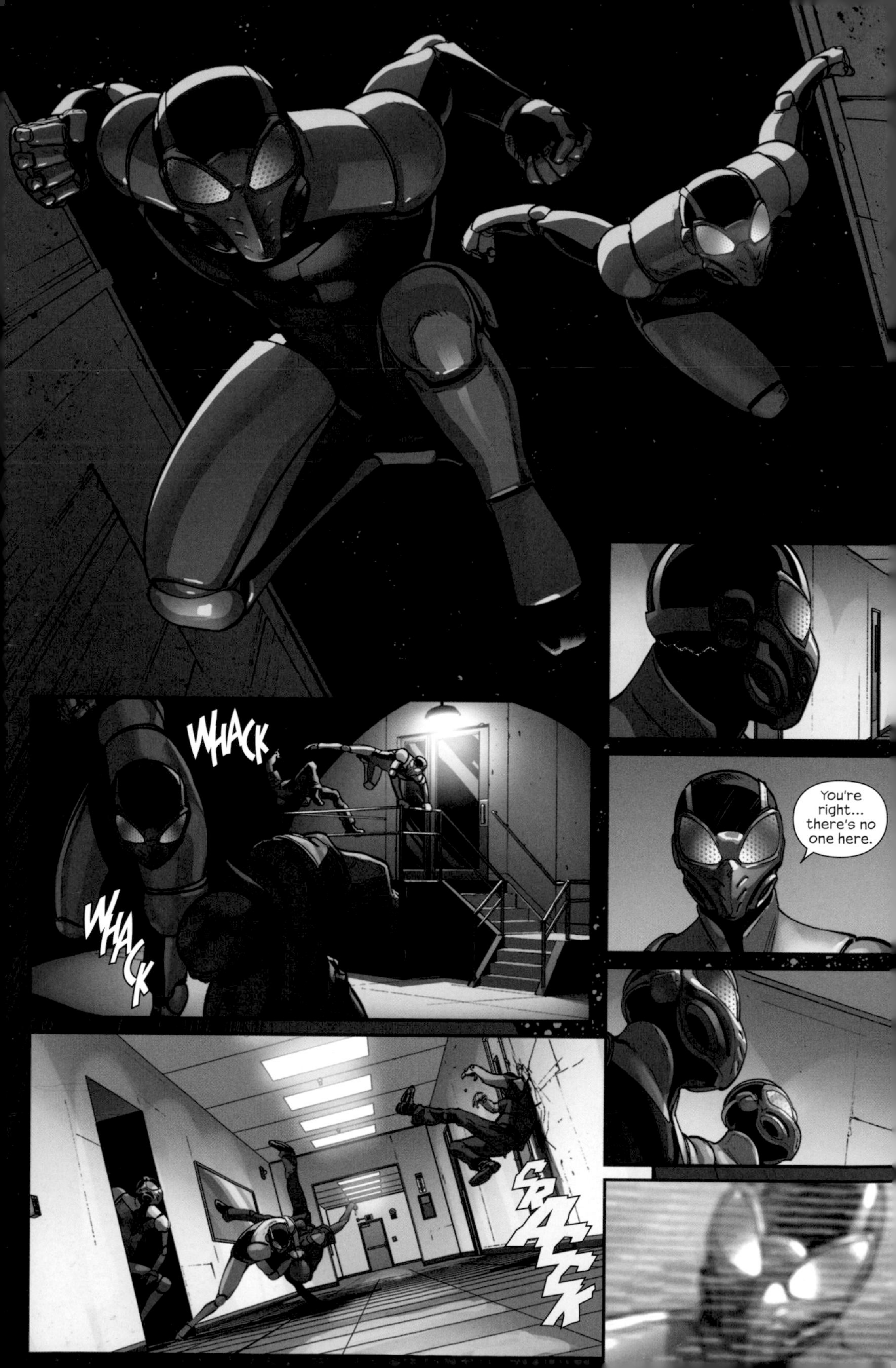
WHACK
WHACK
You're right... there's no one here.
CRACK

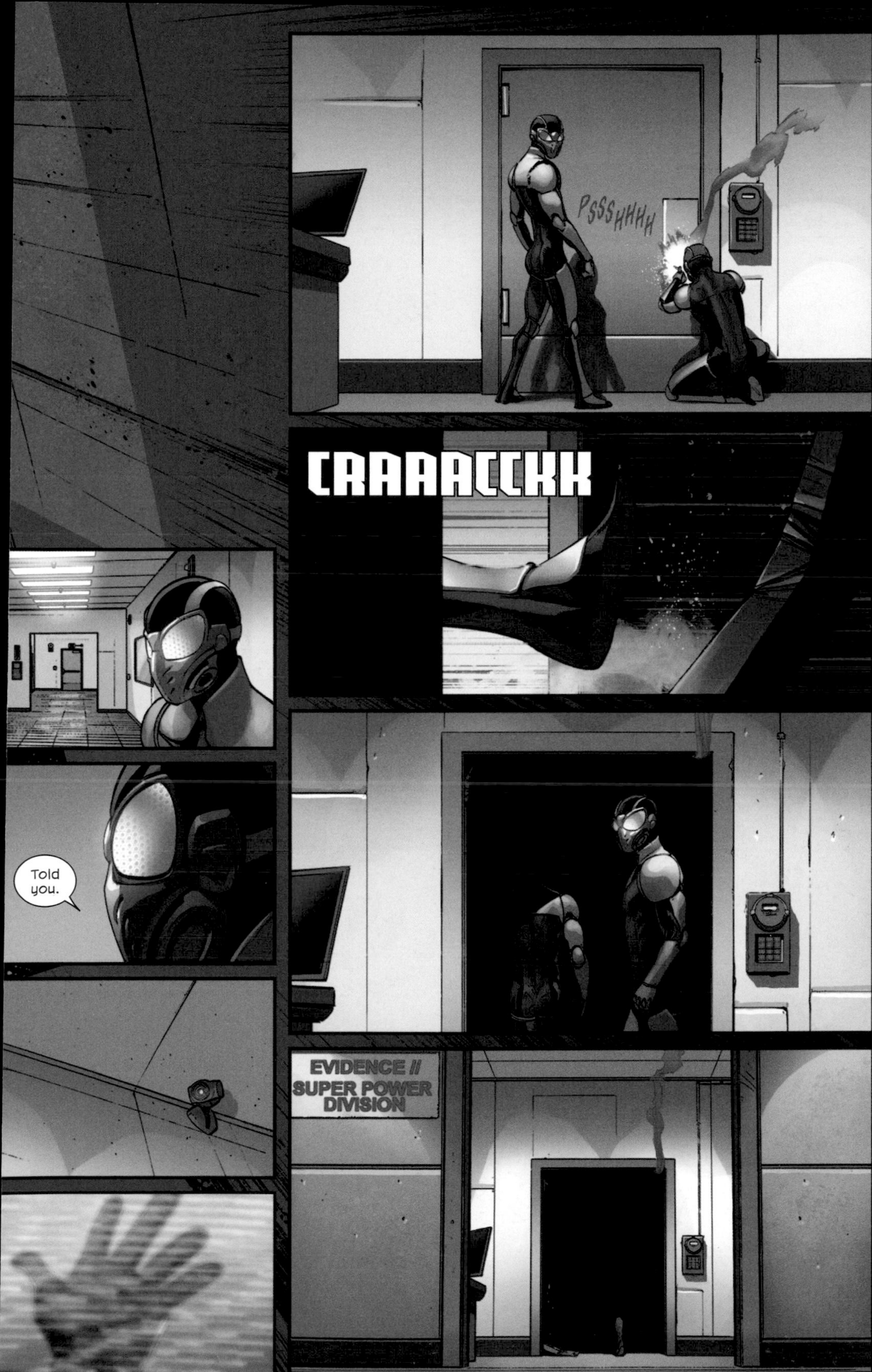
PSSSHHHH
CRAAACCKK
Told you.
EVIDENCE // SUPER POWER DIVISION

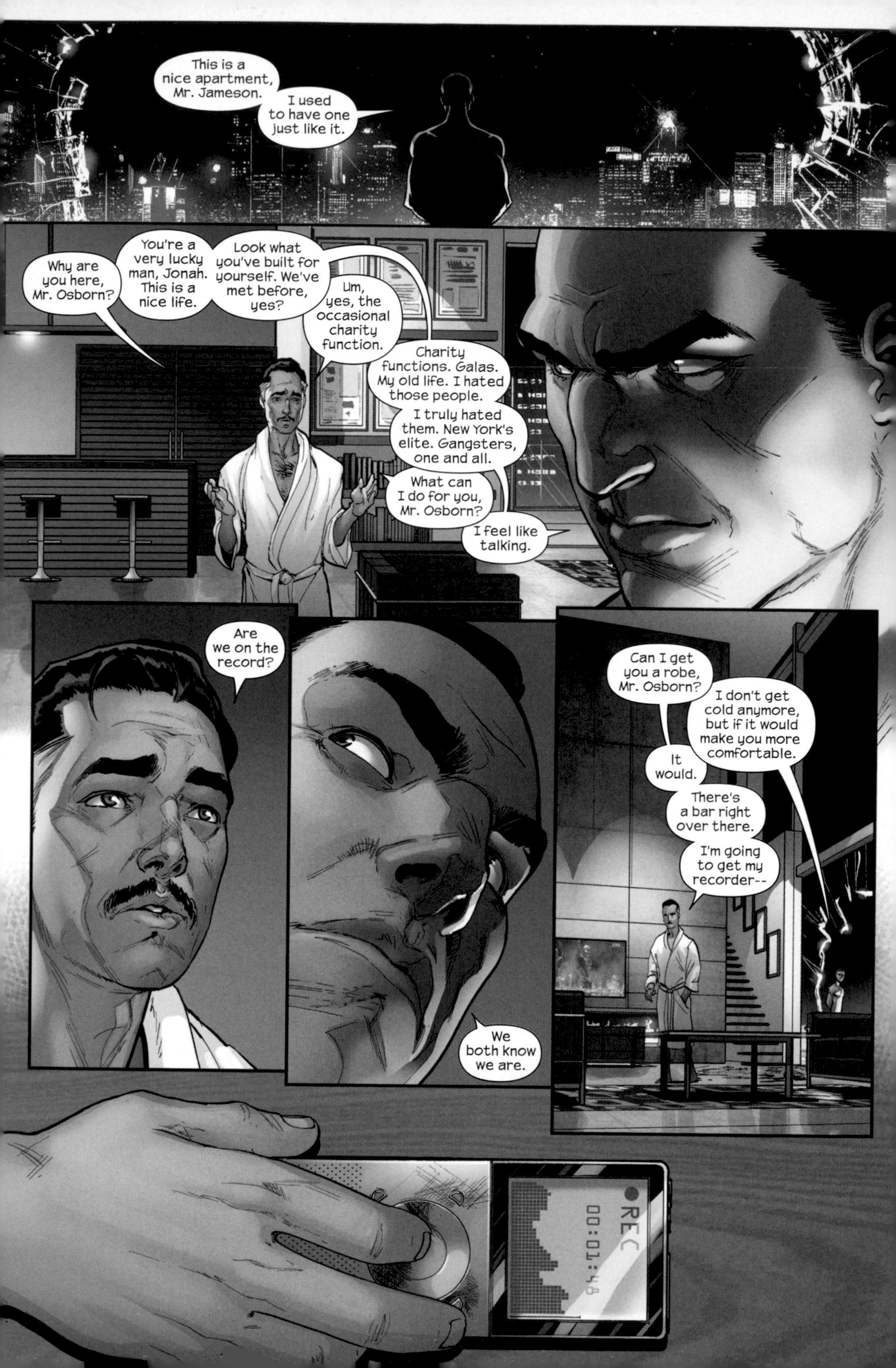
This is a nice apartment, Mr. Jameson.
I used to have one just like it.
Why are you here, Mr. Osborn?
You're a very lucky man, Jonah. This is a nice life.
Look what you've built for yourself. We've met before, yes?
Um, yes, the occasional charity function.
Charity functions. Galas. My old life. I hated those people.
I truly hated them. New York's elite. Gangsters, one and all.
What can I do for you, Mr. Osborn?
I feel like talking.
Are we on the record?
We both know we are.
Can I get you a robe, Mr. Osborn?
I don't get cold anymore, but if it would make you more comfortable.
It would.
There's a bar right over there.
I'm going to get my recorder--
REC
00:01:48

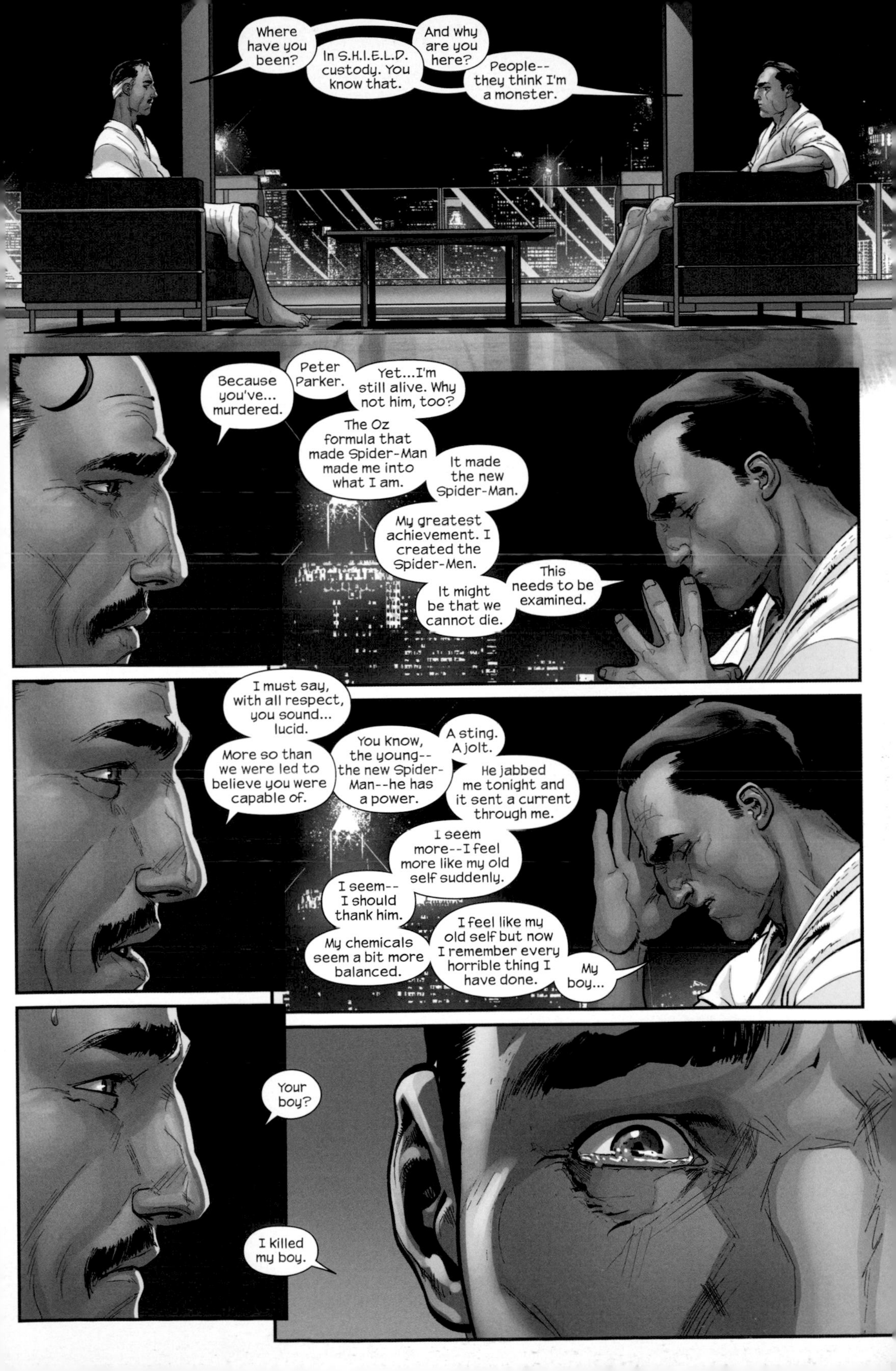
Where have you been?
In S.H.I.E.L.D. custody. You know that.
And why are you here?
People--they think I'm a monster.
Because you've... murdered.
Peter Parker.
Yet...I'm still alive. Why not him, too?
The Oz formula that made Spider-Man made me into what I am.
It made the new Spider-Man.
My greatest achievement. I created the Spider-Men.
It might be that we cannot die.
This needs to be examined.
I must say, with all respect, you sound... lucid.
More so than we were led to believe you were capable of.
You know, the young--the new Spider-Man--he has a power.
A sting. A jolt.
He jabbed me tonight and it sent a current through me.
I seem more--I feel more like my old self suddenly.
I seem--I should thank him.
My chemicals seem a bit more balanced.
I feel like my old self but now I remember every horrible thing I have done.
My boy...
Your boy?
I killed my boy.

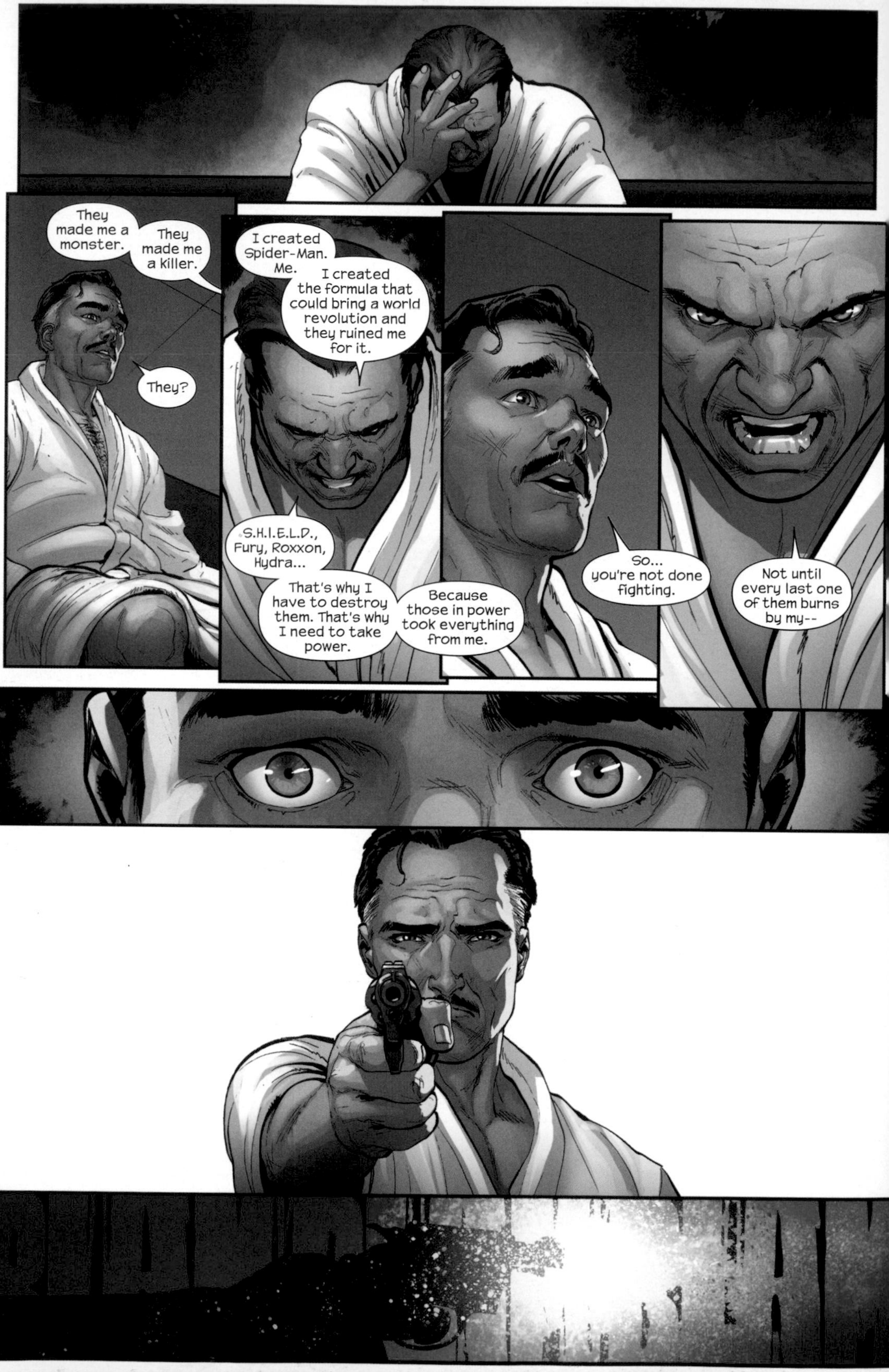
They made me a monster.
They made me a killer.
They?
I created Spider-Man. Me.
I created the formula that could bring a world revolution and they ruined me for it.
S.H.I.E.L.D., Fury, Roxxon, Hydra...
That's why I have to destroy them. That's why I need to take power.
Because those in power took everything from me.
So... you're not done fighting.
Not until every last one of them burns by my--

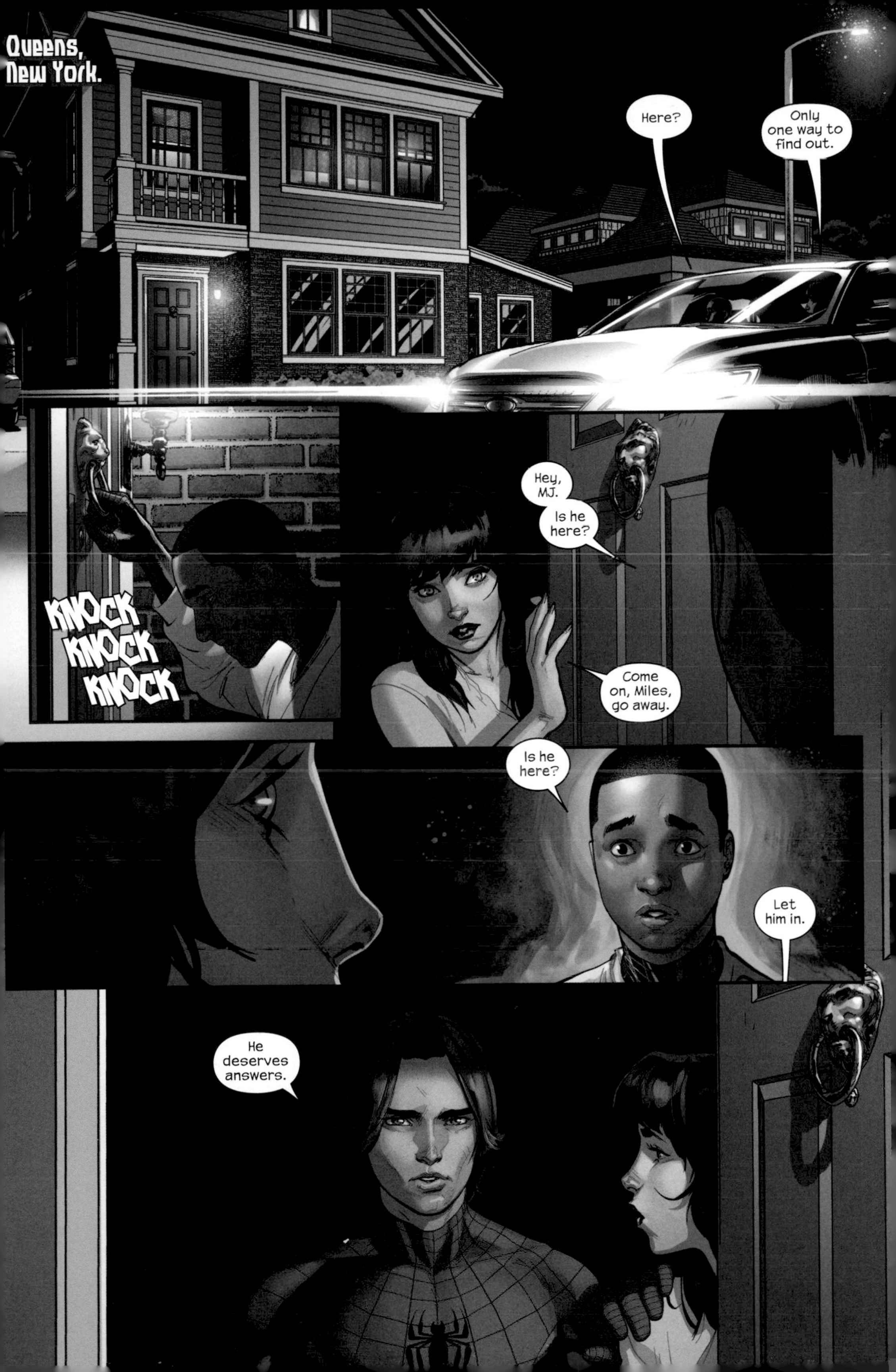
Queens, New York.
Here?
Only one way to find out.
KNOCK KNOCK KNOCK
Hey, MJ.
Is he here?
Come on, Miles, go away.
Is he here?
Let him in.
He deserves answers.

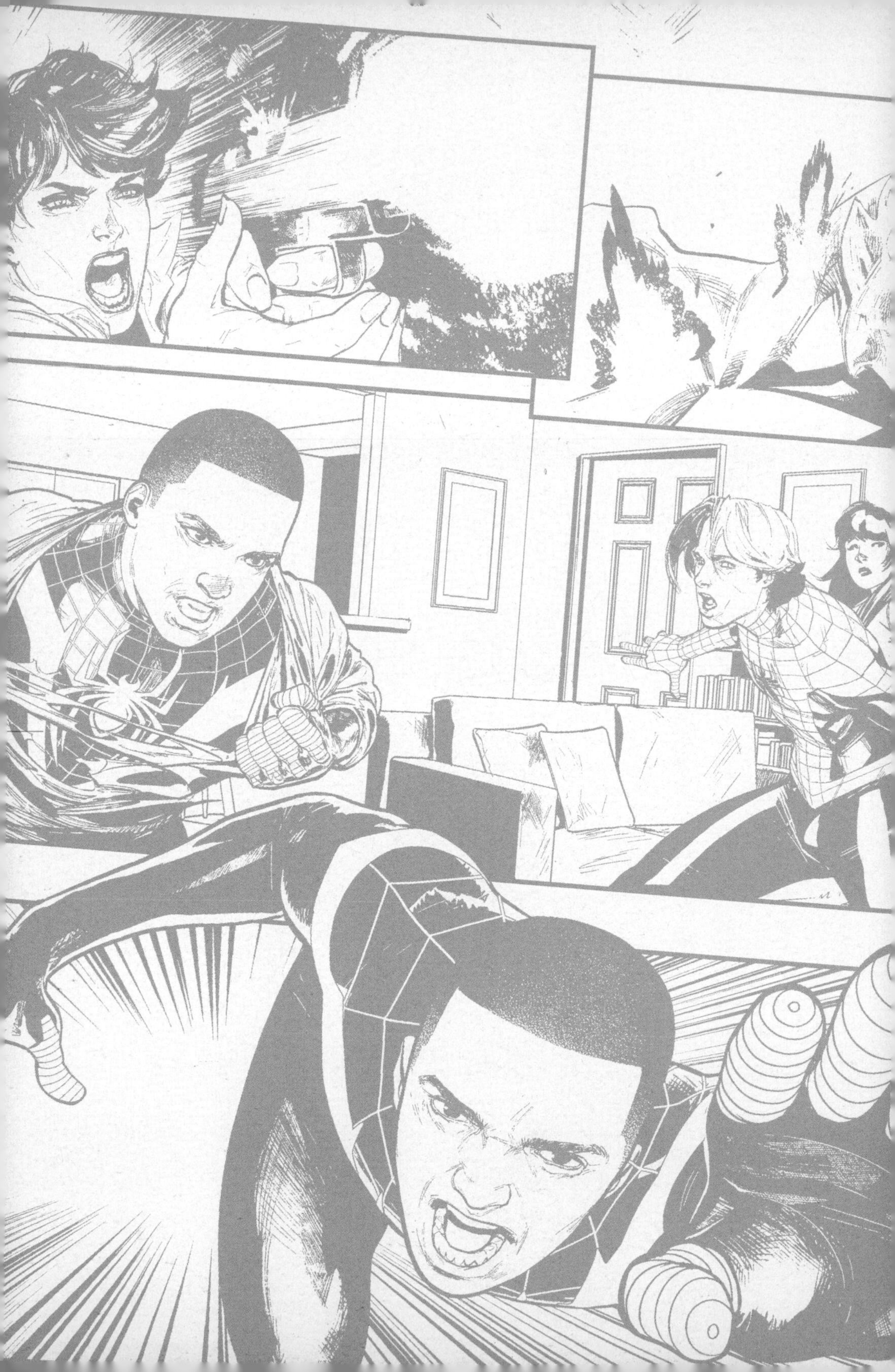

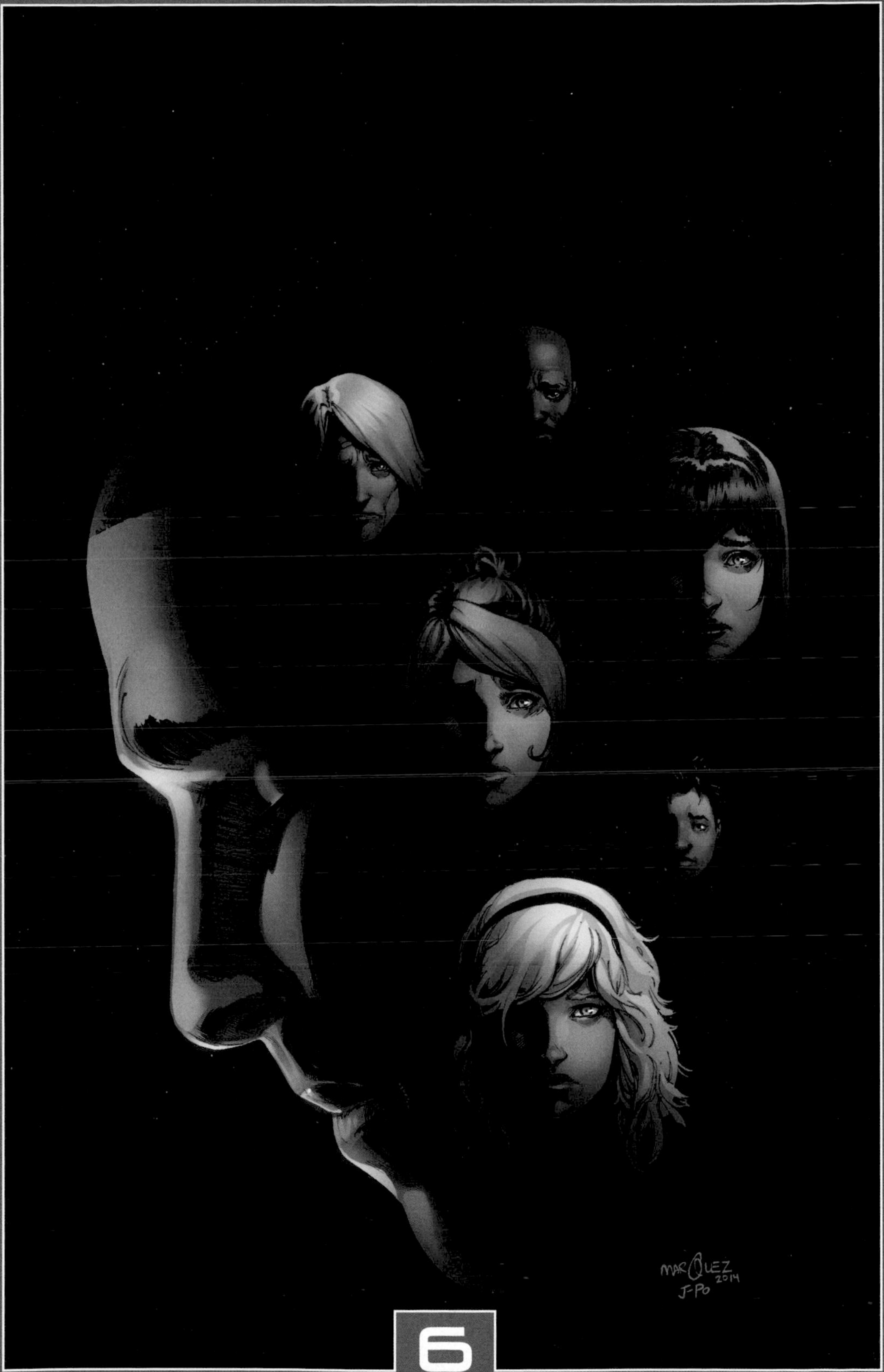
MARQUEZ 2014
J-Po

6

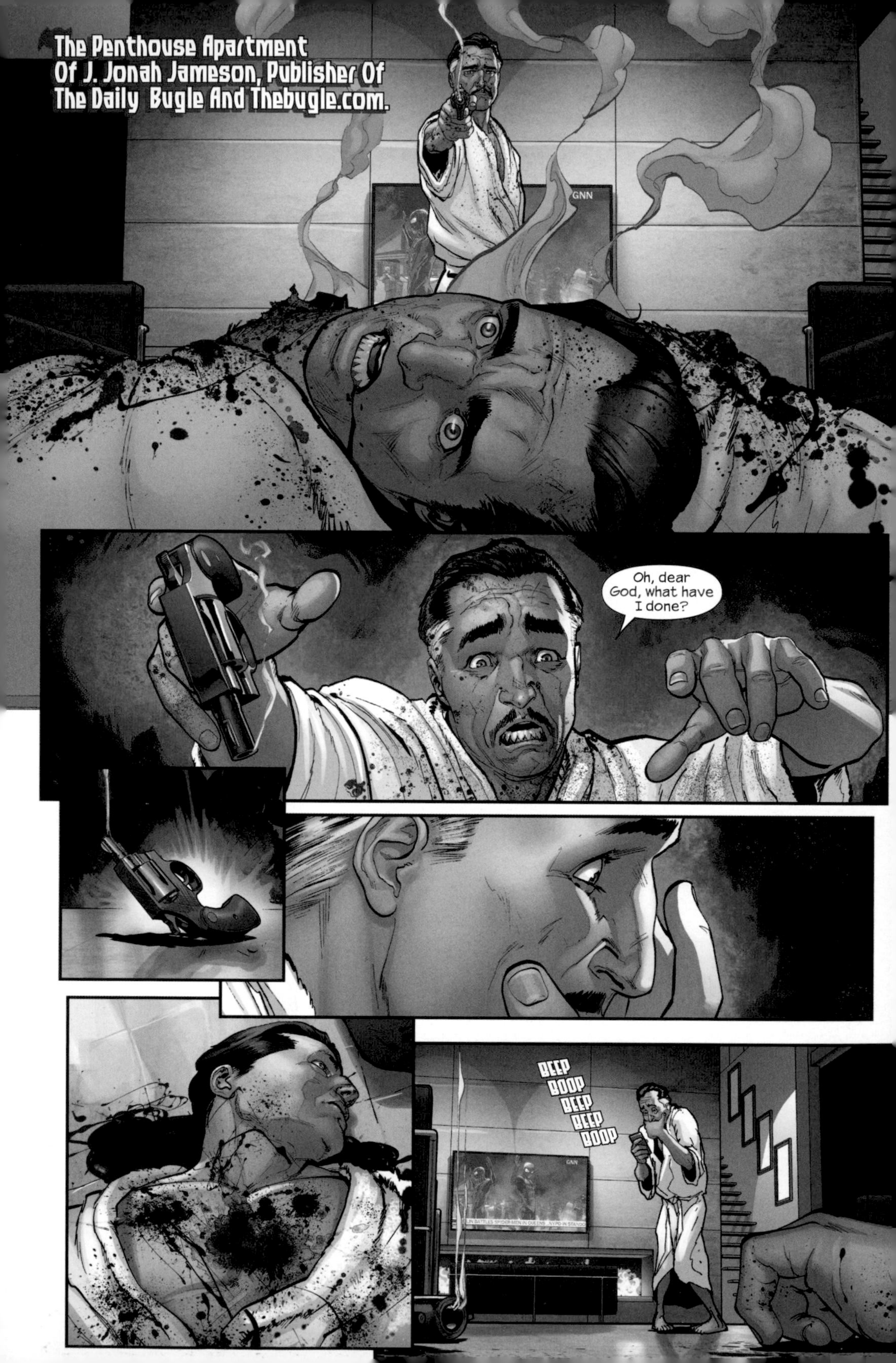
The Penthouse Apartment Of J. Jonah Jameson, Publisher Of The Daily Bugle And Thebugle.com.
GNN
Oh, dear God, what have I done?
BEEP BOOP BEEP BEEP BOOP

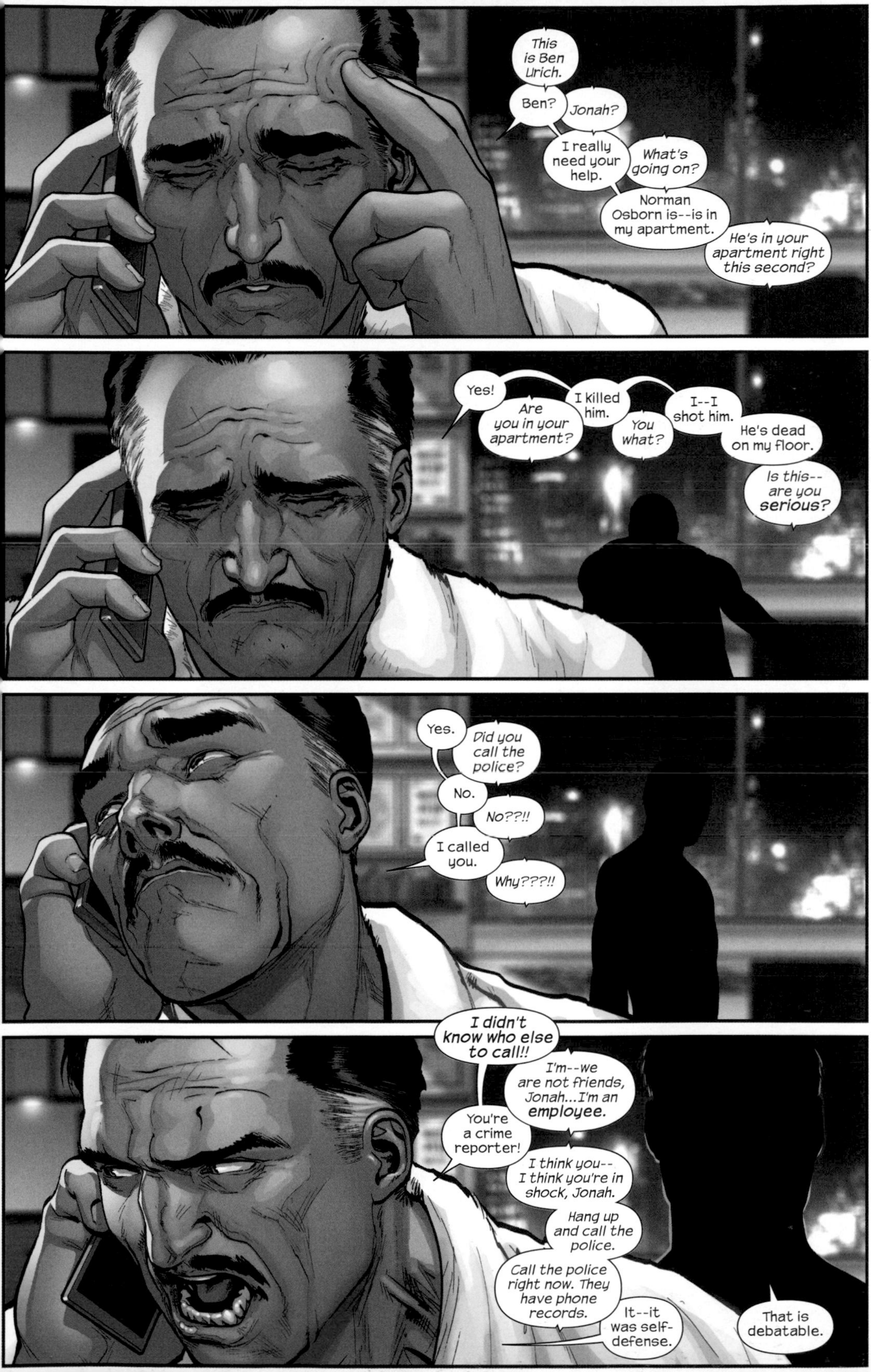
This is Ben Urich.
Ben?
Jonah?
I really need your help.
What's going on?
Norman Osborn is--is in my apartment.
He's in your apartment right this second?
Yes!
Are you in your apartment?
I killed him.
You what?
I--I shot him.
He's dead on my floor.
Is this--are you serious?
Yes.
Did you call the police?
No.
No??!!
I called you.
Why???!!
I didn't know who else to call!!
I'm--we are not friends, Jonah...I'm an employee.
You're a crime reporter!
I think you--I think you're in shock, Jonah.
Hang up and call the police.
Call the police right now. They have phone records.
It--it was self-defense.
That is debatable.

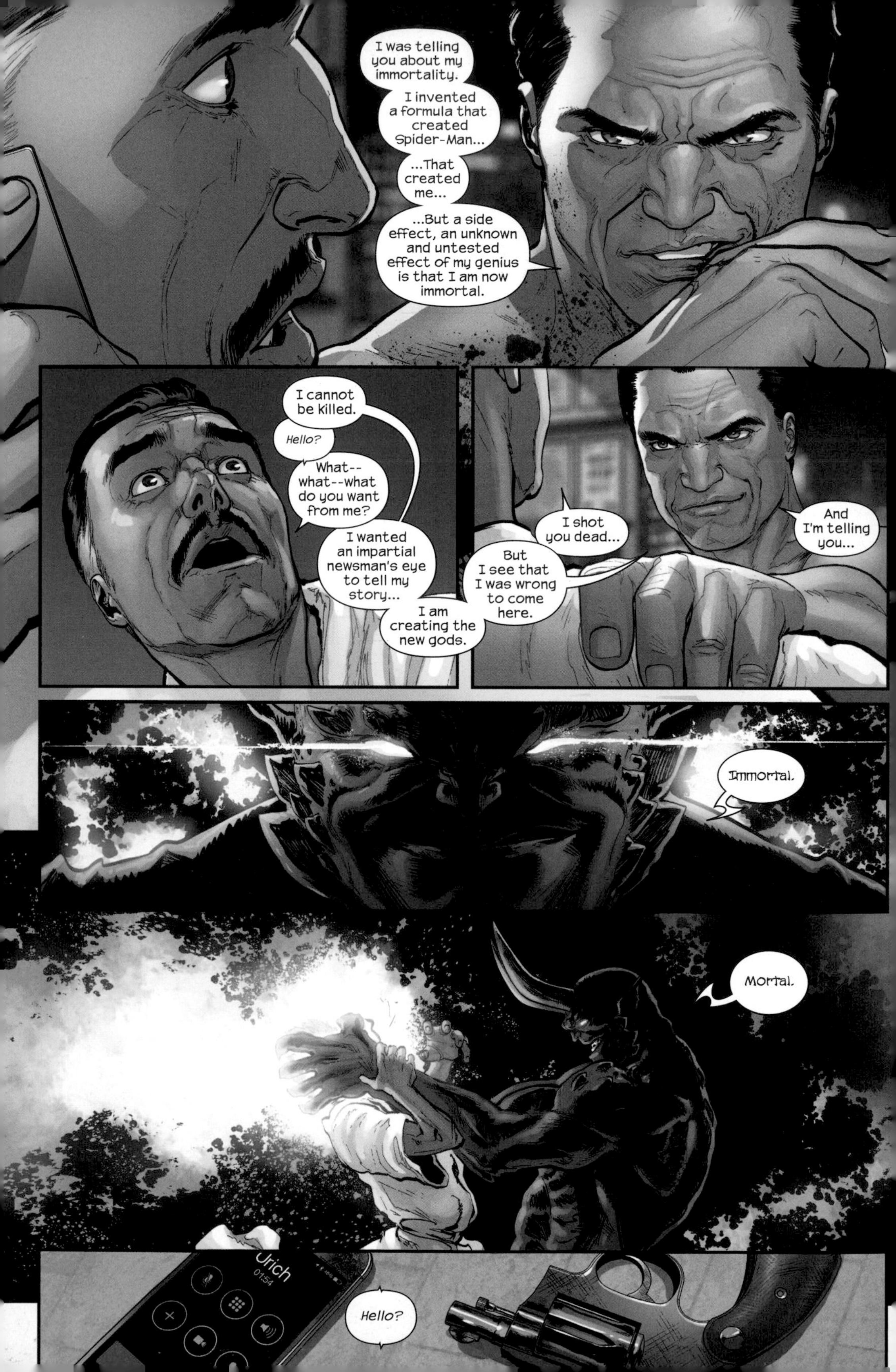
I was telling you about my immortality.
I invented a formula that created Spider-Man...
...That created me...
...But a side effect, an unknown and untested effect of my genius is that I am now immortal.
I cannot be killed.
Hello?
What--what--what do you want from me?
I wanted an impartial newsman's eye to tell my story...
I am creating the new gods.
I shot you dead...
But I see that I was wrong to come here.
And I'm telling you...
Immortal.
Mortal.
Urich
01:54
Hello?

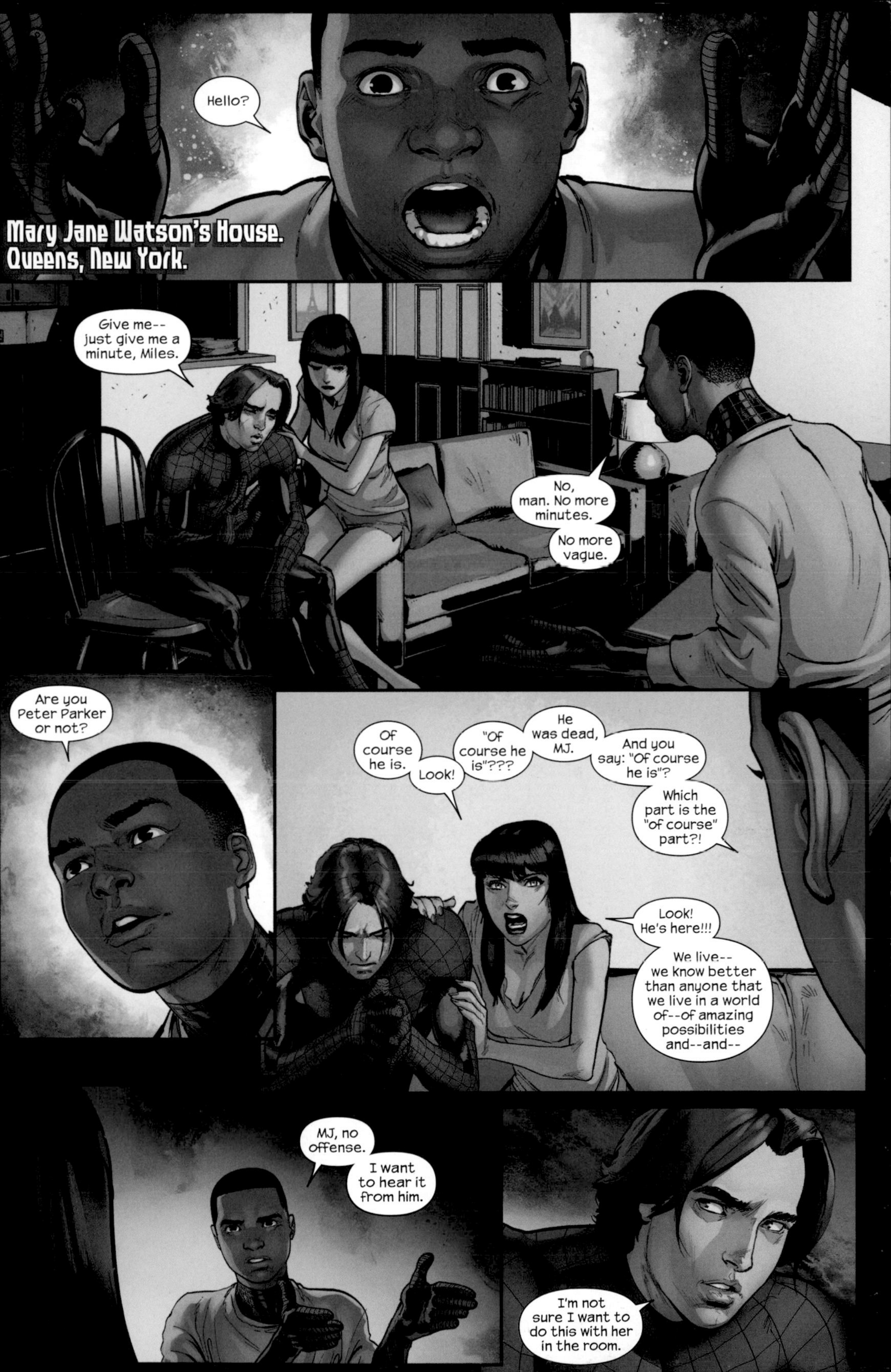
Hello?
Mary Jane Watson's House. Queens, New York.
Give me-- just give me a minute, Miles.
No, man. No more minutes.
No more vague.
Are you Peter Parker or not?
Of course he is.
Look!
"Of course he is"???
He was dead, MJ.
And you say: "Of course he is"?
Which part is the "of course" part?!
Look! He's here!!!
We live-- we know better than anyone that we live in a world of--of amazing possibilities and--and--
MJ, no offense.
I want to hear it from him.
I'm not sure I want to do this with her in the room.

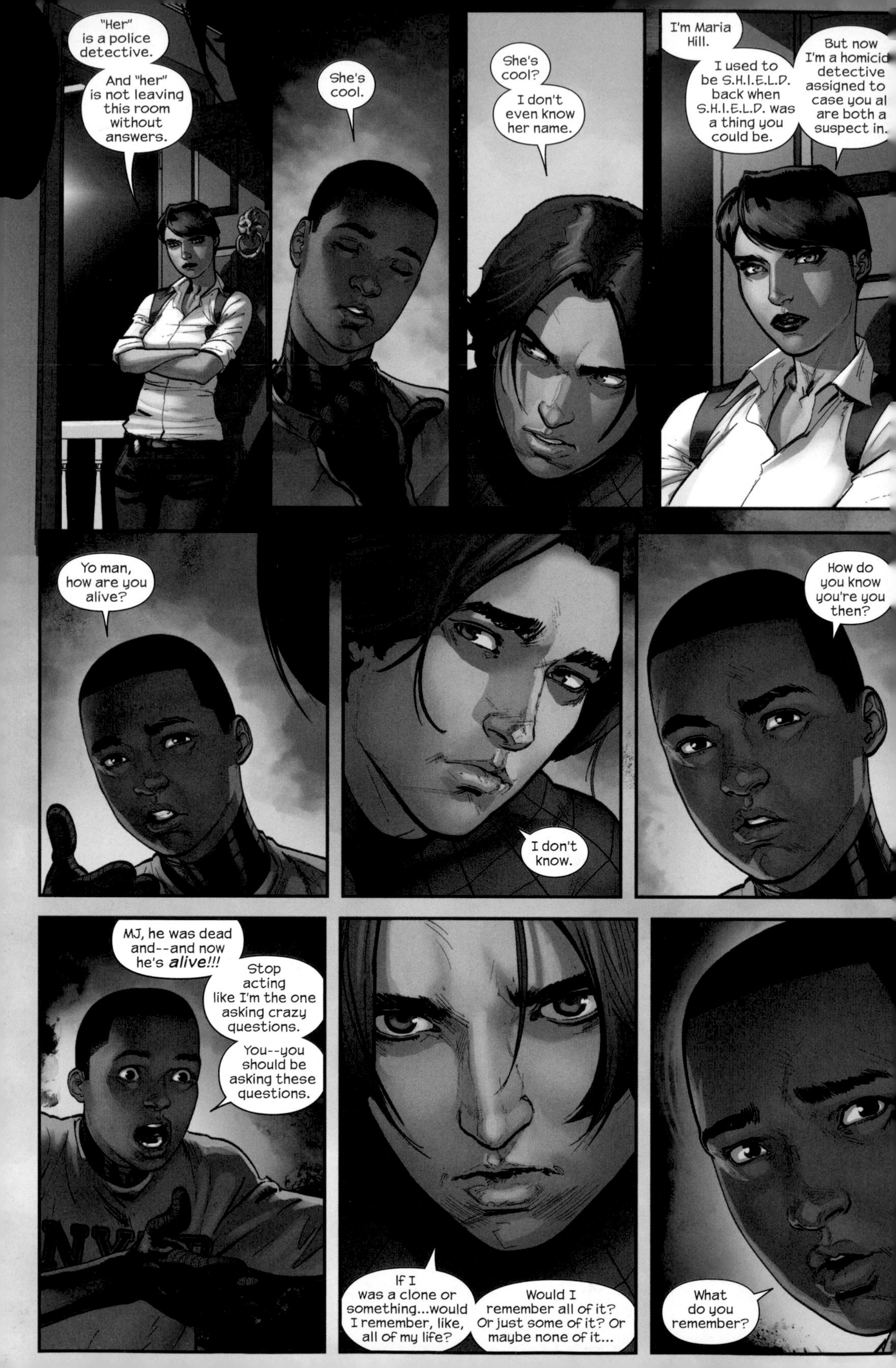
"Her" is a police detective.
And "her" is not leaving this room without answers.
She's cool.
She's cool?
I don't even know her name.
I'm Maria Hill.
I used to be S.H.I.E.L.D. back when S.H.I.E.L.D. was a thing you could be.
But now I'm a homicid detective assigned to case you al are both a suspect in.
Yo man, how are you alive?
I don't know.
How do you know you're you then?
MJ, he was dead and--and now he's *alive!!!*
Stop acting like I'm the one asking crazy questions.
You--you should be asking these questions.
If I was a clone or something...would I remember, like, all of my life?
Would I remember all of it? Or just some of it? Or maybe none of it...
What do you remember?

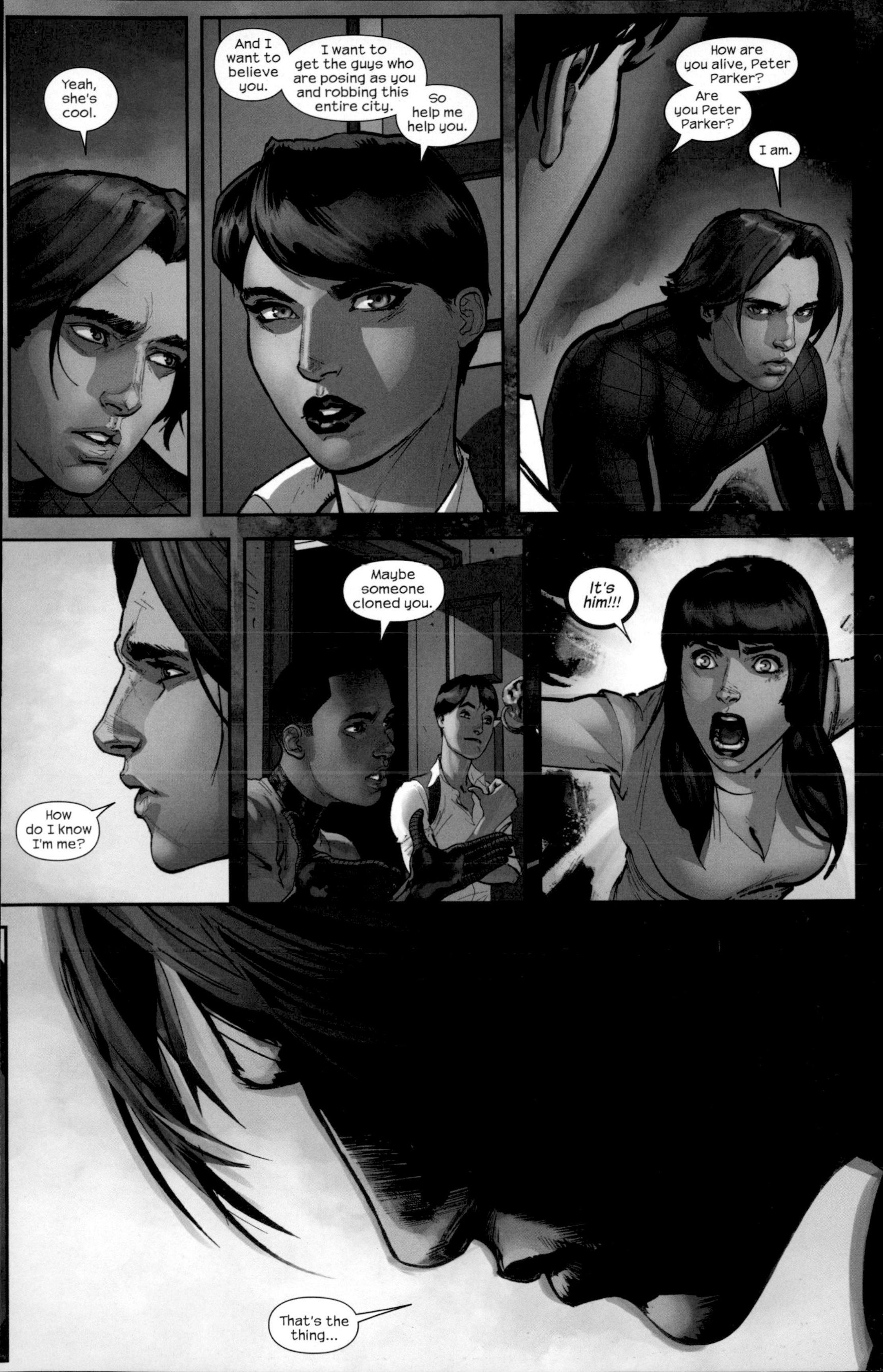
Yeah, she's cool.
And I want to believe you.
I want to get the guys who are posing as you and robbing this entire city.
So help me help you.
How are you alive, Peter Parker?
Are you Peter Parker?
I am.
How do I know I'm me?
Maybe someone cloned you.
It's him!!!
That's the thing...

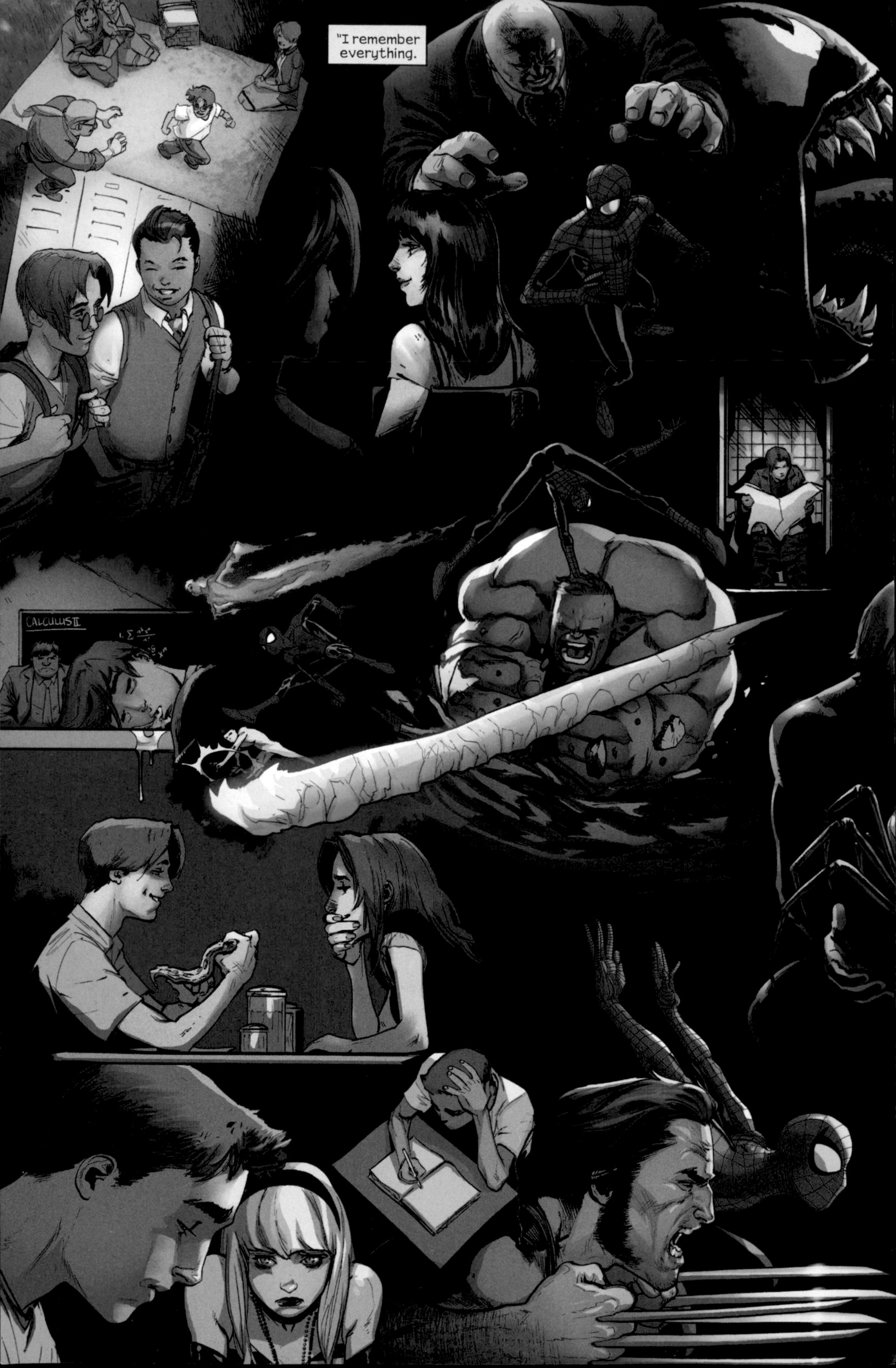
"I remember everything.
CALCULUS II

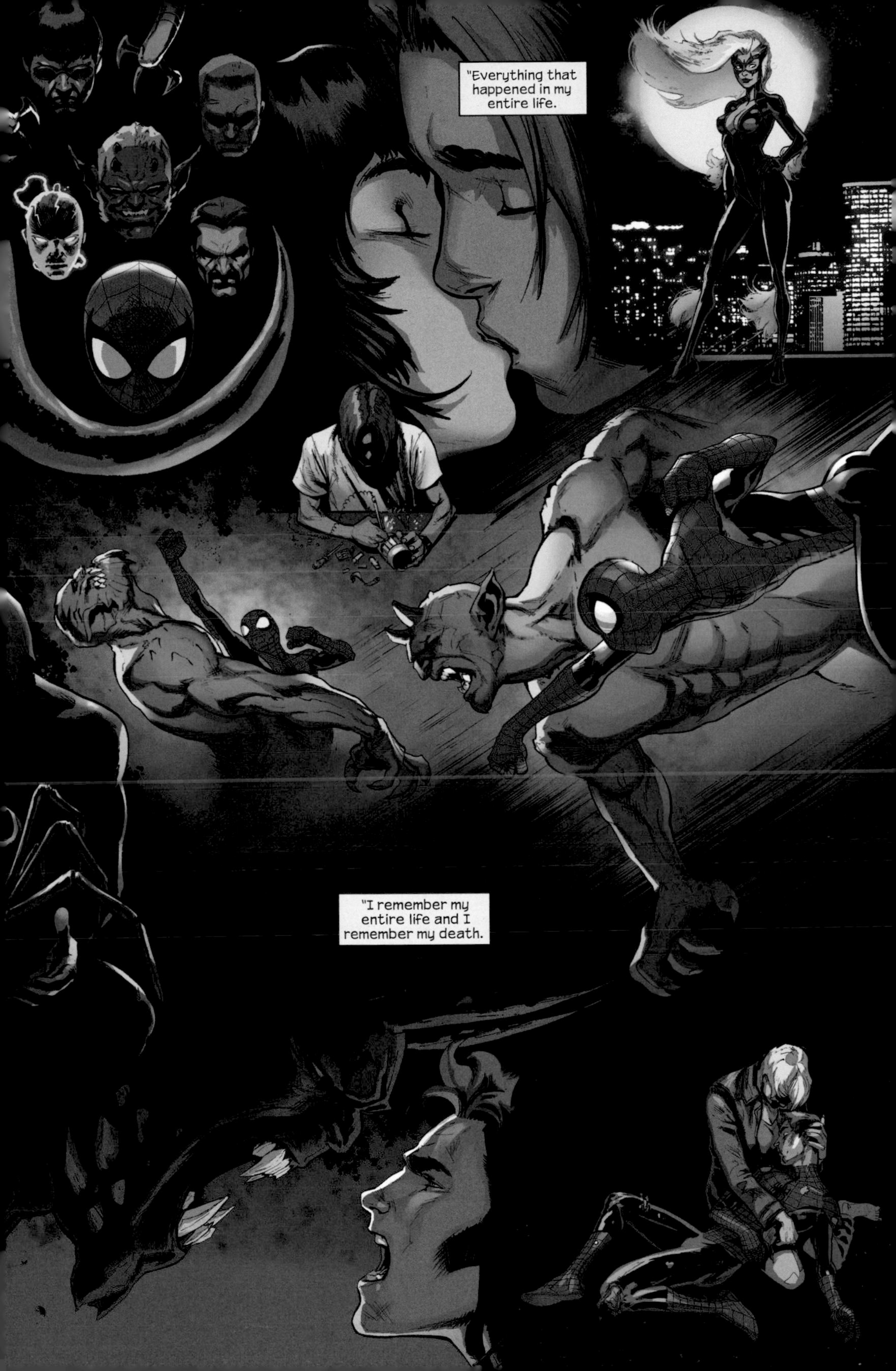
"Everything that happened in my entire life.
"I remember my entire life and I remember my death.

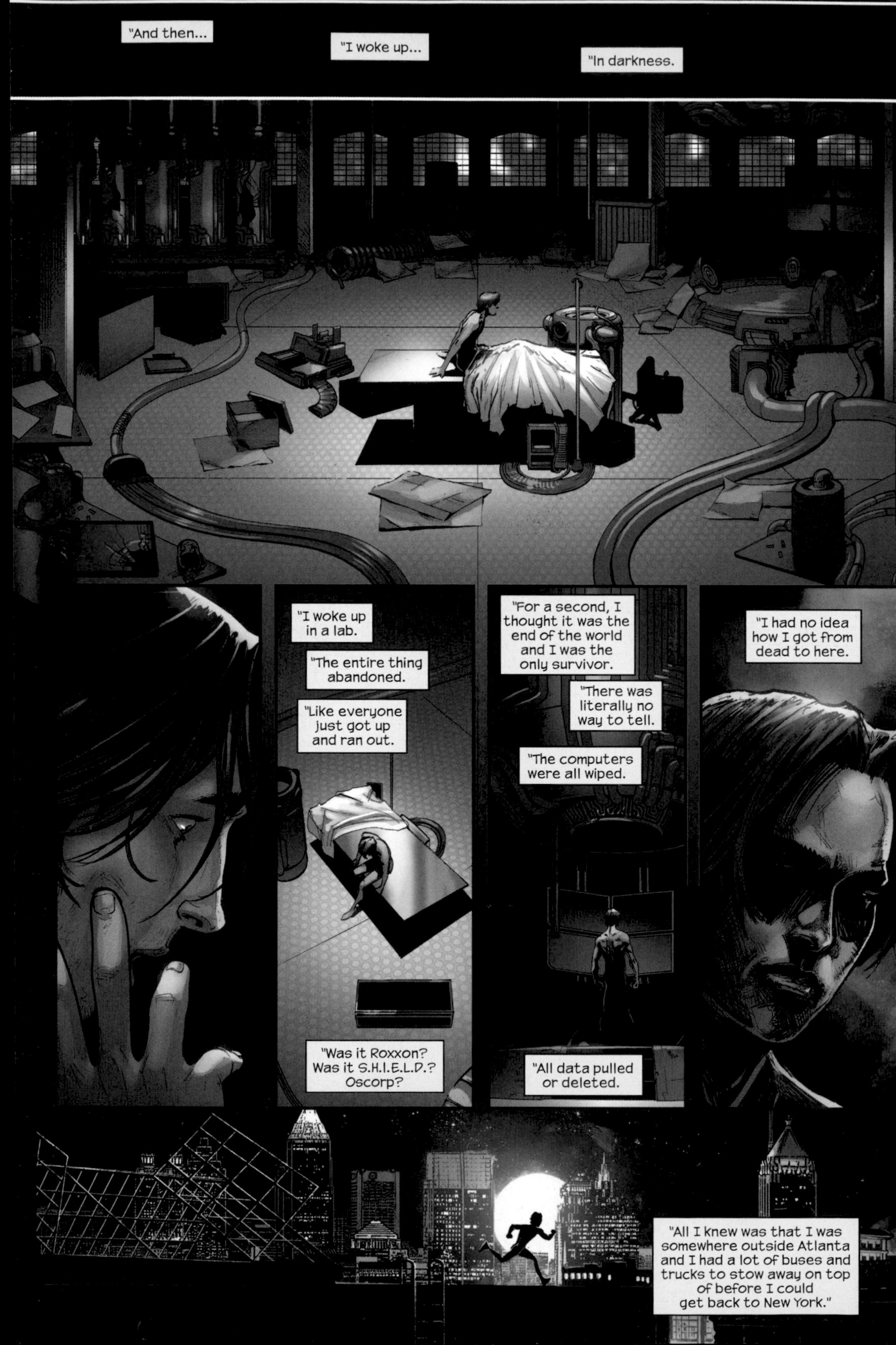
"And then...
"I woke up...
"In darkness.
"I woke up in a lab.
"The entire thing abandoned.
"Like everyone just got up and ran out.
"Was it Roxxon? Was it S.H.I.E.L.D.? Oscorp?
"For a second, I thought it was the end of the world and I was the only survivor.
"There was literally no way to tell.
"The computers were all wiped.
"All data pulled or deleted.
"I had no idea how I got from dead to here.
"All I knew was that I was somewhere outside Atlanta and I had a lot of buses and trucks to stow away on top of before I could get back to New York."

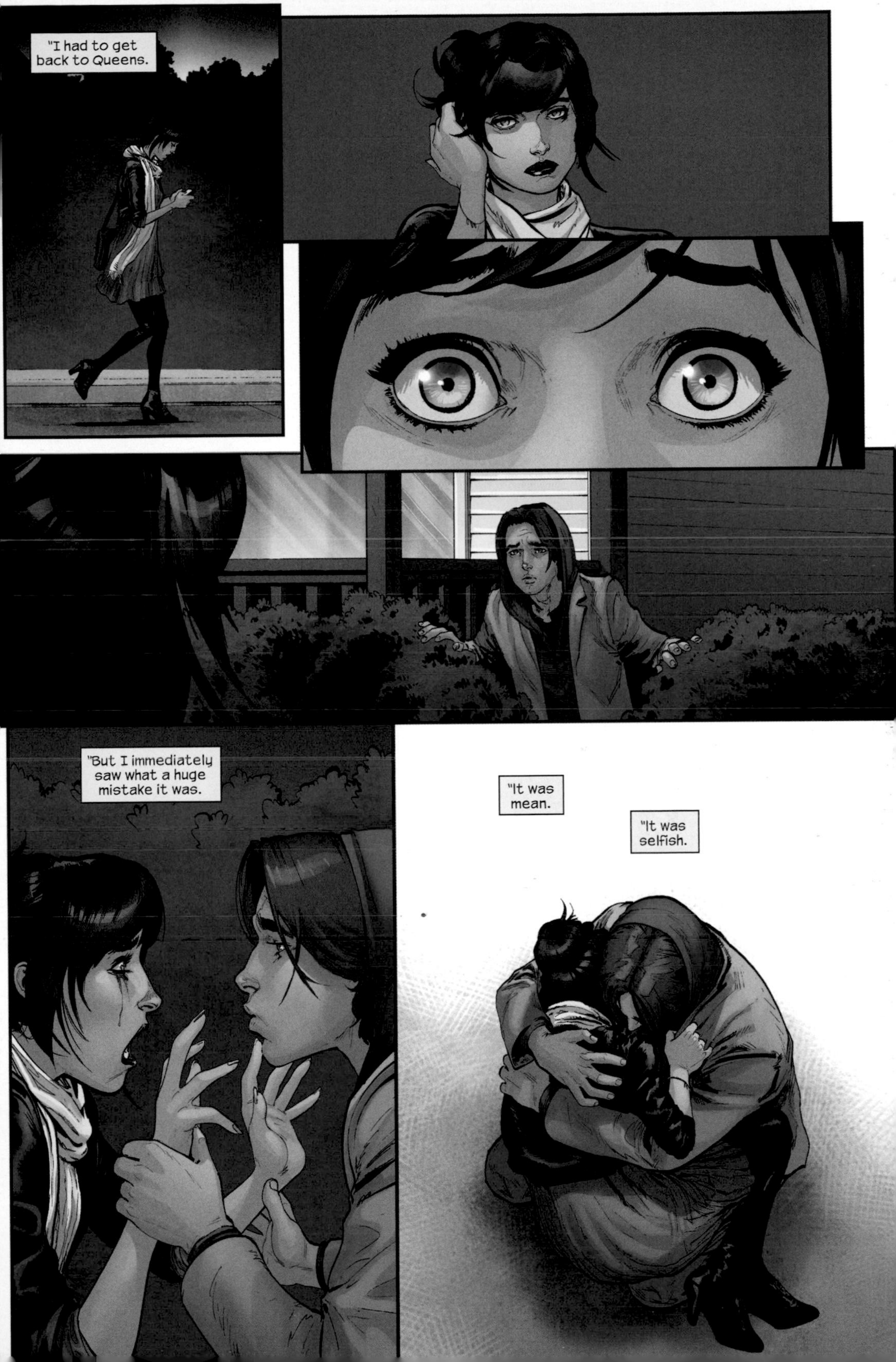
"I had to get back to Queens.
"But I immediately saw what a huge mistake it was.
"It was mean.
"It was selfish.

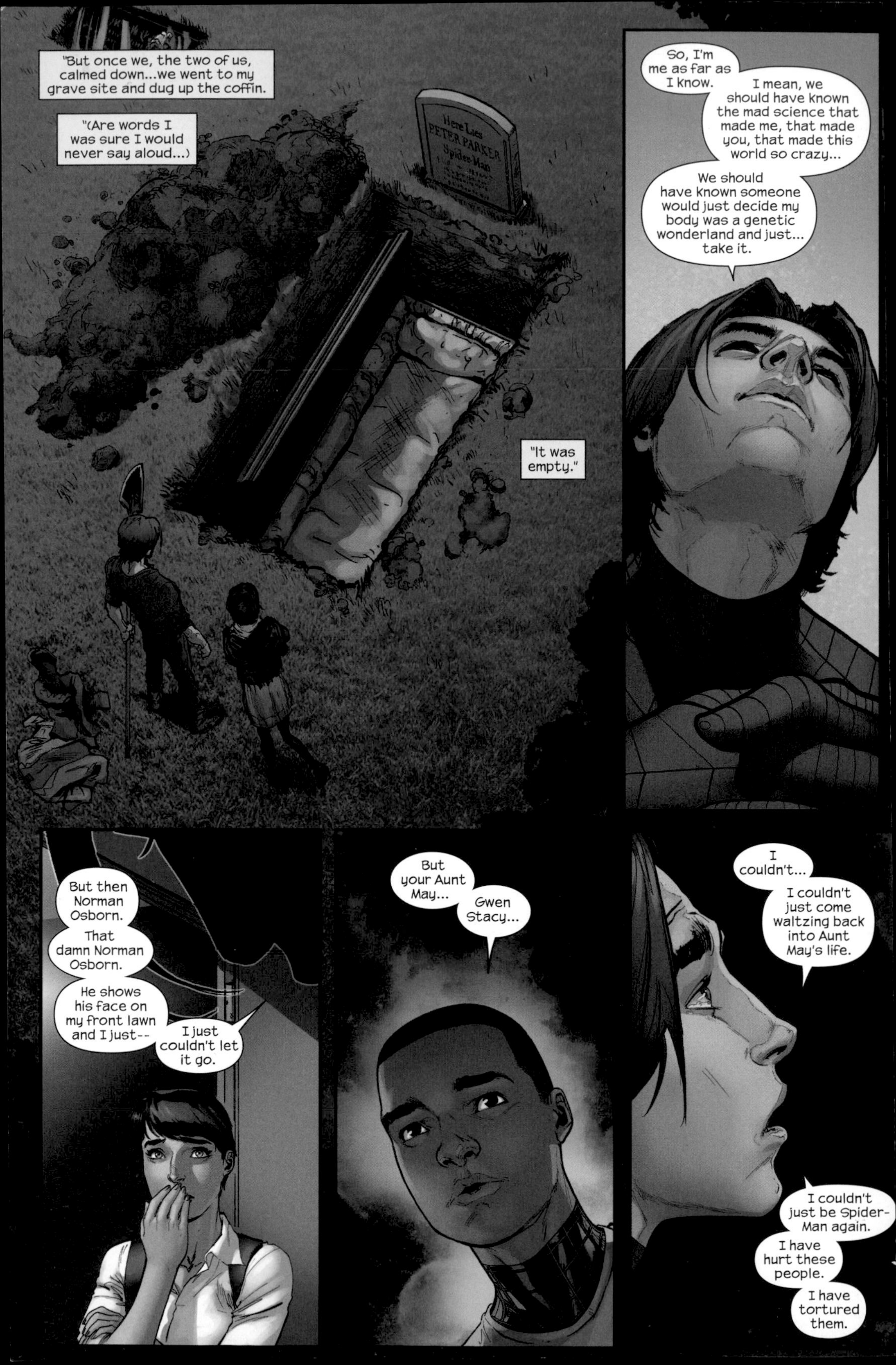

"But once we, the two of us, calmed down...we went to my grave site and dug up the coffin.
"(Are words I was sure I would never say aloud...)
Here Lies PETER PARKER Spider-Man
"It was empty."
So, I'm me as far as I know.
I mean, we should have known the mad science that made me, that made you, that made this world so crazy...
We should have known someone would just decide my body was a genetic wonderland and just... take it.
But then Norman Osborn.
That damn Norman Osborn.
He shows his face on my front lawn and I just--
I just couldn't let it go.
But your Aunt May...
Gwen Stacy...
I couldn't...
I couldn't just come waltzing back into Aunt May's life.
I couldn't just be Spider-Man again.
I have hurt these people.
I have tortured them.

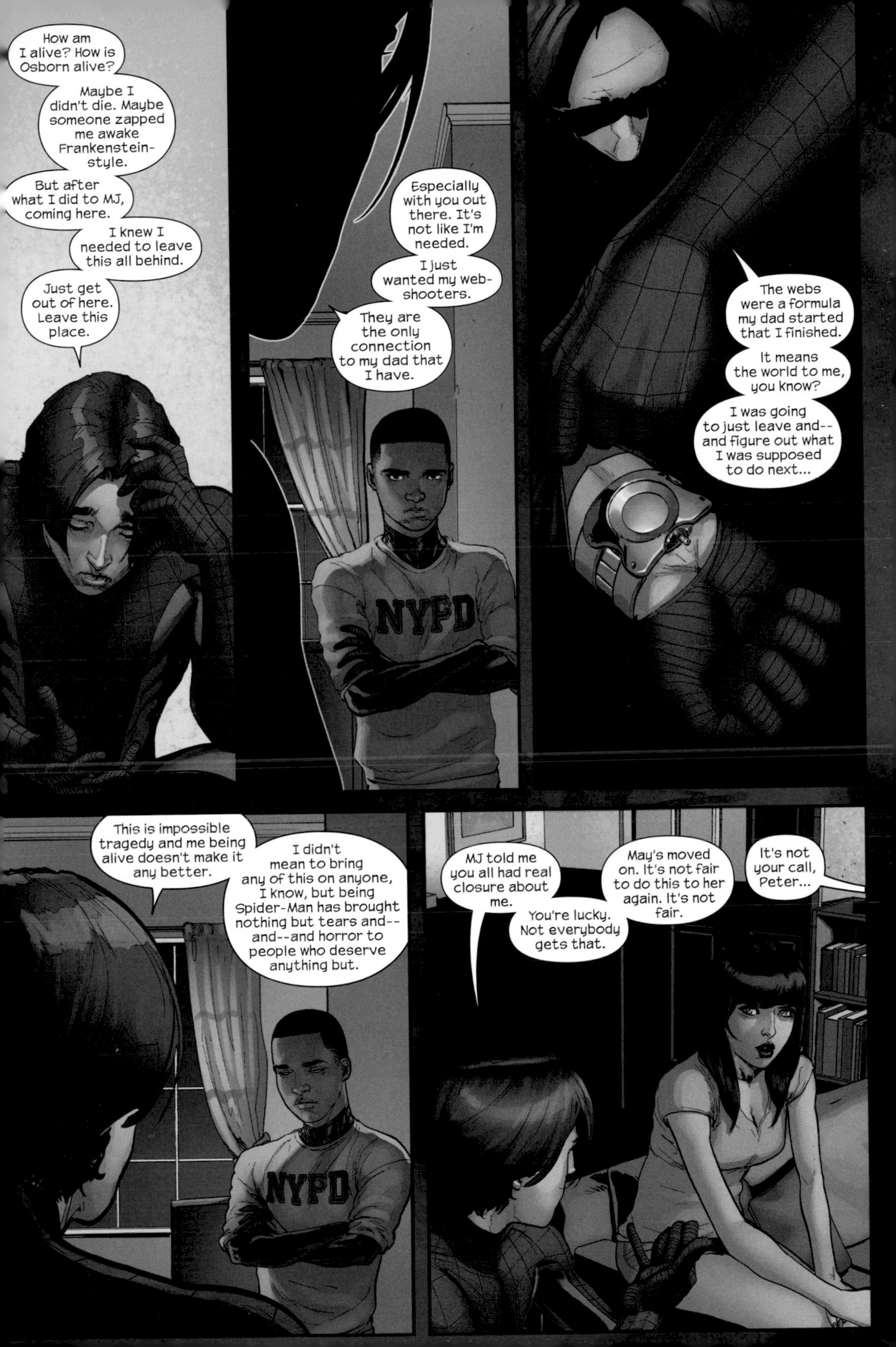

How am I alive? How is Osborn alive?
Maybe I didn't die. Maybe someone zapped me awake Frankenstein-style.
But after what I did to MJ, coming here.
I knew I needed to leave this all behind.
Just get out of here. Leave this place.
Especially with you out there. It's not like I'm needed.
I just wanted my web-shooters.
They are the only connection to my dad that I have.
The webs were a formula my dad started that I finished.
It means the world to me, you know?
I was going to just leave and--and figure out what I was supposed to do next...
This is impossible tragedy and me being alive doesn't make it any better.
I didn't mean to bring any of this on anyone, I know, but being Spider-Man has brought nothing but tears and--and--and horror to people who deserve anything but.
MJ told me you all had real closure about me.
You're lucky. Not everybody gets that.
May's moved on. It's not fair to do this to her again. It's not fair.
It's not your call, Peter...

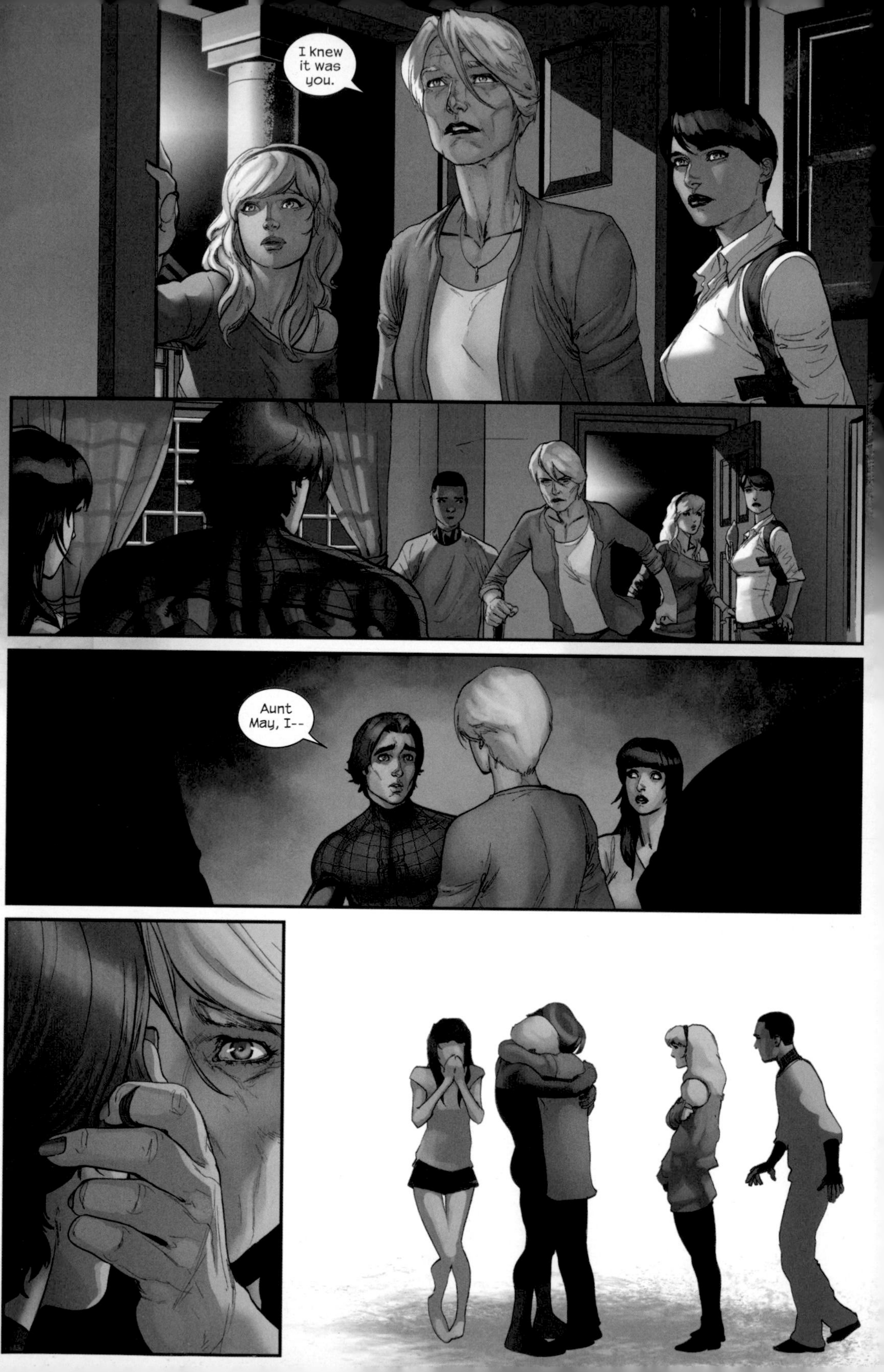
I knew it was you.
Aunt May, I--

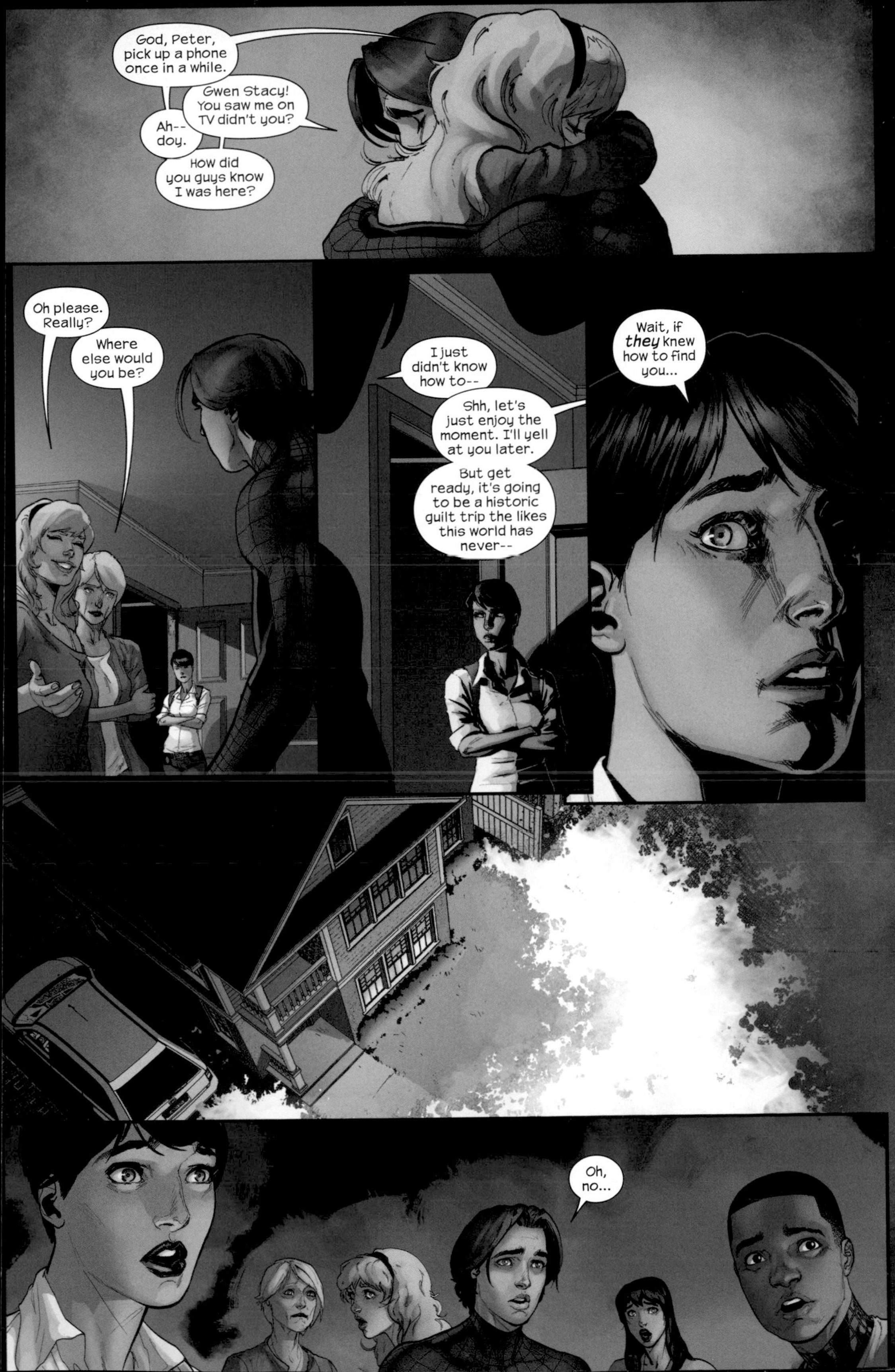
God, Peter, pick up a phone once in a while.
Ah--doy.
Gwen Stacy! You saw me on TV didn't you?
How did you guys know I was here?
Oh please. Really?
Where else would you be?
I just didn't know how to--
Shh, let's just enjoy the moment. I'll yell at you later.
But get ready, it's going to be a historic guilt trip the likes this world has never--
Wait, if *they* knew how to find you...
Oh, no...

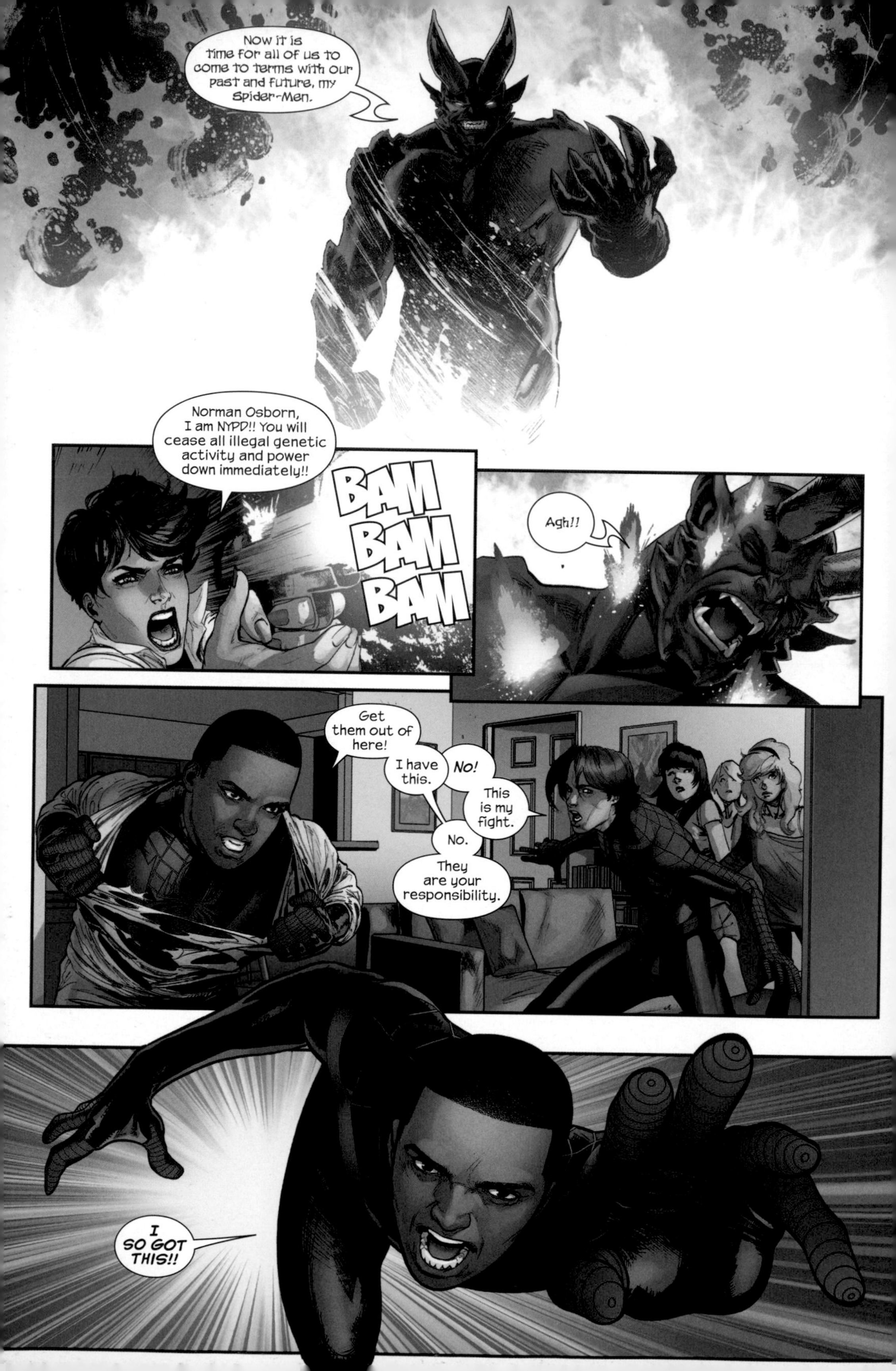
Now it is time for all of us to come to terms with our past and future, my Spider-Men.
Norman Osborn, I am NYPD!! You will cease all illegal genetic activity and power down immediately!!
BAM BAM BAM
Agh!!
Get them out of here!
I have this.
No!
This is my fight.
No.
They are your responsibility.
I SO GOT THIS!!

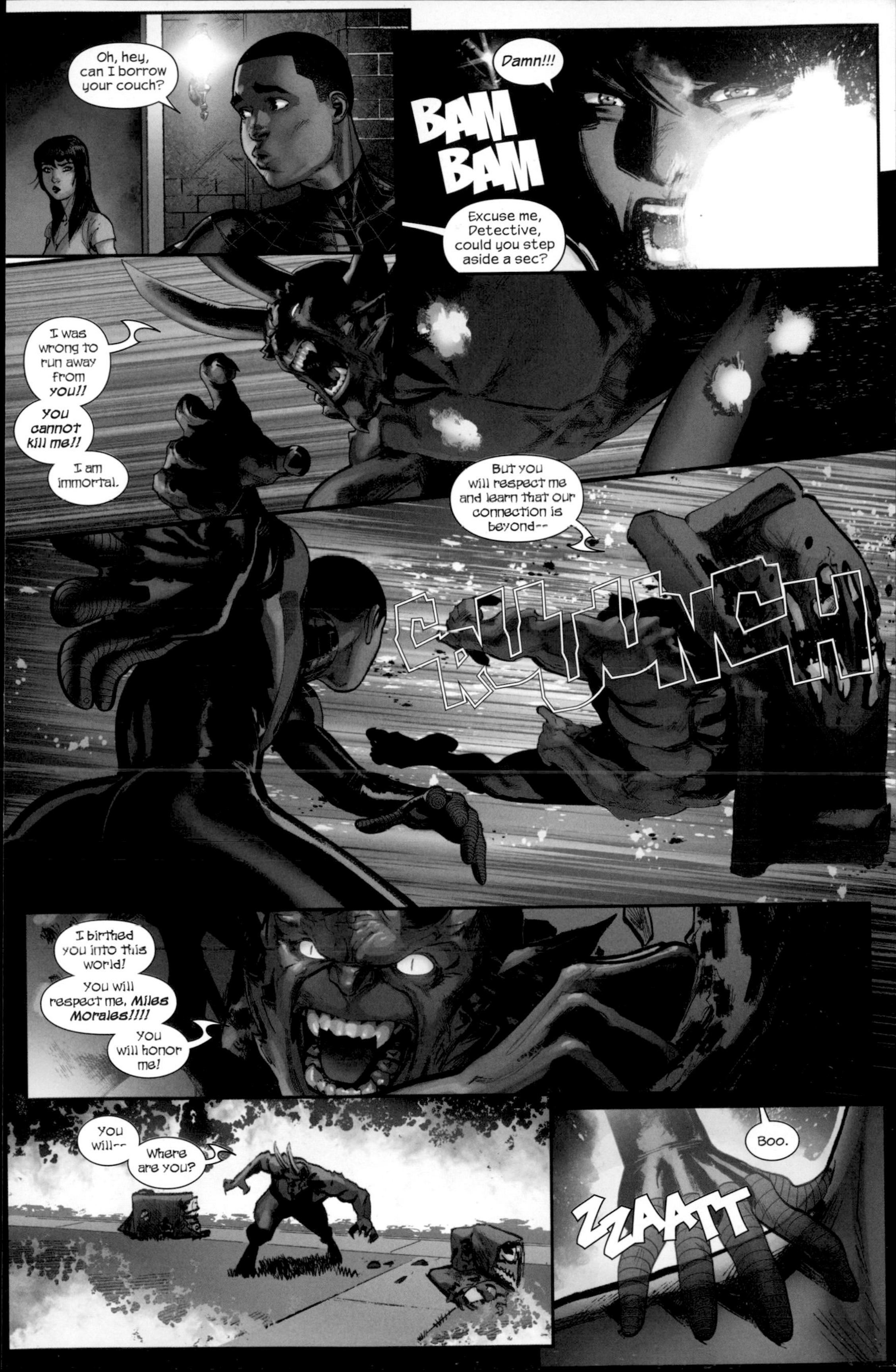

Oh, hey, can I borrow your couch?
Damn!!!
BAM BAM
Excuse me, Detective, could you step aside a sec?
I was wrong to run away from you!!
You cannot kill me!!
I am immortal.
But you will respect me and learn that our connection is beyond--
I birthed you into this world!
You will respect me, Miles Morales!!!!
You will honor me!
You will--
Where are you?
Boo.
ZZAATT

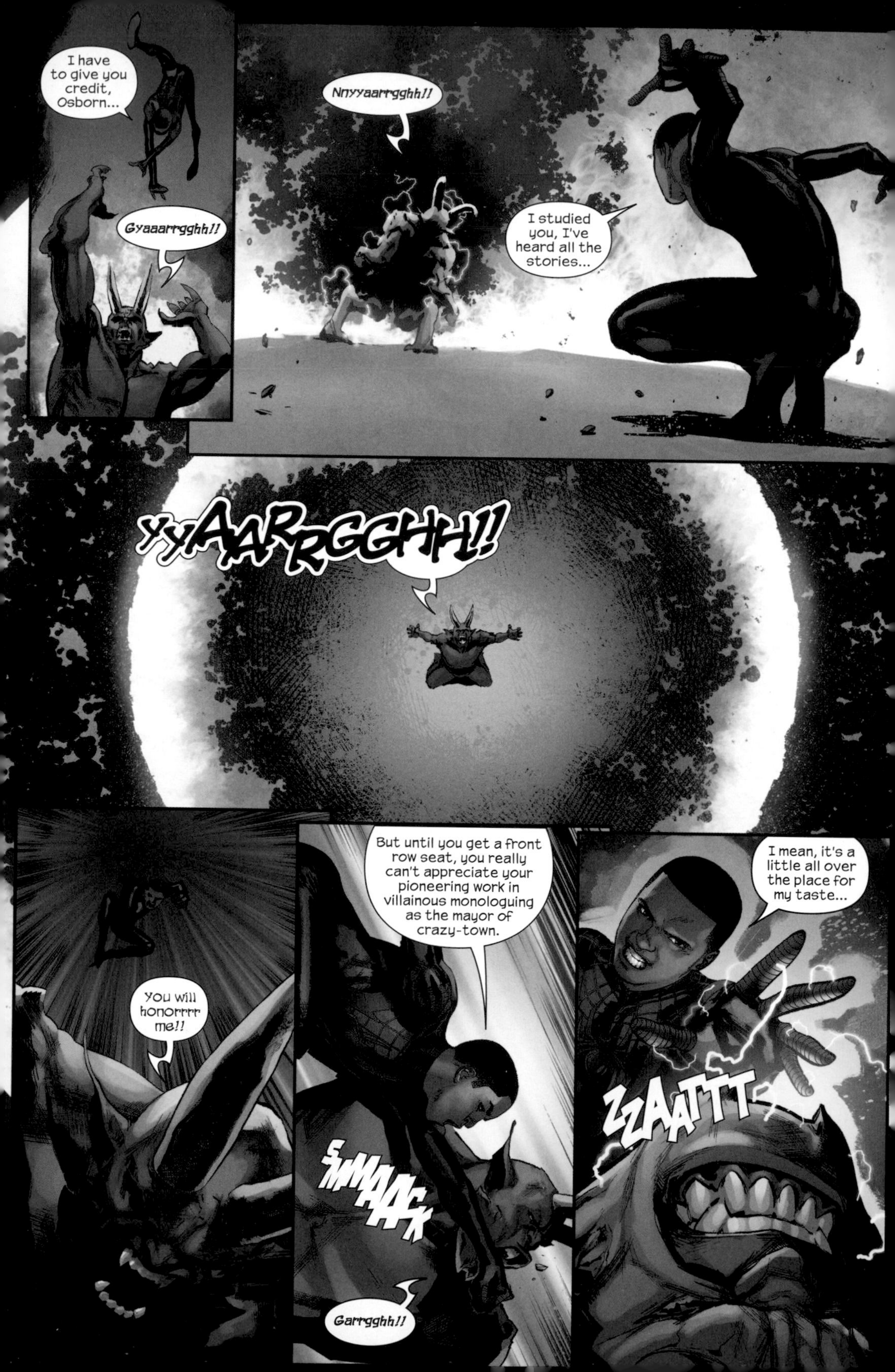
I have to give you credit, Osborn...
Gyaaarrggh!!
Nnyyaarrgghh!!
I studied you, I've heard all the stories...
YYAARRGGHH!!
You will honorrrr me!!
But until you get a front row seat, you really can't appreciate your pioneering work in villainous monologuing as the mayor of crazy-town.
SMAAACK
Garrgghh!!
I mean, it's a little all over the place for my taste...
ZZAATTT

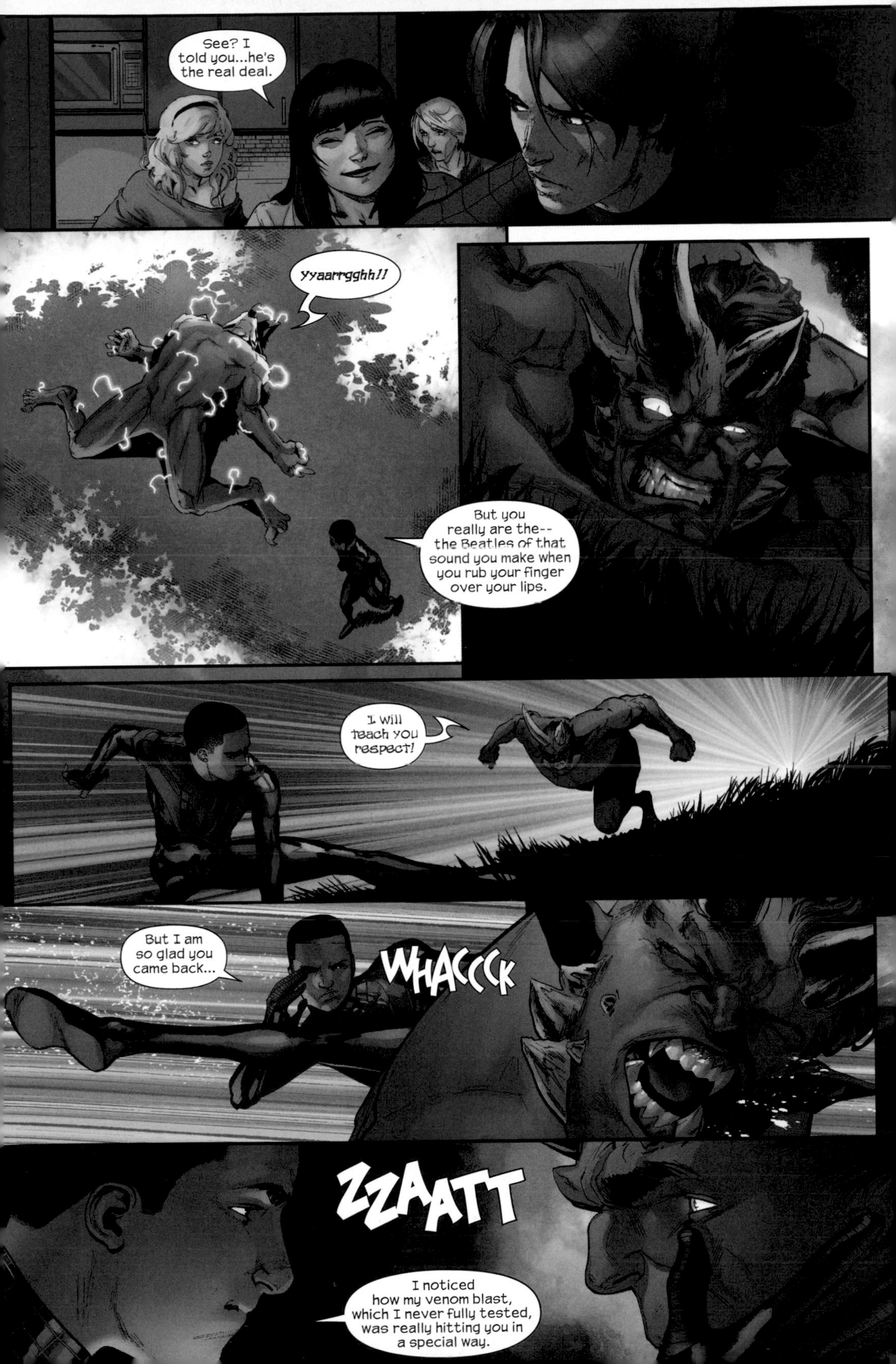
See? I told you...he's the real deal.
Yyaarrgghh!!
But you really are the-- the Beatles of that sound you make when you rub your finger over your lips.
I will teach you respect!
But I am so glad you came back...
WHACCCK
ZZAATT
I noticed how my venom blast, which I never fully tested, was really hitting you in a special way.

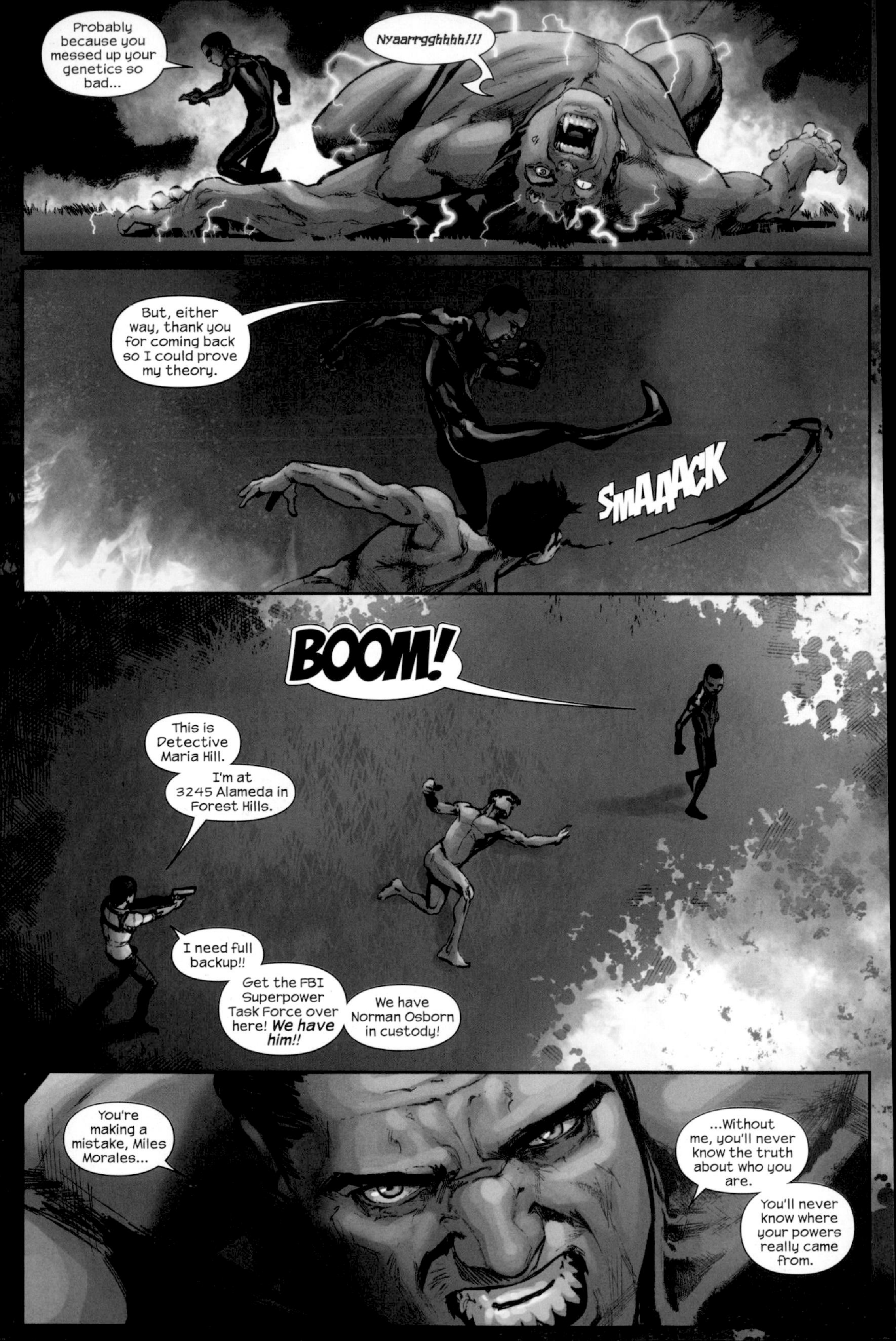
Probably because you messed up your genetics so bad...
Nyaarrgghhhh!!!
But, either way, thank you for coming back so I could prove my theory.
SMAAACK
BOOM!
This is Detective Maria Hill.
I'm at 3245 Alameda in Forest Hills.
I need full backup!!
Get the FBI Superpower Task Force over here! We have him!!
We have Norman Osborn in custody!
You're making a mistake, Miles Morales...
...Without me, you'll never know the truth about who you are.
You'll never know where your powers really came from.

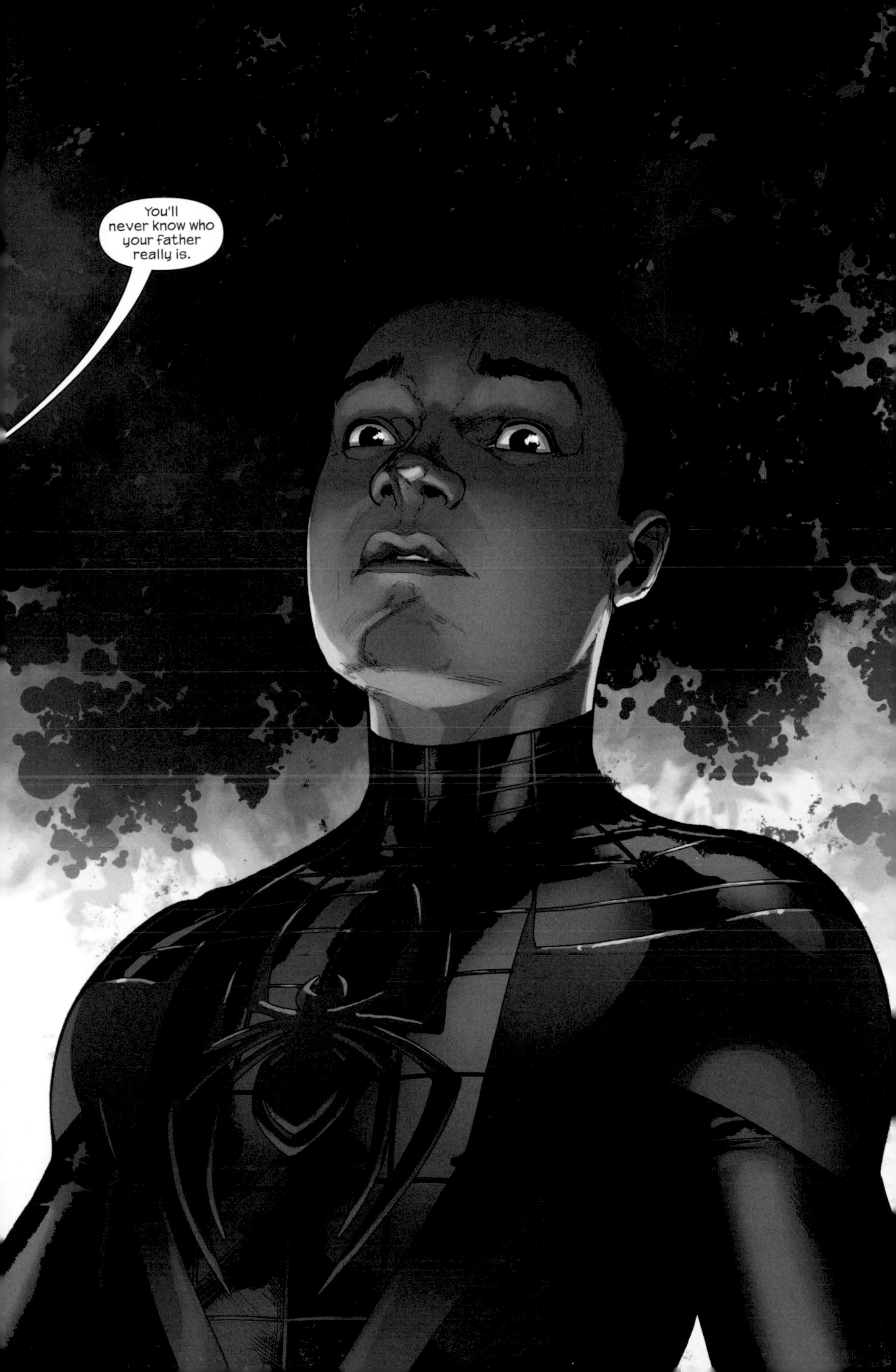
You'll never know who your father really is.

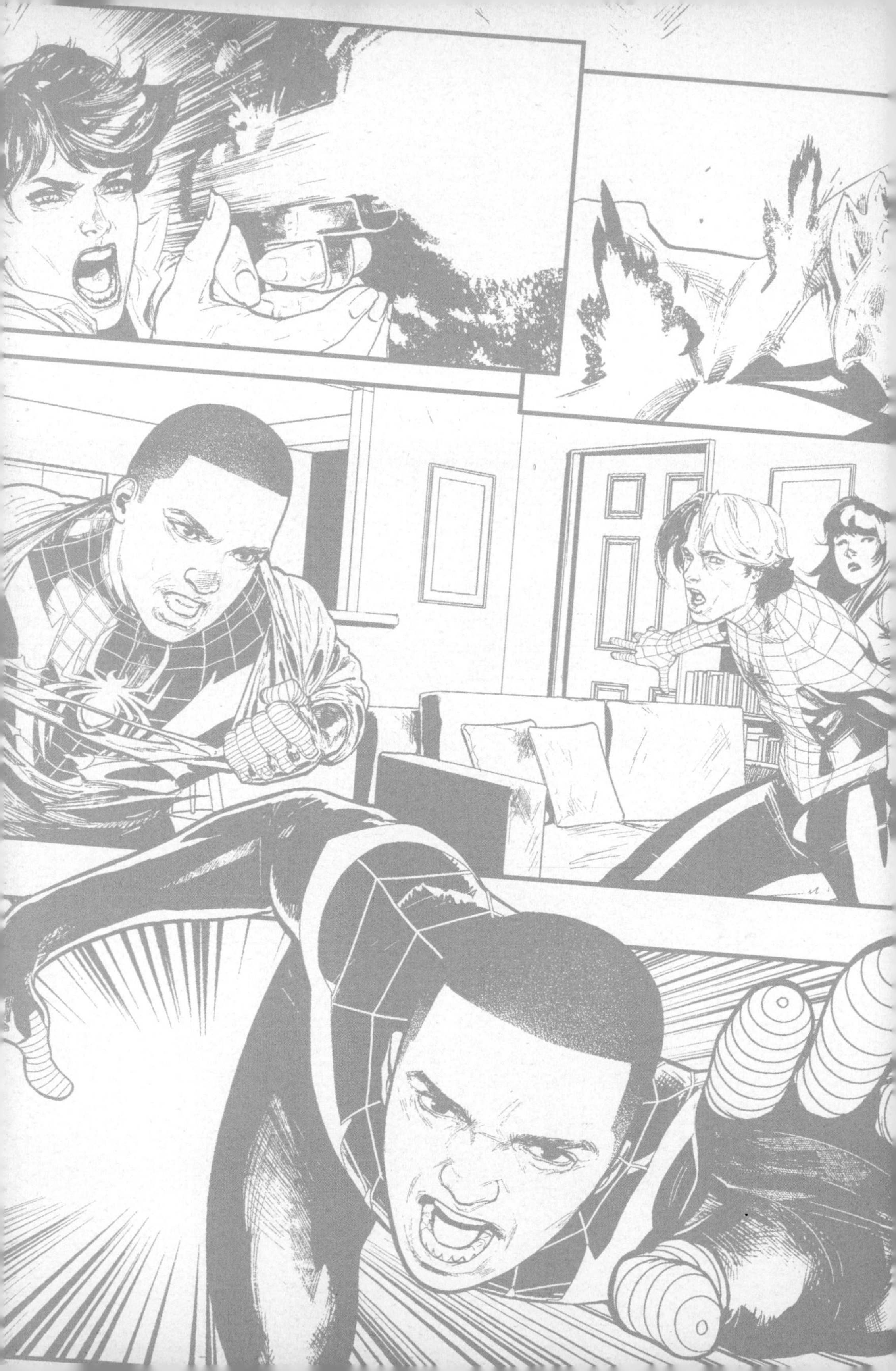

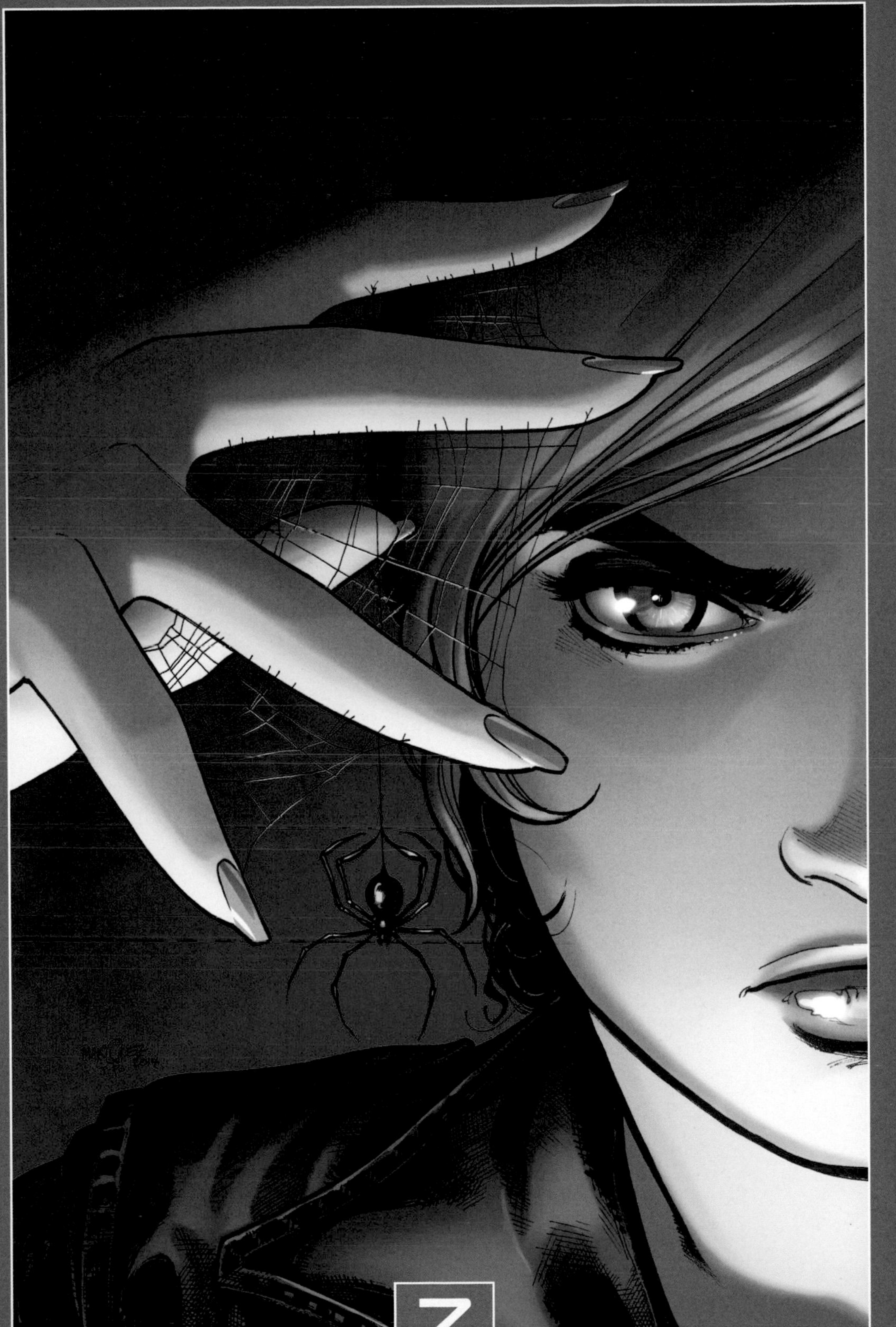
7

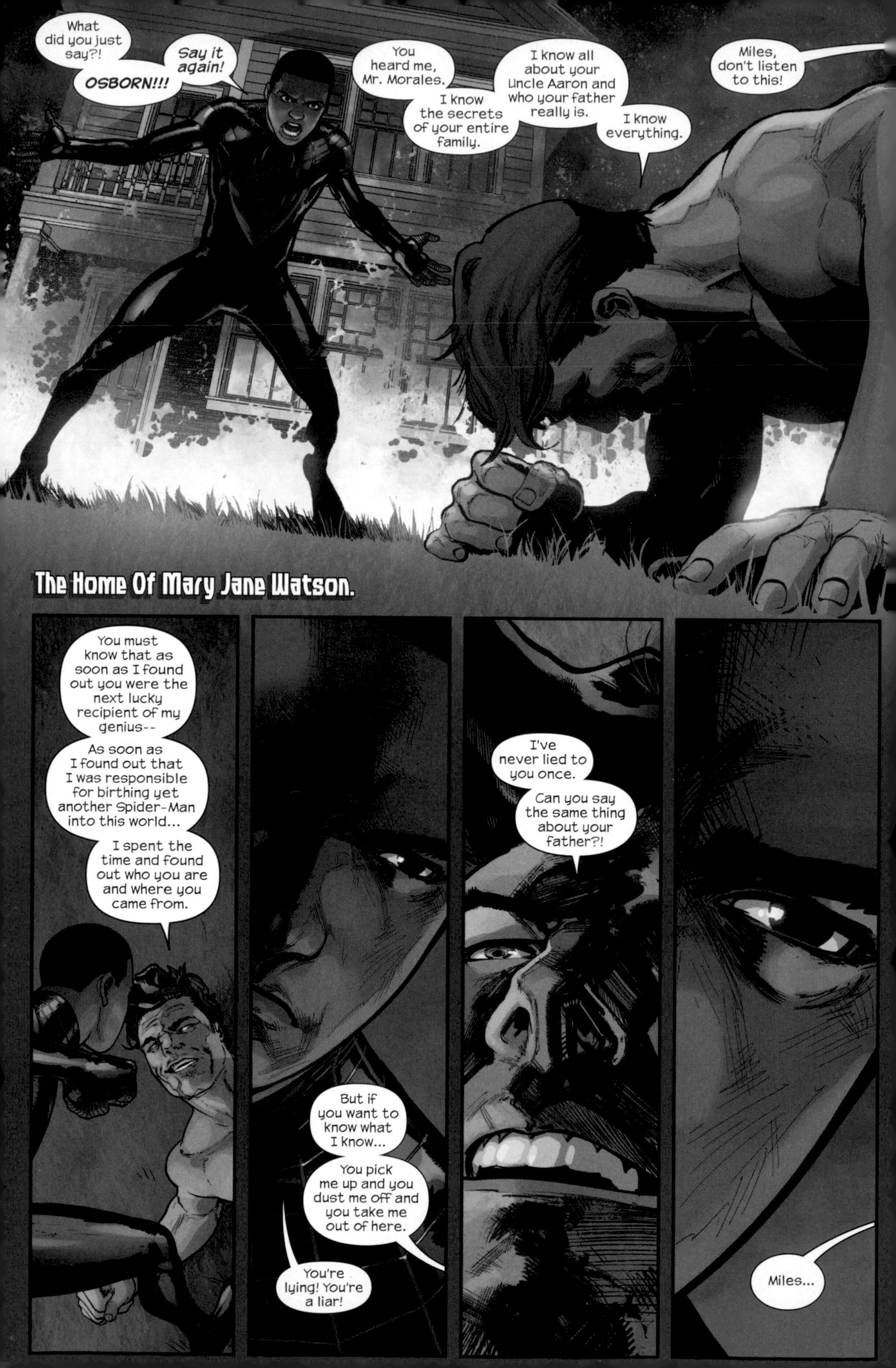
What did you just say?!
OSBORN!!!
Say it again!
You heard me, Mr. Morales.
I know the secrets of your entire family.
I know all about your Uncle Aaron and who your father really is.
I know everything.
Miles, don't listen to this!
The Home Of Mary Jane Watson.
You must know that as soon as I found out you were the next lucky recipient of my genius--
As soon as I found out that I was responsible for birthing yet another Spider-Man into this world...
I spent the time and found out who you are and where you came from.
But if you want to know what I know...
You pick me up and you dust me off and you take me out of here.
You're lying! You're a liar!
I've never lied to you once.
Can you say the same thing about your father?!
Miles...

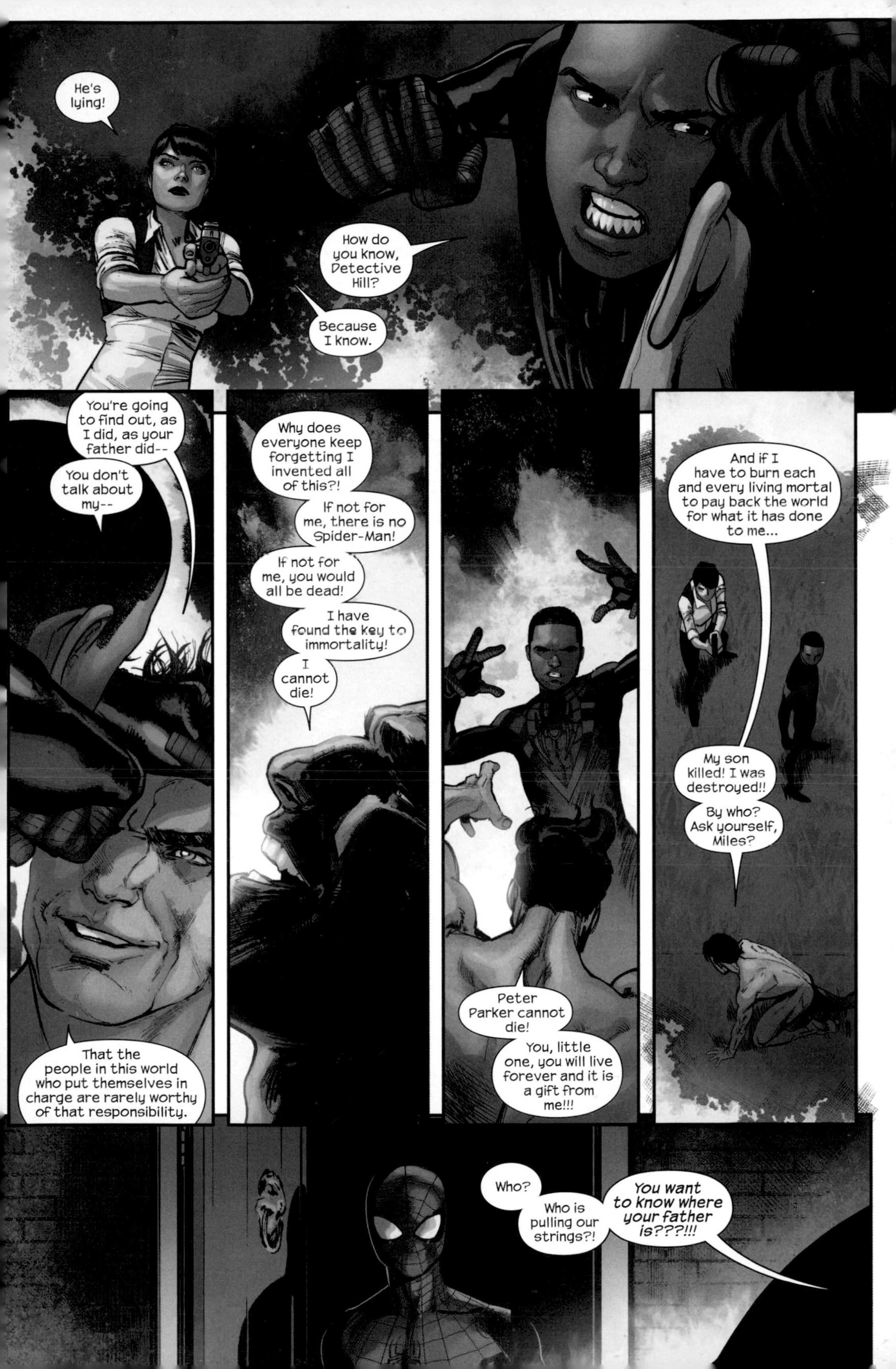
He's lying!
How do you know, Detective Hill?
Because I know.
You're going to find out, as I did, as your father did--
You don't talk about my--
That the people in this world who put themselves in charge are rarely worthy of that responsibility.
Why does everyone keep forgetting I invented all of this?!
If not for me, there is no Spider-Man!
If not for me, you would all be dead!
I have found the key to immortality!
I cannot die!
Peter Parker cannot die!
You, little one, you will live forever and it is a gift from me!!!
And if I have to burn each and every living mortal to pay back the world for what it has done to me...
My son killed! I was destroyed!!
By who? Ask yourself, Miles?
Who?
Who is pulling our strings?!
You want to know where your father is???!!!

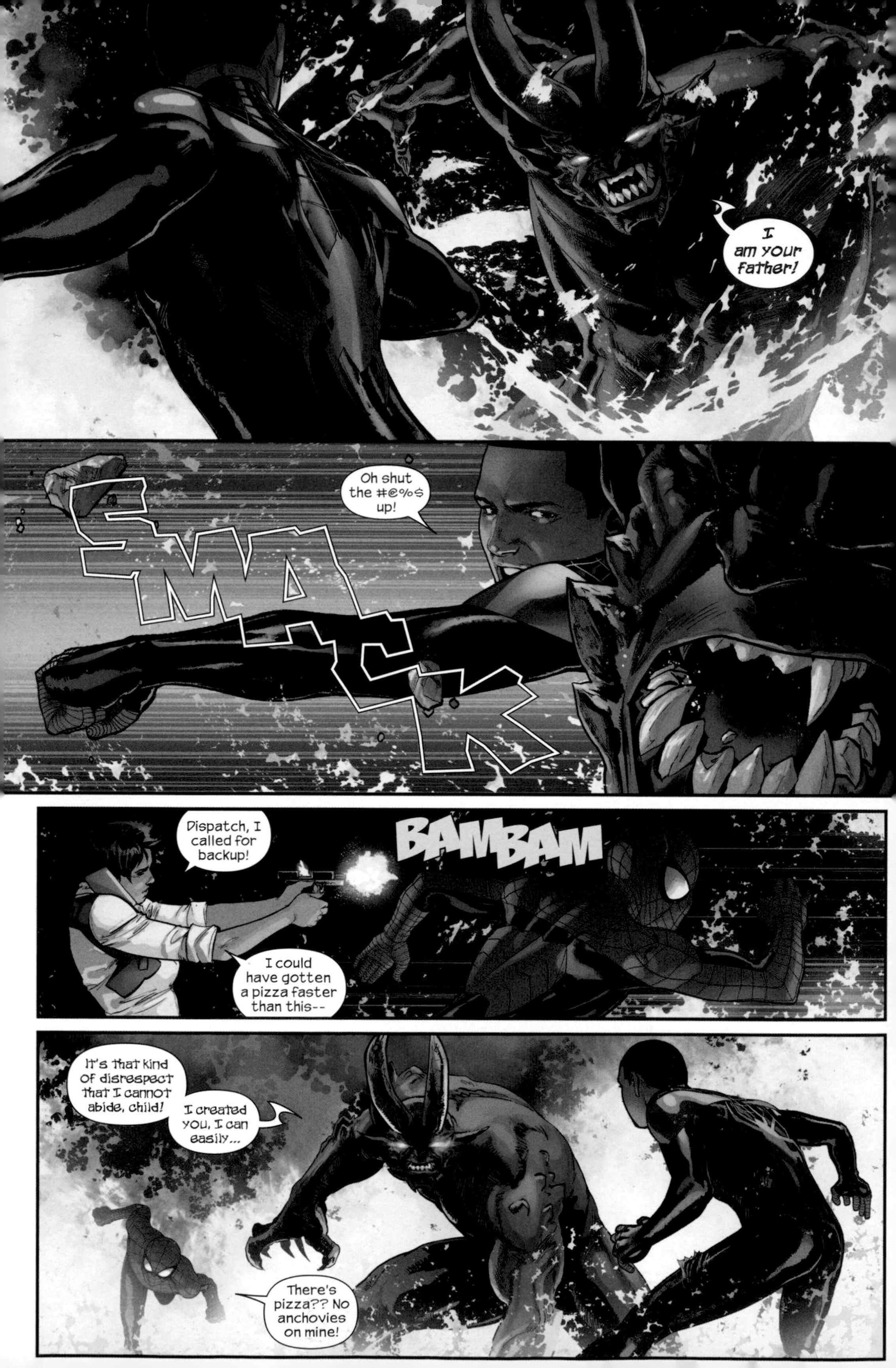
I am your father!
Oh shut the #@%$ up!
SMACK
Dispatch, I called for backup!
BAMBAM
I could have gotten a pizza faster than this--
It's that kind of disrespect that I cannot abide, child!
I created you, I can easily...
There's pizza?? No anchovies on mine!

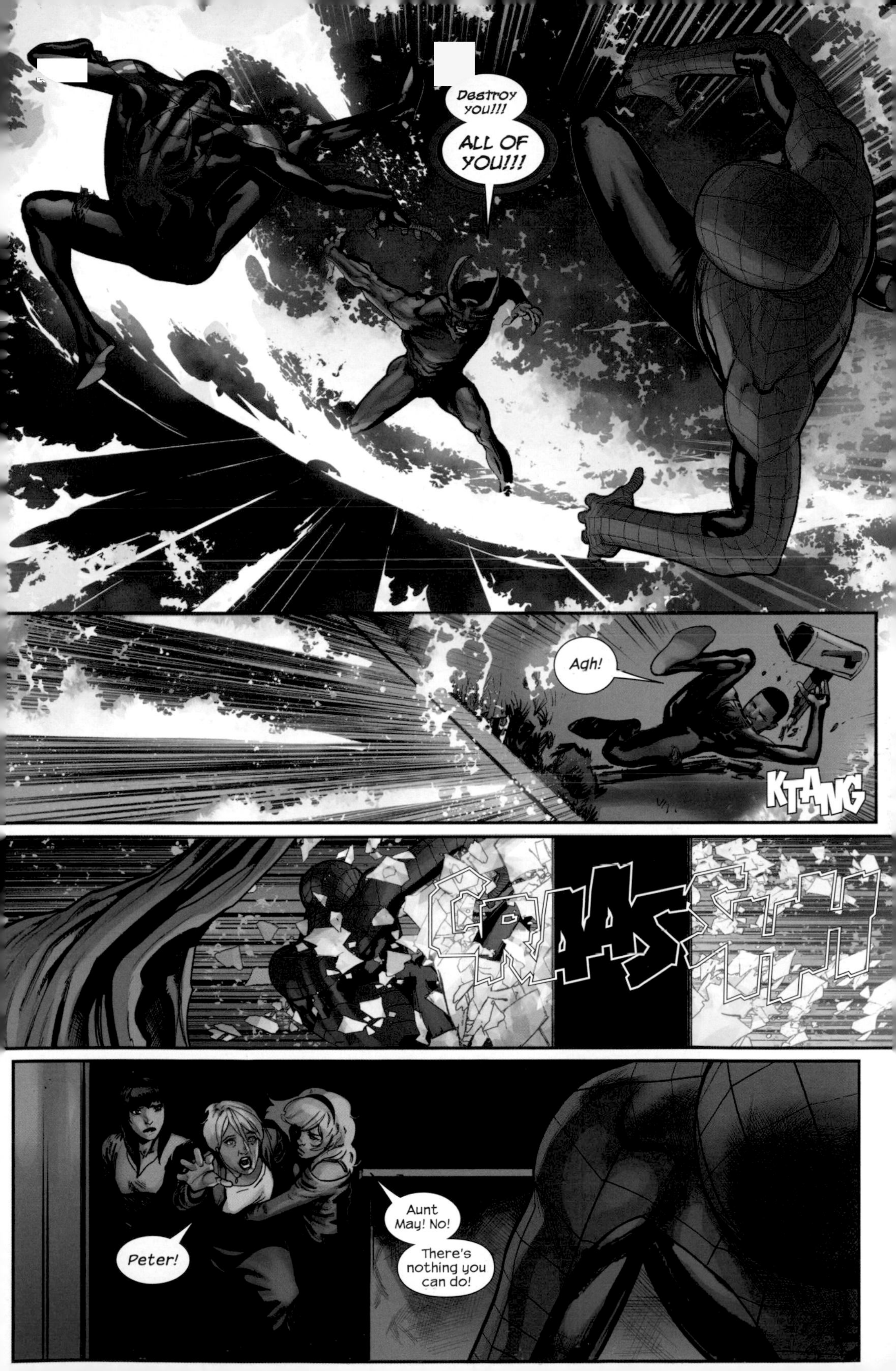

Destroy you!!!
ALL OF YOU!!!
Agh!
KTANG
Peter!
Aunt May! No!
There's nothing you can do!

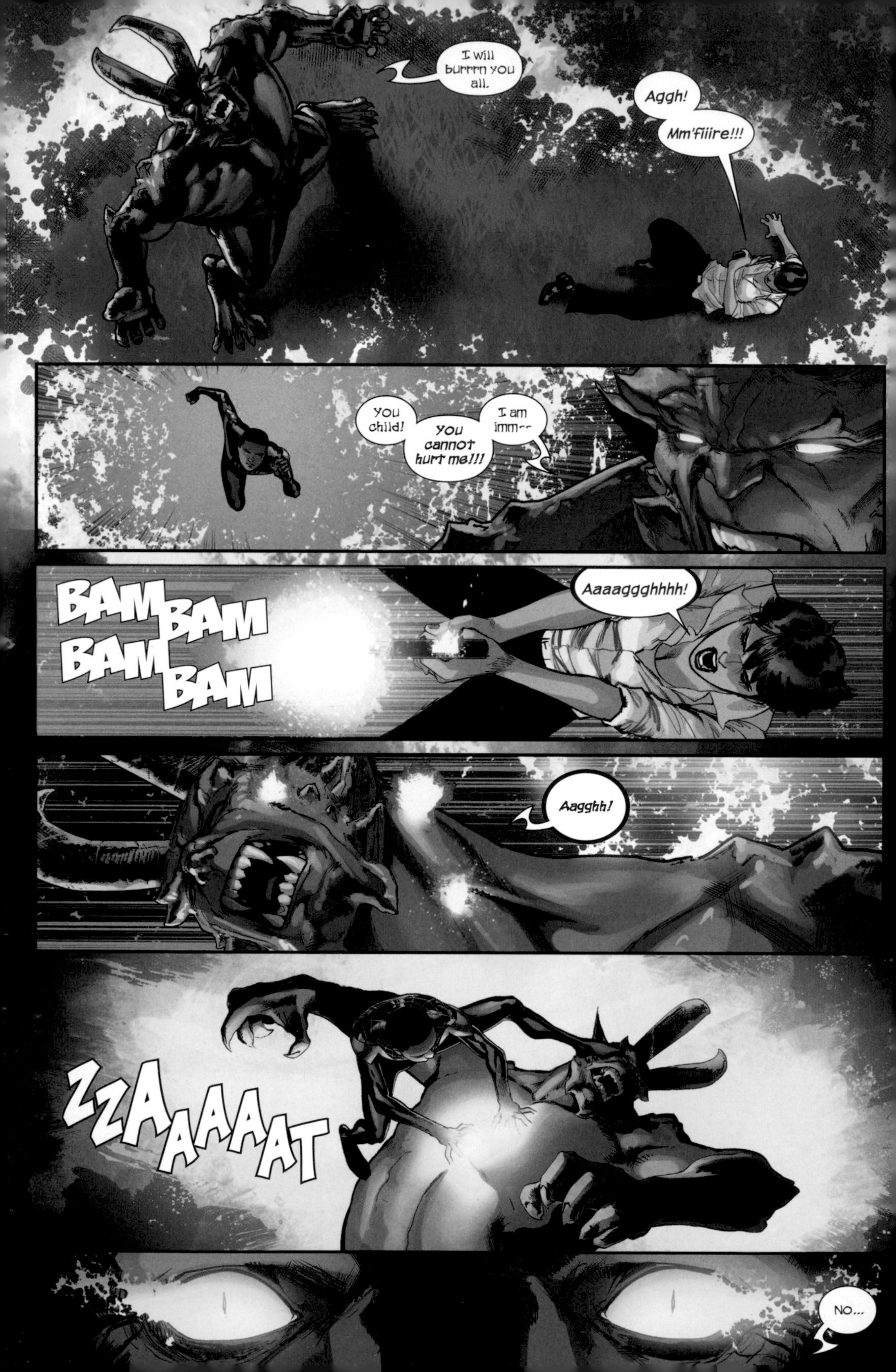

I will burrrn you all.
Aggh!
Mm'fiiire!!!
You child!
You cannot hurt me!!!
I am imm--
BAM BAM BAM BAM
Aaaagggghhhh!
Aagghh!
ZZAAAAAAT
NO...

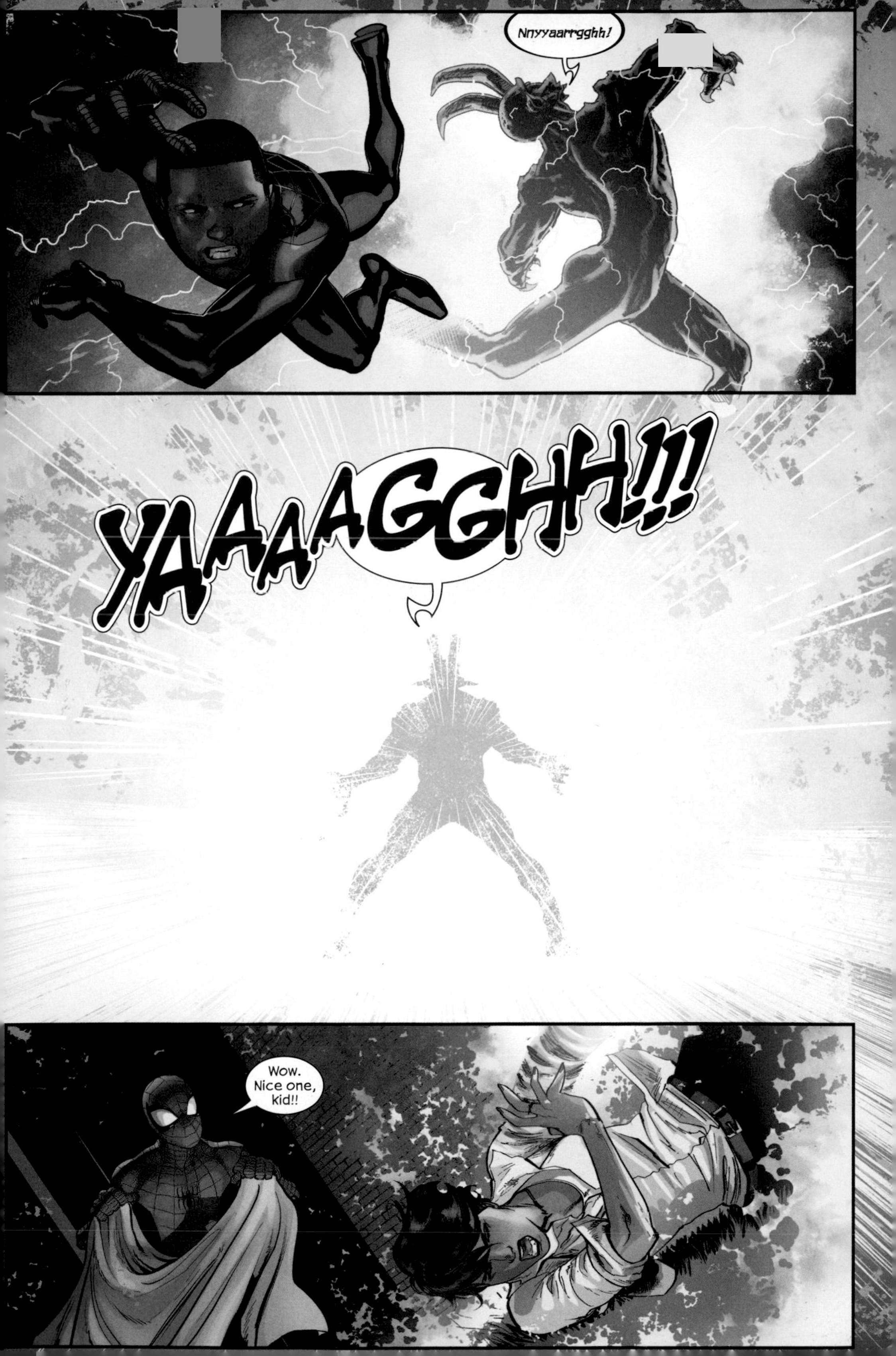
Nnyyaarrgghh!
YAAAAGGHH!!!
Wow. Nice one, kid!!

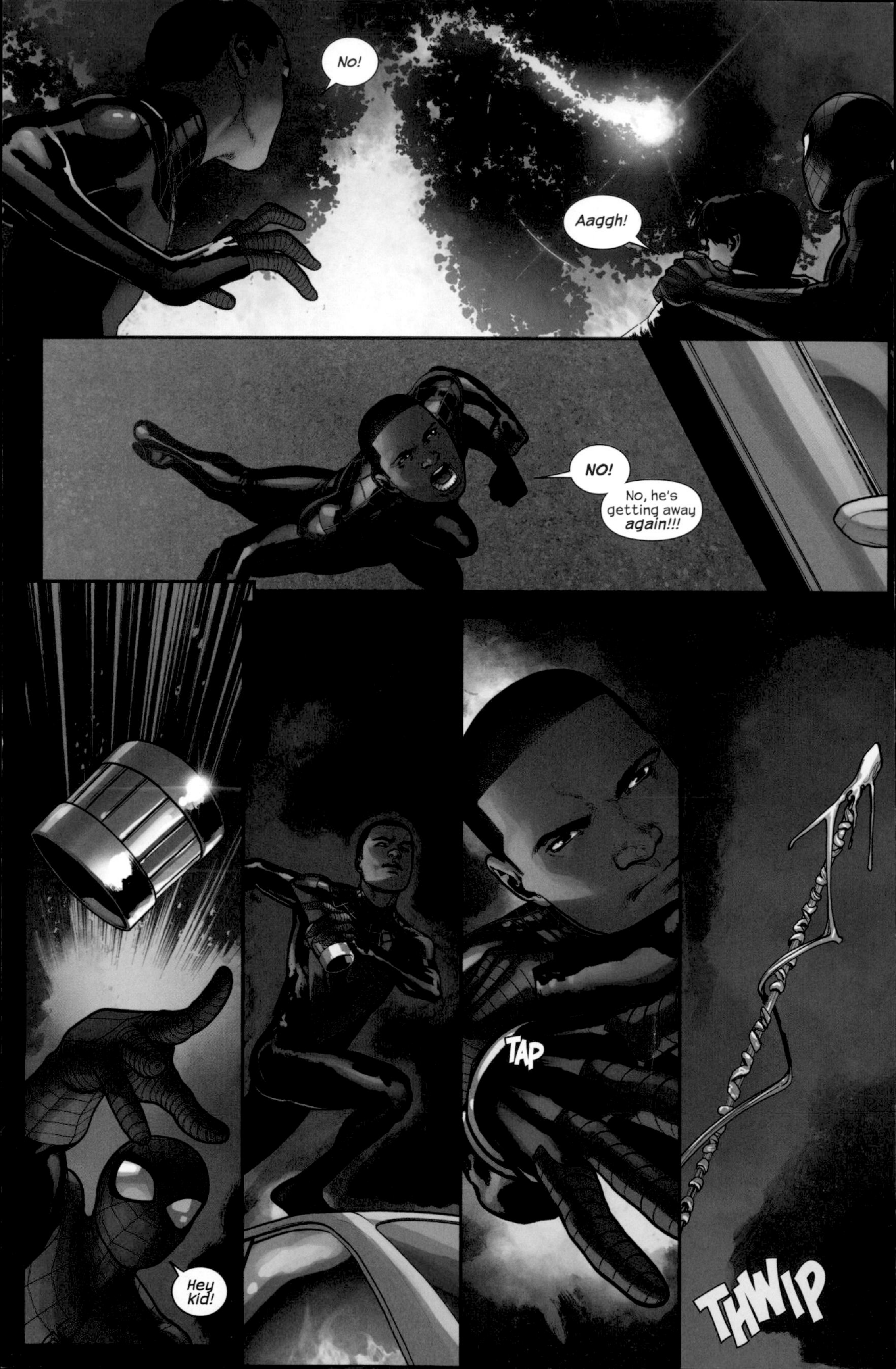
No!
Aaggh!
NO!
No, he's getting away again!!!
Hey kid!
TAP
THWIP

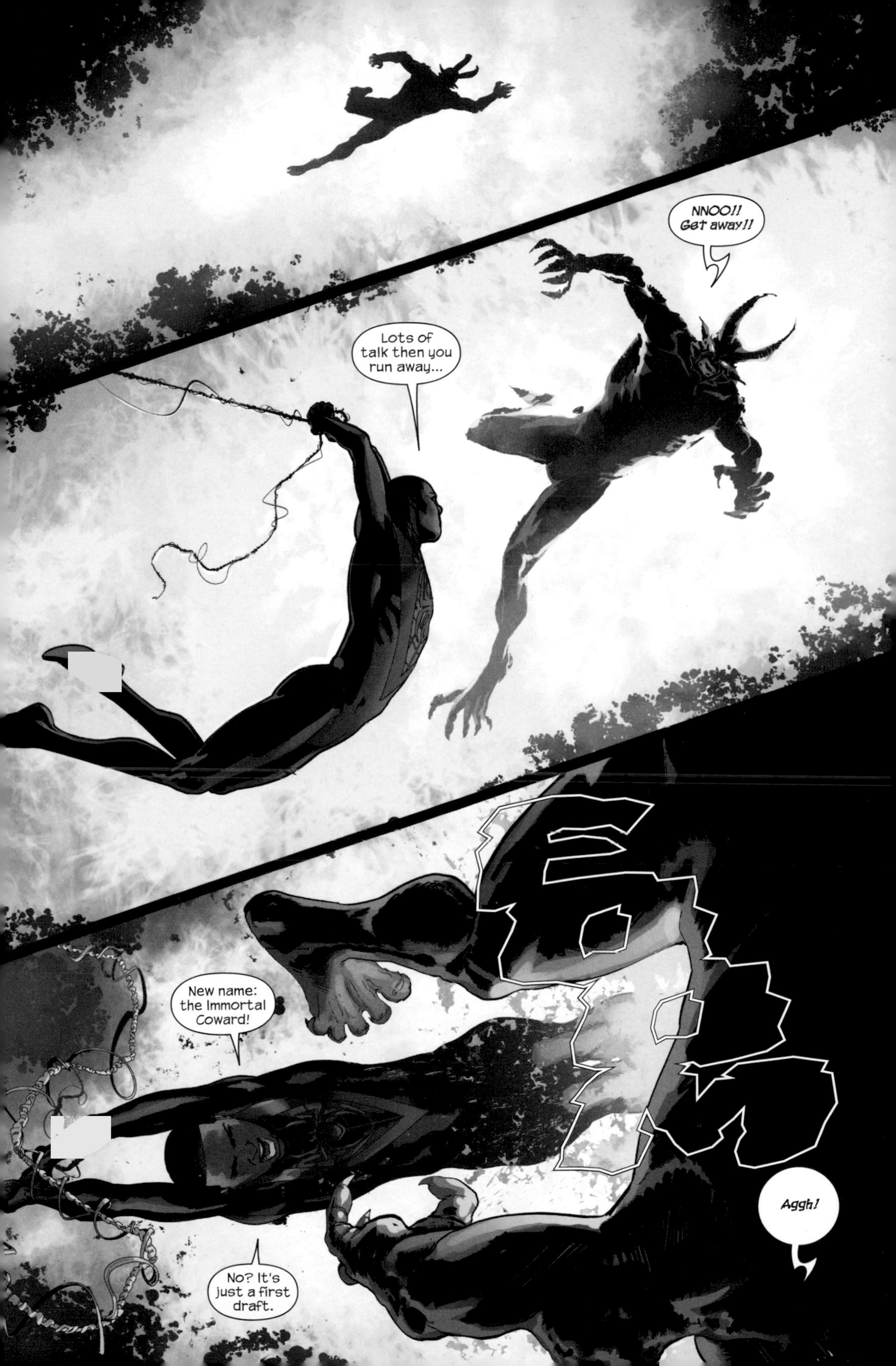
NNOO!! Get away!!
Lots of talk then you run away...
New name: the Immortal Coward!
No? It's just a first draft.
Agghh!

Hey!! Tell me about my father some more!

SMMACK

ZZZZXXAATTTT

Gaaggh!!!

Aaarrgghh!!!

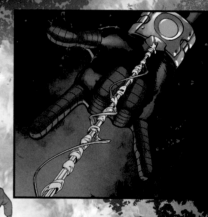

Tell me!

Nyyaagghh!!!

ZZAAATTTXX

Look at him.

I know, right.

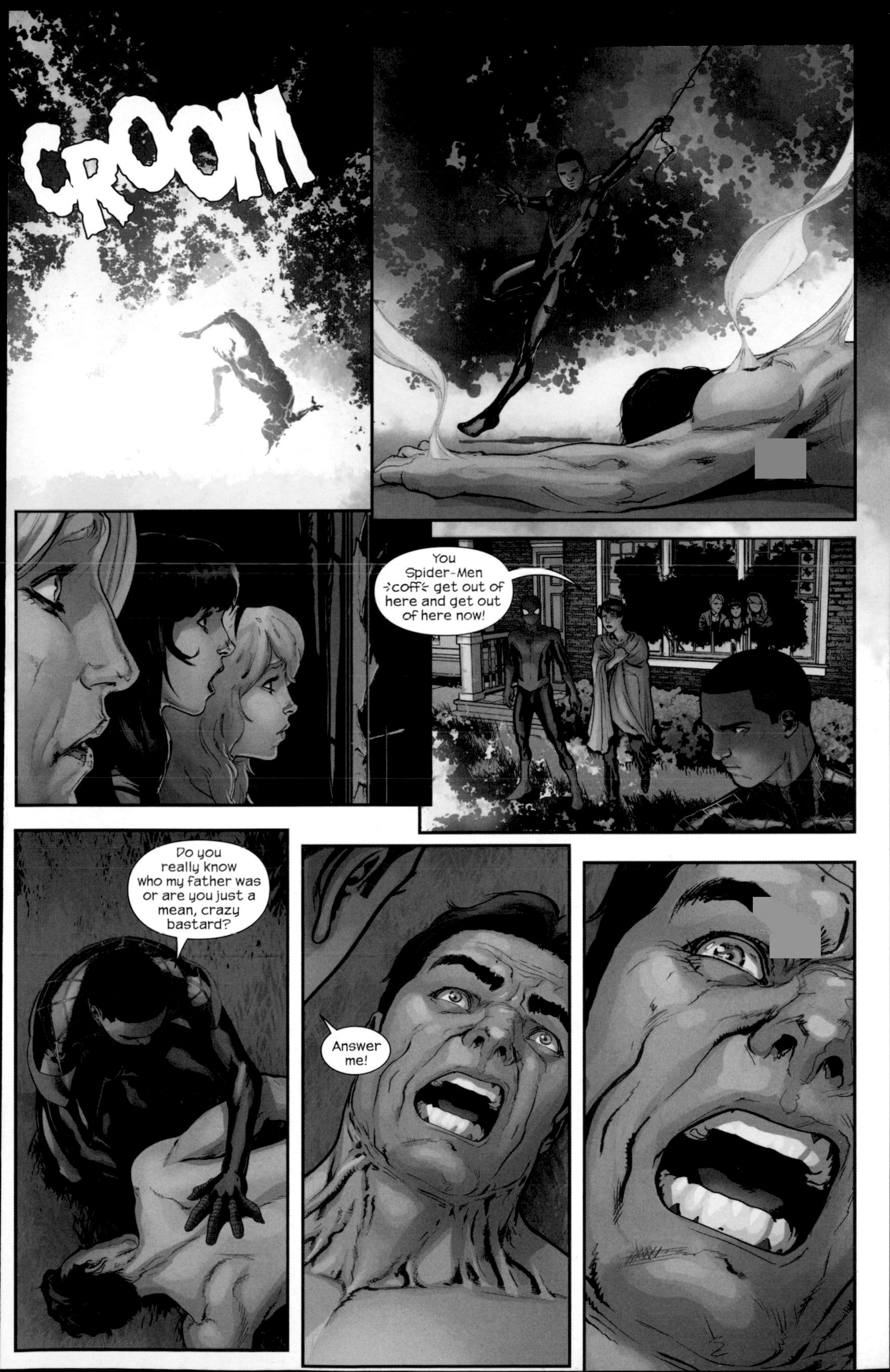
CROOM
You Spider-Men -coff- get out of here and get out of here now!
Do you really know who my father was or are you just a mean, crazy bastard?
Answer me!

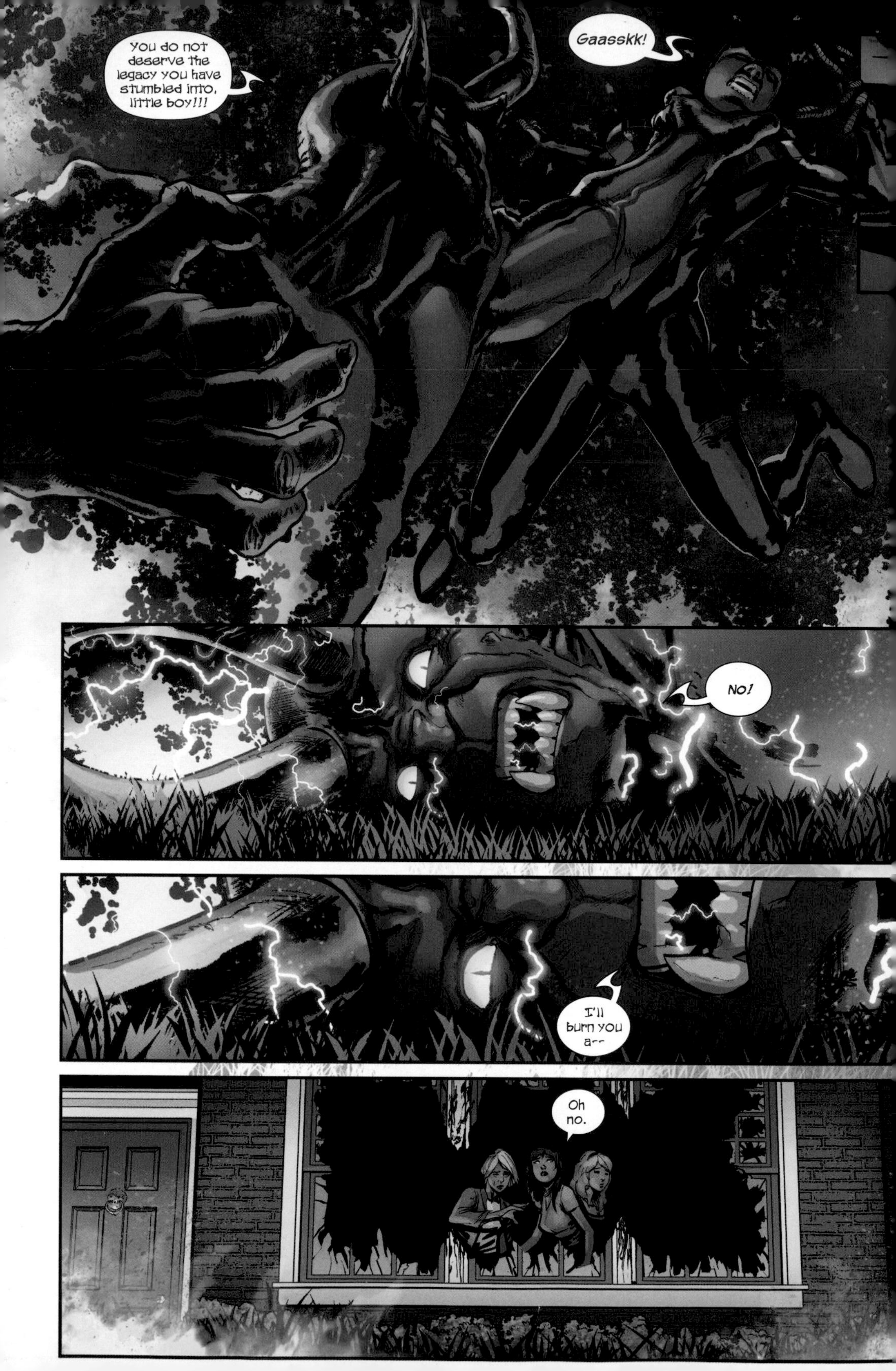

You do not deserve the legacy you have stumbled into, little boy!!!
Gaasskk!
NO!
I'll burn you a--
Oh no.

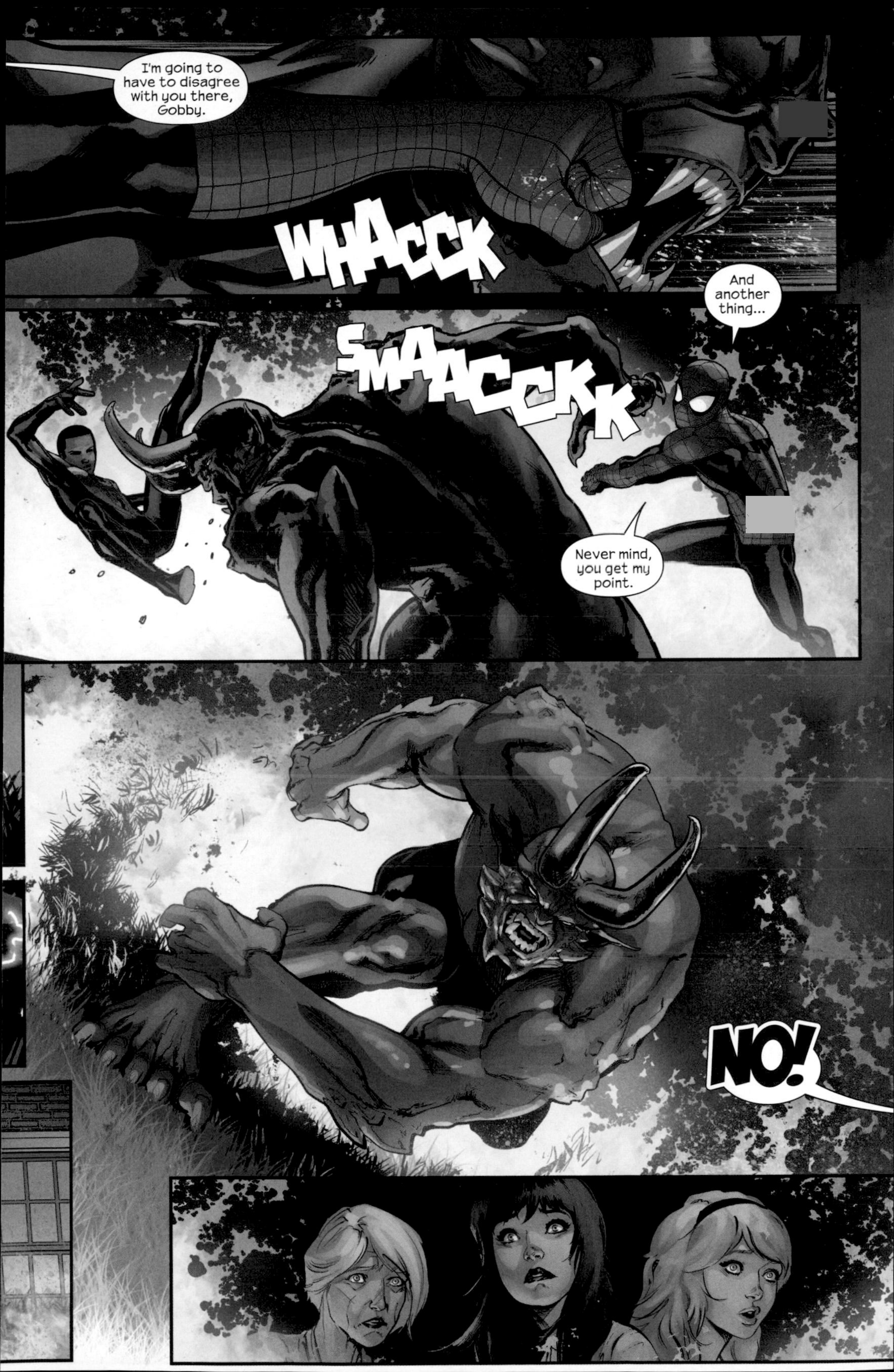
I'm going to have to disagree with you there, Gobby.
WHACCK
And another thing...
SMAACCKK
Never mind, you get my point.
NO!

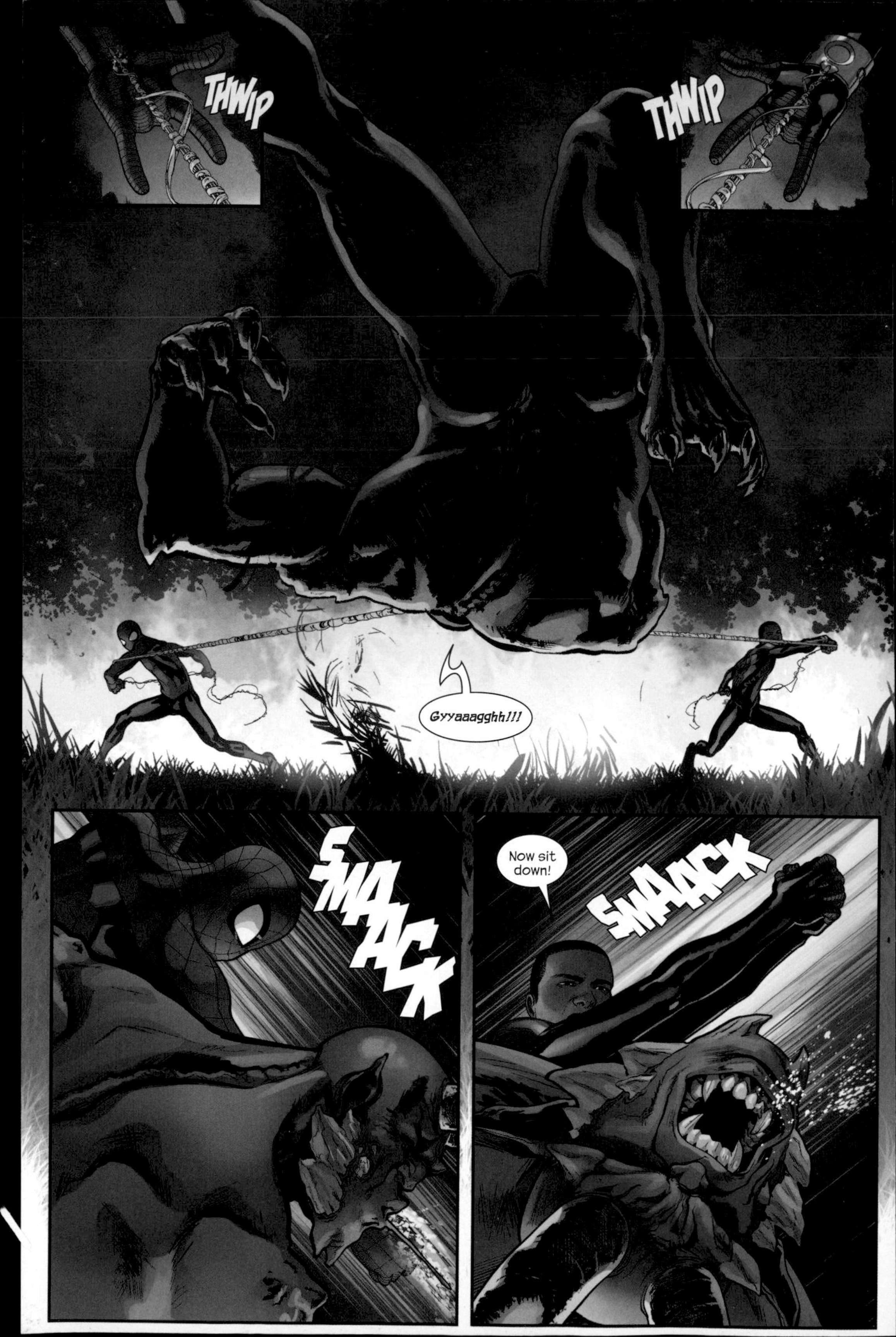
THWIP
THWIP
Gyyaaagghh!!!
SMAACK
Now sit down!
SMAACK

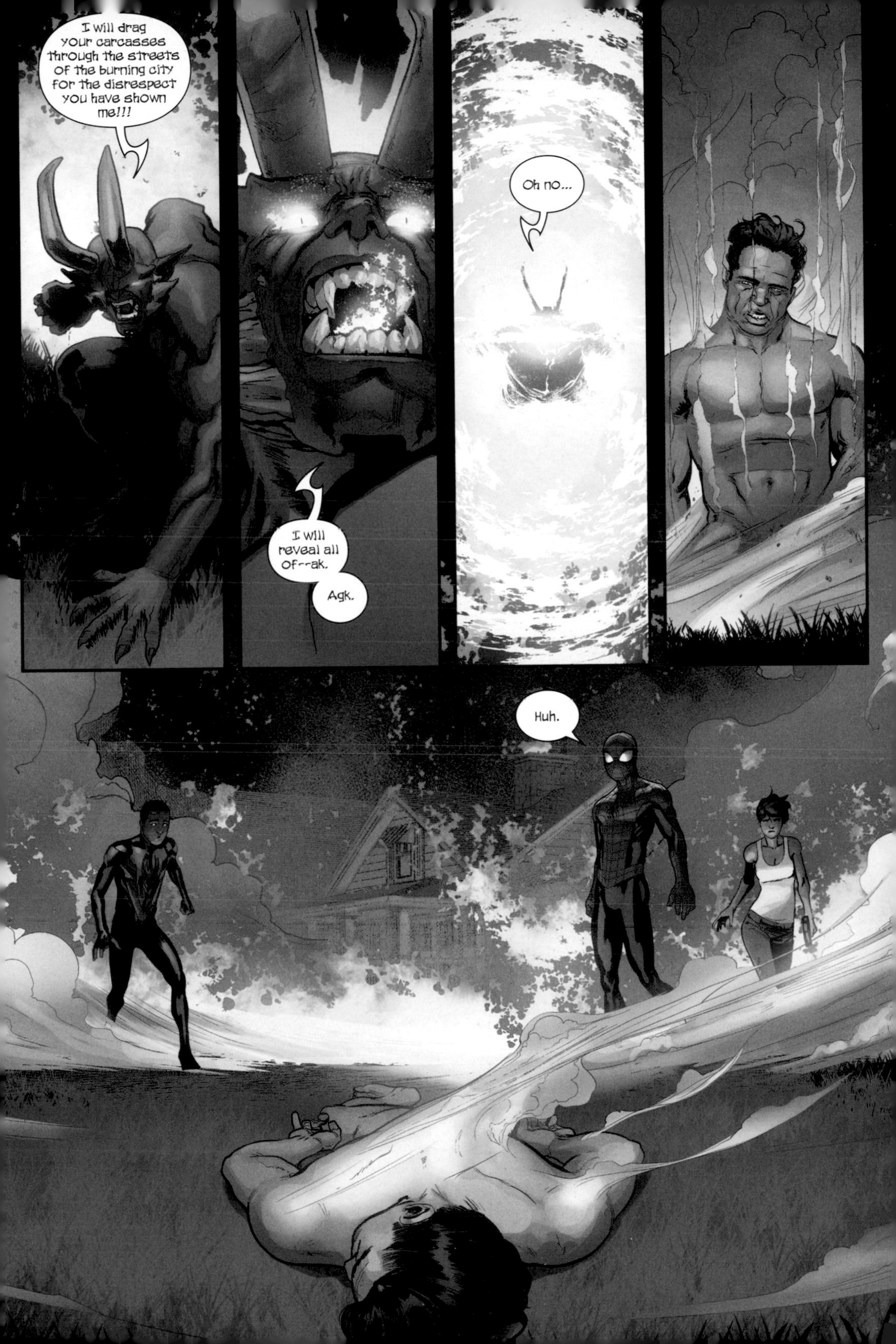
I will drag your carcasses through the streets of the burning city for the disrespect you have shown me!!!
I will reveal all of--ak.
Agk.
Oh no...
Huh.

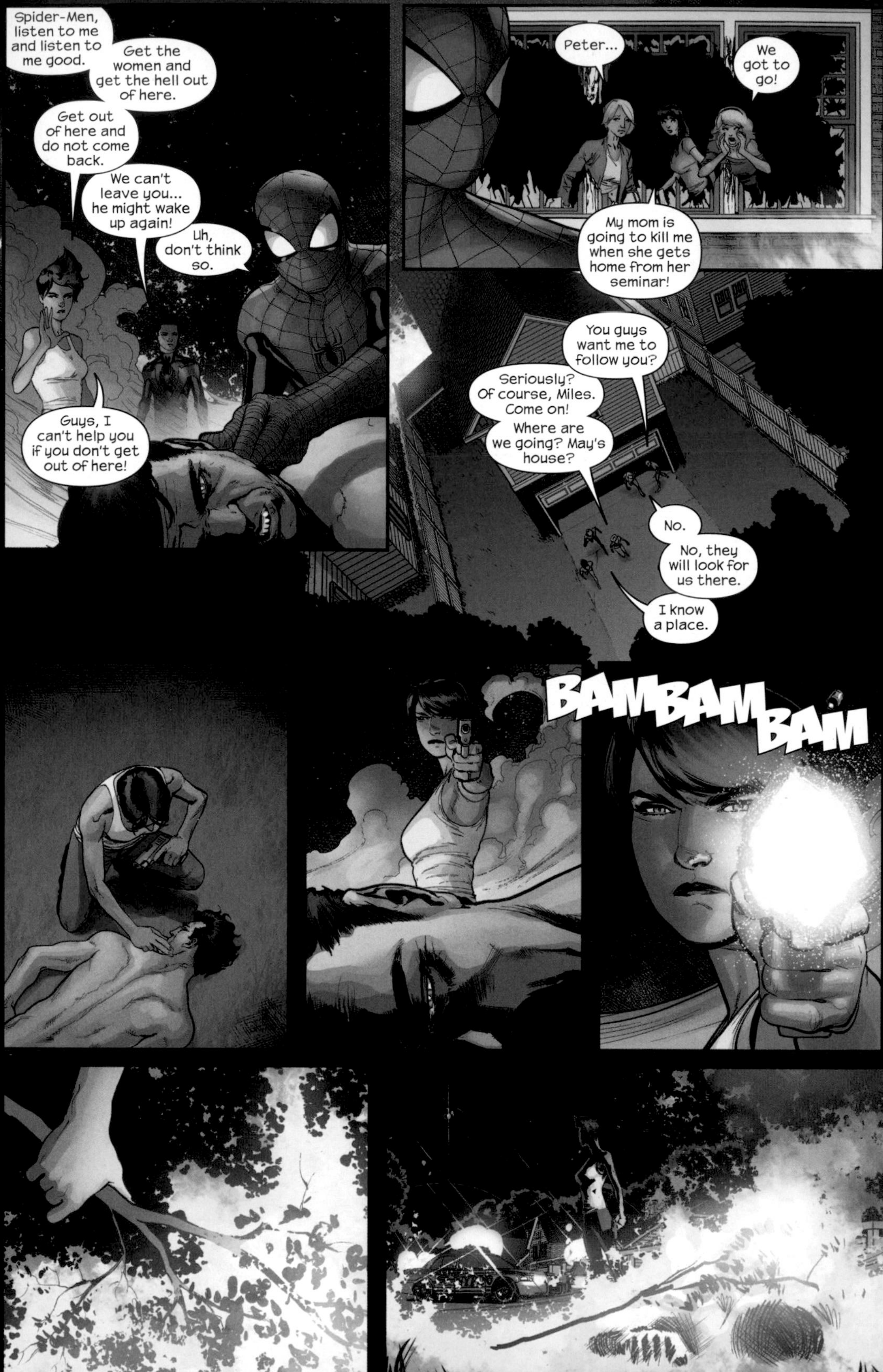
Spider-Men, listen to me and listen to me good.
Get the women and get the hell out of here.
Get out of here and do not come back.
We can't leave you... he might wake up again!
Uh, don't think so.
Guys, I can't help you if you don't get out of here!
Peter...
We got to go!
My mom is going to kill me when she gets home from her seminar!
You guys want me to follow you?
Seriously? Of course, Miles. Come on!
Where are we going? May's house?
No.
No, they will look for us there.
I know a place.
BAMBAMBAM

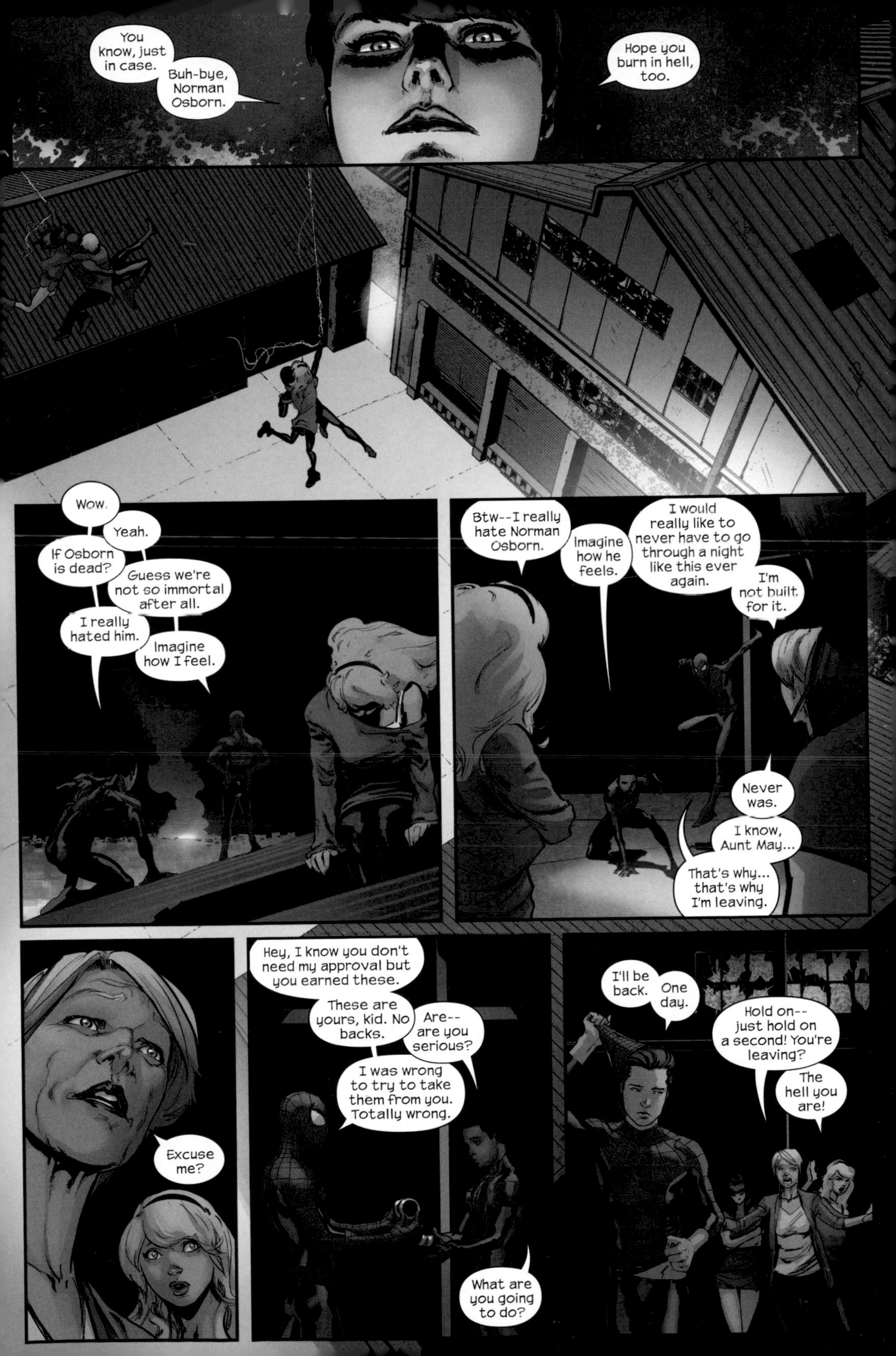

You know, just in case.
Buh-bye, Norman Osborn.
Hope you burn in hell, too.
Wow.
Yeah.
If Osborn is dead?
Guess we're not so immortal after all.
I really hated him.
Imagine how I feel.
Btw--I really hate Norman Osborn.
Imagine how he feels.
I would really like to never have to go through a night like this ever again.
I'm not built for it.
Never was.
I know, Aunt May...
That's why... that's why I'm leaving.
Excuse me?
Hey, I know you don't need my approval but you earned these.
These are yours, kid. No backs.
Are-- are you serious?
I was wrong to try to take them from you. Totally wrong.
What are you going to do?
I'll be back.
One day.
Hold on-- just hold on a second! You're leaving?
The hell you are!

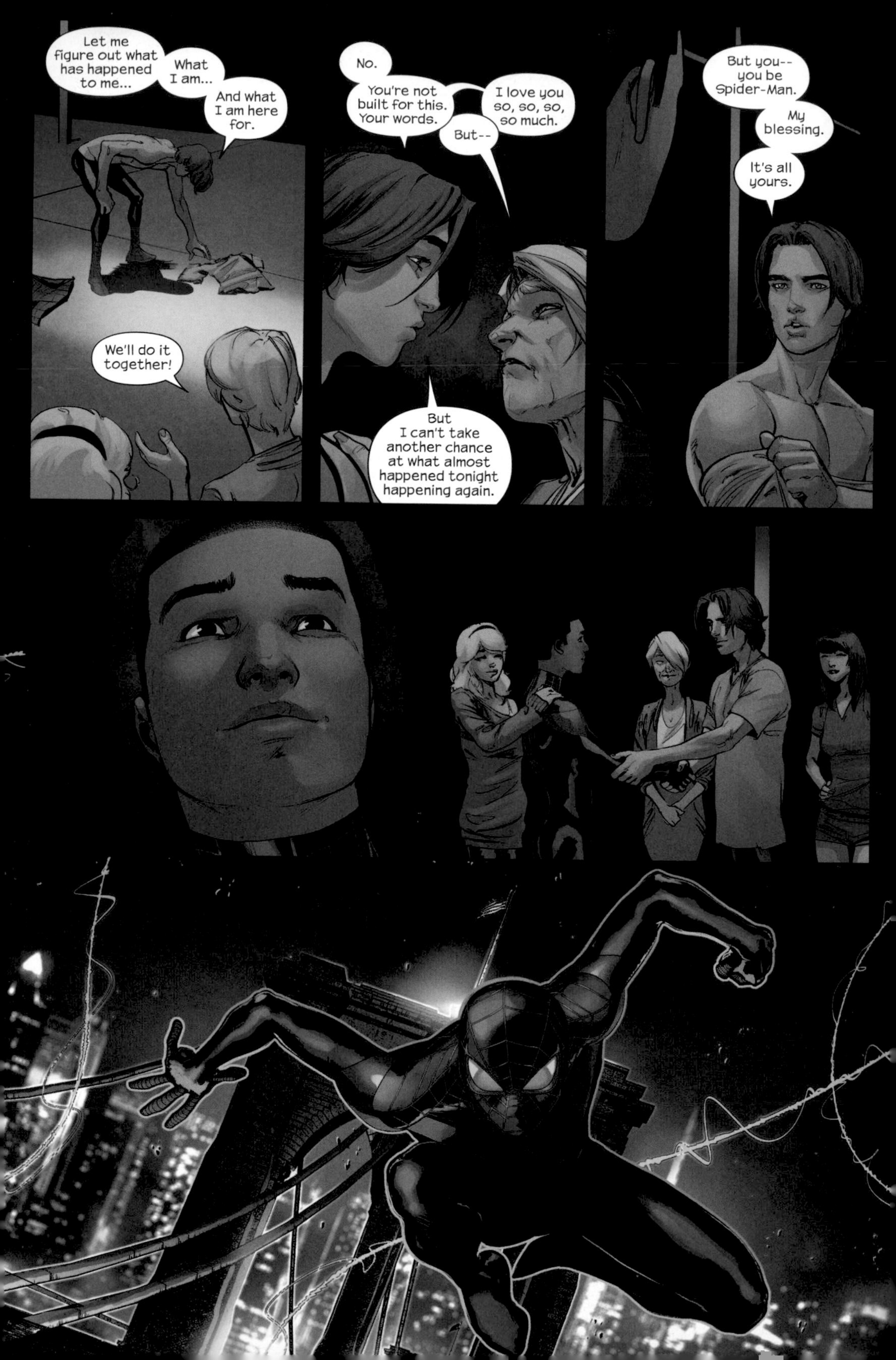
Let me figure out what has happened to me...
What I am...
And what I am here for.
We'll do it together!
No.
You're not built for this. Your words.
I love you so, so, so, so much.
But--
But I can't take another chance at what almost happened tonight happening again.
But you-- you be Spider-Man.
My blessing.
It's all yours.

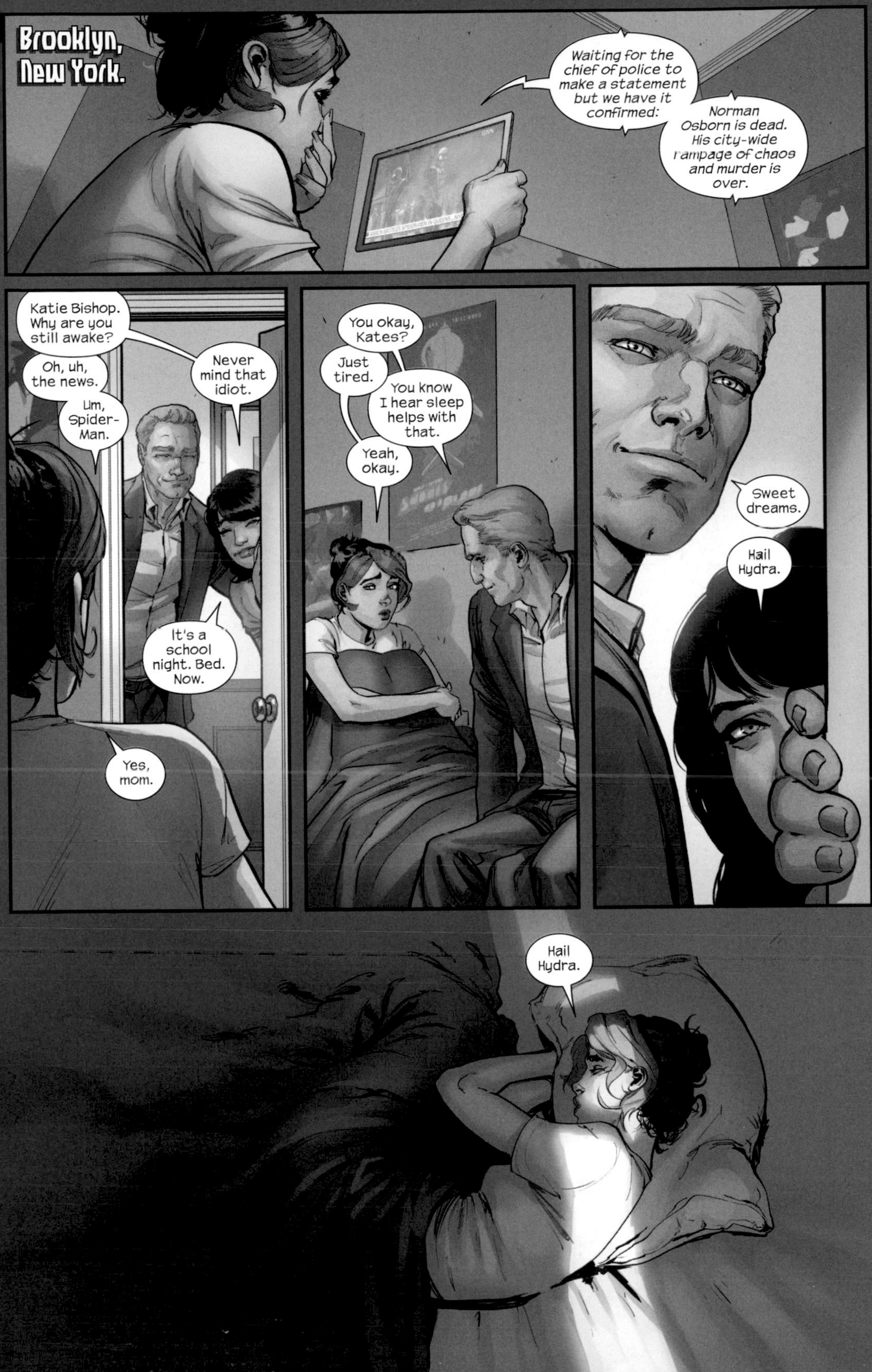
Brooklyn, New York.
Waiting for the chief of police to make a statement but we have it confirmed:
Norman Osborn is dead. His city-wide rampage of chaos and murder is over.
Katie Bishop. Why are you still awake?
Oh, uh, the news.
Um, Spider-Man.
Never mind that idiot.
It's a school night. Bed. Now.
Yes, mom.
You okay, Kates?
Just tired.
You know I hear sleep helps with that.
Yeah, okay.
Sweet dreams.
Hail Hydra.
Hail Hydra.

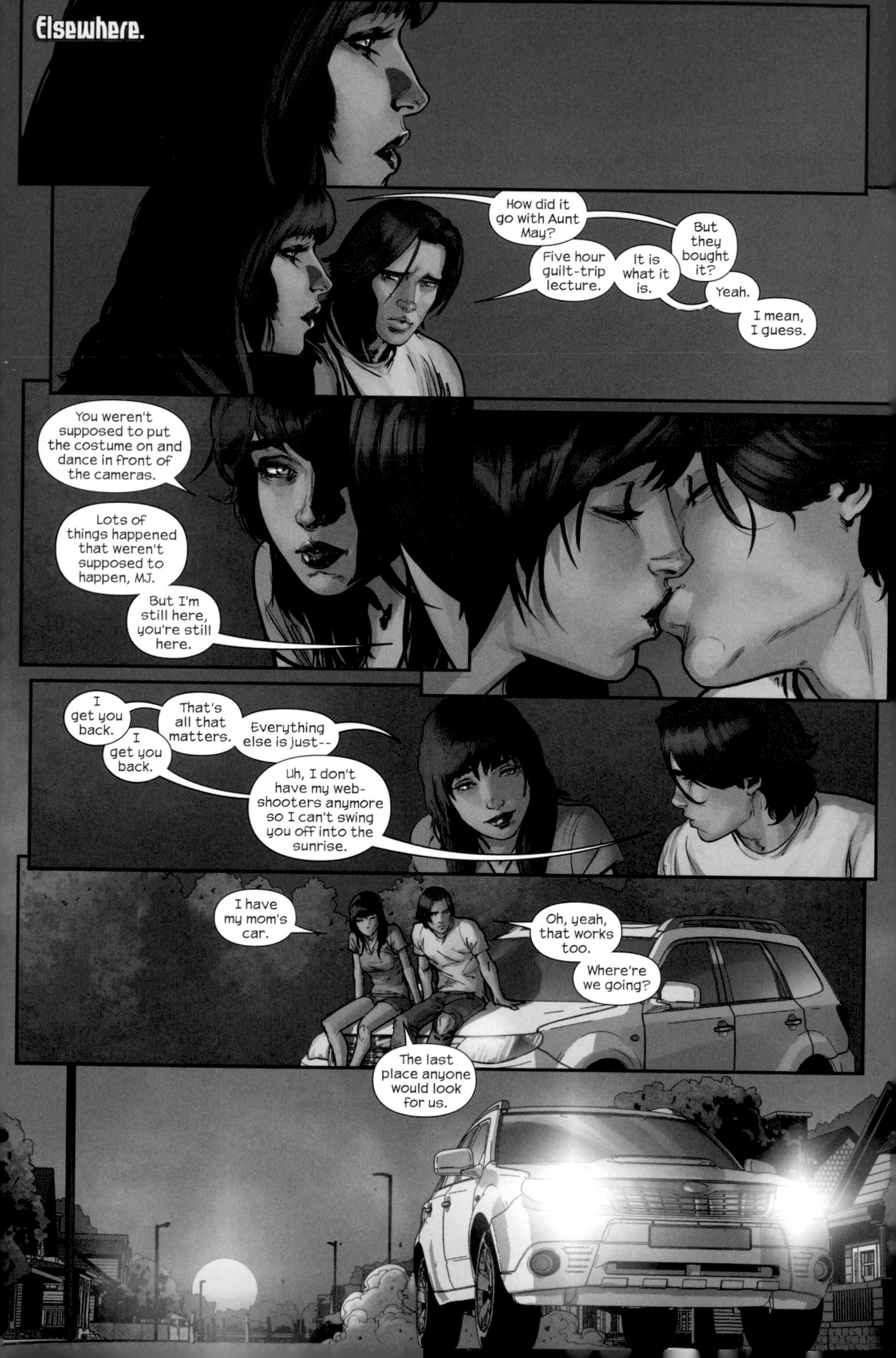
Elsewhere.
How did it go with Aunt May?
Five hour guilt-trip lecture.
It is what it is.
But they bought it?
Yeah.
I mean, I guess.
You weren't supposed to put the costume on and dance in front of the cameras.
Lots of things happened that weren't supposed to happen, MJ.
But I'm still here, you're still here.
I get you back.
I get you back.
That's all that matters.
Everything else is just--
Uh, I don't have my web-shooters anymore so I can't swing you off into the sunrise.
I have my mom's car.
Oh, yeah, that works too.
Where're we going?
The last place anyone would look for us.

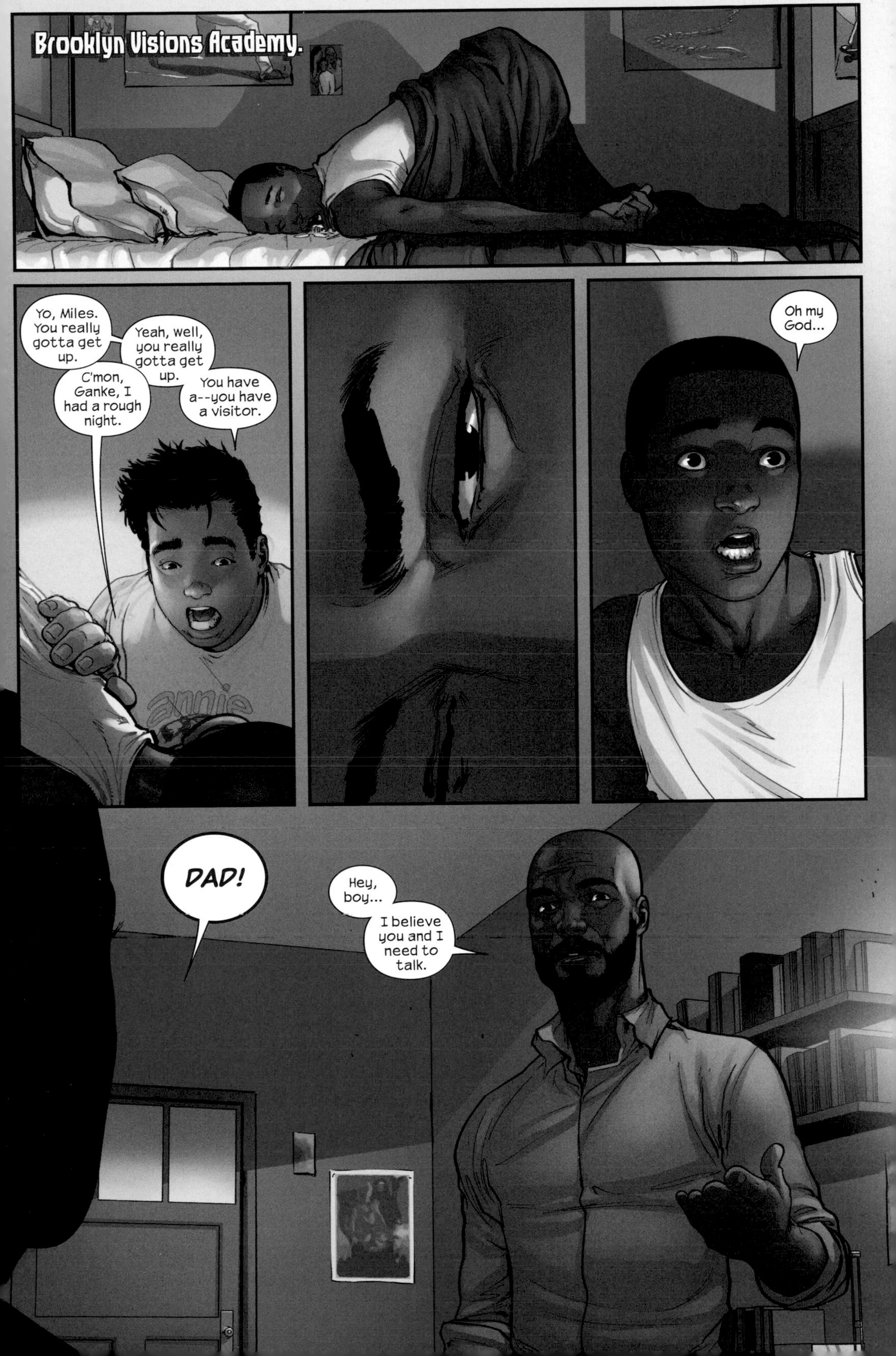
Brooklyn Visions Academy.
Yo, Miles. You really gotta get up.
C'mon, Ganke, I had a rough night.
Yeah, well, you really gotta get up.
You have a--you have a visitor.
Oh my God...
DAD!
Hey, boy...
I believe you and I need to talk.

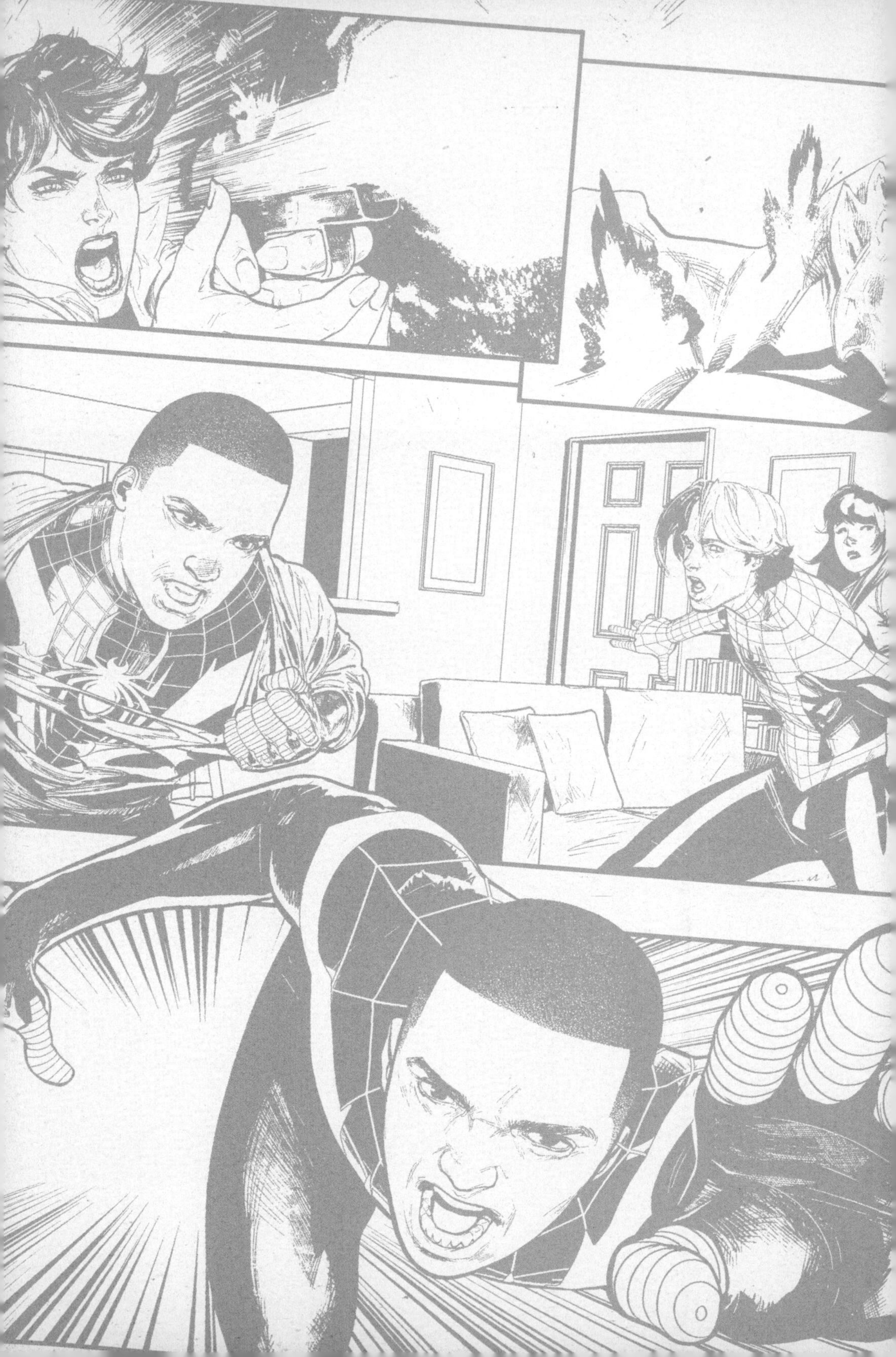

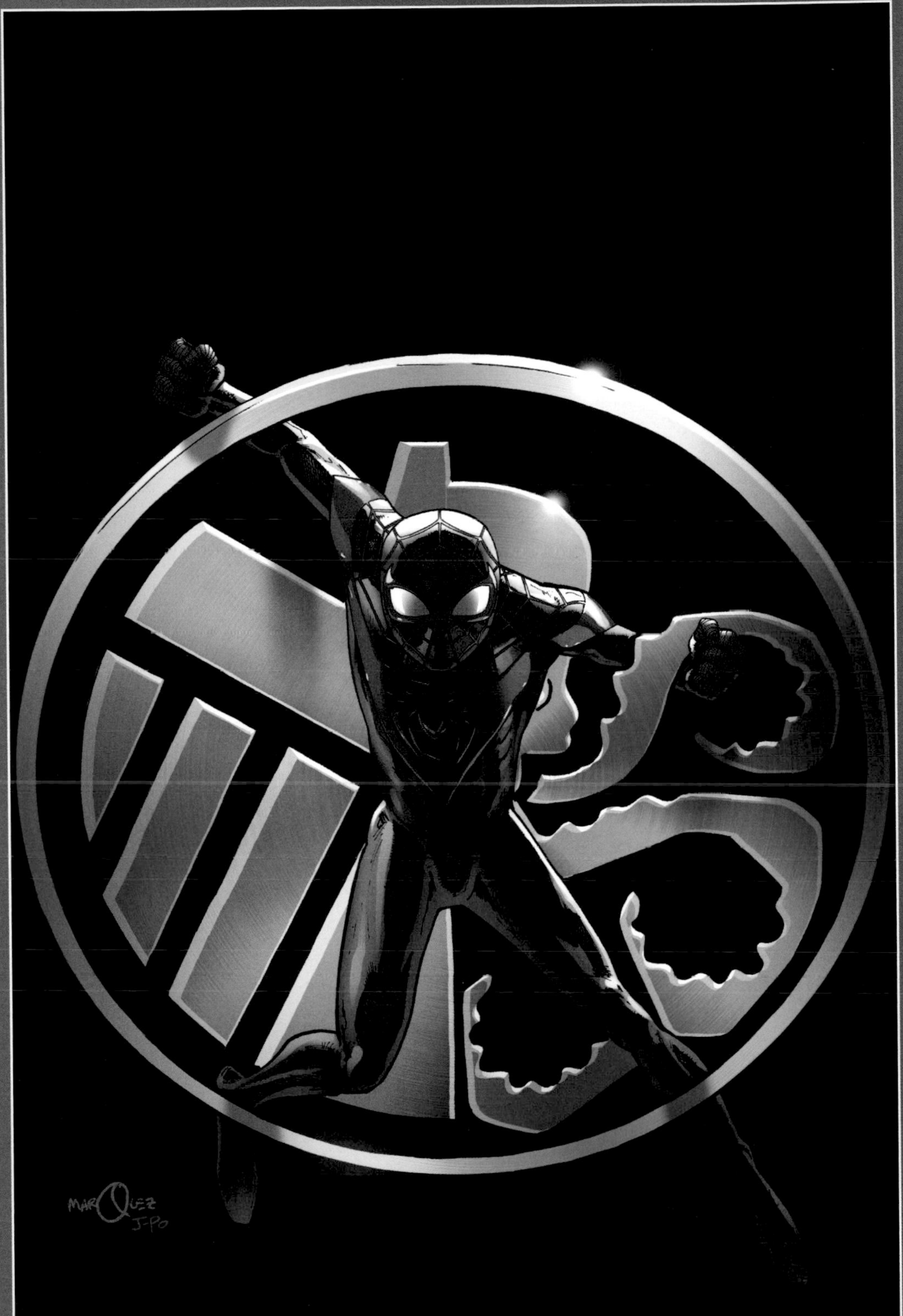

8

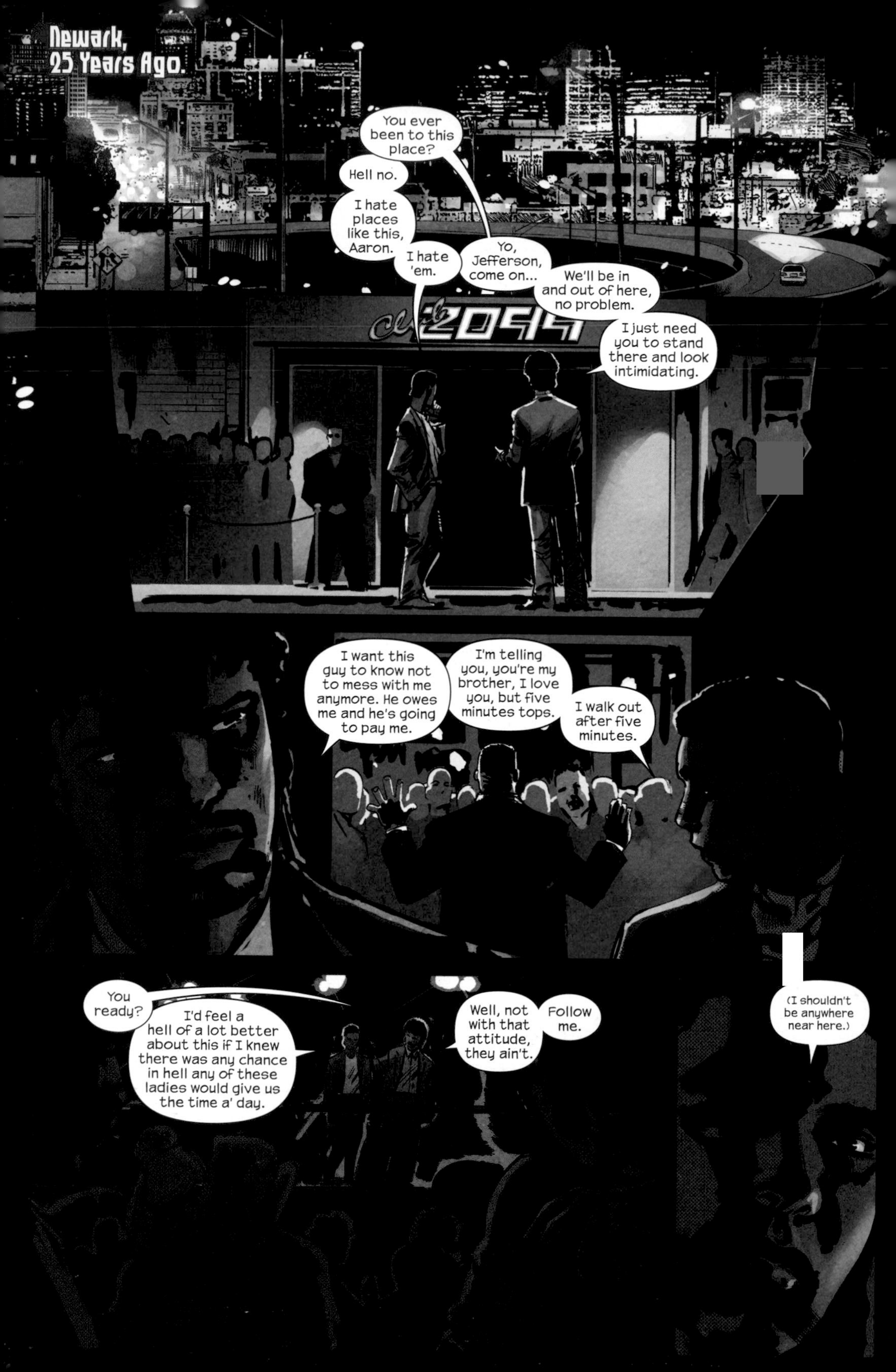
Newark, 25 Years Ago.
You ever been to this place?
Hell no.
I hate places like this, Aaron.
I hate 'em.
Yo, Jefferson, come on...
We'll be in and out of here, no problem.
I just need you to stand there and look intimidating.
I want this guy to know not to mess with me anymore. He owes me and he's going to pay me.
I'm telling you, you're my brother, I love you, but five minutes tops.
I walk out after five minutes.
You ready?
I'd feel a hell of a lot better about this if I knew there was any chance in hell any of these ladies would give us the time a' day.
Well, not with that attitude, they ain't.
Follow me.
(I shouldn't be anywhere near here.)

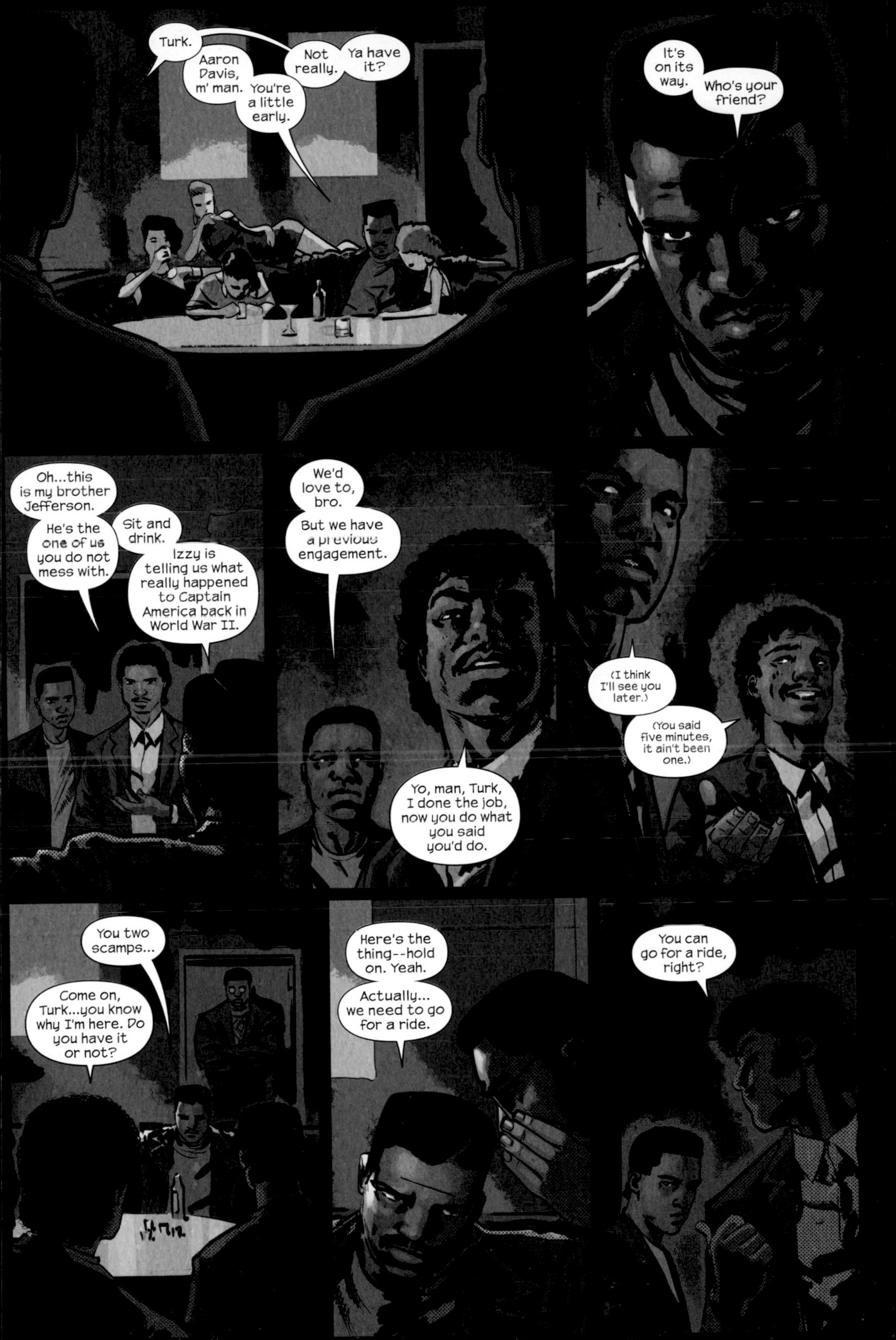
Turk.
Aaron Davis, m' man.
You're a little early.
Not really.
Ya have it?
It's on its way.
Who's your friend?
Oh...this is my brother Jefferson.
He's the one of us you do not mess with.
Sit and drink.
Izzy is telling us what really happened to Captain America back in World War II.
We'd love to, bro.
But we have a previous engagement.
Yo, man, Turk, I done the job, now you do what you said you'd do.
(I think I'll see you later.)
(You said five minutes, it ain't been one.)
You two scamps...
Come on, Turk...you know why I'm here. Do you have it or not?
Here's the thing--hold on. Yeah.
Actually... we need to go for a ride.
You can go for a ride, right?

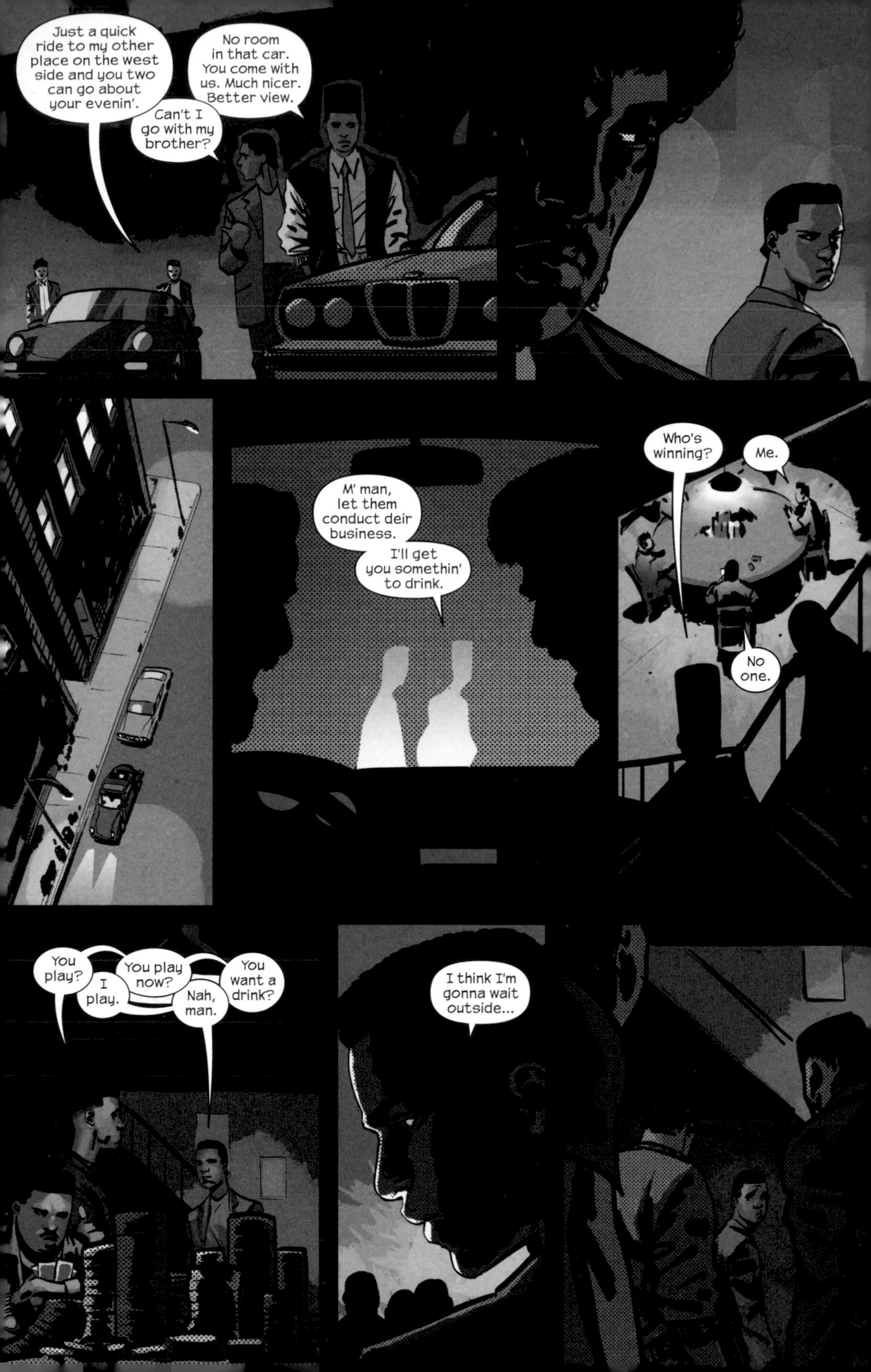
Just a quick ride to my other place on the west side and you two can go about your evenin'.
No room in that car. You come with us. Much nicer. Better view.
Can't I go with my brother?
M' man, let them conduct deir business.
I'll get you somethin' to drink.
Who's winning?
Me.
No one.
You play?
I play.
You play now?
Nah, man.
You want a drink?
I think I'm gonna wait outside...

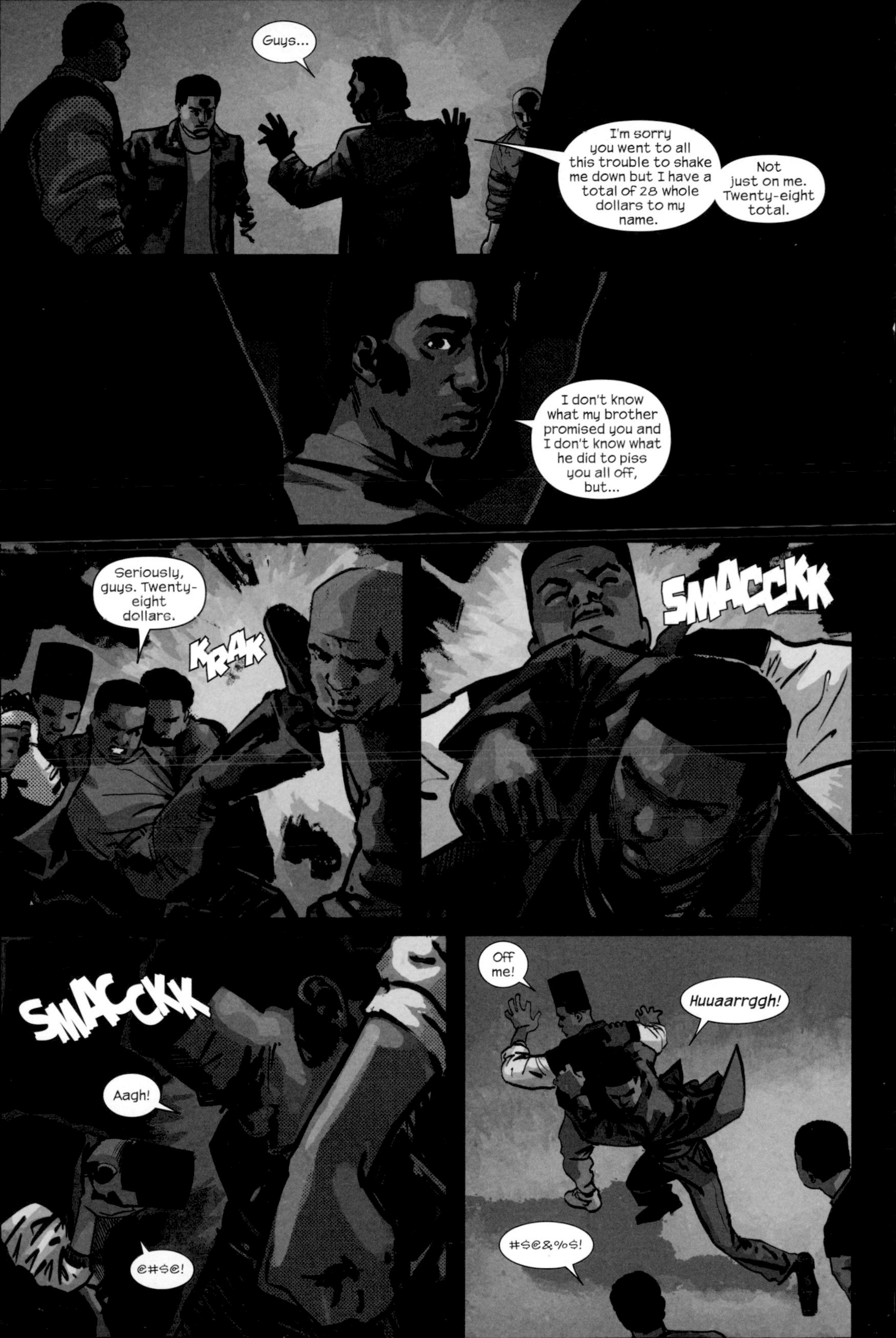
Guys...
I'm sorry you went to all this trouble to shake me down but I have a total of 28 whole dollars to my name.
Not just on me. Twenty-eight total.
I don't know what my brother promised you and I don't know what he did to piss you all off, but...
Seriously, guys. Twenty-eight dollars.
KRAK
SMACCKK
SMACCKK
Aagh!
@#$@!
Off me!
Huuaarrggh!
#$@&%$!

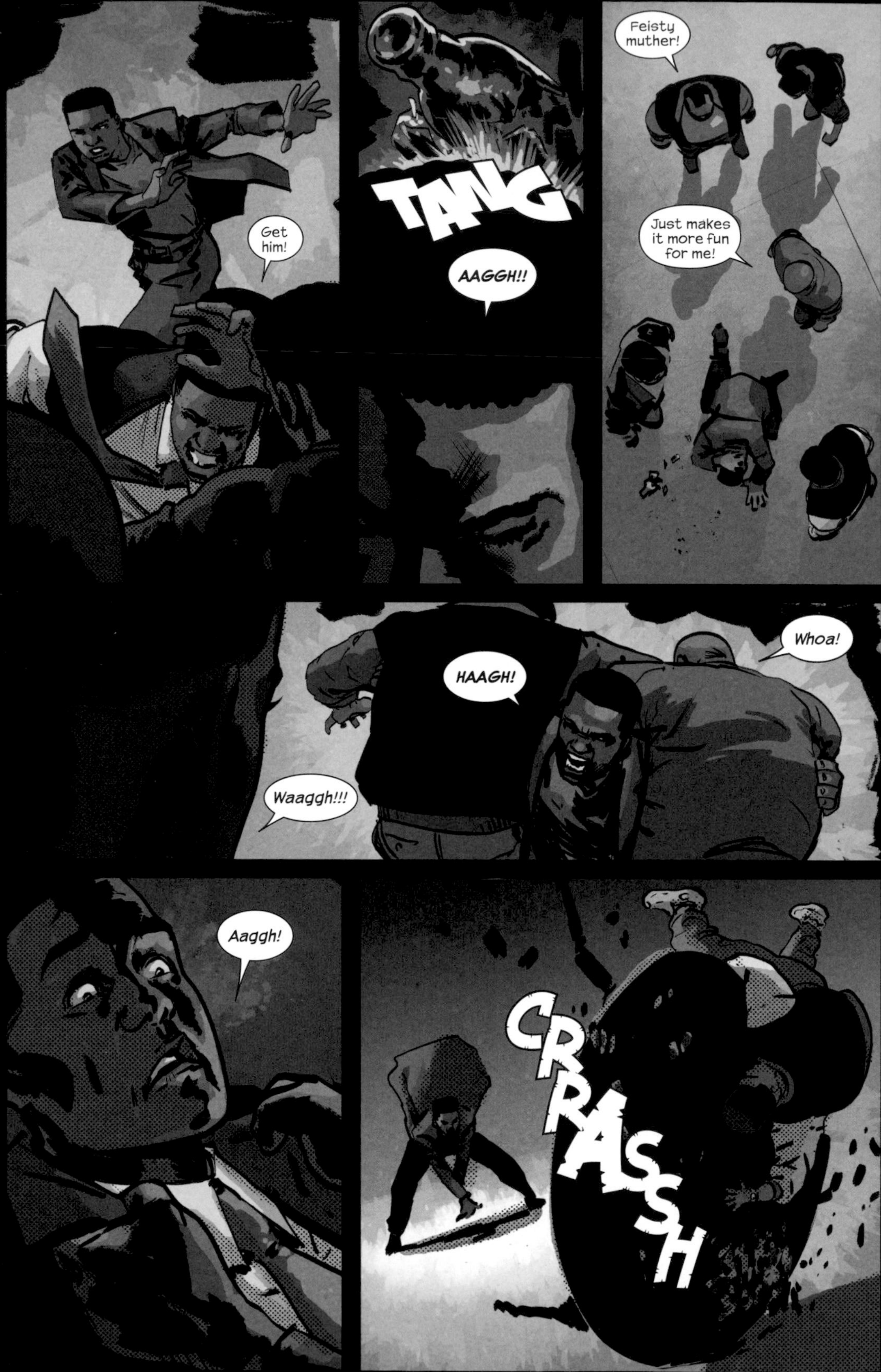
Get him!
TANG
AAGGH!!
Feisty muther!
Just makes it more fun for me!
HAAGH!
Whoa!
Waaggh!!!
Aaggh!
CRASSH

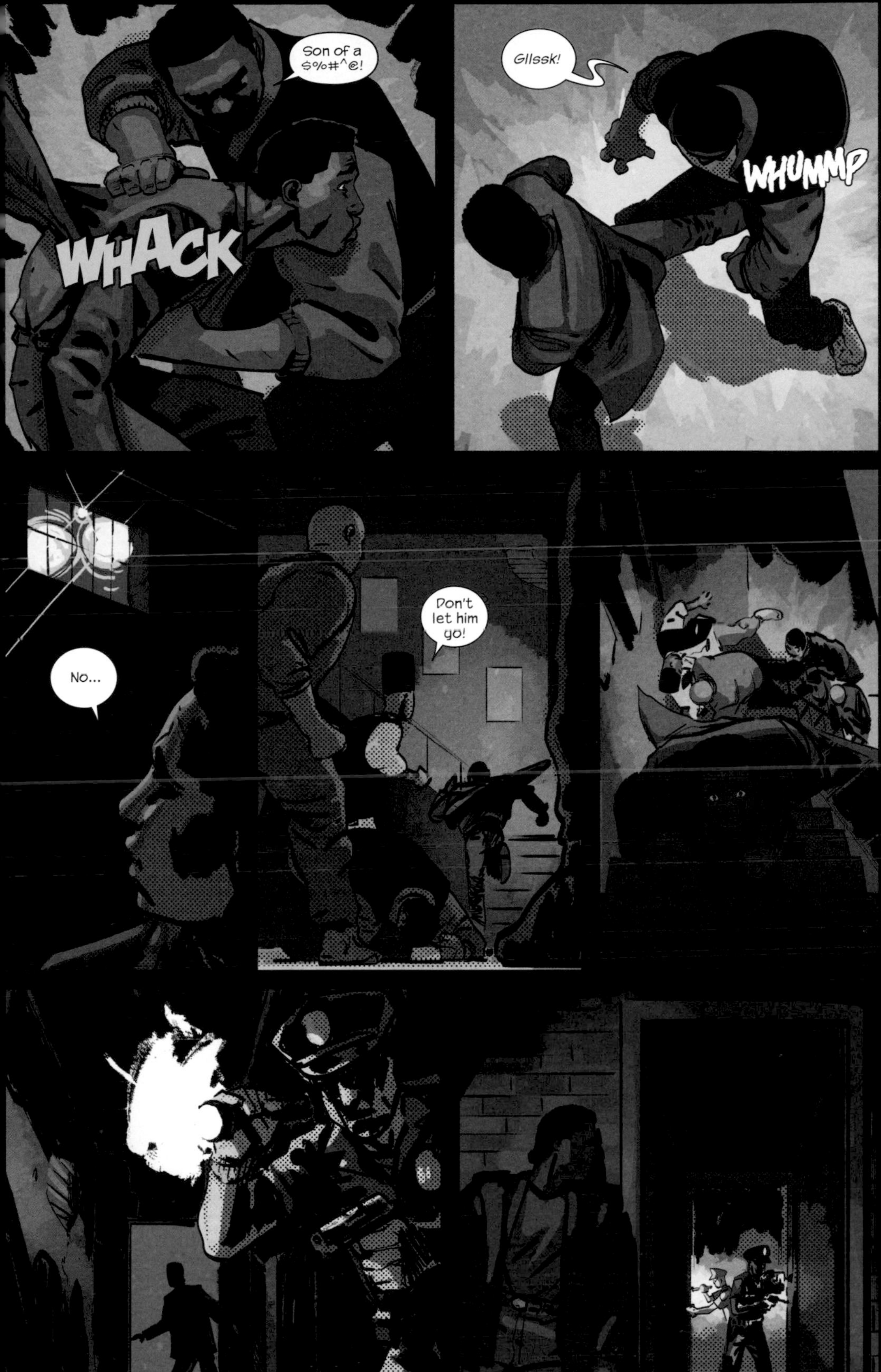
Son of a $%#^@!
WHACK
Gllssk!
WHUMMP
No...
Don't let him go!

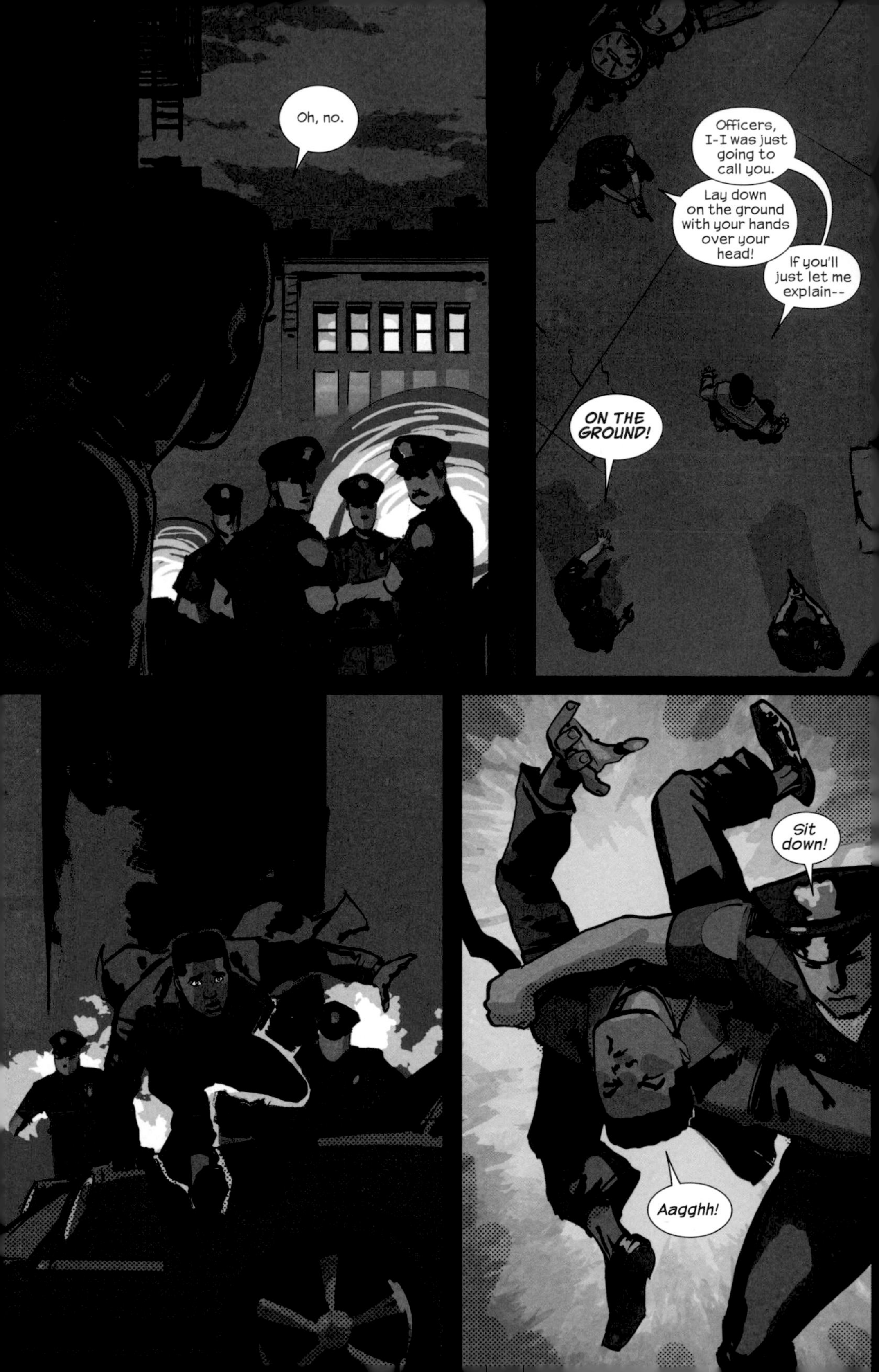
Oh, no.
Officers, I-I was just going to call you.
Lay down on the ground with your hands over your head!
If you'll just let me explain--
ON THE GROUND!
Sit down!
Aagghh!

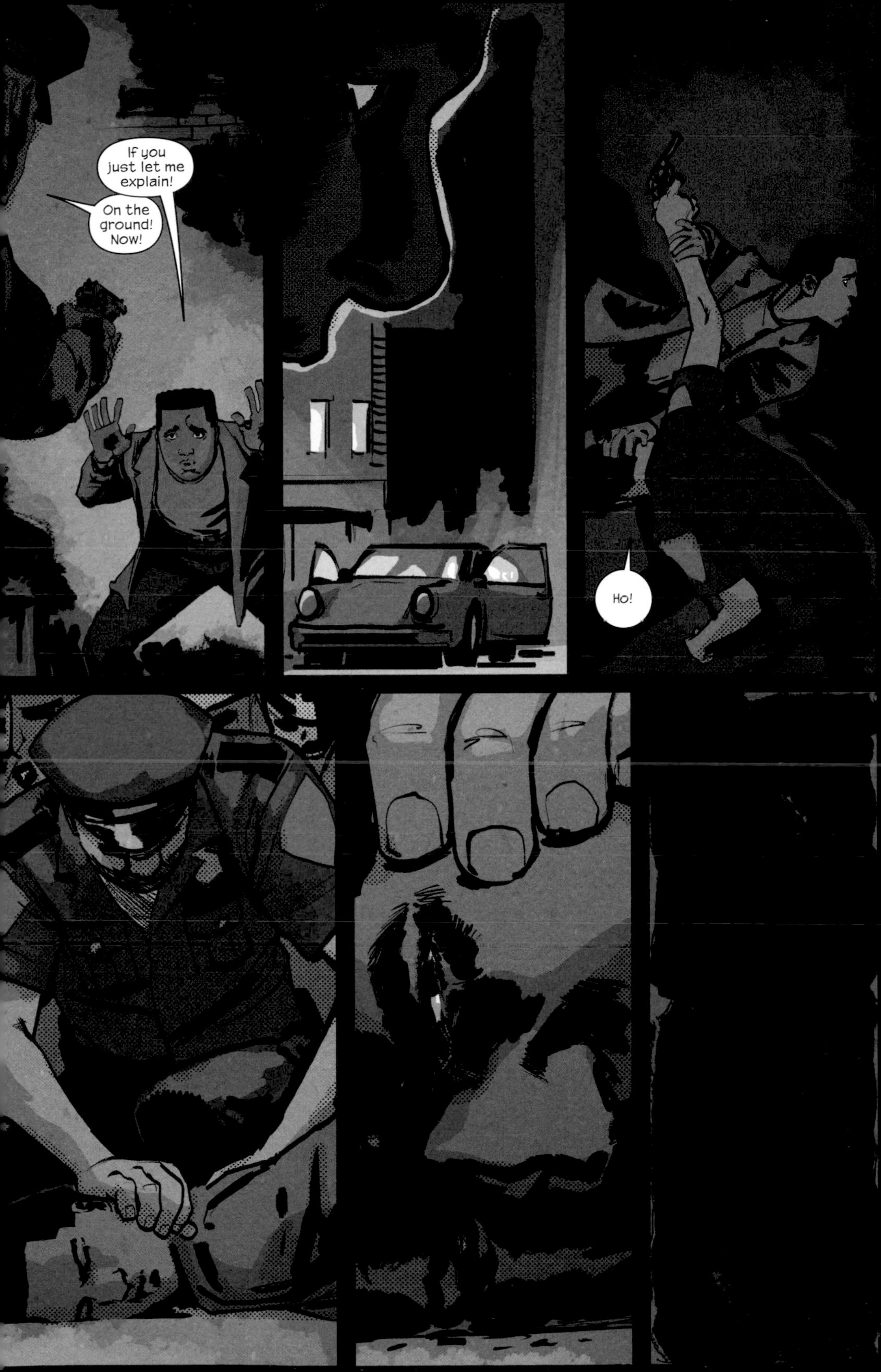
If you just let me explain!
On the ground! Now!
Ho!

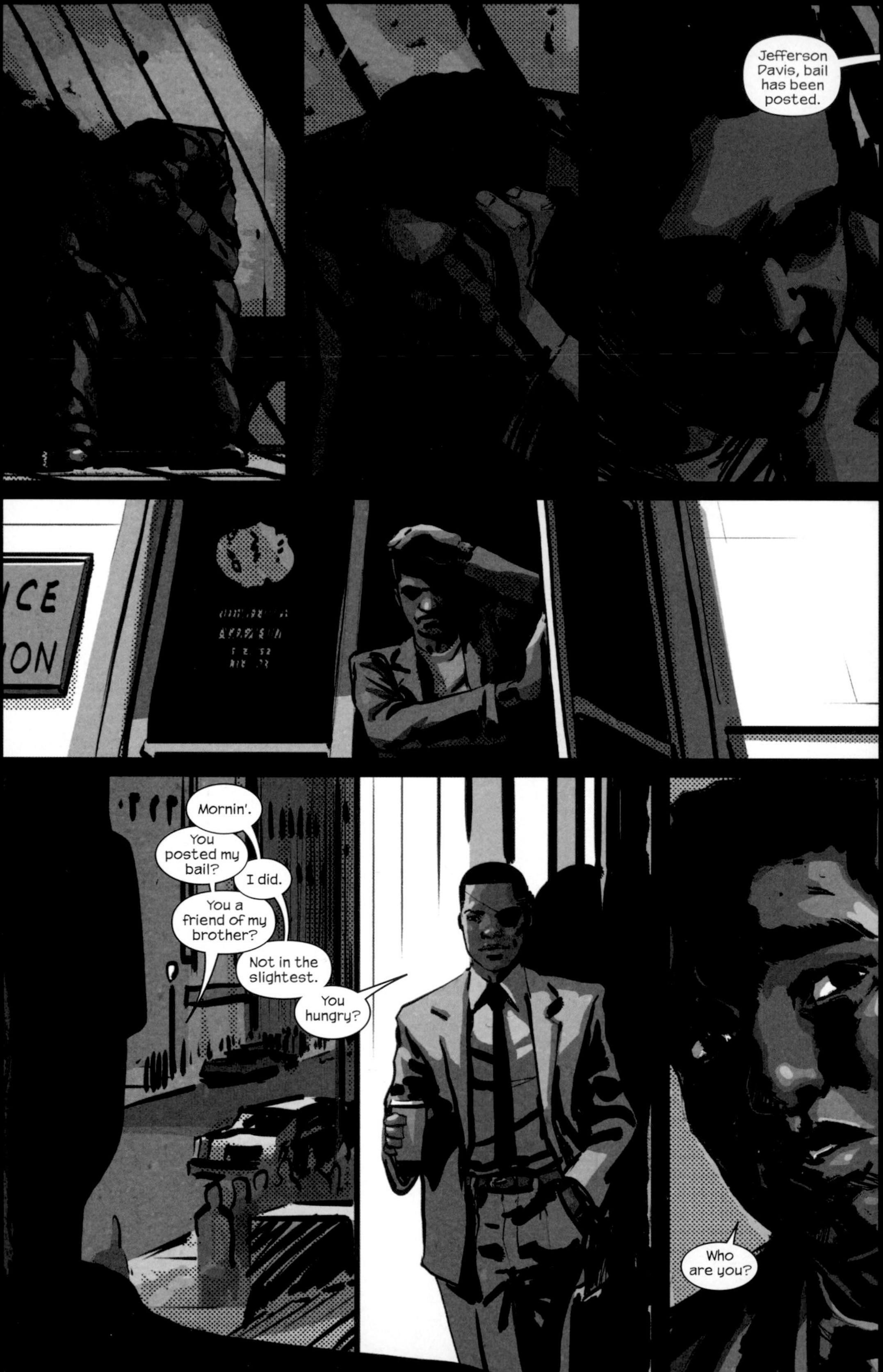
Jefferson Davis, bail has been posted.
Mornin'.
You posted my bail?
I did.
You a friend of my brother?
Not in the slightest.
You hungry?
Who are you?

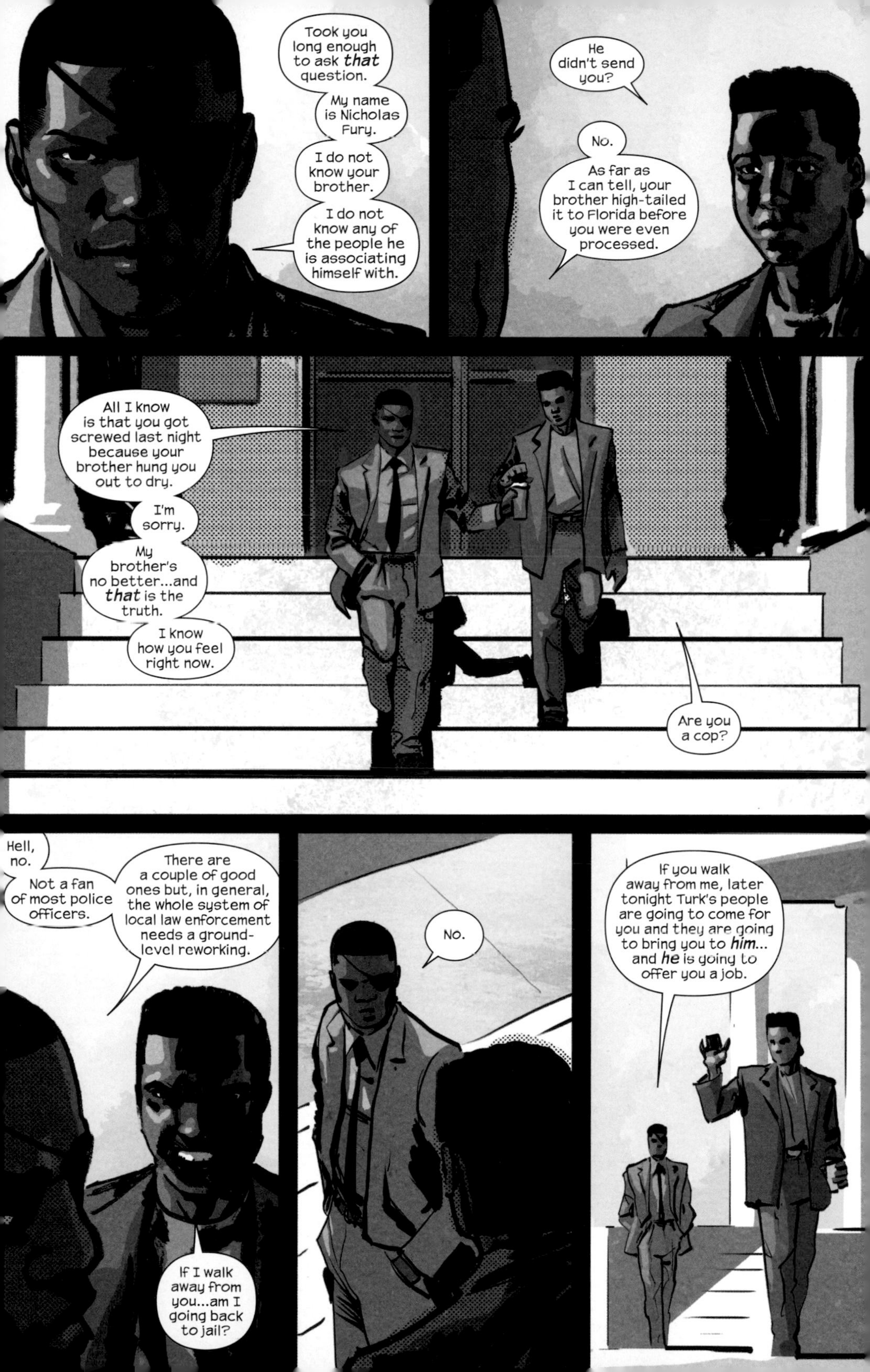
Took you long enough to ask *that* question.
My name is Nicholas Fury.
I do not know your brother.
I do not know any of the people he is associating himself with.
He didn't send you?
No.
As far as I can tell, your brother high-tailed it to Florida before you were even processed.
All I know is that you got screwed last night because your brother hung you out to dry.
I'm sorry.
My brother's no better...and *that* is the truth.
I know how you feel right now.
Are you a cop?
Hell, no.
Not a fan of most police officers.
There are a couple of good ones but, in general, the whole system of local law enforcement needs a ground-level reworking.
If I walk away from you...am I going back to jail?
No.
If you walk away from me, later tonight Turk's people are going to come for you and they are going to bring you to *him*... and *he* is going to offer you a job.

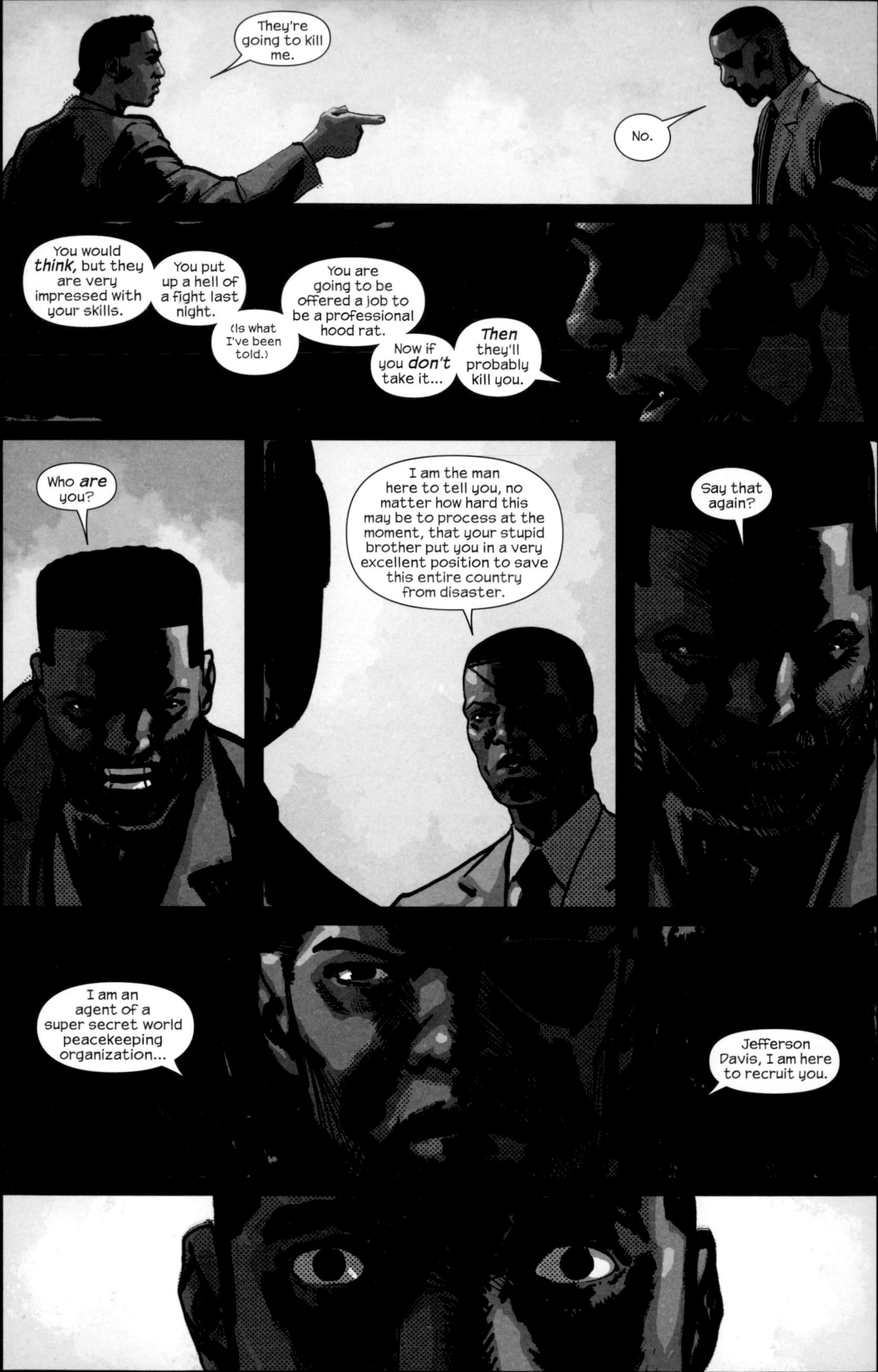
They're going to kill me.
No.
You would *think,* but they are very impressed with your skills.
You put up a hell of a fight last night.
(Is what I've been told.)
You are going to be offered a job to be a professional hood rat.
Now if you *don't* take it...
Then they'll probably kill you.
Who *are* you?
I am the man here to tell you, no matter how hard this may be to process at the moment, that your stupid brother put you in a very excellent position to save this entire country from disaster.
Say that again?
I am an agent of a super secret world peacekeeping organization...
Jefferson Davis, I am here to recruit you.

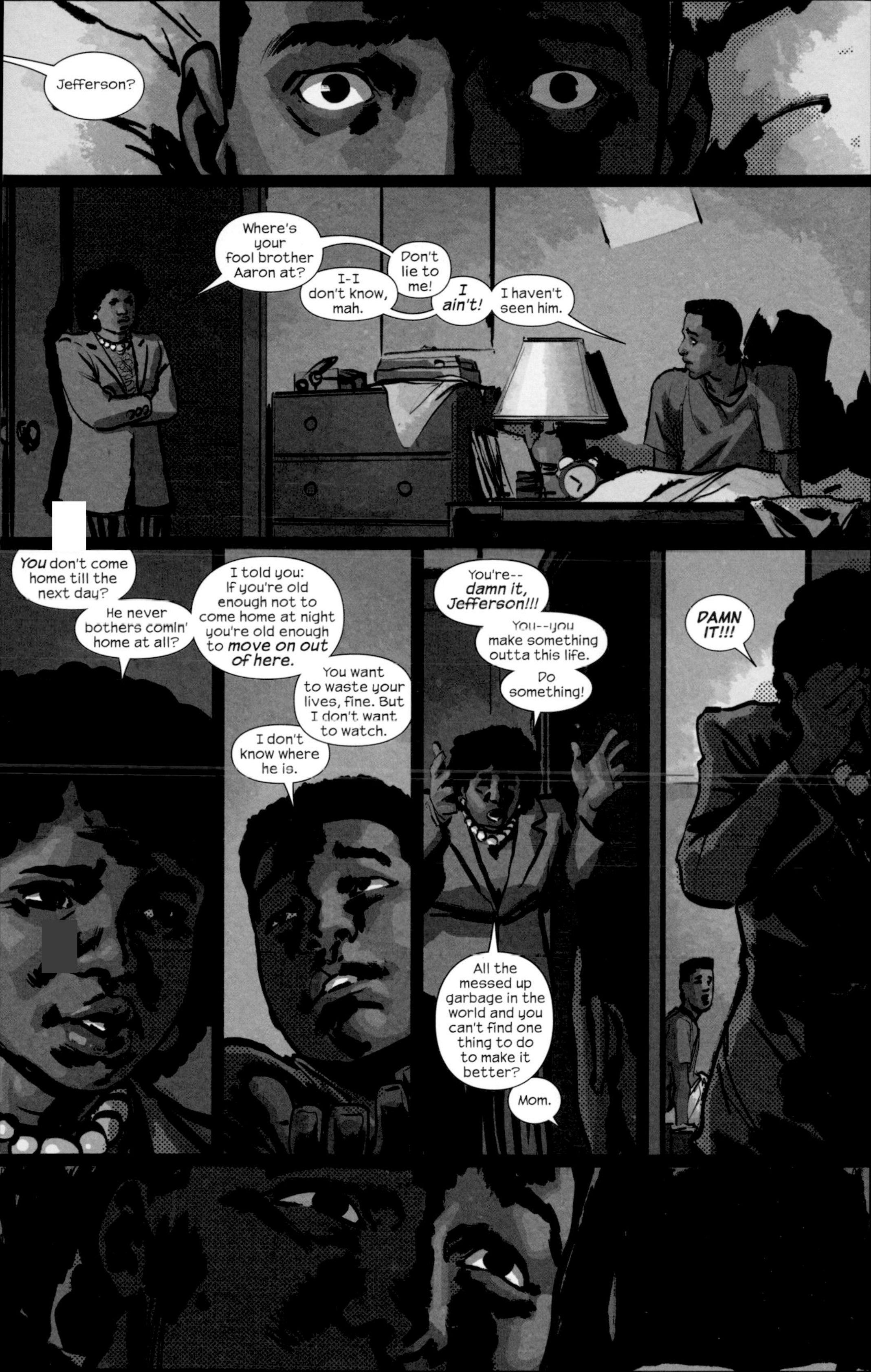
Jefferson?
Where's your fool brother Aaron at?
I-I don't know, mah.
Don't lie to me!
I ain't!
I haven't seen him.
You don't come home till the next day?
He never bothers comin' home at all?
I told you: If you're old enough not to come home at night you're old enough to move on out of here.
You want to waste your lives, fine. But I don't want to watch.
I don't know where he is.
You're-- damn it, Jefferson!!!
You--you make something outta this life.
Do something!
All the messed up garbage in the world and you can't find one thing to do to make it better?
Mom.
DAMN IT!!!

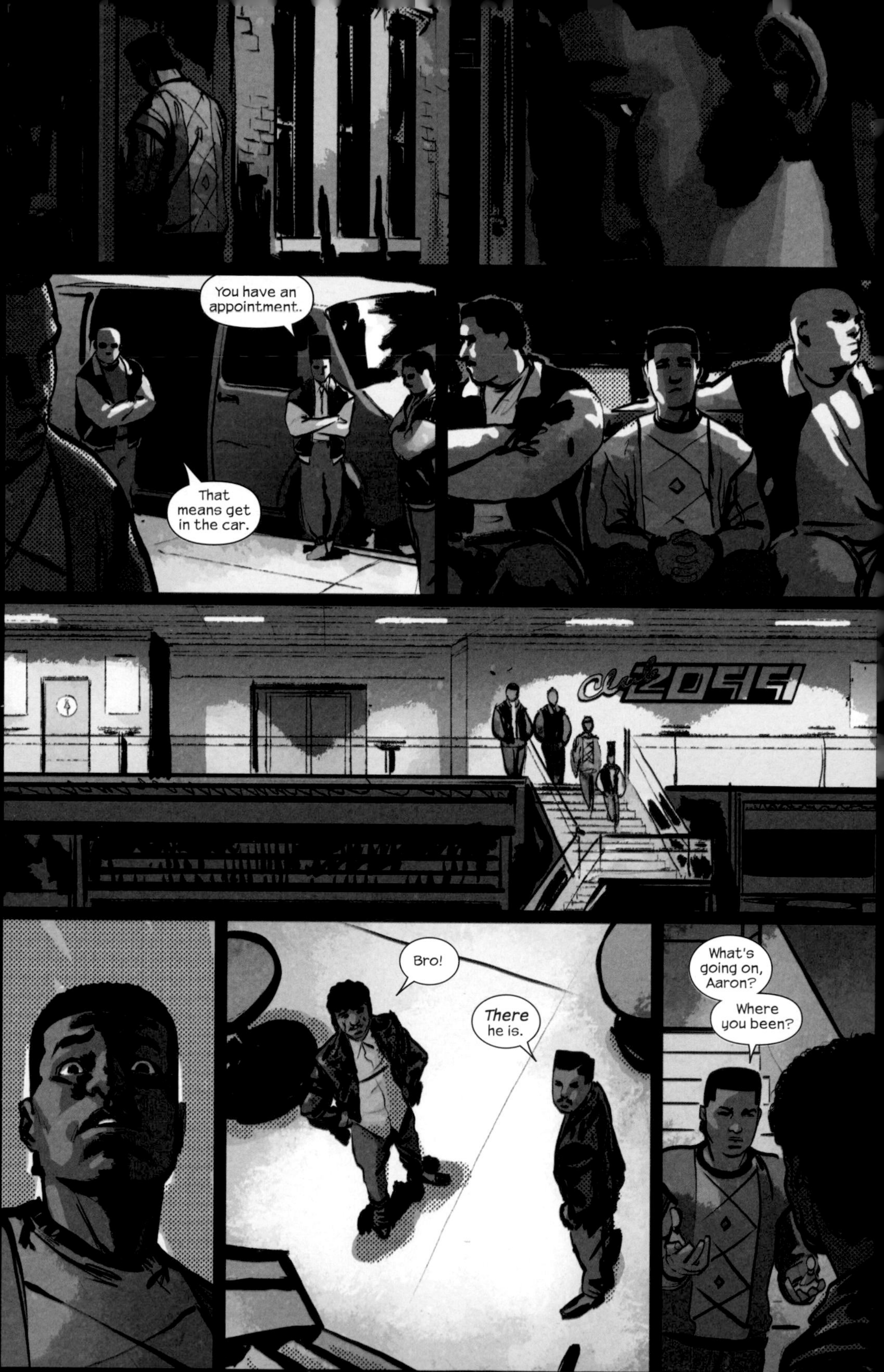
You have an appointment..
That means get in the car.
Bro!
There he is.
What's going on, Aaron?
Where you been?

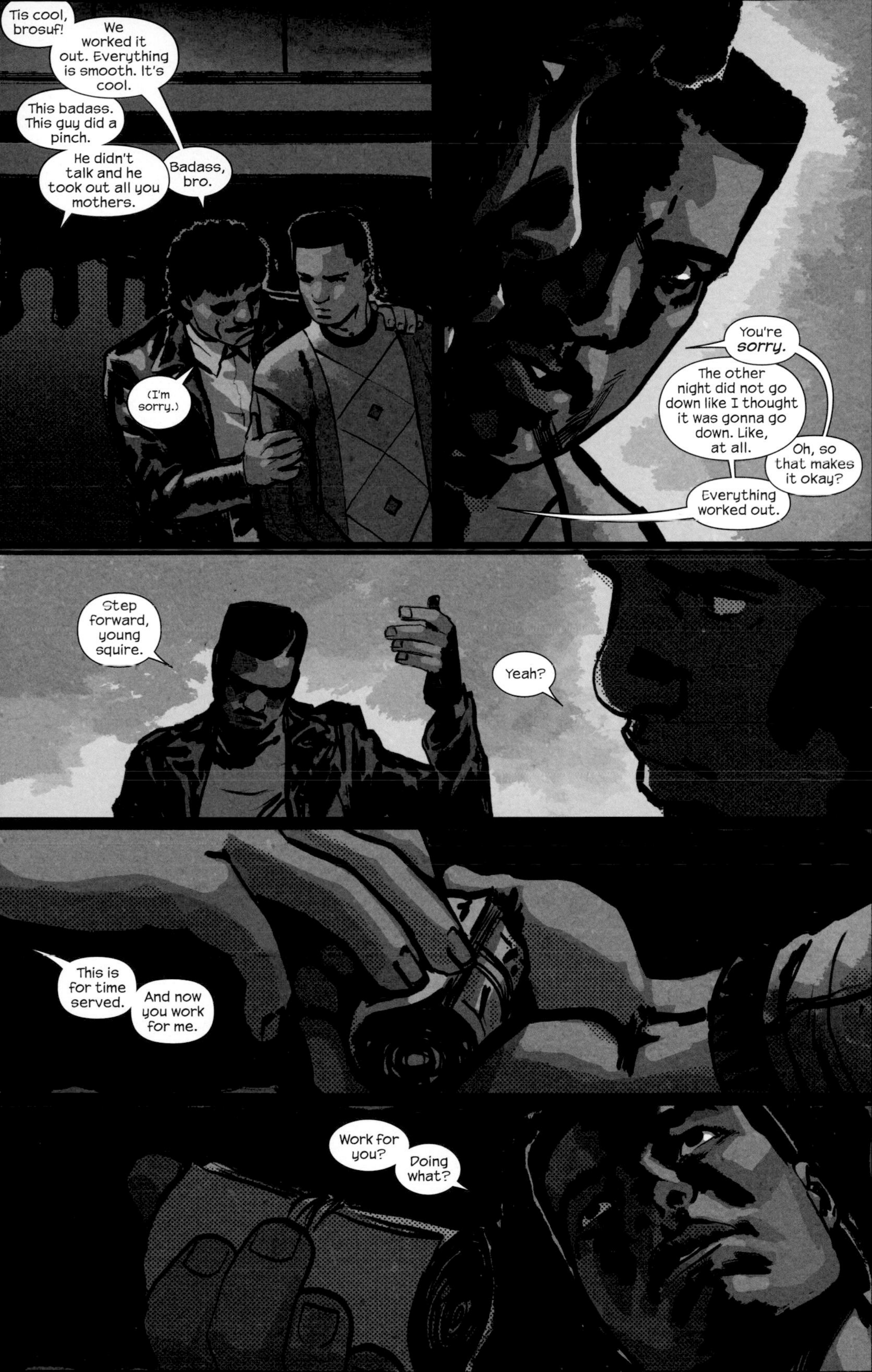
Tis cool, brosuf!
We worked it out. Everything is smooth. It's cool.
This badass. This guy did a pinch.
He didn't talk and he took out all you mothers.
Badass, bro.
(I'm sorry.)
You're *sorry.*
The other night did not go down like I thought it was gonna go down. Like, at all.
Everything worked out.
Oh, so that makes it okay?
Step forward, young squire.
Yeah?
This is for time served.
And now you work for me.
Work for you?
Doing what?

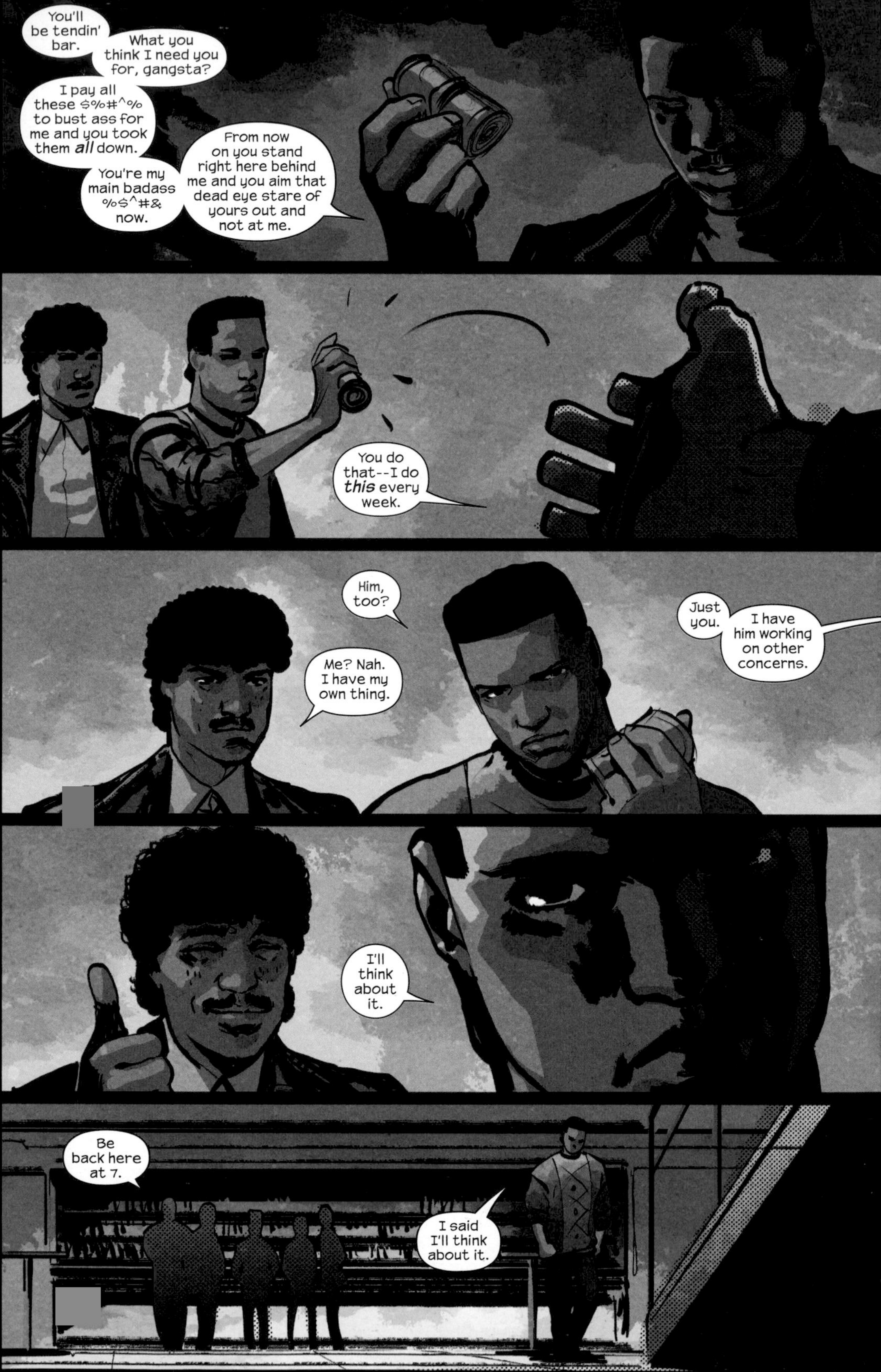

You'll be tendin' bar.
What you think I need you for, gangsta?
I pay all these $%#^% to bust ass for me and you took them *all* down.
You're my main badass %$^#& now.
From now on you stand right here behind me and you aim that dead eye stare of yours out and not at me.
You do that--I do *this* every week.
Him, too?
Me? Nah. I have my own thing.
Just you.
I have him working on other concerns.
I'll think about it.
Be back here at 7.
I said I'll think about it.

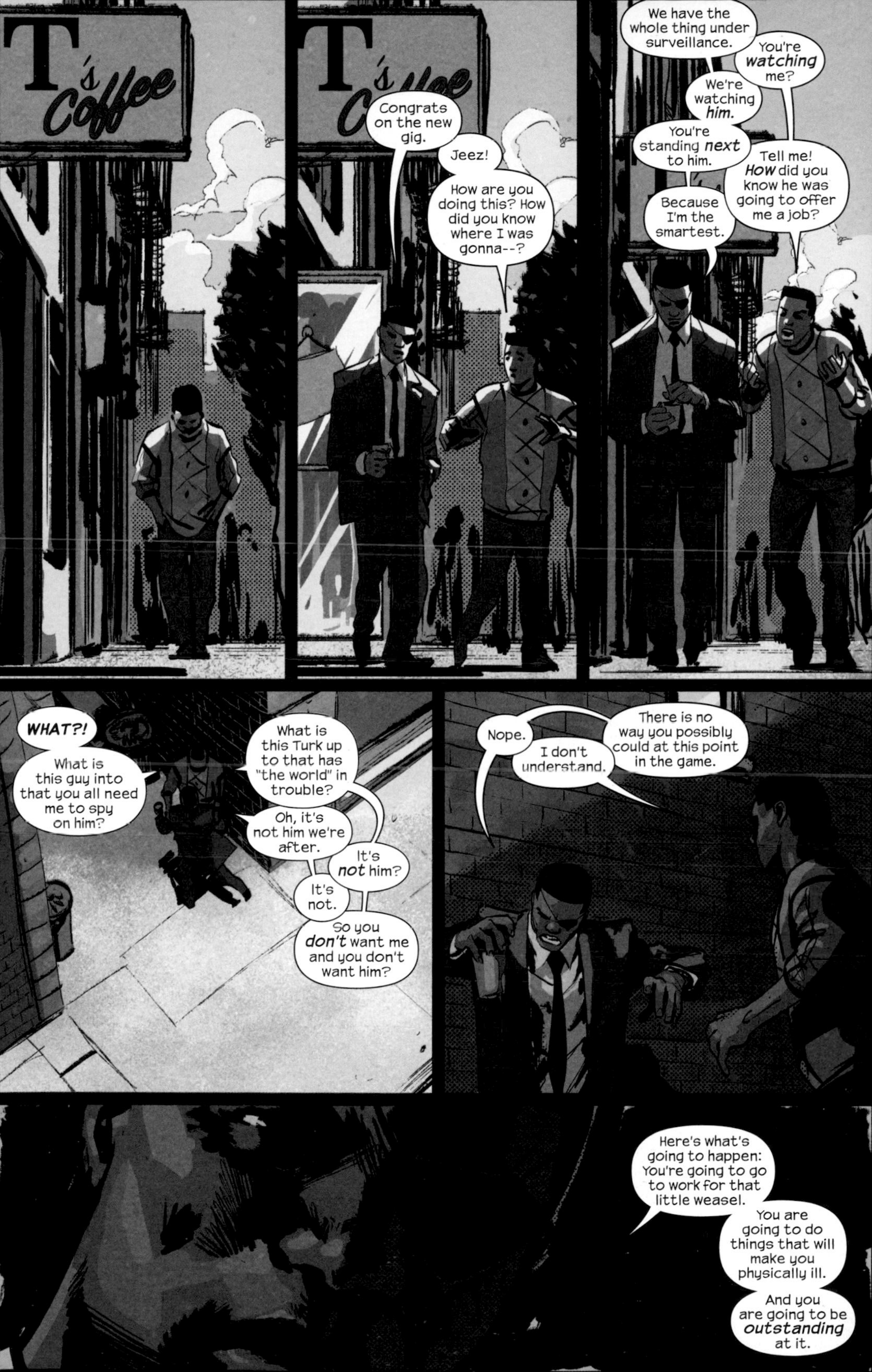

T's Coffee
Congrats on the new gig.
Jeez!
How are you doing this? How did you know where I was gonna--?
We have the whole thing under surveillance.
You're *watching* me?
We're watching *him.*
You're standing *next* to him.
Tell me! *HOW* did you know he was going to offer me a job?
Because I'm the smartest.
WHAT?!
What is this guy into that you all need me to spy on him?
What is this Turk up to that has "the world" in trouble?
Oh, it's not him we're after.
It's *not* him?
It's not.
So you *don't* want me and you don't want him?
Nope.
I don't understand.
There is no way you possibly could at this point in the game.
Here's what's going to happen: You're going to go to work for that little weasel.
You are going to do things that will make you physically ill.
And you are going to be *outstanding* at it.

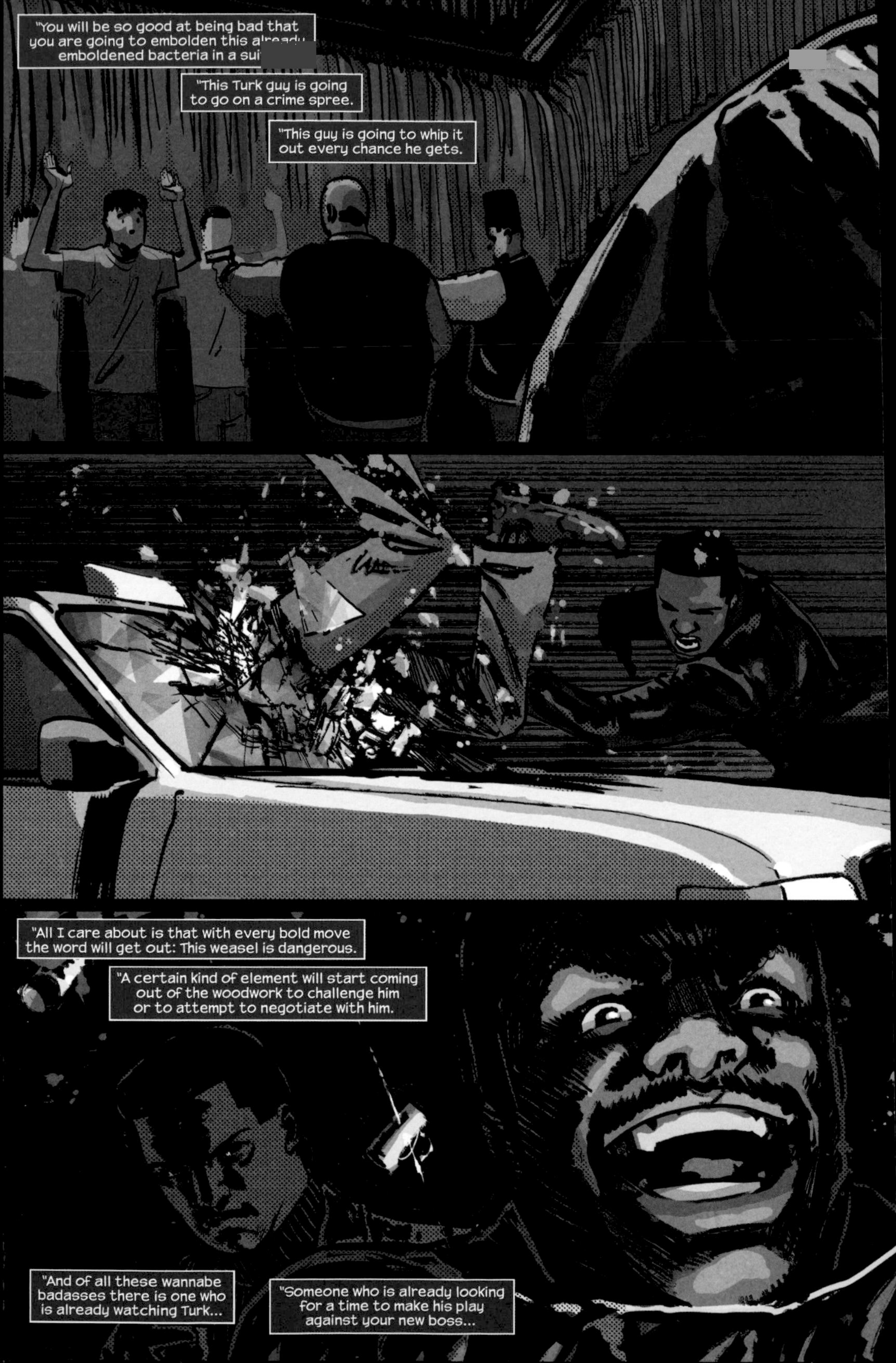
"You will be so good at being bad that you are going to embolden this already emboldened bacteria in a sui
"This Turk guy is going to go on a crime spree.
"This guy is going to whip it out every chance he gets.
"All I care about is that with every bold move the word will get out: This weasel is dangerous.
"A certain kind of element will start coming out of the woodwork to challenge him or to attempt to negotiate with him.
"And of all these wannabe badasses there is one who is already watching Turk...
"Someone who is already looking for a time to make his play against your new boss...

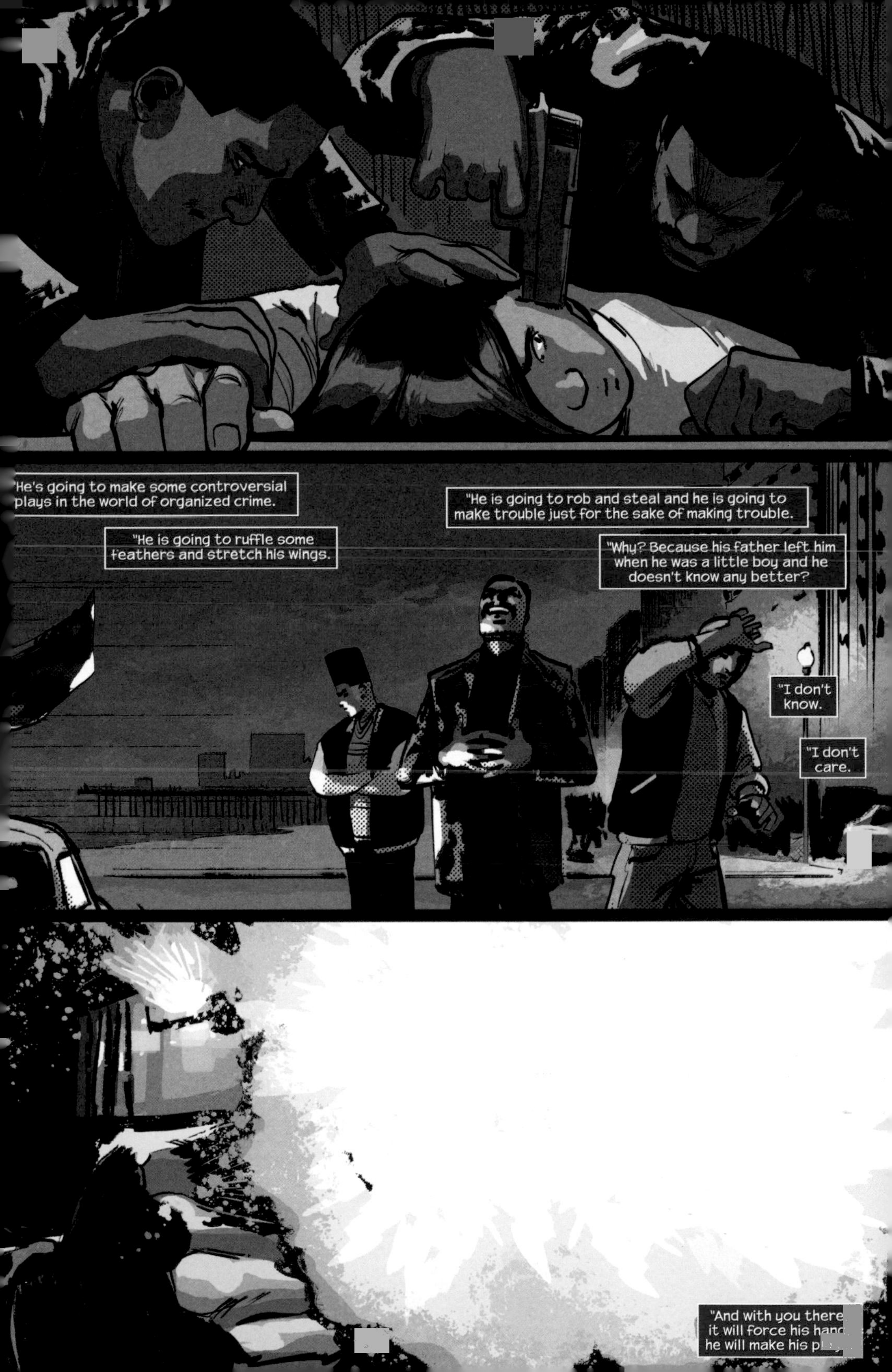
"He's going to make some controversial plays in the world of organized crime.
"He is going to ruffle some feathers and stretch his wings.
"He is going to rob and steal and he is going to make trouble just for the sake of making trouble.
"Why? Because his father left him when he was a little boy and he doesn't know any better?
"I don't know.
"I don't care.
"And with you there
it will force his han
he will make his p

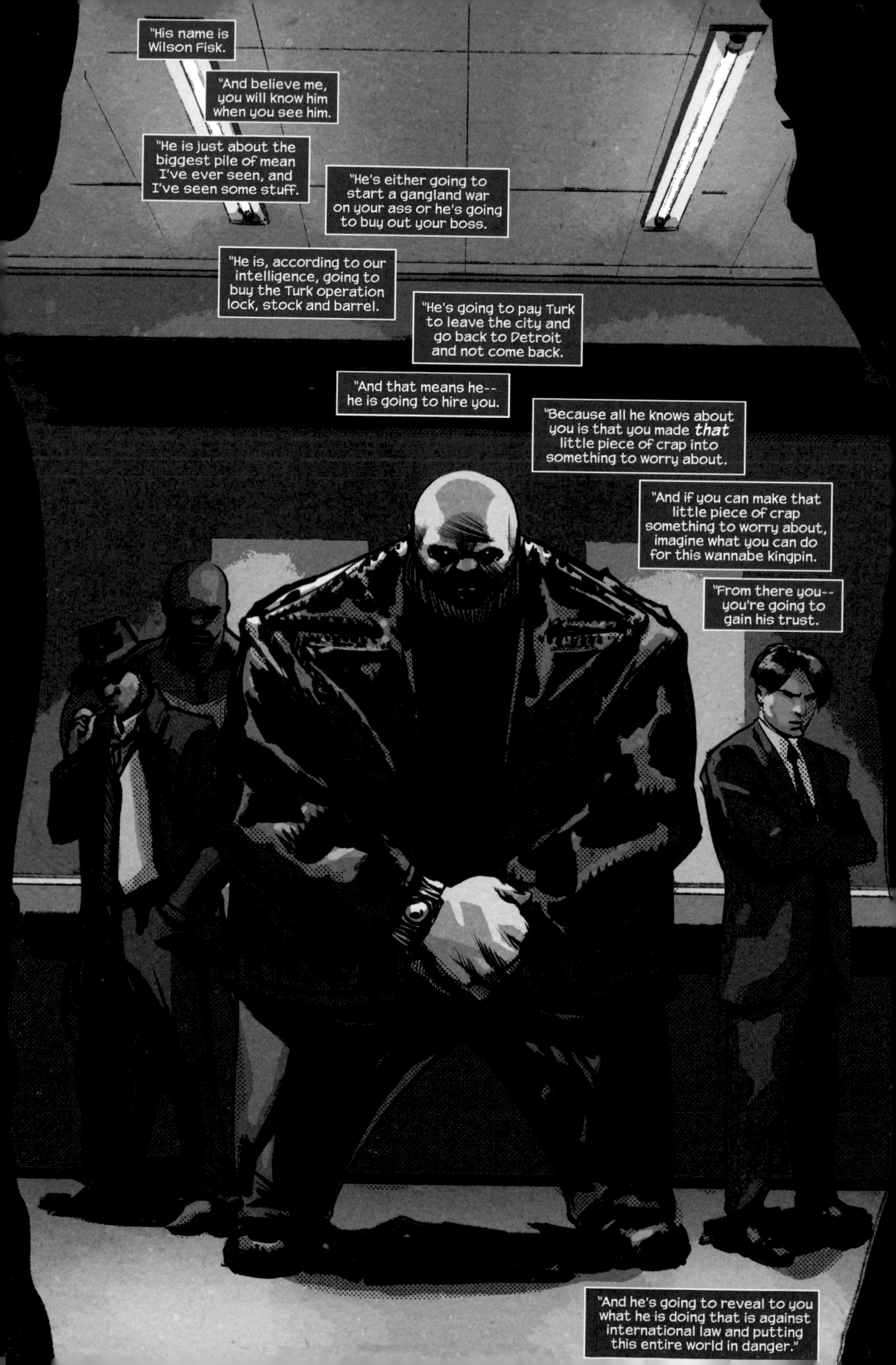
"His name is Wilson Fisk.
"And believe me, you will know him when you see him.
"He is just about the biggest pile of mean I've ever seen, and I've seen some stuff.
"He's either going to start a gangland war on your ass or he's going to buy out your boss.
"He is, according to our intelligence, going to buy the Turk operation lock, stock and barrel.
"He's going to pay Turk to leave the city and go back to Detroit and not come back.
"And that means he-- he is going to hire you.
"Because all he knows about you is that you made *that* little piece of crap into something to worry about.
"And if you can make that little piece of crap something to worry about, imagine what you can do for this wannabe kingpin.
"From there you-- you're going to gain his trust.
"And he's going to reveal to you what he is doing that is against international law and putting this entire world in danger."

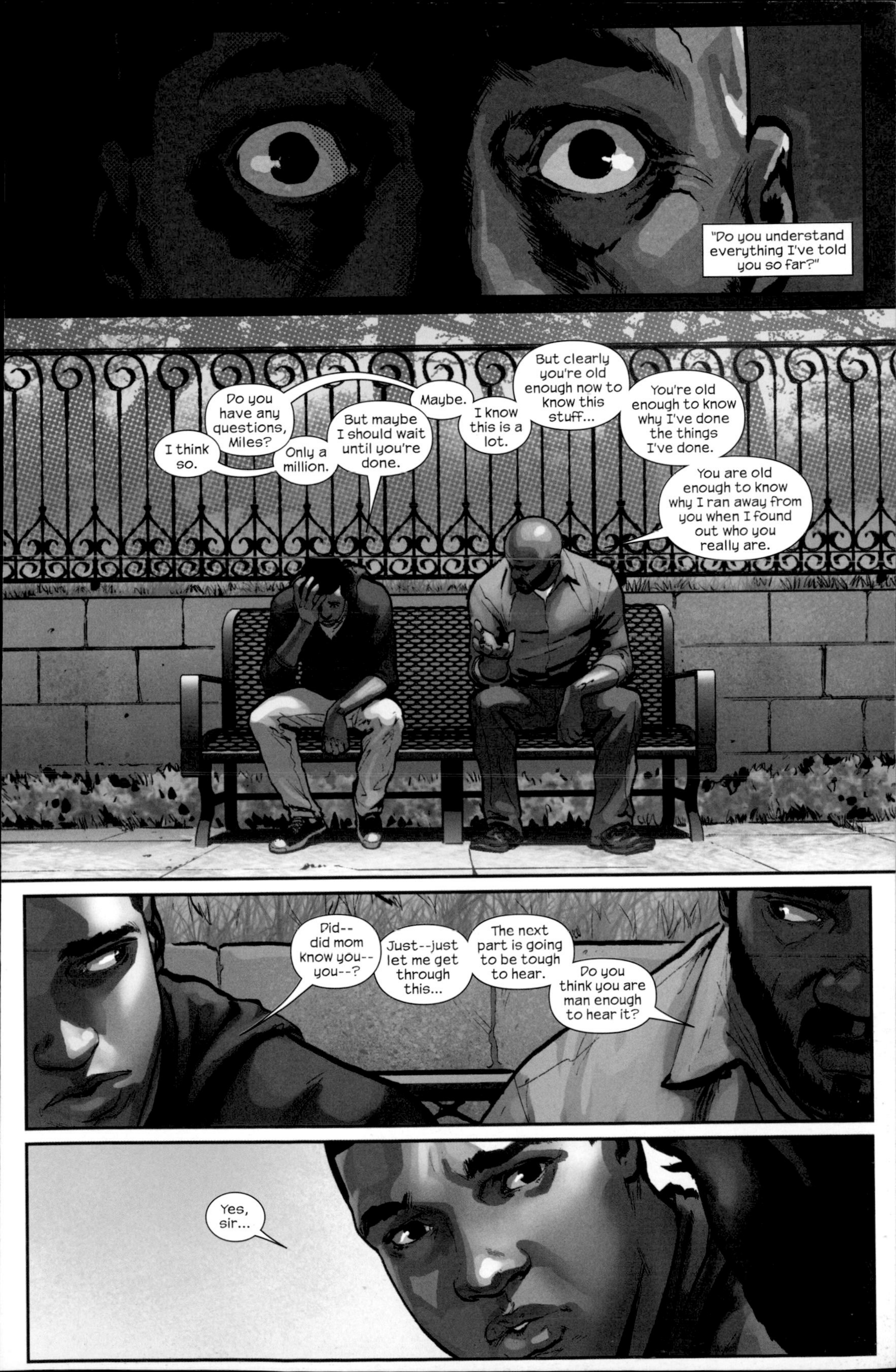
"Do you understand everything I've told you so far?"
I think so.
Do you have any questions, Miles?
Only a million.
Maybe.
But maybe I should wait until you're done.
I know this is a lot.
But clearly you're old enough now to know this stuff...
You're old enough to know why I've done the things I've done.
You are old enough to know why I ran away from you when I found out who you really are.
Did--did mom know you--you--?
Just--just let me get through this...
The next part is going to be tough to hear.
Do you think you are man enough to hear it?
Yes, sir...

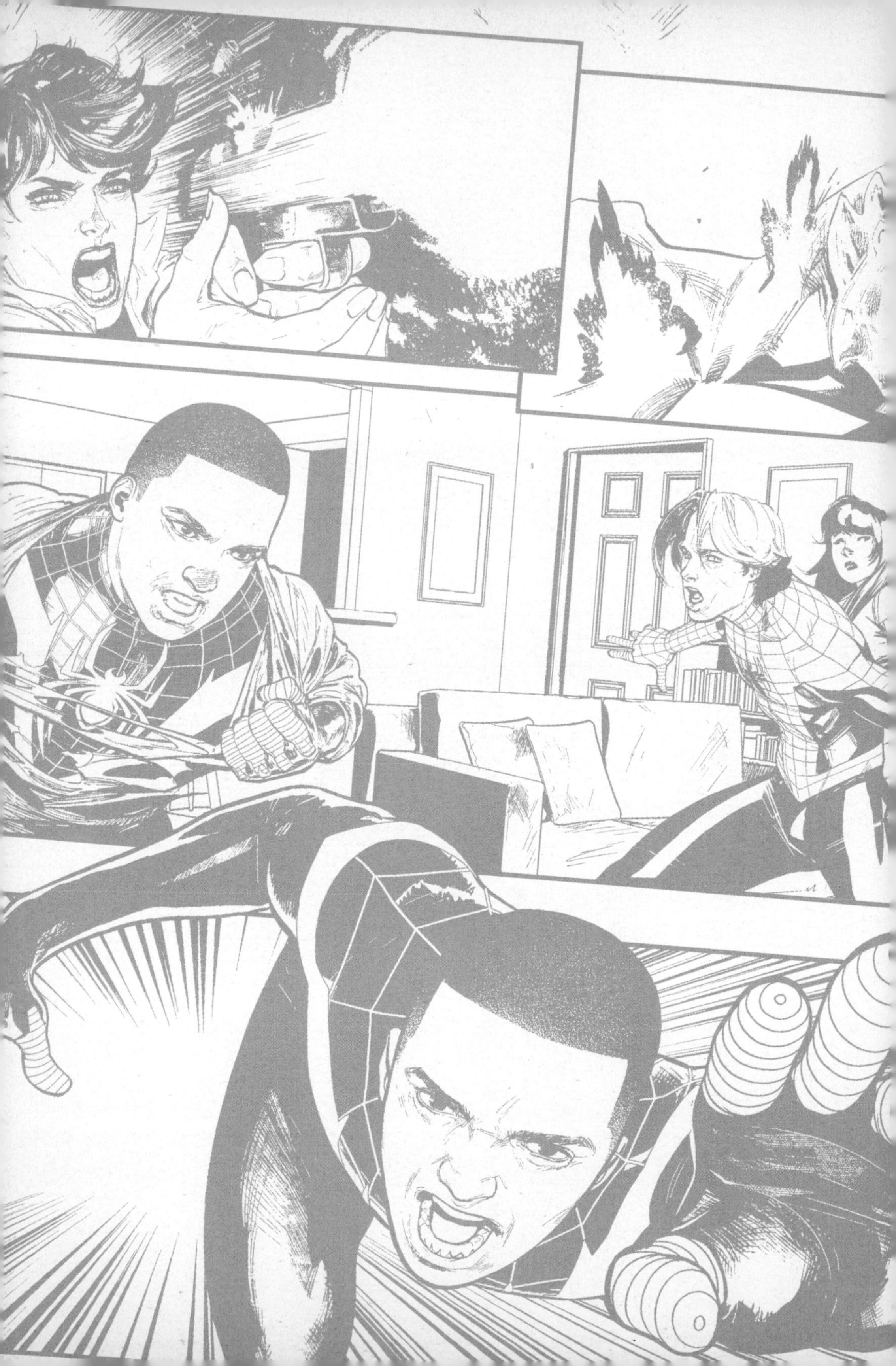

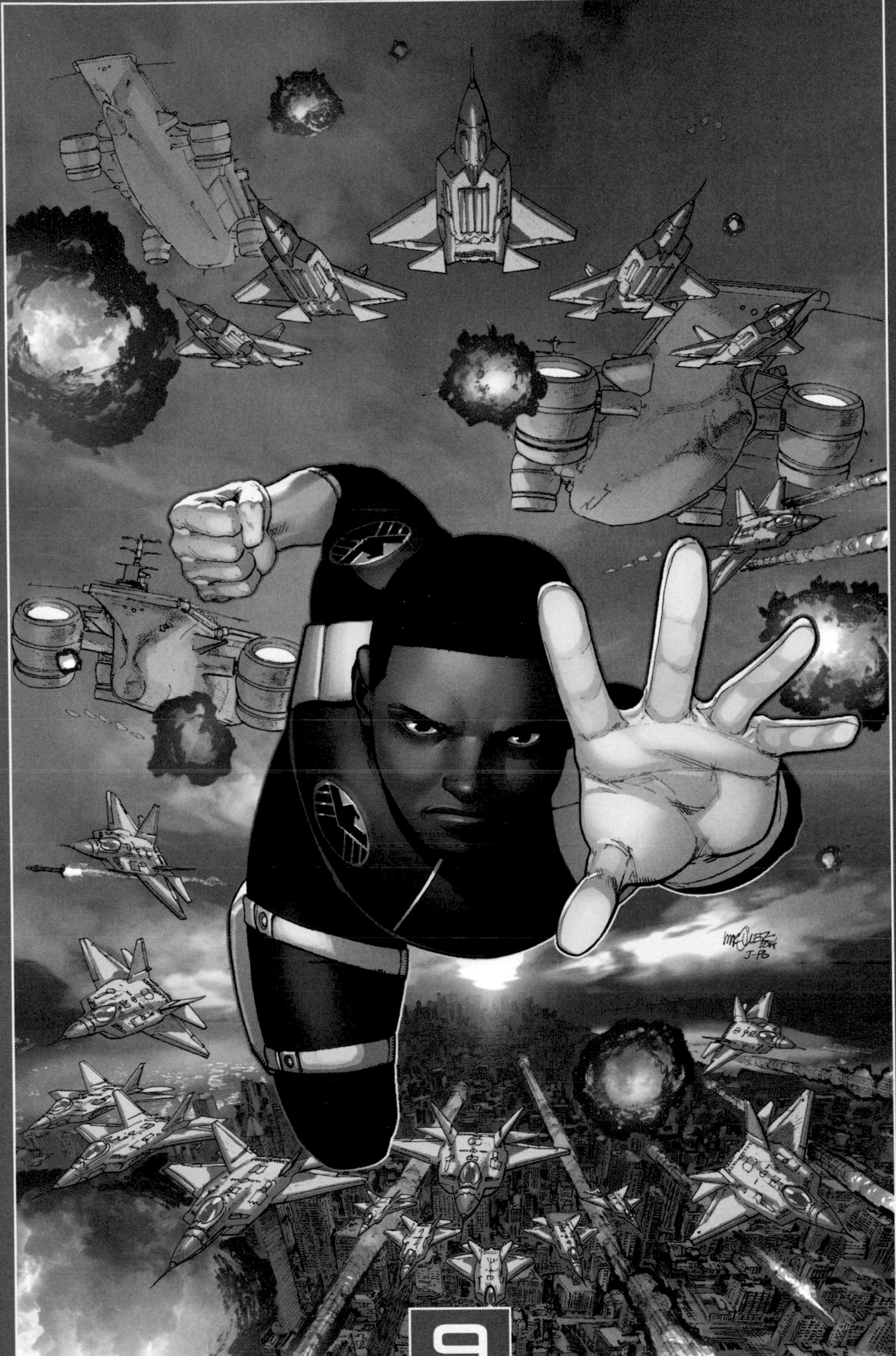

9

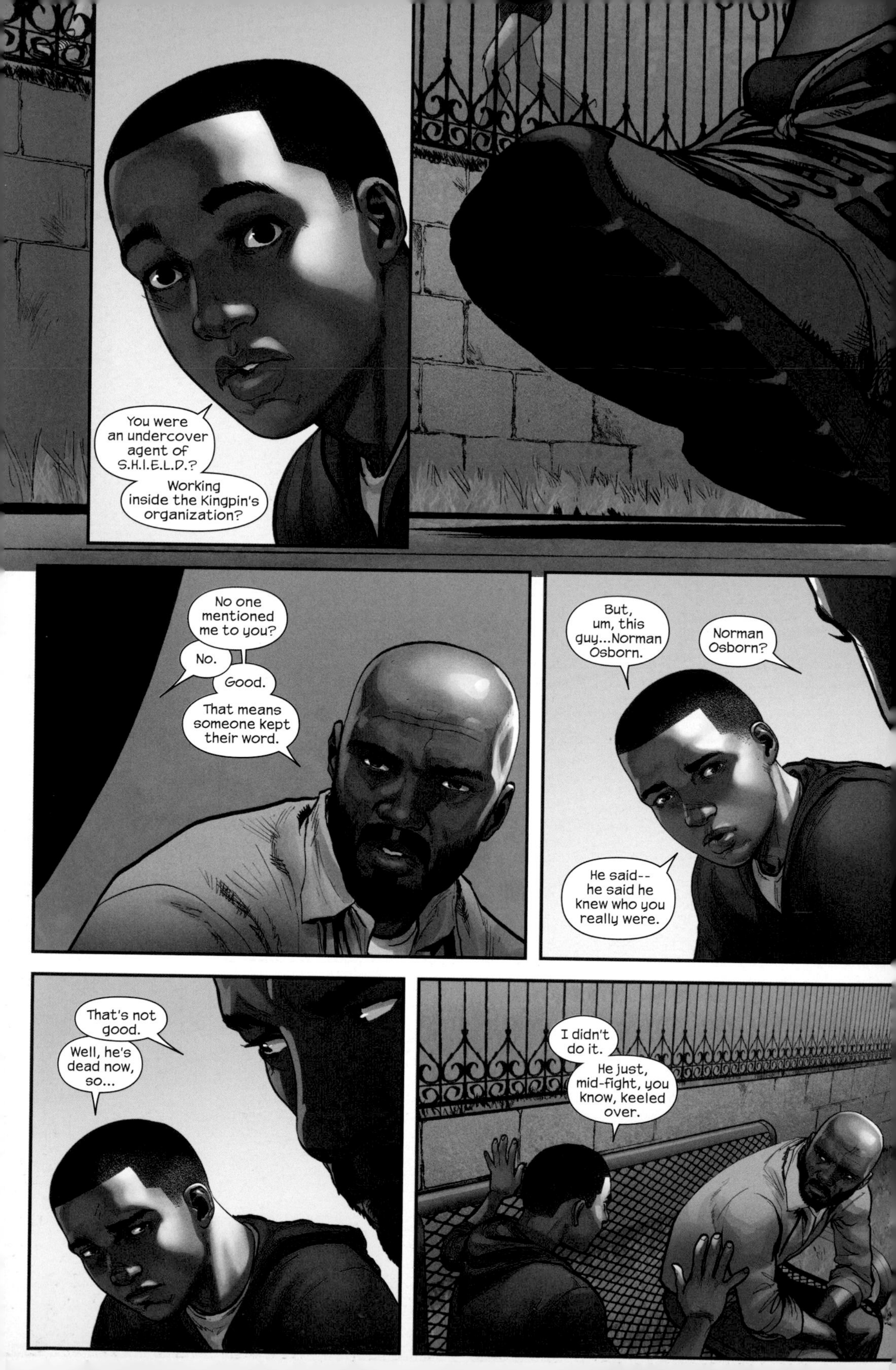
You were an undercover agent of S.H.I.E.L.D.?
Working inside the Kingpin's organization?
No one mentioned me to you?
No.
Good.
That means someone kept their word.
But, um, this guy...Norman Osborn.
Norman Osborn?
He said-- he said he knew who you really were.
That's not good.
Well, he's dead now, so...
I didn't do it.
He just, mid-fight, you know, keeled over.

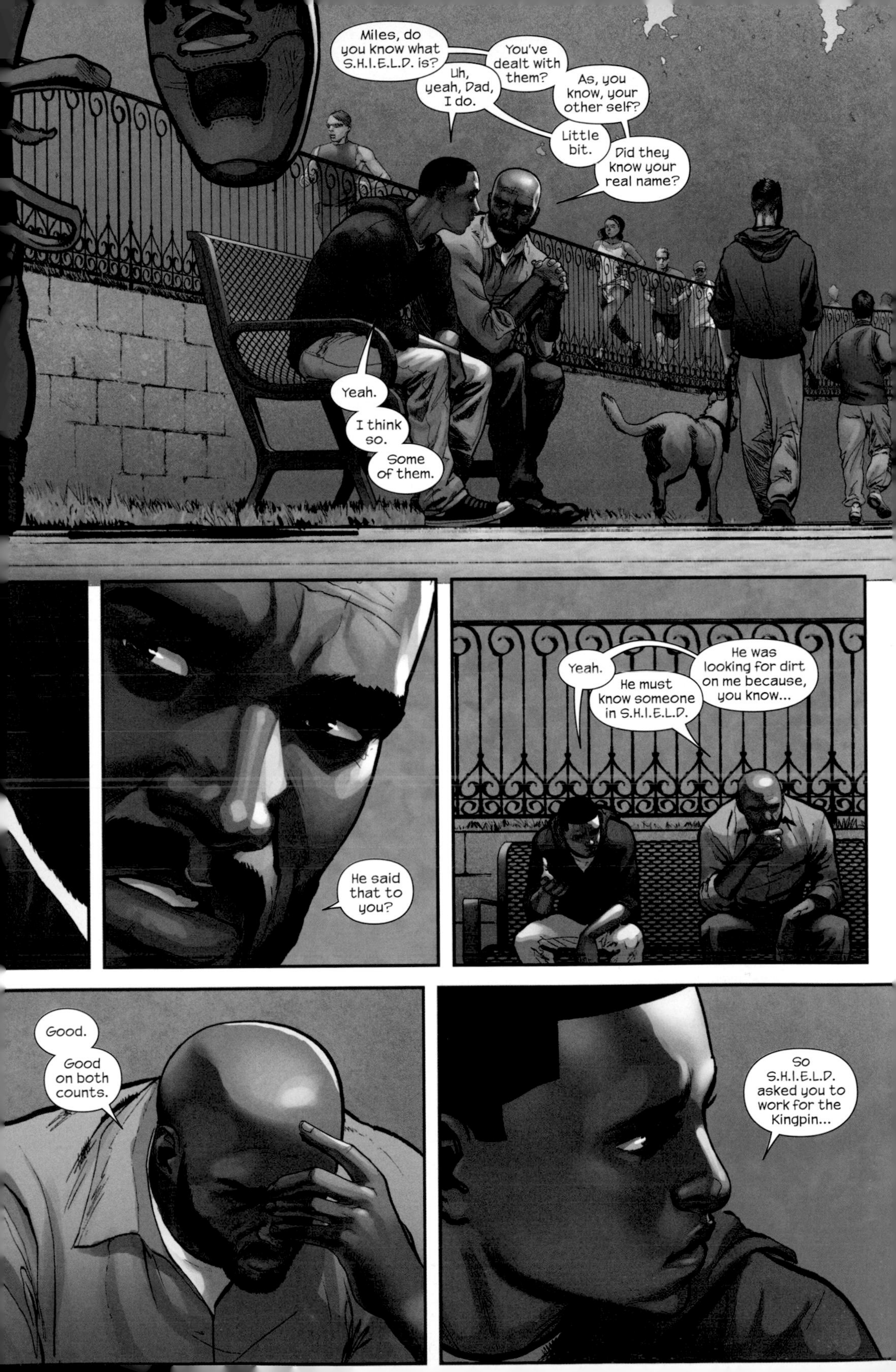
Miles, do you know what S.H.I.E.L.D. is?
Uh, yeah, Dad, I do.
You've dealt with them?
As, you know, your other self?
Little bit.
Did they know your real name?
Yeah.
I think so.
Some of them.
He said that to you?
Yeah.
He must know someone in S.H.I.E.L.D.
He was looking for dirt on me because, you know...
Good.
Good on both counts.
So S.H.I.E.L.D. asked you to work for the Kingpin...

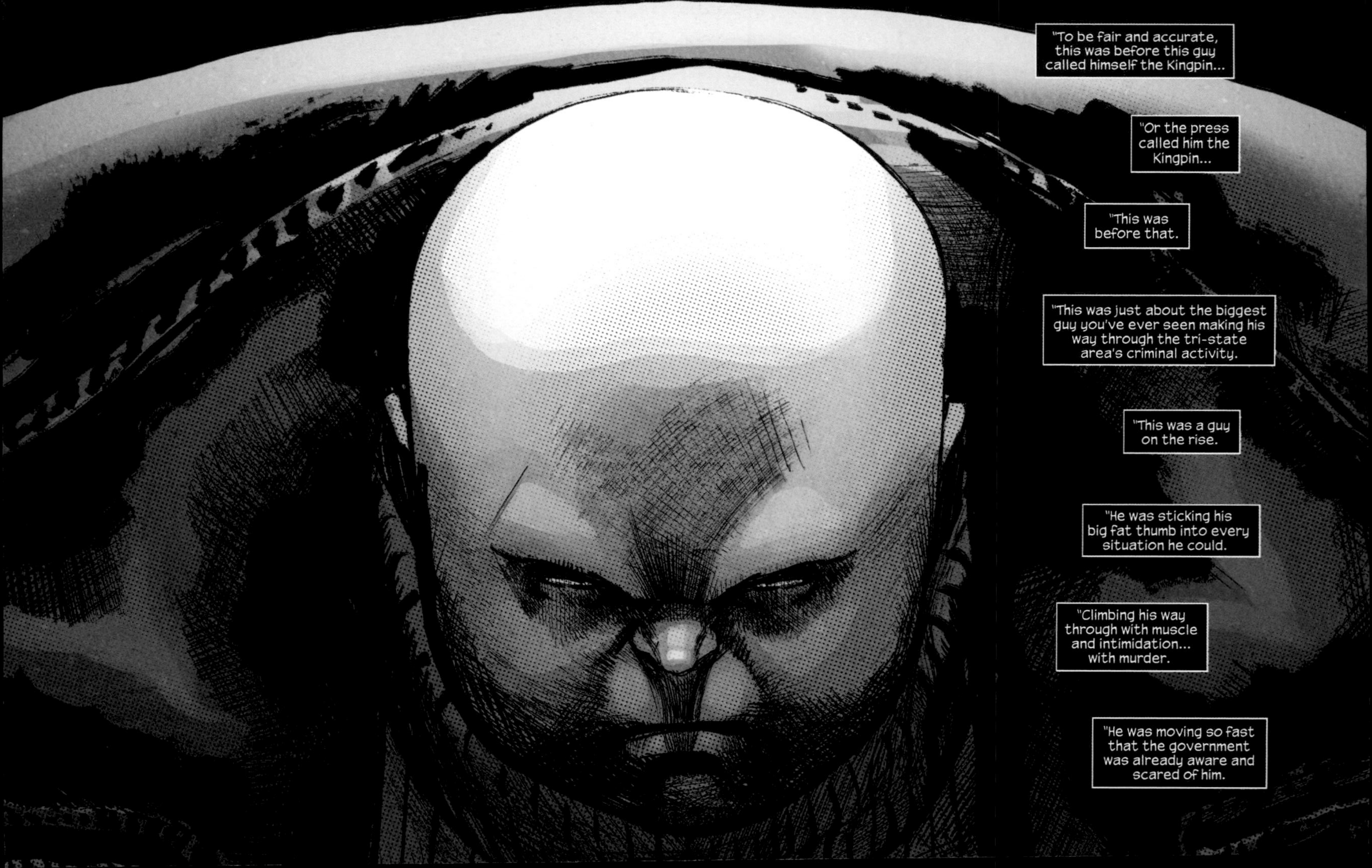
"To be fair and accurate, this was before this guy called himself the Kingpin...
"Or the press called him the Kingpin...
"This was before that.
"This was just about the biggest guy you've ever seen making his way through the tri-state area's criminal activity.
"This was a guy on the rise.
"He was sticking his big fat thumb into every situation he could.
"Climbing his way through with muscle and intimidation... with murder.
"He was moving so fast that the government was already aware and scared of him.

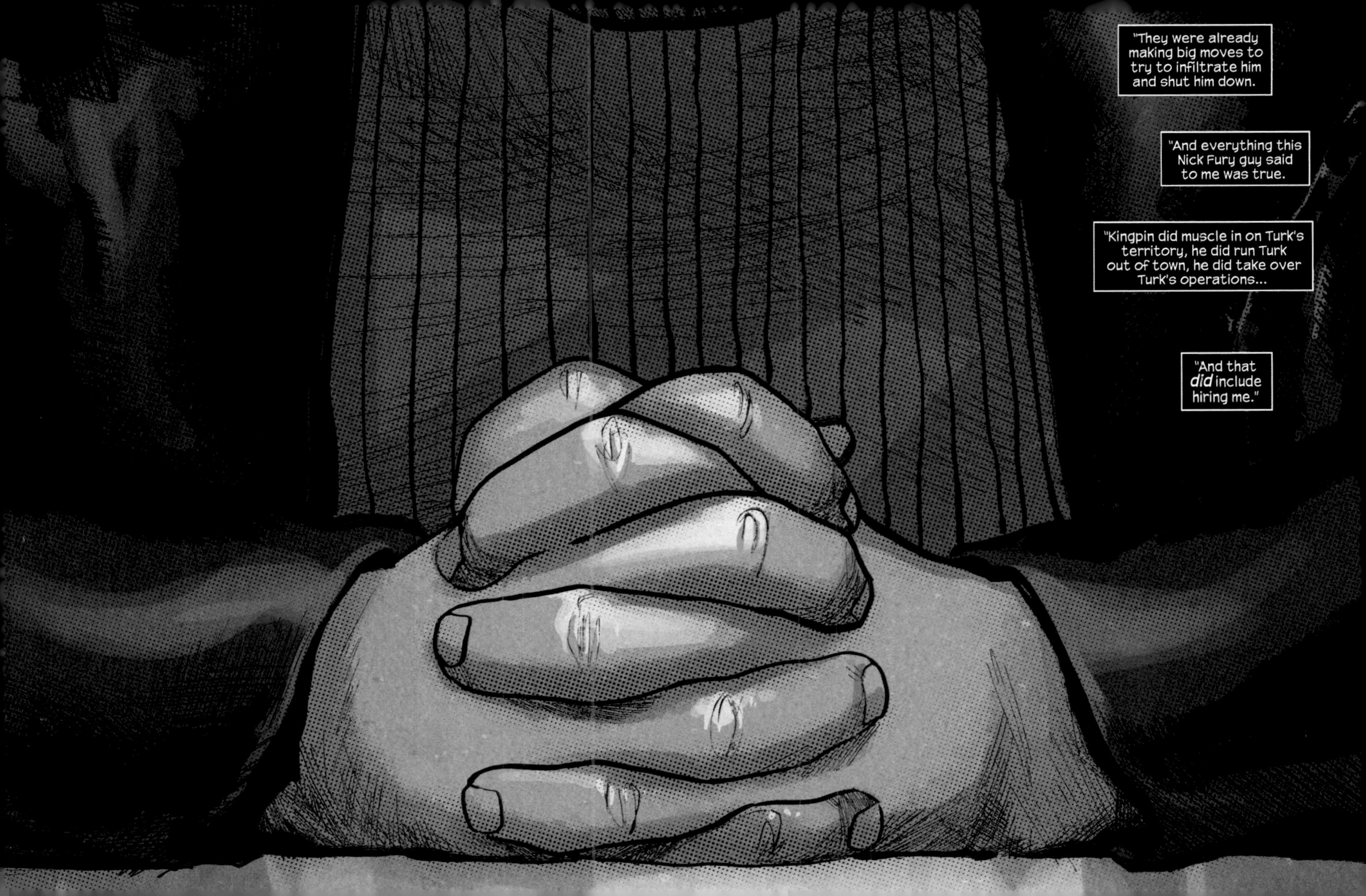

"They were already making big moves to try to infiltrate him and shut him down.
"And everything this Nick Fury guy said to me was true.
"Kingpin did muscle in on Turk's territory, he did run Turk out of town, he did take over Turk's operations...
"And that *did* include hiring me."

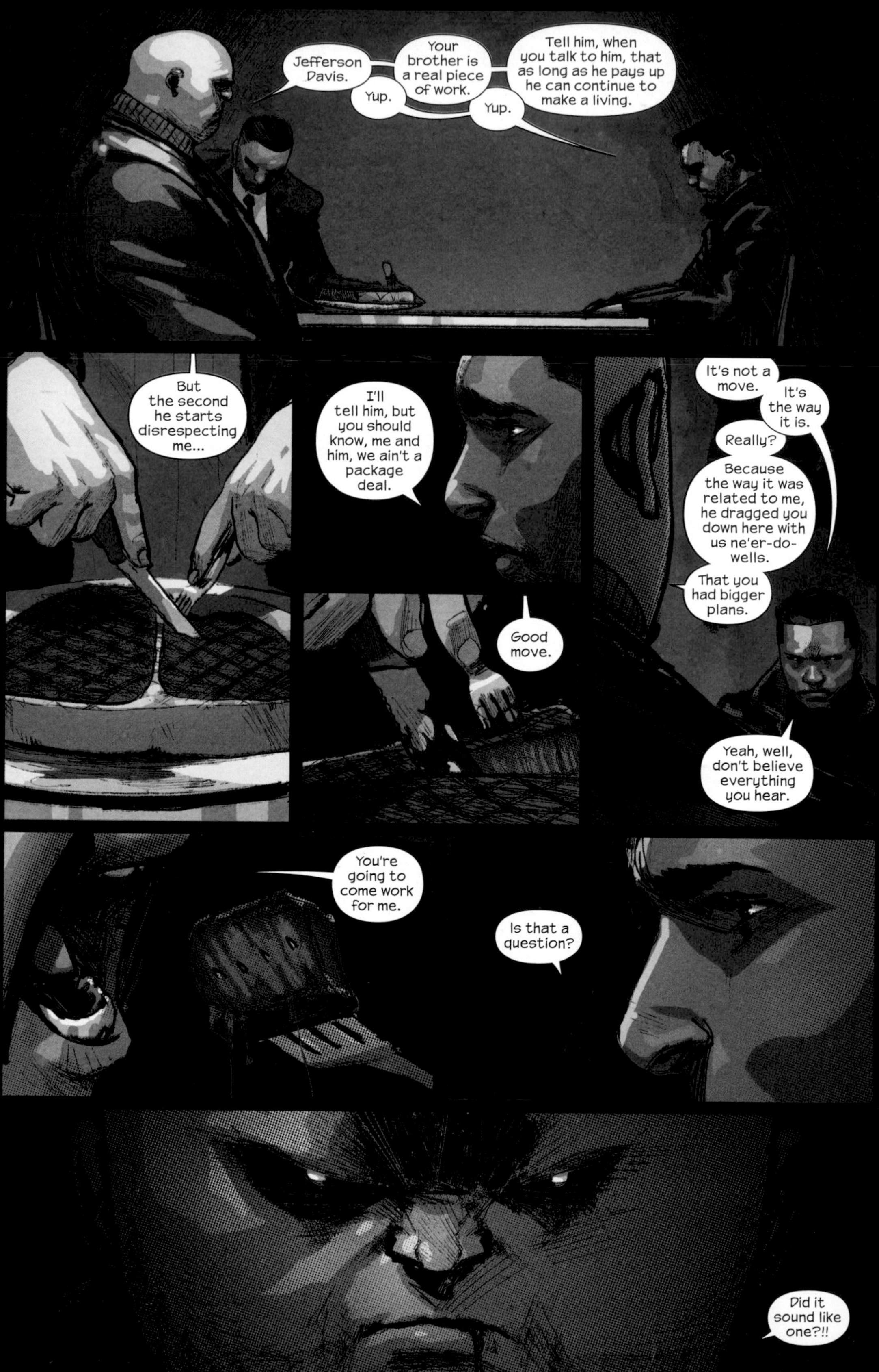
Jefferson Davis.
Your brother is a real piece of work.
Yup.
Tell him, when you talk to him, that as long as he pays up he can continue to make a living.
Yup.
But the second he starts disrespecting me...
I'll tell him, but you should know, me and him, we ain't a package deal.
Good move.
It's not a move.
It's the way it is.
Really?
Because the way it was related to me, he dragged you down here with us ne'er-do-wells.
That you had bigger plans.
Yeah, well, don't believe everything you hear.
You're going to come work for me.
Is that a question?
Did it sound like one?!!

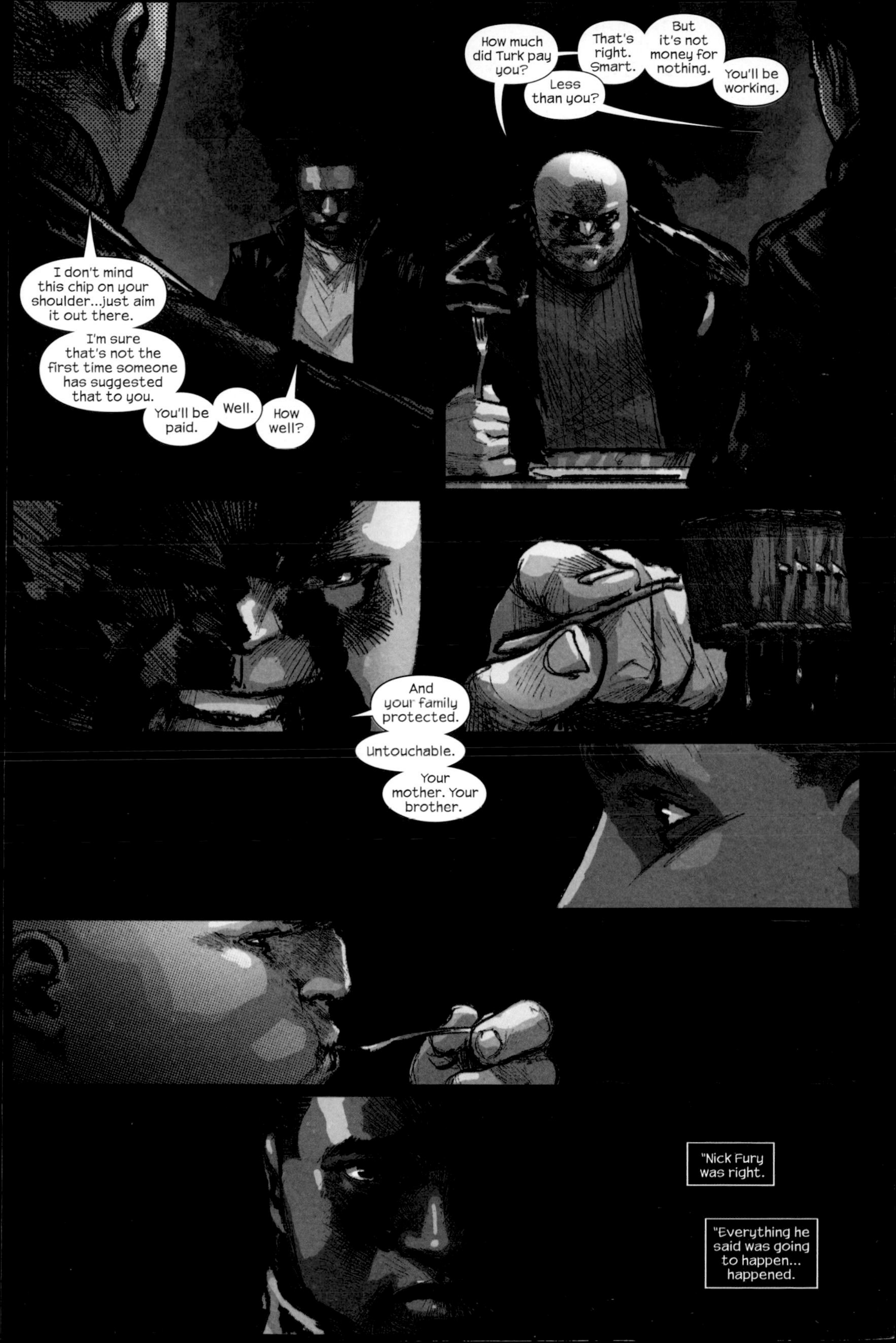
How much did Turk pay you?
That's right. Smart.
But it's not money for nothing.
You'll be working.
Less than you?
I don't mind this chip on your shoulder...just aim it out there.
I'm sure that's not the first time someone has suggested that to you.
You'll be paid.
Well.
How well?
And your family protected.
Untouchable.
Your mother. Your brother.
"Nick Fury was right.
"Everything he said was going to happen... happened.

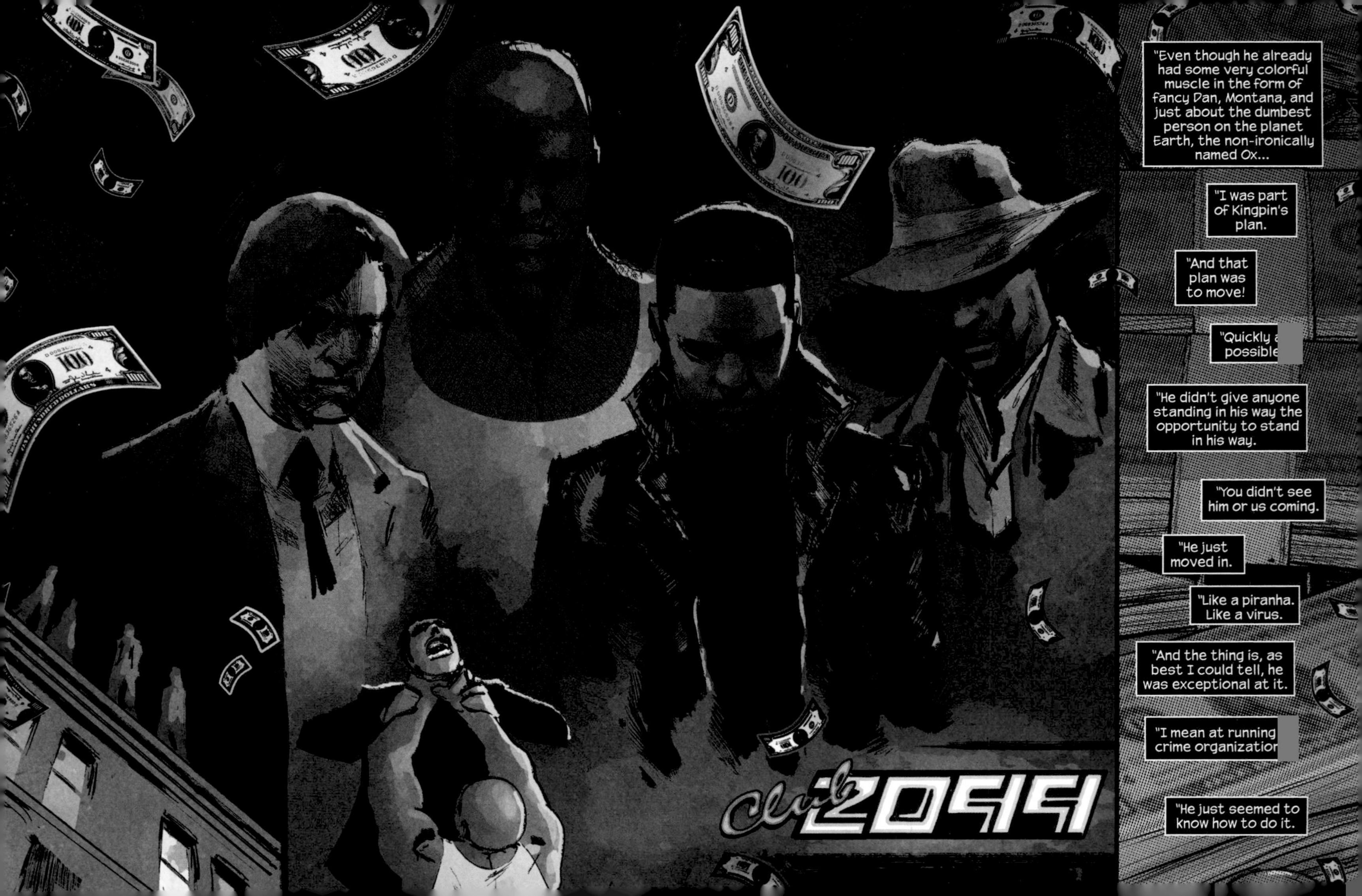

"Even though he already had some very colorful muscle in the form of fancy Dan, Montana, and just about the dumbest person on the planet Earth, the non-ironically named Ox...
"I was part of Kingpin's plan.
"And that plan was to move!
"Quickly a possible
"He didn't give anyone standing in his way the opportunity to stand in his way.
"You didn't see him or us coming.
"He just moved in.
"Like a piranha. Like a virus.
"And the thing is, as best I could tell, he was exceptional at it.
"I mean at running crime organizatior
"He just seemed to know how to do it.
Club 2099

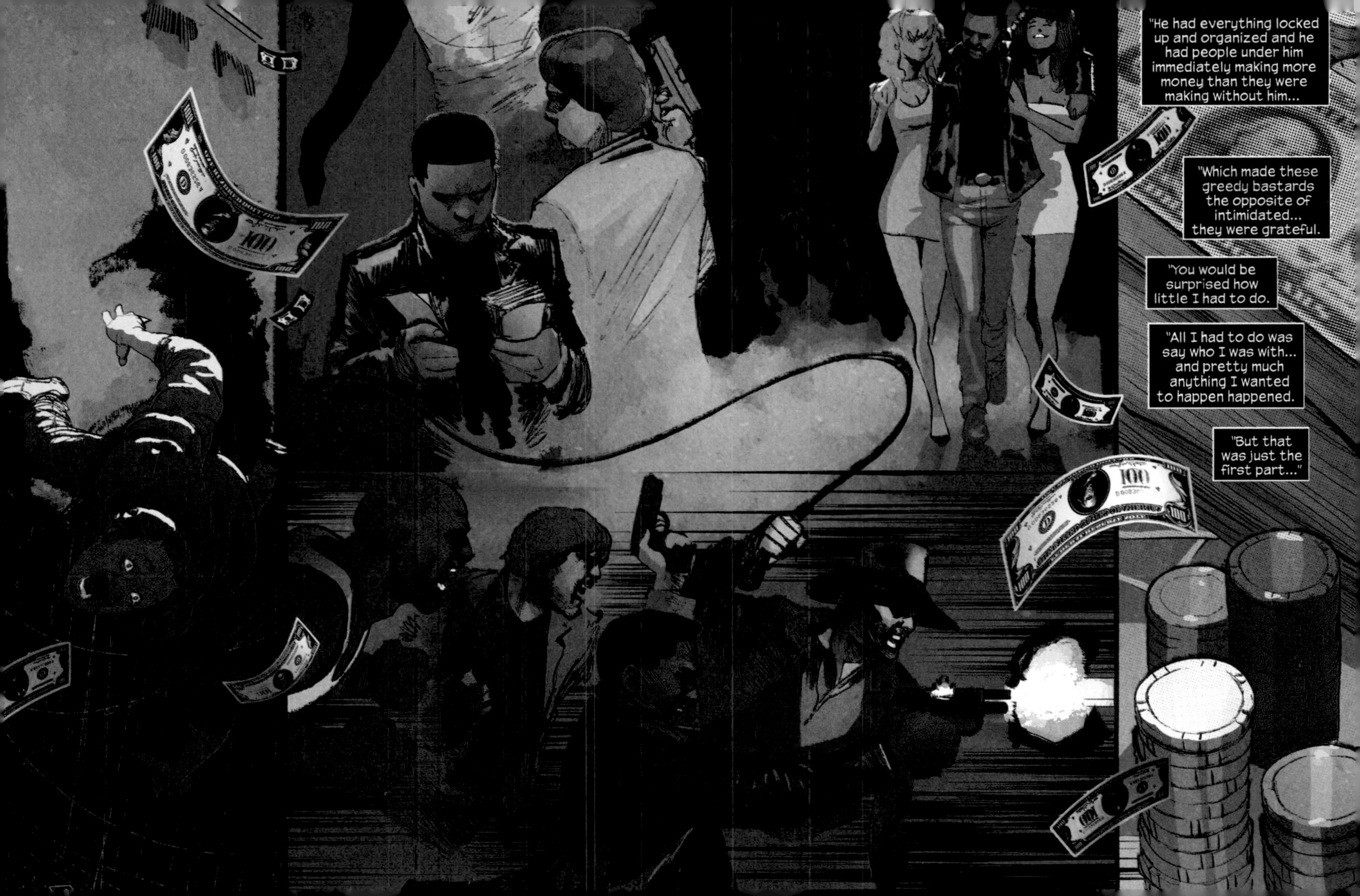
"He had everything locked up and organized and he had people under him immediately making more money than they were making without him...
"Which made these greedy bastards the opposite of intimidated... they were grateful.
"You would be surprised how little I had to do.
"All I had to do was say who I was with... and pretty much anything I wanted to happen happened.
"But that was just the first part..."

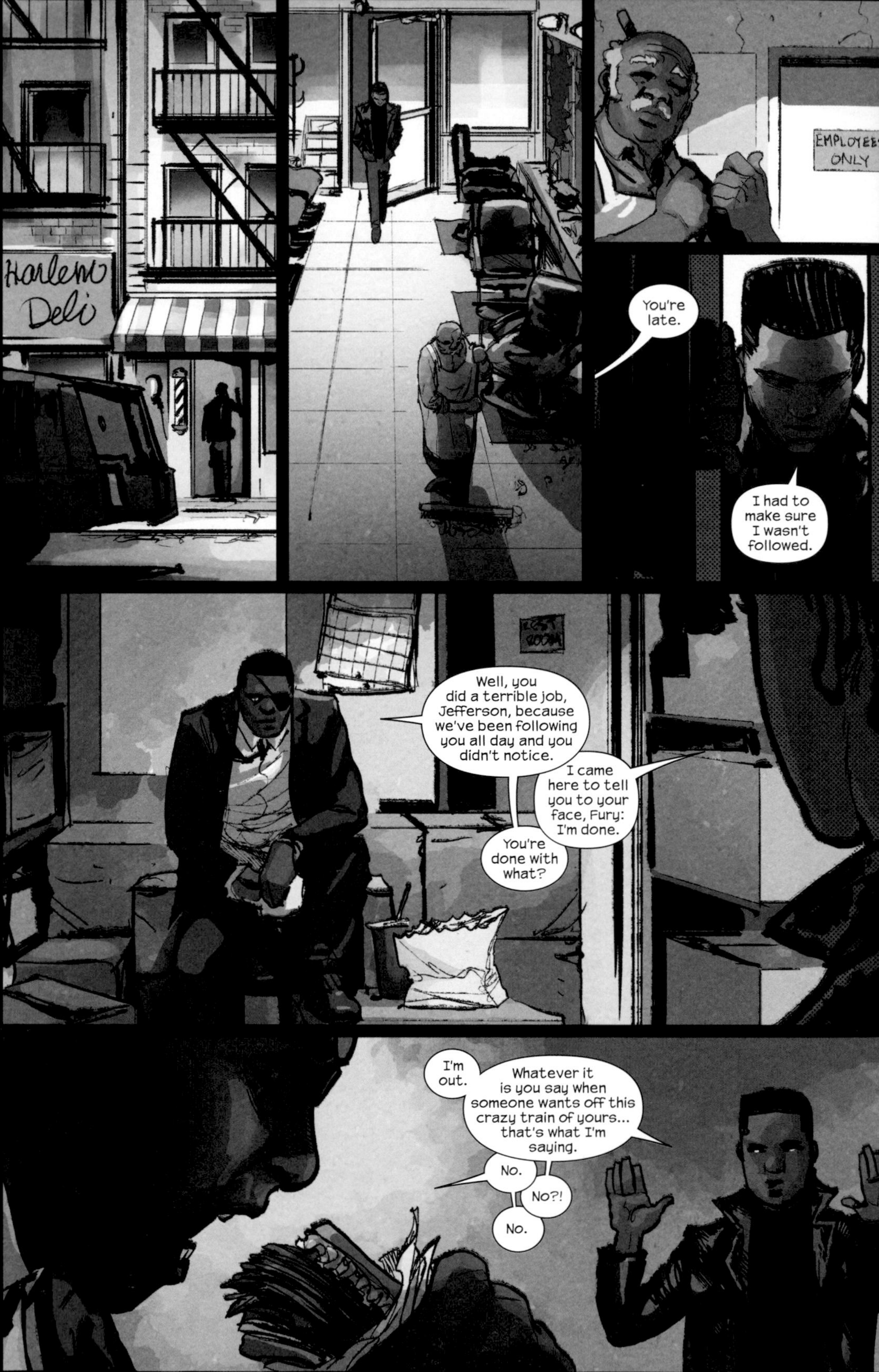
Harlem Deli
EMPLOYEES ONLY
You're late.
I had to make sure I wasn't followed.
REST ROOM
Well, you did a terrible job, Jefferson, because we've been following you all day and you didn't notice.
I came here to tell you to your face, Fury: I'm done.
You're done with what?
I'm out.
Whatever it is you say when someone wants off this crazy train of yours... that's what I'm saying.
No.
No?!
No.

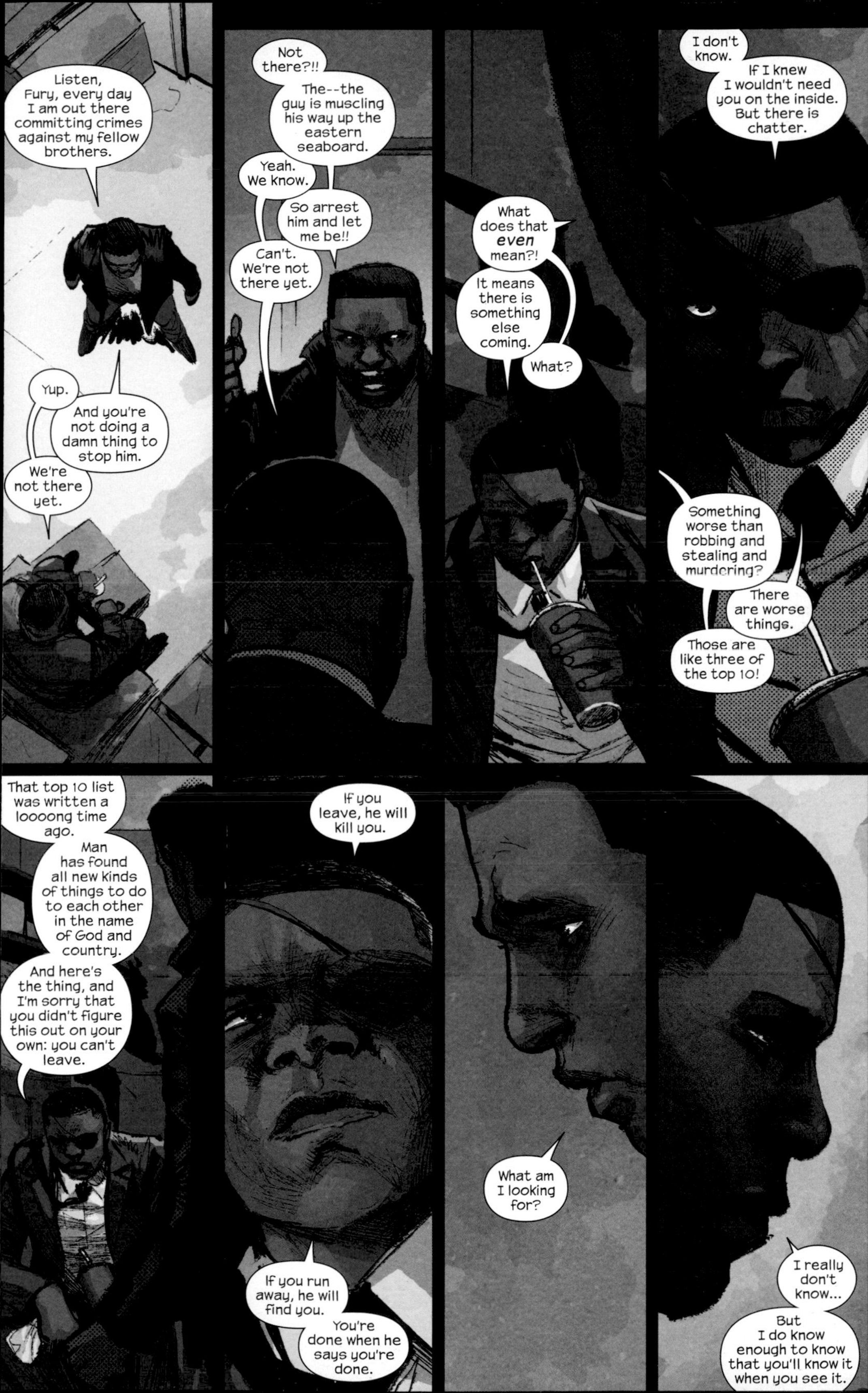
Listen, Fury, every day I am out there committing crimes against my fellow brothers.
Yup.
And you're not doing a damn thing to stop him.
We're not there yet.
Not there?!!
The--the guy is muscling his way up the eastern seaboard.
Yeah. We know.
So arrest him and let me be!!
Can't. We're not there yet.
What does that *even* mean?!
It means there is something else coming.
What?
I don't know.
If I knew I wouldn't need you on the inside. But there is chatter.
Something worse than robbing and stealing and murdering?
There are worse things.
Those are like three of the top 10!
That top 10 list was written a loooong time ago.
Man has found all new kinds of things to do to each other in the name of God and country.
And here's the thing, and I'm sorry that you didn't figure this out on your own: you can't leave.
If you leave, he will kill you.
If you run away, he will find you.
You're done when he says you're done.
What am I looking for?
I really don't know...
But I do know enough to know that you'll know it when you see it.

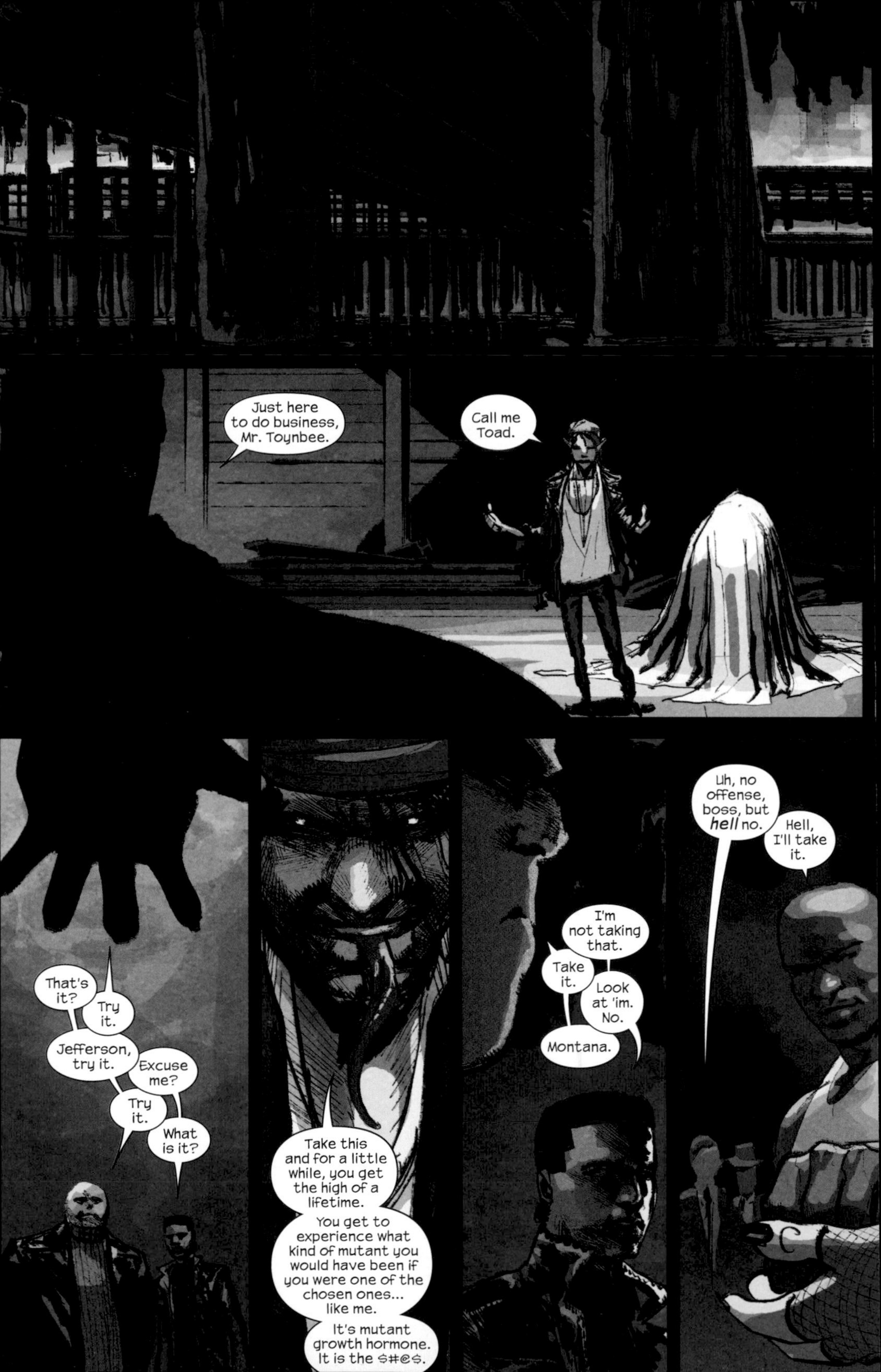

Just here to do business, Mr. Toynbee.
Call me Toad.
That's it?
Try it.
Jefferson, try it.
Excuse me?
Try it.
What is it?
Take this and for a little while, you get the high of a lifetime.
You get to experience what kind of mutant you would have been if you were one of the chosen ones... like me.
It's mutant growth hormone. It is the $#@$.
I'm not taking that.
Take it.
Look at 'im. No.
Montana.
Uh, no offense, boss, but ***hell*** no.
Hell, I'll take it.

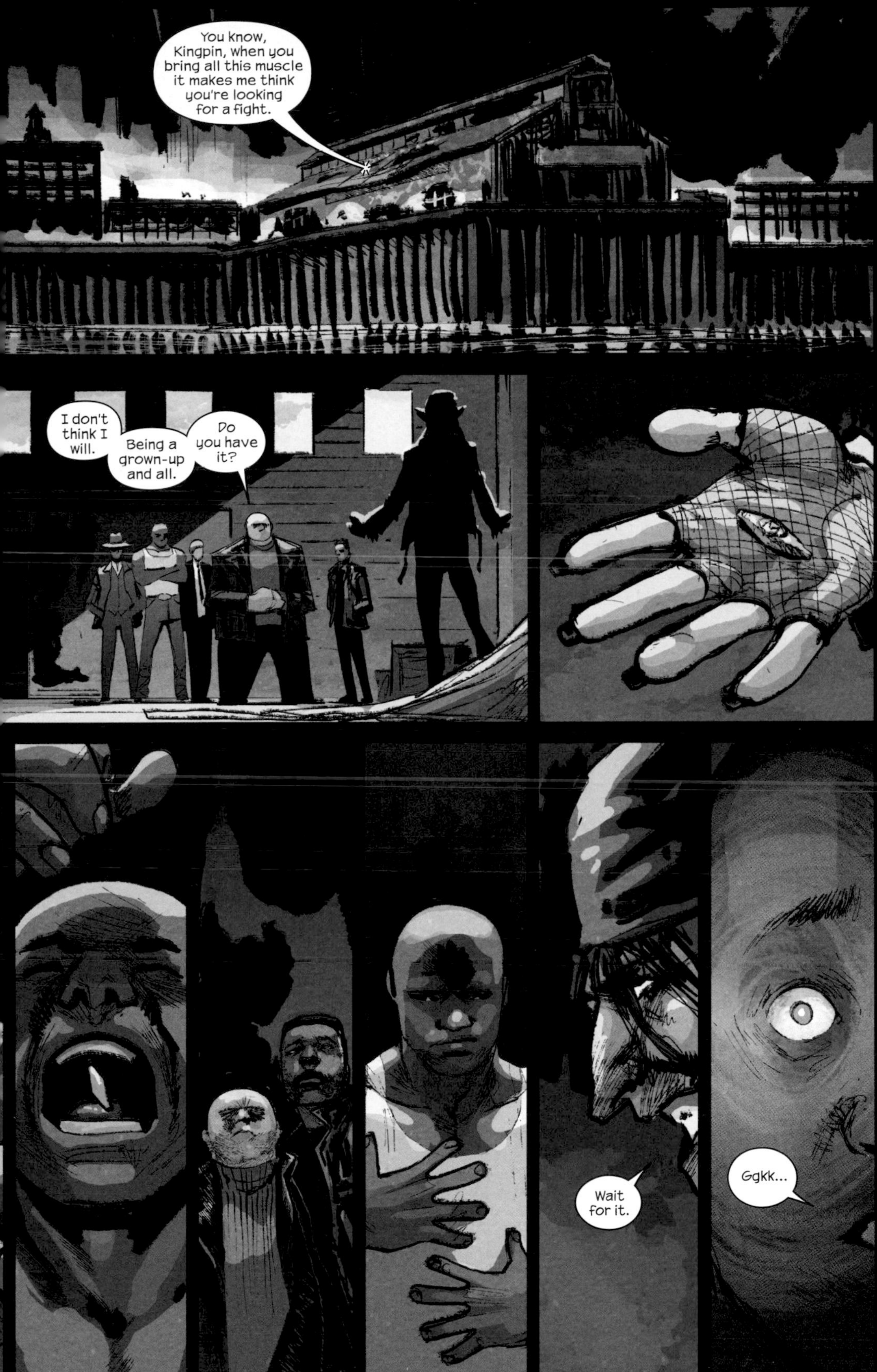
You know, Kingpin, when you bring all this muscle it makes me think you're looking for a fight.
I don't think I will.
Being a grown-up and all.
Do you have it?
Wait for it.
Ggkk...

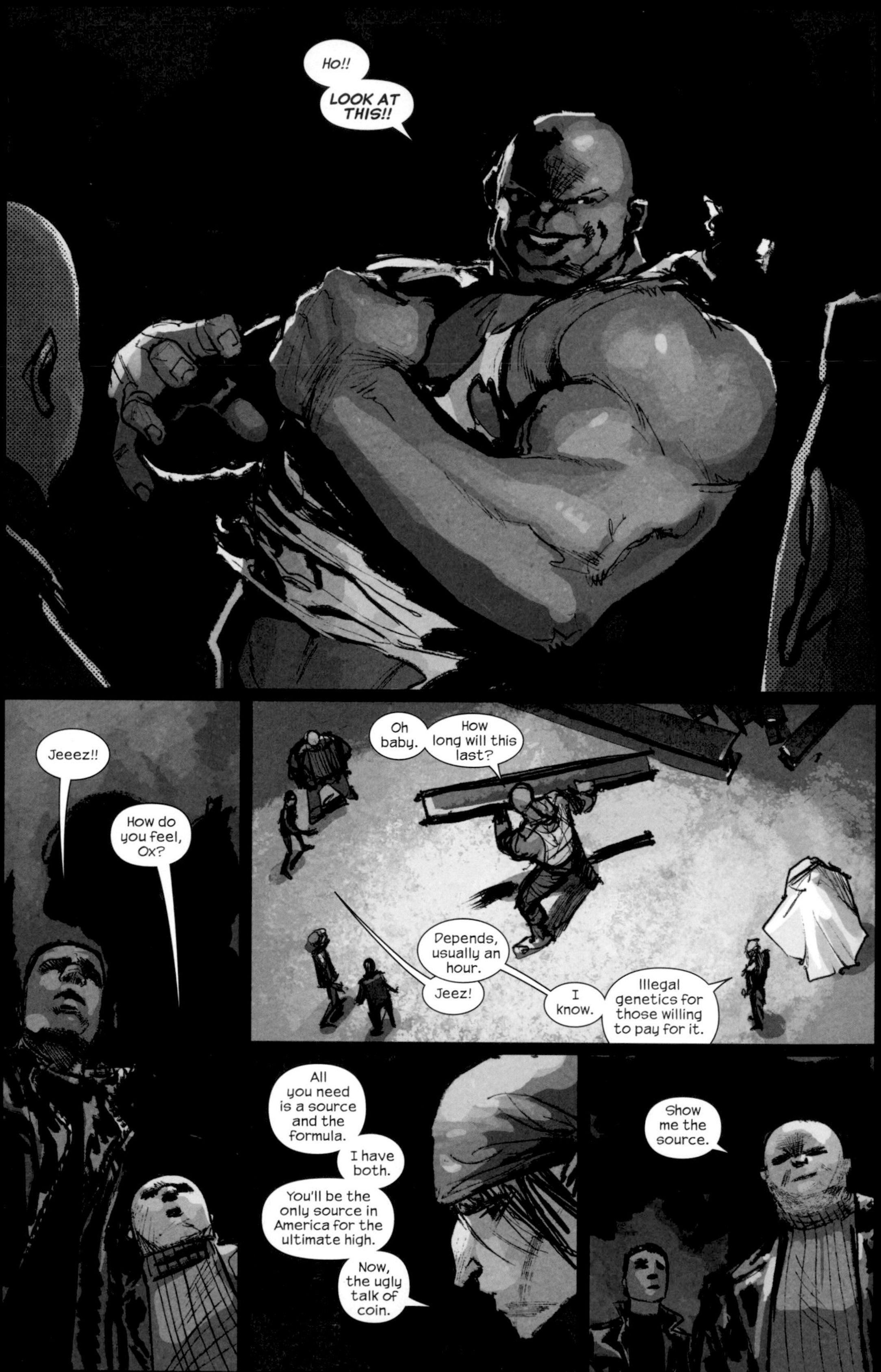
Ho!!
LOOK AT THIS!!
Jeeez!!
How do you feel, Ox?
Oh baby.
How long will this last?
Depends, usually an hour.
Jeez!
I know.
Illegal genetics for those willing to pay for it.
All you need is a source and the formula.
I have both.
You'll be the only source in America for the ultimate high.
Now, the ugly talk of coin.
Show me the source.

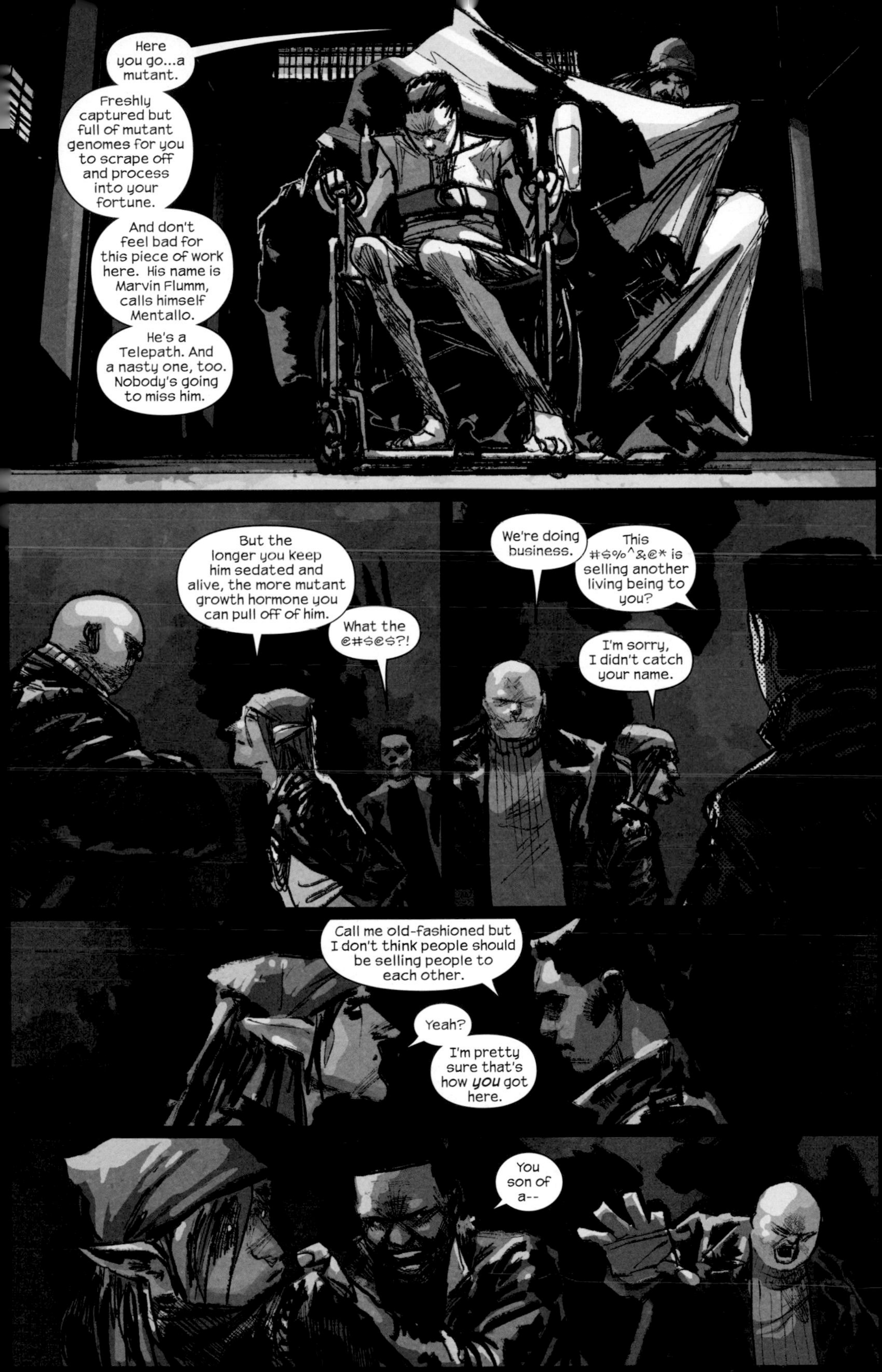

Here you go...a mutant.
Freshly captured but full of mutant genomes for you to scrape off and process into your fortune.
And don't feel bad for this piece of work here. His name is Marvin Flumm, calls himself Mentallo.
He's a Telepath. And a nasty one, too. Nobody's going to miss him.
But the longer you keep him sedated and alive, the more mutant growth hormone you can pull off of him.
What the @#$@$?!
We're doing business.
This #$%^&@* is selling another living being to you?
I'm sorry, I didn't catch your name.
Call me old-fashioned but I don't think people should be selling people to each other.
Yeah?
I'm pretty sure that's how *you* got here.
You son of a--

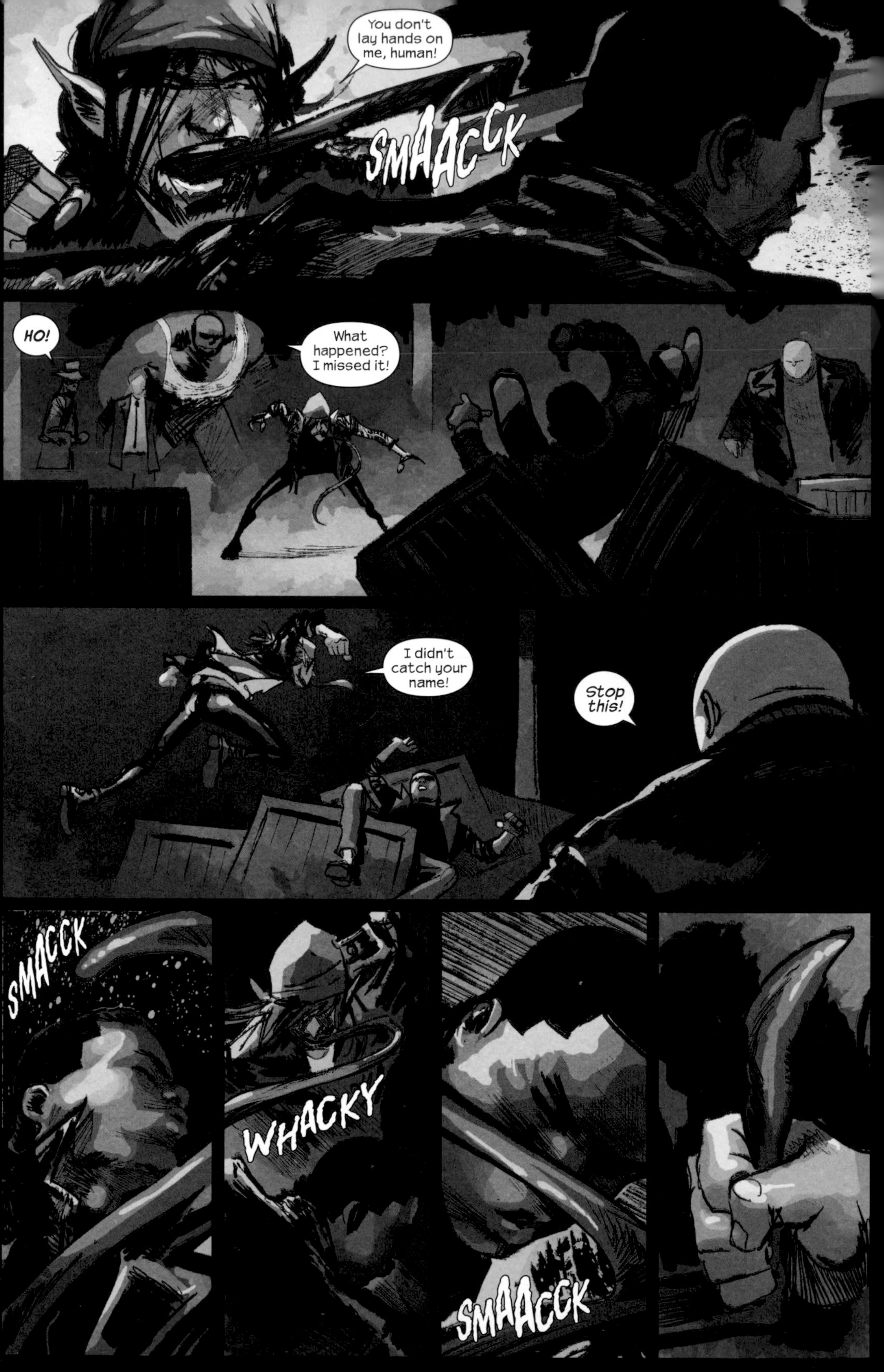
You don't lay hands on me, human!
SMAACCK
HO!
What happened? I missed it!
I didn't catch your name!
Stop this!
SMACCK
WHACKY
SMAACCK

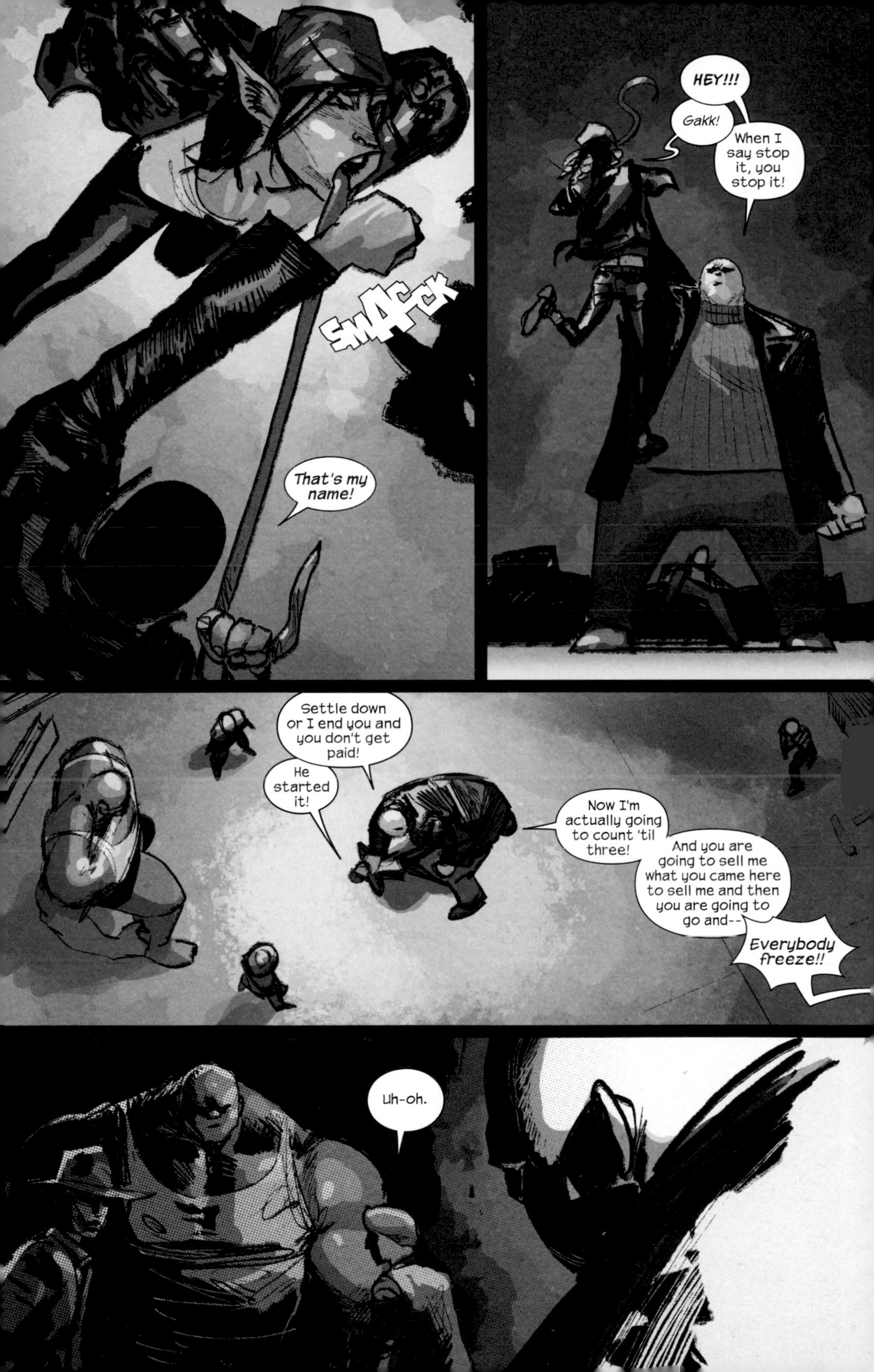
SMACK
That's my name!
HEY!!!
Gakk!
When I say stop it, you stop it!
Settle down or I end you and you don't get paid!
He started it!
Now I'm actually going to count 'til three!
And you are going to sell me what you came here to sell me and then you are going to go and--
Everybody freeze!!
Uh-oh.

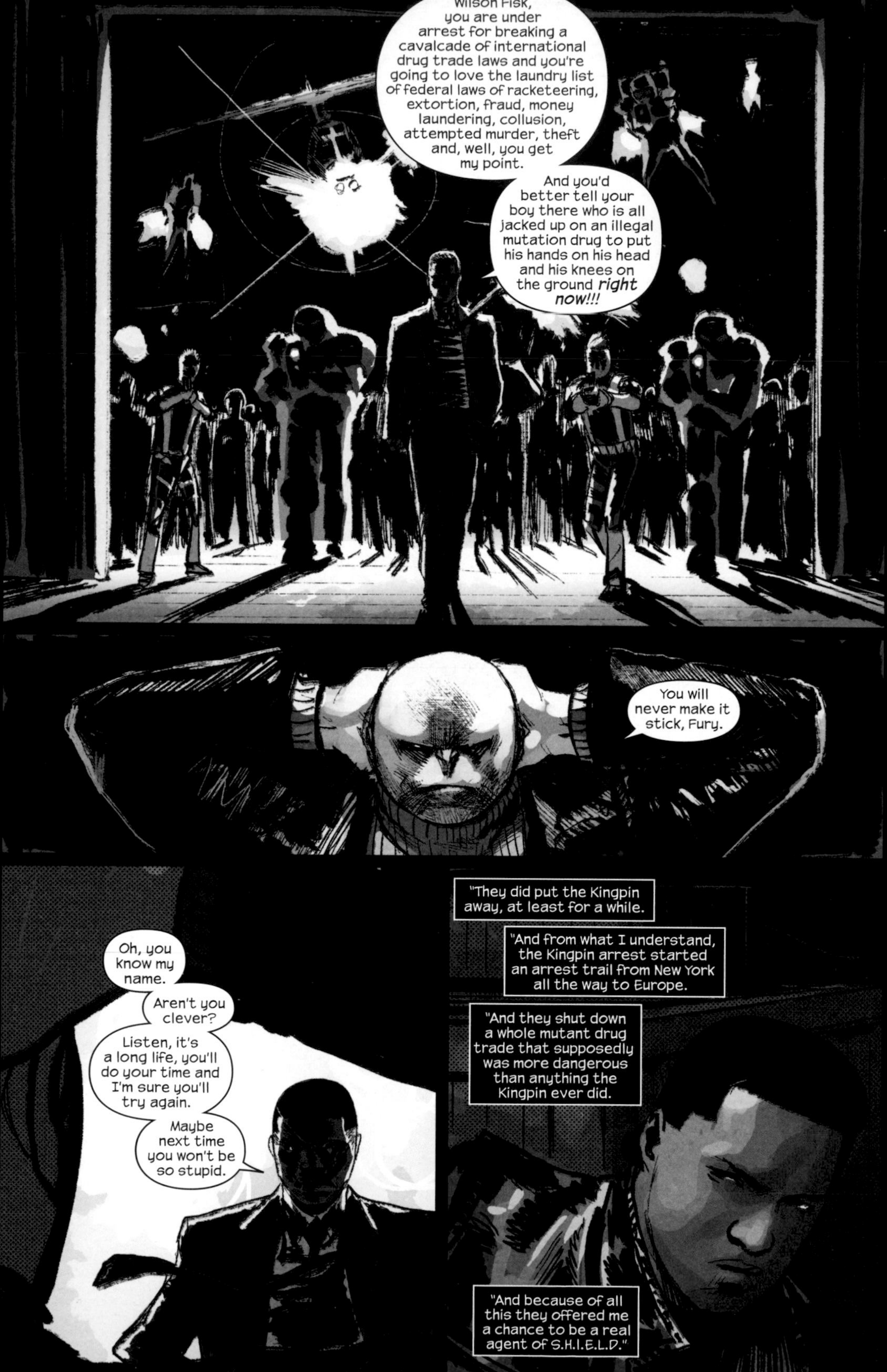
Wilson Fisk, you are under arrest for breaking a cavalcade of international drug trade laws and you're going to love the laundry list of federal laws of racketeering, extortion, fraud, money laundering, collusion, attempted murder, theft and, well, you get my point.
And you'd better tell your boy there who is all jacked up on an illegal mutation drug to put his hands on his head and his knees on the ground *right now!!!*
You will never make it stick, Fury.
Oh, you know my name.
Aren't you clever?
Listen, it's a long life, you'll do your time and I'm sure you'll try again.
Maybe next time you won't be so stupid.
"They did put the Kingpin away, at least for a while.
"And from what I understand, the Kingpin arrest started an arrest trail from New York all the way to Europe.
"And they shut down a whole mutant drug trade that supposedly was more dangerous than anything the Kingpin ever did.
"And because of all this they offered me a chance to be a real agent of S.H.I.E.L.D."

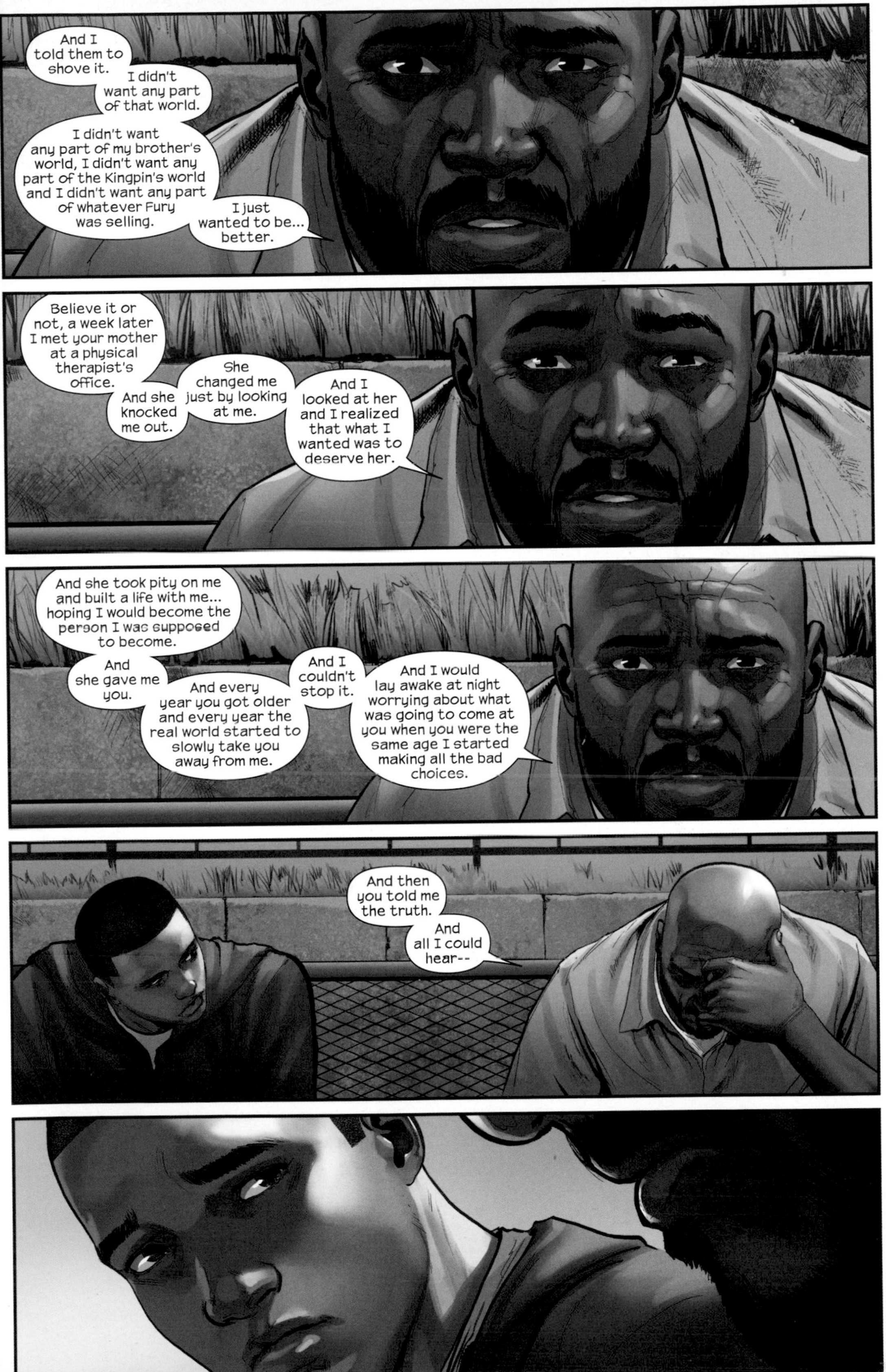

And I told them to shove it.
I didn't want any part of that world.
I didn't want any part of my brother's world, I didn't want any part of the Kingpin's world and I didn't want any part of whatever Fury was selling.
I just wanted to be... better.
Believe it or not, a week later I met your mother at a physical therapist's office.
And she knocked me out.
She changed me just by looking at me.
And I looked at her and I realized that what I wanted was to deserve her.
And she took pity on me and built a life with me... hoping I would become the person I was supposed to become.
And she gave me you.
And every year you got older and every year the real world started to slowly take you away from me.
And I couldn't stop it.
And I would lay awake at night worrying about what was going to come at you when you were the same age I started making all the bad choices.
And then you told me the truth.
And all I could hear--

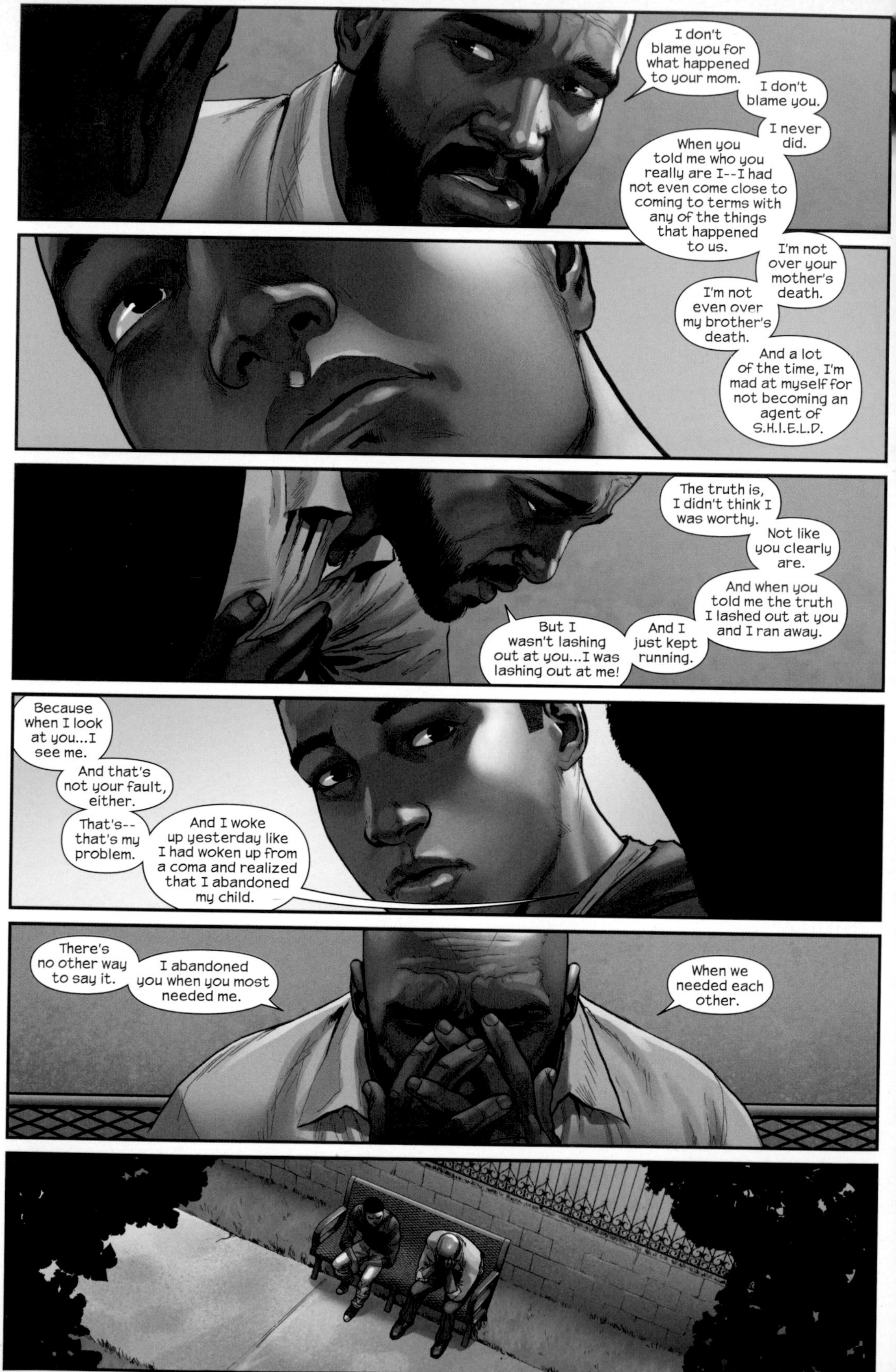

I don't blame you for what happened to your mom.
I don't blame you.
I never did.
When you told me who you really are I--I had not even come close to coming to terms with any of the things that happened to us.
I'm not over your mother's death.
I'm not even over my brother's death.
And a lot of the time, I'm mad at myself for not becoming an agent of S.H.I.E.L.D.
The truth is, I didn't think I was worthy.
Not like you clearly are.
And when you told me the truth I lashed out at you and I ran away.
And I just kept running.
But I wasn't lashing out at you...I was lashing out at me!
Because when I look at you...I see me.
And that's not your fault, either.
That's--that's my problem.
And I woke up yesterday like I had woken up from a coma and realized that I abandoned my child.
There's no other way to say it.
I abandoned you when you most needed me.
When we needed each other.

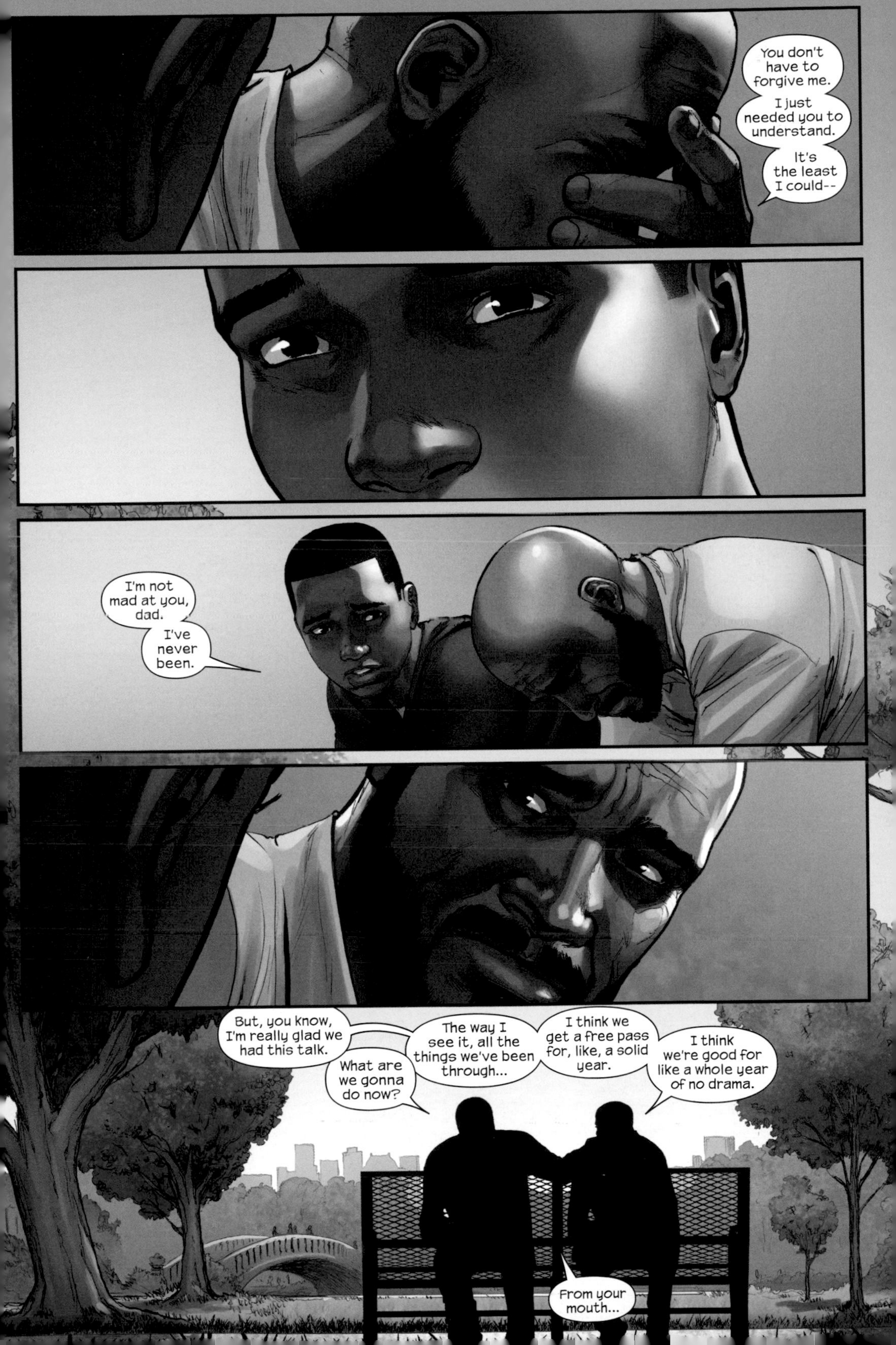
You don't have to forgive me.
I just needed you to understand.
It's the least I could--
I'm not mad at you, dad.
I've never been.
But, you know, I'm really glad we had this talk.
What are we gonna do now?
The way I see it, all the things we've been through...
I think we get a free pass for, like, a solid year.
I think we're good for like a whole year of no drama.
From your mouth...

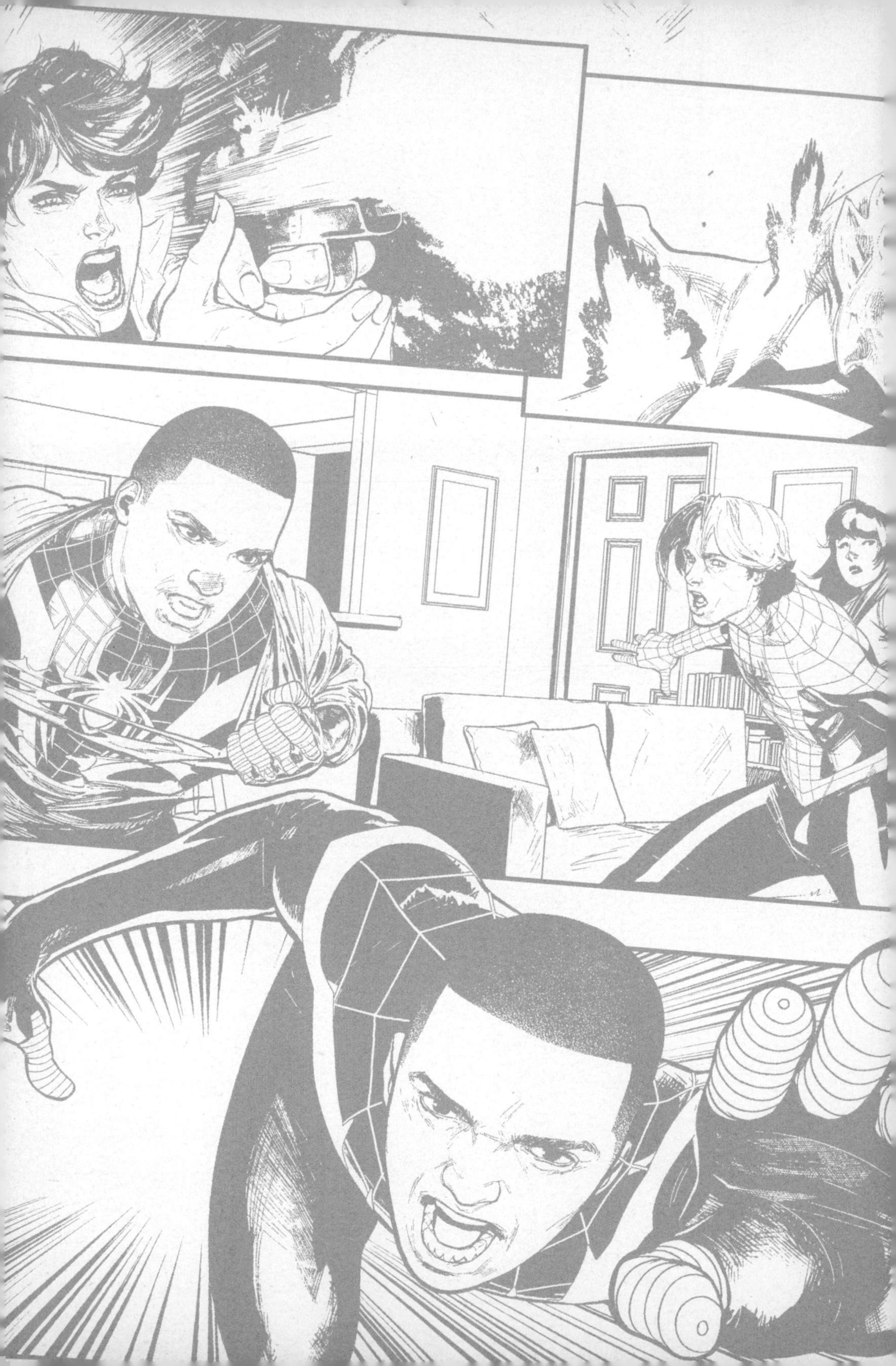

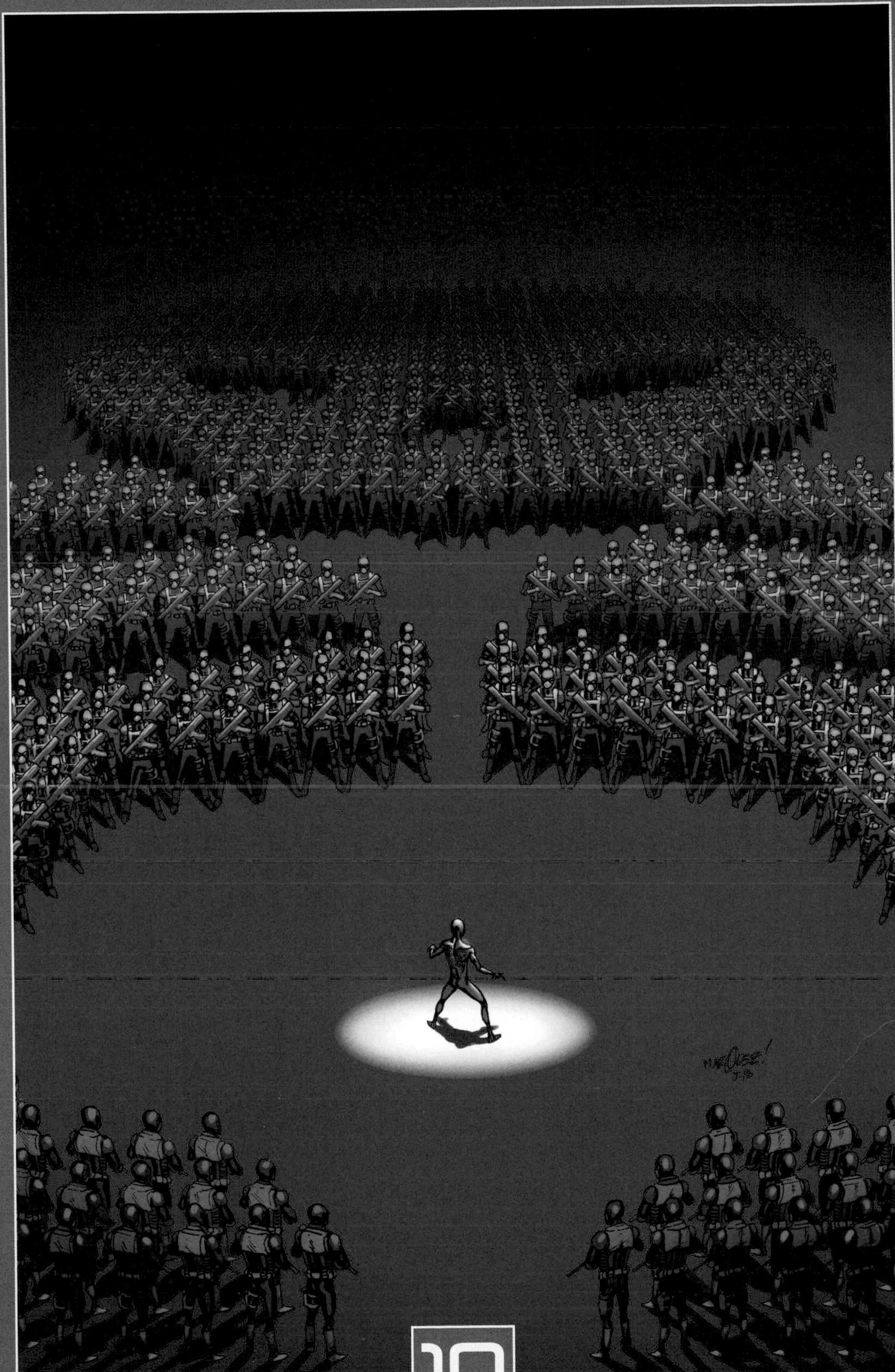

10

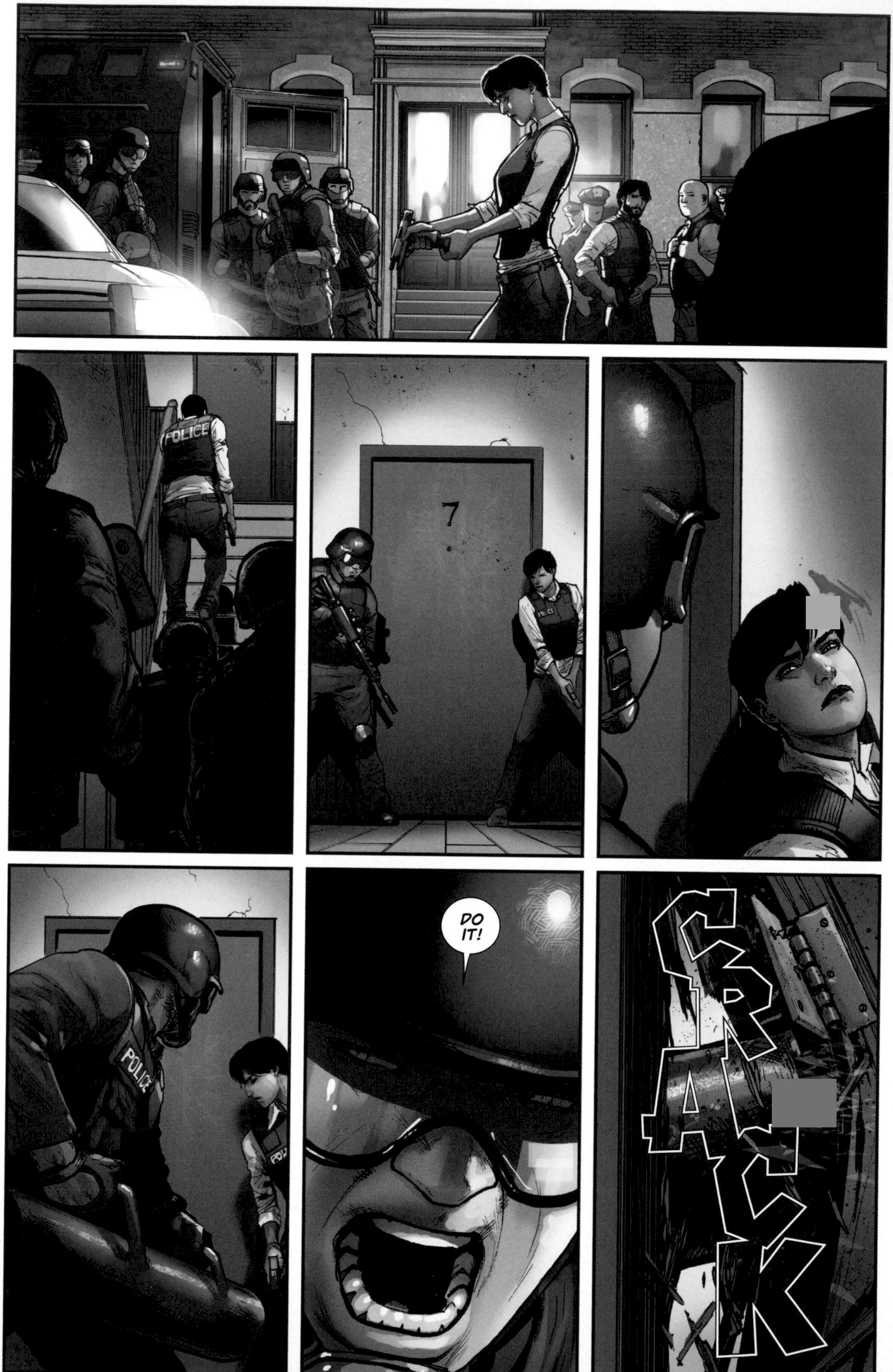
POLICE
7
POLICE
DO IT!
CRACK

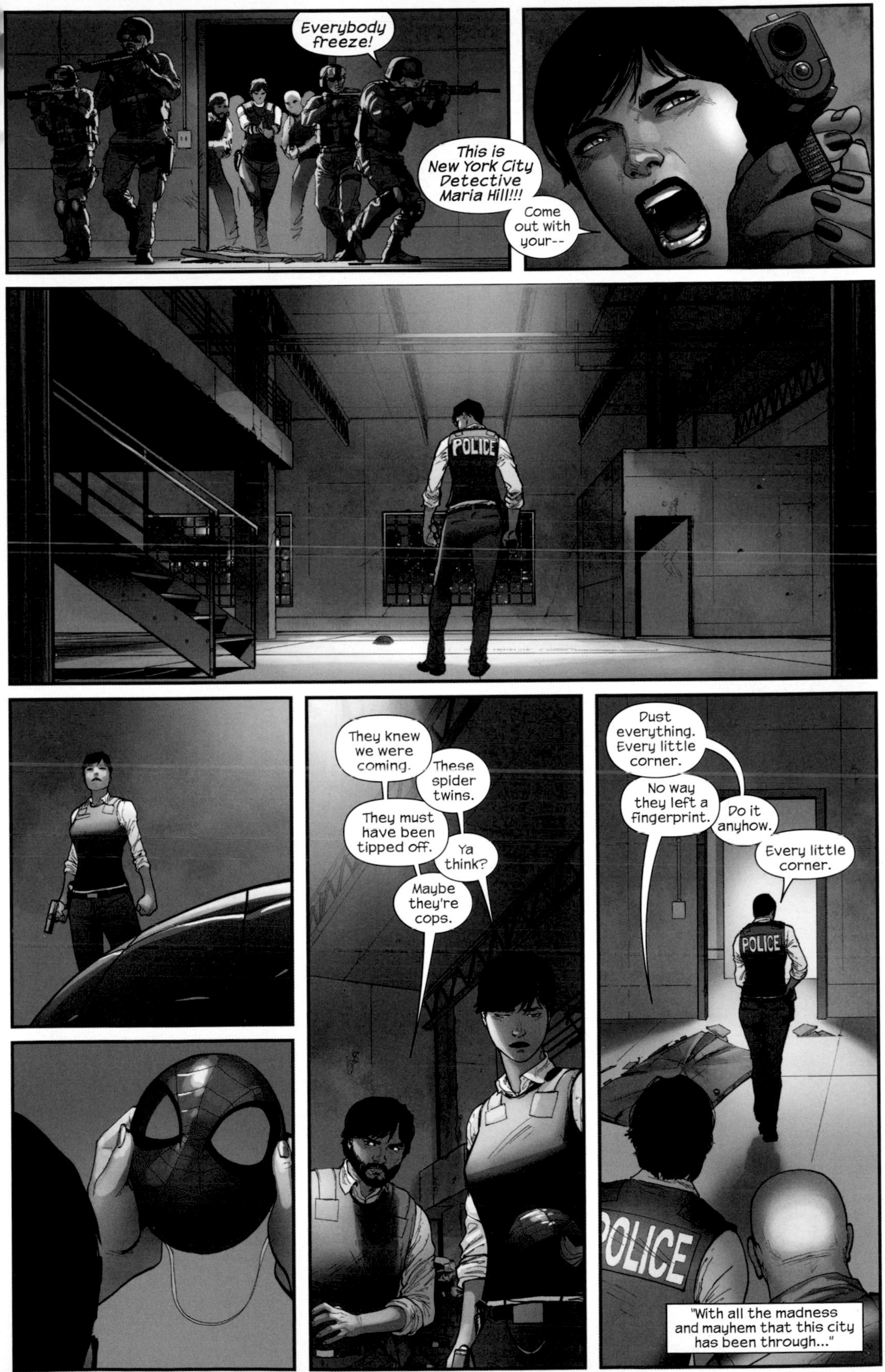

Everybody freeze!
This is New York City Detective Maria Hill!!!
Come out with your--
They knew we were coming.
These spider twins.
They must have been tipped off.
Ya think?
Maybe they're cops.
Dust everything. Every little corner.
No way they left a fingerprint.
Do it anyhow.
Every little corner.
"With all the madness and mayhem that this city has been through..."

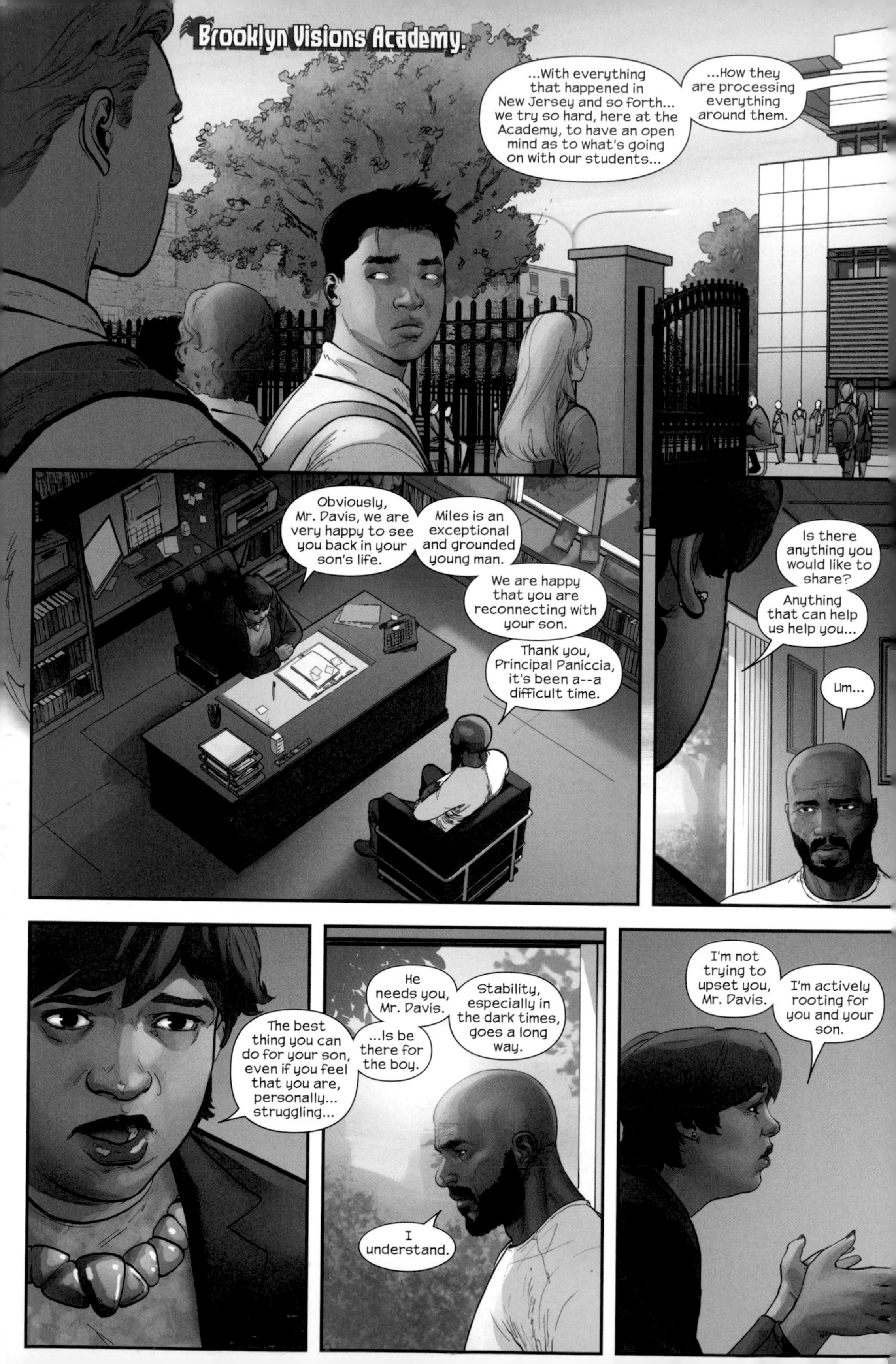
Brooklyn Visions Academy.
...With everything that happened in New Jersey and so forth... we try so hard, here at the Academy, to have an open mind as to what's going on with our students...
...How they are processing everything around them.
Obviously, Mr. Davis, we are very happy to see you back in your son's life.
Miles is an exceptional and grounded young man.
We are happy that you are reconnecting with your son.
Thank you, Principal Paniccia, it's been a--a difficult time.
Is there anything you would like to share?
Anything that can help us help you...
Um...
The best thing you can do for your son, even if you feel that you are, personally... struggling...
He needs you, Mr. Davis.
...Is be there for the boy.
Stability, especially in the dark times, goes a long way.
I understand.
I'm not trying to upset you, Mr. Davis.
I'm actively rooting for you and your son.

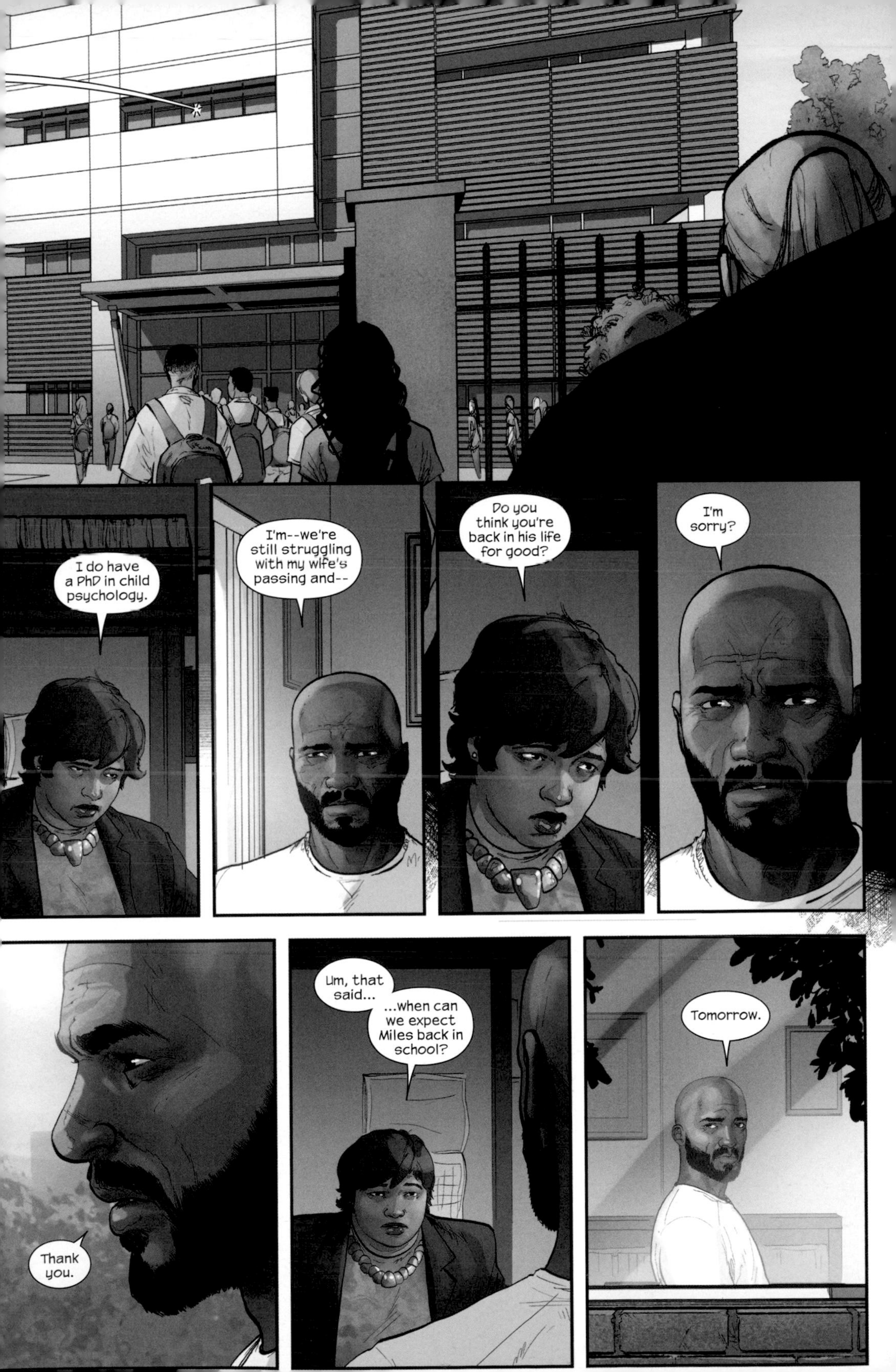

I do have a PhD in child psychology.
I'm--we're still struggling with my wife's passing and--
Do you think you're back in his life for good?
I'm sorry?
Thank you.
Um, that said...
...when can we expect Miles back in school?
Tomorrow.

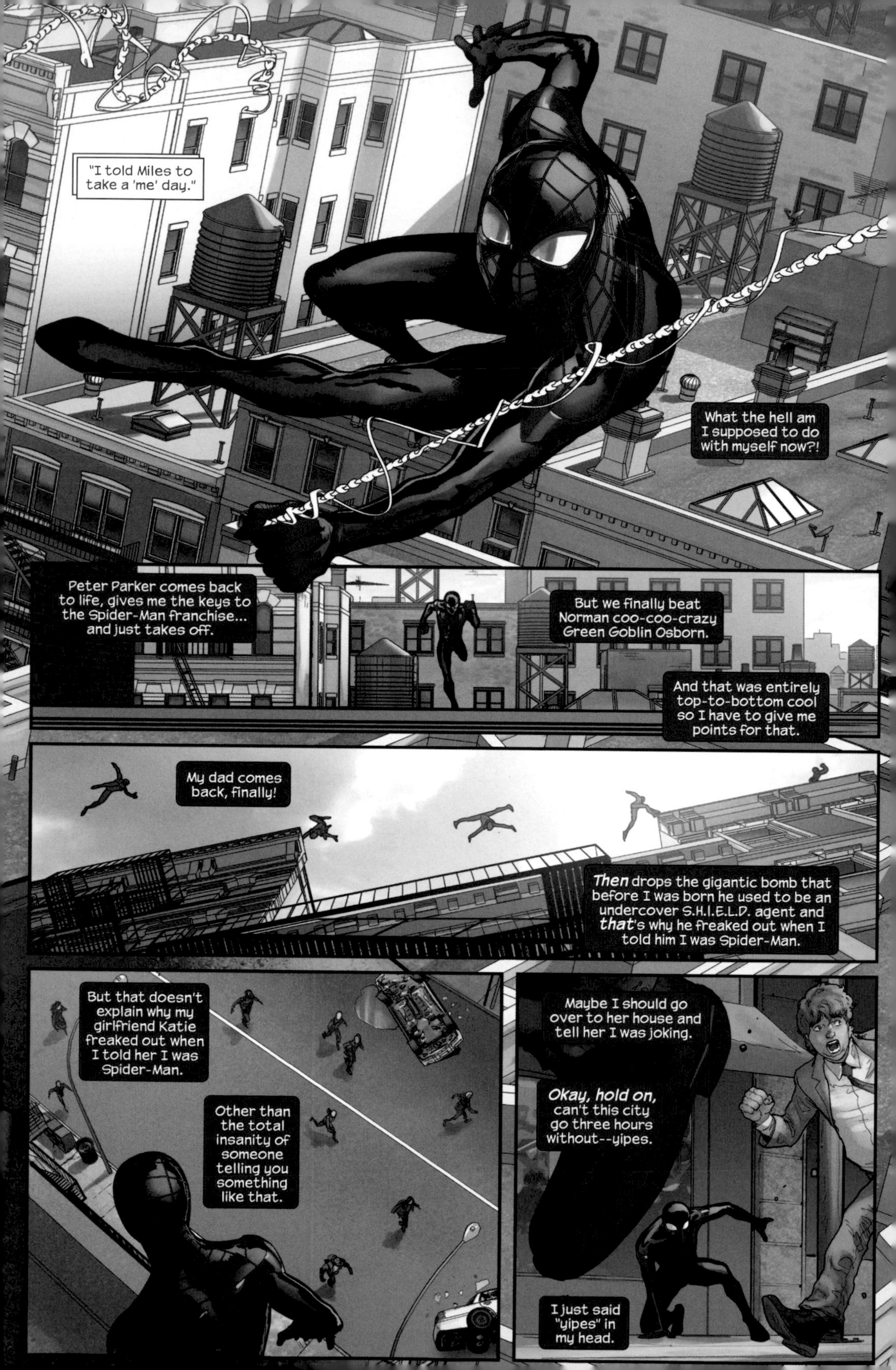
"I told Miles to take a 'me' day."
What the hell am I supposed to do with myself now?!
Peter Parker comes back to life, gives me the keys to the Spider-Man franchise... and just takes off.
But we finally beat Norman coo-coo-crazy Green Goblin Osborn.
And that was entirely top-to-bottom cool so I have to give me points for that.
My dad comes back, finally!
Then drops the gigantic bomb that before I was born he used to be an undercover S.H.I.E.L.D. agent and *that*'s why he freaked out when I told him I was Spider-Man.
But that doesn't explain why my girlfriend Katie freaked out when I told her I was Spider-Man.
Other than the total insanity of someone telling you something like that.
Maybe I should go over to her house and tell her I was joking.
Okay, hold on, can't this city go three hours without--yipes.
I just said "yipes" in my head.

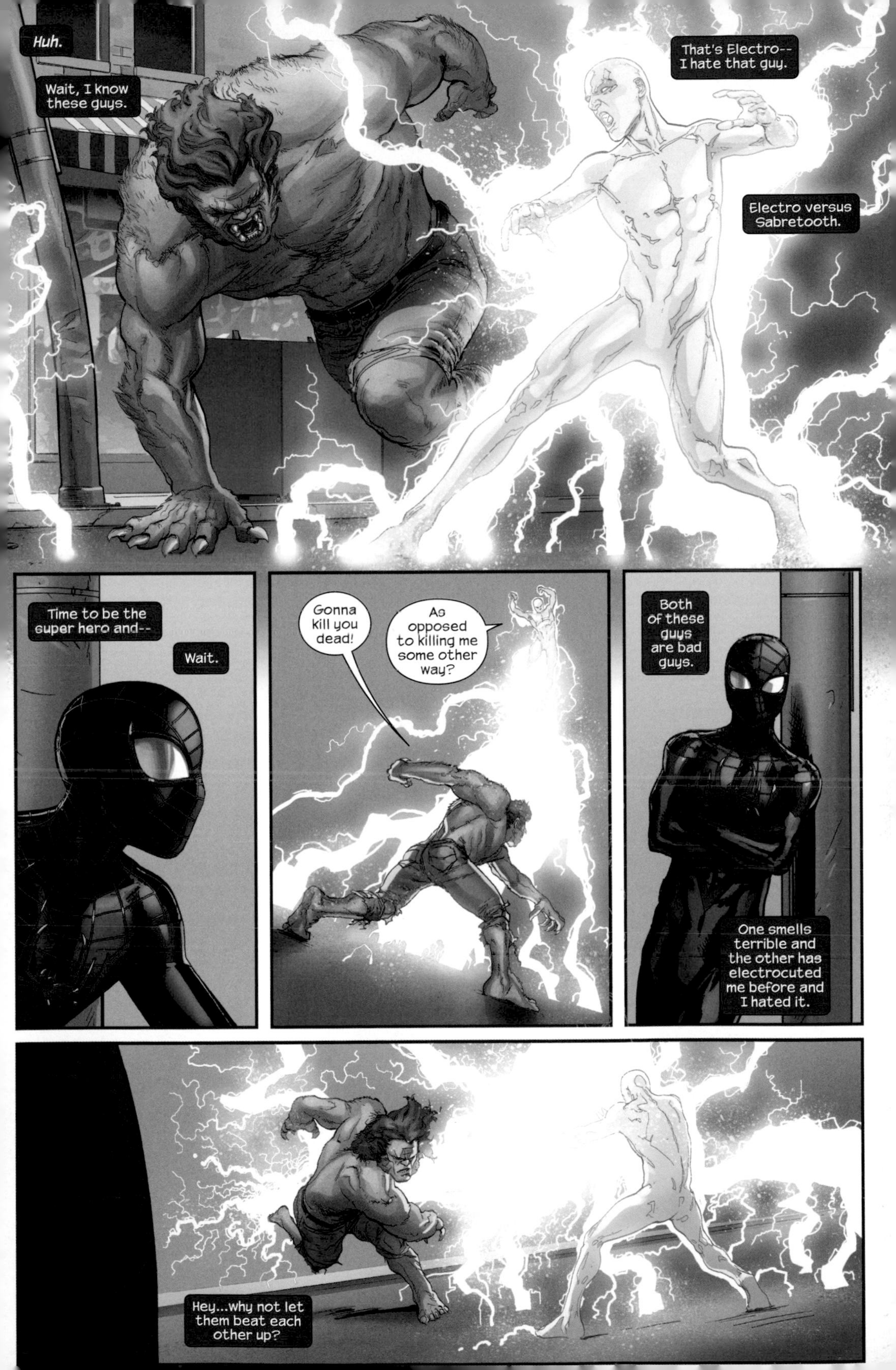
Huh.
Wait, I know these guys.
That's Electro-- I hate that guy.
Electro versus Sabretooth.
Time to be the super hero and--
Wait.
Gonna kill you dead!
As opposed to killing me some other way?
Both of these guys are bad guys.
One smells terrible and the other has electrocuted me before and I hated it.
Hey...why not let them beat each other up?

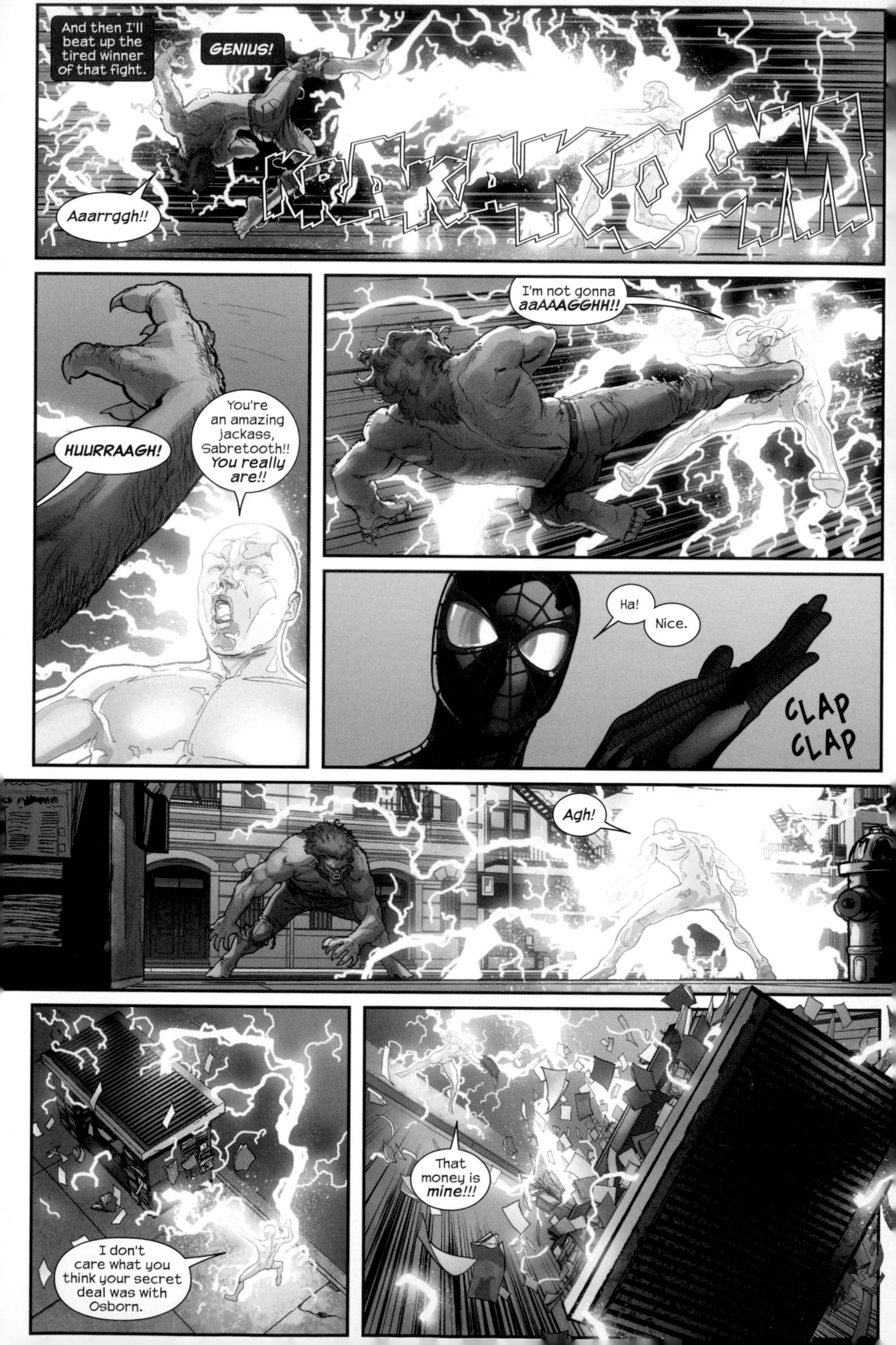
And then I'll beat up the tired winner of that fight.
GENIUS!
KRAKAKOOM
Aaarrggh!!
HUURRAAGH!
You're an amazing jackass, Sabretooth!! You really are!!
I'm not gonna aaAAAGGHH!!
Ha!
Nice.
CLAP CLAP
Agh!
I don't care what you think your secret deal was with Osborn.
That money is mine!!!

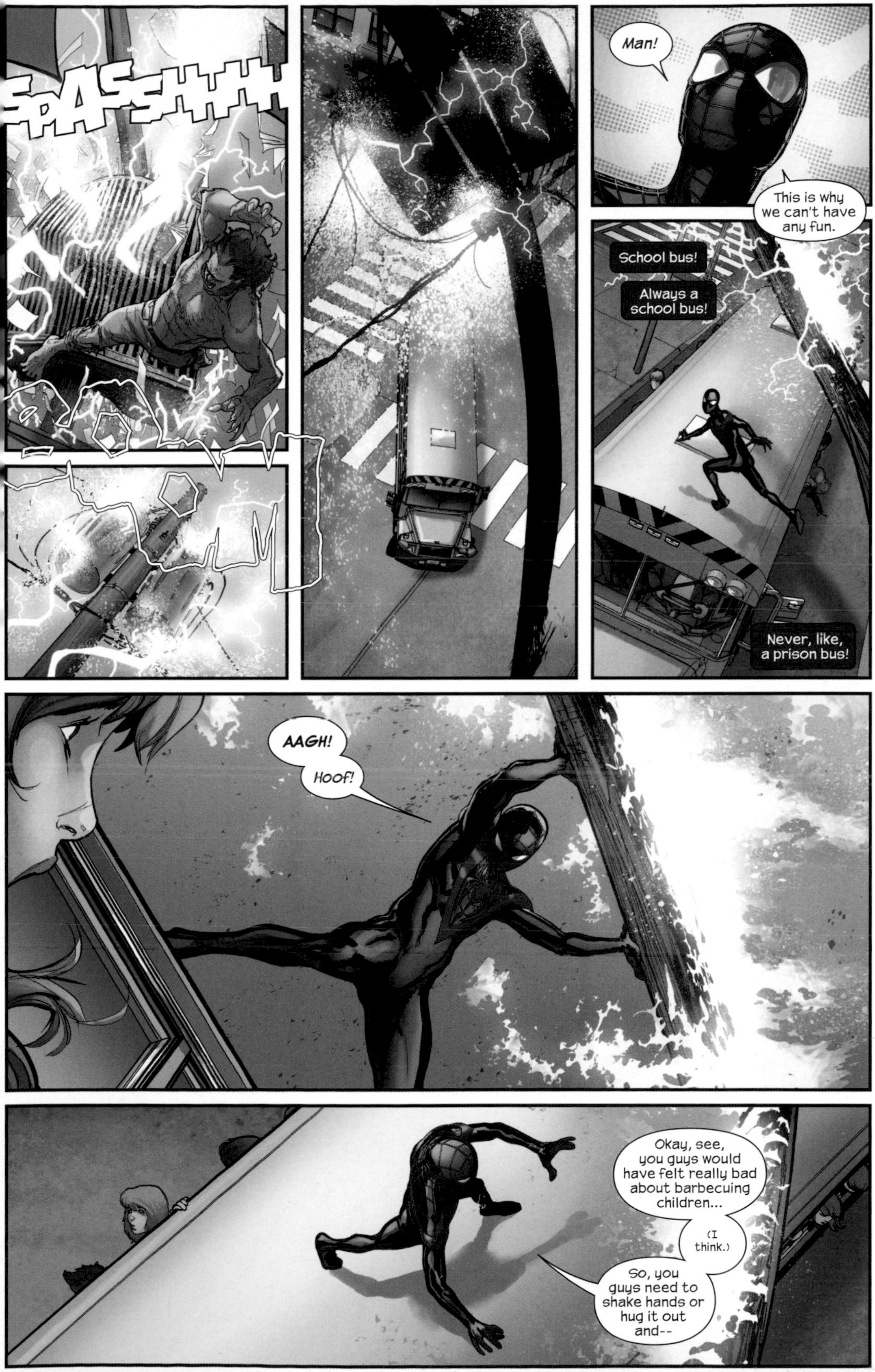
SPASHHHH
BOOOMMM
Man!
This is why we can't have any fun.
School bus!
Always a school bus!
Never, like, a prison bus!
AAGH!
HOOF!
Okay, see, you guys would have felt really bad about barbecuing children...
(I think.)
So, you guys need to shake hands or hug it out and--

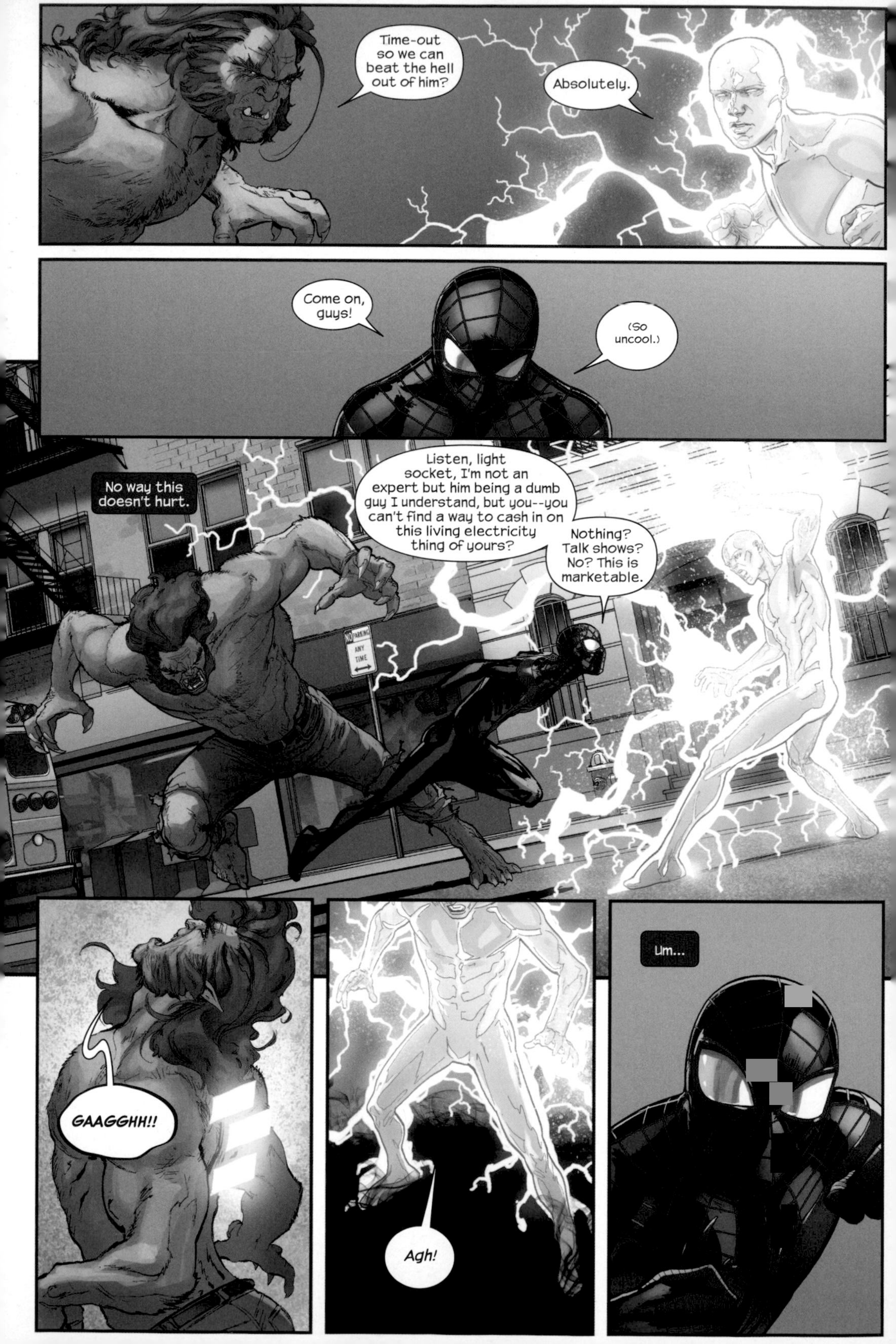
Time-out so we can beat the hell out of him?
Absolutely.
Come on, guys!
(So uncool.)
No way this doesn't hurt.
Listen, light socket, I'm not an expert but him being a dumb guy I understand, but you--you can't find a way to cash in on this living electricity thing of yours?
Nothing? Talk shows? No? This is marketable.
GAAGGHH!!
Agh!
Um...

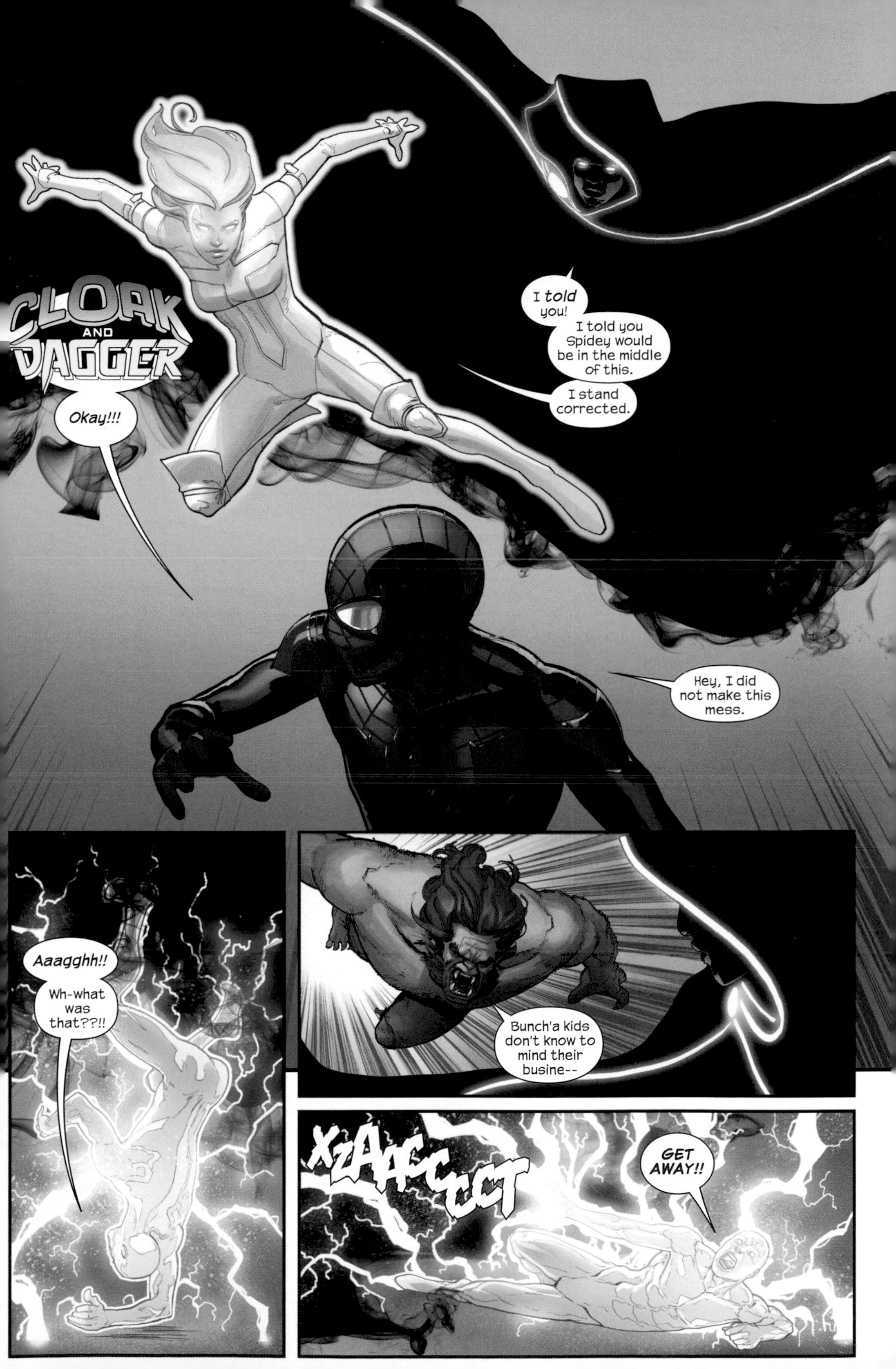
CLOAK AND DAGGER
I told you! I told you Spidey would be in the middle of this.
I stand corrected.
Okay!!!
Hey, I did not make this mess.
Aaagghh!!
Wh-what was that??!!
Bunch'a kids don't know to mind their busine--
XZAACCCCT
GET AWAY!!

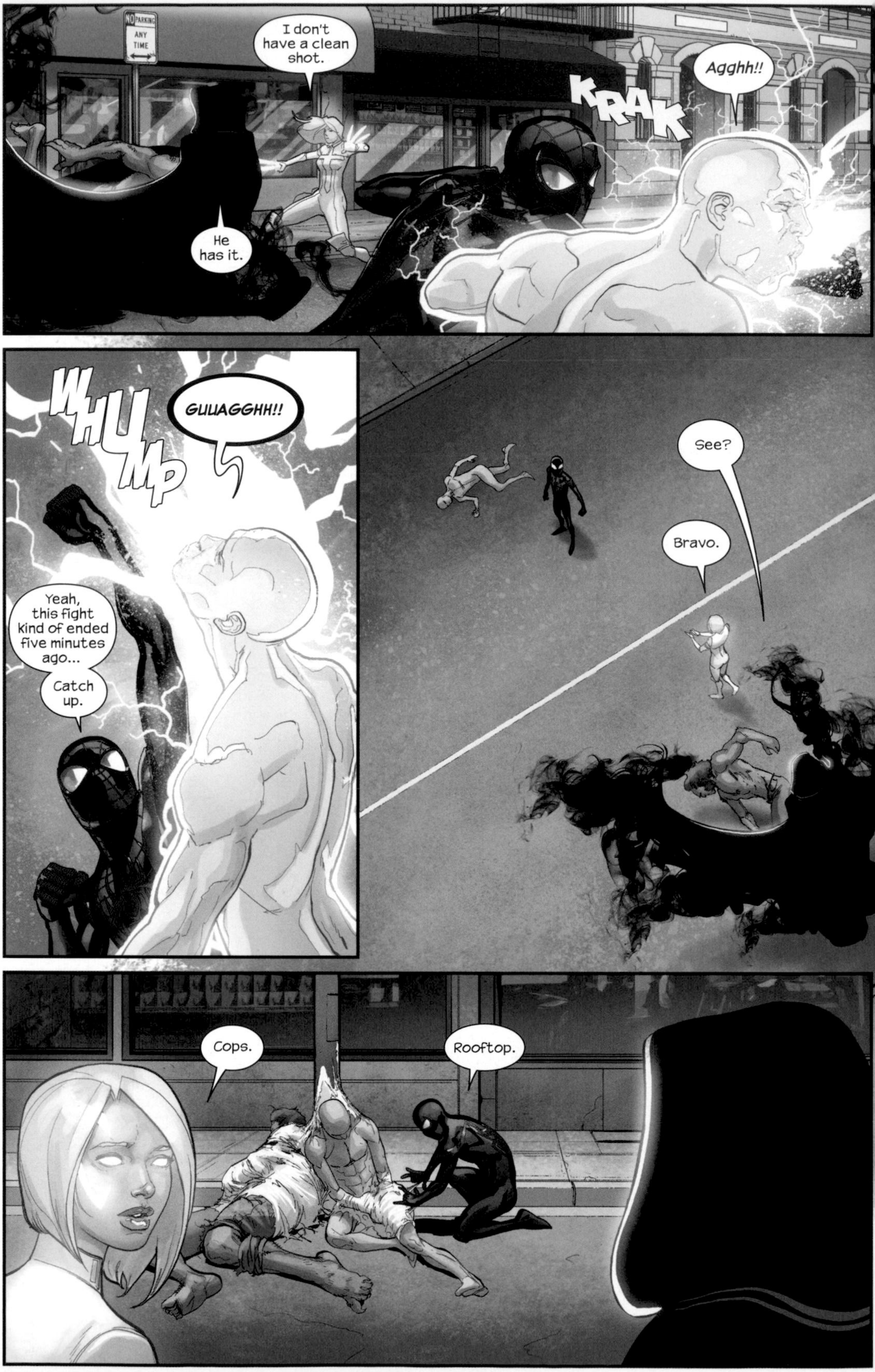
NO PARKING ANY TIME
I don't have a clean shot.
He has it.
KRAK
Agghh!!
WHUMP
GUUAGGHH!!
Yeah, this fight kind of ended five minutes ago...
Catch up.
See?
Bravo.
Cops.
Rooftop.

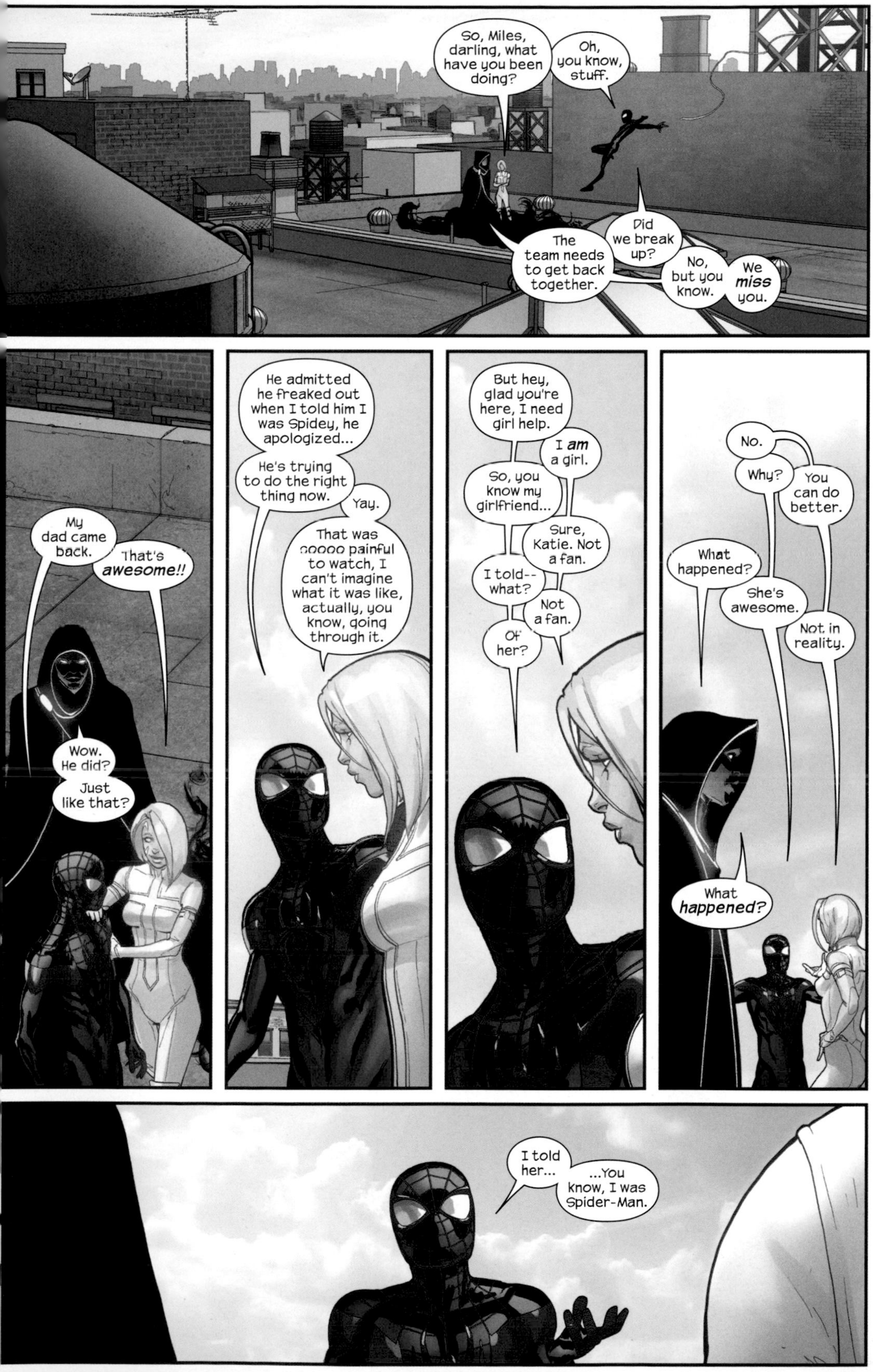

So, Miles, darling, what have you been doing?
Oh, you know, stuff.
The team needs to get back together.
Did we break up?
No, but you know.
We *miss* you.
My dad came back.
That's ***awesome!!***
Wow. He did?
Just like that?
He admitted he freaked out when I told him I was Spidey, he apologized...
He's trying to do the right thing now.
Yay.
That was sooooo painful to watch, I can't imagine what it was like, actually, you know, going through it.
But hey, glad you're here, I need girl help.
I *am* a girl.
So, you know my girlfriend...
Sure, Katie. Not a fan.
I told--what?
Not a fan.
Of her?
No.
Why?
You can do better.
What happened?
She's awesome.
Not in reality.
What ***happened?***
I told her...
...You know, I was Spider-Man.

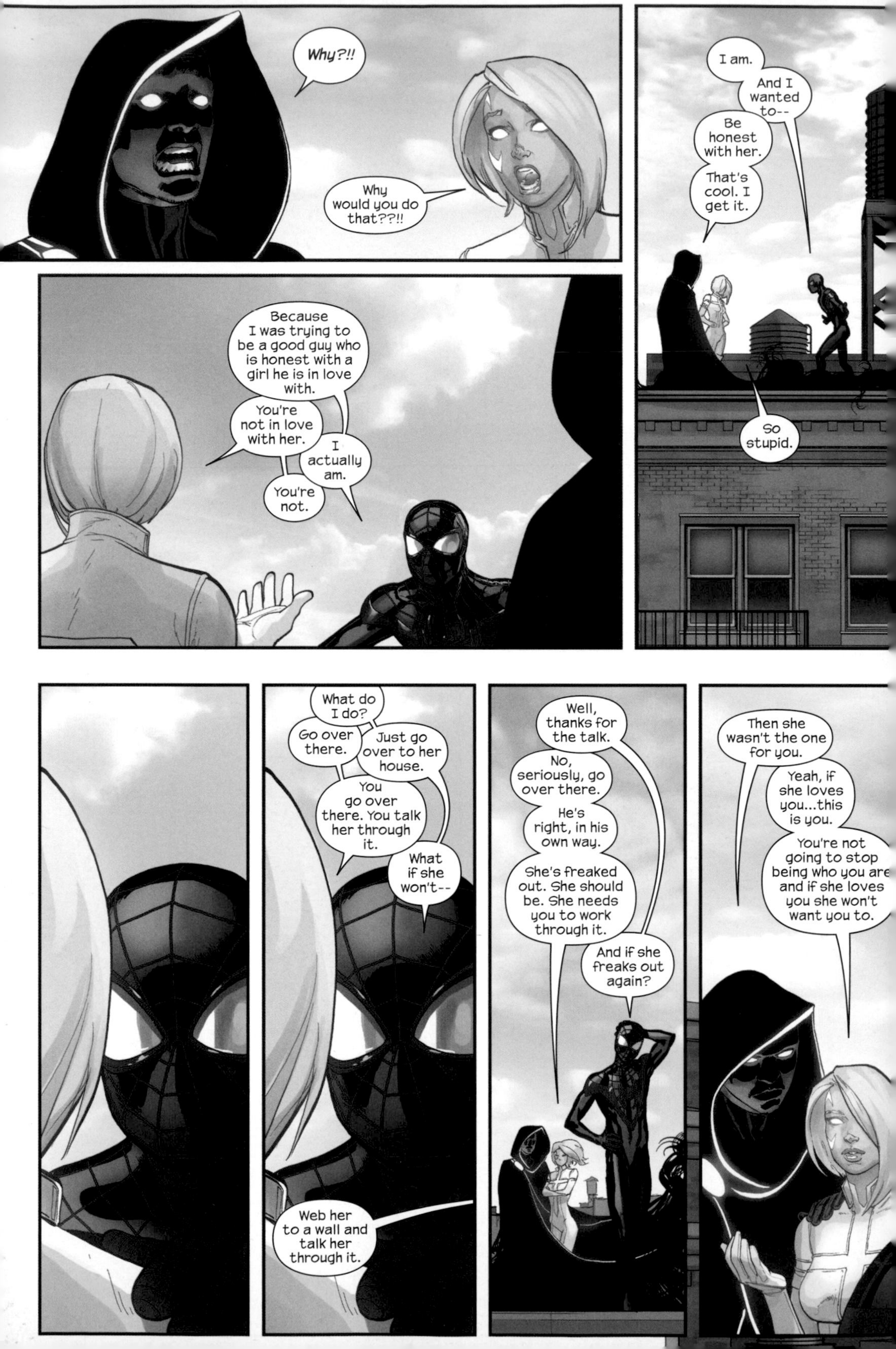
Why?!!
Why would you do that??!!
I am.
And I wanted to--
Be honest with her.
That's cool. I get it.
So stupid.
Because I was trying to be a good guy who is honest with a girl he is in love with.
You're not in love with her.
I actually am.
You're not.
What do I do?
Go over there.
Just go over to her house.
You go over there. You talk her through it.
What if she won't--
Web her to a wall and talk her through it.
Well, thanks for the talk.
No, seriously, go over there.
He's right, in his own way.
She's freaked out. She should be. She needs you to work through it.
And if she freaks out again?
Then she wasn't the one for you.
Yeah, if she loves you...this is you.
You're not going to stop being who you are and if she loves you she won't want you to.

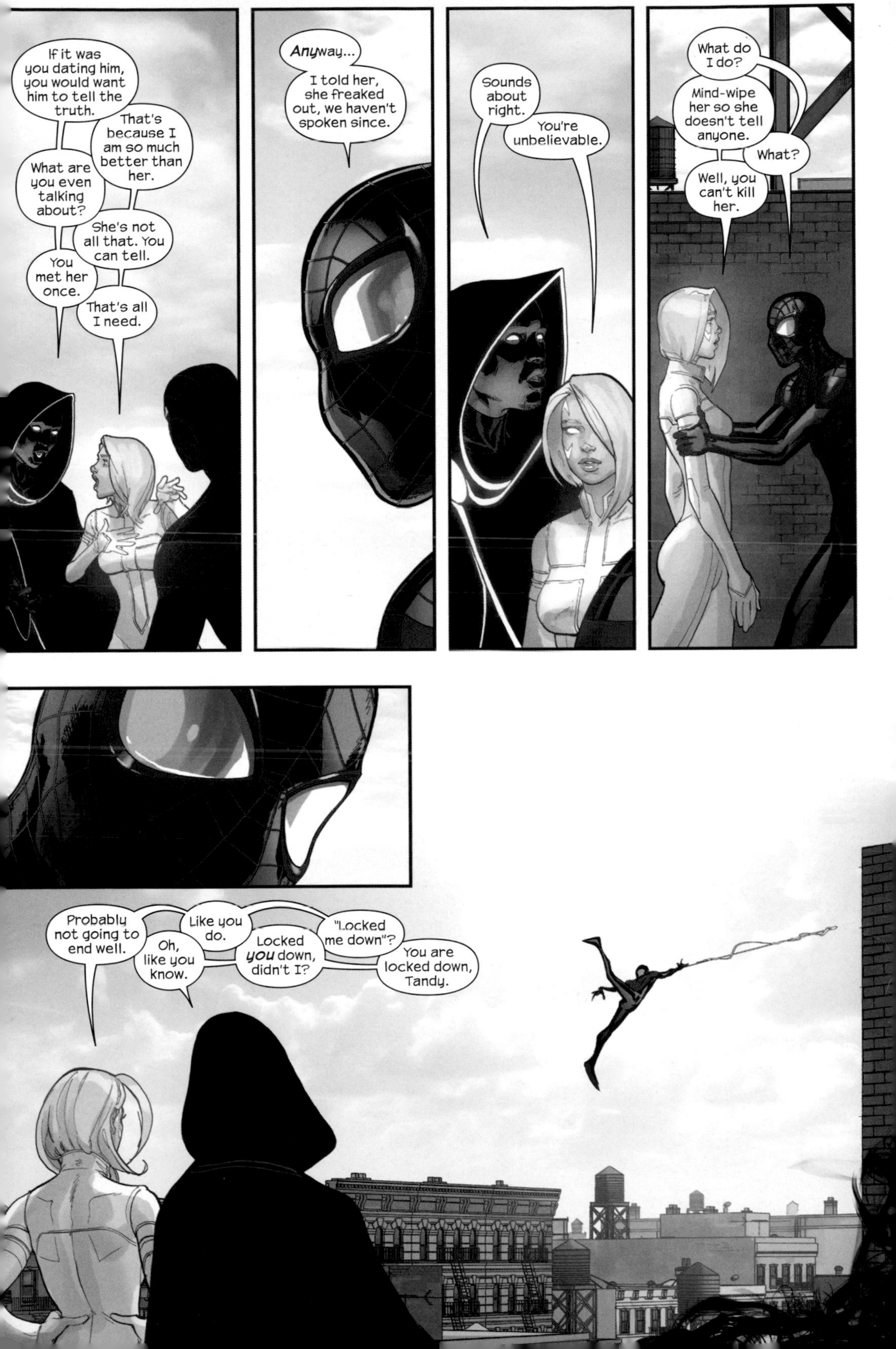
If it was you dating him, you would want him to tell the truth.
That's because I am so much better than her.
What are you even talking about?
She's not all that. You can tell.
You met her once.
That's all I need.
Anyway...
I told her, she freaked out, we haven't spoken since.
Sounds about right.
You're unbelievable.
What do I do?
Mind-wipe her so she doesn't tell anyone.
What?
Well, you can't kill her.
Probably not going to end well.
Oh, like you know.
Like you do.
Locked you down, didn't I?
"Locked me down"?
You are locked down, Tandy.

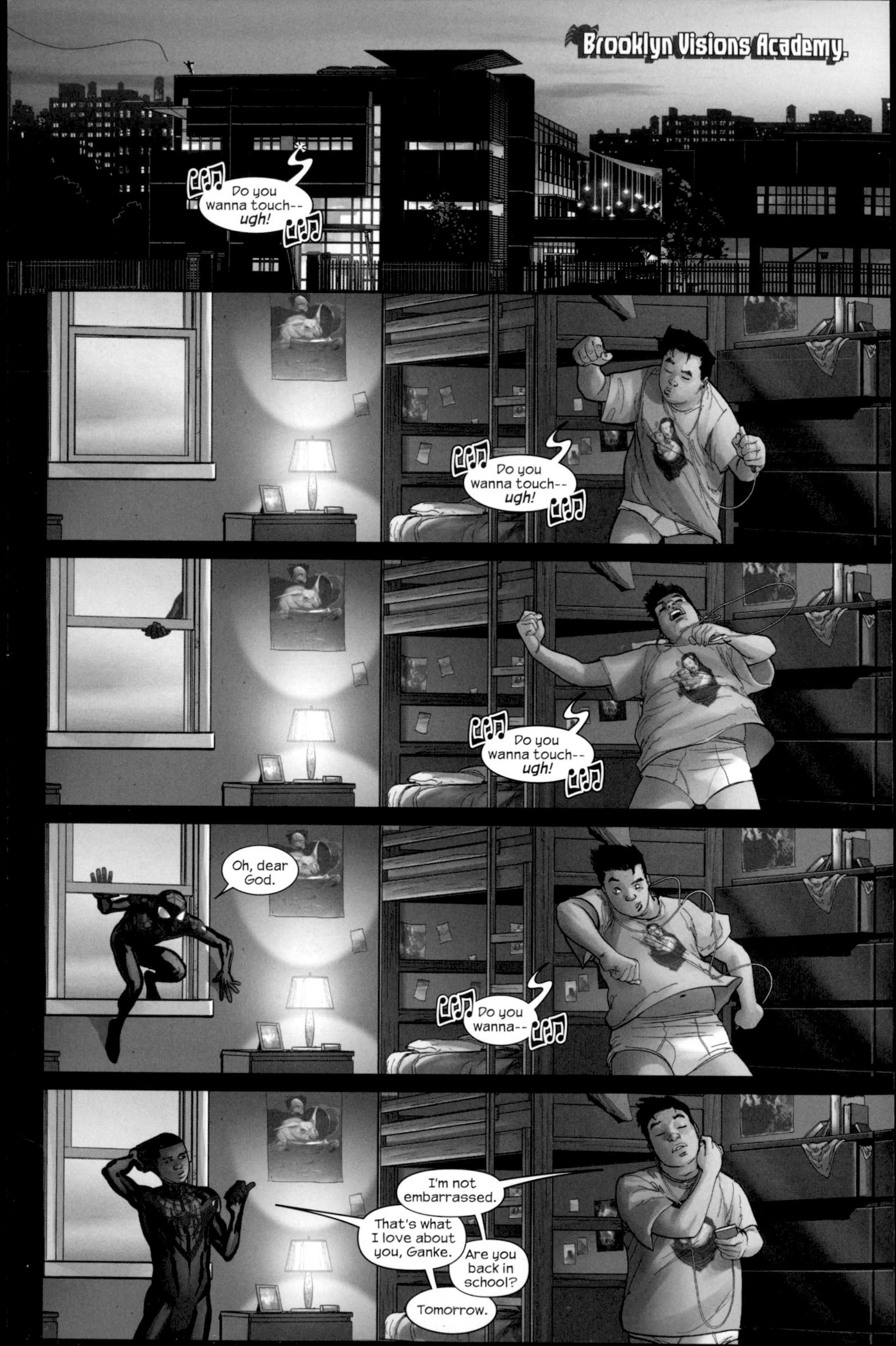
Brooklyn Visions Academy.
Do you wanna touch-- ugh!
Do you wanna touch-- ugh!
Do you wanna touch-- ugh!
Oh, dear God.
Do you wanna--
I'm not embarrassed.
That's what I love about you, Ganke.
Are you back in school?
Tomorrow.

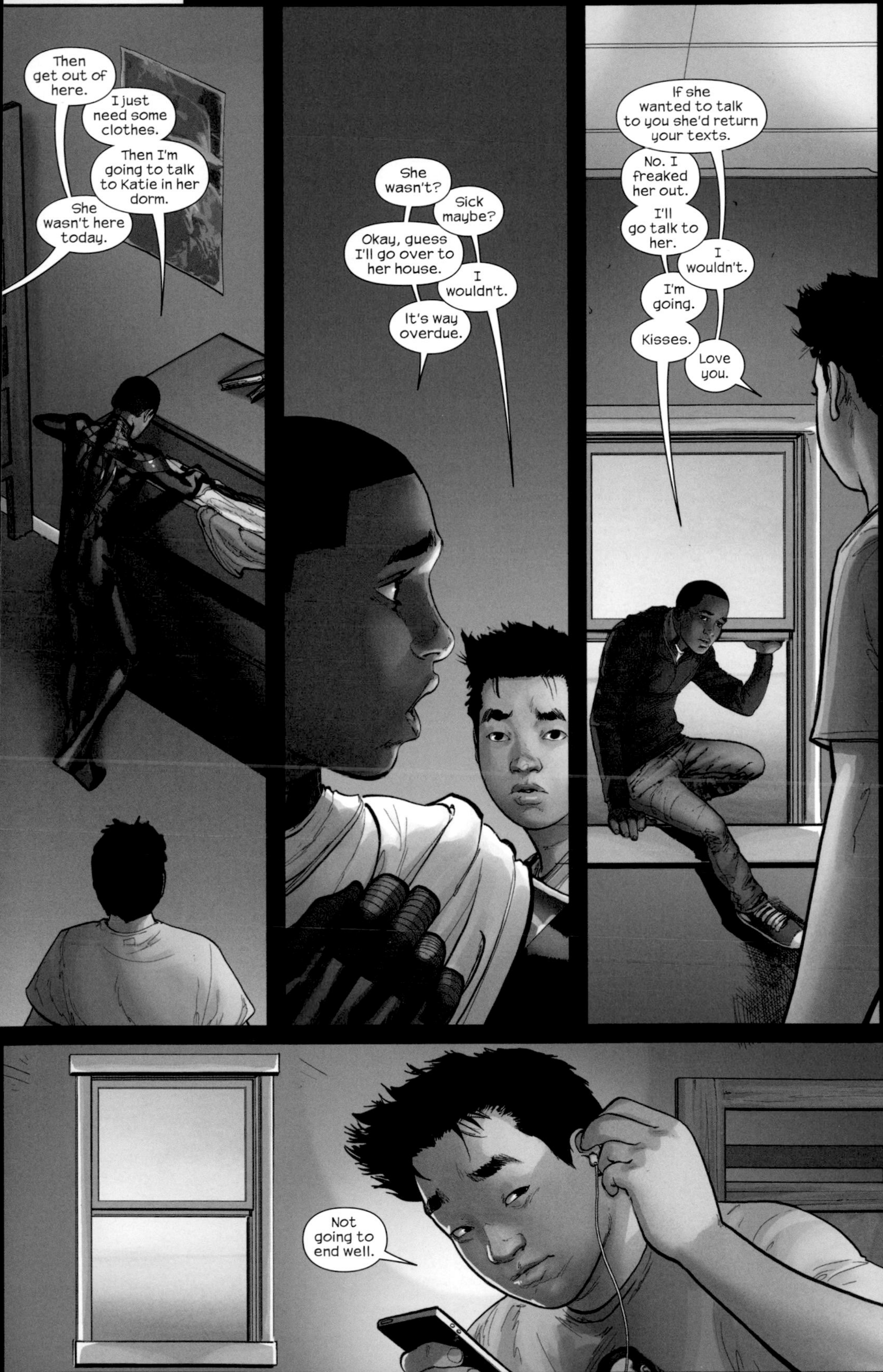

Then get out of here.
I just need some clothes.
Then I'm going to talk to Katie in her dorm.
She wasn't here today.
She wasn't?
Sick maybe?
Okay, guess I'll go over to her house.
I wouldn't.
It's way overdue.
If she wanted to talk to you she'd return your texts.
No. I freaked her out.
I'll go talk to her.
I wouldn't.
I'm going.
Kisses.
Love you.
Not going to end well.

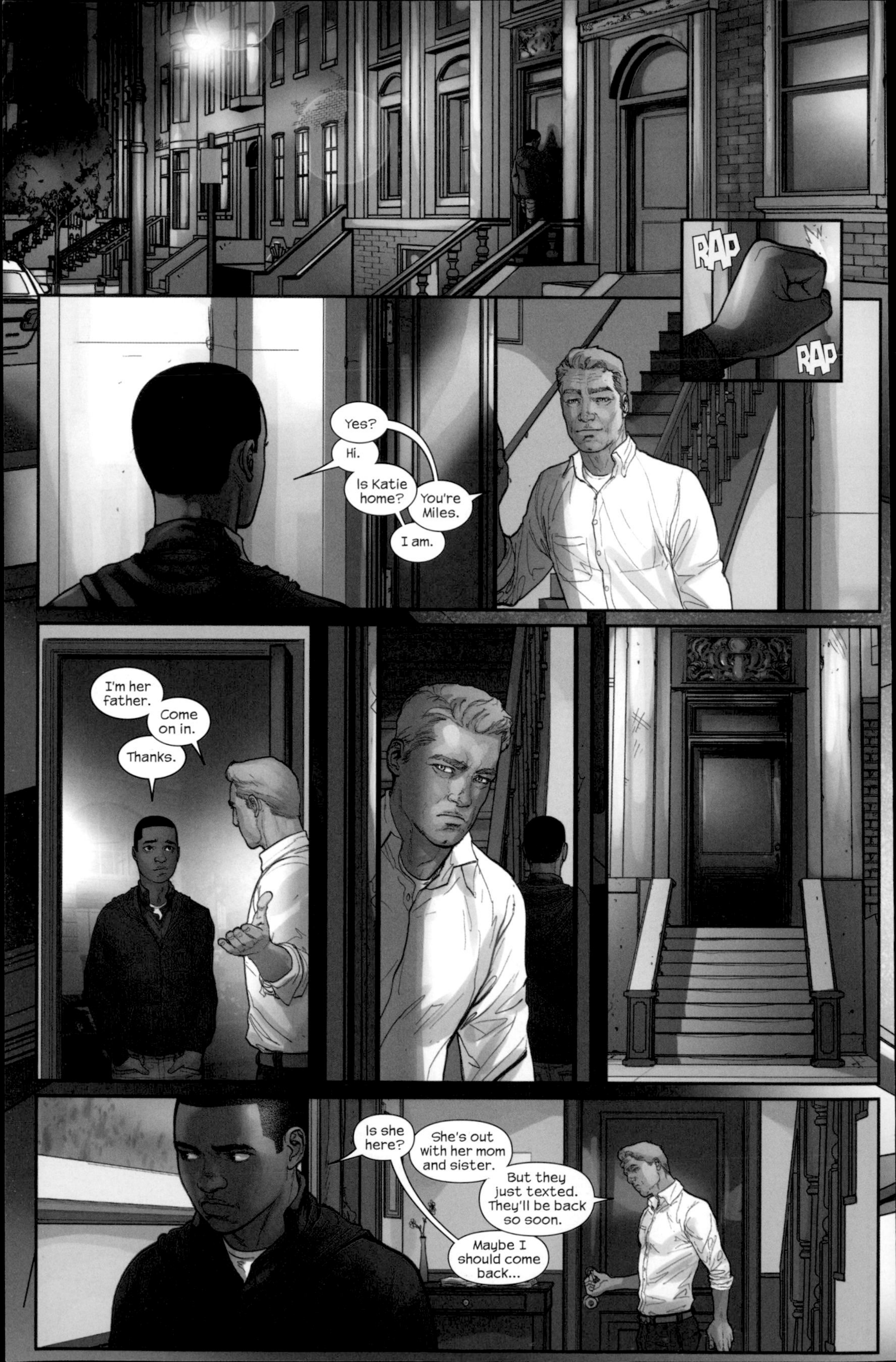

RAP
RAP
Yes?
Hi.
Is Katie home?
You're Miles.
I am.
I'm her father.
Come on in.
Thanks.
Is she here?
She's out with her mom and sister.
But they just texted. They'll be back so soon.
Maybe I should come back...

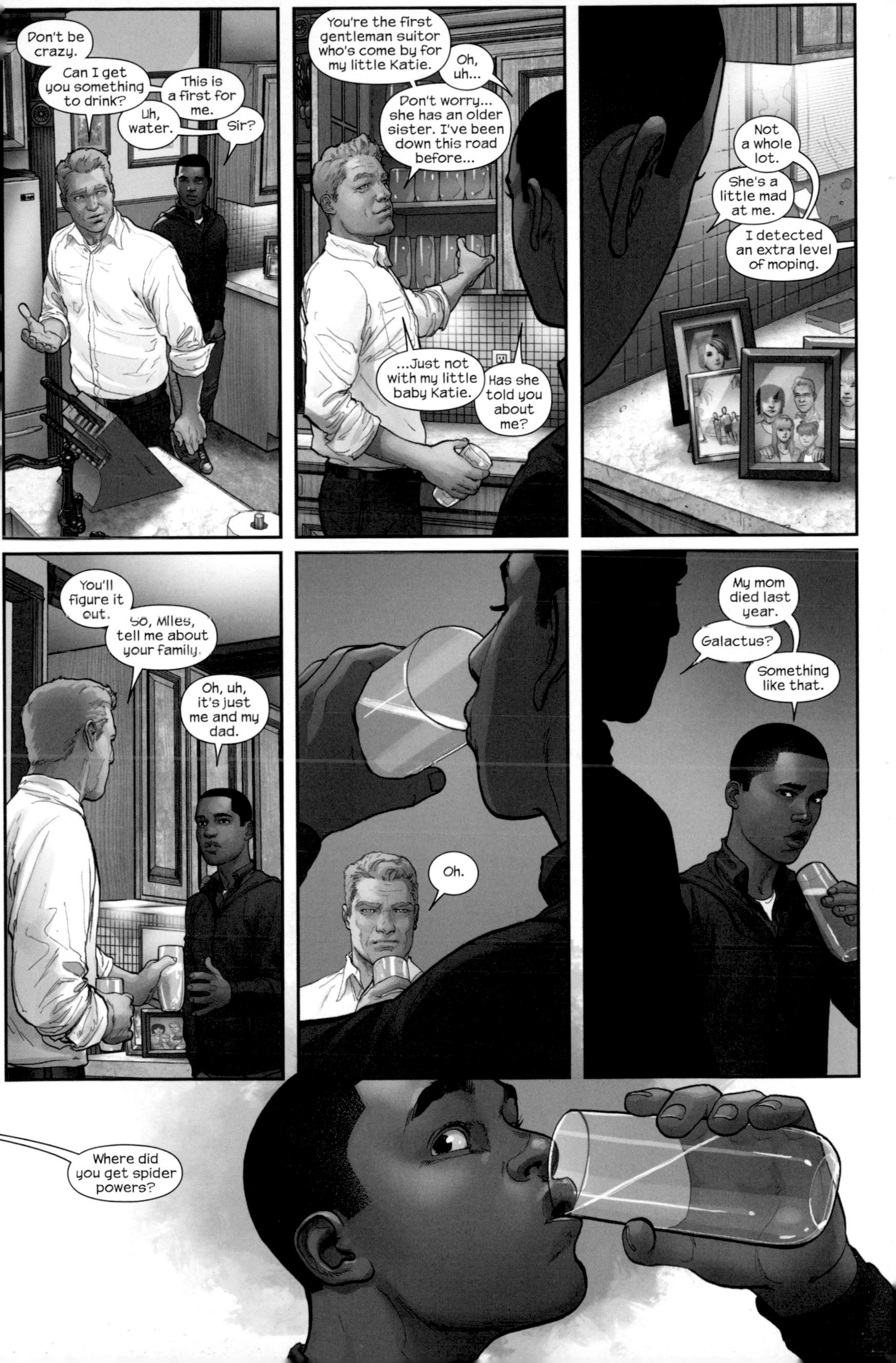
Don't be crazy.
Can I get you something to drink?
This is a first for me.
Uh, water.
Sir?
You're the first gentleman suitor who's come by for my little Katie.
Oh, uh...
Don't worry... she has an older sister. I've been down this road before...
...Just not with my little baby Katie.
Has she told you about me?
Not a whole lot.
She's a little mad at me.
I detected an extra level of moping.
You'll figure it out.
So, Miles, tell me about your family.
Oh, uh, it's just me and my dad.
Oh.
My mom died last year.
Galactus?
Something like that.
Where did you get spider powers?

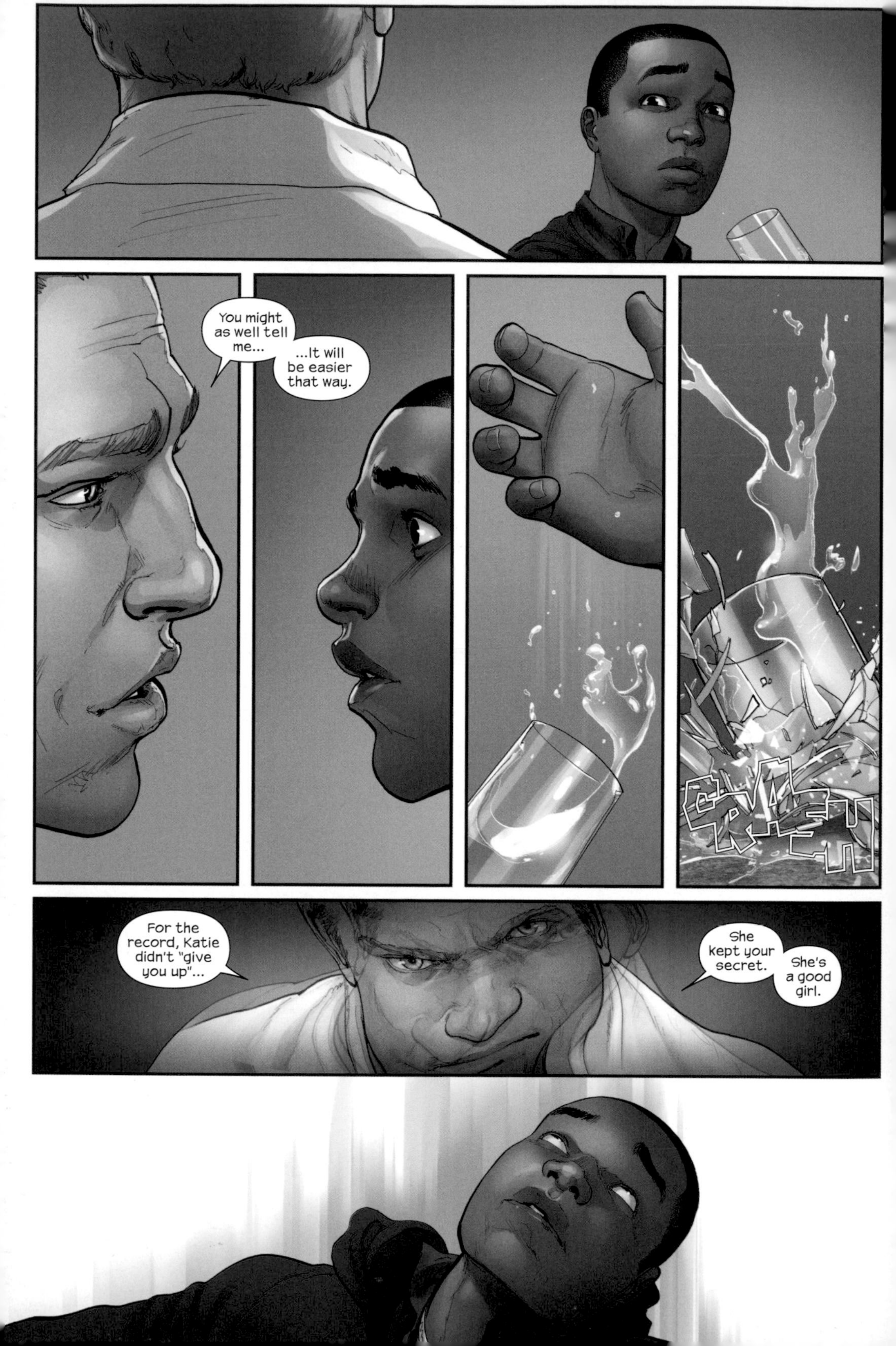
You might as well tell me...
...It will be easier that way.
CRASH
For the record, Katie didn't "give you up"...
She kept your secret.
She's a good girl.

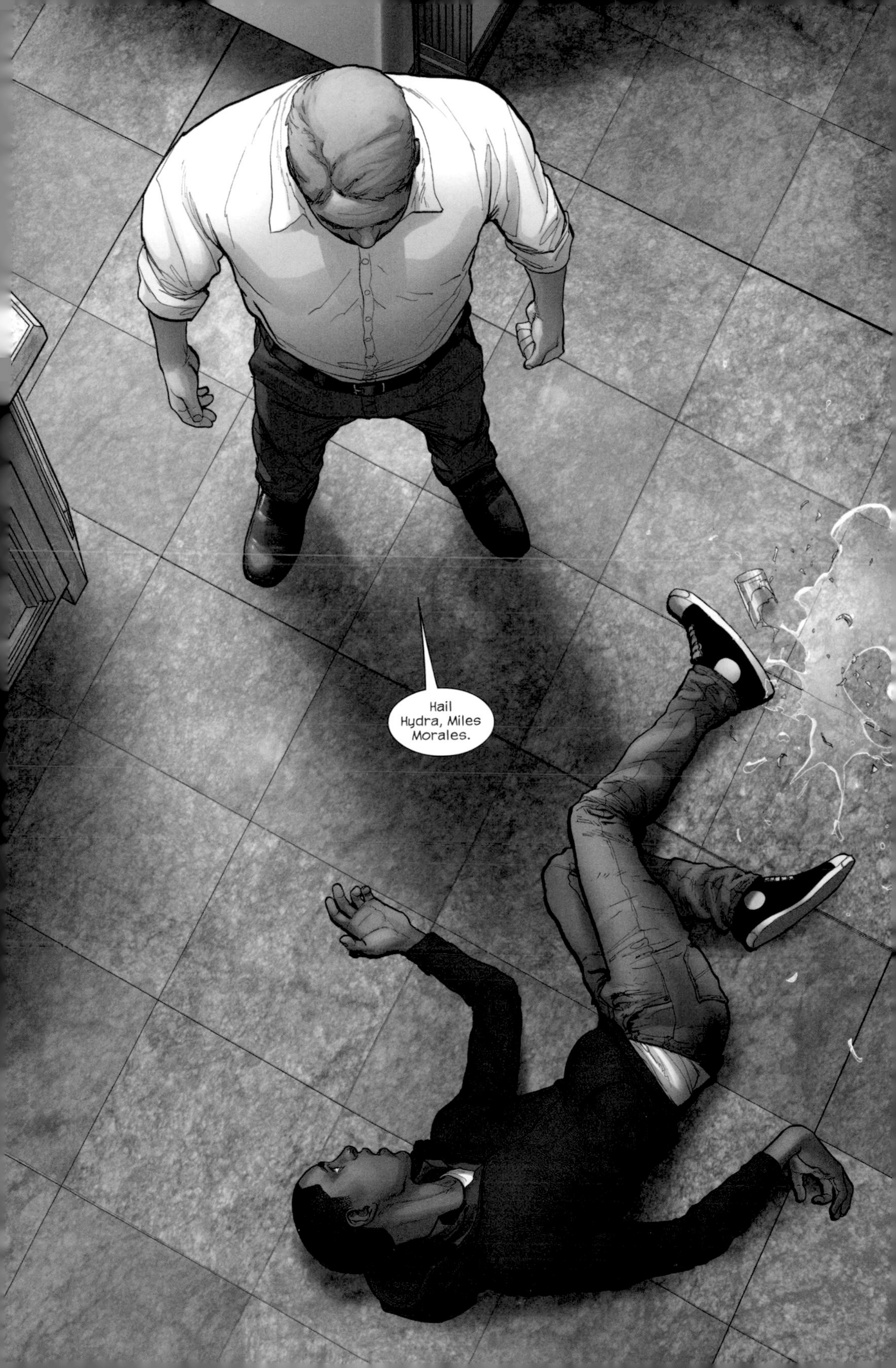
Hail Hydra, Miles Morales.

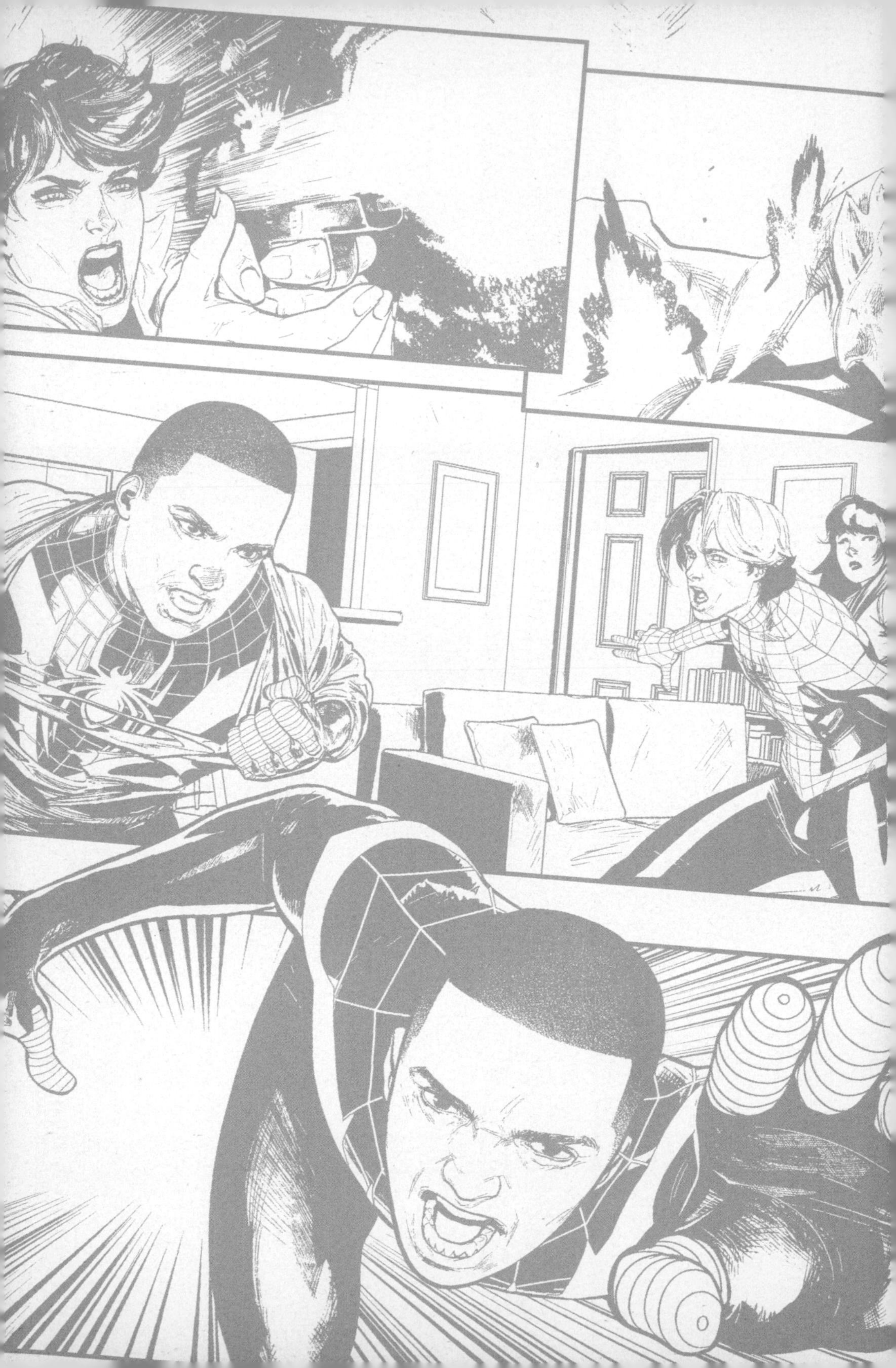

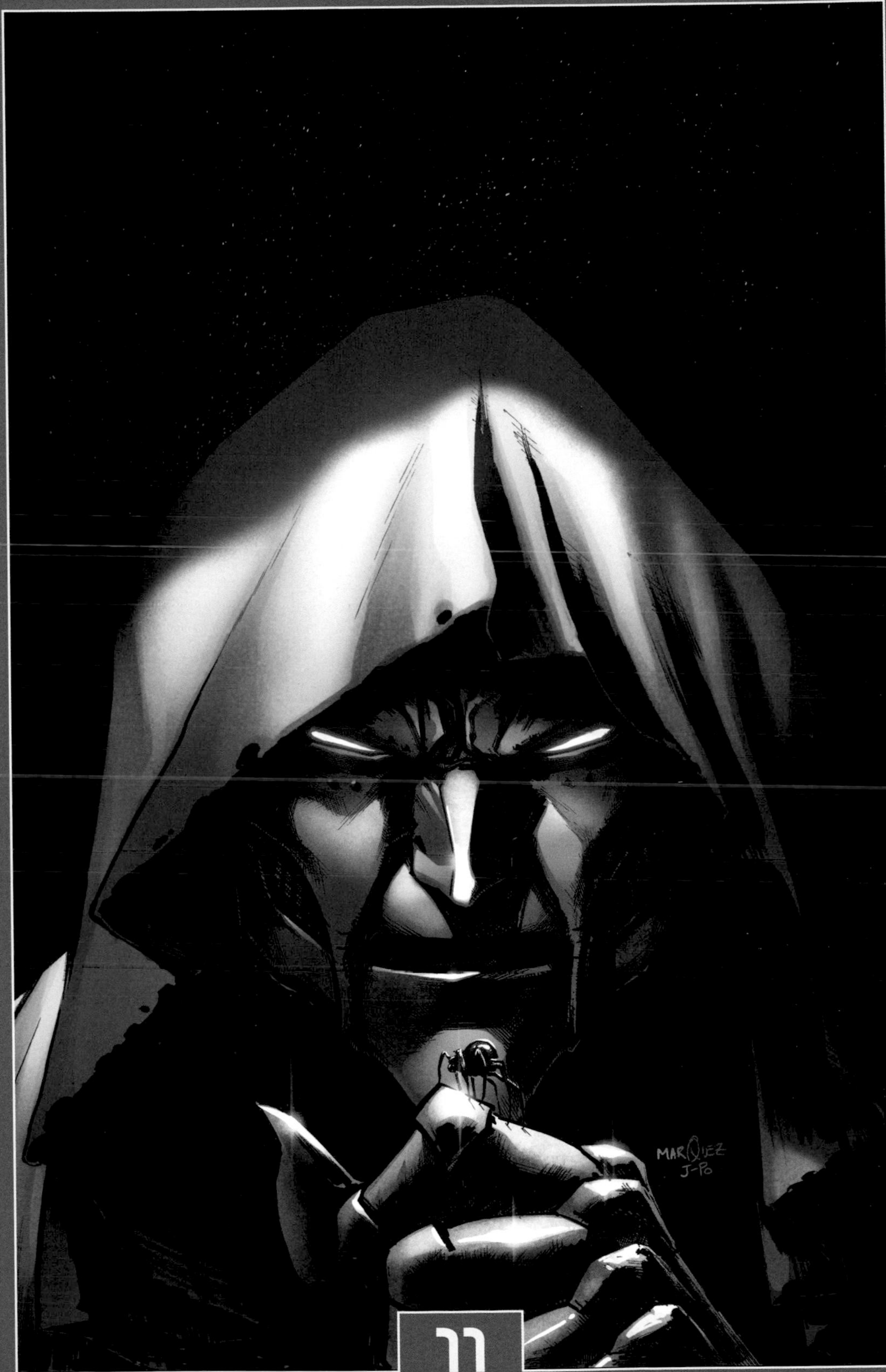
MARQUEZ
J-PO
11

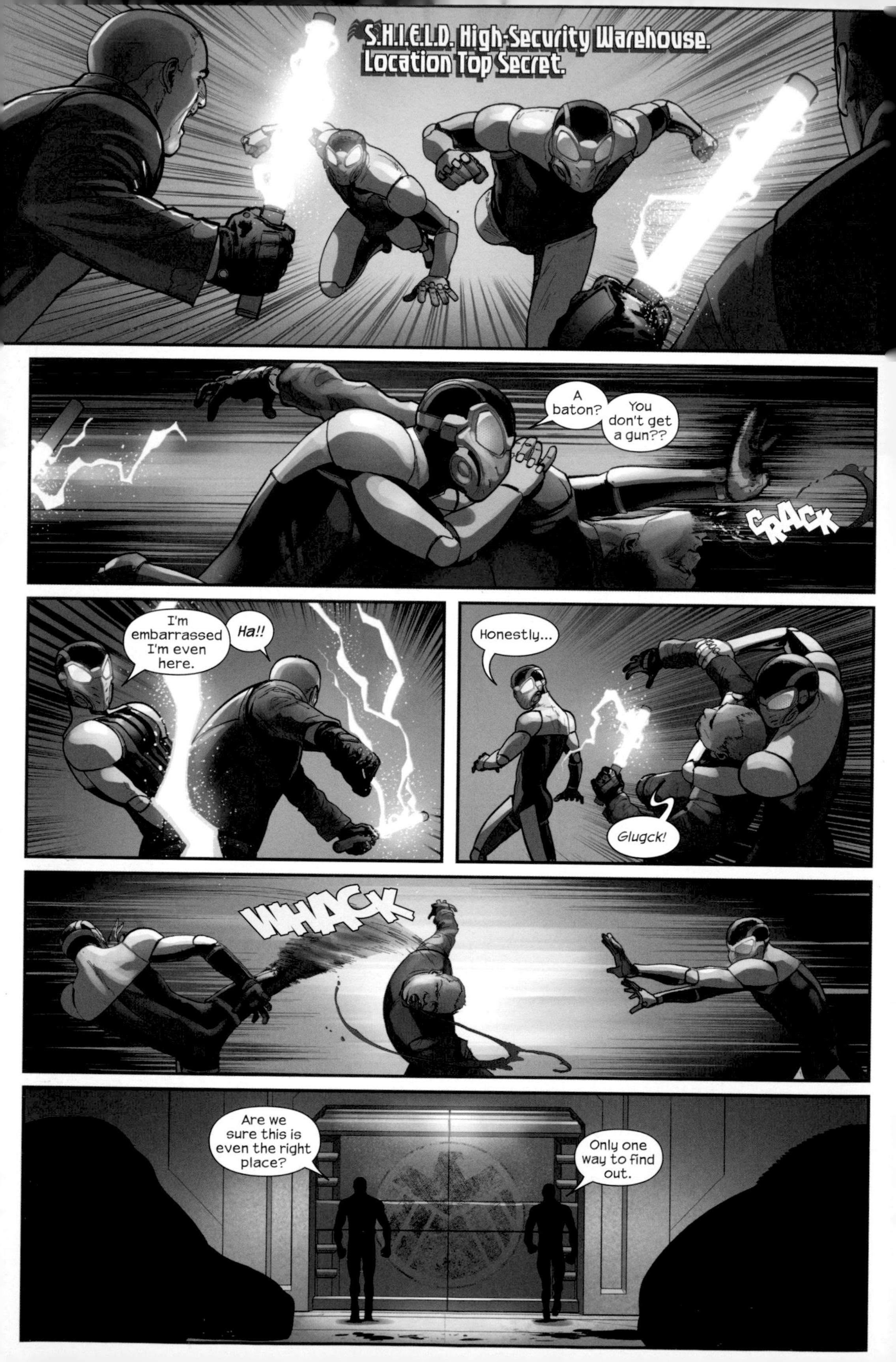
S.H.I.E.L.D. High-Security Warehouse. Location Top Secret.
A baton?
You don't get a gun??
CRACK
I'm embarrassed I'm even here.
Ha!!
Honestly...
Glugck!
WHACK
Are we sure this is even the right place?
Only one way to find out.

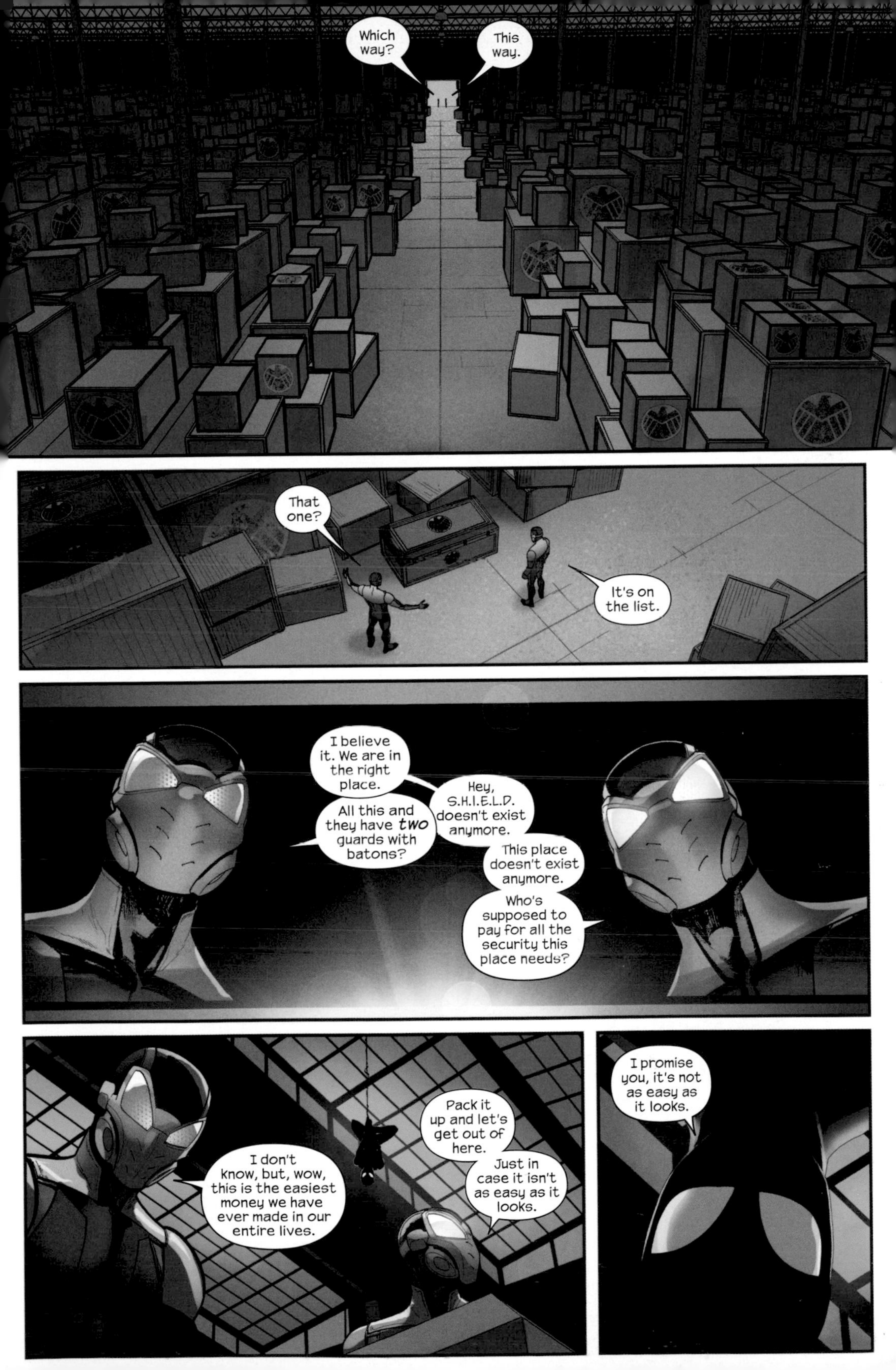

Which way?
This way.
That one?
It's on the list.
I believe it. We are in the right place.
All this and they have *two* guards with batons?
Hey, S.H.I.E.L.D. doesn't exist anymore.
This place doesn't exist anymore.
Who's supposed to pay for all the security this place needs?
I don't know, but, wow, this is the easiest money we have ever made in our entire lives.
Pack it up and let's get out of here.
Just in case it isn't as easy as it looks.
I promise you, it's not as easy as it looks.

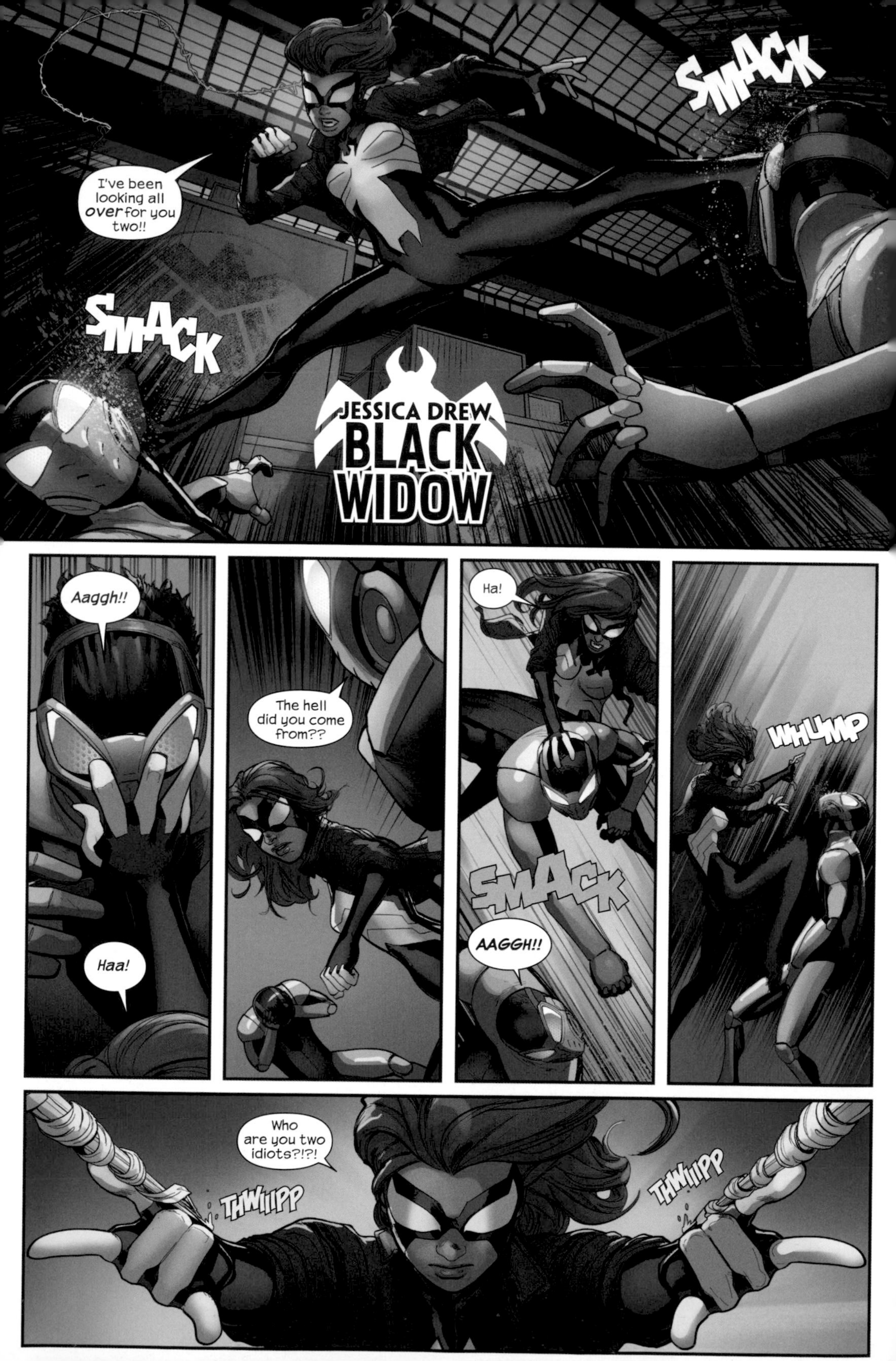
SMACK
I've been looking all over for you two!!
SMACK
JESSICA DREW
BLACK WIDOW
Aaggh!!
Haa!
The hell did you come from??
Ha!
SMACK
AAGGH!!
WHUMP
Who are you two idiots?!?!
THWIIIPP
THWIIIPP

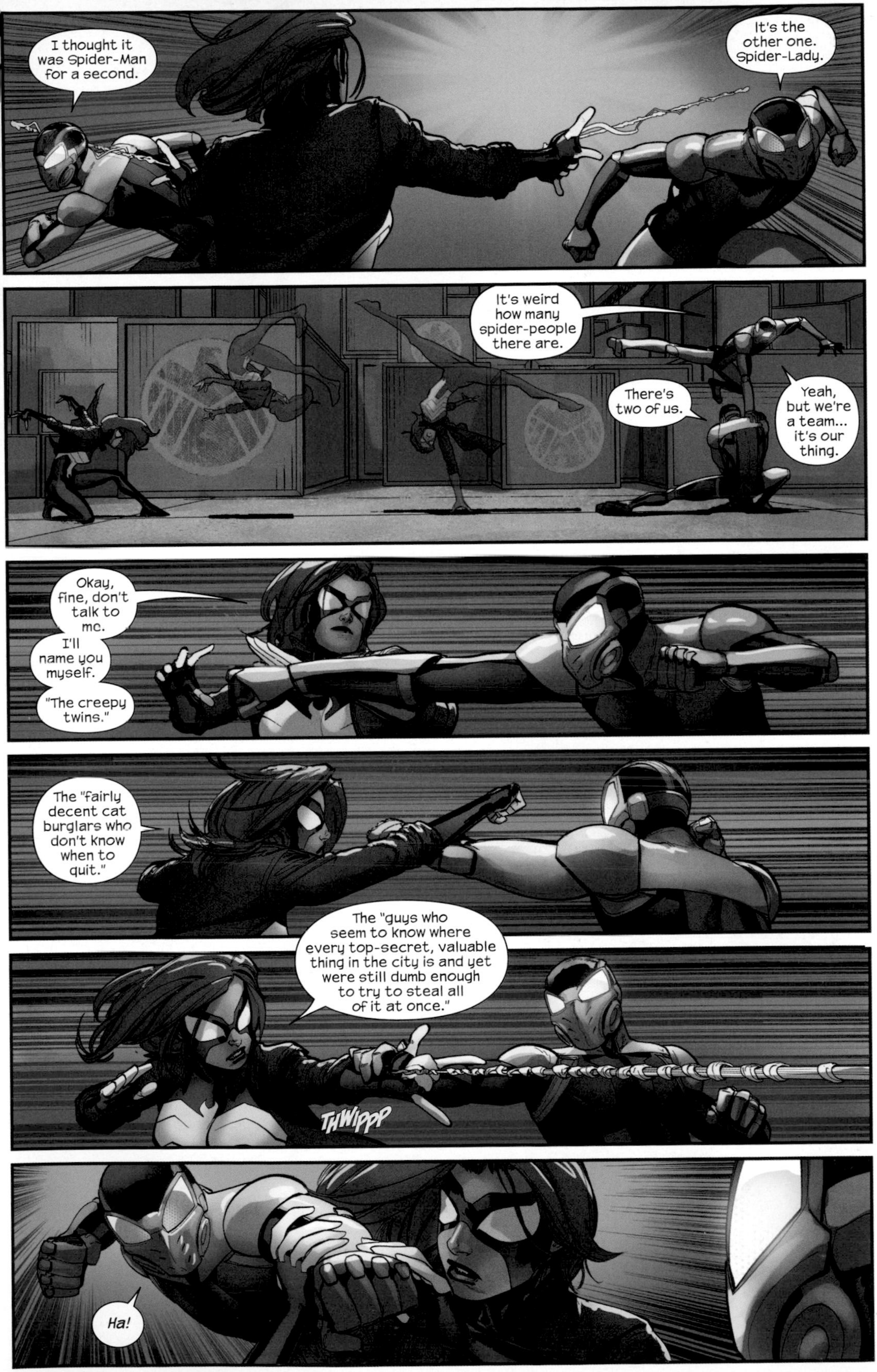
I thought it was Spider-Man for a second.
It's the other one. Spider-Lady.
It's weird how many spider-people there are.
There's two of us.
Yeah, but we're a team... it's our thing.
Okay, fine, don't talk to me.
I'll name you myself.
"The creepy twins."
The "fairly decent cat burglars who don't know when to quit."
The "guys who seem to know where every top-secret, valuable thing in the city is and yet were still dumb enough to try to steal all of it at once."
THWIPPP
Ha!

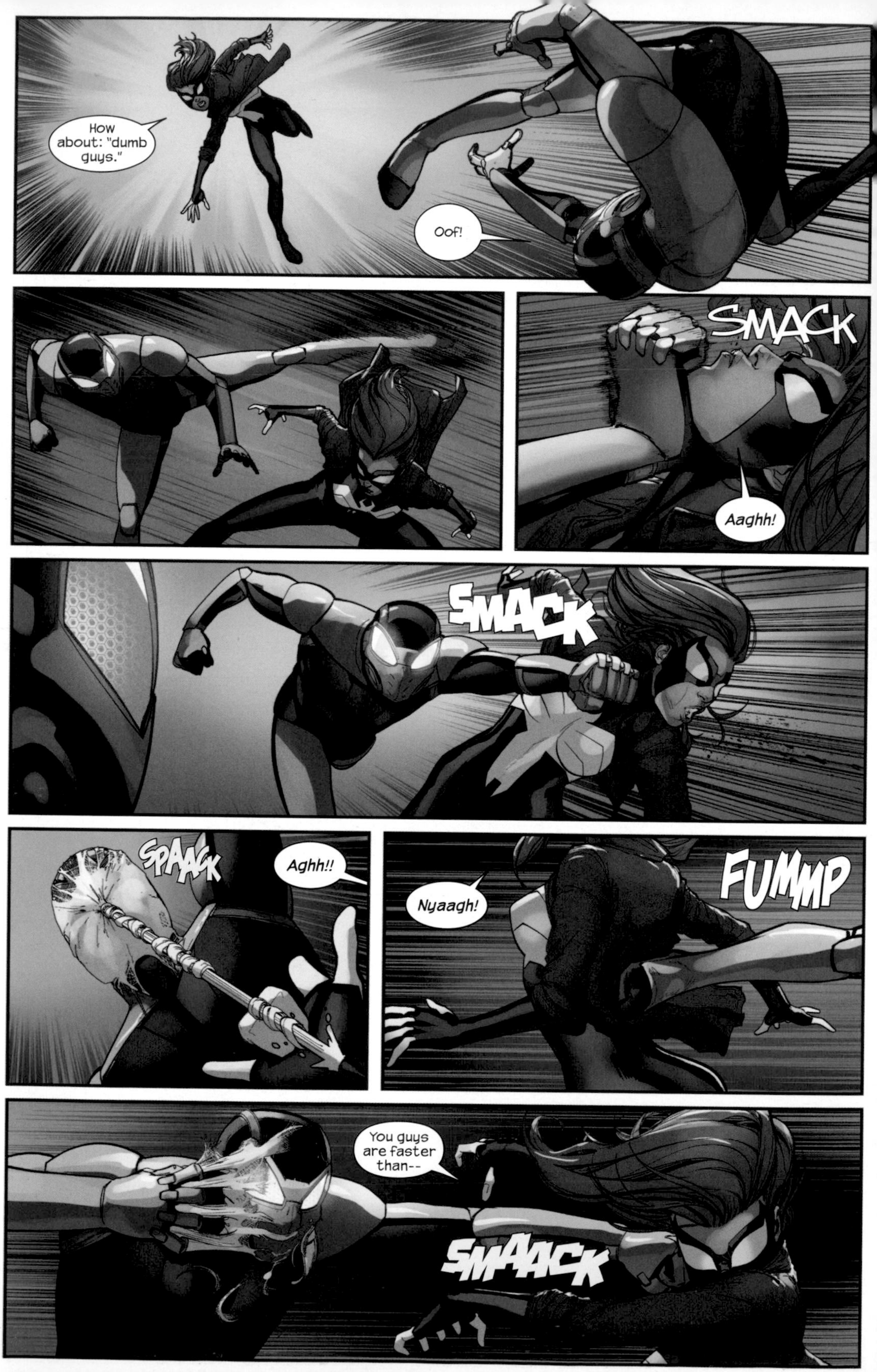
How about: "dumb guys."
Oof!
SMACK
Aaghh!
SMACK
SPAACK
Aghh!!
Nyaagh!
FUMMP
You guys are faster than--
SMAACK

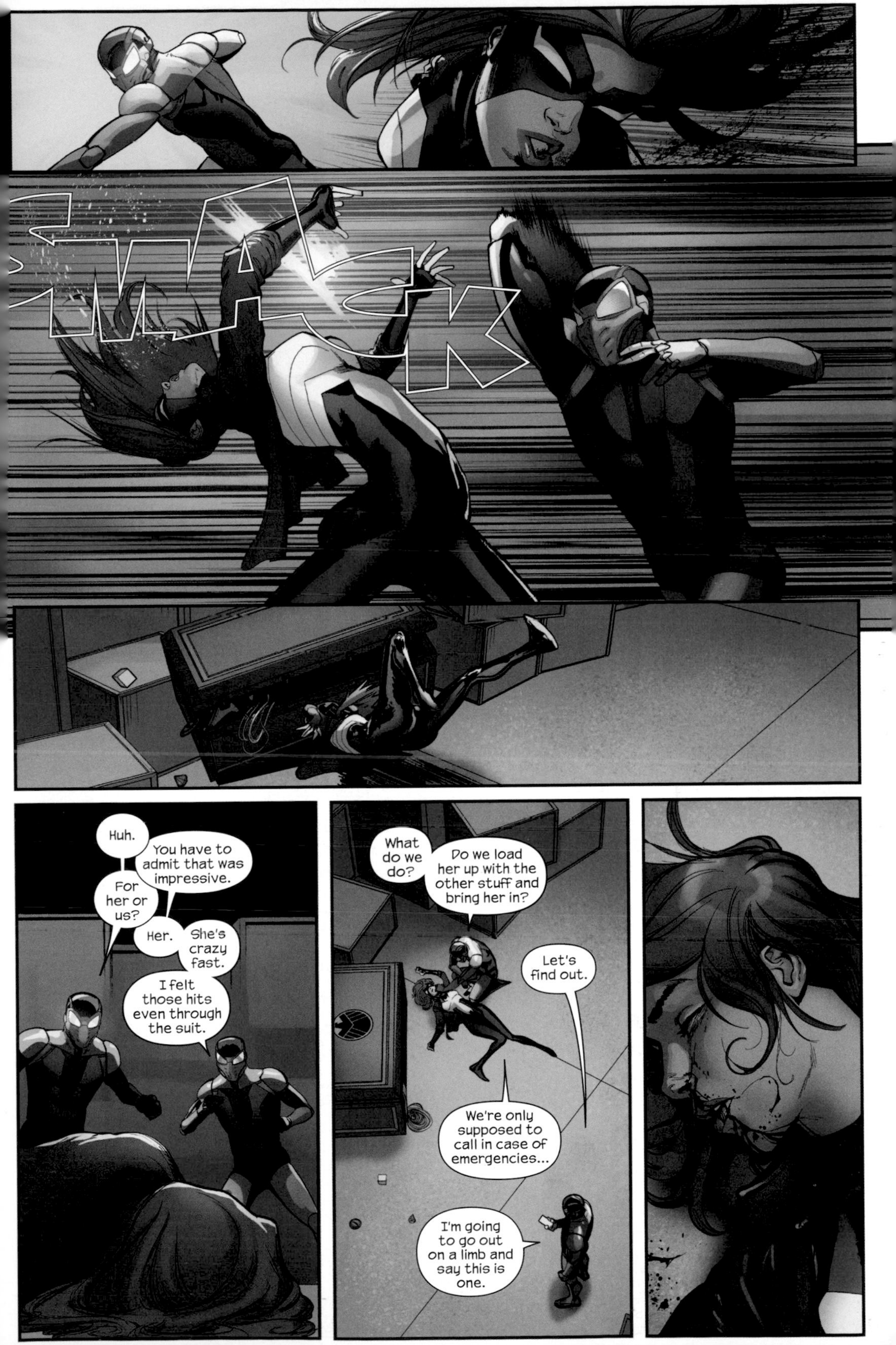
WHACK
Huh.
You have to admit that was impressive.
For her or us?
Her.
She's crazy fast.
I felt those hits even through the suit.
What do we do?
Do we load her up with the other stuff and bring her in?
Let's find out.
We're only supposed to call in case of emergencies...
I'm going to go out on a limb and say this is one.

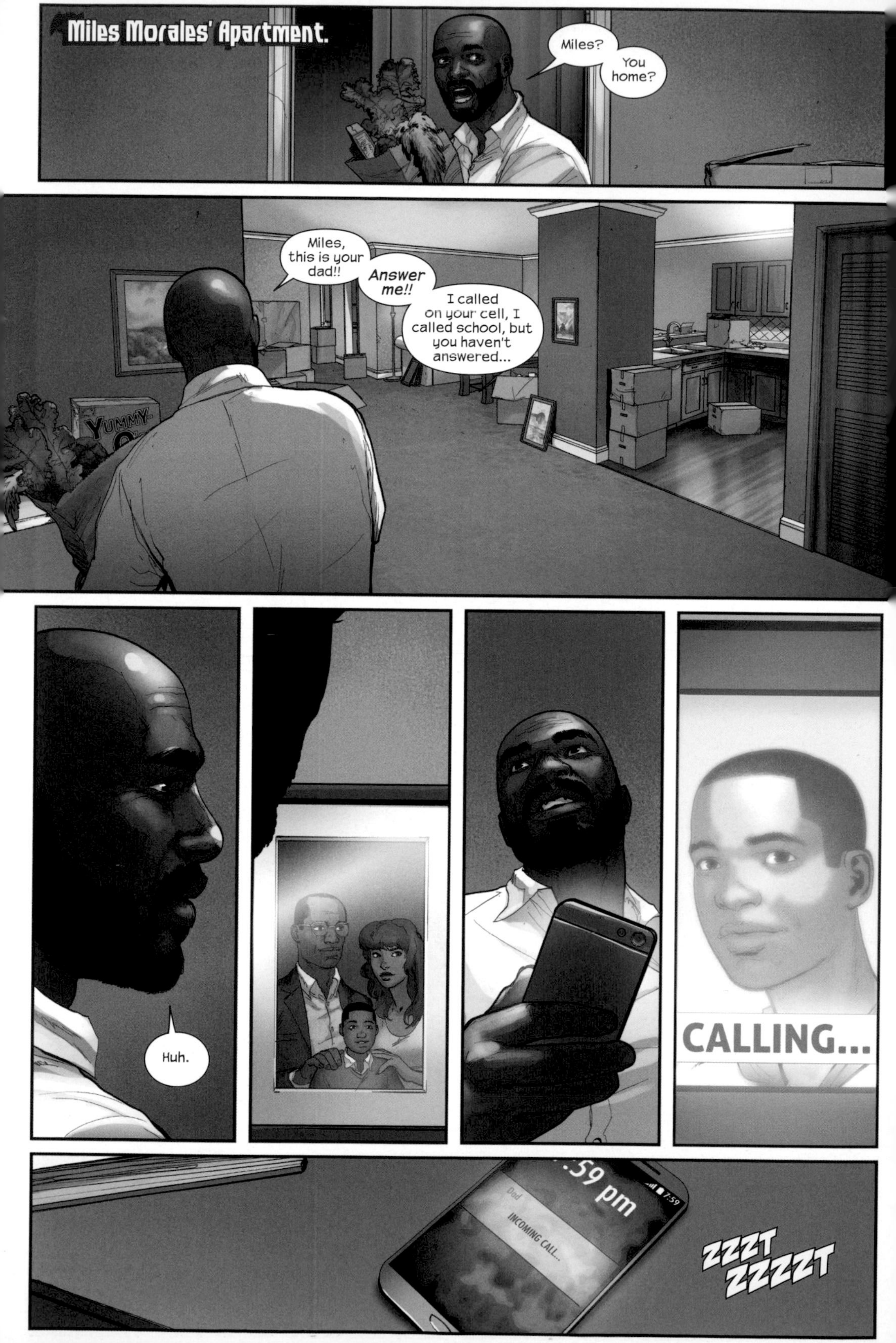
Miles Morales' Apartment.
Miles?
You home?
Miles, this is your dad!!
Answer me!!
I called on your cell, I called school, but you haven't answered...
Huh.
CALLING...
:59 pm
7:59
Dad
INCOMING CALL...
ZZZT ZZZZT

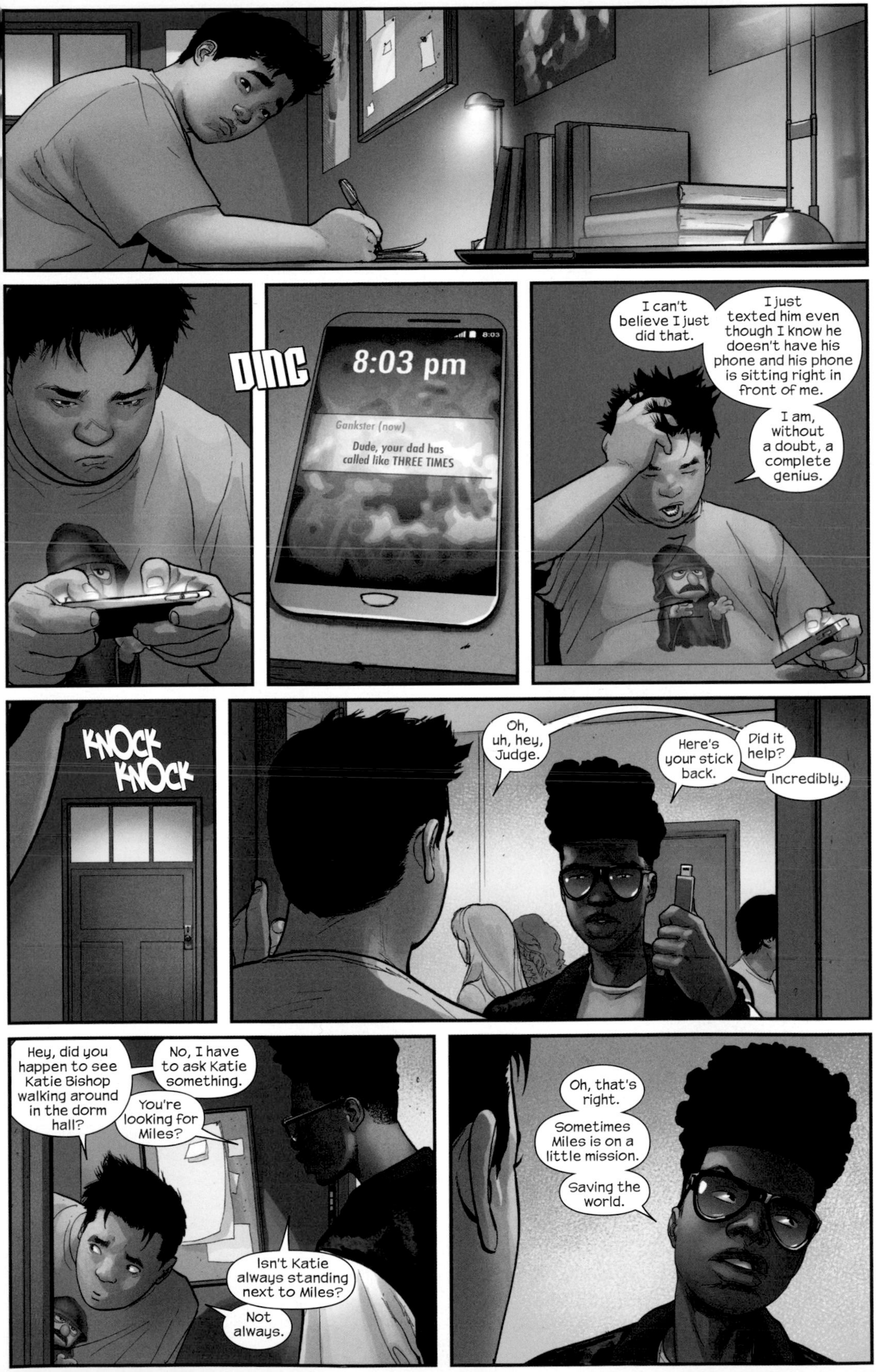
DING
Gankster (now)
Dude, your dad has called like THREE TIMES
8:03 pm
I can't believe I just did that.
I just texted him even though I know he doesn't have his phone and his phone is sitting right in front of me.
I am, without a doubt, a complete genius.
KNOCK KNOCK
Oh, uh, hey, Judge.
Here's your stick back.
Did it help?
Incredibly.
Hey, did you happen to see Katie Bishop walking around in the dorm hall?
No, I have to ask Katie something.
You're looking for Miles?
Isn't Katie always standing next to Miles?
Not always.
Oh, that's right.
Sometimes Miles is on a little mission.
Saving the world.

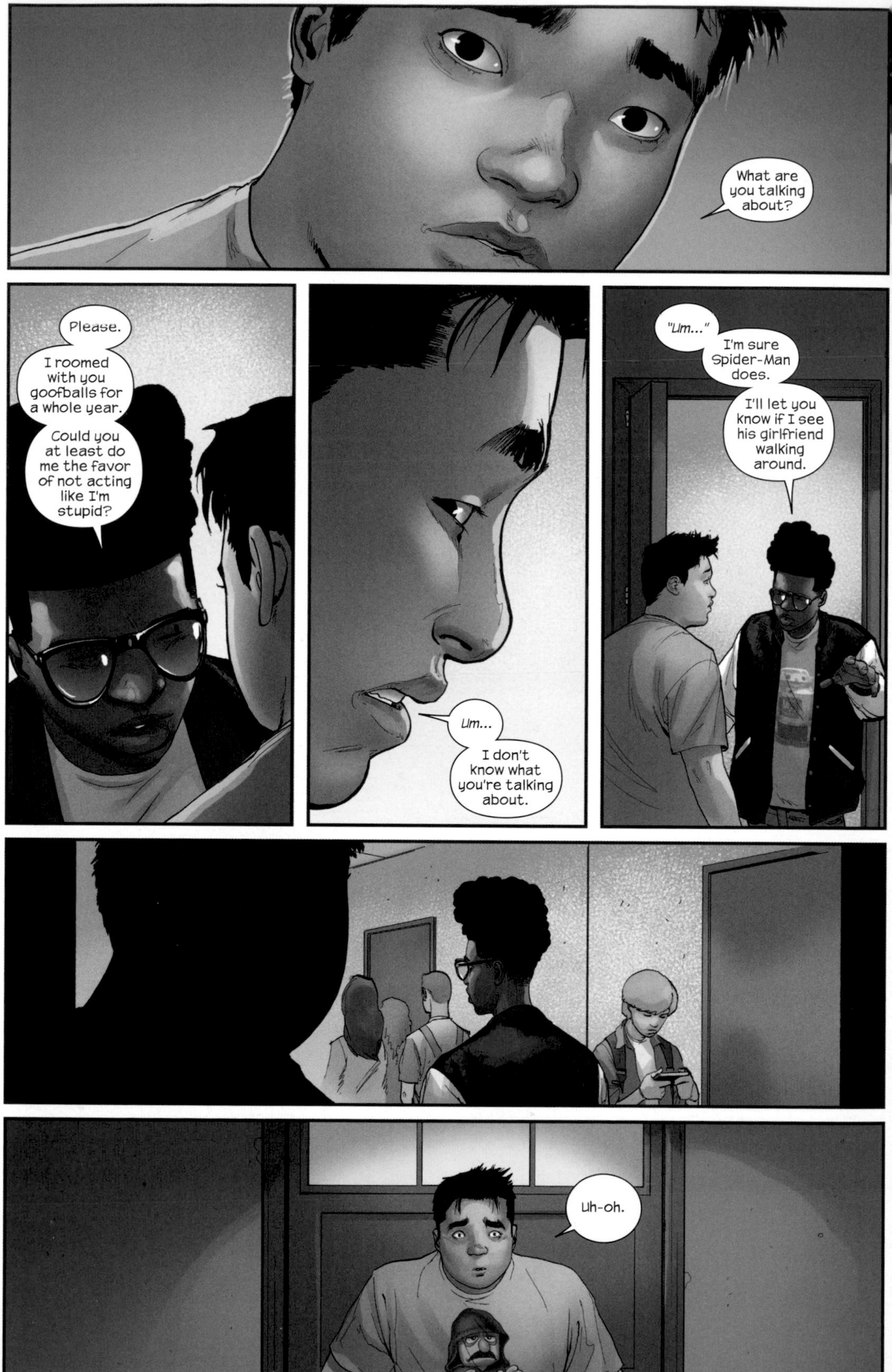
What are you talking about?
Please.
I roomed with you goofballs for a whole year.
Could you at least do me the favor of not acting like I'm stupid?
Um...
I don't know what you're talking about.
"Um..."
I'm sure Spider-Man does.
I'll let you know if I see his girlfriend walking around.
Uh-oh.

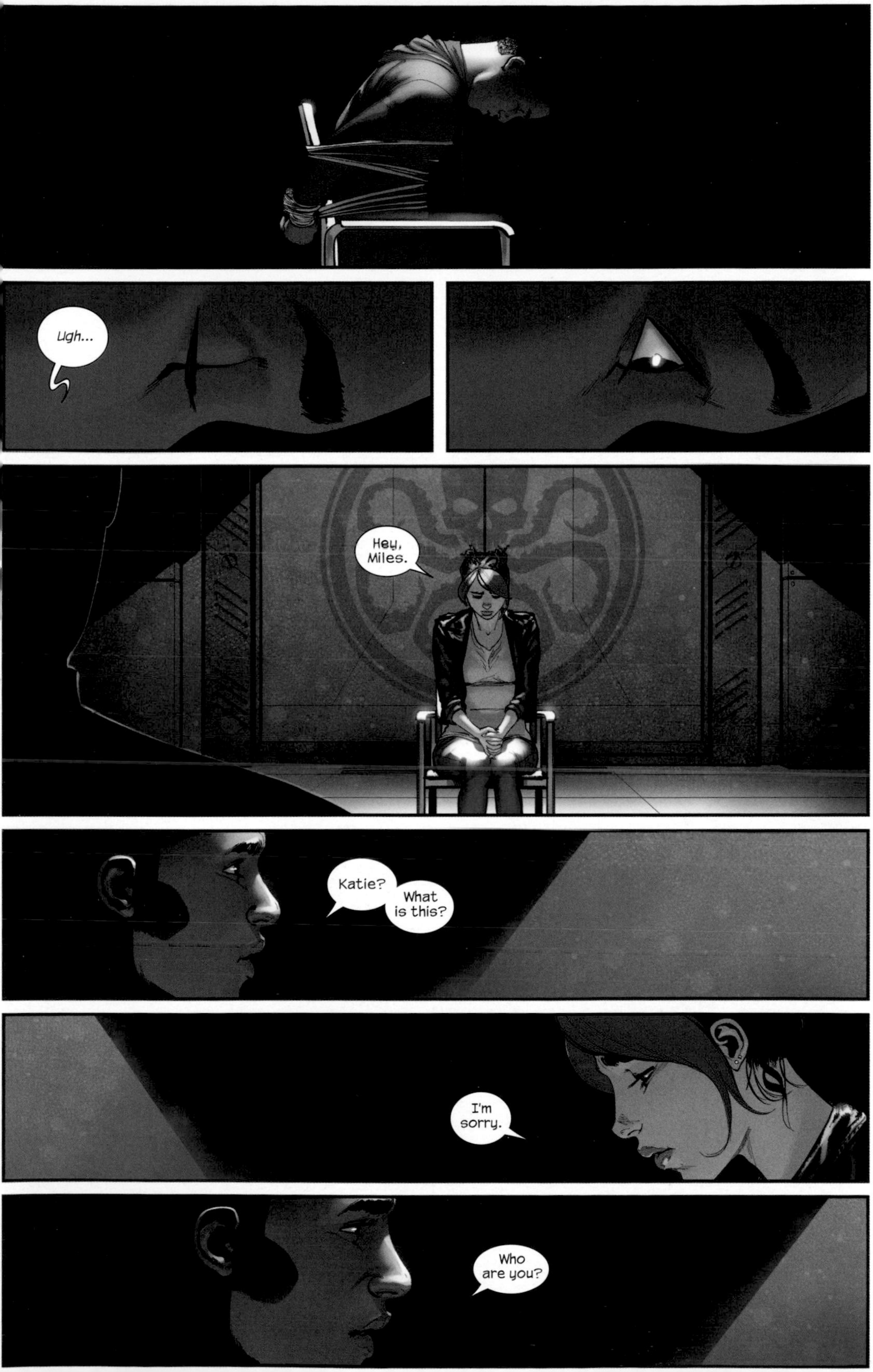
Ugh...
Hey, Miles.
Katie?
What is this?
I'm sorry.
Who are you?

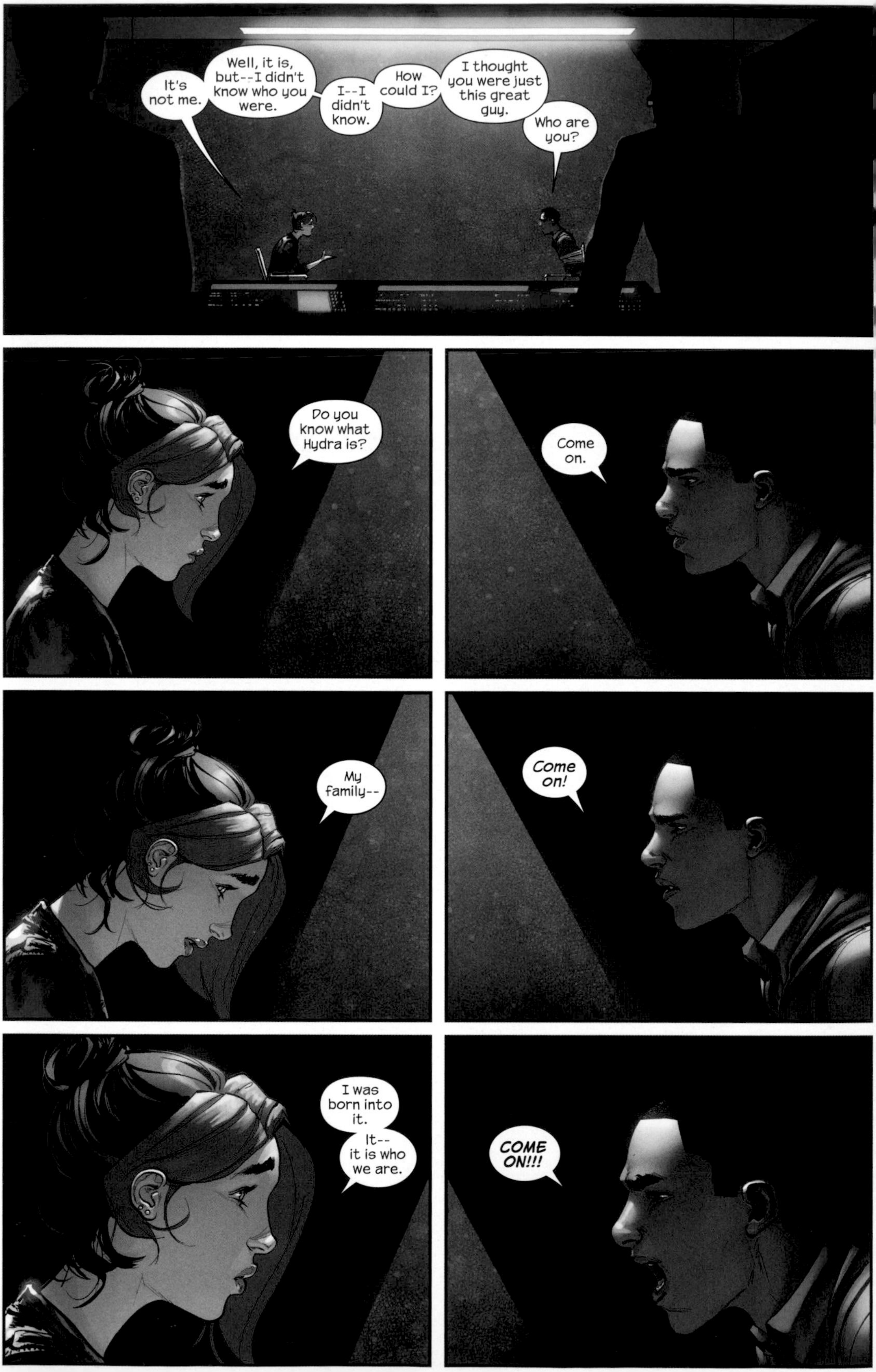
It's not me.
Well, it is, but--I didn't know who you were.
I--I didn't know.
How could I?
I thought you were just this great guy.
Who are you?
Do you know what Hydra is?
Come on.
My family--
Come on!
I was born into it.
It--it is who we are.
COME ON!!!

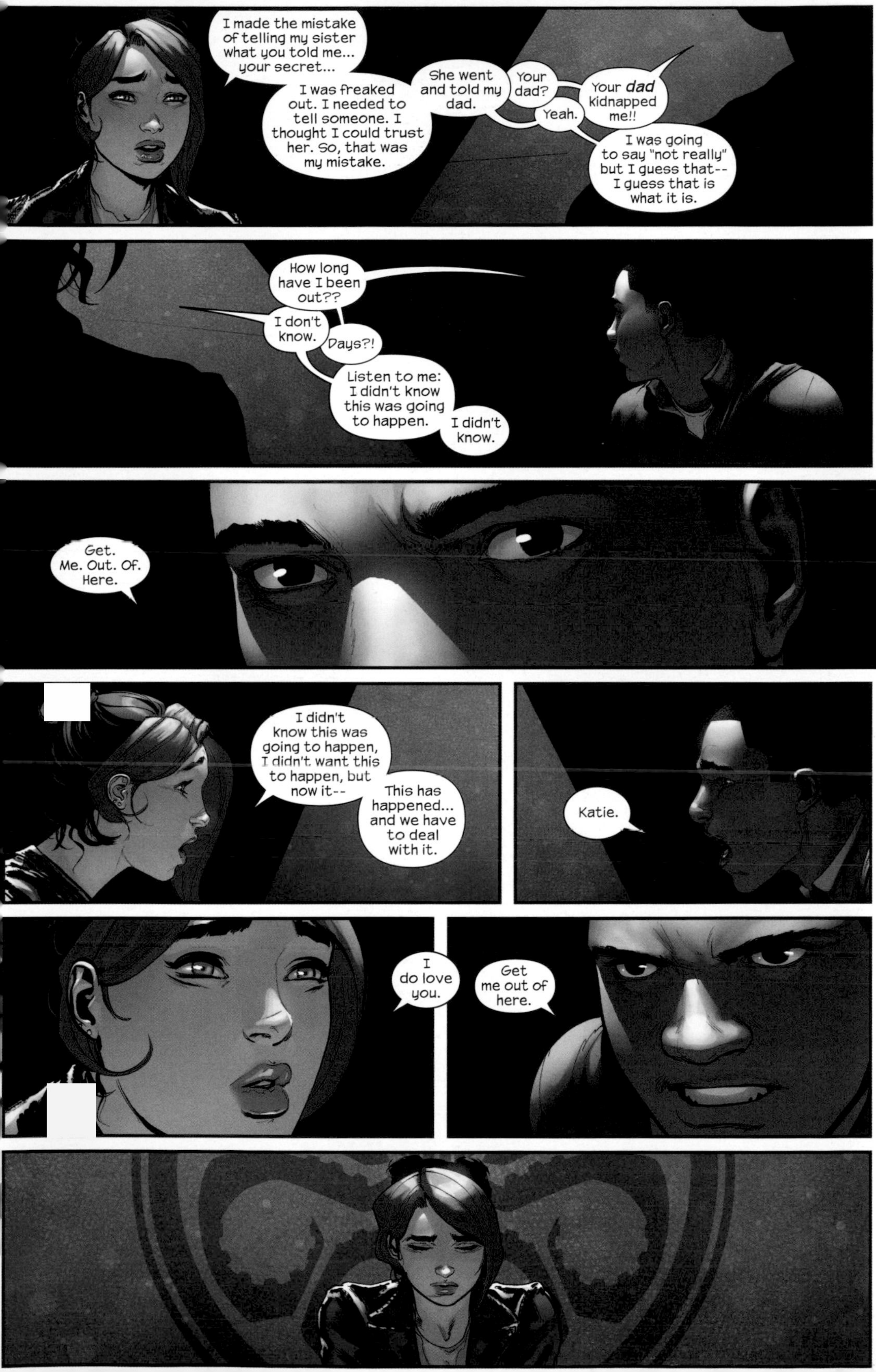

I made the mistake of telling my sister what you told me... your secret...
I was freaked out. I needed to tell someone. I thought I could trust her. So, that was my mistake.
She went and told my dad.
Your dad?
Yeah.
Your *dad* kidnapped me!!
I was going to say "not really" but I guess that-- I guess that is what it is.
How long have I been out??
I don't know.
Days?!
Listen to me: I didn't know this was going to happen.
I didn't know.
Get. Me. Out. Of. Here.
I didn't know this was going to happen, I didn't want this to happen, but now it--
This has happened... and we have to deal with it.
Katie.
I do love you.
Get me out of here.

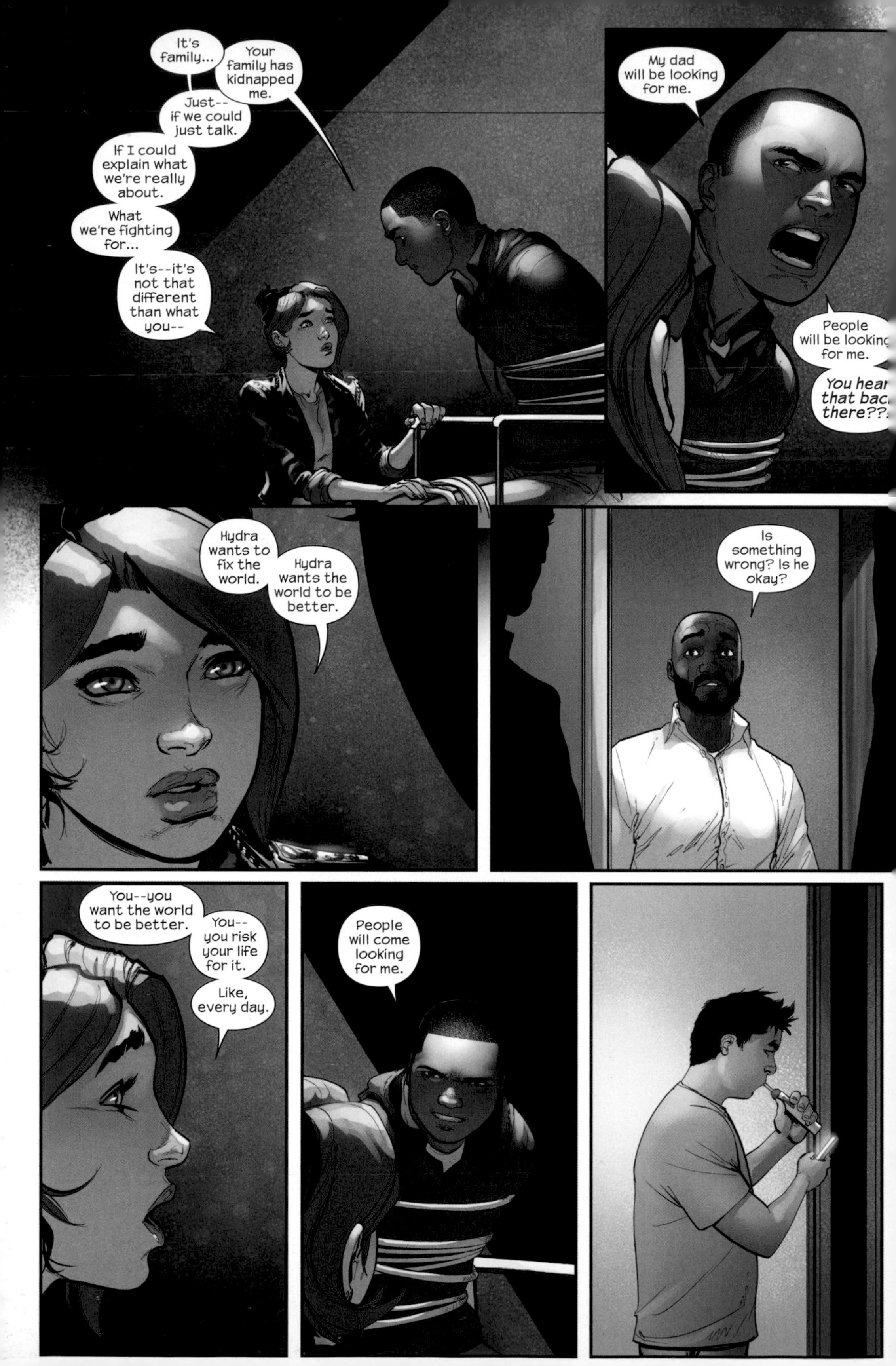
It's family...
Your family has kidnapped me.
Just-- if we could just talk.
If I could explain what we're really about.
What we're fighting for...
It's--it's not that different than what you--
My dad will be looking for me.
People will be lookin
You hear that bac there??
Hydra wants to fix the world.
Hydra wants the world to be better.
Is something wrong? Is he okay?
You--you want the world to be better.
You-- you risk your life for it.
Like, every day.
People will come looking for me.

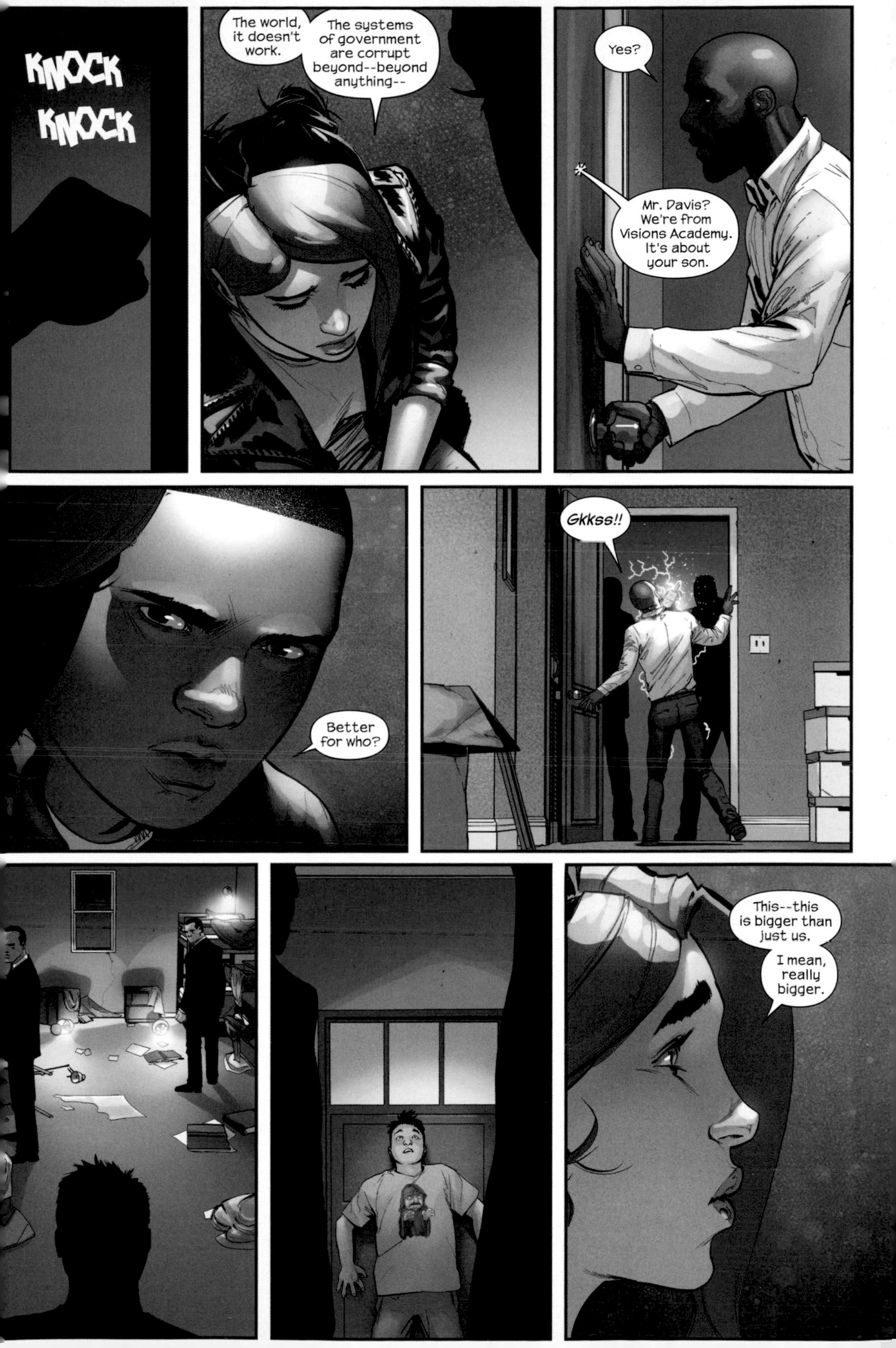
KNOCK KNOCK
The world, it doesn't work.
The systems of government are corrupt beyond--beyond anything--
Yes?
Mr. Davis? We're from Visions Academy. It's about your son.
Better for who?
Gkkss!!
This--this is bigger than just us.
I mean, really bigger.

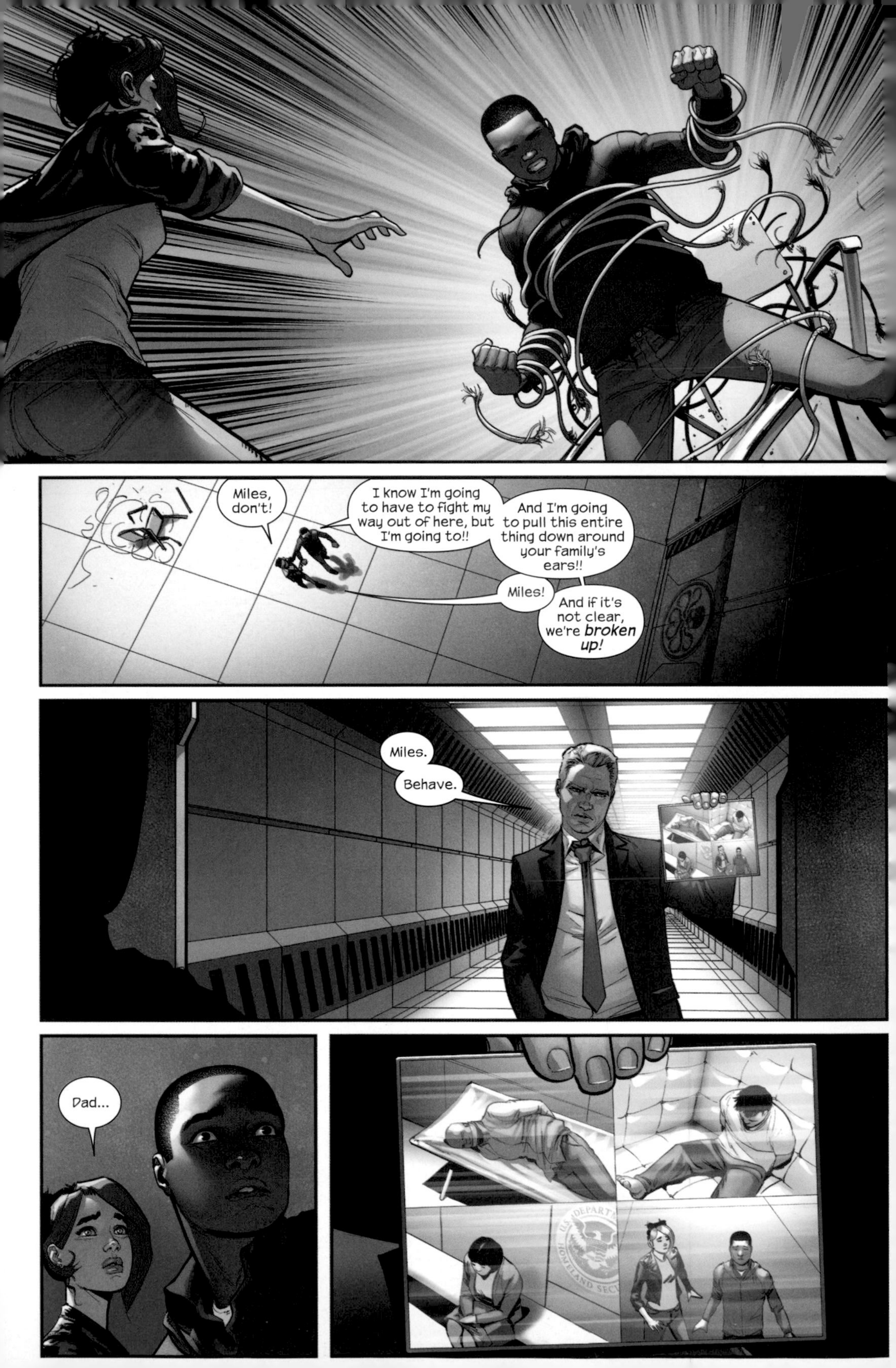
Miles, don't!
I know I'm going to have to fight my way out of here, but I'm going to!!
And I'm going to pull this entire thing down around your family's ears!!
Miles!
And if it's not clear, we're **broken up!**
Miles.
Behave.
Dad...

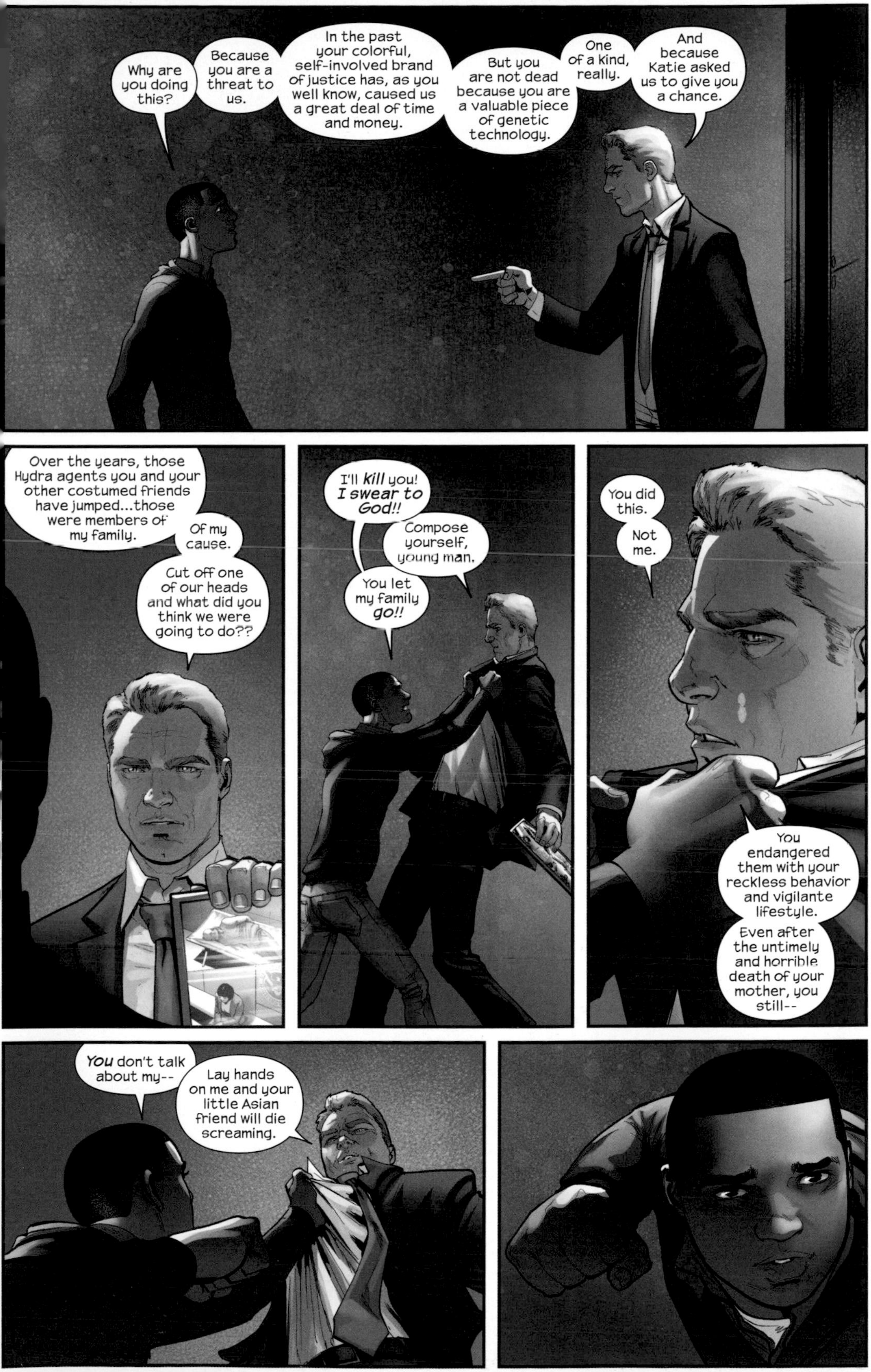

Why are you doing this?
Because you are a threat to us.
In the past your colorful, self-involved brand of justice has, as you well know, caused us a great deal of time and money.
But you are not dead because you are a valuable piece of genetic technology.
One of a kind, really.
And because Katie asked us to give you a chance.
Over the years, those Hydra agents you and your other costumed friends have jumped...those were members of my family.
Of my cause.
Cut off one of our heads and what did you think we were going to do??
I'll *kill* you! *I swear to God!!*
Compose yourself, young man.
You let my family *go!!*
You did this.
Not me.
You endangered them with your reckless behavior and vigilante lifestyle.
Even after the untimely and horrible death of your mother, you still--
You don't talk about my--
Lay hands on me and your little Asian friend will die screaming.

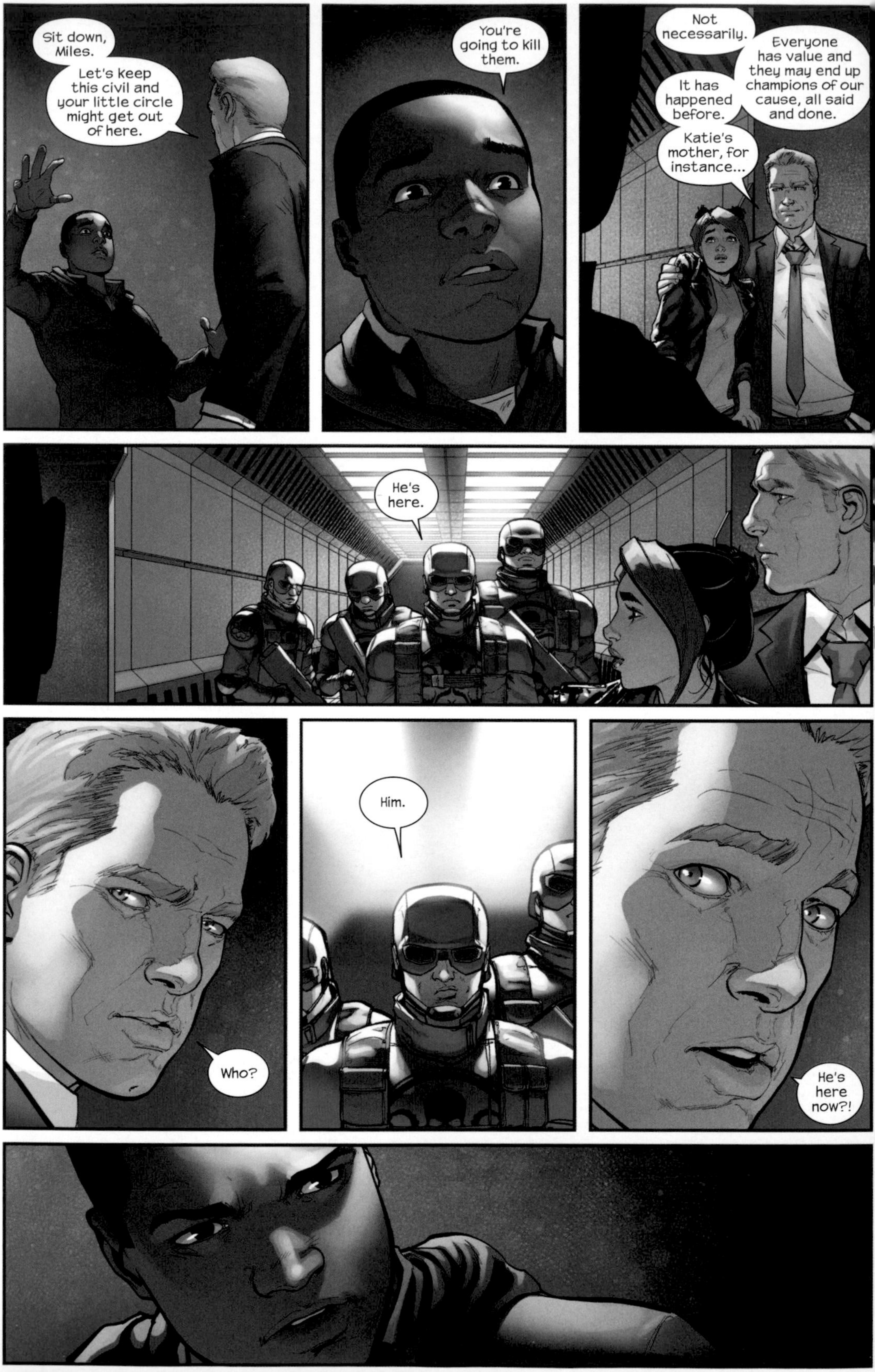
Sit down, Miles.
Let's keep this civil and your little circle might get out of here.
You're going to kill them.
Not necessarily.
Everyone has value and they may end up champions of our cause, all said and done.
It has happened before.
Katie's mother, for instance...
He's here.
Who?
Him.
He's here now?!

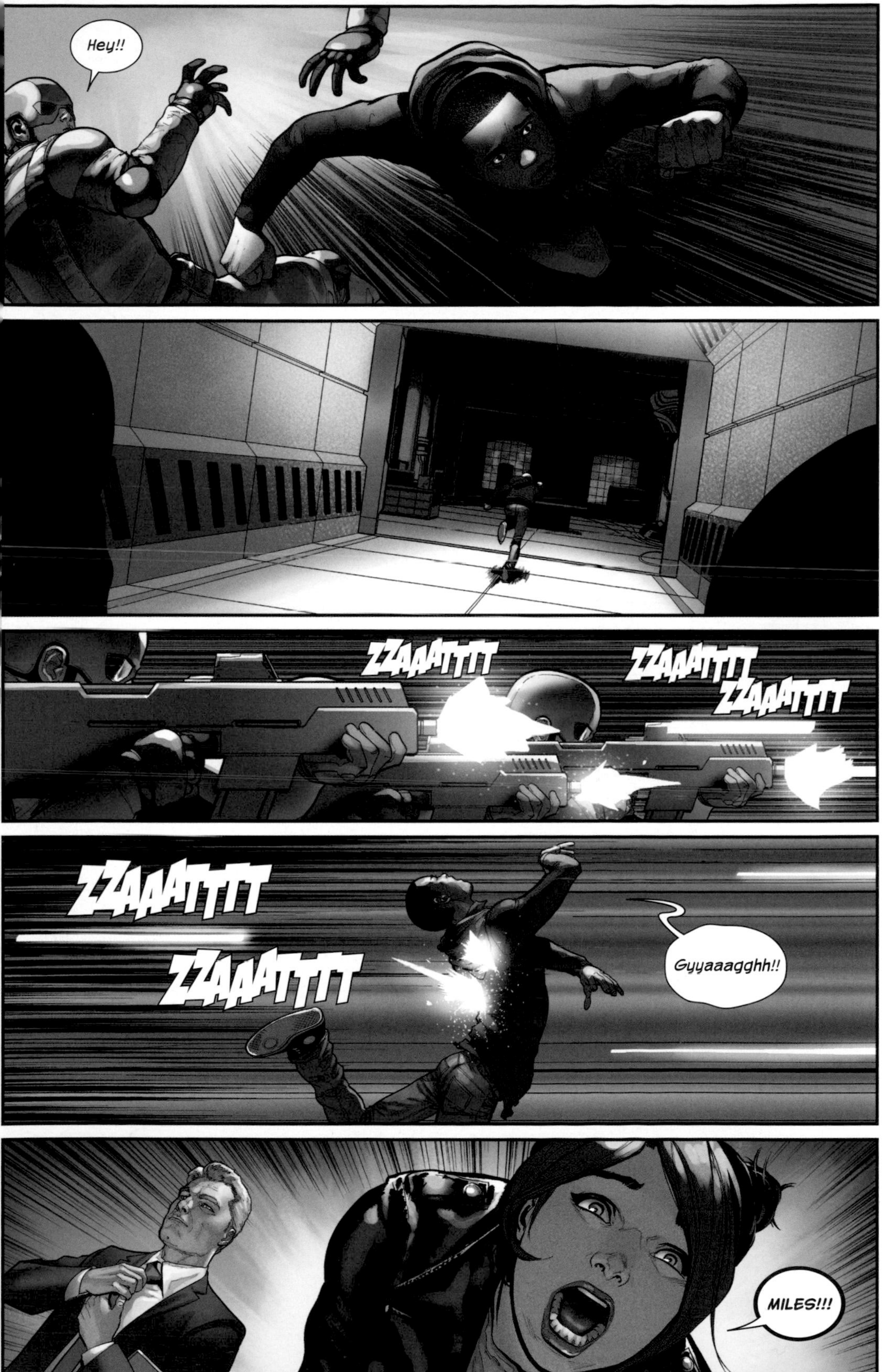

Hey!!
ZZAAATTTT
ZZAAATTTT
ZZAAATTTT
ZZAAATTTT
ZZAAATTTT
Gyyaaagghh!!
MILES!!!

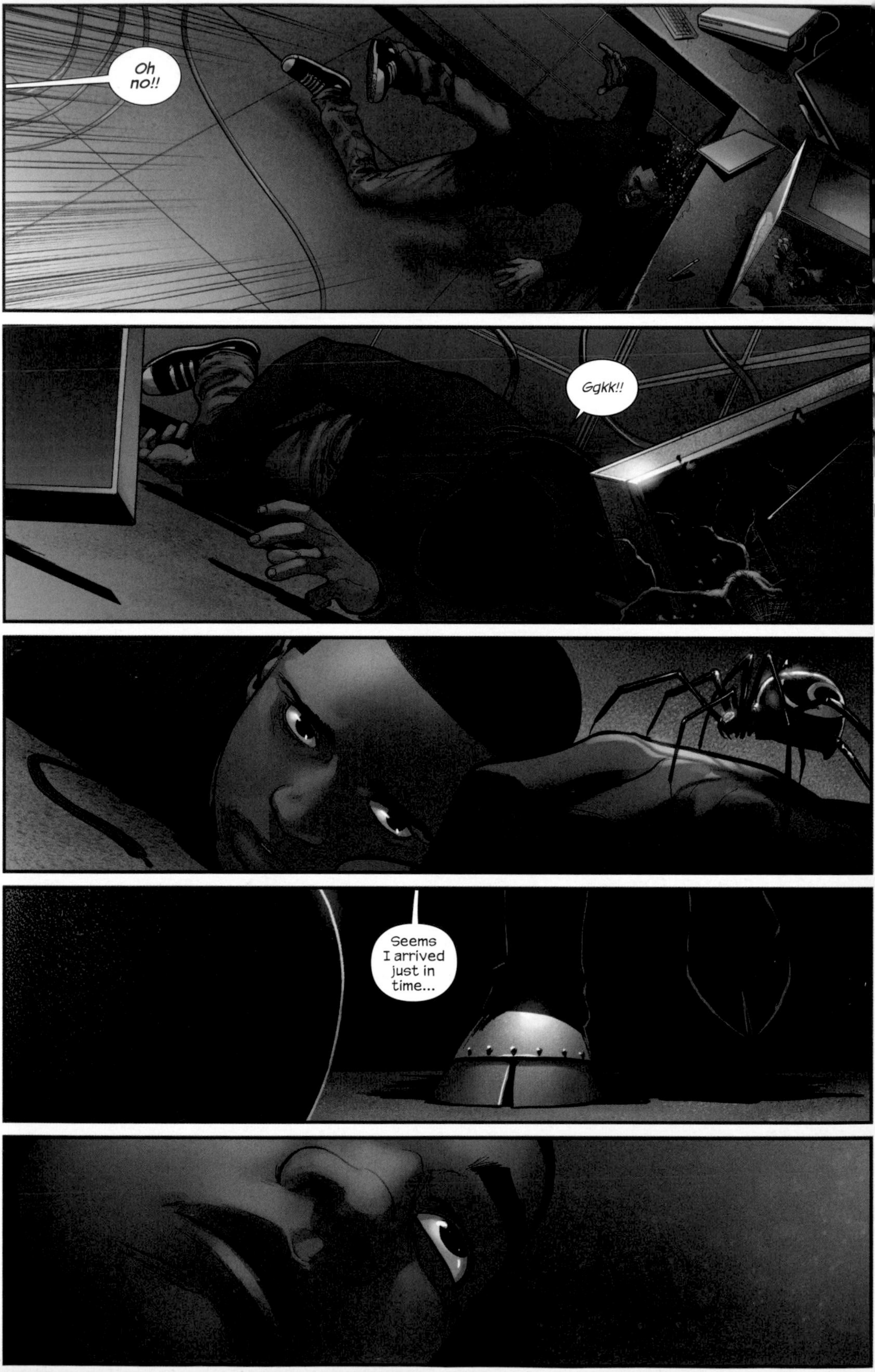
Oh no!!
Ggkk!!
Seems I arrived just in time...

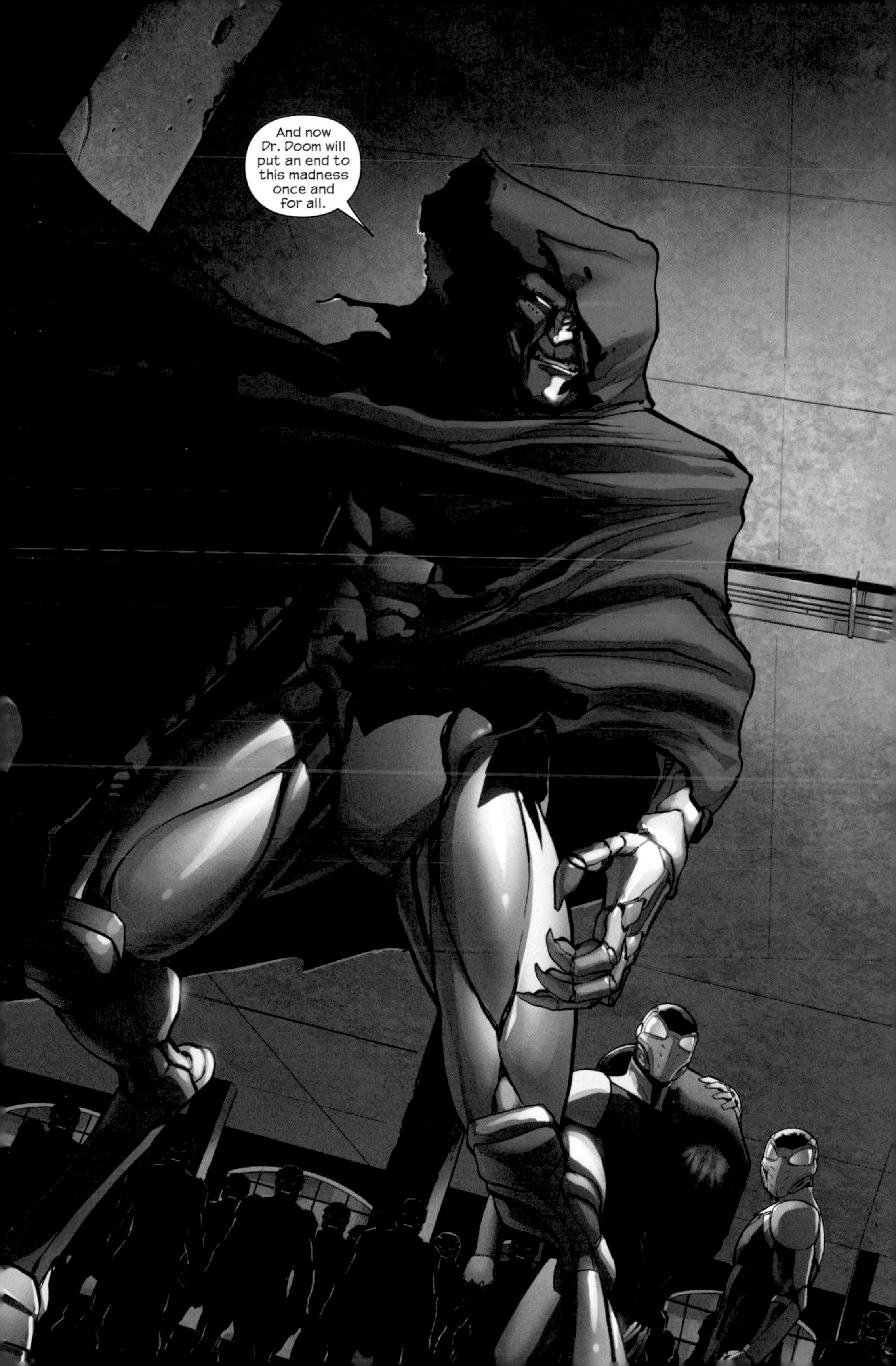
And now Dr. Doom will put an end to this madness once and for all.

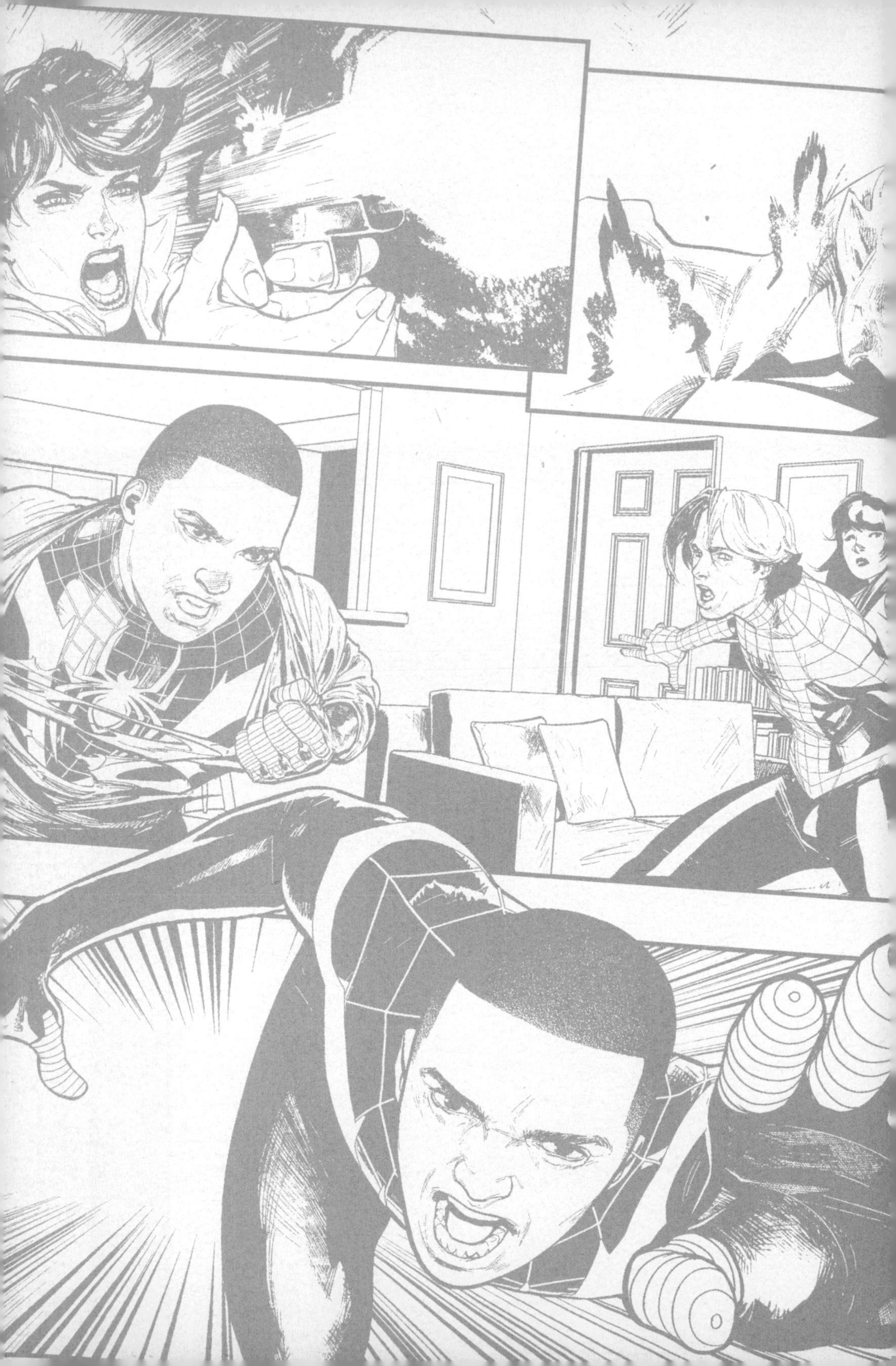

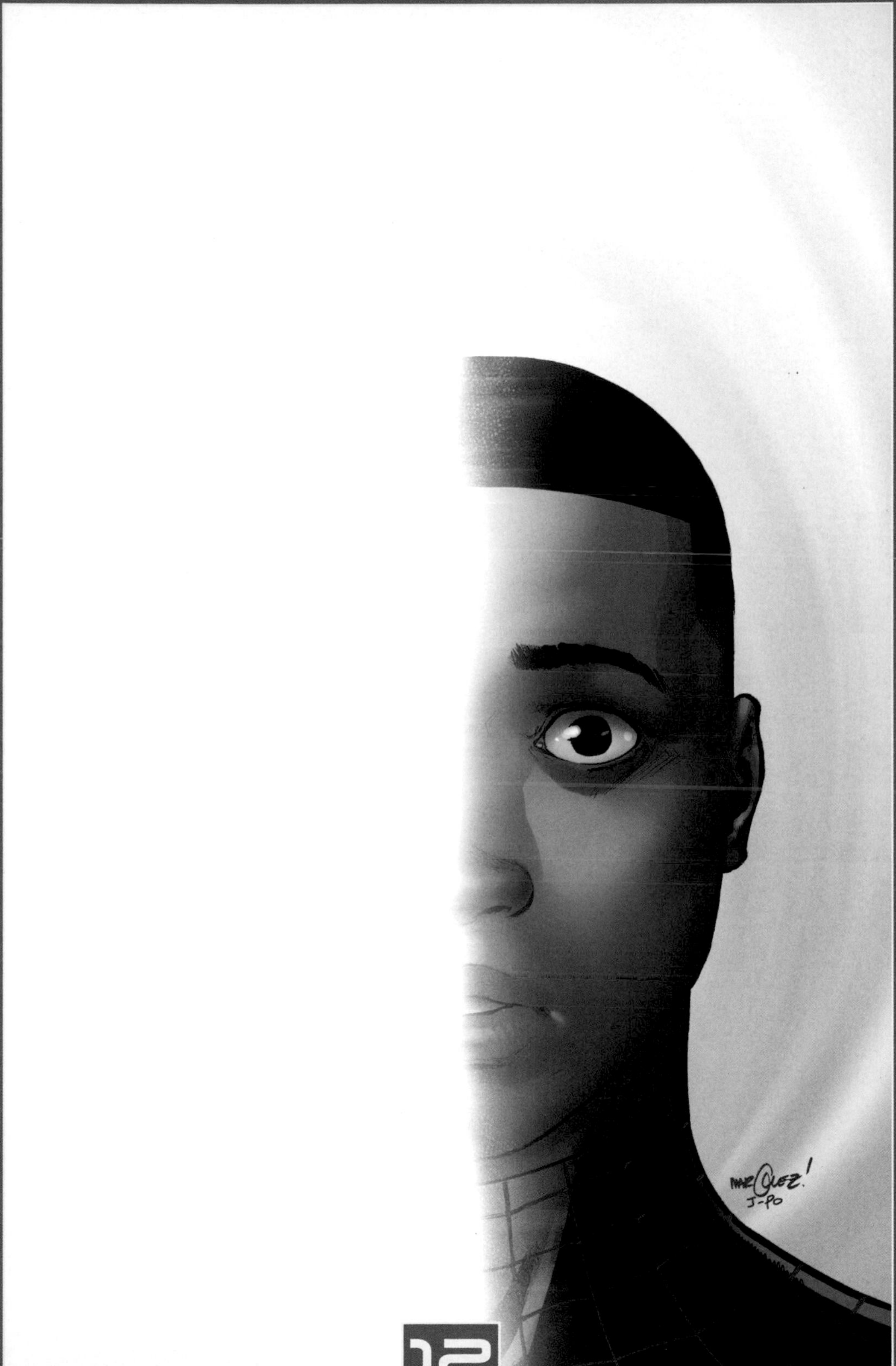
12

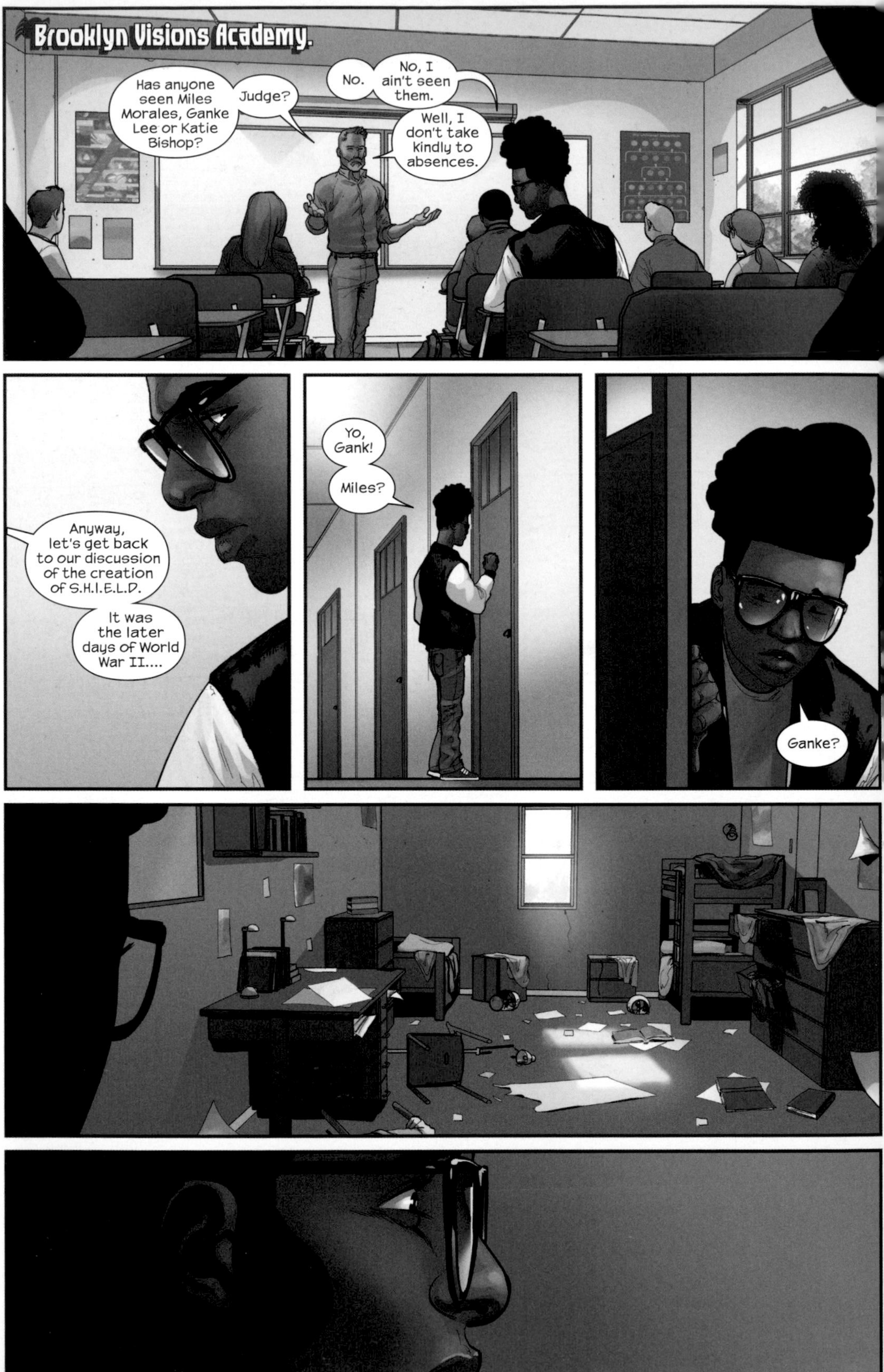
Brooklyn Visions Academy.
Has anyone seen Miles Morales, Ganke Lee or Katie Bishop?
Judge?
No.
No, I ain't seen them.
Well, I don't take kindly to absences.
Anyway, let's get back to our discussion of the creation of S.H.I.E.L.D.
It was the later days of World War II....
Yo, Gank!
Miles?
Ganke?

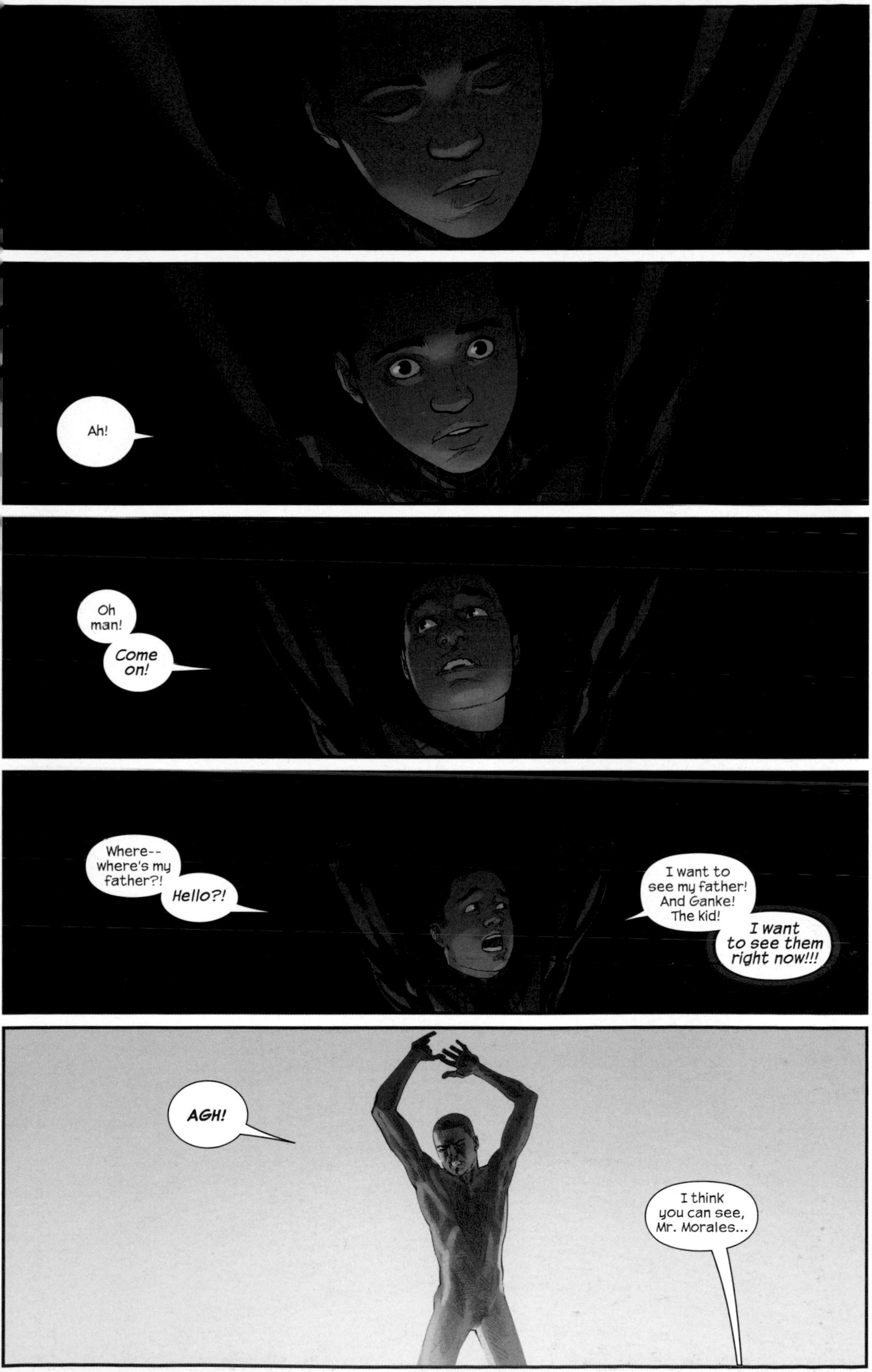
Ah!
Oh man!
Come on!
Where-- where's my father?!
Hello?!
I want to see my father! And Ganke! The kid!
I want to see them right now!!!
AGH!
I think you can see, Mr. Morales...

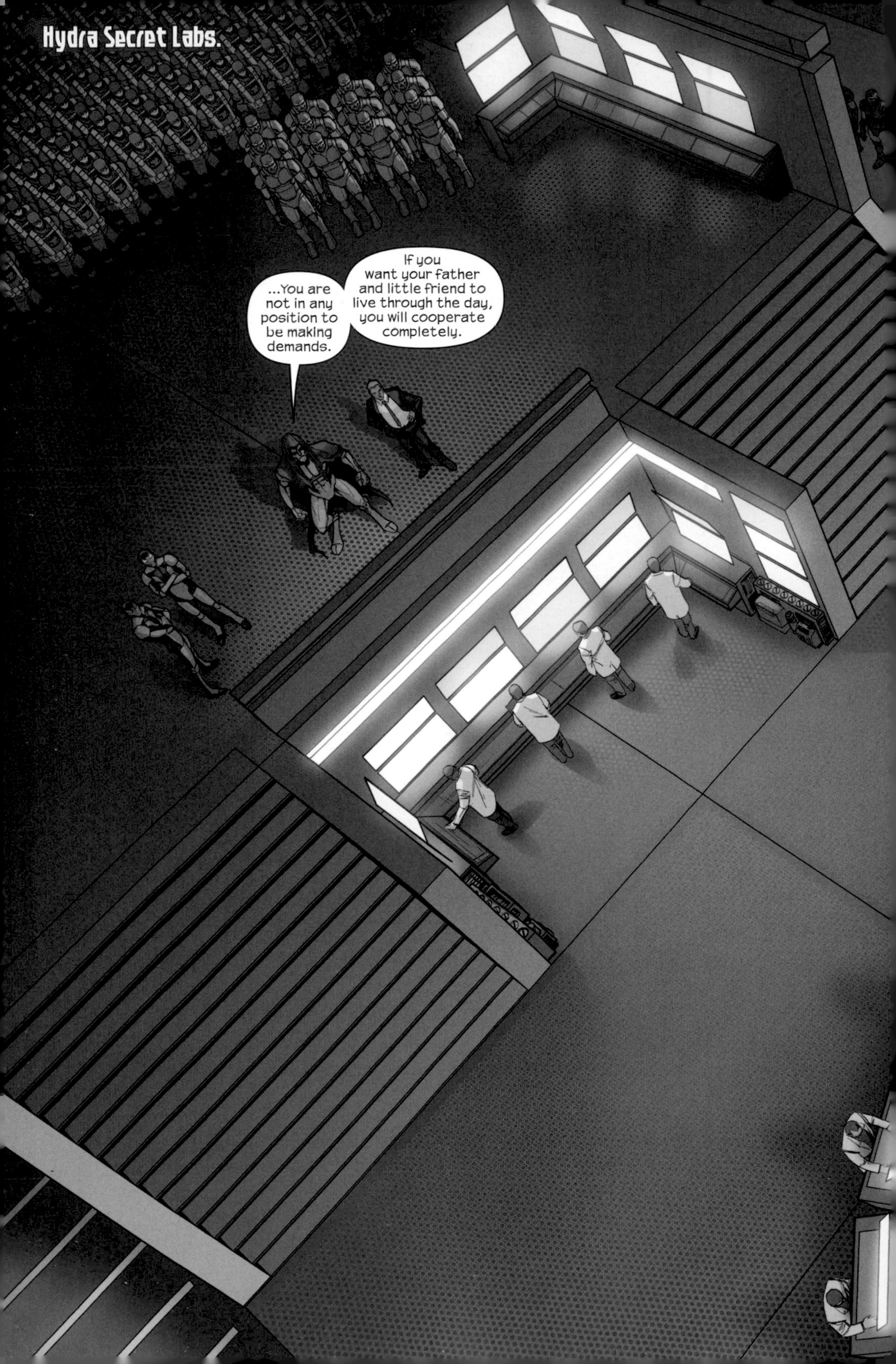
Hydra Secret Labs.
...You are not in any position to be making demands.
If you want your father and little friend to live through the day, you will cooperate completely.

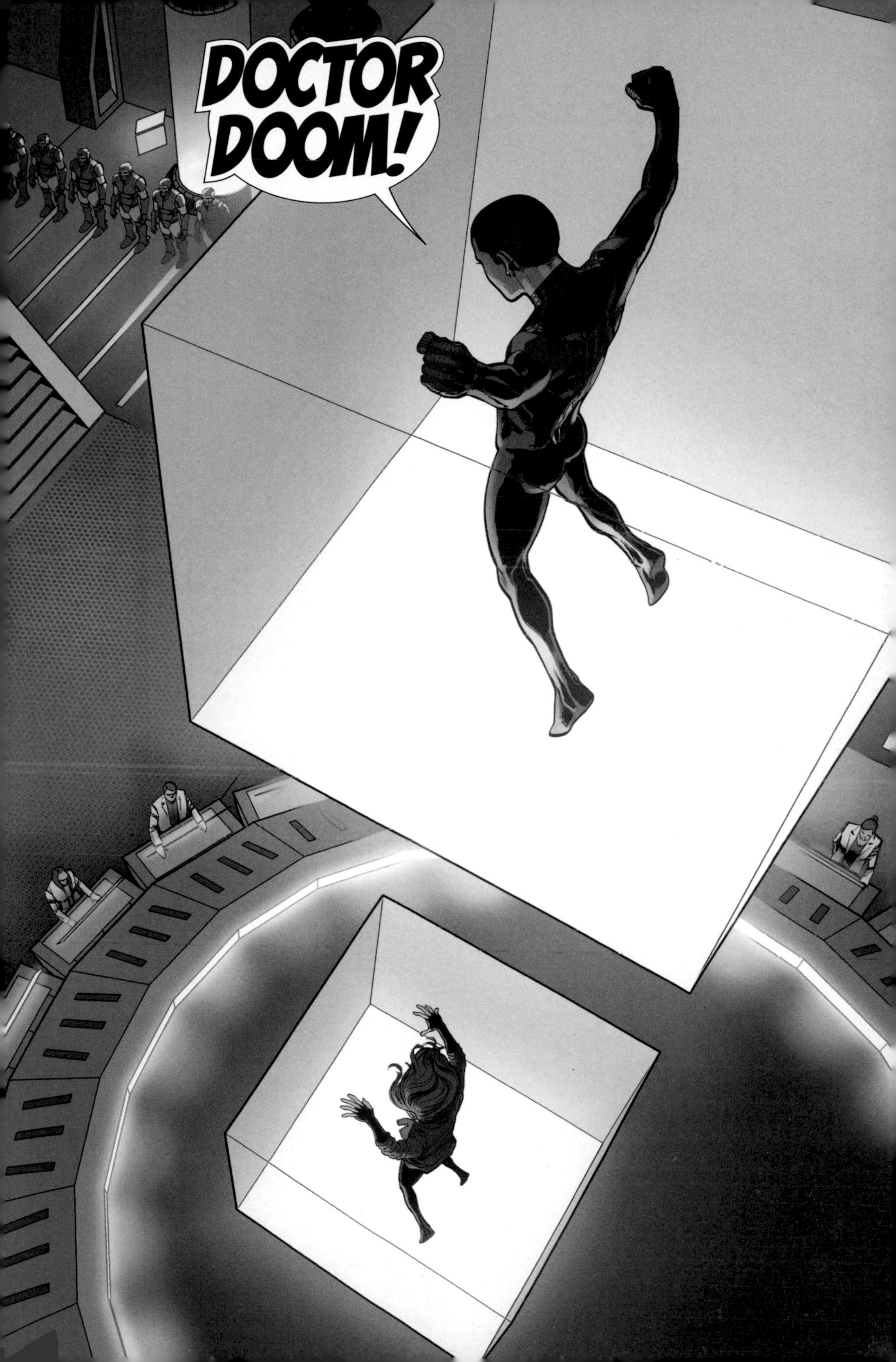
DOCTOR DOOM!

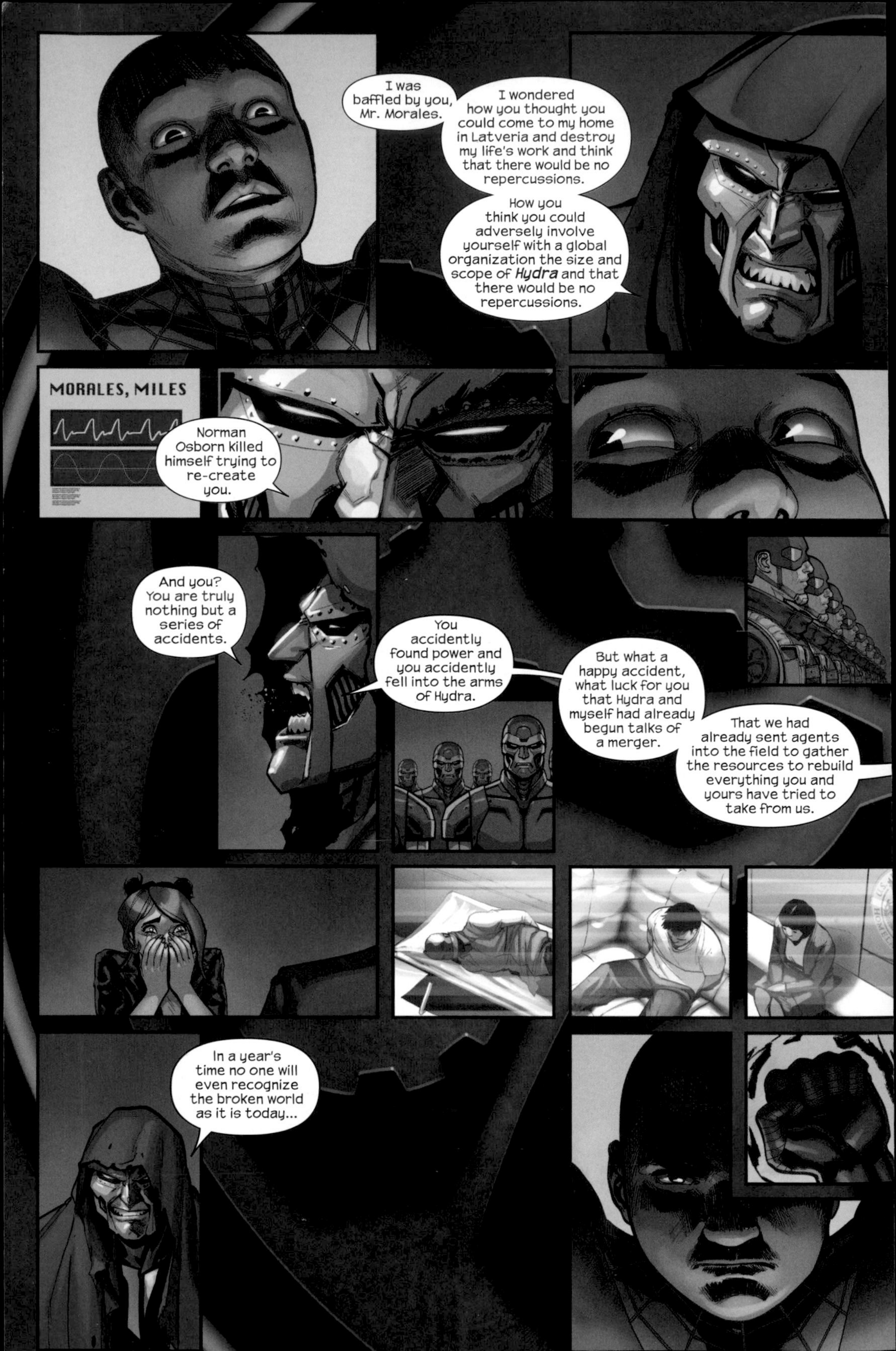
I was baffled by you, Mr. Morales.
I wondered how you thought you could come to my home in Latveria and destroy my life's work and think that there would be no repercussions.
How you think you could adversely involve yourself with a global organization the size and scope of *Hydra* and that there would be no repercussions.
MORALES, MILES
Norman Osborn killed himself trying to re-create you.
And you? You are truly nothing but a series of accidents.
You accidently found power and you accidently fell into the arms of Hydra.
But what a happy accident, what luck for you that Hydra and myself had already begun talks of a merger.
That we had already sent agents into the field to gather the resources to rebuild everything you and yours have tried to take from us.
In a year's time no one will even recognize the broken world as it is today...

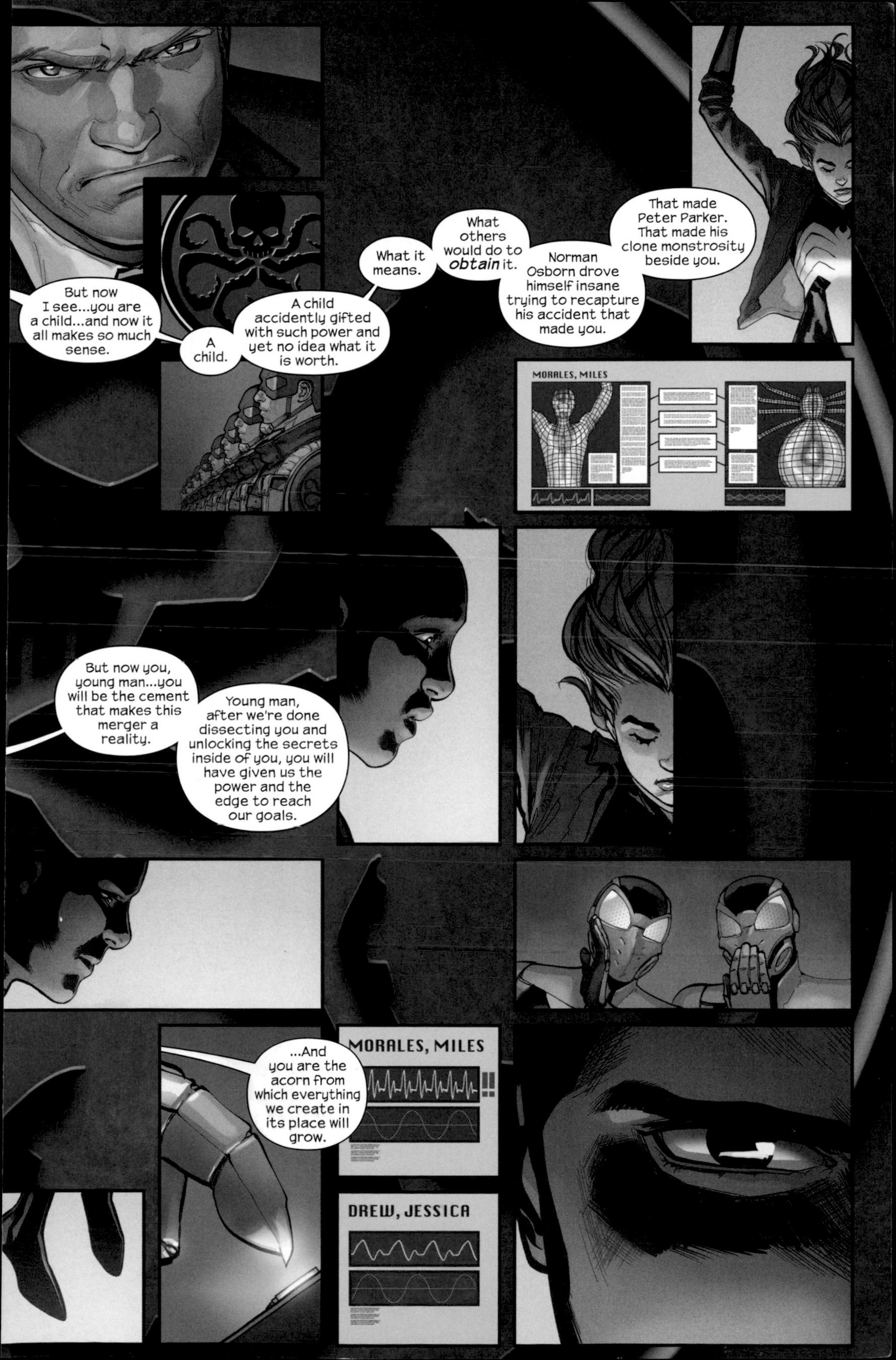
But now I see...you are a child...and now it all makes so much sense.
A child.
A child accidently gifted with such power and yet no idea what it is worth.
What it means.
What others would do to *obtain* it.
Norman Osborn drove himself insane trying to recapture his accident that made you.
That made Peter Parker. That made his clone monstrosity beside you.
MORALES, MILES
But now you, young man...you will be the cement that makes this merger a reality.
Young man, after we're done dissecting you and unlocking the secrets inside of you, you will have given us the power and the edge to reach our goals.
...And you are the acorn from which everything we create in its place will grow.
MORALES, MILES
DREW, JESSICA

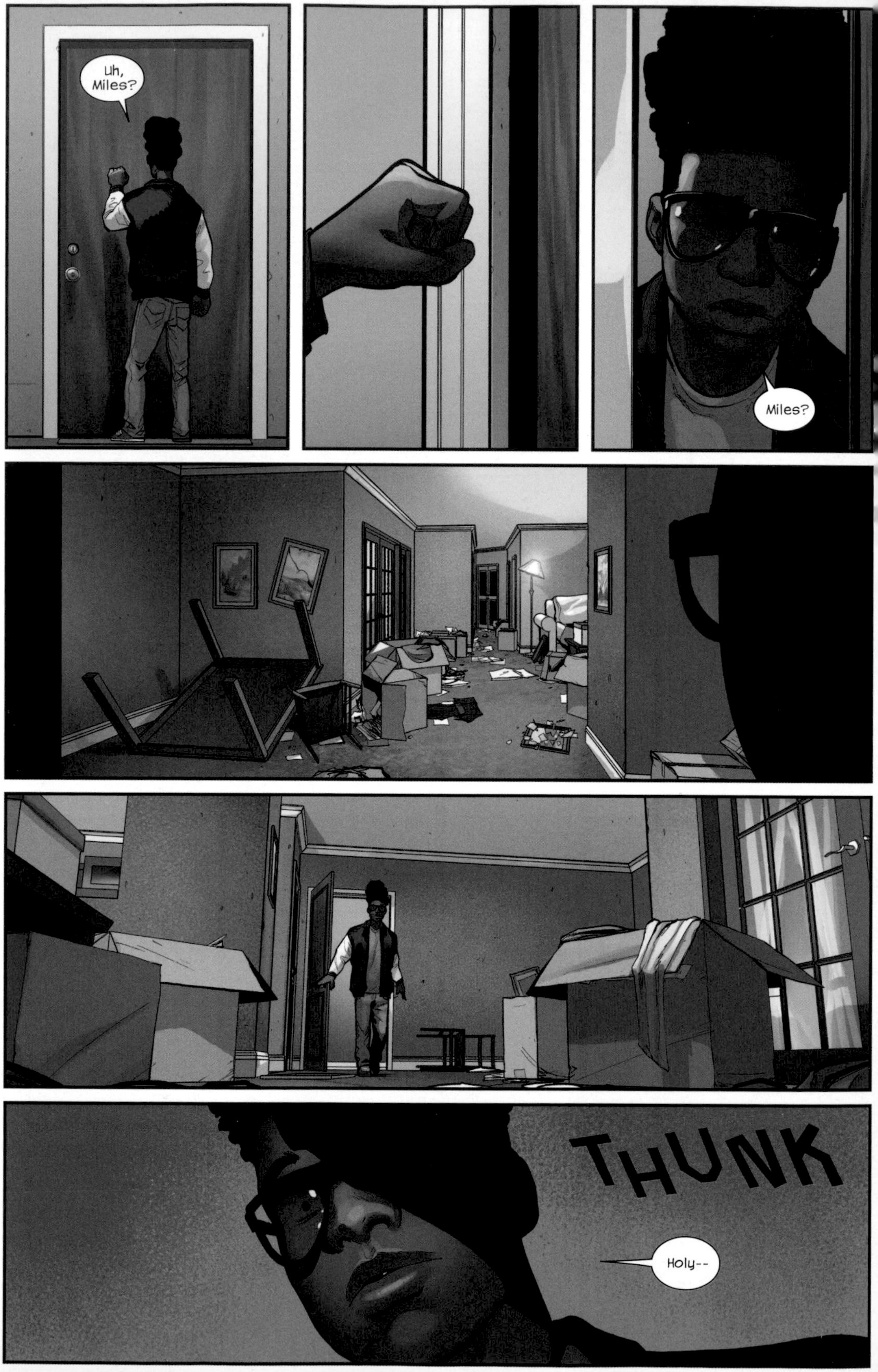
Uh, Miles?
Miles?
THUNK
Holy--

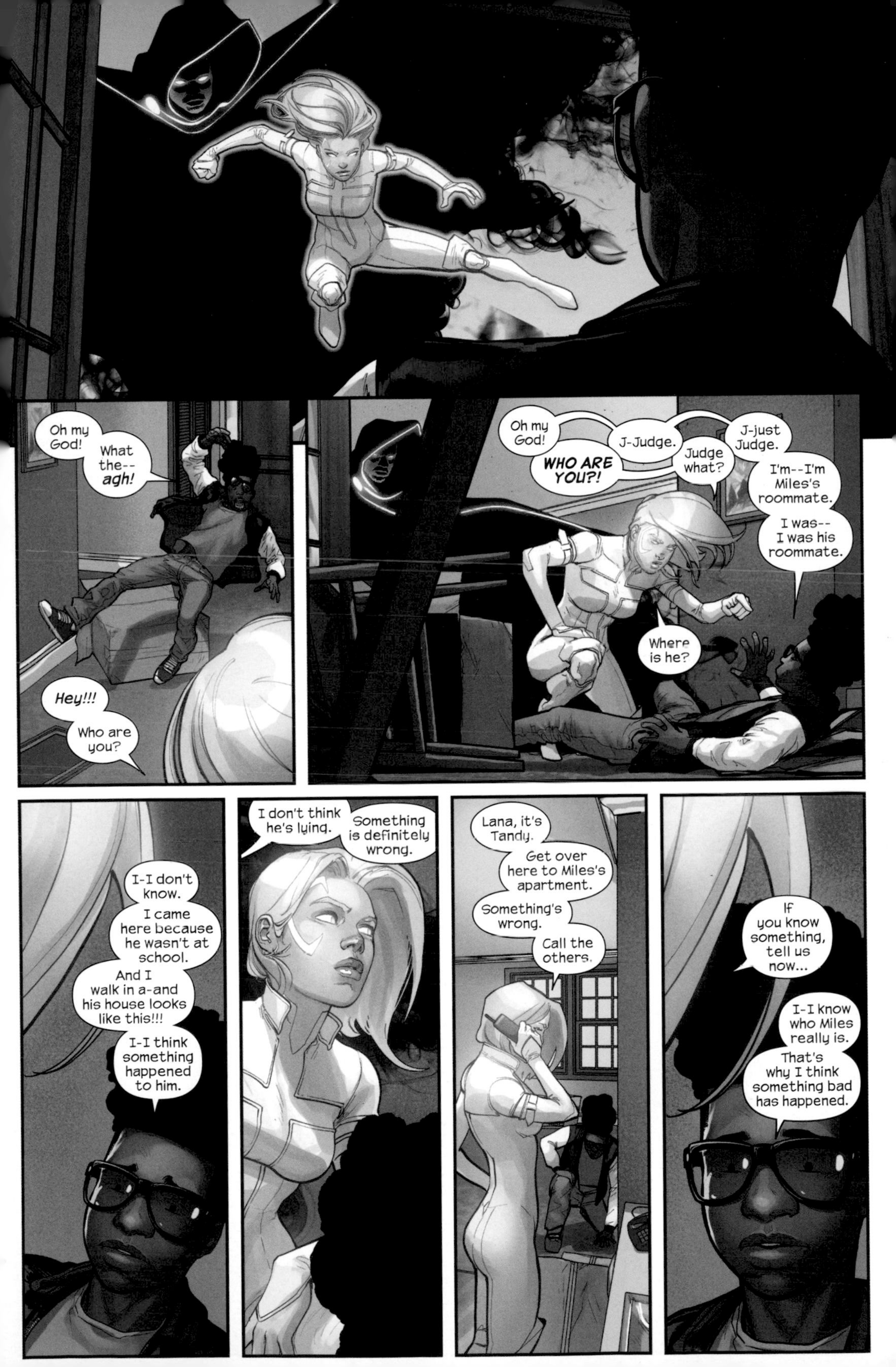
Oh my God!
What the-- agh!
Hey!!!
Who are you?
Oh my God!
WHO ARE YOU?!
J-Judge.
Judge what?
J-just Judge.
I'm--I'm Miles's roommate.
I was-- I was his roommate.
Where is he?
I-I don't know.
I came here because he wasn't at school.
And I walk in a-and his house looks like this!!!
I-I think something happened to him.
I don't think he's lying.
Something is definitely wrong.
Lana, it's Tandy.
Get over here to Miles's apartment.
Something's wrong.
Call the others.
If you know something, tell us now...
I-I know who Miles really is.
That's why I think something bad has happened.

AAAGGHH!!

This needleless sample process is entirely fascinating.

We developed a mix of zero-point energy and microscopic laser fields.

We get to take living tissue samples without any unnecessary interaction with the subject.

His vital signs are elevated, but within range.

It reduces sample contamination.

Why can't you get what you need from him when he's dead?

We'll do that too.

Comparing the living and dead tissues of both subjects will be very illuminating.

Bishop, this will make reverse-engineering what makes a Spider-Man a very simple task.

Your dream of an army of Hydra super-soldiers will finally be a reality.

I'd hug you, but you don't seem the type.

You are correct.

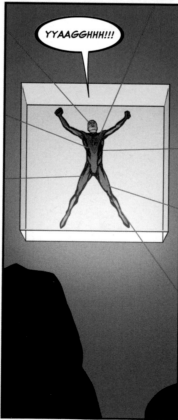

YYAAGGHHH!!!

His vitals are rising!

AAAAARRRGGH!

Rrrr!!!

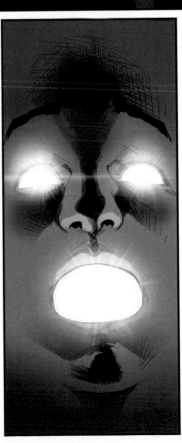

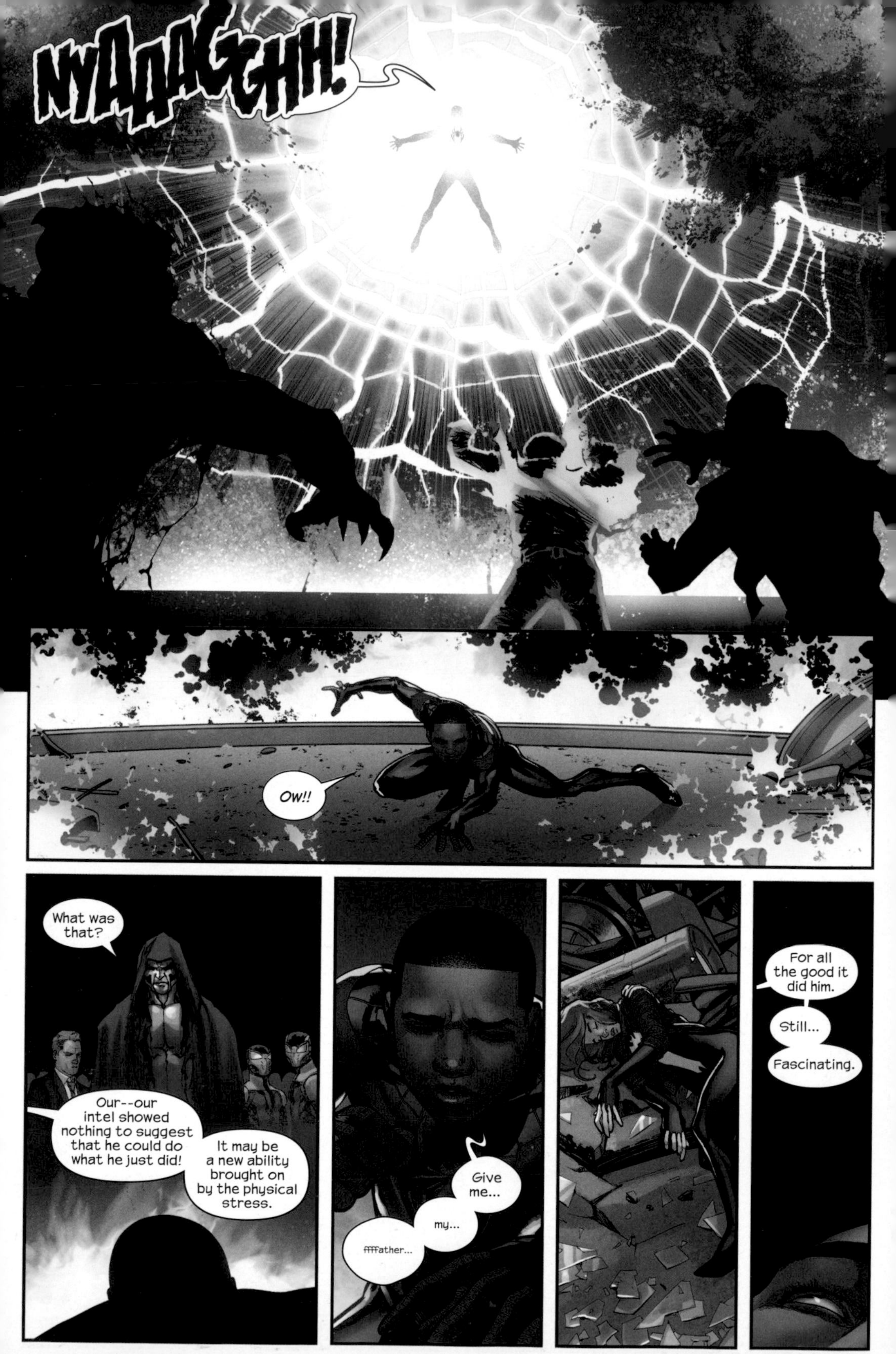
NYAAAGGHH!
Ow!!
What was that?
Our--our intel showed nothing to suggest that he could do what he just did!
It may be a new ability brought on by the physical stress.
Give me...
my...
ffffather...
For all the good it did him.
Still...
Fascinating.

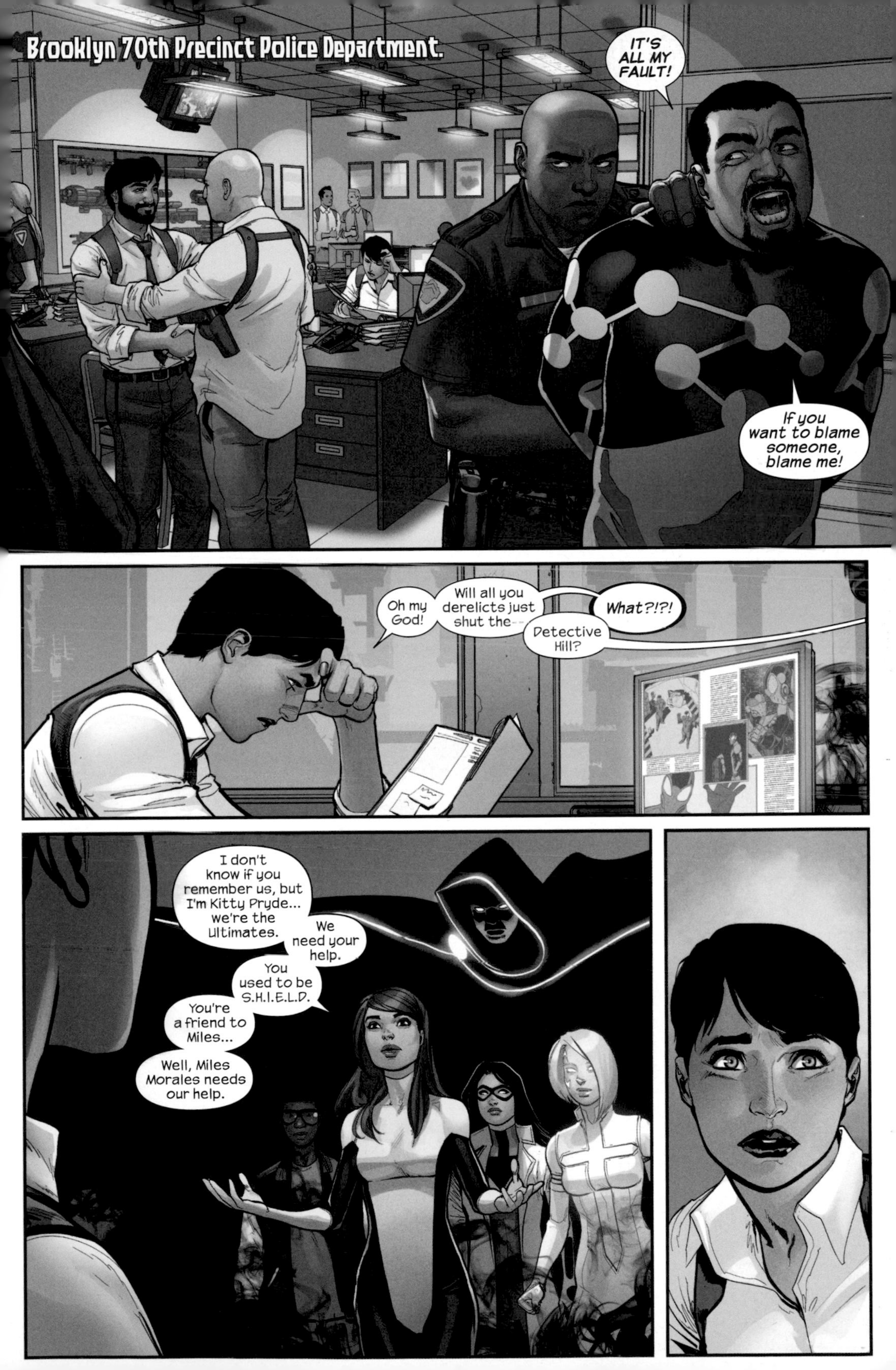
Brooklyn 70th Precinct Police Department.
IT'S ALL MY FAULT!
If you want to blame someone, blame me!
Oh my God!
Will all you derelicts just shut the--
What?!?!
Detective Hill?
I don't know if you remember us, but I'm Kitty Pryde... we're the Ultimates.
We need your help.
You used to be S.H.I.E.L.D.
You're a friend to Miles...
Well, Miles Morales needs our help.

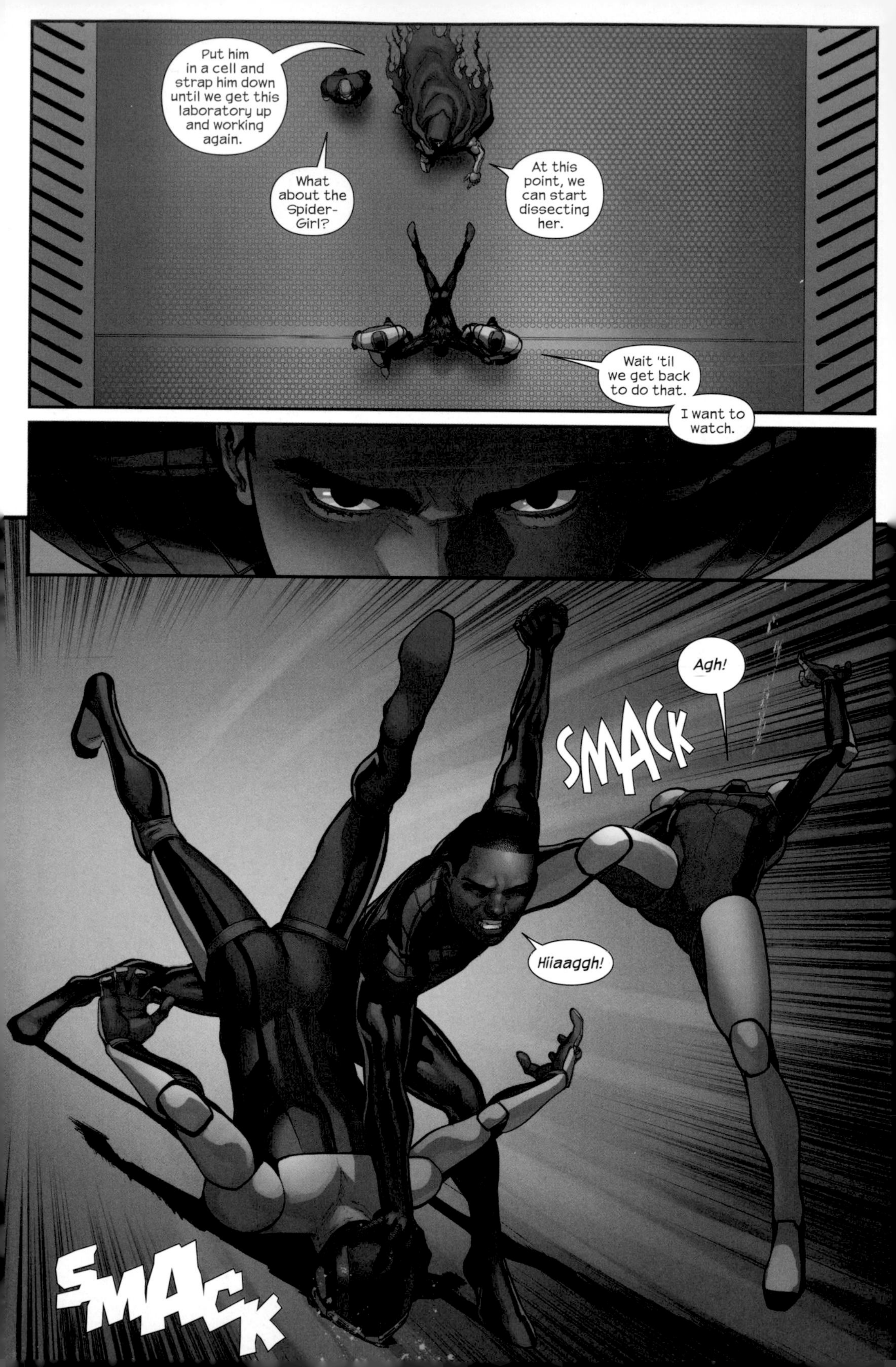
Put him in a cell and strap him down until we get this laboratory up and working again.
What about the Spider-Girl?
At this point, we can start dissecting her.
Wait 'til we get back to do that.
I want to watch.
SMACK
Agh!
Hiiaaggh!
SMACK

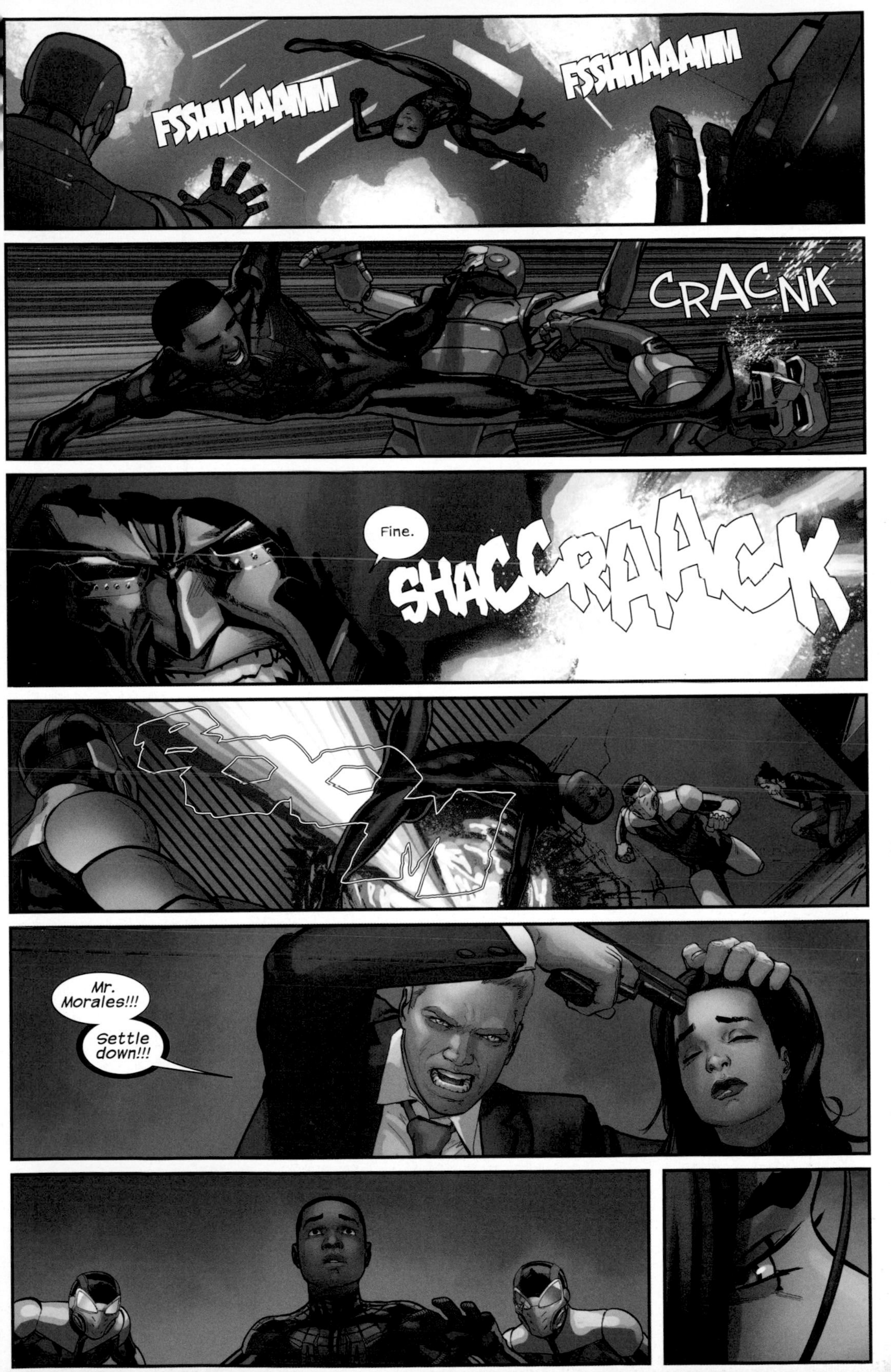
FSSHHAAAMM
FSSHHAAAMM
CRACNK
Fine.
SHACCRAACK
Mr. Morales!!!
Settle down!!!

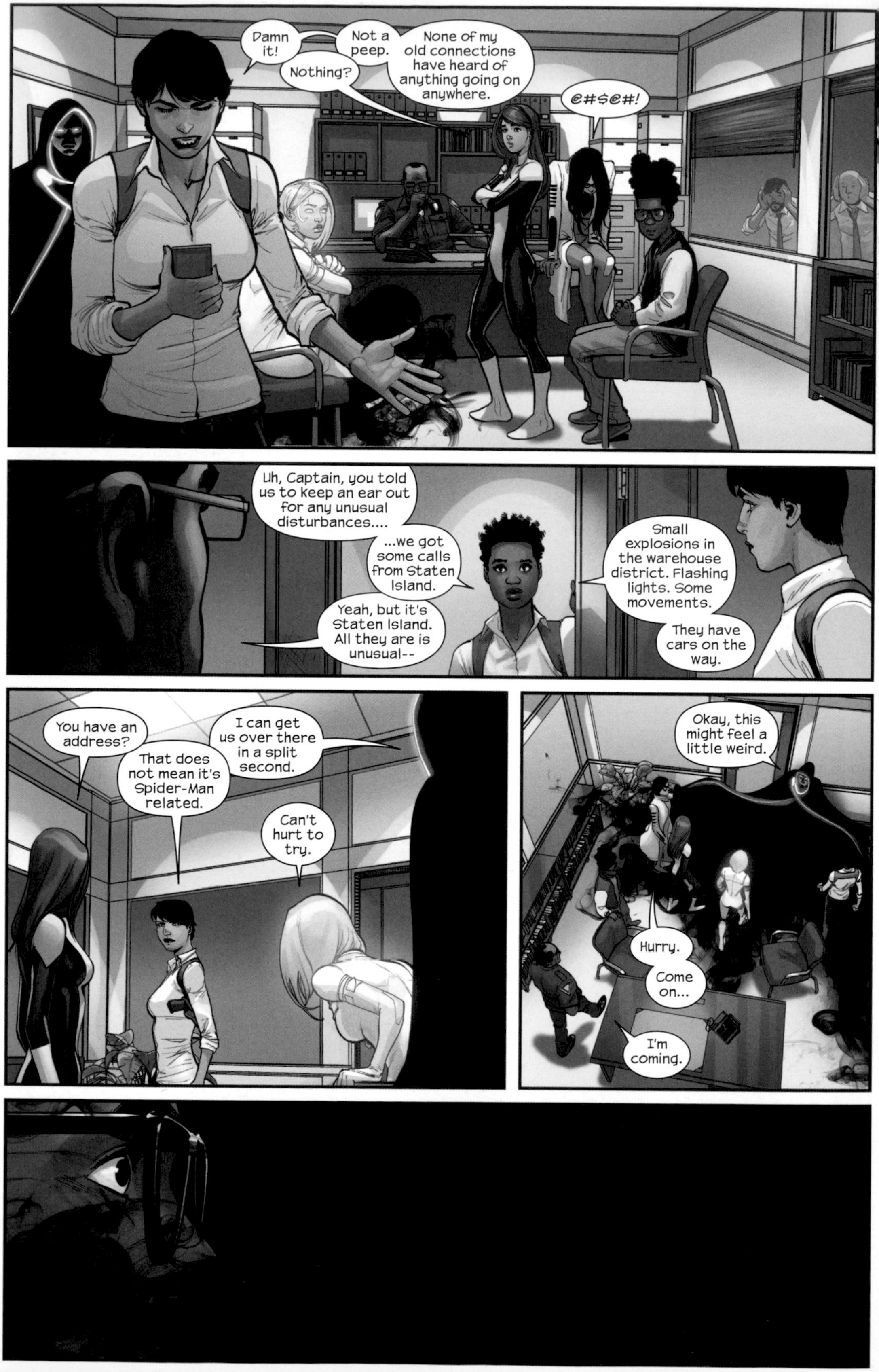
Damn it!
Nothing?
Not a peep.
None of my old connections have heard of anything going on anywhere.
@#$@#!
Uh, Captain, you told us to keep an ear out for any unusual disturbances....
...we got some calls from Staten Island.
Yeah, but it's Staten Island. All they are is unusual--
Small explosions in the warehouse district. Flashing lights. Some movements.
They have cars on the way.
You have an address?
That does not mean it's Spider-Man related.
I can get us over there in a split second.
Can't hurt to try.
Okay, this might feel a little weird.
Hurry.
Come on...
I'm coming.

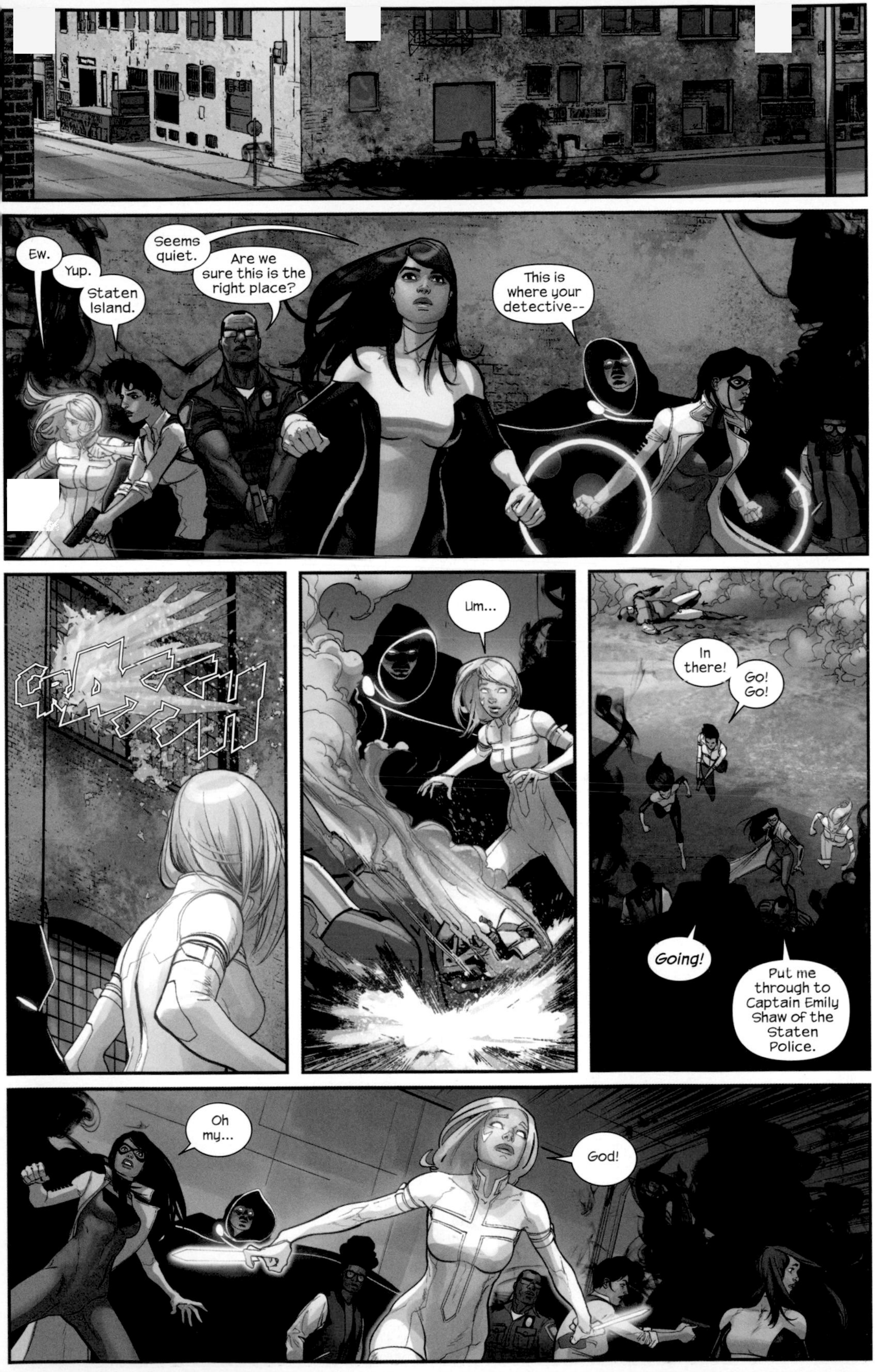

Ew.
Yup.
Staten Island.
Seems quiet.
Are we sure this is the right place?
This is where your detective--
Um...
In there!
Go! Go!
Going!
Put me through to Captain Emily Shaw of the Staten Police.
Oh my...
God!

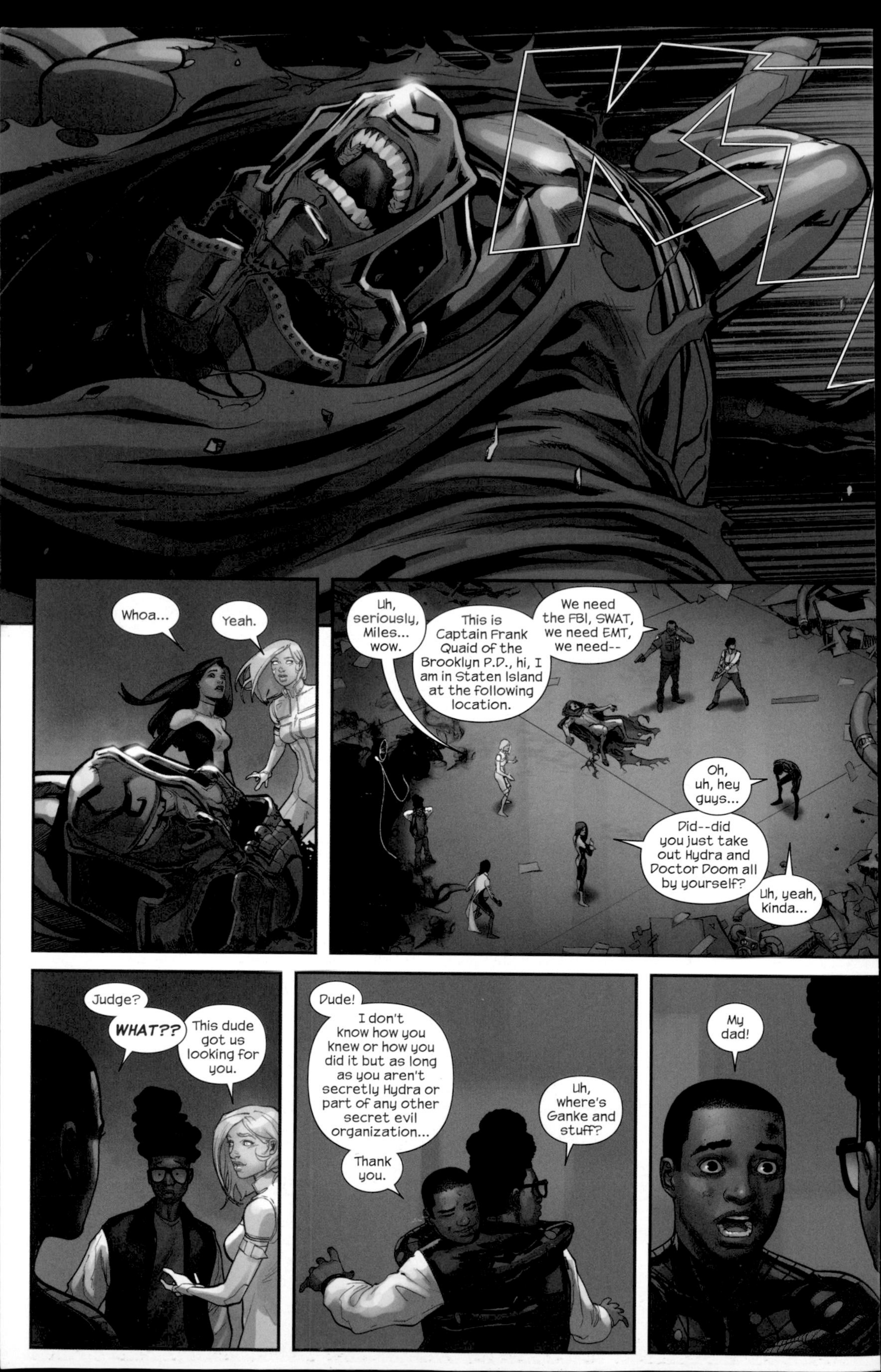
Whoa...
Yeah.
Uh, seriously, Miles... wow.
This is Captain Frank Quaid of the Brooklyn P.D., hi, I am in Staten Island at the following location.
We need the FBI, SWAT, we need EMT, we need--
Oh, uh, hey guys...
Did--did you just take out Hydra and Doctor Doom all by yourself?
Uh, yeah, kinda...
Judge?
WHAT??
This dude got us looking for you.
Dude!
I don't know how you knew or how you did it but as long as you aren't secretly Hydra or part of any other secret evil organization...
Thank you.
Uh, where's Ganke and stuff?
My dad!

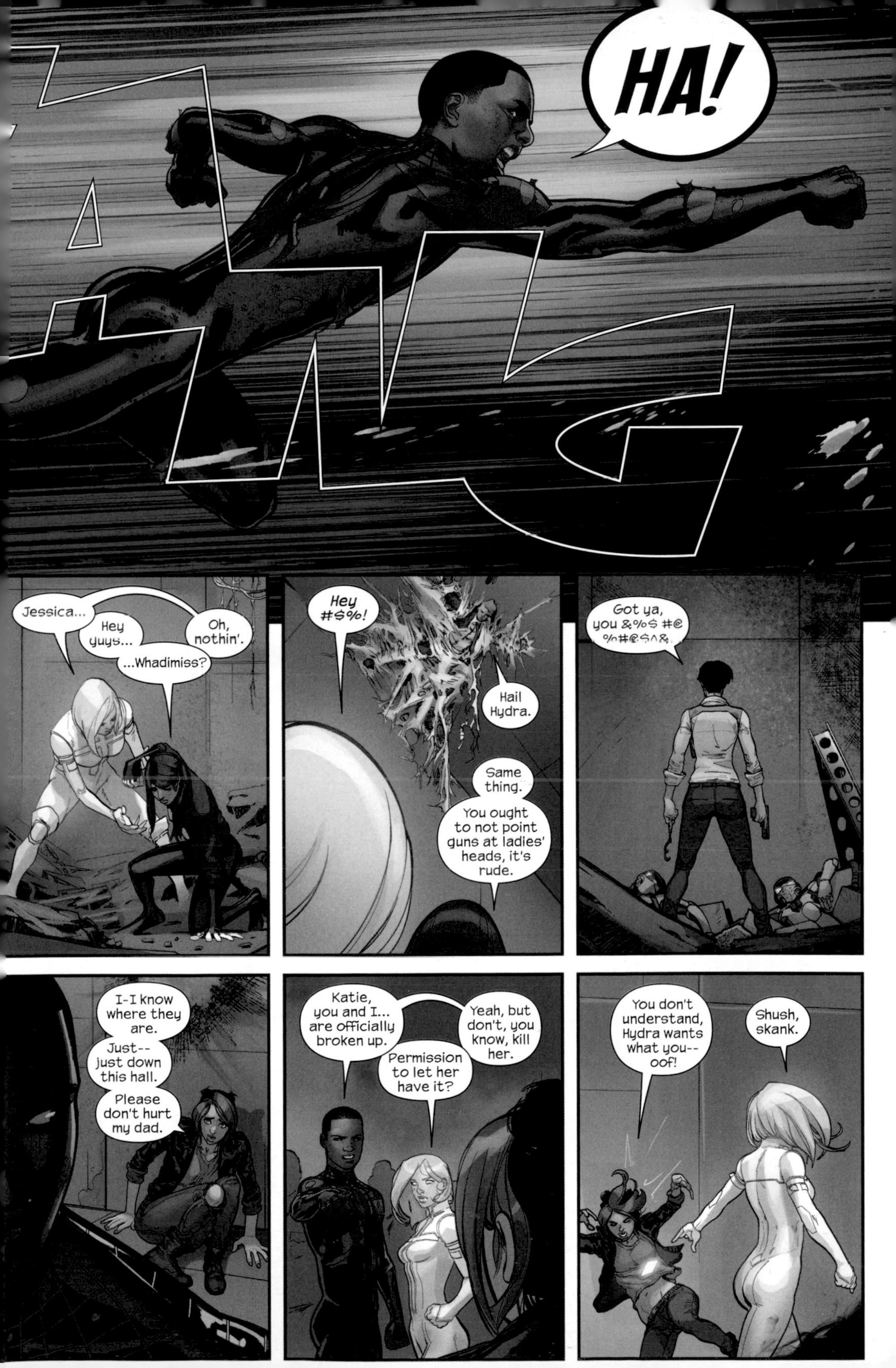
HA!
Jessica...
Hey guys...
...Whadimiss?
Oh, nothin'.
Hey #$%!
Hail Hydra.
Same thing.
You ought to not point guns at ladies' heads, it's rude.
Got ya, you &%$ #@ %#@$^&
I-I know where they are.
Just-- just down this hall.
Please don't hurt my dad.
Katie, you and I... are officially broken up.
Permission to let her have it?
Yeah, but don't, you know, kill her.
You don't understand, Hydra wants what you-- oof!
Shush, skank.

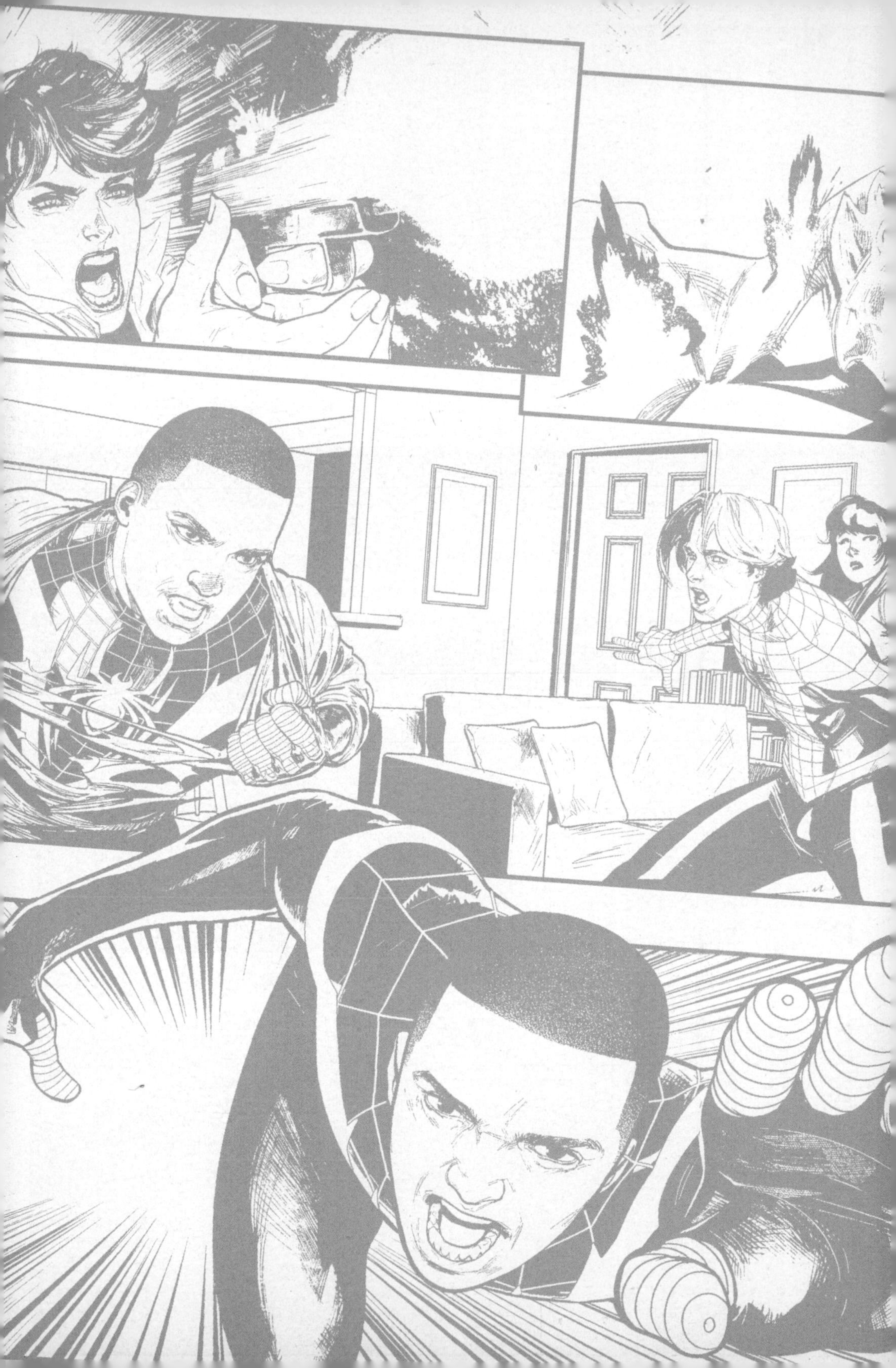

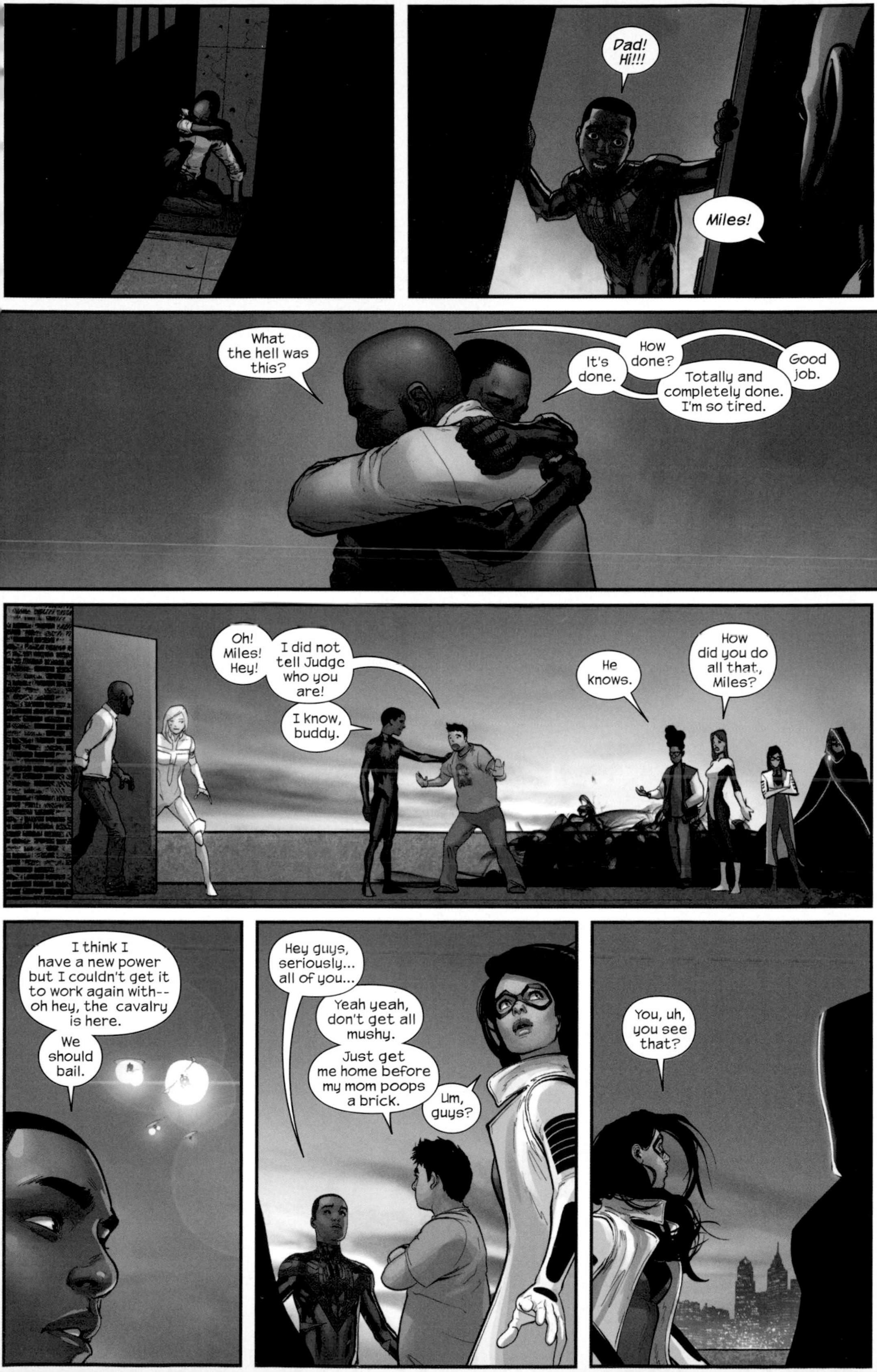

Dad! Hi!!!
Miles!
What the hell was this?
It's done.
How done?
Totally and completely done. I'm so tired.
Good job.
Oh! Miles! Hey!
I did not tell Judge who you are!
I know, buddy.
He knows.
How did you do all that, Miles?
I think I have a new power but I couldn't get it to work again with-- oh hey, the cavalry is here.
We should bail.
Hey guys, seriously... all of you...
Yeah yeah, don't get all mushy.
Just get me home before my mom poops a brick.
Um, guys?
You, uh, you see that?

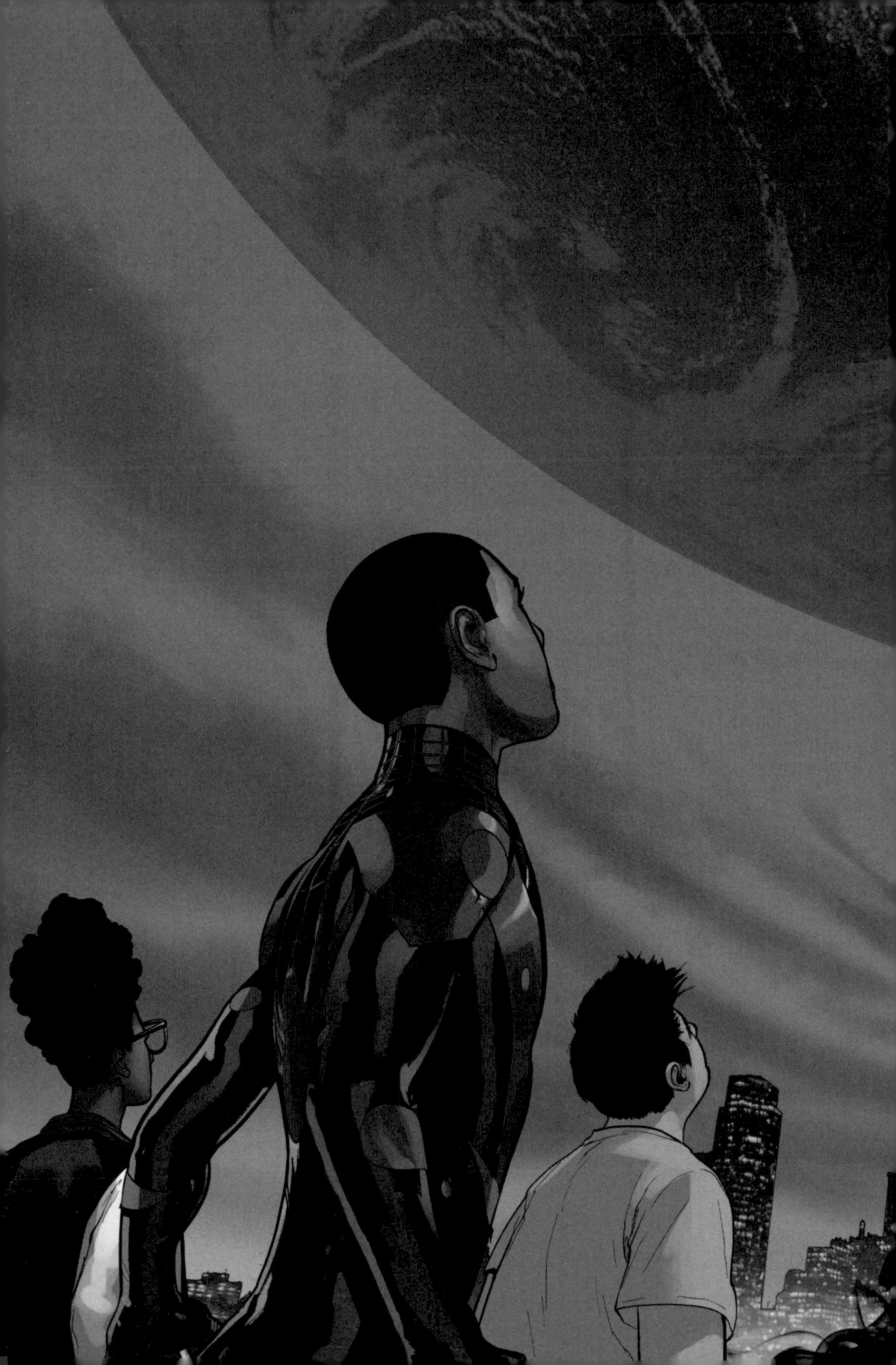

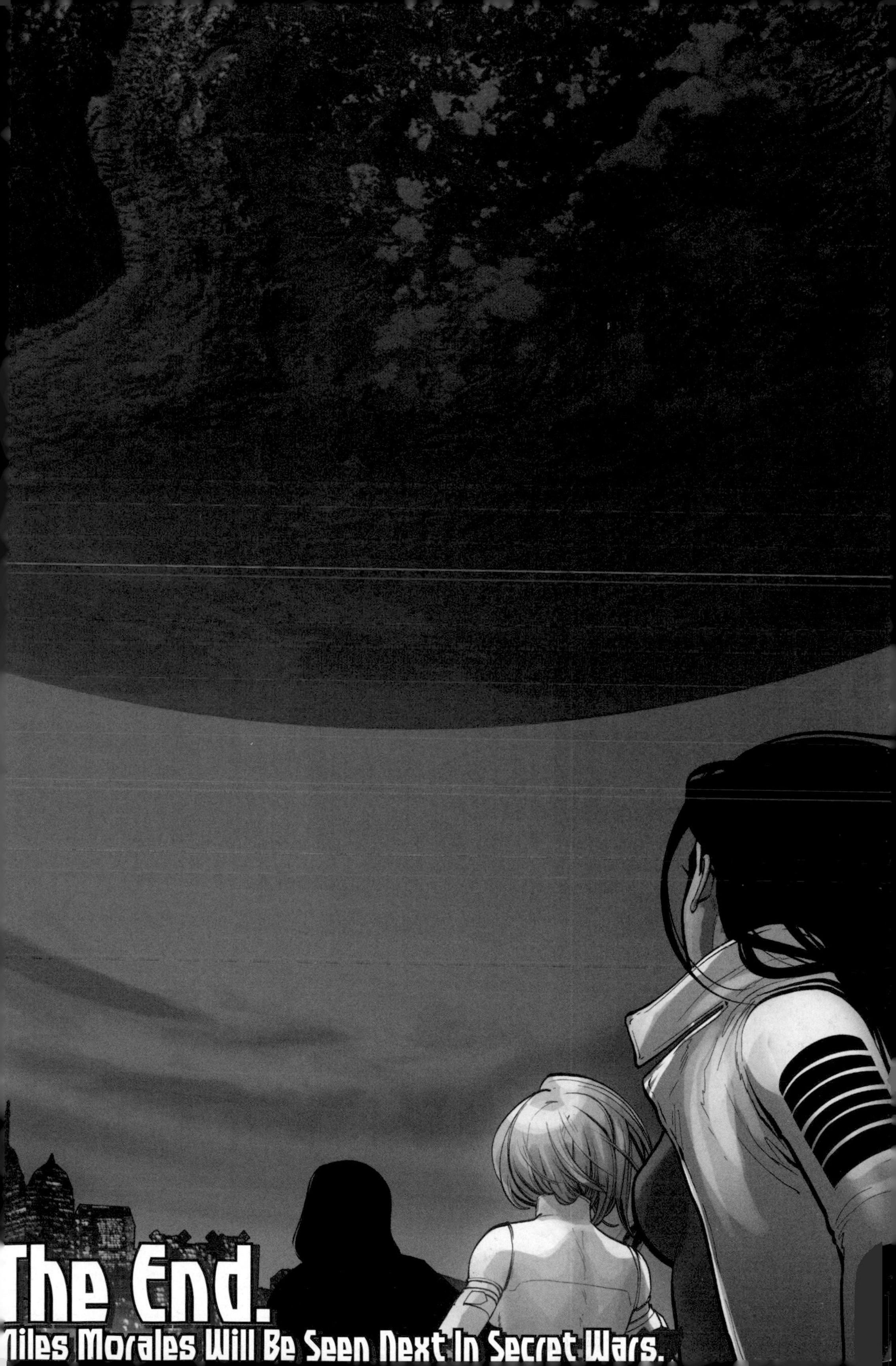
The End.
Miles Morales Will Be Seen Next In Secret Wars.

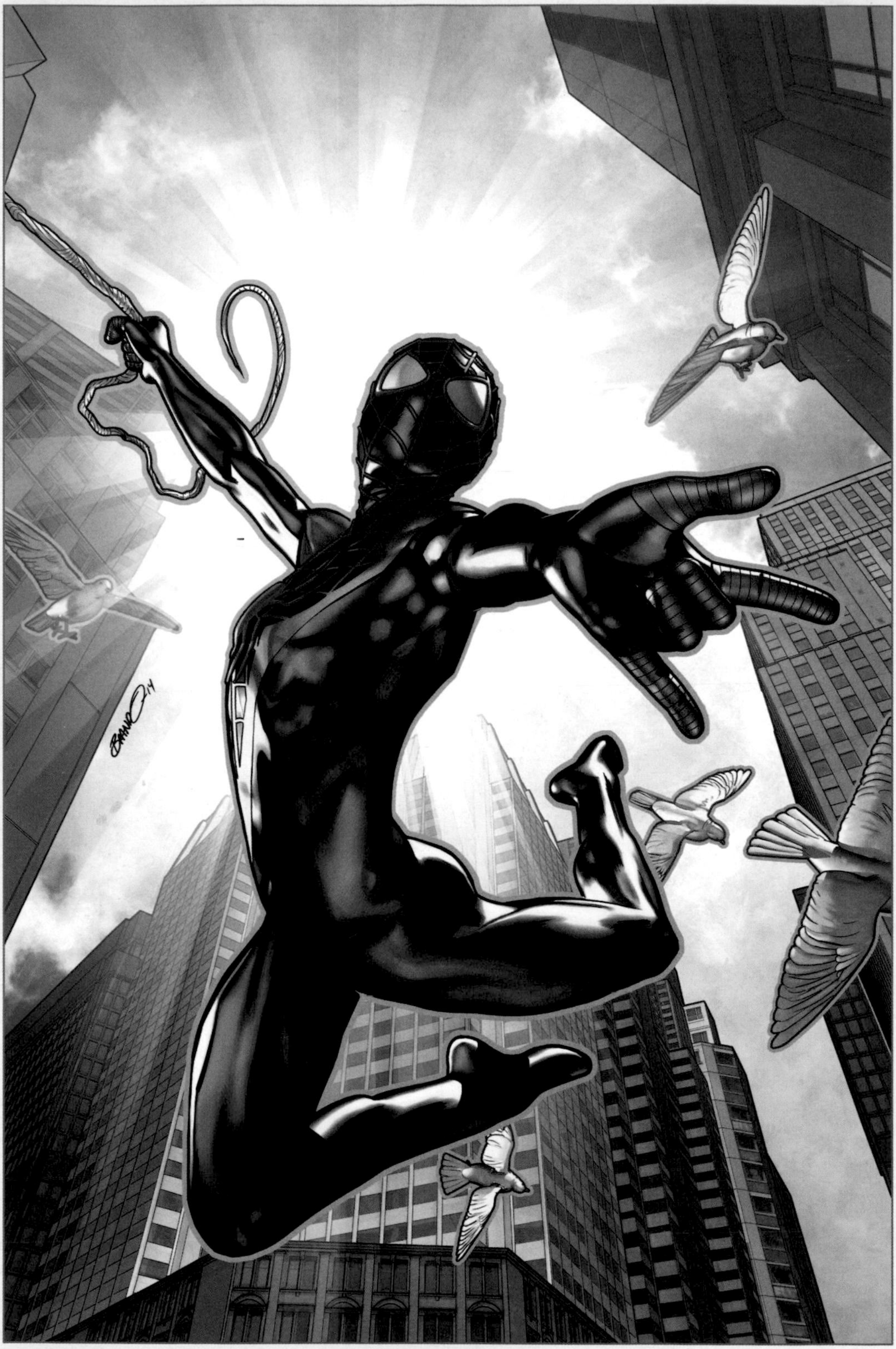

#1 VARIANT
BY BRANDON PETERSON

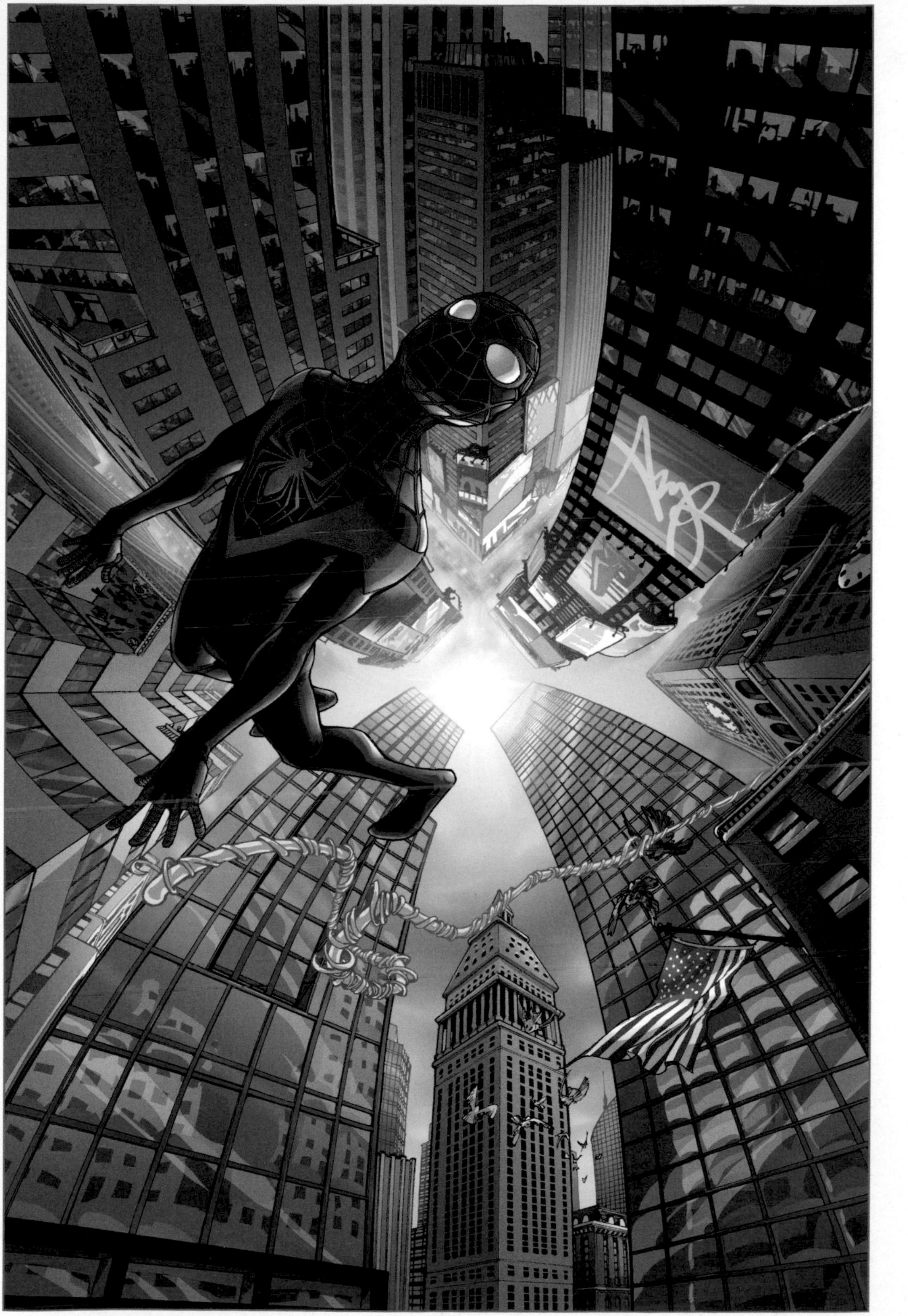

#2 VARIANT
BY AMY REEDER

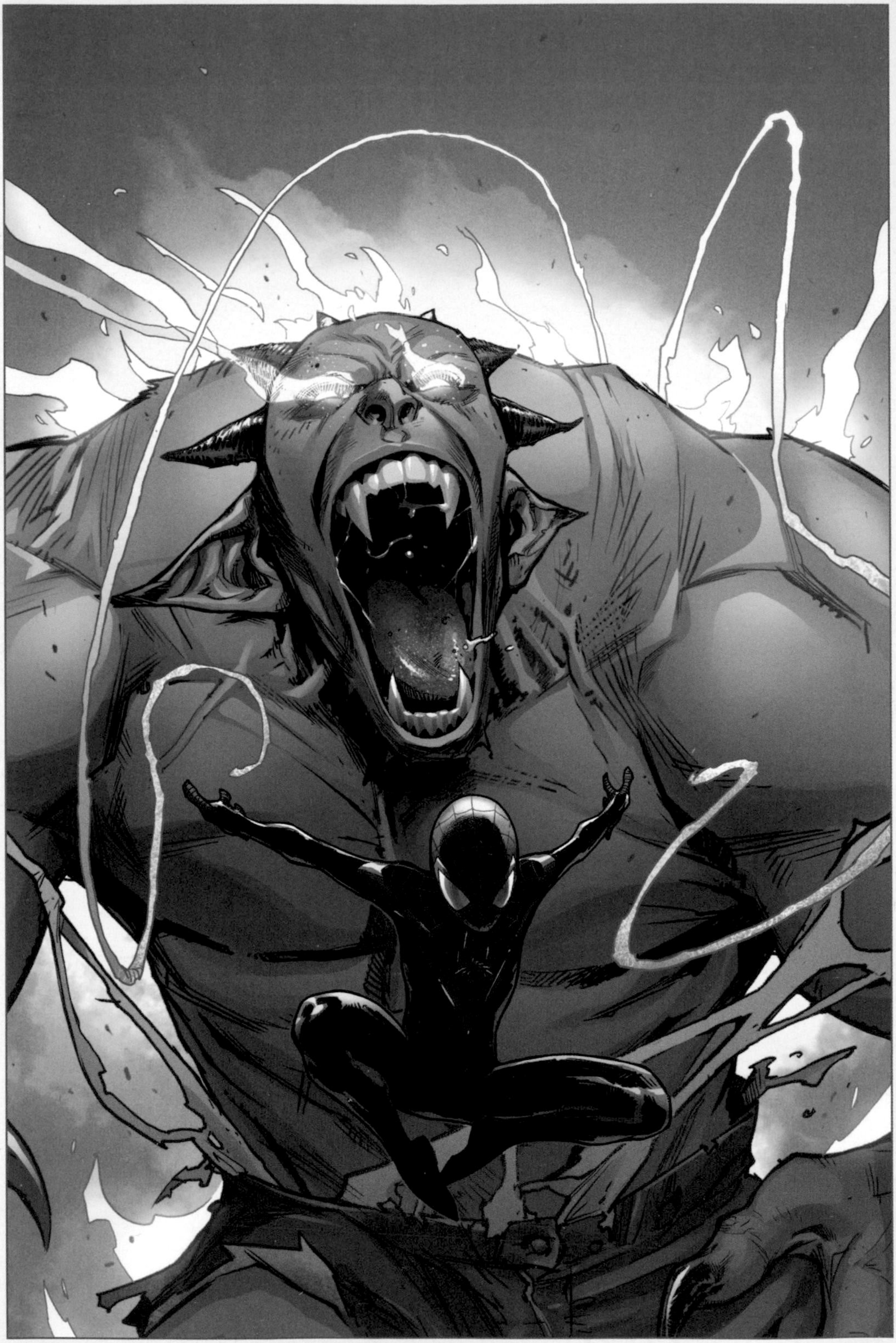

#3 VARIANT
BY SARA PICHELLI & JUSTIN PONSOR